Shaman's Crossing

THE SOLDIER SON TRILOGY
ONE

D0714308

By Robin Hobb

The Farseer Trilogy
ASSASSIN'S APPRENTICE
ROYAL ASSASSIN
ASSASSIN'S QUEST

The Liveship Traders
SHIP OF MAGIC
THE MAD SHIP
SHIP OF DESTINY

The Tawny Man
FOOL'S ERRAND
THE GOLDEN FOOL
FOOL'S FATE

Writing as Megan Lindholm

THE REINDEER PEOPLE
WOLF'S BROTHER

HARPY'S FLIGHT
THE WINDSINGERS
THE LIMBRETH GATE
LUCK OF THE WHEELS

CLOVEN HOOVES
ALIEN EARTH

Voyager

ROBIN HOBB

Shaman's Crossing

THE SOLDIER SON TRILOGY
ONE

HarperCollins*Publishers*

Voyager
An Imprint of HarperCollins*Publishers*
77–85 Fulham Palace Road,
Hammersmith, London W6 8JB

www.voyager-books.co.uk
www.voyageronline.com.au

Published by *Voyager* 2006
1

Map by Andrew Ashton

A catalogue record for this book
is available from the British Library

ISBN-13 978 0 00 719614 2
ISBN-10 0 00 719614 8

Typeset in Sabon by
Palimpsest Book Production Limited
Polmont, Stirlingshire

Printed and bound in Great Britain by
Clays Limited, St Ives plc

ONE

Magic and Iron

I remember well the first time I saw the magic of the plains-people.

I was eight and my father had taken me with him on a trip to the outpost on Franner's Bend. We had arisen before the dawn for the long ride; the sun was just short of standing at noon when we finally saw the flag waving over the walls of the outpost by the river. Once, Franner's Bend had been a military fort on the contested border between the plainspeople and the expanding Kingdom of Gernia. Now it was well within the Gernian border, but some of its old martial glory persisted. Two great cannons guarded the gates, but the trade stalls set up against the mud-plastered stockade walls behind them dimmed their ferocity. The trail we had followed from Widevale now joined a road that picked its way among the remains of mud-brick foundations. Their roofs and walls were long gone, leaving the shells gaping at the sky like empty tooth sockets in a skull. I looked at them curiously as we passed, and dared a question. 'Who used to live here?'

'Plainspeople,' Corporal Parth said. His tone said that was his full reply. Rising early did not suit his temperament, and I suspected already that he blamed me for having to get out of bed so early.

I held my tongue for a time, but then the questions burst out of me. 'Why are all the houses broken and gone? Why

1

did they leave? I thought the plainspeople didn't have towns. Was this a plainspeople town?'

'Plainspeople don't have towns, they left because they left, and the houses are broken because the plainspeople didn't know how to build any better than a termite does.' Parth's low-voiced answer implied that I was stupid for asking.

My father has always had excellent hearing. 'Nevare,' he said.

I nudged my horse to move up alongside my father's taller mount. He glanced at me once, I think to be sure I was listening, and then said, 'Most plainspeople did not build permanent towns. But some folk, like the Bejawi, had seasonal settlements. Franner's Bend was one of them. They came with their flocks during the driest part of the year, for there would be grazing and water here. But they didn't like to live for long in one place, and so they didn't build to last. At other times of the year, they took their flocks out onto the plains and followed the grazing.'

'Why didn't they stay here and build something permanent?'

'It wasn't their way, Nevare. We cannot say they didn't know how, for they did build monuments in various locations that were significant to them, and those monuments have weathered the tests of time very well. One day I shall take you to see the one named Dancing Spindle. But they did not make towns for themselves as we do, or devise a central government or provide for the common good of their people. And that was why they remained a poor, wandering folk, prey to the Kidona raiders and to the vagaries of the seasons. Now that we have settled the Bejawi and begun to teach them how to have permanent villages and schools and stores, they will learn to prosper.'

I pondered this. I knew the Bejawi. Some of them had settled near the north end of Widevale, my father's holdings. I'd been to the settlement once. It was a dirty place, a random tumble of houses without streets, with rubbish and sewage and offal scattered all around it. I hadn't been impressed. As if my father could hear my thoughts, he said, 'Sometimes it takes a while for people to adapt to civilization. The learning process can be hard. But in the end it will be of great benefit to them. The Gernian people have a duty to lift the Bejawi folk and help them learn civilized ways.'

Oh, that I understood. Just as struggling with mathematics would one day make me a better soldier. I nodded and continued to ride at his stirrup as we approached the outpost.

The town of Franner's Bend had become a traders' rendezvous, where Gernian merchants sold overpriced wares to homesick soldiers and purchased hand-made plainsworked goods and trinkets from the bazaar for the city markets in the west. The military contingent had a barracks and headquarters there which was still the heart of the town but the trade had become the new reason for its existence. Outside the fortified walls a little community had sprung up around the riverboat docks. A lot of common soldiers retired there, eking out their existence with hand-outs from their younger comrades. Once, I suppose, the fort at Franner's Bend had been of strategic importance. Now it was little more than another backwater on the river. The flags were still raised daily with military precision and a great deal of ceremony and pomp. But, as my father told me on the ride there, duty at Franner's Bend was a 'soft post' now, a plum given to older or incapacitated officers who did not wish to retire to their family homes yet.

Our sole reason for visiting was to determine if my father would win the military contract for sheepskins to use as saddle padding. My family was just venturing into sheep herding at that time, and he wished to assess the market potential for them before investing too heavily in the silly creatures. Much as he detested playing the merchant, he told me, as a new noble he had to establish the investments that would support his estate and allow it to grow. 'I've no wish to hand your brother an empty title when he comes of age. The future Lord Burvelles of the East must have income to support a noble lifestyle. You may think that has nothing to do with you, young Nevare, since as a second son you will go to be a soldier. But when you are an old man, and your soldiering days are through, you will come home to your brother's estate to retire. You will live out your days at Widevale, and the income of the estate will determine how well your daughters will marry, for it is the duty of a noble first son to provide for his soldier brother's daughters. It behooves you to know about these things.'

I understood little, then, of what he was telling me. Of late, he talked to me twice as much as he ever had, and I felt I understood only half as much of what he said. He had only recently parted me from my sisters' company and their gentle play. I missed them tremendously, as I did my mother's attentions and coddling. The separation had been abrupt, following my father's discovery that I spent most of my afternoons playing 'tea-party' in the garden with Elisi and Yaril, and had even adopted a doll as my own to bring to the nursery festivities. Such play alarmed my father for reasons my eight-year-old mind could not grasp. He had scolded my mother in a muffled 'discussion' behind the closed doors of the parlour, and instantly assumed total responsibility for my upbringing. My schoolbook lessons were suspended, pending the arrival of a new tutor he had hired. In the intervening days he kept me at his side for all sorts of tedious errands and constantly lectured me on what my life would be like when I grew up to be an officer in the King's Cavalla. If I was not with my father, and sometimes even when I was, Corporal Parth supervised me.

The abrupt change had left me both isolated and unsettled. I sensed I had somehow disappointed my father, but was unsure of what I had done. I longed to return to my sisters' company. I was also ashamed of missing them, for was I not a young man now and on my path to be my father's soldier son? So he often reminded me, as did fat old Corporal Parth. Parth was what my mother somewhat irritably called a 'charity hire'. Old, paunchy, and no longer fit for duty, he had come to ask my father's aid and been hired as an unskilled groundskeeper. He was now the temporary replacement for the nanny I had shared with my sisters. He was supposed to school me in 'the basics of military bearing and fitness' each day until my father could find a more qualified instructor. I did not think much of Parth. Nanny Sisi had been more organized and demanded more discipline of me than he did. The slouching old man who had carried his corporal's rank into retirement with him regarded me as more of a nuisance and a chore than a bright young mind to be shaped and a body to be built with rigor. Often, when he was supposed to be teaching me riding, he spent an hour napping while I practised 'being a good little sentry and keeping watch', which meant that I sat in the branches of a shady tree while he slept beneath it. I had not told my father any of that, of course. One thing that Parth had already instructed me in was that he was the commander and I was the soldier, and a good soldier never questioned his orders.

My father was well known at Franner's Bend. We rode through the town and up to the gates of the fortress. There he was saluted and welcomed without question. I looked curiously about me as we rode past an idle smith's shop, a warehouse, and a barracks before we reined in our horses before the commander's headquarters. I gaped up at the grand stone building, three storeys tall, as my father gave Parth his instructions regarding me.

'Give Nevare a tour of the outpost and explain the layout. Show him the cannon and talk to him about their placement and range. The fortifications here are a classic arrangement of defences. See that he understands what that means.'

If my father had looked back as he ascended the steps, he would have seen how Parth rolled his eyes. My heart sank. It meant that Parth had little intention of complying with my father's orders, and that I would later be held accountable for what I had not learned, which had happened before. I resolved, however, that it would not happen this time.

I followed him as we walked a short distance down the street. 'That's a barracks, where soldiers live,' he told me. 'And that's a canteen, tacked onto the end of it, where soldiers can get a beer and a bit of relaxation when they aren't on duty.'

The tour of the fort stopped there. The barracks and canteen were constructed of wooden planks, painted green and white. It was a long, low building with an open porch that ran the length of it. Off-duty soldiers idled there, sewing, blacking their boots, or talking and smoking or chewing as they sat on hard benches in the paltry shade. Outside the canteen, another porch offered refuge for a class of men I knew well. Too old to serve or otherwise incapacitated, these men wore a rough mix of military uniform and civilian garb. A lone woman in a faded orange dress slouched at one table, a limp flower behind her ear. She looked very tired. Mustered-out soldiers often approached my father in the hope of work and a place to live. If he thought they had any use at all he usually hired them, much to my lady mother's dismay. But these men, I immediately knew, my father would have turned away. Their clothes were unkempt, their unshaven faces smudged with dirt. Half a dozen of them loitered on the benches, drinking beer, chewing tobacco and spitting the brownish stuff onto the earth floor. The stink of tobacco juice and spilled beer hung in the air.

As we passed by, Parth glanced longingly into the low windows, and then delightedly hailed an old crony of his, one he evidently hadn't seen in years. I stood to one side, politely bored, as the two men exchanged reports on their current lives through the window opening, Parth's friend leaning on the sill to talk to us as we stood in the street. Vev had only recently arrived at the fort with his wife and his two sons, having been mustered out after he injured his back in a fall from his horse. Like many a soldier when his soldiering days were done, he had no resources to fall back on. His wife did a bit of sewing to keep a roof over their heads, but it was rocky going. And what was Parth doing these days? Working for Colonel Burvelle? I saw Vev's face lighten with interest. He immediately invited Parth to join him in a beer to celebrate their reunion. When I started to follow him up the steps, Parth glared at me. 'You wait outside for me, Nevare. I won't be long.'

'You're not supposed to leave me alone in town, Corporal Parth,' I reminded him. I'd heard my father reiterate that carefully on the ride here; young as I was, I was still a bit surprised that Parth had forgotten it already. I waited for him to thank me for the reminder. I considered that my due, for whenever my father had to remind me of a rule I had forgotten, I had to thank him and accept the consequences of my lapse.

Instead Parth scowled at me. 'You ain't alone out here, Nevare. I can see you right from the window, and there's all these old sojers keeping an eye on you. You'll be fine. Just sit yourself down by the door and wait like I told you.'

'But I'm supposed to stay with you,' I objected. My order to stay in Parth's company was a separate order from his to watch me and show me the fort. He might get in trouble for leaving me alone outside. And I feared my father would do more than rebuke me for not following Parth as I was supposed to.

His drinking companion came up with a solution. 'My boys Raven and Darda are out there, laddie. They're down by the corner of the smithy, playing knife toss with the other lads. Whyn't you go and see how it's done, and play a little yourself? We won't be gone long. I just want to talk to your

7

Uncle Parth here about what it takes to find a cushy job like what he's found for himself, nursie-maiding for old Colonel Burvelle.'

'Keep a civil tongue in your head when you speak of the boy's pa in front of him! Do you think he hasn't got a tongue of his own, to wag on about how you talk? Shut it, Vev, before you put my job on the block.'

'Well, I didn't mean anything, as I'm sure Colonel Laddie knew, right, lad?'

I grinned uncertainly. I knew that Vev was needling Parth on purpose, and perhaps mocking my father and me into the bargain. I didn't understand why. Weren't they friends? And if Vev were insulting Parth, why didn't we just walk away like gentlemen, or demand satisfaction of him, as often happened in the tales my eldest sister read aloud to my younger sister when my parents were not about? It was all very confusing, and as there had been much talk over my head of late that I must be taught how men did things now or I should grow up to be effeminate, I hesitated long over what response I should make.

Before I could, Parth gave me a none-too-gentle push in the direction of some older boys lounging at the corner of a warehouse and told me to go and play, for he'd only be a moment or two, and immediately clomped up the steps and vanished into the tavern, so that I was left unchaperoned on the street.

A barracks town can be a rough place. Even at eight I knew that, and so I approached the older boys cautiously. They were, as Vev had said, playing a knife toss game in the alley between the smithy and a warehouse. They were betting half-coppers and pewter bits as each boy took a turn at dropping the knife, point first, into the street. The bets wagered were on whether or not the knife would stick and how close each boy could come to his own foot on the drop without cutting himself. As they were barefoot, the wagers were quite interesting apart from the small coins involved, and a circle

8

of five or so boys had gathered to watch. The youngest of them was still a year or two older than me, and the eldest was in his teens. They were sons of common soldiers, dressed in their father's cast-offs and as unkempt as stray dogs. In a few more years, they'd sign their papers and whatever regiment took them in would dust them off and shape them into foot soldiers. They knew their own fortunes as well as I knew mine, and seemed very content to spend the last days of their boyhoods playing foolish games in the dusty street.

I had no coins to bet and I was dressed too well to keep company with them, so they made a space in their huddle to let me watch but didn't speak to me. I learned a few of their names only by listening to them talk to each other. For a time, I was content to watch their odd game, and listen intently to their rough curses and the crude name-calling that accompanied bets lost or won. This was certainly a long way from my sisters' tea parties, and I recall that I wondered if this were the sort of manly company that of late my father had been insisting I needed.

The sun was warm and the game endless as the bits of coin and other random treasure changed hands over and over. A boy named Carky cut his foot, and hopped and howled for a bit, but soon was back in the game. Raven, Vev's son, laughed at him and happily pocketed the two pennies and three marbles Carky had bet. I was watching them intently and would scarcely have noticed the arrival of the scout, save that all the other boys suddenly suspended the game and fell silent as he rode past.

I knew he was a scout, for his dress was half-soldier and half-plainsman. He wore dark-green cavalla trousers like a proper trooper, but his shirt was the loose linen of a plainsman, immaculately clean. His hair was not cropped short in a soldier's cut nor did he wear a proper hat. Instead, his black hair hung loose and long and moved with his white kaffiyeh. A rope of red silk secured his headgear. His arms were bare that summer day, the sleeves rolled to his biceps, and his forearm was circled with tattooed wreaths and trade-bracelets of silver beads and pewter charms and gleaming yellow brass. His horse was a good one, solid black, with long straight legs and jingle charms braided into his mane. I watched him with intent interest. Scouts were a breed apart, it was said. They were ranked as officers, lieutenants usually and frequently were nobly born, but they lived independent lives, outside the regular ranks of the military and often reported directly to the commander of an outpost. They were our first harbingers of any trouble, be it logjams on the river, eroding roads or unrest among the plainspeople.

A girl of twelve or thirteen on a chestnut gelding followed the scout. It was a smaller animal with a finely sculptured brow that spoke of the best nomadic stock. She rode astraddle as no proper Gernian girl would, and by that as much as by her garb I knew her for a mixed blood. It was not uncommon, though still deplored, for Gernian soldiers to take wives from among the plainspeople. It was less common for a scout to stoop so low. I stared at the girl in frank curiosity. My mother often said that the products of cross-unions were abominations before the good god, so I was surprised to see that such a long and ugly-sounding word described such a lovely creature. She was dressed in brightly layered skirts, one orange, one green, one yellow, that blossomed over the horse's back and covered her knees, but not her calves and feet. She wore soft little boots of antelope skin, and silver charms twinkled on their laces. Loose white trousers showed beneath her bunched skirts. Her shorter kaffiyeh matched her father's and displayed to advantage the long brown hair that hung down her back in dozens of fine braids. She had a high, round brow and calm grey eyes. Her white blouse bared her neck and arms, displaying the black torc she wore around her throat and a quantity of bracelets, some stacked above her elbows and others jingling at her wrist. She wore the woman's wealth of her family proudly for all to see. Her naked arms were brown from the sun and as muscled as a boy's. As she rode, she looked round boldly, very unlike my sisters' modest manner and downcast eyes when in public.

Her stare met mine, and we exchanged looks of honest appraisal. She had probably never seen a noble's soldier son, and I stood a bit straighter, well aware that I was finely turned out in my dark green trousers and crisp blouse and black boots, and especially so in the company of the ragged street-jay boys. I was not so young that the attention of a girl was not flattering. Looking back, perhaps it annoyed the others that she looked so intently at me, for they stared at her like hungry dogs studying a plump kitten.

She and the scout dismounted outside the same building that my father had entered. The scout had a clear, carrying voice, and we all heard him tell her that he would join her as soon as he'd delivered his report to the commander. He gave her some coins and told her she might go down the street to the bazaar and get some sweets or fresh caralin juice or ribbons for her hair, but not to go beyond the line of stalls there. 'Yes, Papa. I will.' She promised her father quickly, her eagerness to get to the market evident in her voice. The scout glanced over at my cluster of lads and scowled at us absent-mindedly, and then hurried up the steps into the command quarters.

His daughter was left alone in the street.

In such a circumstance, I know my sisters would have been terrified. My parents would never have left Elisi and little Yaril in a barracks town without an adult chaperone. I wondered if her father did not care for her. Then, as she strode smiling down the street, heading past the knot of boys and toward the vendors' stores on the market square just outside the outpost gates, I saw that she was not frightened or cowed in the least. She walked with confidence and

11

grace, intent on exploring the many delights of the bazaar. My gaze followed her.

'Look at her, will you?' one of the older boys hissed to his friend.

Raven grinned knowingly. 'That hinny's tamed. See that iron thing round her neck? Long as she wears that, her charms don't work.'

I looked from one leering young face to the other, confused. 'Her charms?' I asked.

It was flattering when Raven deigned to notice me. 'Little silver jingly things, woven in her hair, supposed to protect her. Plains magic. But someone tamed her. Put an iron collar on a plainswoman, and she can't use her charms against you. She's ripe for the picking, that hinny is.'

'Picking what?' I boldly asked. There was no hinny to be seen, only the girl walking past us. I was confused and resolved to get an explanation. I did not know at that time that my bold assumption of not only equality but superiority to these sons of common soldiers would be resented by the older boys. Raven brayed a laugh out, and then said to me earnestly, 'Why, to picking out her friends, of course. You seen how she looked at you? She wants to be your friend. And you want her to be friends with us, right, 'cause we're your friends, too. Whyn't you just go out there and catch her by the hand and lead her back here to us?'

Raven's voice was sugary, but his words fell somewhere between a compliment and a dare. As he spoke, he gestured to the other boys, and they all retreated more deeply into the alley between the buildings. I stared up at him for a moment longer. His cheek was downy, and the fine hair held the dust of the street. The corners of his mouth were caked with dust that had been trapped there by stray, sticky crumbs. His hair was shaggily cut, his clothing dirty. But he was older than I was, and he'd been playing with a knife, and thus I yearned to distinguish myself in his eyes.

12

The girl walked like a gazelle going down to water. She was intent on her quest, and yet both wary and aware of what was around her. She did not look at us, but I knew she had seen us. She probably knew we were talking about her. I darted out a few steps into the street to intercept her, and when she looked at me, I smiled at her. She smiled down at me. It was all the encouragement I needed. I hurried up to her, and she halted in the street.

'Hello. My friends want you to come and meet them.' Such an ingenuous way for me to greet her. I had no idea I was leading her into a vile trap.

I think she did. She looked past me at the loitering boys inside the alley mouth, and then back at me again. I hope she saw I was innocent of their scheme. She smiled again but her words dismissed me. 'I don't think so. I'm going to the market. Goodbye.' Her voice was clear and unaccented, and obviously intended to reach my playmates' ears.

They heard her words and saw how she strode off. One of my erstwhile companions gave a catcall and Raven laughed at me. I couldn't stand it. I ran after her and seized her hand. 'Please? Just come over and say hello.'

She did not react with alarm, or take her hand from mine. She considered me kindly for a moment and then offered, 'You're a friendly little cub, aren't you? Why don't you come to the market with me instead?'

Her invitation instantly attracted me more than the company of the boys. I loved going to market almost as much as my sisters did. Exotic goods and trinkets demanded to be handled and explored. Market food was always exciting; I loved plains food, the spicy root-paste rolled in terna seed, sweet and peppery meat sticks, and little buns of salty ember-bread, each with a lump of carrada in the middle. My gaze met her grey eyes and I found myself nodding and smiling. I forgot the boys and their stick-knife game. For the moment, I ignored the knowledge that not only Parth but

13

also my father would disapprove of me wandering off with a half-breed plainsgirl to saunter through the market.

We had gone less than five paces when my earlier companions suddenly ringed us. They were smiling, but their grins were wolfish, not friendly. Raven stood directly in front of us, forcing us to stop. Carky, his cut foot tied with a rag, stood at Raven's elbow. The girl's fingers twitched in mine, and as clearly as if she had voiced it, I felt the little jolt of fear that shot through her. My half-formed honour came to the fore and I said importantly, 'Please step out of our way. We are going to the market.'

Raven grinned. 'Well, listen to him! We're not in your way, colonel's son. In fact, we're here to guide you. There's a short cut to the market. We'll show you. Right down that alley.'

'But I can see the market from here!' I protested stupidly. The girl tried to take her hand from mine, but I held on tightly. I suddenly knew my duty. A gentleman always protected women and children. I instinctively knew that these fellows meant my companion some sort of harm. Innocent as I was, I did not know what they intended for her, or perhaps I would have been more sensibly frightened. Instead, I only grew more determined to guard her. 'Step out of our way,' I commanded them again.

But they were bunching closer, and unwillingly both the girl and I stepped back, trying to gain space. They came on and again we stepped back. We were being herded toward the alley mouth as surely as dogs herd sheep into a pen. I glanced over my shoulder at the boys behind me, and Carky laughed an ugly laugh. At the sound, the girl beside me halted. Despite my grip on her fingers, she drew her hand free of mine. The boys advanced another step on us. They suddenly loomed larger and uglier than they had when I had watched them play. I could smell them, the cheap food on their breath, their unwashed bodies. I glanced quickly around, seeking some adult who would intervene, but the sun was hot and this part of the street was deserted. People were either inside the cooler buildings, or at the market. Down the street, the lounging soldiers on the canteen porch were talking amongst themselves. Even if I shouted for help, I doubted that anyone would respond. We were very near the alley mouth; we could quickly be dragged out of sight. I summoned the last of my quavering authority. 'My father will be very angry if you do not let us pass.'

Carky showed his teeth. 'Your father won't even find your body, officer's brat.'

I had never before been called such a name, let alone threatened with it. My father had always assured me that a good officer earned his troopers' affection and loyalty. Somehow, I had thought that meant that all soldiers loved their officers. In the face of this youngster's schooled hostility, I was struck dumb.

The girl, however, was not. 'I don't want to hurt anyone,' she said quietly. She strove for calm, but her voice broke slightly.

Raven laughed. 'Think we don't know nothing, hinny-breed? You're collared. Iron-tamed. You can't do no more to us than any other woman. And a little kicking and screaming won't bother none of us.'

He must have given some sort of signal. Or perhaps, like a flock of birds or a pack of wild dogs, the boys acted in concert by instinct. Two of the younger boys, both larger than I, tackled me and bore me, kicking and shouting, toward the alley's mouth. Raven and Carky seized hold of the girl, one on either side of her. I had one horrible glimpse of their dirty fingers clenching hard against her soft white sleeves. They gripped her upper arms and near lifted her off her feet as they moved her toward the alley. The other boys followed in a mob, their eyes bright, laughing excitedly. For a second, she looked delicate as a frightened bird in their grasp and

15

then instantly furious. As I was dragged backwards, she gave one of her arms a twist and a shrug, snapping it free of her captor's grip. I saw her slender fingers weave a small sign in the air. It reminded me of the little charm my father always performed above his cinch-buckle whenever he saddled a horse. But it was not the familiar 'keep-fast' charm. This was something older and much more powerful.

It is hard to describe the magic she did. There was no lightning flash, no roar of thunder, no green sparks, nothing like the old Gernian tales of magic. All she did was move her hand in a certain way. I cannot describe it, I could never imitate it and yet some old part of my soul knew and recognized that sign. Even though she had not targeted me, I saw the sign and I had to react to it. Every muscle in my body gave an involuntary twitch, and for a terrible moment, I feared I had lost control of my bowels. I jerked in my captors' grip and if I'd had my wits about me, I probably could have escaped them, for they, too, twitched as if jabbed with pins.

The two boys holding her reacted far more strongly. At the time, I had never seen a man fall in a seizure, so I did not realize until years later what I was witnessing. Their bodies contorted as their muscles spasmed wildly; Raven and Carky literally flung themselves away from her, landing several feet away and hitting the ground hard enough to raise dust from the street. One of the younger boys, Raven's brother Darda from the resemblance, gave a howl of dismay and scampered off toward the canteen.

She stumbled as they dropped her, nearly going to her knees, but in an instant she was on her feet again. She tugged at her blouse, for they had dragged her sleeves down her arms to expose her shoulders and part of her bosom. Covered again, she took two swift strides forward. 'Let him go!' she commanded the two young ruffians who held me, and her voice was low and threatening through her clenched white teeth.

16

'But . . . your iron collar!' Only the one boy objected. He gaped at her, dismayed and offended, as if she had broken the rules of a game. The other released my arm and fled, howling like a kicked dog, although I am almost certain nothing had been done to him. She made no reply to the boy's protest. Her fingers began to weave, and the protesting boy did not wait for her to complete the charm. He knew as well as I did that a plains charm had a limited range. He thrust me at her so suddenly that I dropped into the dust at her feet, and then he raced full tilt after his friend. Carky had already disappeared, scrabbling to his feet and darting around the corner of a building. As Raven got to his feet, she helped me to mine. Then she turned to him, and as if she were wishing him good day, said, 'Black paint over bronze. Not iron. My father would never put iron on any of us. He docs not even bring his iron into our home.'

Raven backed slowly away from us. His face was flushed with fury, and his black eyes gleamed with it. I knew exactly when he thought he was beyond the range of her magic. He stopped there, and cursed her with the foulest names I'd ever heard, names I did not know the meaning of, only that they were vile. He finished with, 'Your father shamed himself when he dipped his rod in your mother. Better he had done it with a donkey, and produced a true mule. That's what you are, hinny. A mule. A cross-breed. A freak. You can do your dirty little magic on us, but one day one of us will ride you bloody. You'll see.'

He grew braver as he spoke, and perhaps he thought my gaping mouth indicated shock at his words. Then the scout, who had walked up behind Raven in utter silence, seized the boy. In one fluid motion, he spun Raven around and backhanded him across the face. The scout held nothing back from that blow, did not temper it at all for the sake of it being a boy he hit instead of a man. I heard the crack as Raven went down, and knew he had mouthed his last foul words until his jaw healed. As if the sound were a charm to bring witnesses, men left the shaded porches of the barracks and canteen to gather in the street. Darda was there, pulling his father Vev along by the hand. My father was suddenly there, striding up angrily, spots of colour on his cheeks.

It seemed that everyone spoke at once. The girl ran to her father. He put his arms around her shoulders, and bending his head, spoke quietly to her. 'We'll be leaving now, Sil. Right away.'

'But . . . I never got to go to the market! Papa, it wasn't my fault!'

Vev had knelt by Raven. He turned and shouted angrily, 'Damn it all, he's broke my boy's jaw! He's broken it!'

Other men were flowing out of the canteen now, blinking in the daylight like a pack of nocturnal animals stirred to alarm. Their faces were not kindly as they looked at the scout and then the boy writhing on the ground.

My father demanded, 'Nevare, why are you involved in this? Where is Parth?'

Parth, his moustache still wet with beer, was behind my father, a latecomer to the scene. I suspected he had stayed to down the last of his mug, and perhaps Vev's, too, when the man had abruptly left the table. Parth shouted, loudest of all, 'Praise to the good god! There's the boy. Nevare, come here at once! I've been looking all over for you. You know better than to run off and hide from old Parth. That's not a funny trick to play in a rough town like this.'

My father's voice, pitched for command, would have carried through a battlefield. Yet he did not shout. It was the way he said, 'Praise whoever you like, Parth, but I'm not deceived. Your time in my employ is finished. Take your saddle off my horse.'

'But sir, it were the boy! He run off, almost as soon as you went inside . . .'

Parth's voice trailed away. My father was no longer listening to him. No one was. The commander of the outpost had come down the steps of his headquarters and was striding down the street toward us, his aide speaking quietly and rapidly as he trotted alongside the older, taller man. The aide pushed ahead of his chief, clearing a way through the gawkers until the commander reached the front of the crowd. The commander, to his credit, did not look or sound the least bit excited as he halted and demanded, 'What is going on here?'

Everyone fell silent, save for Vev, who howled, 'He hit my boy, he busted his jaw, sir! That scout done it! Just walked up on my lad and hit him!'

'Scout Halloran. Would you care to explain yourself?'

Halloran's face had gone carefully blank. Something in me felt shamed at the change in the man's demeanour, although I did not understand it in a way I could put words to. The scout said carefully, 'Sir, he insulted and threatened my daughter.'

The commander scowled. 'That was all?' he asked, and awaited clarification. The silence grew long. I squirmed, confused. Insulting a girl was a serious thing. Even I knew that. Finally, I did my duty. My father had always told me it was a man's duty to speak the truth. I cleared my throat and spoke up plainly.

'They grabbed her arms, sir, and tried to pull her into the alley. Then Raven called her a hinny, after she threw him off, and said he would ride her bloody.' I repeated only the words I had understood, not knowing that the adult context of them escaped me. To my childish interpretation, he had called the girl a mule. I knew I would have received a whipping if I called my sisters any such animal name. Plainly, the boy had been rude and been punished for it. I spoke my piece loud and clear, and then added, more to my father than to the commander, 'I was trying to protect her. You told me that it's always wrong to hit a girl. They nearly tore off her blouse.'

A silence followed my words. Even Vev stopped his

caterwauling, and Raven muffled his groans. I looked round at all the eyes focused on me. My father's face confused me. Pride warred with embarrassment. Then the scout spoke. His voice was tight. 'I'd say that's a fair summation of what my daughter was threatened with. I acted accordingly. Does any father here blame me?'

No one spoke against him, but if he had hoped for support, no one gave that, either. The commander observed coldly, 'All this could have been avoided if you'd had the good sense to leave her at home, Halloran.'

That statement seemed to give Vev permission to be angry again. He leapt up from where he had been cradling Raven, wringing a yelp from the boy as he jostled him in passing. He advanced on the scout, hands hanging loose at his side, his knees slightly bent and all knew that at the slightest provocation, he would fling himself on the man. 'It's all your fault!' he growled at him. 'All your fault, bringing that girl to town and letting her loose to wander, tempting these lads.' Then, his voice rising to a shout, 'You ruined my boy! That jaw don't heal right, he'll never go for a soldier! And then what's left for him, I want to know? The good god decreed he'd be a soldier; the sons of soldiers is always soldiers. But you, you've ruined him, for the sake of that half-breed hinny!' The man's fists shook at the end of his arms, as if a mad puppeteer were tugging at his strings. I feared that at any second they would come to blows. By common accord, men were moving back, forming a ring. The scout glanced once, sideways, at the commander. Then he gently set his daughter behind him. I looked about wildly, seeking shelter for myself, but my father was on the opposite side of the circle and not even looking at me. He stared at the commander, his face stiff, waiting, I knew, for him to give the orders that would bring these men to heel.

He did not. The soldier swung at the scout. The scout leaned away from the swing, and hit Vev twice in the face in quick succession. I thought he would go right down. I think the scout did too, but Vev had deliberately faked his awkwardness and accepted the blows to bring Halloran to him. The scout had misjudged him, for the soldier now struck him back, an ugly blow, his fist coming fast and hard, to strike the scout solidly in the midsection and push up, under his ribs. The blow lifted Halloran off his feet and drove the wind out of him. He clutched at his opponent as he came down and staggered forward, and Vev hammered in two more body blows. They were solid, meaty hits. The girl gave a small scream and cowered, covering her face with her hands as her father's eyes rolled up. Vev laughed aloud.

He fell to his own trick. The scout was not close to falling; he suddenly came to life again. He fisted Vev in the face, a solid crack. Vev gave a high breathless cry. Halloran took him down with a sweep of his foot that knocked Vev's feet from under him and sent him sprawling in the dirt. Several men in the crowd shouted aloud at that, and surged forward. Vev wallowed in the dust for a moment, then curled up on his side, hands to his face. Blood streamed between his fingers. He coughed weakly.

'Halt!' The commander finally intervened. I do not know why he had waited so long. His face had gone dark with blood; this was not something any commander wanted happening at his post. Halloran might be only a scout, but he was a noble's soldier son and an officer all the same. Surely the commander could not have deliberately permitted a common soldier like Vev to strike him. From somewhere, uniformed soldiers had appeared. The aide had gone to fetch them, I suddenly saw. Backed by his green-coated troops, the commander issued terse orders.

'Round them up, every man here. If they're ours, confine them to barracks. If they're not, put them outside the walls and instruct the sentries that none of them are to re-enter for three days. Sons to follow their fathers.'

21

I knew he had the right. Soldier's sons would one day be soldiers. As he commanded their fathers, so could he order their sons in times of need.

'He struck an officer.' My father spoke quietly. He was not looking at the commander or the scout or me. His eyes were carefully focused on nothing. He said the words aloud, but there was no indication he was intending them for the commander.

The commander responded anyway. 'You there!' He pointed at Vev. 'You are to pack up yourself and your whelps and take them all out of my jurisdiction. Because I am a merciful man and the result of your actions will fall on your wife and daughters as well, I will allow you time to take your boy to a doctor and have his jaw bound before you depart and gather what goods you rightfully own. But by nightfall tomorrow, I want you on your way!'

The crowd muttered, displeased. It was a severe punishment. There was no other settlement for several days journey. It was effectively an exile to the arid plains. I doubted the family had a wagon, or even horses. Vev had, indeed, brought a severe hardship down on himself and his family. One of his friends came forward to help him with his son. They glared at the scout and at the commander as they picked up the moaning Raven, but they did as they were told. The ranks of uniformed soldiers had fanned out to be sure it was so. The crowd began to disperse.

The scout was standing silently, his arm around his daughter's shoulders. He looked pale, his face greenish from the blows he had taken to his gut. I did not know if he sheltered his daughter or leaned on her. She was crying, not quietly, but in great sobs and gulps. I didn't blame her. If someone had hit my father like that, I'd have wept, too. He spoke low, comfortingly, 'We're going home now, Sil.'

'Halloran.' The commander's voice was severe.

'Sir?'

22

'Don't bring her to my post ever again. That's an order.'

'As if I would.' Insubordination simmered in his voice. Belatedly, he lowered his eyes and voice. 'Sir.' It was at that moment that I suddenly knew how much the scout now hated his commander. And when the commander ignored it, I wondered if he feared the half-wild soldier.

Nothing more was said that I heard. I think all sound and motion stopped for me as I stood in the street and tried to make sense of what I had seen that day. Around me, the uniformed troopers were dispersing the mob, harrying them along with curses and shoves. My father stood silently by the commander. Together they watched the scout escort his daughter to their horses. She had stopped crying. Her face was smooth and emotionless now, and if they spoke to one another, I did not hear it. He mounted after she did, and together they rode slowly away. I watched them for a long time. When I looked back to my father, I realized that he and the commander and I were the only ones left standing in the alley mouth.

'Come here, Nevare,' my father said, as if I were a straying pup, and obediently I came to his side. When I stood there, he looked down at me and setting his hand on my shoulder, asked, 'How did you come to be mixed up in this?'

I did not even imagine I could lie to him about it. I told him all, from the time Parth had shooed me into the street until the moment that he had come on the scene. The commander listened as quietly as he did. When I repeated the threat that he'd never even find my body, my father's eyes went flinty. He glanced at the post commander, and the man looked ill. When I was through, my father shook his head.

I felt alarm. 'Did I do wrong, Father?'

The commander answered before my father could. But he spoke to my father, not me. 'Halloran brought the trouble to town when he brought his half-breed daughter here, Keft. Don't trouble your boy's head over it. If I'd known that Vev was such an insubordinate rascal, I'd never have let him or his family on my post. I'm only sorry your lad had to see and hear what he did.'

'As am I,' my father agreed tersely. He did not sound mollified.

The commander spoke on, hastily. 'At the end of the month, I'll send a man with the forms to fill out for the military requisition of the sheepskins. You'll not have any competition for the bid. And when I deal with you, I'll know I'm dealing with an honest man. Your son's honesty speaks for that.' The commander seemed anxious to know he had my father's regard. My father seemed reluctant to give it.

'You honour me, sir,' was all that my father said, and gave a very small bow at the compliment. They bid each other farewell then. We walked to our horses. Parth was standing a short distance away, his saddle at his feet and a look of forlorn hope on his face. My father didn't look at him. He helped me to mount, for my horse was tall for me. He led the horse that Parth had ridden and I rode beside him. He was silent as the sentries passed us out of the gates. I looked wistfully at the market stalls as we rode past them. I would have liked to explore the vendors' booths with the scout's pretty daughter. We hadn't even stopped for a meal, and I knew better than to complain about that. There were meat sandwiches in our saddlebags, and water in our bags. A soldier was always prepared to take care of himself. A question came to me.

'Why did they call her a hinny?'

My father didn't look over at me. 'Because she's a cross, son. Half-plains, half-Gernian, and welcome nowhere. Just like a mule is a cross between a horse and a donkey, but isn't really one or the other.'

'She did magic.'

'So you said.'

His tone indicated he didn't really care to talk about that

with me. It made me uncomfortable, and I finally asked him again, 'Did I do wrong, back there?'

'You shouldn't have left Parth's side. Then none of this would have happened.'

I thought about that for a time. It didn't seem quite fair. 'If I hadn't been there, they couldn't have sent me out to the girl. But I think they would have tried to get her in the alley, even if I wasn't there.'

'Perhaps so,' my father agreed tightly. 'But you wouldn't have been there to witness it.'

'But . . .' I tried to work it through my mind. 'If I hadn't been there, she would have been hurt. That would have been bad.'

'It would,' my father agreed, after the clopping of our horses' hooves had filled the silence for some time. My father pulled his horse to a stop, and I halted with him. He took a breath, licked his lips and then hesitated again. Finally, as I squinted up at him, he said, 'You did nothing shameful, Nevare. You protected a woman, and you spoke the truth. Both of those traits are things I value in my son. Once you had witnessed what was happening, you could have done no different. But your witnessing that, and your speaking up caused, well, difficulties for all the officers there. It would have been better if you had obeyed my command and stayed with Parth.'

'But that girl would have been hurt.'

'Yes. That is likely.' My father's voice was tight. 'But if she had been hurt, it would not have been your fault, or our business at all. Likely, no one would have questioned her father's right to punish the offender. The scout hurt that soldier's son over a mere threat to his daughter; his right to punish the man was less clear to the men. And Commander Hent is not a strong commander. He seeks his men's permission to lead rather than demands their obedience. Because you protected her and offered testimony that the threat was real, the

25

situation had to be dealt with. That man and his family had to be banished from the fort. The common soldiers didn't like that. They all imagined the same happening to them.'

'The commander let the soldier hit the scout,' I slowly realized.

'Yes. He did it so he would have a clear reason to banish him, independent of the insult to the scout's daughter. And that was wrong of the commander, to take such a coward's way out. It was shameful of him. And I witnessed it, and a bit of that shame will cling to me, and to you. Yet there was nothing I could do about it, for he was the commander. If I had questioned his decision, I would only have weakened him in the sight of his men. One officer does not do that to another.'

'Then. . . did Scout Halloran behave honourably?' It suddenly seemed tremendously important to me to know who had done the right thing.

'No.' My father's reply was absolute. 'He could not. Because he behaved dishonourably the day he took a wife from among the plainspeople. And he made a foolish decision to bring the product of that union to the outpost with him. The soldier sons reacted to that. She displayed herself, with her bright skirts and bare arms. She made herself attractive to them. They know she will never be a Gernian's rightful wife, and that most plainspeople will not take her. Sooner or later, it is likely she will end up a camp whore. And thus they treated her that way, today.'

'But—'

My father nudged his horse back into motion. 'I think that is all there is for you to learn from this today. We shall not speak of it again, and you will not discuss it with your mother or sisters. We've a lot of road to cover before dusk. And I wish you to write an essay for me, a long one, on the duty of a son to obey his father. I think it an appropriate correction, don't you?'

'Yes, sir,' I replied quietly.

26

TWO

Harbinger

I was twelve when I saw the messenger who brought the first tidings of plague from the east.

Strange to say, it left little impression on me at the time. It was a day like many other days. Sergeant Duril, my tutor for equestrian skills, had been putting me through drills with Sirlofty all morning. The gelding was my father's pride and joy, and that summer was the first that I was given permission to practise manoeuvres on him. Sirlofty himself was a well-schooled cavalla horse, needing no drill in battle kicks or fancy dressage, but I was green to such things and learned as much from my mount as I did from Sergeant Duril. Any errors we made were most often blamed on my horsemanship and justifiably so. A horseman must be one with his mount, anticipating every move of his beast, and never clinging nor lurching in his saddle.

But that day's drill was not kicks or leaps. It involved unsaddling and unbridling the tall black horse, then demonstrating that I could still mount and ride him without a scrap of harness on him. He was a tall, lean horse with straight legs like iron bars and a stride that made his gallop feel as if we were flying. Despite Sirlofty's patience and willingness, my boy's height made it a struggle for me to mount him from the ground, but Duril had insisted I practise it. Over and over and over again. 'A horse soldier has got to be able

27

to get on any horse that's available to him, in any sort of circumstances, or he might as well admit he has the heart of a foot soldier. Do you want to walk down that hill and tell your da that his soldier son is going to enlist as a foot soldier rather than rise up to a commission in the cavalla? Because if you do, I'll wait up here while you do it. Better that I not witness what he'd do to you.'

It was the usual rough chivvying I received from the man, and I flatter myself that I handled it better than most lads of my years would have. He had arrived at my father's door some three years ago, seeking employment in his declining years, and my father had been only too relieved to hire him on. Duril replaced a succession of unsatisfactory tutors, and we had taken to one another almost immediately. Sergeant Duril had finished out his many long years of honourable military service, and it had seemed only natural to him that when he retired he would come to live on my father's lands and serve Lord Burvelle as well as he had served Colonel Burvelle. I think he enjoyed taking on the practical training of Nevare Burvelle, Colonel Burvelle's second boy, the soldier son born to follow his father's example as a military officer.

The sergeant was a shrivelled little man, with a face as dark and wrinkled as jerky. His clothing was worn to the point of comfort, holding the shape of a man who was most often in the saddle. Even when they were clean, his garments were always the colour of dust. On his head, he wore a battered leather hat with a floppy brim and a hatband decorated with beads and animal fangs. His pale eyes always peered watchfully from under the brim of his hat. What hair he had left was a mixture of grey and brown. Half his left ear was missing and he had a nasty scar where it should have been. To make up for that lack he carried a Kidona ear in a pouch on his belt. I'd only seen it once, but it was unmistakably an ear. 'Took his for trying to take mine. It was a barbaric thing to do, but I was young and I was angry, with blood running

28

down the side of my neck when I did it. Later that evening, when the fighting was over I looked at what I'd done, and I was ashamed. Ashamed. But it was too late to put it back with his body and I couldn't bring myself to just throw it away. I've kep' it ever since to remind me of what war can do to a young man. And that's why I'm showing it to you now,' he had told me. 'Not so you can run tell your little sister and have your lady ma complain to the colonel that I'm learning you wild ways, but so that you can think on that. Before we could teach the plainspeople to be civilized, we had to teach them they couldn't beat us in a fight. And we had to do that without getting down on their level. But when a man is fighting for his life that's a hard thing to remember. Especially when you're a young man and out on your own, 'mongst savages. Some of our lads, good honest lads when they left home, well, they wound up little better than the plainspeople we fought against before we were through. A lot of them never went home. Not jus' the ones who died, but the ones who couldn't remember how to be civilized. They stayed out there, took plains wives, some of 'em, and became part of what we'd gone out there to tame. Remember that, young Nevare. Hold on to who you are when you're a man grown and an officer like the Colonel.'

Sometimes he treated me like that, as if I were his own son, telling me stories of his days as a soldier and passing on the homespun wisdom that he hoped would see me through. But most days he treated me as something between a raw recruit and a rather dim hound. Yet I never doubted his fondness for me. He'd had three sons of his own, and raised them and sent them off to enlist years before he'd got to me. In the way of common soldiers and their get, he'd all but lost track of his own boys. From year to year he might receive a message from one or another of them. It didn't bother him. It was what he had always expected his boys to do. The sons of common soldiers went for soldiers, just as the Writ tells us they should.

'Let each son rise up and follow the way of his father.'

Of course it was different for me. I was the son of a noble. 'Of those who bend the knee only to the King, let them have sons in plenitude. The first for an heir, the second to wear the sword, the third to serve as priest, the fourth to labour for beauty's sake, the fifth to gather knowledge…' and so on. I'd never bothered to memorize the rest of that passage. I had my place and I knew it. I was the second son, born to 'wear the sword' and lead men to war.

I'd lost count that day of how many times I'd dismounted and then mounted Sirlofty and ridden him in a circle around Duril, without a scrap of harness to help me. Probably as many times as I'd unsaddled and unbridled the horse, and then replaced the tack. My back and shoulders ached from lifting the saddle on and off of the gelding's back, and my fingertips were near numb from making the cavalryman's 'keep fast' charm over the cinch. I was just fastening the cinch yet again when Sergeant Duril suddenly commanded, 'Follow me!' With those words, he gave his mare a sharp nudge with his heels and she leapt forth with a will. I had no breath for cursing him as I finished tightening the strap, hastily did the 'keep fast' charm over it and then flung myself up and into the saddle.

Those who have not ridden the plains of the Midlands will speak of how flat and featureless they are, how they roll on endlessly forever. Perhaps they appear so to passengers on the riverboats that wend their way down the waterways that both divide and unite the plains. I had grown up on the Midlands, and knew well how deceptive their gentle rises and falls could be. So did Sergeant Duril. Ravines and sudden crevasses smiled with hidden mouths, waiting to devour the unwary rider. Even the gentle hollows were often deep enough to conceal mounted men or browsing deer. What the unschooled eye might interpret as scrub brush in the distance could prove to be a shoulder-high patch of sickle-berry, almost impenetrable to a man on horseback. Appearances were deceiving, the sergeant always warned me. He had often told me tales of how the plainspeople could use tricks of perspective in preparing an ambush, how they trained their horses to lie down, and how a howling horde of warriors would suddenly seem to spring up from the earth itself to attack a careless line of cavalrymen. Even from the vantage of tall Sirlofty's back, Sergeant Duril and his mount had vanished from my view.

The gentle roll of prairie around me appeared deserted. Few real trees grew in Widevale, other than the ones which Father had planted. Those that did manage to sprout on their own were indications of a watercourse, perhaps seasonal, perhaps useful. But most of the flora of our region was sparsely leaved and dusty grey-green, holding its water in tight, leathery leaves or spiny palms. I did not hurry, but allowed myself to scan the full circle of horizon, seeking any trace of them. I saw none; I had only the dry dents of Chafer's hoofprints in the hard soil to guide me. I set out after them. I leant down beside Sirlofty's neck, tracking them and feeling proud of my ability to do so until I felt the sudden thud of a well-aimed stone hit me squarely in the back. I pulled in Sirlofty and sat up, groaning as I reached back to rub my new bruise. Sergeant Duril rode up from behind me, his slingshot still in his hand.

'And you're dead. We circled back. You were too busy following our sign, young Nevare, and not wary enough about your surroundings. That pebble could just as easily have been an arrow.'

I nodded wearily. There was no use in denying his words. Useless to complain that when I was grown, I could expect to have a full troop of horsemen with me, with some men to keep watch while others tracked. No. Better to endure the bruise and nod than to bring an hour of lecture down on myself as well. 'Next time, I'll remember,' I told him.

31

'Good. But only good because this time it was just a little rock and so there *will* be a next time for you. With an arrow, that would have been your last time to forget. Come on. Pick up your rock before we go.'

He kneed Chafer again and left me. I dismounted and searched the ground around Sirlofty's feet until I found the stone. Duril had been 'killing' me several times a month since I was nine years old. Picking up the stones had been my own idea at first; I think the first few times I was slain, I had taken to heart the concept that, had Duril truly been a hostile, my life would have ended in that moment. When Duril realized what I was doing, he began to take pains to find interesting stones to use in his sling. This time it was a river-worn piece of crude red jasper half the size of an egg. I slipped it into my pocket to add to my rock collection on the shelf in the schoolroom. Then I mounted and nudged Sirlofty to catch up with Chafer.

We rode on, stopping on a tall scarp that looked out over the lazily flowing Tefa River. From where we sat our mounts we could look down at my father's cotton fields. There were four of them, counting the one that rested fallow this year. It was easy to tell which field was in its third year of cultivation and close to its end of agricultural usefulness. The plants there were stunted and scrubby. Prairie land seldom bore well for more than three years running. Next year, that field would lie fallow, in the hope of reviving it.

My father's holdings, Widevale, were a direct grant to him from King Troven. They spanned both sides of the Tefa River and many acres beyond in all directions. The land on the north side of the river was reserved for his immediate family and closest servants. Here he had built his manor house and laid out his orchards and cotton fields and pasturage. Some day, the Burvelle estate and manor would be a well-known landmark like the 'old Burvelle' holdings near Old Thares. The house and grounds and even the trees were younger than I was.

My father's ambition extended beyond having a fine manor house and agricultural holdings. On the south side of the river, my father had measured out generous tracts of land for the vassals he recruited from amongst the soldiers who had once served under his command. The town had become a much-needed retirement haven for foot soldiers and non-commissioned officers when they mustered out of the service. My father had intended that it be so. Without Burvelle's Landing, or simply Burvelle as it was most often called, many of the old soldiers would have gone back west to the cities, to become charity cases or worse. My father often said that it was a shame that no system existed to utilize the skills of soldiers too old or too maimed to soldier on. Born to be a soldier and an officer, my father had assumed the mantle of lord when the king granted it, but he wore it with a military air. He still held himself responsible for the well-being of his men.

The 'village' his surveyors had laid out on the south bank of the river had the straight lines and the fortification points of a fortress. The dock and the small ferry that operated between the north and south banks of the river ran precisely on the hour. Even the six-day market there operated with a military precision, opening at dawn and closing at sundown. The streets had been engineered so that two wagons could pass one another, and a horse and team could turn round in any intersection. Straight roads like the spokes of a wheel led out of the village to the carefully measured allotments that each vassal earned by toiling four days a week on my father's land. The village thrived and threatened soon to become a town, for the folk had the added benefit of the traffic along the river and on the river road that followed the shoreline. His old soldiers had brought their wives and families with them when they came to settle. Their sons would, of course, go off to become soldiers in their days. But the daughters stayed, and my mother was instrumental in bringing to the town young men skilled in needed trades who welcomed the idea of brides who came with small dowries of land. Burvelle Landing prospered.

Traffic between the eastern frontier and old Fort Renalx to the west of us was frequent along the river road. In winter, when the waters of the river ran high and strong, barges laden with immense, sap-heavy spond logs from the wild forests of the east moved west with the current, to return later laden with essential supplies for the forts. Teams of barge mules had worn a dusty trail on the south bank of the river. In summer, when the depleted river did not offer enough water to keep the barges from going aground, mule-drawn wagons replaced them. Our village had a reputation for honest taverns and good beer; the teamsters always stopped there for the night.

But today the seasonal traffic that crawled the road was not so convivial. The slow parade of men and wagons stretched out for half a mile. Dust hung in the wake of their passage. Armed men rode up and down the lines. Their distant shouts and the occasional crack of a whip were carried to us on the light wind from the river.

Three or four times each summer, the coffle trains would pass along the river road. They were not welcome to stop in the village. Not even the guards who moved the coffle along could take the ferry across to my father's well-run town. Hours down the road, out of view of both my home and the village, there were six open-sided sheds, a fire pit and watering troughs set up for the coffle trains. My father was not without mercy, but he distributed it on his own terms.

My father had strictly forbidden my sisters to witness the passing of the penal trains, for the prisoners included rapists and perverts as well as debtors, pickpockets, whores, and petty thieves. There was no sense in exposing my sisters to such rabble, but on that day Sergeant Duril and I sat our horses for the better part of an hour, watching them wend their dusty way along the river road. He did not say that my

34

father had wished me to witness that forced emigration to the east, but I suspected it was so. Soon enough, as a cavalry trooper, I'd have to deal with those whom King Troven had sentenced to be settlers on the lands around his eastern outposts. My father would not send me to that duty ignorant.

Two supply wagons led the penal coffle making its centipedian way toward us. Mounted men patrolled the length of the winding column of shackled prisoners. At the very end, choking their way through the hanging dust, teams of mules pulled three more wagons laden with the women and children that belonged to the convicts trudging their way toward a new life. When a trick of the wind carried the sounds of the prisoners to us, they sounded more animal than human. I knew that the men would be chained, day and night, until they reached one of the King's far posts on the frontier. They'd be fed bread and water, and know a respite from their journey only on the Sixday of the good god.

'I feel sorry for them,' I said softly. The heat of the day, the chafing shackles, the dust; sometimes it seemed a miracle to me that any of the criminal conscripts survived their long march to the borderlands.

'Do you?' Sergeant Duril was disdainful of my soft sentiment. 'I feel sorrier for the ones left behind in the city, to continue being scum the rest of their lives. Look at them, Nevare. The good god decrees for every man what he is to do. But those down there, they scoffed at their duty, and ignored the skills of their fathers. Now the King offers them a second chance. When they left Old Thares, they were prisoners and criminals. If they weren't caught and hanged, they'd probably be killed by their fellows, or live out their lives like rats in a wall. But King Troven has sent them away from all that. They'll walk a long hard way, to be sure, but it's a new life that awaits them in the east. By the time they get there, they'll have built some muscle and endurance. They'll work on the King's Road for a year or so, pushing it across the plains and then they'll have earned the right to their freedom and two acres of land. Not bad wages for a couple of years of toil. King Troven's given them all a new chance to be better than they were, to own land of their own and to live a clean life, to follow in their fathers' trades as they should have done, with their old crimes forgotten. You feel sorry for them? What about the ones who refuse the King's mercy, and end up with the chopping block taking their thieving hands off, or living in debtors' prison with their wives and little ones alongside them? Those are the ones I pity, the ones too stupid to see the opportunity our king offers them. No. I don't pity those men down there. They walk a hard road, and no mistake, but it's a better road than the one they originally chose for themselves.'

I looked down at the ragged line of chained men and wondered how many truly felt it had been their own decision to choose this course. And what of the women and children in the wagons? Had they had any choice at all? I might have pondered longer if Duril had not distracted me with the terse word, 'Messenger!'

I lifted my eyes and looked toward the east. The river snaked off into the distance, and the river road followed its winding course beside it. Passenger coaches, freight wagons and the post travelled that road. Ordinary mail travelled in wagons for the most part; letters to soldiers from their families and sweethearts in the west and their replies. But King Troven's couriers travelled that road as well, bearing important dispatches between the far outposts and the capital in Old Thares. Part of my father's duty to his king as a landed noble was to maintain a relay station and the change of horses for the messengers. Often the dispatch riders were invited up to my father's manor for the evening after they had passed on their messages, for my father enjoyed being kept up to date on events at the frontier, and the messengers were glad of his generous hospitality in the harsh land. I hoped we would have company for the evening meal; it always enlivened the conversation.

Along the river road a man and horse were coming at a gallop. A thin line of dust hung in the still air behind them, and the horse was running heavily in a way that spoke more of spurs and quirt than willing effort. Even at our distance, I could see the billowing of the rider's short yellow cape that marked him as the King's courier, and notified every citizen of the duty to speed him on his way.

The watcher at the relay station below us had spotted the oncoming rider. I heard the clanging of the bell and in the next moment the inhabitants of the station sprang into action. One ran into the stable, to emerge almost immediately leading a long-legged horse wearing a tiny courier's saddle. He held the fresh mount at the ready, while another man dashed out from the station bearing a waterskin and a packet of food for the rider. A fresh rider emerged, his face already swathed against the dust, his short bright yellow cape flapping in the river wind. He stood by his mount and waited for the message to be passed to him.

We watched as the messenger approached the station and then saw a frightening thing. The messenger only pulled in when his horse was abreast of the fresh mount. His feet never touched the ground as he lunged from one saddle to the next. He shouted something to the waiting men, leaned down to snatch up the packet of provisions and waterskin, and then set spurs to the new horse. In an instant he was gone, galloping down the centre of the road and through the penal coffle. Shackled men and mounted guards surged out of his way as he passed. There were angry shouts and cries as a section of the chained men were trampled by one of the mounted guards when they did not get out of the way quickly enough to avoid the horse. Heedless of the milling chaos in his wake, the courier was already dwindling to a tiny figure on the ribbon of road leading west. I stared after him for a moment, and then glanced back down at the relay station. A stable-man was trying to lead the messenger's horse, but the animal went suddenly down on his front knees, and then rolled onto his side in the dust. He lay there, kicking vaguely at the air.

'His wind's broke,' Duril said sagely. 'He'll never carry a courier again. Poor beast will be lucky if he lives.'

'I wonder what desperate message he bore, that he rode his horse to death and could not pass it on to a fresh rider.' My mind was already full of possibilities. I visualized night attacks by the Specks on the Wildlands border towns, or fresh uprising amongst the Kidona.

'King's business,' Sergeant Duril said tersely.

As we watched, we saw one of the men break free of the group, running toward the manor with something in his hand. A separate message for my father? He knew most of the commanders of the forts on the eastern boundary, and he was kept almost as well appraised of conditions on the frontier as the King himself. I saw curiosity light in the old sergeant's eyes. Duril glanced at the sun and announced abruptly, 'Time for you to go in to your books. We don't want Master Quills-and-Ink to be looking at me nasty again, do we?'

And with that, he turned his horse's head away from the river, the road, and the relay station and led me at an easy lope back to the trail that led down to my father's manor house.

My boyhood home was set on a gentle rise of land that overlooked the river. In an indulgence of my mother, my father had planted scattered trees for two acres around it, poplar and oak and birch and alder. Water hauled up from the river irrigated the trees that both shaded the house and grounds and provided a windbreak from the constant wind. It was a little island of trees in the vast expanse of prairie all around us, green and shady and inviting. Sometimes I thought it looked small and isolated. At other times, it seemed like a green fortress of welcome in the windswept, arid lands. We rode toward it, the horses eager now for cool water and a good roll in the paddock.

As Sergeant Duril had predicted, my tutor was standing outside the manor awaiting us. Master Rissle's arms were crossed on his narrow chest and he was trying to look forbidding. 'Hope he don't wallop ye too hard for being late, young Nevare. Looks like he could be cruel harsh, him so big and all,' Duril said in quiet derision before we were in earshot of the man. I kept my face straight at his gentle gibe. He knew he should not mock my tutor, an earnest but scrawny young scholar come all the way from Old Thares to teach me penmanship and history and figuring and astronomy. Although Duril would not curb his own disrespectful tongue, he would freely cuff me for daring to smile at it. So I held my amusement inside as I dismounted. I called a farewell to Sergeant Duril as he led our mounts away, and he answered with a vague wave of his hand.

I longed to run and find my father, to discover what news had been so urgent, but I knew that if I did, I would only bring punishment down on myself. A good soldier did his duty, and waited for orders from above without speculating. If I ever hoped to command men, I must first learn to accept authority. I sighed and followed my tutor off to my lessons. The academics seemed more tedious than ever that day. I tried to apply myself, knowing that the foundation I built now would support my studies at the King's Academy.

When the long afternoon of lessons were over and my tutor finally released me, I dressed for dinner and descended. We might live far from any cities or polite society on the plains, but my mother insisted that all of us observe the proprieties appropriate to my father's station. Both my parents had been born into noble houses. As younger offspring, they had never expected to hold titles themselves, but their upbringing had left them with a keen awareness of what my father's elevation to lordship required of them. Only later would I appreciate all the courtesy and manners that my mother had instilled in me, for those lessons enabled me to move more easily at the Academy than did many of my rustic counterparts.

Our family gathered in the sitting room until my father entered. Then he escorted my mother into the dining room and we children followed. I seated my younger sister Yaril while Rosse, my elder brother, held a chair for my elder sister Elisi. Vanze, the youngest at nine years old and my father's priest son, said the blessing for all of us. Then my mother rang the tiny silver bell beside her place setting, and the servants began to bring in the food.

Our family was 'new nobility', my father elevated by the King himself to lordship for his valour in the wars against the plainspeople. For this reason, we had no dynasty of family servants. My mother was afraid of plainspeople and my father did not approve of them mingling with his daughters as servants in our household, so unlike many of the new nobility we had no servants from the conquered peoples. Instead, he offered house and grounds employment to the cream of his retired soldiers and their wives and daughters. This meant that most of the male servants in our household were elderly or crippled in some way that had left them unfit for military service. My mother would have preferred to hire servants from the cities in the west, but in this my father prevailed, saying that he felt a duty to provide for his men and give them a share of his own good fortune, for without them to lead to glory he never would have merited the King's notice. So, my mother bowed her head to his will and did her best to school them in the proper ways of serving. She had taken it upon herself, in a few instances, to advertise in the western cities for suitable husbands from the serving classes for the soldiers' daughters, and in this way we had acquired two young men who could properly wait a table, a valet for my father, and a butler.

I managed to contain my curiosity throughout most of the meal. My father spoke to my mother of his orchards and crops and she nodded gravely. She asked his permission to send to Old Thares for a proper tiring-maid for my sisters, now that they were both becoming young ladies. He replied that he would think about it, but I saw him looking at my sisters with a sudden awareness that Elisi was approaching marriageable age and would benefit from greater sophistication in her manners.

As he did at every evening meal, he asked each of his off-spring in turn how we had employed our day. Rosse, my elder brother and the heir, had ridden down with our steward to visit the Bejawi settlement at the far north end of Widevale. The remnants of one branch of the formerly migratory people lived there at my father's sufferance. When my father had first taken them in, the villagers had been mostly women, children and grandfathers too old to have fought in the Plains War. Now the children were young men and women, and my father wished to be sure they had useful tasks to occupy them and content them. There had been news from the Swick Reaches of an uprising of young warriors who had become discontented with settled ways. My father had no desire to see a similar restlessness in his nomads. He had recently gifted the Bejawi with a small herd of milk goats, and Rosse was pleased to report that the animals were thriving and providing both occupation and sustenance for the former hunters.

Elisi, my elder sister was next. She had mastered a difficult piece of music on her harp, and begun an embroidery of a Writ verse on a large hoop. She had also sent a letter to the Kassler sisters at Riverbend, inviting them to spend Midsummer week with us, planning a picnic, music, and fireworks in the evening of her sixteenth birthday. My father agreed that it sounded like a most pleasant holiday for Yaril and her and their friends.

Then it was my turn. I spoke first of my studies with my tutor, and then of my exercises with Duril. And then, almost as an afterthought, I mentioned that we had seen the messenger and cautiously added that I was very curious as to what could prompt such cruel haste. It was not quite a question, but it hung in the air, and I saw both Rosse and my mother hoping for an answer.

My father took a sip of his wine. 'There is an outbreak of disease in the east, at one of the farthest outposts. Gettys is in the foothills of the Barrier Mountains. The messenger asks for reinforcements to replace the victims, healers to nurse the sick and guards to bury the dead and patrol the cemetery.'

Rosse was bold enough to speak. 'It seems an urgent message and yet not, perhaps, one of such urgency to require the messenger to continue with the task himself.'

My father gave him a disapproving look. He obviously regarded rampant sickness and men dying in droves as inappropriate topics for discussion at table with his wife and young daughters. Quite possibly he considered it a military matter, and not a topic to be lightly discussed until King Troven had decided how best to deal with it. I was surprised when he actually replied to Rosse's observation. 'The medical officer for Gettys is, I fear, a superstitious man. He has sent a separate report, to the Queen, full of his usual speculations about magical influences from the native peoples of that region, stipulating that it not leave the messenger's hand until he delivered it to her. Our queen, it is said, has an interest in matters of the supernatural, and rewards those who send her new knowledge. She has promised a lordship to anyone who can offer her proof of life beyond the grave.'

My mother made bold to speak, I think for the benefit of my sisters. 'I do not regard such topics as appropriate for a lady to pursue. I am not alone in this. I have had letters from my sister and from Lady Wrohe, expressing the discomfort they felt when the Queen insisted they join her for a spirit-summoning session. My sister is a sceptic, saying it is all a trick by the so-called mediums who hold these sessions but Lady Wrohe wrote that she witnessed things she could not explain and it gave her nightmares for a month.' She looked from Elisi, who appeared properly scandalized to Yaril, whose grey-blue eyes were round with interest. To Yaril, she added the comment, 'We ladies are often considered to be flighty, ignorant creatures. I would be shamed if any of my daughters became caught up in such unnatural pursuits. If one wishes to study metaphysics, the first thing one should do is read the holy texts of the good god. In the Writ is all we need to know of the afterlife. To demand proof of it is presumptuous and an affront to the deity.'

That seemed properly to quench Yaril. She sat silent while my younger brother Vanze reported that he had worked on reading a difficult passage in the holy texts in the original Varnian and then meditated for two hours on it. When my father asked how Yaril had employed her day, she spoke only of mounting three new butterflies in her collection and of tatting enough lace to trim her summer shawl. Then, looking at her plate, she asked timorously, 'Why must they guard the cemetery at Gettys?'

My father narrowed his eyes at her circling back to a topic he had dismissed. He answered curtly, 'Because the Specks do not respect our burial customs and have been known to profane the dead.'

Yaril's little intake of breath was so slight that I am sure I was the only one who heard it. Like her, my interest was more piqued than satisfied by my father's reply, but as he immediately asked my mother how her day had progressed, I knew it was hopeless even to wonder.

And so that dinner came to a close, with coffee and a sweet, as all our dinners did. I wondered more about the Specks than I did about the mysterious plague. None of us could know then that the plague was not a one-time blight of disease, but would return to the outposts, summer after summer, and would gradually strike deeper and deeper into the western plains country.

During that first summer of contagion, awareness of the Speck plague slowly seeped into my life and coloured my concept of the borderlands. I had known that the farthest outposts of the King's cavalry were now at the foothills of the Barrier Mountains. I knew that the ambitious King's Road being built across the plains pushed ever closer to the mountains, but it was expected to take four more years to be completed. Since I was small I had heard tales of the mysterious and elusive Specks, the dappled people who could only live happily in the shadows of their native forest. Tales of them were, to my childish ears, little different to the tales of pixies and sprites that my sisters so loved. The very name of the people had crept into our language as a synonym for 'inattentive'; to do a Speck's day of work meant to do almost nothing at all. If I were caught day-dreaming over my books, my tutor might ask me if I were Speck-touched. I had grown up in the belief that the distant Specks were a harmless and rather silly folk who inhabited the glens and vales of the thickly forested mountains that, to my prairie-raised imagination, were almost as fantastic as the dappled folk who dwelt there.

But in that summer, my image of the Specks changed. They came to represent insidious disease, a killing plague that came, perhaps, simply from wearing a fur bought from a Speck trader or wafting one of the decorative fans they wove from the lace vines that grew in their forest. I wondered what they did to our graveyards, how they 'profaned' the dead. Instead of elusive, I now thought of them as furtive. Their mystery became ominous rather than enchanting, their lifestyle grubby and pest-ridden rather than primitively idyllic. A sickness that merely meant a night or two of fever for a Speck child devastated our outposts and outlying settlements, slaughtering by the score hearty young men in the prime of their youth.

Yet horrifying as the rumours of widespread death were to us, it was still a distant disaster. The stories we heard were like the tales of the violent windstorms that sometimes struck coastal cities far to the south of Gernia. We did not doubt the truth of them but we did not feel dread. Like the occasional uprisings amongst the conquered plainspeople, we knew they brought death and disaster, yet it was something that happened only on the new borders of the wild lands, out where our king's horse still struggled to man the outposts, manage the more savage plainspeople and push back the wilderness to make way for civilization. It did not threaten our croplands and flocks in Widevale. Deaths from violence and privation and disease and mishap were the lot of the soldier. They entered the service, well aware that many would not live to retire from it. The plague seemed but another enemy that they must face stout-heartedly. I had faith that, as a people, we would prevail. I also knew that my current duty was to worry about my studies and training. Problems such as plainspeople uprising, Speck plagues and rumours of locusts were for my father to manage, not me.

In the weeks that followed, my father discouraged discussion of the plague, as if something about the topic were obscene or disgusting. His discouragement only fired my curiosity. Several times, Yaril brought me gossip from her friends, tales of Specks unearthing dead soldiers to perform hideous rites with the poor bodies. Some whispered of cannibalism and even more unspeakable desecration. Despite my mother's discouragement, Yaril was as avariciously inquisitive about Specks and their wild magic as I was, and there were evenings when we passed our time in the shadowy garden, frightening one another with our ghoulish speculations.

The closest I came to having that curiosity indulged was one night the next summer when I overheard a conversation between my father and my elder brother Rosse. I was feeling a boy's pique at being excluded from the domain of men. A scout had ridden in that morning and stopped to pass the day with my father. I had learned that he was taking his three-years leave, and intended to spend his three months of earned leisure in a journey to the cities of the west and back again. Scout Vaxton knew my father from years back, when they had served together in the Kidona campaign. They had both been young men then. Now my father was a noble and retired from the military, but the old scout toiled on for his king.

Scouts held a unique place in the King's Cavalla. They were officers without official rank. Some were ordinary soldiers whose abilities had advanced them through the ranks to the duty of scouts. Others, it was rumoured, were noble-born soldier sons who had disgraced themselves, and had to find a way to serve the good god as soldiers without using their family names. There was an element of romance and adventure to everything I'd ever heard about scouts. Uniformed officers were supposed to treat them with respect, and my father seemed to hold Scout Vaxton in esteem, yet did not think him a worthy dining companion for his wife, daughters, and younger sons.

The grizzled old man fascinated me, and I had longed to listen to his talk, but only my eldest brother had been invited to take the noon meal with Scout Vaxton and my father. By mid-afternoon, the scout had ridden on his way, and I had looked longingly after him. His dress was a curious combination of cavalry uniform and plainspeople garb. The hat he wore was from an older generation of uniform, and supplemented with a bright kerchief that hung down the back of his neck to keep the sun off. I'd only glimpsed his pierced ears and tattooed fingers. I wondered if he'd adopted plainspeople ways in order to be accepted amongst them and learn more of their secrets, the better to scout for our horse soldiers in times of unrest. I knew he was a ranker, and truly not a fit dinner companion for my mother and sisters, and yet I had hoped that as a future officer, my father would include me at their meal. He hadn't. There was no arguing with him about it, and even at dinner that evening he'd said little of the scout, other than that Vaxton now served at Gettys and found the Specks far more difficult to infiltrate than the plainspeople had been.

Rosse and my father had retired to my father's study for brandy and cigars after dinner. I was still too young to be included in such manly pursuits, so I was walking off my meal with a sullen stroll about the gardens. As I passed the tall windows of the study, open to the sultry summer night, I overheard my father say, 'If they indulge in filthy practices, then they deserve to die of them. It's that simple, Rosse, and the good god's will.'

The repugnance in my father's voice brought me to a silent halt. My father was a man satisfied with his life, content with his land and his gentleman farming. He had survived his hard days as a soldier son and a cavalla officer, had risen to become one of King Troven's new nobles and wore that mantle well. I seldom heard him speak with anger about anything, and even more rare was it to hear him so thoroughly disgusted. I drew closer to the house until I stood outside the gently blowing curtains and listened, aware that it was gravely rude to do so but still fascinated. Around me, the dry warm evening was filled with the chirring of insects from the fields.

'Then you think the rumours are true? That the plague comes from sexual congress with the Specks?' My brother, usually so calm a fellow, was horrified. I found myself creeping closer to the window. At that age, I had no personal experience of sexual congress at all. I was shocked to hear my brother and father bluntly speaking of such perversions as coupling with a lesser race. Like any lad of my years, I was consumed with curiosity about such things. I held my breath and listened.

'How else?' my father asked heavily. 'The Specks are a vermin-ridden folk, living in the deep shadows under the trees until their skin mottles from lack of sunlight, like cheese gone to mould. Turn over a log in a bog and you'll find better living conditions than what the Specks prefer. Yet their women, when young, can be comely, and to those soldiers of low intellect and less breeding they seem seductive and exotic. The penalty for such congress was a flogging when I was stationed on the edge of the Wilds. Distances were kept, and we had no plague.

'Now that General Brodg has taken over as commander in the east, discipline is more lax. He is a good soldier, Rosse, a damn fine soldier, but blood and breeding have thinned in his line. He made his rank honestly and I do not begrudge him that, though some still say that the King insulted the nobly born soldier sons when he raised a common soldier to the rank of general. I myself say that the King has the right to promote whom he pleases, and that Brodg served him as well as any living man. But as a ranker rather than an officer born, he has far too much sympathy for the common soldier. I suspect he hesitates to apply proper punishment for transgressions that he himself may once have indulged in.'

My brother spoke but I could not catch his words. My father's disagreement was in his tone. 'Of course, one can sympathize with what the common soldier must endure. A good commander must be aware of the privations his men face, without condoning their plebeian reactions to them. One of the functions of an officer is to raise his men's standards to his own; not to make so many allowances for their failings that they have no standards to aspire to.'

I heard my father rise and I shrank back into the shadows under the window, but his ponderous steps carried him to the sideboard. I heard the chink of glass on glass as he poured. 'Half our soldiery these days are conscripts and slum scrapings. Some see little honour in commanding such men, but I will tell you that a good officer can make a silk purse out a sow's ear, if given a free hand to do so! In the old days, any noble's second son was proud to have the chance to serve his king, proud to venture into the wilds and drag civilization

48

along in his footsteps. Now the Old Nobles keep their soldier sons close to home. They "soldier" by totting up columns of numbers and patrolling the grounds of the summer palace at Thares as if those were true tasks for an officer. The common foot soldiers are worse, as much rabble as troops these days, and I've heard tales of gambling, drinking and whoring in the border settlements that would have made old General Prode weep with fury. He never permitted us to have anything to do with the plainspeople beyond trade, and they were an honourable warrior folk before we subdued them. Now some regiments employ them as scouts, and even bring the females into their households as maids for their wives or nursemaids for their children. No good can come of that mingling, neither to the plainspeople nor us. It will make them hungry for all they don't have, and envy can lead to an uprising. But even if it doesn't come to that, the two races were never meant to traffic with one another in that way.'

My father was gathering momentum as he spoke. I am sure he did not realize that he had raised his voice. His words carried clearly to my ears.

'With the Specks, it is even more true. They are a slothful people, too lazy even to have a culture of their own. If they can find a dry spot to sleep at night and dig up enough bugs to fill their bellies by day why, then they are well content. Their villages are little more than a few hammocks and a cook fire. Little wonder that they have all sorts of diseases amongst them. They pay such things no more mind than they do to the shiny little parasites that cling to their necks. Some of their children die, the rest live, and they go on breeding as happily as a tree full of monkeys. But when their diseases cross over to our folk, well . . . Well, then you have just what you have heard from that scout: an entire regiment sickened, half of them like to die, and the plague now spreading among the women and children of the settlement. And probably all because some low-born conscript wanted something a bit stranger or stronger than the honest whores at the fort brothel.'

My brother said something I could not quite hear, a query in his voice. My father gave a snort of laughter in reply. 'Fat? Oh, I've heard those tales for years. Scare stories, I think, told to new troopers to keep them out of the forest edge of an evening. I've never seen one. And if the plague indeed works so, well, then, good. Let them be marked by it, so all may know or guess what they've been doing. Perhaps the good god in his wisdom chooses to make an example of them, that all may know the wages of sin.'

My brother had risen and followed my father to the sideboard. 'Then you don't believe,' and I heard the caution in my brother's voice, as if he feared my father would think him foolish, 'that it could be a Speck curse, a sort of evil magic they use against us?' Almost defensively, he added, 'I heard the tale from an itinerant priest who had tried to take the word of the good god to the Specks. He was passing through the Landing on his way back west. He told me that the Specks drove him away, and one of their old women threatened that if we did not leave them in peace, their magic would loose disease amongst us.'

I, too, thought my father would laugh at him or rebuke him. But my father replied solemnly, 'I've heard tales of Speck magic, just as you have, I'm sure. Most of those stories are nonsense, son, or the foolish beliefs of a natural people. Yet, at the bottom of each, there may be some small nugget of truth. The good god who keeps us left pockets of strangeness and shadow in the world he inherited from the old gods. Certainly, I've seen enough of plains magic to tell you that, yes, they have wind-wizards who can make rugs float upon the wind and smoke flow where they command it, regardless of how the wind blows, and I myself have seen a garrotte fly across a crowded tavern and wrap around the throat of a soldier who had insulted a wind-wizard's woman. When the old gods left this world, they left bits of their magic behind for the folk who preferred to dwell in their dark rather than accept the good god's light. But bits of it are all that they have left. Cold iron defeats and contains it. Shoot a plainsman with iron pellet, and his charms are worthless against us. The magic of the plains-people worked for generations, but in the end, it was just magic. Its time is past. It wasn't strong enough to stand against the forces of civilization and technology. We are coming up on a new age, son. Like it or not, all of us must move into it, or be churned into the muck under the wheels of progress. The introduction of Shir bloodlines to our plough horses coupled with the new split-iron ploughs has doubled what a farmer can keep under cultivation. Half of Old Thares has pipe drains now, and almost every street in the city is cobbled now. King Troven has put mail and passenger coaches on a schedule, and regulated the flow of trade on all the great rivers. It has become quite the fashion to travel up the Soudana River to Canby, and then enjoy the swift ride down on the elegant passenger jank-ships. As travellers and tourists venture east, population will follow. Towns will become cities in your lifetime. Times are changing, Rosse. I intend that Widevale change with them. A disease like this Speck plague is just a disease. Nothing more. Eventually, some doctor will get to the root of it, and it will be like shaking fever or throat rot. For the one, it was powdered kenzer bark, for the other, gargling with gin. Medicine has come a long way in the last twenty years. Eventually, a cure will be found for this Speck plague, or a way to avoid catching it. Until then, we mustn't imagine it is anything more than an illness, or like a child turning a stray sock into a bugaboo under his cot, we'll become too frightened of it to look at it closely.' Almost as an aside, he added, 'I wish our monarch had chosen a mate a bit less prone to flights of fancy. Her majesty's fascination with hocus-pocus and "messages from beyond" has done much to spur the popular interest in such nonsense.'

I heard my brother's lighter tread as he approached the

window. He spoke carefully, well aware that my father tolerated no treasonous criticism of our king. 'I am sure that you are right, Father. Disease must be fought with science, not charms and amulets. But I fear that some of the guilt for the conditions that welcome disease must be laid at our own door. Some say that our frontier towns have become foul places since the King decreed that debtors and criminals might redeem themselves by becoming settlers. I've heard that they are places of crime and vice and filth, where men live like rats amidst their own waste and garbage.'

My father was silent for a time, and I've no doubt that my brother held his breath, awaiting a paternal rebuke. But instead my father replied reluctantly, 'It may be that our king has erred on the side of mercy with them. You would think that given the opportunity to begin anew, in a new land, all past sins and crimes erased, they would choose to build homes and raise families and leave their dirty ways behind. Some do, and perhaps those few are worth the trouble and expense of the coffles. If one man in ten can rise above a sordid past, maybe we should be willing to accept failure with the other nine as the price of saving the one. After all, can we expect King Troven to succeed with scum who will not heed even the teachings of the good god? What can one do with a man who will not reach out to save himself?'

My father's voice had hardened, and I well knew what lecture would follow. He believed that a man determined his own fate, regardless of the class or circumstances he was born into. He himself was an example of this. He was the second son of a noble family, and thus society expected only that he become an officer in the military and serve his king and his country. And so he had, but with service so exemplary that he had been one of those the King had chosen to elevate to the status of lord. He was not asking of any man any more than that which he had demanded of himself.

I waited for him to explain this, yet again, to my brother,

but instead it was my mother's raised voice that reached my ears. She was calling to my sisters in their garden retreat. 'Elisi! Yaril! Come in, my dears! The mosquitoes will make you all over blotches if you stay out much later tonight!'

'Coming, Mother!' my sisters called, their obedience and reluctance both evident in their tone. I did not blame them. Father had had an ornamental pond dug for them that summer, and it had become their favourite evening retreat. Strings of paper lanterns provided a pleasant glow without drowning out the stars above them. There was a small gazebo, the latticed walls laced with vines, and the walks around it had been landscaped with all sorts of fragrant night-blooming bushes. It had been quite an engineering project to find a way to keep the pond filled, and one of the gardener's boys had to guard it nightly to keep the little wild cats of the region from devouring the expensive ornamental fish that now inhabited it. My sisters took great pleasure in sitting by the pond, weaving dreams of the homes and families that they would some day possess. Often I shared those evening conversations with them.

I knew that mother calling them meant that she would next be wondering what had become of me, and so I slipped from my hiding place and followed the gravel path around to the main door of our manor house and slipped inside and up to my schoolroom. I gave no more thought to the Speck plague at that time, but the next day I had many questions for Sergeant Duril about whether he thought the quality of foot soldiers had declined since the days when he and my father had served together along the borders. As I might have expected, he told me that the quality of the soldier directly reflected the quality of the officer who commanded him, and that the best way for me to ensure that those who followed me were upright was to be an upright man myself.

Even though I had heard such advice before, I took it to heart.

THREE

Dewara

The seasons turned and I grew. In the long summer of my twelfth year, it had taken all of Sirlofty's patience and every bit of spring that my boyish legs possessed for me to fling myself onto his back from the ground. By the time I was fifteen, I could place my hands flat on my mount's back and lever myself gracefully onto him without scrabbling my feet across him. It was a change that we both enjoyed.

There had been other changes as well. My scrawny, petulant tutor had been replaced twice over as my father's requirements for my education had stiffened. I had two instructors now for my afternoon lessons, and I no longer dared to be tardy for them. One was a wizened old man with severely bound white locks and yellow teeth, who taught me tactics, logic, and to write and speak Varnian, the formal language of our ancient motherland, all with the liberal use of a very flexible cane that never seemed to leave his hand. I believe that Master Rorton's diet consisted mostly of garlic and peppers and he nearly drove me mad by constantly standing at my shoulder watching every stroke of my pen as I hunched at my desk.

Master Leibsen was a hulking fellow from the far west who taught me both the theory and practice of my weapons. I could shoot straight now, both standing and mounted, with pistol and long gun. He taught me to measure powder as accurately by eye as most men could with a balance, and how to pour my own ball shot as well as maintain and repair my weapons. That was only lead ball, of course. The more expensive iron shot that had helped us defeat the plainspeople had to be turned out by a competent smith. My father saw no reason for me to be using it up on targets. From Master Leibsen I also learned boxing, wrestling, staves, fencing and, very privately after many entreaties on my part, to both throw and fight with knives. I relished my lessons with Leibsen as much as I detested the long afternoons with Master Rorton of the foul breath.

I had one other teacher in the spring of my sixteenth year. He did not last long and yet he was the most memorable of them. He stayed briefly, pitching his small tent in the shelter of a hollow near the river and never once approached the manor house. My mother would have been both terrified and offended if she had known of his presence, scarcely two miles away from her tender daughters. He was a plains savage and my father's ancient enemy.

On the day I was to meet Dewara, I rode out innocently with my father and Sergeant Duril. Occasionally my father invited us on his morning rounds. I thought my ride that morning was such an outing. Usually it was a pleasant ride. We would move leisurely, lunch with one of his overseers, and halt at various cottages and tents to consult with the shepherds and the orchard workers. I took no more than I would usually carry on a pleasure ride. As the spring day was mild, I did not even take a heavy coat, but only my light jacket and my brimmed hat against the bright sunlight. The sort of country we lived in meant that only a fool set out on any ride unarmed. I carried no gun with me that day, but I did have a cavalry sword, worn yet serviceable, at my hip.

My father rode on one side of me, with Sergeant Duril on the other. It felt odd, as if they escorted me somewhere. The sergeant looked sullen. He was often taciturn, but his silence that day was weighted with suppressed disapproval. It was not often that he disagreed with my father about anything, and it filled me with both dread and intense curiosity.

Once we were well away from the house, my father told me that I would meet a Kidona plainsman that day. As he often did when we spoke of specific clans, my father discussed Kidona courtesy, and cautioned me that my meeting with Dewara was a matter for men, not to be discussed later with my mother or sisters, nor even mentioned in their hearing. On the rise above the plainsman's camp, we halted and looked down upon a domed shelter made from humpdeer skins pegged to a wicker frame. The hides had been cured with the hair on so that they shed water. His three riding beasts were picketed nearby. They were the famous black-muzzled, round-bellied, striped-legged mounts that only the Kidona bred. Their manes stood up stiff and black as hearth brushes and their tails reminded me of a cow's more than a horse's. A short distance away, two Kidona women stood patiently next to a two-wheeled cart. A fourth animal shifted disconsolately between the shafts of the high-wheeled vehicle. The cart was empty.

A small smokeless fire burned in front of the tent. Dewara himself, arms folded on his chest, stood looking up at us. He did not notice us as we arrived; he was already standing, looking toward us, as we came into view. The man's prescience made the hair on my arms stand up and I shivered.

'Sergeant, you may wait here,' my father said quietly.

Duril chewed at his upper lip, then spoke. 'Sir, I'd rather be closer. In case I'm needed.'

My father looked at him directly. 'Some things he cannot learn from me or from you. Some things can't be taught to you by a friend; they can only be learned from an enemy.'

'But, sir—'

'Wait here, Sergeant,' my father repeated, and that closed the subject. 'Nevare, you will come with me.' He lifted a hand, palm up, in greeting and the plainsman below returned the sign. Father stirred his horse to a leisurely walk and started down the rise to the Kidona's camp. I glanced at Sergeant Duril, but he was staring past me, mouth set in a flat line. I gave him a nod anyway and then followed my father. At the bottom of the rise, we dismounted and dropped our horses' reins, trusting our well-trained mounts to stand. 'Come when I motion to you,' my father said softly. 'Until then, stand still by the horses. Keep your eyes on me.'

My father approached the plainsman solemnly, and the old enemies greeted one another with great respect. Privately, my father had cautioned me to treat the Kidona with the solemn deference I extended to any of my tutors. As a youth, I should bow my head to my left shoulder when I first greeted him, and never spit in his presence or show my back to him, for such were the courtesies of his people. As my father had bid me, I stood still and waited. I could almost feel Sergeant Duril's stare on us, but I did not look back at him.

The two spoke to one another for a time. Their voices were lowered and they spoke in the trade language, so I caught little of what they said. I could tell only that they spoke of a bargain. At length my father gestured to me. I walked forward and remembered to bow my head to my left shoulder. Then I hesitated, wondering if I should offer to shake hands as well. Dewara did not offer his hand, and so I kept mine by my side. The plainsman did not smile but looked me over frankly as if I were a horse he might buy. I took the opportunity to appraise him as bluntly. I had never before seen a Kidona.

He was smaller and more wiry than the plainsmen I was familiar with. The Kidonas had been hunters, raiders and scavengers rather than herders. They had regarded all the other peoples of the plains as their rightful prey. The other plainsmen had dreaded their attacks. Of all our enemies, the Kidonas had been the most difficult to subdue. They were a hard-natured people. Once, after the Gernian horse troops had defeated the Rew tribe, the Kidona had swept in to raid the demoralized people and carry off what little was left to them. My father spoke of them with head-shaking awe at their savagery. Sergeant Duril still hated them.

During his raiding years, a Kidona man would eat only meat, and some filed their front teeth to points. Dewara had. He wore a cloak woven from narrow strips of light leather, perhaps from rabbits. Some of the strands had been dyed to form a pattern like hoofprints. He wore loose brown trousers and a long-sleeved white robe that came just past his hips. It was belted with a bright strip of beaded braiding. He was shod in low boots of soft grey leather. His head was uncovered, and his steel-grey hair stood out from his head in a short stiff brush that reminded me of a dog's lifted hackles, or perhaps his horse's mane. At his hip hung a short curved blade, the deadly bronze swanneck of his people, as much tool as weapon. The hilt was wrapped in fine braids of human hair in varying shades. When I first met him, I thought they were battle trophies. Later he would explain that such weapons were passed down from father to son, and that the braids of hair were the blessing of his ancestors passed down with the swanneck. Such a blade was sharp enough to be flourished in a battle charge, but sturdy enough to chop meat for the pot. It was a formidable weapon and a utilitarian tool, the finest weapon a Kidona could use without resorting to iron.

After perusing me in silence, Dewara gave his full attention back to my father. They bargained in fluent Jindobe, haggling over the fee the plainsman would charge to instruct me. It was the first time I understood that teaching me was what this encounter was about. My fledgling knowledge of the trade language meant that I had to listen carefully to understand their conversation. First, Dewara demanded guns for his people. My father refused him, but made it a compliment, saying that his warriors were still far too deadly with their swannecks, and that my father's own people would turn on him if he offered the Kidonas distance weapons. That was perfectly true. My father did not mention that the King's law forbade the selling of such weapons to any plainsmen. Dewara would have thought less of him if he had admitted bowing to any rule but his own. Curiously, he did not remind the Kidona that the use of iron would cripple his magic. Though I am certain the man needed no such reminder.

Instead of guns and powder, my father offered loom-woven blankets, bacon, and copper cooking pots. Dewara replied that the last time he had looked, he himself was not a woman to care about blankets and food and cooking. He was surprised that my father bothered about such things. And surely a respected warrior such as my father could obtain at least powder as he wished. My father shook his head. I kept silent. I knew that the law forbade selling gunpowder to any plainsmen. They finally came to an accommodation that involved one bale of the best western tobacco, a dozen skinning knives, and two sacks of lead ball suitable for slings. Despite his expressed disdain for such things, I saw that what really finalized the bartering was my father's offer of a hogshead of salt and one of sugar. Many of the conquered plainspeople had acquired a taste for sugar, an item almost unknown in their diets before then. Added to the previous goods, they made a handsome fee. I risked a sideways glance at his women and found they were gleefully nudging one another and talking behind their splayed hands.

My father and Dewara finalized the agreement Kidona-style, by each tying a knot in a trade thong. Then Dewara turned to me and added a personal codicil to the contract in gruff Jindobe. 'If you complain, I send you home to your mother's house. If you refuse or disobey, I send you home to your mother's house with a notch in your ear. If you flinch or hesitate, I send you home to your mother's house with a notch in your nose. I teach you no more then, and I keep the tobacco, salt, sweet, knives and shot. To this, *you* must agree, stripling.'

My father was looking at me. He did not nod, but I read in his eyes that I should assent. 'I agree,' I told the plainsman. 'I will not complain or disobey or refuse your orders. I will neither hesitate nor flinch.'

The warrior nodded. Then he slapped me hard in the face. I saw the blow coming. I could have dodged it or turned my head to lessen it. I had not expected it, and yet some instinct bade me accept the insult. My cheek stung and I felt blood start from the corner of my mouth. I said nothing as I straightened from the blow. I looked Dewara in the eye. Beyond him, I saw my father's grim look. There were little glints in his eyes. I thought I read pride there as much as anger.

'My son is neither a weakling nor a coward, Dewara. He is worthy of the teaching you will give him.'

'We will see,' Dewara said quietly. He looked at his women and barked something in Kidona. Then he turned back to my father. 'They follow you, get my goods and go back to my home. Today.'

He was challenging my father to question his honour. Would Dewara keep his end of the bargain once he had his trade goods? My father managed to look mildly surprised. 'Of course they will.'

'I keep your son then.' The look he gave me was a measuring one, more chilling than anything I had ever beheld. I'd endured my father's stern discipline and Sergeant Duril's physical challenges and chastisement. This look spoke of colder things. 'Take his horse. Take his knife, and his long knife. You leave him here with me. I will teach him.'

I think that if I could have begged quarter of my father then without humiliating both of us in front of the plainsman, I would have. It was as if I stripped myself to nakedness as I took my sheath knife from my belt and handed it over to my father. I felt numb all over, and wondered what Dewara could teach me that was so important that my father would leave me weaponless in the hands of his old enemy. My father accepted my knife from me without comment. He had spoken of the Kidona ways of survival and understanding one's enemy as being the greatest weapon that any soldier could have. But the cruelty of the Kidona was legendary, and I knew that Dewara himself still bore the scar of the iron ball that had penetrated his right shoulder. My father had shot him, manacled him with iron and then held him as prisoner and hostage during the final months of King Troven's war with the Kidona. It was only due to the cavalry doctor's effort that Dewara had survived both his wound and the poisoning of his blood that followed it. I wondered if he felt a debt of mercy or of vengeance toward my father.

I unbuckled the worn belt that supported the old cavalry sword. I bundled it around the sword to offer it to my father, but at the last moment Dewara leaned forward to seize it from my hands. It was all I could do to keep myself from snatching it back. My father stared at him, his eyes expressionless, as Dewara drew the blade from the sheath and ran his thumb along the flat of it. He gave a sniff of disdain. 'This will do you no good where we go. Leave it here. Maybe, some day, you come back for it.' He took a tight grip on the hilt and thrust the blade into the earth. When he let go of it, it stood there like a grave marker. He dropped the sheath beside it in the dust. A chill went up my spine.

My father did not touch me as he bade me farewell. His paternal gaze reassured me even as he told me, 'Make me proud of you, son.' Then he mounted Steelshanks and led Sirlofty away. He rode away along a gentler path than we had come by, out of consideration for the women who followed him in their high-wheeled cart. I was left standing beside the Kidona with no more than the clothes on my back. I wanted to gaze after them, to see if Sergeant Duril abandoned his watch post and followed them, but I dared

61

not. For all the times I had resented the sergeant's eagle-eyed supervision, that day I longed for a guardian to be looking down on me. Dewara held my gaze, measuring me with his steely grey eyes. After what seemed a long time, for the sound of departing hoofbeats and wheels had faded, he pursed his lips and spoke to me, 'You ride good?'

He spoke broken Gernian. I replied in my equally awkward Jindobe, 'My father taught me to ride.'

Dewara snorted disdainfully, and again spoke to me in Gernian. 'Your father show you, sit on saddle. I teach you ride on *taldi*. Get on.' He pointed at the three creatures. As if they knew we spoke of them, they all lifted their heads and gazed at us. Every single one laid its ears back in displeasure.

'Which *taldi*?' I asked in Jindobe.

'You choose, soldier's boy. I teach you to talk, too, I think.' This last comment he delivered in the trade language. I wondered if I had gained any ground with him by trying to use the trade language. It was impossible to tell from his implacable face.

I chose the mare, thinking she would be the most tractable of the three beasts. She would not let me approach her until I seized her picket line and forced her to stand. The closer I got to them, the more obvious it became to me that these were not true horses, but some similar beast. The female did not whinny, but squealed in protest, a sound that did not seem horse-like at all to me. She bit me twice while I was mounting, once on the arm and once on my leg as I swung onto her. Her dull teeth didn't break the skin but I knew the bruises would be deep and lasting. She snorted, plunged and then wheeled in the midst of my mounting her. With difficulty, I managed to get a seat on her. She turned her head to snap at me again and I moved my leg out of reach. As I did so, she wheeled again, and I felt sure she was deliberately trying to unseat me. I gripped her firmly with my legs and made no sound. She plunged twice more but I stayed on her. I tried to ignore her bad manners, for I did not know how Dewara would react to me disciplining one of his mounts.

'Keeksha!' Dewara exclaimed and she abruptly quieted. I did not relax. Her belly was round and her hide was slick. The only harness she wore was a hackamore. I had ridden bareback before, but not on a creature shaped like her.

Dewara gave a grudging nod. Then he said, 'Her name is Keeksha. You tell her name before you get on, she knows obey you. You don't tell name, she knows you are not allowed. All my horses are so. This way.' He turned to one of the other taldi. 'Dedem. Stand.'

The beast he spoke to put his ears forward and came to meet Dewara. The plainsman mounted the round-bellied stallion casually. 'Follow,' he said, and slapped his animal on the rump. Dedem surged forward, leaping out in an instant gallop. I stared in surprise, and then copied him, giving Keeksha a slap that set her into motion.

For a time, all I could do was cling to Keeksha's mane. I jolted and flopped about on her back like a rag doll tied to a dog's tail. Every time one of her hooves struck, my spine was jolted in a different direction. Twice I was sure I was going to hit the ground, but the mare knew her business better than I did. She seemed to shrug herself back under me. The second time she did it, I abruptly decided to trust her. I shifted my weight and my legs, swaying into her stride and suddenly we moved as one creature. She surged forward and I felt that we almost doubled our speed. Dewara had been dwindling in the distance, headed away from the river and into the wastelands that bordered my father's holding. The land rose there, the rocky hillsides cut by steep-sided gullies prone to sudden flooding during storms. Wind and rain had carved that place. Spindly bushes with grey-green leaves grew from cracks in the rocks carpeted with dull purple lichen. The hooves of his mount cut into the dry earth and left dust hanging in the air for me to breathe. Dewara kept his horse at a dead run across country where I never would have risked Sirlofty. I followed him, sure that soon he must rein in his mount and let the animal breathe, but he did not.

My little mare steadily gained on them. As we entered rougher country, climbing toward the plateaus of the region, it was harder to keep them in constant view. Hollows and mounds rumpled the plain like a rucked blanket. I suspected he was deliberately trying to lose me, and set my teeth, resolved that he would not. I well knew that one misplaced step could break both our necks, but I made no effort to pull Keeksha in and although her sides heaved with her effort, she did not slow on her own but followed the stallion's lead. Her rolling gait ate up the miles.

We had been climbing, in the almost imperceptible way of the plains, and now emerged onto the plateau country. The flats gave way to tall outcroppings of red or white rock in the distance. Scattered trees, stunted and twisted by the constant wind and the erratic rains, offered clues to watercourses long dry. We passed disconnected towers of crumbling stone like rotted teeth in a skull's jaw or the worn turrets of the wind's castle. Hoodoos, my father called them. He'd told me that some of the plainspeople said they were chimneys for the underworld of their beliefs. Dewara rode on. I was parched with thirst and coated with dust when we finally topped a small rise and I saw Dewara and his taldi waiting for us. The plainsman stood beside his mount. I rode Keeksha down and halted before him. I was grateful to slide from her sweaty back. The mare moved three steps away from me, and then dropped to her knees. Horrified, I thought I had foundered the beast, but she merely rolled over onto her back and scratched herself luxuriously on the short, prickly grass that grew in the depression. I thought longingly of my waterskin, still slung on Sirlofty's saddle. Useless to wish for it now.

If Dewara was surprised that I had caught up with him,

he gave no sign of it. He said nothing at all until I cautiously asked, 'What are we going to do now?'

'We are here,' was all he replied.

I glanced about and saw nothing to recommend 'here' over any other arid hollow in the plains. 'Should I tend to the horses?' I asked. I knew that if I had been riding Sirlofty, my father's first admonition would be to look after my mount. 'A horse soldier without his horse is an inexperienced foot soldier,' he'd told me often enough. But Dewara just wet his lips with his tongue and then casually spat to one side. I recognized that he insulted me, but held myself silent.

'Taldi were taldi long before men rode on them,' he observed disdainfully. 'Let them tend to themselves.' His expression implied I was something of a weakling to have been concerned for them.

But the Kidona animals did seem well able to care for themselves. After her scratch, Keeksha heaved herself to her feet and joined Dedem in grazing on the coarse grass. Neither seemed any the worse for their long gallop. Had I put Sirlofty through a similar run, I would have walked him to cool him off and then rubbed him down thoroughly and given him water at careful intervals. The Kidona taldi seemed content with their rough forage and the grit they had rubbed into their wet coats. 'The animals have no water. Neither do I,' I told Dewara after a time.

'They won't die without it. Not today.' He gave me a measuring look. 'And neither will you, soldier's boy.' Coldly he added, 'Don't talk. You don't need to talk. You are with me to listen.'

I started to speak again, but a brusque gesture from him quieted me. An instant later, I recalled his earlier warnings about what he would do if I disobeyed. I sealed my dry lips and, for lack of anywhere to perch, hunkered down on the bare earth. Dewara seemed to be listening intently. He

65

bellied quietly up the side of our hollow, not so far that his head would show over the lip of it, and lay flat there. He closed his eyes and was so still that, except for his expression, I would have thought him sleeping. His intensity warned me to keep still in body as well as voice. After a time, he sat up slowly and turned to me. He gave me a very self-satisfied smile; the row of pointed white teeth in his mouth was a bit unnerving. 'He is lost,' he said.

'Who?' I asked, bewildered.

'Your father's man. Set to watch over you, I think.' His smile was cruel. I think he waited for an expression of dismay from me.

Instead, I was puzzled. Sergeant Duril? Would my father have commanded him to watch over me? Would Duril have done it on his own? Some of my doubts must have shown on my face because Dewara's look became more considering. He came to his feet and walked slowly down the sloping bank toward me. 'You are mine now. The student pays best attention when his life depends on it. Is it so?'

'Yes,' I replied, feeling certain it was true. I wondered uneasily what he meant.

For a long time, it seemed he meant nothing at all. He hunkered down on his heels not far from me. The taldi grazed on the dry forage. The only sounds were the wind blowing over the plain and the occasional crunch of a hoof as the animals shifted and the ceaseless chirring of small insects. In the hollow, the air was still, as if the plain cupped us in the palm of its hand. Dewara seemed to be waiting, but I had no idea for what. I felt I had no choice save to emulate him and wait also. I folded my legs and sat on the hard ground, my face and eyelashes still thick with the fine dust from our ride, and tried to ignore my thirst. He stared at me. From time to time, I met his eyes, but mostly I studied the fine pebbles on the dirt in front of me or gazed at the surrounding terrain. The shadows grew shorter and then began

66

to lengthen again. At last he stood, stretched and walked over to his mount. 'Come,' he said to me.

I followed him. The mare sidled away until I said, 'Keeksha. Stand.' Then she came to me and waited for me to mount. Dewara hadn't waited for us, but at least this time he was walking Dedem instead of galloping away. For a time we trailed him, and then he irritably motioned me to move up and ride beside him. I thought he would want to talk, but that was not it. I suspect he simply didn't like having someone at his back.

We rode on through the rest of the afternoon. I thought he was taking us to water or a better camping site, but when we halted, I saw nothing to recommend the spot. At least our previous stopping place had offered us shelter from the relentless wind. Here, outcroppings of reddish rock nudged up out of the scant soil. Released, the ponies dispiritedly went to browse on some leathery-leaved shrubs. They, too, seemed to think little of Dewara's choice of a stopping place. I turned in a slow circle, surveying the surrounding terrain. Most of what I could see was very similar to what was right at my feet. Dewara had sat down, his back propped against one of the large rocks.

'Should I gather brush for a fire?' I asked him.

'I have no need of a fire. And you have no need to talk.'

That was our evening's conversation. He sat, his back against the rock, while the shadows lengthened and then night flowed slowly across the land. There was no moon that night and the distant stars sparkled ineffectually against the black sky. When it became apparent that Dewara was not moving from where he sat, I found a place where a ledge of rock jutted up from the sand. I scratched out a hollow in the sand beside it, a place big enough for me to lie with my back against the rock, mostly for the warmth that it would hold after the sun went down. I lay down, cushioned my head with my hat and crossed my arms on my chest. For a time I listened to the wind, the horses and the insects.

I woke twice in the night. The first time, I had dreamed of smoked meat so vividly that I could still smell it. The second time it was because I was shivering. I shouldered deeper into my hollow, for there was little else I could do. I wondered exactly what I was supposed to be learning, and then fell asleep again.

Before dawn, sleep vanished and I opened my eyes to lucid awareness. I was chilled, hungry and thirsty, yet none of those things had awakened me. Without moving my head, I shifted my eyes. Dewara had awakened and was standing, a blacker shadowing against the steel grey sky. As I watched, he took another stealthy step toward me. I lowered my eyelids, keeping them only a slit open, wondering if his sight was keen enough to know I was awake. Another step closer. The man could flow like a snake on a dune.

I weighed my options. If I lay still and feigned sleep, I would have the element of surprise on my side. If I lay still and feigned sleep, he would have the element of being above me with his feet under him and his swanneck at his hand. I mentally tested all my muscles, and then came to my feet. Dewara halted where he stood. His expression was guileless. I kept mine as smooth. I bowed my head to my left shoulder and greeted him with, 'It's nearly morning.'

My voice came out as a croak. I cleared my dry throat and added, 'Will we find water today?'

He fluttered his hands, a plainsman's equivalent of a shrug. 'Who can say? That is with the spirits.'

It would have been a silent blasphemy and a coward's choice to let his words stand alone. 'The good god may have mercy on us,' I replied.

'Your good god lives up beyond the stars,' he replied disdainfully. 'My spirits are here, in the land.'

'My good god watches over me and protects me from harm,' I countered.

68

He gave me a withering glance. 'Your good god must be very bored, soldier's boy.'

I took a breath. I did not wish to argue theology with a savage. I decided that the insult was to me, for having a boring life, rather than to the good god. I could let it pass, if I chose to do so. I said nothing, and after a long pause Dewara cleared his throat. 'There is no reason to stay here,' he said. 'It's light enough to ride.'

I had seen no reason to be there at all, but again, I smothered my opinion. I had been riding since I was a small child, but I ached in unexpected muscles from his beast's odd shape. Nevertheless, I dutifully mounted up and followed him, still wondering what it was this man was supposed to be teaching me. I worried that my father was getting a very poor exchange for his trade goods.

Dewara led and I rode beside him. By noon, my need for water had surpassed thirst and was venturing toward privation. My sturdy taldi followed Dewara's gamely, but I knew that she, too, needed water. I had employed every trick that I knew to stave off my thirst. The smooth pebble in my mouth had become more annoying than helpful. I had picked it up when I had dismounted to strip the fleshy leaves from a mules-ear plant. I chewed the thick leaves to fibres, and then spat them out. They did little more than moisten my mouth. My lips and the inside of my nose were dry and cracking. My tongue felt like a piece of thick leather in my mouth. Dewara rode on without speaking to me or betraying any sign of thirst. Hunger returned to pester me, but thirst retained my attention. I watched anxiously for the water signs that Sergeant Duril had taught me – a line of trees, a depression where the plants were thick and greener than usual or animal tracks converging – but I saw only that the land was becoming more barren and even stonier.

There was little I could do other than follow Dewara and trust that he must have some end in mind. When shadows began to lengthen again with still no water in sight, I spoke up. My lips cracked as I formed my words. 'Will we reach water soon?'

He glanced at me, and then made a show of looking all around us. 'It does not seem so.' He smiled at me, showing no effects from our water privation. Without words, we rode on. I could feel the little mare's flagging energy, but she seemed as willing as ever. Evening had begun to ooze across the plains when Dewara reined his mount and looked around. 'We'll sleep here,' he announced.

The location was worse than the previous one. There was not even a rock to sleep against, and only dry browse for the horses, no grass at all.

'You're daft!' I croaked out before I recalled that I was to show this man respect. It was hard to recall anything just then except how thirsty I was.

He was already off his horse. He looked up at me, his face impassive. 'You are to obey me, soldier's boy. Your father said so.'

At the time it seemed that I had no choice except to do as he said. I dismounted from the tubby little mare and looked around. There was nothing to see. If this was some sort of test, I feared I was failing it. As he had the evening before, Dewara sat down cross-legged on the dry earth. He seemed perfectly content to sit there and watch evening turn to full night.

My head ached and I felt my stomach clench with the nausea of unanswered hunger. Well, it would go away soon enough, I told myself. I decided I would make my bed a bit more comfortable than it had been the night before. I picked a place that looked more sandy than stony, at a good distance from Dewara. I had not forgotten his sneaking approach that morning. With my hands, I dug a slight depression in the sand about the size of my body. Curled in it, I could trap my body warmth during the chill of night. I was picking the larger rocks out of the bottom when Dewara stood and stretched.

He walked over to my hole and looked at it disdainfully. 'Planning to lay your eggs soon? It's a fine nest for a sage hen.'

Replying would have required moving my cracked lips, so I let his jibe pass. I could not understand how thirst and hunger affected me so strongly and left him untouched. As if in answer to my thought, he muttered, 'Weakling.' He turned and walked back to his post and squatted down again. Feeling childish, I curled into my hole and closed my gritty eyes. I said my evening prayers silently, asking the good god to grant me strength and help me to discern what my father thought this man could teach me. Perhaps this endurance of privation was how he wished to measure me. Or perhaps this old enemy of my father planned to break his bargain with my father and torment me to my death.

Perhaps my father had been wrong to trust him.

Perhaps I *was* a weakling and a traitor to my father to doubt his judgment. 'Make me proud, son,' he had said. I prayed again for strength and courage, and sought sleep.

In the dark of night, I came awake. I smelled sausages. No. I smelled smoked meat. Foolishness. Then I heard a very small sound: the gurgle of a waterskin. My mind was playing tricks on me. Then I heard it again, and the slosh as it was lowered from Dewara's mouth. It occurred to me that his loose robes could easily conceal such things as a waterskin and a wallet of dried meat. My sticky eyelids clung together as I opened my eyes. There is nothing darker than full night on the Midlands. The stars were distant and uninterested. Dewara was completely invisible to me.

Sergeant Duril had often counselled me that thirst, hunger, and sleeplessness can lead to a man making poor decisions. He said I could add lust to that list when I was a few years closer to full manhood. So now I pondered and then pondered again. Was this a test of my perseverance and endurance? Or had my father been deceived by his old enemy? Should I obey Dewara even if he was leading me to my death? Should I trust my father's judgment or my own? My father was older and wiser than I. But he was not here and I was. I was too weary and too thirsty to think coherently. Yet I must make the decision. Obey or disobey. Trust or distrust.

I closed my eyes. I prayed to the good god for guidance, but heard only the sweep of wind across the plains. I slept fitfully. I dreamed that my father said that if I were worthy to be his son, I could endure this. Then the dream changed, and Sergeant Duril was saying that he'd always known I was stupid, that even the youngest child knew better than to venture out on the plains without water and food. Idiots deserved to die. How many times had he told me that? If a man couldn't figure out how to take care of himself, then let him get himself killed and get out of the way before he brought down his whole regiment. I wandered out of my dream to sleeplessness. I was in the control of a savage who disliked me. I had no food or water. I doubted that there was water within a day's walk of here, or that I could walk a full day without water. Grimness settled on me. I decided to sleep on my decision.

In the creep of dawn, I arose from my hollow in the sand. I went to where Dewara slept. He did not sleep. His eyes were open and watching me. It hurt even to try to speak but I croaked out the words. 'I know you have water. Please give me some.'

He sat up slowly. 'No.' His hand was already on the haft of his swanneck. I had no weapon at all. He grinned at me. 'Why don't you try to take it?'

I stood there, anger, hatred and fear fighting for control of me. I decided I wanted to live. 'I'm not stupid,' I said. I turned away from him and walked toward the taldi.

He called after me, 'You say you are "not stupid". Is that another way to say "coward"?'

The words were like a knife in my back. I tried to ignore them. 'Keeksha. Stand.' The mare came to me.

'Sometimes a man has to fight for what he needs to live.

72

He has to fight, no matter what the odds.' Dewara stood up, pulling his swanneck from its sheath. The bronze blade was gold in the rising sun. His face darkened with anger. 'Get away from my animal. I forbid you to touch her.'

I grasped the mane at the base of her neck and heaved myself onto her.

'Your father said you would obey me. You said you would obey me. I said that if you disobeyed me, I would notch your ear.'

'I am going to find water.' I don't know why I even said those words.

'You are not a man of your word. Neither is your father. But I am!' he shouted after me as I rode off. 'Dedem. Stand!' At that, I kicked Keeksha into a run. Deprivation had weakened her as much as it had me, but she seemed to share my mind. We fled. I heard Dedem's strong hoofbeats behind us. 'It can't be helped,' I thought to myself. I leaned into Keeksha's gallop and hung on.

The stallion was bigger and hardier than the mare. They were gaining on us. I had two objectives: to get away from Dewara and to find water before the mare's strength gave out. I knew I would need her to get home. To those ends, I urged her to speed, guiding her back the way we had come. My somewhat rattled assessment of the situation was that by going back the way we had come, I knew that water was only two days away. A man can survive four days without food or water. Sergeant Duril had told me so. Yet he had added, kindly, that such survival was made more unlikely by exposure and exertion, and that a man who trusted his judgment after two days without food and water was as likely to die of foolishness as deprivation. I knew the horse could not run for two days straight, nor could I ride for that long. Yet my thinking was badly disordered by the fact that I was fleeing for my life, a new experience for me, and defying my father's authority as I did so. The one seemed equally as terrifying as the other.

73

I did not get far. I had only a small lead over the Kidona. Urge the mare as I might, Dewara gained steadily until he was riding beside us. I clung grimly to Keeksha's back and mane, for there was little else I could do. I saw him draw his swanneck and slapped the mare frantically, but she had no more speed to give. The deadly curved blade swiped the air over my head. I risked a kick at him, hoping more to distract him than unseat him. I nearly unseated myself as well, and I felt the mare's pace falter. The shining metal swept past me again, and such was Dewara's skill that, true to his threat, I felt the harsh bite of the blade as it passed through my ear. The act dealt me a scalp wound as well, one that immediately began to pour blood down the side of my neck. I screamed as the blade sliced through my flesh, both in pain and in terror. The shameful memory of that girlish shriek has never left me. Pain and the warm seep of thick blood down my neck became one sensation, making it impossible for me to assess how badly I was injured. I could only cling tighter to Keeksha and ride hard. I knew I had no chance of survival. The next pass of Dewara's swanneck would finish me.

Astonishingly, he let me go.

It took a short time for me to realize that. Or perhaps a long time. I rode, my wound burning and my heart hammering so that I thought it would burst from my body. At any moment, I expected the swish of the blade and the quenching of light. The drumming of my own blood in my ears was such that at first I did not realize that his hoofbeats were fading. I ventured a glance to the side and then back. He was pulling his stallion in. As I fled, he sat, unmoving on his horse, watching me go. He laughed at me. I did not hear it, could not see his smile, and yet I knew it. He flourished his golden blade over his head and flapped his free arm derisively at me. The knowledge of his mockery seared me.

Shamed and bleeding, I fled like a kicked cur. I did not have the water in my body to weep, or I probably would have. My scalp wound bled thickly for a short time, and then crusted over with dust. I rode on. Keeksha's pace slowed, and I lacked the will or energy to urge her to go faster. For a time, I tried to guide her, hoping to go back the way we had come, but we were already off course, and the little taldi was determined to have her own way. I gave in to her, excusing myself on the grounds that Sergeant Duril had often urged me to trust my horse when I had no better guide.

Afternoon found me slumping on Keeksha's back, letting her pick her way where she would. Our pace was little more than an amble. I felt dizzy. The sky was a clear blue and the sun was bright and warm. My hunger that had abated for a time had returned, and with it a retching nausea very painful to my dry throat. I felt completely adrift. When I had followed Dewara, I had believed that there was some destination that we sought, and despite my doubts, I'd felt safer with him. Now I was as good as lost until nightfall and the stars came out. Worse, I was lost in my life. I'd disobeyed my father and Dewara. I'd put my inexperienced judgment above theirs, and if I died out here, I'd have only myself to blame. Perhaps it had been a test of endurance, and I'd fled it too soon. Perhaps if I'd tried to take the water from him, he would have been impressed with my courage and rewarded me with a drink. Perhaps my fleeing had earned me a coward's death. My body would rot out here, insect and bird bait until my bones turned to sand. My father would be ashamed of me when Dewara told him how I had run away. I rode hopelessly on.

Midmorning of the next day, Keeksha found water. I claim no credit for helping her.

People who say our plains are arid are only partially correct. There is water, but for the most part it moves beneath the surface, and breaks through to the top only when the terrain forces it there. Keeksha found such a sike. The rocky watercourse she followed was dry as a bone that spring, but she kept with it until we reached a place where an outcropping of rock had forced the hidden flow up, to briefly break above ground as a marshy little pond, not much bigger than two box stalls. The sike stank of life, and was the virulent green of desperation. She walked into it and began drinking in the thick water.

I slid from her back, walked two steps from her and lay down on my belly in the muck. I put my face in the thin layer of water and sucked it up, straining it through my teeth. After I had drunk, I lay there still, my mouth open to the liquid, trying to soak my leather tongue and frayed lips back to a semblance of normalcy. Above me, Keeksha drank and then breathed and then drank some more. Finally I heard the heavy splashes of her hooves as she moved out of the shallow pond and to the cracked earth at the muddy edge of it. She began grazing greedily on the ring of grass that surrounded the sink. I envied her.

I stood slowly and wiped a scum of slime from my chin and then shook it from my hands. I could feel the water in my belly, and felt almost sickened by the sudden plenitude of it. I waded out of the muck and inspected our tiny sanctuary. The cut of the watercourse meant that we were below the windswept plain. I could hear the constant mutter of the never-still air above us. Our tiny hollow cupped silence. Then, as I stood still, the chorus of life slowly took up its song again. Insects spoke to one another. A dragonfly hovered over the water. The gore frogs that had gone into hiding during our splashing began to emerge once more. Bright as gobbets of spilled blood, they were blots of scarlet on the floating scum and stubby reeds of our pond. I knew a moment's relief that they had gone into hiding at our arrival. They were toxic little creatures. When I was small, one of our dogs had died from picking a gore frog up in his mouth. Even to touch one caused a tingling on the skin.

I picked and ate some water plants that I recognized. They were something in my belly, but hunger growled around them. I found nothing that I could fashion into a vessel for carrying water. I dreaded the thought of the hunger and thirst I'd have to endure during my journey home, but not as deeply as I dreaded my confrontation with my father when I returned. I'd failed him. The thought made me return to the water's edge. I washed the thick blood from my neck and ear. Notched. My ear would never be whole again. I'd carry the reminder of my broken promise to the end of my days. For the rest of my life, whenever anyone asked me about it, I'd have to admit that I'd disobeyed my father and gone back on my own word.

The mucky edges of the pond gave way to plates of roughly cracked earth that showed how the pond had shrunken since winter. I studied the tracks in them. When the ground had been moist, a little shrub-deer had visited the water. One blurry set of tracks could have been a big cat or the slopped prints of a wild dog. Beyond the cracked edge of the bare ground, dry grass stood in the skeletal shade of a dead sapling. I picked several double handfuls of the grass, and then approached Keeksha. She seemed apprehensive when I started rubbing the dust and sweat from her back and flanks, but soon decided she enjoyed it. It was not just that she'd found water for us. I did it to remind myself that the wisdom of my early training was to take good care of my mount. I should never have listened to Dewara about anything.

Afterwards, I made my bed among the grass tussocks, resolving to sleep the afternoon away, then awaken, drink as much water as I could hold, and then ride as the stars pointed me. I broke the dead sapling down, and broke the skinny branches away from it. It was a feeble weapon, but anything might come to water in the night. It was better than nothing. I placed it by my side as I lay down to sleep. As much as I dreaded confessing to my father, I also longed to be home again. I closed my eyes to the chirring of the insects and the peeping of the gore frogs.

FOUR

Crossing the Bridge

I opened my eyes. The dark had not yet thickened into the full blackness of a night on the plains. I remained motionless, pushing my senses to their limits to discover what had awakened me. Then I knew. The silence. I had dozed off to the relentless chorus of insects and frogs. Now they were still, concealing themselves from something.

My stick was still beneath my hand. I tightened my grip on it and rolled my eyes to find Keeksha. The mare stood, ears pitched forward, intently aware. I shifted my gaze to follow hers. There was nothing to see, and then there was. Dewara stood outlined against the darkening sky. I instantly rolled to my feet to face him, bringing my stick up into the guard position as if it were a proper pike instead of a brittle pole. The surge of hatred and fear that I felt surprised me. Dewara's swanneck was sheathed at his side. I suspected it was still slick with my blood. I had only the stick, and I was suddenly painfully aware of my gangly fifteen years pitted against the mature and solidly muscled warrior.

He did not make a sound, but stalked slowly down the incline to my pond. I held myself ready, and felt suddenly very calm as I knew I would die here. He met my gaze as he advanced and then a slow smile bared his pointed teeth. 'You learn the lesson I teach, I think,' he said.

I kept my silence.

'Nice ear notch,' he said. 'I marked you like a woman marks a goat.' He laughed aloud. I hated him then with a hate that boiled my blood. He knew it, and didn't care. He hunkered down as if I were no threat to him at all. He scratched his shoulder, and then reached inside his loose robe. He pulled out a packet and opened it, and shook out a stick. My nose told me it was smoked meat. He made a show of holding it up for me to see. My deprived belly growled loudly at the smell of it. He stuffed it into his mouth and chewed noisily, smacking his lips. 'You hungry, soldier's boy?' He waved the packet of jerky at me.

'Give me meat,' I demanded. I had not known I would say the words and regretted them. I was powerless to force him to obey my command. My mouth had filled with saliva at the sight of the food, and I swallowed it almost painfully. Need for what he had swept through me and I suddenly knew that I was going to fight him for it. I would rather die fighting than starving and defeated, I decided. I began to move toward him in a slow but purposeful way, keeping my pathetic weapon at the ready. He marked my intent and smiled his carnivorous smile again. I saw that gentling of his muscles as he relaxed into his body and readied it for my onslaught. I kept one eye on his swanneck as I moved toward him.

I was within ten feet of him when he abruptly stood up straight. I had not seen him draw it, but his swanneck gleamed in his hand. 'You want the meat? Come and take it, soldier's boy,' he taunted me.

I do not know which of us was more surprised when I charged at him with my stick. I tried to sweep his feet from under him, but the brittle sapling cracked off when it connected with his shin. He roared, more in anger than in pain, and a swipe of his swanneck chopped what remained of my stick into two useless pieces.

I threw the two pieces of stick at his head, missing with both of them. Then I charged him, hoping feebly that I could get inside the sweep of his swanneck and do some damage before he killed me. To my shock, he reversed his grip on his blade and rammed the short haft of it directly into my belly. The force of the blow lifted me off my feet and threw me backward. I lit on my back, my head striking the packed earth hard enough to blast light into my eyes. His strike had driven the air from my lungs. Pain radiated from the centre of my body.

I gasped for air and black spots swam at the edge of my vision. I sprawled on the sand, almost too frightened to be humiliated as I tried to pull air into my emptied lungs. He walked a few steps away from me, straightened his robes and sheathed his swanneck. All that he did with his back to me. I could not miss the meaning of that; I was too feeble an enemy to be considered a threat. When he turned back toward me, he laughed, as if we had shared some joke, and then pulled out a strip of the smoked meat. I had rolled to my side and was struggling to rise. He tossed the jerky at me, and it landed in the dirt beside me. 'You learned the lesson. Eat, soldier's boy. Tomorrow's lessons will be more challenging for you.'

It was several more minutes before I could even sit up. Nothing that had happened to me before had ever hurt as bad as this. Compared to this, the bruises from Sergeant Duril's rocks were a mother's kisses. I knew there would be blood in my piss; I only hoped there was no serious damage inside me. Dewara was moving unconcernedly about my pond. He picked up a broken piece from my stick and stirred the water thoughtfully, perhaps to disperse the gore frogs.

I had never felt more defeated and humiliated in my life. I hated him passionately and hated my own ineffectualness even more. I stared at the meat in the dirt, wanting it desperately and shamed that I'd even think of taking food from my enemy. After a time, I picked up the jerky. I remembered Sergeant Duril telling me that in a dangerous situation, a man must do all he can to keep his strength up and his mind clear. Then I wondered if I was just making excuses for my weakness. I still feared a trick. I sniffed the jerky, wondering if I'd be able to smell poison. At the smell of it, my stomach lurched with hunger and I felt dizzy. I heard Dewara chuckle. Then he called across to me, 'Better eat, soldier's boy. Or did you learn the lesson too strong?'

'I learned nothing from you,' I snarled, and bit into the meat. It was too tough to rip a bite free. I had to chew it soft and then tear it off. I swallowed it in half-chewed bites that scraped down the inside of my throat. It was too soon gone. Never once had I taken my gaze from Dewara. It grated on me that he seemed to regard me with approval. He made a noise, a clicking of his teeth, and a moment later I heard the thud of his mount's hooves. Dedem appeared at the lip of the hollow, and came down in haste. He waded out into the shallow water and began sucking noisily.

Dewara moved toward the other side of the small pond. I watched him kneel. He used his hands to smooth the coating of plantlets away from the water's surface before he bent his head and drank. I hoped that he would suck up a frog.

Having drunk, he moved back onto drier ground and settled himself for the night that was now closing around us in earnest. I watched him, seething. His bland assumption that I was no danger to him, his mocking dismissal of how he had mistreated and maimed me affronted me beyond insult. I choked on the indignity of it. 'Why did you follow me?' I burst out at last, and hated that I sounded like a child.

He didn't even open his eyes. 'You had my taldi. And I told you. Kidonas keep their word. I must take you back safely to your mother's house.'

'I want no help from you,' I hissed.

He leaned up on his elbows and looked at me. 'Not even my Keeksha, that you ride? Not even the meat you just ate?' He leaned back, scratched his chest and made the small sounds of a man settling for the night. 'Eat your pride tomorrow, I think. You have lots. Very filling. Tomorrow we start to make you Kidona.'

'Make me Kidona? I don't want to be Kidona.'

He laughed briefly. 'Of course you do. Every man wants to become the man who has bested him. Every youth with a thread of war in him wishes to be Kidona in his heart. Even those who do not know what Kidona is yearn for it, like a dream still to be dreamed. You wish to be Kidona. I will waken that dream in you. It is what your father wanted me to do, I think, even if he dared not say it.'

'My father wishes me to be an officer and a gentleman in his majesty's cavalla, follow the ancient traditions of knight-hood and bring honour to my family name as the men of my line have always done, since ever we fought for the kings of Gernia. I am a soldier son of the Burvelle line. I desire only to do my duty to my king and my family.'

'Tomorrow, we will make you Kidona.'

'I will never be Kidona. I know what I am!'

'So do I, soldier's son. Sleep, now.' He cleared his throat and coughed once. Then he fell silent. His breathing deep-ened and evened. He slept.

Full of fury, I walked up to him and stood over him for a time. He opened one eye, looked up at me, yawned elabo-rately and closed his eyes again. He did not even fear that I'd kill him in his sleep. He used my own honour as weapon against me. That stung like an insult, even though I never would have stooped to such a dastardly act. I stood over him, aching for him to make some sort of threatening move so that I could fling myself on him and try to throttle the life out of him. To attack a sleeping man who had just by-passed the opportunity to kill me while I sprawled at his feet was beyond dishonourable. Humiliated as I was, I would not and could not do it. I walked away from him.

I made my bed a good distance away from him and huddled in my nest of dry grass, feeling queasy still. I thought my anger and hatred would keep me awake, but I fell asleep surprisingly quickly. At fifteen, the body demands rest regardless of how sore the heart may be. Somehow I had completely forgotten my plans to ride in the darkness, letting the stars guide me home. Years later, I would begin to comprehend how neatly Dewara had put me under his control again. I would comprehend, and see how it was done to me, but I would never understand it.

The next morning, Dewara greeted the new day with enthusiasm and extended his good wishes and warm fellowship to me. He behaved as if all differences between us were settled. I was mystified. I ached still and a private inspection of my chest and belly showed me the deep bruise I bore. My slit ear still burned from my morning ablutions. I itched to carry on my feud with the man; I almost hoped Dewara would somehow abuse or challenge me so that I could fight him. But he was suddenly all good-natured jests and companionable conversation. When I reacted to his friendly overtures with suspicion, he praised me for my caution. When I maintained a surly silence, he praised my warrior's quiet demeanour. No matter what I did to express my defiance of him, he found something in it to compliment. When I sat absolutely still, refusing to respond to him in any way, he commended my self-control, and said it was the wise warrior who conserved his energy until he understood his situation.

In every imaginable way, he was a different man from the one he had been the day before. I vacillated between being stunned by the change in his demeanour to being certain that his apparent sincerity was a mask for his contempt of me. His friendly behaviour made my hostility seem childish, even to myself. His affability made it difficult for me to maintain my antagonism toward him, especially as he endeavoured to include me in every one of his activities, beckoning me repeatedly to come closer while he explained his actions in detail. Nothing in my life experience had prepared me for something like this. I wondered if he were mad, and then wondered if I were.

A confused boy is easy to manipulate.

That morning, he offered me meat without my asking, and showed me how he used the water plants as a filter when he filled his long tubular waterskins. I think they were made of gut. He also caught several of the gore frogs, taking great care not to touch them with his bare hands. He carried them away from the sike to a large flat rock and marooned them there. The little red creatures swiftly baked flat and brown in the hot sun of the day. He made a packet from the tough, flat leaves of a swort bush and carefully stored the dried frogs in one of the inner pockets of his loose robe. I was beginning to realize that although I had believed we had both ridden away from his camp empty-handed, Dewara had actually been very well supplied for our sojourn. He had with him all we both needed to survive. To get it from him, he would force me to admit my dependency on him.

He was so cheerful and affable with me, it was bewildering for me to sustain my wariness, but I managed. He suddenly stepped into the role of instructor, as if he had finally decided he would teach me the things my father had wanted me to learn. When we mounted up that first morning by the pond, I thought we would go straight back to his camp on my father's lands near the river. Instead, he led and I followed. We stopped at mid-day, and he gave me a small sling, showed me the Kidona style of using it and told me to practise with it. Then we left our taldi and moved into scrub brush along the edge of a ravine. He stunned the first prairie grouse we flushed and I raced up to wring its neck before it recovered. His second one, he broke the wing, and the bird led me a merry chase before I caught it. I could not hit a bird for the life of me until the late afternoon, when I actually killed one with my stone.

That night we had fire and cooked meat and shared his waterskin as if we were companions. I said little to him, but he had become suddenly garrulous. He told me a number of battle tales from his day as a warrior, back in the time when the Kidona raided their fellow plainsmen. They were full of blood and rape and pillaging, and he laughed aloud as he joyously recalled those 'victories'. From those tales, he went on to 'sky legends' about the constellations. Most of his hero tales seemed to involve deceit, theft or wife stealing. I perceived that a successful thief was admired among the Kidona, while a clumsy one often paid with his life. It seemed an odd morality to me. I fell asleep as he told a story about seven lovely sisters and the trickster who seduced them in succession and had a child with each one of them while marrying none of them.

His people had no writing, yet they kept their history in their oral accounts. I was to hear many of them in the long nights that followed. Sometimes when he told tales, I could hear the echo of the years of repetition in the measured way he spoke. The oldest tales of his people spoke of when they were a settled folk and lived in the skirts of the mountains. The Dappled People had driven them out from their homes and farms, and a curse from the Dapples had made his people wanderers, doomed to live by raids and thefts and blood instead of tending plants and orchards. The way he spoke of the Dapples as immensely powerful sorcerers who lived in ease among their vast riches confused me for several days. Who were these people with patterned skins and magic that could cause a wind of death to blow upon their enemies? When I finally realized that he was speaking of the Specks, it was almost like seeing double of a familiar image. The image and opinion I had of the Specks as a primitive woodland tribe of simple-minded people was suddenly overlaid with Dewara's image of them as a complex and formidable foe. I mentally resolved it by deciding that the Specks had, somehow, forced the Kidona to retreat from their settled lands and become wanderers and scavengers. Therefore Dewara's people had endowed them with tremendous and legendary power to excuse their failure to prevail against the Specks. This 'solution' troubled me, for I knew it didn't quite fit. It was like rough boards nailed over a broken window. The cold winds of another truth still blew through it and chilled me even then.

I never felt any warm glow of friendship or true trust of Dewara, but in the days that followed, he taught and I learned. From Dewara, I learned to ride as the Kidona did, to mount one of his taldi by running alongside it, to cling to the mare's bare smooth back and guide her by tiny thuds of my heels, to slide off my mount, even at a gallop, into a tumbling roll, from which I could either fling myself flat or come easily to my feet. My Jindobe, the trade language of all the plainspeople, became more fluent.

I had never been a fleshy youth, always rangy and, thanks to my father and Sergeant Duril, well muscled. But in the days that I was in Dewara's care, I became ropy and tough as jerky. We ate only meat or blood. At first, I knew a terrible hunger, and dreamed of bread and sweets and even turnips, but those hungers passed like ill-advised lusts. A sort of euphoria at my reduced need for food replaced them. It was a heady sensation, difficult to describe. After my fifth or sixth day with Dewara, I lost count of the days, and moved into a time where I belonged to him. It was ever after difficult for me to describe the state of mind and body that I entered into, even to the trusted few with whom I discussed my sojourn with the Kidona warrior.

Almost every day we hunted pheasant and hare with slings, and drank blood drawn from our mounts when our hunt failed to produce a meal for us. He shared his water and dried meat with me, but sparingly. We often made camp without water or fire, and I stopped regarding such lacks as a hardship. He told stories every night and I began to have a sense of what passed for wrong and right amongst his people. To get another man's wife with child, so that another warrior laboured to feed your get, was a riotously good jest upon that fellow. To steal and not be caught was the mark of a clever man. Thieves who were caught were fools and deserved no man's mercy or sympathy. If a man had taldi, a wife and children, then he was wealthy and beloved of the gods, and the others of his tribe should pay heed to his counsel. If a man was poor, or if his taldi or wife or children sickened or died, then he was either stupid or cursed by the gods, and in either case, it was a waste of time to hark to him.

Dewara's world was harsh and unforgiving, bereft of all the gentler virtues. I could never accept his people's ways, yet in some curious fashion, I became more capable of seeing the world as he saw it. By the harsh logic of the Kidona, my people had defeated his and forced them to settle. They resented and hated us for it, and yet by their traditions, we could only do those things because the gods favoured us over them. Therefore, our wisdom was to be considered when we spoke. Dewara had been honoured when my father sent word that he wished him to be my instructor. That during the course of teaching me he could bully and mistreat me was a great honour to him, one that all his fellow Kidona would envy. Dewara had the son of his enemy at his mercy, and he would have no mercy for me. Freely he rejoiced before me, that I would carry a notch in my ear from his swanneck to the end of my days.

He teased me often, telling me that I was not bad, for a Gernian cub, but no Gernian cub would ever grow to be as strong as a Kidona plateau bear. Every day he taunted me with that, not cruelly, but as an uncle might, several times, holding his full acceptance of me always just out of my reach. I thought I had won his regard when he began to teach me how to fight with his swanneck. He grudgingly conceded that I attained some skill with it, but would always add that that evil metal had ruined my 'iron-touched' hands, and thus I could never regain the purity of a true warrior.

I challenged him on that. 'But I heard you asking my father to trade guns for what you are teaching me. Guns are made of iron.'

He shrugged. 'Your father ruined me when he shot me with an iron ball. Then he bound my wrists with iron, so that all my magic was still inside me. It has never fully come back. I think a little bit of his iron stayed in me.' And here he slapped his shoulder, where I knew he still bore the scar of my father's shot. 'He was smart, your father. He took my magic from me. So, of course, I try to trick him. If I could, I would take his kind of magic from him, and turn it against his people. He said "no", this time. He thinks he can keep it from me always. But there are other men who trade. We will see how it ends.' Then he nodded to himself in a way I didn't like. In that moment, I was completely my father's son, the son of a cavalla officer of King Troven, and I resolved that when I returned, I would warn my father that Dewara still meant him harm.

The longer I stayed with him, living by his rules, the more I felt that I straddled two worlds, and that it would not take much to step fully into his. I had heard of that happening to troopers or those who interacted too freely with the plainspeople. Our scouts routinely camouflaged themselves in the language, dress and the customs of the indigenous people. Travelling merchants who traded with the plainspeople, exchanging tools and salt and sugar for furs and handicrafts, spanned the boundaries of the cultures. It was not uncommon to hear of Gernians who had gone too far and crossed over into plainspeople ways. Sometimes they took wives from amongst them, and adopted their way of dress. Such men were said to have 'gone native'. It was recognized that they were useful as go-betweens, but they were accorded little respect, less trust and almost no acceptance into gatherings of polite company, and their half-breed children could never venture into society at all. I wondered what had become of Scout Halloran and his half-breed daughter.

I could never conceive what would prompt any man to go native, but now I began to understand. Living alongside Dewara, I sometimes felt the urge to do something that would impress him, according to his own standards. I even considered stealing something from him, in some clever way that would force him to admit I was not dull-witted. Theft ran against all the morality I had ever been taught, and yet I found myself thinking about it often, as a way to win Dewara's respect. Sometimes I would snap out of such pondering with a jolt, surprised at myself. Then I began to wonder whether stealing something from Dewara would truly be an evil act, when he seemed to regard it as a sort of contest of wits. He made me want to cross that line. In Dewara's world, only a Kidona warrior was a whole man. Only a Kidona warrior was tough, of body and mind, and brave past any instinct for self-preservation. Yet self-preservation was high on a warrior's priority list, and no lie, theft, or cruelty was inexcusable if it was done with the goal of preserving one's own life.

Then one night he offered me the opportunity to cross over completely to his world.

Each day of our hunting and wandering had carried us closer to my father's lands. I more felt this than knew it. One night we camped on an outcropping of rocky plateau that fell away in gouged cliffs. The altitude gave us a wide view of the plains below us. In the distance, I saw the Tefa River carving its way through Widevale. I made our fire Kidona-style, as Dewara had taught me, with a strip of sinew and a curved stick as my fire-bow. I was much quicker at it than I had been. The narrow-leaved bushes that edged our campsite were resinous, but even though the branches were green they burned well. The fire crackled and popped and gave off a sweet smoke. Dewara leaned close to breathe in the fumes and then sat back, sighing them out in pleasure. 'That is how the hunting grounds of Reshamel smells,' he told me.

I recognized the name of a minor deity in the Kidona pantheon. So I was a bit surprised when Dewara went on, 'He was the founder of my house. Did I tell you that? His first wife had only daughters, so he put her aside. His second wife bore only sons. The daughters of his line wed the sons of his line, and thus I have the god's blood in me twice.' He thumped his chest proudly and waited for me to respond. He'd taught me this game of bragging, where each of us tried to top the other's previous claim. I could think of no reply to his claim of divine descent.

He leaned closer to the fire, breathed the sweet smoke and then said, 'I know. Your "good god" lives far away, up past the stars. You are not the descendants of his loins but of his spirit. Too bad for you. You have no god's blood in your veins. But,' he leaned closer to me, and pinched me hard on the forearm, a physical gesture I'd become accustomed to. 'But I could show you how to become part god. You are as much Kidona as I can make you, Gernian. It would be up to Reshamel to judge you and see if he wished to take you to be one of us. It would be a hard test. You might fail. Then you would die, and not just in this world. But if you passed the test, you would win glory. Glory. In all worlds.' He spoke of it as another man might gloat over gold.

'How?' The word popped out of me, a query that he took as assent.

He looked at me a long time. His grey eyes, unreadable even in the day, were a mystery in the twilight. Then he nodded, more to himself than to me, I think.

'Come. Follow me where I will lead you.'

I stood to obey him, but he did not seem in a hurry to go

anywhere. Instead, he bid me gather more leafy branches and build the fire up until it burned like a beacon. Sparks rose on its smoke whenever I threw more fuel on, and the heat of it made the sweat run down my face and back while the resinous aroma wrapped me. Dewara sat and watched me while I worked. Then, when the fire was roaring like a beast, he slowly stood. Walking to a nearby bush, he tore a fresh branch free, and then wrapped the leafy ends of it in several smaller branches. He wove the smaller branches deftly in and out of the larger one until he had a stick with a dense wad of foliage on one end. When he thrust it into the fire, it kindled almost immediately. Bearing this torch, he led me to the edge of our rocky campsite. For a very brief time he paused at the drop-off, staring out over the plain. In the distance, the land slowly swallowed the sun. Then, as full inky blackness poured over the low lands before us, he turned to me. The torch made his face a shifting mask of shadow and highlights. He spoke in a singsong voice, very different from his usual tone.

'Are you a man? Are you a warrior? Would Reshamel welcome you to his hunting grounds, or feed your flesh to his dogs? Have you courage and pride, stronger than your desire to live? For that is what makes a Kidona warrior. A Kidona warrior would rather be brave and proud than alive. Would you be a warrior?'

He paused, awaiting my answer. I stepped into his world. 'I would be a warrior.' Around me, the wide plateaus and the prairie below seemed to catch their breath and wait.

'Then follow me,' he said. 'I go to open a way for you.' He lifted his free hand and seemed to touch his lips. For two breaths, he stood there, the flame-light etching his aquiline features into the night.

He stepped off the cliff's edge.

In shock, I watched him fall, the flames of his torch streaming in the wind of his descent. Abruptly, he vanished.

I saw the glow from the torch, but could not see the flame itself. Then even that faded to only a vague nimbus of light. Dewara was gone.

I stood alone on the cliff's edge. Night was black around me. The wind pushed at me gently but insistently, bringing the sweet scent and heat of the roaring bonfire. It urged me toward the edge of the cliff. What I did I cannot explain, save by saying that Dewara had led me slowly into his world and his way of thinking and his beliefs. What would have been insane and unthinkable a month earlier now seemed my only possible path. Better to fall to my death than be seen as a coward. I stepped off the cliff's edge.

I fell. I did not scream or even shout. I made that passage in silence, the wind ripping at my worn clothing as I fell. I cannot now judge how long or how far I fell. My feet struck something, and my knees buckled under the impact. I wind-milled my arms wildly, trying as much to fly as to catch my balance. In the darkness, a hand caught me by the front of my shirt and jerked me close. A voice I did not recognize as Dewara's said, 'You have passed the first gate. Open your mouth.'

I did.

He thrust something inside it, something small and flat and leathery hard. For a second, it tasted not at all, and then my saliva wet it, and a pungent taste filled my mouth. It was so strong that I smelled it as much as I tasted it. I felt it, too, a strange tingling that sent saliva cascading and made my nose run. An instant later, I heard the taste as well, as my ears began to ring. All my skin stood up in gooseflesh, and I felt the press of the night, not the air, but the darkness, touching my body. Darkness was not the absence of light, I suddenly knew. Darkness was an element that flowed in to fill spaces such as the one I now occupied. The hand that gripped my shirtfront pulled, and I stumbled forward. Somehow, I walked out of darkness and into another world.

Light and the sweet scent of the burning torch overwhelmed my senses. I tasted light and heard the smell of the torch. I felt Dewara was there, but I could not see him. I could not see any distinct object. All distance around me faded to an equal blue. All of my senses were aware of every sensation.

A god spoke to me. 'Open your mouth.'

Again, I obeyed.

Fingers reached between my lips and took a frog from my mouth. The man who smelled like Dewara set the frog on the flames of the torch that was suddenly a tiny campfire on a hearth of seven flat black stones. The frog burned and sizzled, and sent fine threads of fiery red smoke up along with the sweet smoke. The man pushed my head forward, so that I leaned over the tiny fire, breathing the fumes. The smoke stung my eyes. I closed them.

Again, I closed them.

But the landscape that had opened up around me the moment I shut my eyes did not disappear. I could not close my eyes to this world, for it existed inside me. We were on a steep hillside. Huge trees surrounded us, blocking the twilight that filtered down to us, and the forest floor was almost bare of plant life. It was carpeted instead with centuries of fallen leaves. A fine rain of dewdrops fell from the leaves above. A fat yellow snake slithered by, sparing us not a glance. The air was cool and full of moisture. The world smelled rich and alive.

'This is an illusion,' I said to Dewara. He stood beside me in that twilight world. I knew it was he, even though he was several feet taller than I was and wore a hawk's head on his shoulders.

'Gernian!' He spat the word at me. 'You are the one who is not real here. Do not profane the hunting grounds of Reshamel with your disbelief. Go.'

'No,' I begged him. 'No. Let me stay. Let me be real here.'

He just looked at me. His hawk's eyes were gold and

round. His beak looked very sharp. His fingernails were black and curved like talons. I knew he could reach into my breast and lift out my beating heart if he chose to do so. Instead, he waited, giving me time to think.

Suddenly the right words came to me. 'I would be a man. I would be a warrior. I would be Kidona.'

In some distant place, I was ashamed of myself for disowning my heritage and becoming a savage. Then like a bubble popping, that life no longer mattered. I was Kidona.

We journeyed in that place. I do not remember what time passed, and yet I do. I cannot, for the most part, summon up what we saw or did or spoke there. It is like trying to recall a dream after one has fully awakened. Yet to this day there are moments when I smell a resinous fragrance or hear a distant roar of rapids, and it will bring a sudden vivid recall of a moment in that place and time. I recall that Dewara wore a hawk's head, and that I sometimes rode on a horse with two heads, one the bristle-maned head of a Kidona pony and one very like to my own Sirlofty. The memories come, sharp as broken glass and then ripple away like a disturbance in a pond. Sometimes I wake from ordinary sleep, grieving that I cannot recall the dreams of that place.

Only one incident remains clear in my mind from that experience. There was a time, neither evening nor morning, yet twilight all the same, as if twilight were the only time that place knew. Dewara and I stood on a bare bluff of deep blue stone. It was the place we had been journeying to, all that time. The forest on the steep hills behind us was a crouching guardian that watched over us. Before us was a chasm, sculpted more by wind than water. Within it, like strange towers of churches built to a wild god, tall pinnacles of stone rose from the distant floor of the canyon. The blustering air had carved spiralling towers and bulging knobs from the rock as neatly as a good cabinet-maker might turn a spindled leg for a chair. The freestanding spires of deeply swirled blue stood like a stony forest in the chasm before us. In the distance, I saw the sag and swoop of the wandering bridges that led from the stony cap of one hoodoo to the next, a meandering pathway across the divide. Dewara pointed across the rift that blocked us, to a land where slices of yellow light revealed stripes of ancient forest and rippling meadowland. The light moved across the land in the same way that cloud shadows dapple over a hill when the wind blows them.

'There,' he said, speaking loudly above the whispering sweep of a fragrant wind. He pointed with a long hand, and there were tufts of feathers at his wrist. 'Over there, you behold the dream home of my people. To get there, one must make a leap, and then cross the six spirit bridges of the Kidona tribe. All it once meant to be a Kidona lived in those bridges. They were built from the stuff of our souls. To cross them was to affirm to our gods that we were Kidona.

'It was never an easy crossing; always it required courage, but we are a courageous people. And we knew that beyond the challenge of the shaman's crossing was our homeland, the birthplace of our souls, our place of dreaming, the place to which our spirits ultimately return. But now it has been generations since any Kidona could complete the journey. The bridge was stolen from us. The Dappled Ones robbed us, and made the passage their own. They will suffer none of us to pass.

'Once, it was our custom that every young warrior and maiden should make this journey. From here, each would cross to the dream place, and sojourn there until a beast of that world chose him. Ever after, that beast would be the guardian of his spirit, offering him wisdom and advice. Our warriors were mighty, and our fields were fertile. In that time, the gentle hills were ours, and we lived well. Our cattle increased every year until they covered the foothills like stones beside a watercourse. We raided far, but for honour

95

and treasures rather than sustenance, for we had a home that yielded all we needed. The Kidona were a mighty people, content with our blessings and a glory to our gods. All that, all that, was taken from us by the Dappled Ones and we were doomed to become nomads, herders of the dust storms, planting only bodies and reaping only death.'

He dropped his hand to his side. He bowed his bird's head, expressing a sorrow beyond words and stared with longing across the divide.

'What befell your people?' I asked at last, when it was plain he intended to say no more.

He heaved a great sigh. 'In those days, we lived far to the west, in the foothills of what Gernians call the Barrier Mountains. A foolish name. They are not a barrier, but a bridge. The mountains are full of game and rich with trees bearing flowers, fruit and running with sweet sap. Their thick forests are shady and cool in the heat of summer. When the storms of winter blow, the tree canopies are shelter from deep snow and the sweep of the wind. The forests gave us everything we needed. The streams that run down from the high snows teem with fish, frogs, and turtles. Once, they were ours, our land to hunt and forage, and we were a wealthy people. In the forests, we hunted and harvested the same lands as the Dappled Folk. But we also ventured out onto the plains, standing out in the full sun, as they did not dare to do, for their eyes and skin cannot tolerate the full brightness of day. They are creatures of the shadows and twilight times. On the plains at the foot of the mountains, the Kidona kept our herds and flocks in the summer. There we built our towns and cities, our monuments and roads. In the winters, our herdsmen took our beasts up into the shelter of the forest. We prospered. Our herds increased. Our women were thriving, our men full of vigour and so many children were born to us that yearly we had to build new rearing temples to house them.

'All would have been well, save for the Dappled Folk who infested the mountain forests above us. They resented the increase of our herds, and strove to prevent our expansion of our grazing lands and our taking of timber for our towns. They said that our sheep and our kine ate too much, and that our taldi trampled the winding forest paths into wide roads. They complained of the land that we cleared for fields and mourned every tree that fell to our axes. They claimed the forest as their own, and wanted it to remain as if no man had ever trod there. We wished only to be allowed to have our children, to hunt and harvest as our fathers and grand-fathers had done before us. We argued with the Dappled Folk. And eventually, we fought with them.

'The Dappled Folk are a loathsome race, sly and slick as yellow and black salamanders under a rotting log. We did not seek a grievance with them. We were willing to exchange goods with them, but when we traded with them, they cheated us. Their women are lustful as war chiefs, but will not keep to one man's bed nor acquire cattle and manage wealth as befits a woman. They ruined our young warriors with random bedding and children they could not know were truly theirs. They set our warriors to fighting amongst themselves. The Dappled men are worse than their women. They would not fight warrior to warrior with swannecks and spears, but struck from a distance, with arrows and stones, so that the souls of the warriors they killed did not reach the territory of the gods, but fell unaware, disgraced as slain prey, like rabbits and grouse, no more than meat. We did not seek grievance with the Dappled Folk but when they forced it upon us, we did not shrink from it. When we rode through their villages and slew all those who did not flee, they vowed revenge on us. The winds of death they sent to us, so that men died coughing, huddled in their own filth. They orphaned our children and left them to die instead of taking them into their families. They set disease on us like

97

dogs on wounded deer. Such deaths end a man completely; there is no after life for men who are betrayed by their own bodies.'

Dewara fell silent, but his feathered chest surged with his emotion. It was the brooding, seething silence of a man who hates and hates without hope of satisfaction. Then he spoke softly, saying, 'The warriors of your people are on the edges of the mountain forests claimed by the Dappled Folk. Your warriors are strong. They defeated the Kidona, when no other plainspeople could stand against us. I speak to you of our ancient defeat by the Dappled Folk. I reveal to you this shame of my people, so that you may understand that the Dappled Ones deserve none of your good god's mercy. You should show them the same sword's edge you showed us. Use your iron weapons, to slay them from a distance, and never go near their people or their homes, or they will work their sorcery upon you. They should be trampled underfoot like dung-worms. No humiliation is undeserved by them, no atrocity too vicious to inflict on them. Do not ever regret anything your folk do to them, for behold what they did to my people. They severed our bridge to the dream world.' His hands fell to his sides. 'When I die, my being will end. There is no passage for me to the birth lands of the spirits of my people.

'When I was a young man, before our war with your people, I vowed I would reopen this passage. I made my vow before my people and my gods. I captured and shed the blood of a hawk to bind me to it. And so I am bound.' He gestured at his bird form. 'Twice I attempted this passage. I crossed and did battle with the terrible guardian they have set upon our way. Twice, I was defeated. But I did not sur-render, nor did I give up. Not until your father shot me with his iron, not until he sank the magic of your people deep into my chest, crippling my Kidona magic, did I know that I could not do this myself. I thought I had failed.'

98

He paused in his account and shook his beaked head. 'I had no hope. I knew I was condemned to the torment of the oath-breaker when I died. But then the gods revealed to me their way. This is why they allowed your people to make war upon us and conquer us. This is why they showed up the power of your iron magic. This is why your father sought me out and gave you to me. The gods sent me my weapon. I have trained you and taught you. The iron magic belongs to you, and you belong to me. I send you to open the way for the Kidona. It has taken all the strength of the feeble magic that remains in me to bring you this far. I can go no further. I redeem my oath in you and bring great glory to my name forever. You will slay their guardian with the cold iron magic. Go now. Open the way.'

'I have no weapon,' I said. My own words made me a coward in my eyes.

'I will show you how, now. This is how you summon your weapon to you.'

He stooped impatiently and dragged his finger in a crescent in the dust. It left a line. He stooped, and blew upon the dusty stone, and as the dust flew away from his breath, a shining bronze swanneck was revealed. He gestured at it proudly. Then he lifted it from the ground; its outline remained in the stone of the cliffs, like the imprint of an animal's hoof near a streambed. With a powerful blow, he drove the gleaming blade into the blue stone at our feet. 'There. That will hold this end of the bridge for the Kidona people. Now, you must summon your own weapon, to use against the guardian. I cannot call iron.'

I pushed my doubts away. I stooped and in the dust, I drew an image I knew well. It was an image I had idly drawn a thousand times in my boyhood. I drew a cavalla sword, proud and straight, with a sturdy haft and dangling tassel. As my fingers traced it against the stone, I suddenly hungered for the weapon to be within my hand again. And when

I stooped and blew my breath across the dusty stone, the sword I had left at Dewara's campsite was suddenly there at my feet. Triumphant, yet wondering, I lifted the blade from the earth. Its imprint remained behind beside the swanneck's. When I proudly flourished it aloft, Dewara shrank from it, lifting his arm-wing to shield himself from the steel in my hand.

'Take it and go!' he hissed, his arms lifted to mimic the aggressive stance of a bird. 'Slay the guardian. But bear it away from me before it can weaken the magic that holds us here. Go. My swanneck anchors this end. Your iron will hold the other.'

I had become so much his creature that I could not think of any alternative to doing what he had commanded. In that time and place and uncertain light, there was no room for me to think of disobeying him. So I turned from him and walked along the stone ledge to the cliff's edge. The rocky chasm gaped bottomlessly before me. The standing hoodoos of stone and the flimsy bridges that connected them were my only possible passage to the other side. My destination was faded by distance, as if smoke or fog hung in the air and curtained it. I could see no detail of it. The sculpted pinnacles varied in size; the tops of some were no bigger than tables, whilst others could have supported a mansion. The capstones of each spire were a slightly different grey-blue, a harder stone than that of the softer columns that the wind had eroded away beneath them. There was no bridge between the cliff edge and the first hoodoo. I would have to leap to it. It was not an impossible distance, and my landing place was large, as big as the beds of two wagons. If I had been leaping over solid ground, it would not have been so daunting. But below me gaped the seemingly bottomless ravine. I gathered my courage and my strength for the leap.

Then, as I watched, a bronze path, no wider than the blade of the swanneck, flowed from the embedded weapon to the top of the first hoodoo. Like an unfurling ribbon, the tongue of shimmering metal reached out across the void until it touched the first hoodoo. It was not a wide bridge, but it spanned it. I thrust my cavalla sabre into my belt, spread my arms for balance, and stepped out onto the bronze path.

Almost immediately, I lost my footing. The sword in my belt suddenly seemed to weigh as much as an anvil. I wrenched my whole body against the drag, started to topple the other way, and responded by sprinting forward along the length toward the hoodoo. Its top was slightly rounded, like a very large bed-knob. A gritty layer of sand coated the capstone and I skidded in it and fell to my knees as I tried to stop, halting less than an arm's length from the edge. For an instant I crouched there, catching my breath and calming my heart. Grinning foolishly at my near mishap, I glanced back at Dewara. He was unimpressed. Impatiently, he gestured me on.

The scant layer of sand crunched under my feet as I stood. I looked down at the footbridge that awaited me. It was narrow and insubstantial. Bits of brightly painted pottery floated in a net of spider web. At my feet, three hawk feathers stood upright, their shafts wedged in tiny heaps of sand. The wind stirred them and they swayed. Gossamer threads reached from these foolish anchors to the footbridge that spanned the gap. I did not think a mouse could safely cross such a frail construction, let alone a man. I looked again to Dewara for guidance. He opened one wing wide and pointed at a gap in his flight feathers. This magic belonged to him, then. He obviously had full faith in it, for he flapped his arms at me, shooing me on. Later, it would seem foolhardy to me, but at the moment, I felt I had no choice. I stepped out onto the bridge. It gave beneath me, sagging so that my foot sank, just as if I had stepped out onto netting. It was the weight of my iron, I knew, that burdened the bridge. On my next step, it sagged even more, and swayed. It was like trying to walk across an insubstantial hammock that was decorated with shards of ceramic and stretched beneath my weight. Yet even that does not describe it at all. I suppose it was an experience of that world, and thus untranslatable to this one.

There was nothing certain about my footing. The bits of pottery sank unevenly beneath me and the bridge swayed with every step I took. Sometimes I sank so deeply that I had to lift my foot unnaturally high to step to the next stone, as if I were climbing a very steep stair. The pottery fragments that floored the path were marked with distinctive patterns that I had never seen before. Some of them were fire-blackened, as if from much use. Sometimes I sank almost waist deep in the netted path so that I had to wallow onto the next section of trail, which in turn sank under me. It was more exhausting than breaking trail in deep wet snow, and yet I pushed on, for I could not turn around and go back. It was a narrow way, and to either side, the bottomless chasm yawned. Once, panting, I rested and looked down. I had thought to see a river carving its way amongst those natural monuments. Instead, the spiral stone pillars seemed to descend endlessly into a shadowy distance. If I fell, I might die of starvation before my bones were ever shattered by the impact. I shook my head at that thought, and forced myself to go on.

After a long struggle, I reached the second hoodoo of turned blue stone. I dragged myself up from the path onto the rounded top of the spire and lay there, catching my breath. When I looked back, I was shocked to find I had come a very short way. Dewara stood on the cliffs, staring at me, his hawk's beak ajar. He shifted from foot to foot uncertainly.

'The path seems difficult but sound.' I said the words first and the air swallowed them. Then I shouted them, and saw

Dewara cock his head, as if he knew I had spoken but could not hear my voice. And yet it did not seem he was that far away from me.

Slowly I got to my feet. I was not rested yet I felt driven to go on, as if I only had a certain amount of time in which to accomplish my task. I eyed the new section of trail before me. Fine threads, braided and interwoven, made a softly gleaming trail. I knelt and touched it. Hair. Human hair, I judged, in every shade from blackest ebony to pale gold. I patted it with my hand. It seemed sound. I rose and again stepped from the dome of stone onto the strange floating pathway. I walked out feeling relieved at the sturdiness of this new path. But three steps from the rock, it swayed beneath me as if I stood in a swing.

My sisters used to play a game with tops, trying to make one walk the length of a tautly strung ribbon. I was the top, and the ribbon I traversed was not taut. The farther I went from the rock spire, the more it sagged beneath my weight. I drew my sword and gripped it, holding it horizontally with both hands as if it were a balance pole. Briefly it made a small improvement. Then the bridge began to swing, like the lazy swinging of a girl's jump rope. I felt sick with dizziness, but pressed on, now edging upward on the sag of matted hair. Behind me, Dewara shouted something, but his words seemed distant and I dared not look back at him.

When I reached the third pinnacle of stone, I clawed my way onto it and sat down to catch my breath. I glanced back at Dewara then, but he had sunk his hawk's head down upon his hunched shoulders and perched motionless on the edge of the chasm. I could read nothing in his bird's eyes, and his arms were clapped to his sides. There was no help or advice for me there.

I looked to the next hoodoo. A longer path separated it than the three I had trodden. That next resting place looked smaller, too, and even more rounded. The path to it was an interlocking web of plants. Tiny white flowers, smaller than my smallest fingernail, blossomed thickly on the matted vines. Suspicious, I pushed hard on it with my hand before venturing forth. The tough roots held. When I poked at them with my sword, they browned and shrivelled away. That would not do. I had no desire to weaken the path by killing the plants. I placed my sabre once again through my belt. This path was wider, also, and the roots of the plants seemed anchored to the pillar on which I stood, reminding me of ivy climbing up the trunks of trees and the walls of houses.

I set out across the path more boldly than I had the previous two. It bore me up firmly and although the plants and their tough vines crunched underfoot as I stepped on them, it did not sway nor give beneath my stride. The fragrance of the crushed flowers and foliage was oddly pungent, but surely a smell could not harm me. I was halfway across before my hands burst into tiny white blisters. They itched painfully and I longed to scratch them. Even clutching my hands into fists caused the tiny blisters to burst. The liquid that flowed from them seared my skin, and left a second crop of white blisters in its wake. I held my hands away from my body and tried to ignore the searing pain. How grateful I was that I wore boots and not the low, soft shoes of a plainsman. If the plants had affected my feet, I do not think I could have gone on. As it was, my eyes began to burn and my nose to run. It took stern discipline to keep my hands away from my face. I stumbled on, and when I reached the next stone support, I found it as small as it had appeared. I stepped away from the loathsome plants and perched on a hoodoo cap no larger than a dinner platter.

Almost as soon as I had stepped onto the stone cap, my agonies ceased. The sores on my hands ceased burning. I still dared not touch my face, but when I turned my face to my shoulder and rubbed my streaming eyes on my upper arm, my symptoms began to clear. I would have felt much better, had I not been perched on such a tiny island. There was not room enough to sit down and rest, and so I moved on.

The next bridge was made of bird bones, cleverly bored and bound together with fine thread ligaments. Occasional beads of shell or polished stone glittered in the network. Perhaps they had been bracelets or necklaces before they had been re-wrought into a suspension bridge. The tiny bones clicked together as I ventured over them. Despite the fragility of the fine white bones, none of them gave way beneath me, nor did the bridge sway or give to my weight. Only the rising wind gave me pause as it tugged at my clothing and whispered past my ears. The wind carried a strange and distant music. I paused to listen to it. The distant whistling of flutes and rattle of bone castanets marked it as Kidona music. It was foreign to me and yet I sensed its significance. I looked down at the bridge beneath my feet and suddenly knew the bird bones were parts of a musical instrument. The music sang to me in a language I almost knew. I stood still, trying to comprehend its meaning. I think if I had truly been a plainsman, it would have been more compelling in its efforts to lull me. As it was, I was able to shake off its influence and walk on. I completed that leg of the journey, reaching a much larger pinnacle of stone.

This refuge was as generous as the last one had been mean; I could have stretched out and slept upon it with no fear of tumbling off. The very temptation to do so warned me against it. I had finally sensed something about the bridges that I should have suspected all along. This pathway was not for me. Dewara had done all he could to make me think like a Kidona, but I was not truly Kidona. I traversed stretches of meaning that eluded me. I suspected there was great significance to each crossing, symbolism and subtext that did not reach my Gernian soul. For some reason, that made me feel diminished and ashamed, like an uneducated man unable to comprehend the cultural significance of a lovely poem. I did not even understand the full significance of the challenges I faced, and thus they did not truly challenge me. Chastened, I did not even glance back at Dewara, but crossed the capstone to where the next bridge began.

This bridge was all of ice, not the solid ice of a frozen pond in the dead of winter, but the fantastic ice that festoons glass into a garden of fern fronds. It seemed no thicker than window glass, and I could see through it into the deep blue distance below me. I was only a few steps out onto it before the cold bit deeply into my bones. I listened for the sound of running cracks. I shivered as I went, and my footing was slippery and uncertain. Memories not my own shivered around me. There had been a time of great hardship, a time when the old and the young died, and even the strong faced desperate decisions in order to survive. Had I truly been Kidona, the heartbreak of those recollections might have driven me to my knees with weeping. But those horrors had happened to a people not my own in a distant time. I could sympathize with their sorrows, but they were not my sorrows. I walked on, past that season of heartbreak and reached the next pinnacle of respite.

Bridge after bridge, each a test of my courage, had zigzagged me slowly across the chasm. Yet as I stood facing the next bridge, I had the uneasy feeling that I had cheated, as if I had strode unchecked through a child's hopping game. Did my lack of roots in the Kidona culture or my cold iron make me impervious to the challenges of this task? I looked back to Dewara. He perched still and distant at the beginning of the bridge. Suspicion tapped softly on my shoulder, breathed chill down my neck. Did he hope I would succeed, or was I a stalking horse for some incomprehensible plan of his foreign mind? I stood at the lip of the next bridge and doubted all he had ever told me. Nonetheless, I went on.

The next bridge was of mud brick, solid and ancient. The

bridge had block walls along each side and towers at the midpoint. It was wide enough for an oxcart to traverse. It did not swing nor sway. I should have felt safe crossing it, yet the hair stood up on my head, arms and neck. Haunted. That was the word that came to me. The bridge spoke of a time when the Kidona had built things that would stand in place for generations. Dim memories of lively towns tried to reach me. I could not believe them. As I walked out onto the bridge, its ruin was revealed to me. Rain and wind had rounded the corners of the mud bricks. Cracks wandered through the walls that edged it. Time had sucked on this structure, softening and dissolving the decorative carvings that had once stood in bas-relief on its balustrades and arches. This mighty work of the Kidona people was dwindling away, one layer of red dust at a time, just as the Kidona people were dwindling away. I felt a sudden awareness of the connection. When this weakening bridge was gone, eaten by wind and rain and time, the Kidona people would also be gone, not just from this world but from my own as well.

The farther I went, the more obvious was the decay. There were gaps in the paving under my feet, and blue distance showed in the holes. I began to encounter thin runners of vine twining along the walls of the bridge. Tiny, flowering plants had found homes in the hollows of the disintegrating bricks: Their roots pried into the cracks, and their crawling foliage snaked over the Kidona bricks, obscuring them.

I walked on, into a strange dusk. When I looked back, the long afternoon seemed to linger in the distance. The sun's warm light shone on Dewara's crouching figure. But the light faded gently around me as I ventured on. Plant life grew thicker on the bridge. Small trees had found places to root, and tussocks of grass grew around them. I began to hear insects and to smell the fragrance of the blossoms. Less and less of the brickwork was visible; the encroaching forest had swallowed it, cloaking it with greenery and taking it over. The walkway beneath me became ropy with vines and crawling creepers. They engulfed the turrets of the bridge and reached out over my head to tangle with one another. The bridge had become a tunnel of greenery. The twilight sky and the depths below me peeked at me from irregular openings in the foliage.

At some point, I halted, feeling more than seeing that I had left the Kidona bridge behind. I now stood upon the forest that had enveloped and devoured it. It felt oddly foreign to me, as if I had left the last vestiges of a familiar world behind and now ventured into a place where I had no right to be. A pervasive sense of wrongness thrummed through me. My body as much as my mind commanded me to turn back. The passage before me radiated hostility. All of those sensations reached me through a sense I had no name for. I saw a lovely woodland path before me in the evening twilight. A cool sweet wind blew, carrying the scent of evening flowers. I could hear birdcalls in the distance.

I lifted my eyes and looked ahead. The dimming light revealed to me a grandfather tree at the end of the tunnel. The gnarled roots snaked out from that cliff's edge and crossed what remained of the chasm to become the foundation of the path I now walked. Red flowers the size of dinner plates peeped out from the tree's thick foliage. Butterflies played lazily about the crown of the big-leaved tree, and grass grew thick beneath it. It beckoned me as a place of peace and rest. Yet I regarded the great tree with suspicion. Was this the final guardian that Dewara had spoken about? I wondered if the sylvan serenity before me were a trap. Did it lure me to carelessness? Once I had trusted myself to the pathway of tangling roots, would it twist and tumble me into the abyss?

I looked more closely at the network of living vines and roots that would be the final link in my trail. Part of a skull, a yellow-brown dome of bone, protruded from the moss and vines. Beyond it, a skinny root snaked in and then out of a shattered leg bone, as if it had sucked the marrow there and gained sustenance from it. The bones were old but I took no comfort from that. Farther along the pathway, I glimpsed the corroded stump of a broken swanneck. I turned and looked back toward Dewara. He was a tiny figure at the end of a green tube. He perched on the edge of the bluff, watching me. I lifted my arm in greeting to him. He lifted his, not in response but to wave me on.

I took my sabre from my belt and held it at the ready. Some small part of me saw the innate foolishness of this. If I attacked the bridge and cut it through, would I have won? I wanted to look back at Dewara again, but I deemed that he would judge such hesitation as cowardice. Would I or would I not be Kidona? If I finished the crossing, would I have won the way for them again?

I stepped out onto the bridge of roots and tested my weight on it. It was sound. It did not sway nor creak, but held me as firmly as the brick walkway had. I moved forward in the warrior's crouch Dewara had taught me. I kept my weight low and centred, my sword going before me.

When I was a third of the way across the living section of the bridge, the roots began to creak under me, very slightly, like straining ropes. I continued to move forward, placing each foot as securely as I could on the uneven surface of the root web and holding myself ready for the expected attack. My senses strained against their limits as I strove to be wary. The tree was the sentry, Dewara had said. I fixed my attention on it, searching it for signs of hidden attackers or unnatural activity as I eased toward it.

It did nothing.

I felt a bit foolish by the time I had traversed two-thirds of the forest bridge with absolutely no signs of hostility from the tree. I began to wonder if this were one of Dewara's practical jokes. Usually, they were physically painful, but perhaps he simply meant to humiliate me. Or perhaps there was something about the tree that he wished me to see. I stopped watching it and studied it instead. The closer I came to it, the more immense it was. The trees I knew were the trees of the plains, bent by the constant winds. They grew very slowly, and the oldest ones I'd seen did not have a quarter of the girth of the tree before me. This tree stood straight and tall; she was thick of trunk and limb, reaching her branches wide to the nourishment of the sun. Her fallen leaves carpeted the earth below her, a thick, rich litter of humus and leaf skeletons and last year's leaves gone brown but still recognizable. The red flowers had tall yellow stamens in their centres. When the wind puffed past them, they released their yellow pollen to drift like smoke. The wind blew some toward me; it smelled earthy and rich, but stung my eyes. I blinked to clear the pollen from my lashes, and when my watering vision cleared, a woman stood before the tree. I halted.

She was no guardian warrior! I stared at her, aghast. She was very old and very fat. She was someone's fat old granny, save that I had never before seen a woman so corpulent. Her bright eyes were hooded with flesh and wrinkles. Both her nose and ears had grown with her years. Her lips were plumped and pursed at me as if she considered me in as much bewilderment as I did her.

I continued to stare, to try to make sense of what confronted me. Dewara wanted me to do battle with *this*? Her flesh girdled her arms and doubled her chin. Many rings were sunken into her plump fingers, and heavy earrings, thick with gemstones, had stretched the lobes of her ears. Her fallen bosom was enormous and rested on the rolling swell of her belly. Her hair, long and streaky grey as a horse's mane, hung like a cloak over her shoulders and down her back. The persistent breeze toyed with its uneven ends. Her robe looked as if it had been woven from grey-green lichen.

It hung nearly to the ground, tenting her immense girth, and her thick ankles and plump feet showed beneath it. She was barefoot. The sunlight breaking through the tree's leafy canopy dappled her skin and garment with shadow.

Then she moved, and my image of her changed. When she shifted, the shadowy patterns on her skin and robe moved with her, independent of the true shadows of the leaves. Her feet, like her bare arms and face, were patterned with splotches of pigment. Even at that distance, I recognized it was neither paint nor tattoo. She was dappled, speckled with colour. It took an instant before I realized that, for the first time in my life, I was seeing a Speck.

The reality was far different from the images I had formed in my mind. I had thought a Speck would be speckled with small marks, like freckles. Instead, the colour that patterned her skin was uneven. It reminded me of the dappling of some cats, as if their stripes were left unfinished to become splotches and dots. Her dapples gave me that sense of a pattern interrupted. A dark stripe ran down her nose. Dark streaks radiated from the corners of her eyes. The backs of her hands and fingers were dark, like a cat's sooty feet, but the colour faded on her forearms.

Entranced, I drew closer to her, almost forgetting Dewara's warnings. My approach had become the cautious creep of the fascinated cat rather than the wary stalking of a warrior. Her face was still, her expression both serene and dignified. Now she seemed, not old, but ageless. Her face was lined but they were the kindly lines of a woman who smiled often and enjoyed life. In a woman of my own kind, I would have found her bulging flesh repulsive, but because she was a Speck, it seemed just another difference between us.

She spoke, asking in Jindobe, 'Who approaches?' Her expression remained grave, but her low voice was courteously neutral. It was the question that anyone might ask of a stranger approaching her door.

111

I halted. I wanted to answer her, but I could not remember my name. I felt that I had left it behind when I entered the Kidona world. I reminded myself that I had taken Dewara's challenge in order to become Kidona. To become a warrior and gain Dewara's respect, I had to defeat the enemy in front of me. Yet he had not warned me that the sentry might be an old woman. The part of me that was not Kidona felt shamed by the bare blade in my hand and my failure to reply to her courteous question. A Gernian soldier did not bear weapons against women and children. I felt a strong tug from that self, and found myself lowering my sword. I tried to be chivalrous and yet warrior-like as I said, 'The one who brought me here calls me "soldier's son".'

She cocked her head to one side and smiled at me as if I were very young. Her voice rebuked me gently, as a kindly old woman might recall manners to a youngster. 'That is not your proper name, nor any way to introduce yourself. What is the name your father gave you?'

I took a breath and found a truth I had not previously known. 'I do not think I can say that name here. I came here to be Kidona. But as of yet, I have no name in Kidona.' After I spoke, I felt suddenly childishly foolish, to have confided this information to my enemy. I hardened my muscles and brought my blade up to readiness again.

She seemed singularly unimpressed with my sabre. She leaned closer, and as she did so, I perceived that her loose hair was snagged on the tree's trunk, as if binding her to it. She peered at me and I felt that she looked deep inside me. In a quiet, almost confidential voice, she informed me, 'I see your difficulty. He thinks to use you to force his way past me. He has made you believe that you must kill me to gain a man's respect and standing. That is not true. Killing is only killing. The respect that Kidona will give you if you kill me is real only to him. No one else believes in it, least of all you. And you don't have to kill me to earn true respect. My blood

112

will only buy you that fool's regard. I will pay a high price for you to be respected by a churl. Nothing bought with blood is worth having, young man.'

I thought about what she said. They were an idealist's words that made sense as a lofty philosophy. But on a day-to-day level, I knew that much of my world had been bought with blood. My father often spoke of that, that our soldiers, especially the cavalla officers, had 'bought the new Gernia with their lives, made these lands ours when the soils of them were watered with the blood of our soldier sons.'

'I don't agree with you!' I called out to her, and then realized I need not have spoken so loud. Somehow I had drawn much closer to her without being aware of it. I wondered if the root path had drawn me closer, unperceived by me. I glanced around but had no way to tell.

She smiled then, an elder's smile. 'The truth doesn't need you to recognize it, young man, for it to be so. You need the truth to recognize you. Until you do, you are not real. But let us set aside the truth of the worthlessness of things bought with blood. Let us try to recall who you are in another way. We are not defined by what we die for, but by what we live for. Will you acknowledge that truth?'

Somehow, the whole situation had changed. She was testing me now, rather than meeting my warrior's challenge. I felt that she guarded the bridge, demanding that I prove myself worthy to cross. If I earned her regard, she would permit me passage. I did not have to be Kidona to cross.

Distant as a bird's call on a hot summer day, Dewara's voice reached me. 'Do not talk with her! She will twist your thoughts like a twining vine. Ignore her words. Rush forward and kill her! It is your only hope!'

She did not lift her voice to reply to him. She spoke almost quietly as she said, 'Be quiet, Kidona man. Let your "warrior" speak for himself.'

'Kill her now, soldier's son! She seeks to possess you!'

113

But like a distant birdcall, the sound of his voice seemed a territorial challenge that did not apply to me. I let his words go by me, my mind mulling over the tree woman's words. Defined by what we live for. Was that how I defined myself? Should a soldier ponder such things?

'The same things I live for are the things I would die for,' I said, thinking of my king, my country and my family.

She nodded slowly, like the canopy of a tree swaying in a flurry of wind.

'I see that. There is much in you that wants to live for those things. More of you wishes to live for them than to die for the Kidona man's respect. He is the one who sends you to kill me. You do not have that quest in your true heart, but only in the heart he has tried to give you. He thinks he cannot lose. You are, still, the son of his enemy. If I die, you have served him well. If you die, he takes no real loss. But I think either death would be a loss for you. What was your real quest, soldier's son? Why have the gods sent you to me, why have you managed to come past every trap unscathed? I do not think you are meant to die trying to kill me. There is more to you than that. You come as a weapon. Are you a weapon from the gods given as a gift to me?'

'I do not understand.'

'It's a simple question.' She leaned toward me, studying me intently. 'Did you make the crossing to this world to take life or to give it?'

'What do you mean?'

'What do I mean? Isn't it clear? I ask you to make a choice: life or death. Which do you worship?'

'I don't . . . that is . . . I want . . . I don't know! I don't know what you mean!' I groped within myself but found no good answer to her question. I suddenly knew that I was in very great danger, the sort of danger that lasts not a moment, but an eternity, and threatens not the body but the soul. All I wanted was to go back to my own world, to be my father's

114

son and live to be a soldier for my king. The answer came to me too late. I had no chance to utter a syllable.

'I shall have to find out for you, I think. Live or die, soldier's son.'

The roots parted and the bridge opened under me. The twining tendrils did not break; they opened their network to allow me to plunge through. As they gave way, I desperately lunged forward, running over roots that gave way beneath my feet, hoping against hope to reach solid ground.

I fell short. Suddenly there was nothing under my feet. My left hand scrabbled at roots that squirmed away from my touch, refusing me a grip. All the roots had fled, opening wide a gap in their web, leaving only bare stone cliff before me. In a stupidly futile act I jabbed my sabre toward the ground that the tip of the blade could barely reach.

It sank in, with a jolt that sent a shock up my arm, gripped unnaturally by the stone that had given way before it. It defied all physical laws I knew, and the fright of that was stunning. The tree woman gasped, in surprise or pain, I don't know which. But I was still falling, and in foolish desperation, I grabbed the blade of my sabre with my left hand as my right came free of the hilt. The blade cut into my fingers, but that pain was nothing compared to the terror I felt at falling into that abyss. In an instant, I'd wrapped my right hand around the blade as well. I clung there, the weight of my body suspended from my hands gripping that carefully honed edge, the toes of my boots scrabbling against the undercut cliff. I knew it would soon be over. My mind's command to my hands to grip would either give way to pain or be futile when I'd severed my own fingers from my hands.

'Help me!' I cried, neither to the tree woman who stood looking down at me mercilessly nor to Dewara who had sent me to this doom. Rather, I shouted to the uncaring universe, a desperate plea that something would take pity on this dangling bit of life.

The pain was agonizing and the blade was slippery with my own blood. I wanted to let go with one hand and try for a handhold on the bluish stone, but it was smooth and featureless. I closed my eyes, not wishing to see my fingers fall from my hands before I plunged to my doom.

'Shall I take you up?' the tree woman asked me.

'Help me! Please!' I begged suddenly, no longer caring if she was friend or foe. She was my sole chance for survival. My eyes flew open. She had come closer but was still out of reach. She stood, looking down at me curiously. I could see the fronds of ferns growing from her mossy dress.

'Please, what?' she asked me, gently, implacably.

'Please help me up!' I gasped.

'Please take you up?' she asked, as if she had to be certain she had heard me correctly. 'You wish to live, then? To cross the bridge and complete it?'

'Please! Take me up!' I all but shrieked the words. Blood was running down my wrists. The edge of the blade had found the joints in my fingers and was slicing through them. I feared I would faint from the pain even if my fingers did not detach.

She was implacable. 'I must give you the choice. You can say you wish to die, rather than have your life taken up. If you so choose, so shall it be. But if you wish to be taken up to this life, then you must choose it clearly. The magic does not take anyone against his will. Do you choose the bridge?' She knelt at the edge of the cliff, leaning over me but still out of my reach. I could smell her odour, old woman and humus mingled in a sickening richness.

'I . . . choose . . . life!' My heart was pounding in my ears. I could barely find breath to get the words out. I could claim that I did not know what I was saying, but a part of me did. The tree woman was not speaking of death and life as I knew it; those words conveyed something else when she spoke them. I suppose I could have dangled there longer, and

116

demanded that she explain herself. I feared I made a coward's choice, choosing my life at some hideous expense that I could not yet comprehend. At the time, with blackness at the edges of my vision, demanding the exact terms of her bargain did not seem an option. I would live first, and then do whatever I must to make it right.

In the vast distance, I heard Dewara shout. 'Fool! Fool! She has you now! You've become hers! You've opened the way and condemned us all!' The words came tiny but clear to my ears. I thought my fear was as fierce as it could get, but Dewara's warning sent a fresh rush of dread surging through my body. To what had I agreed? What would the tree woman's victory mean to me?

Yet there was no triumph in the tree woman's voice, only acquiescence to my wish when she spoke. 'As you have asked it, so shall it be. I take you up. Come and join us.'

I had expected that she would grasp my wrists and pull me up. Instead, she reached down and I felt her fingers touch the top of my head. My father always kept my hair cut short, no longer than the tops of my ears, as befitted a soldier son, but in my time with Dewara, it had grown out. She gripped me by the hair on the top of my head. Even then, she did not pull me up, but seemed to twine my hair in her fingers, as if getting a better grip on it.

Dimly, I became aware that Tree Woman was speaking in a raised voice. She ignored me, and sent her words over the abyss to Dewara. 'Was this your weapon, Kidona man? This boy from the west? Ha. The magic has chosen him, and given him to me. I will use him well. Thank you for such a fine weapon, Kidona man!'

Then her voice went very soft. I think I only heard it in my mind. The words reached me as I struggled to keep my grip. She pulled relentlessly upward on my hair now, but it did not seem to lift me.

'Grab my wrists!' I begged her, but she did not heed me.

She spoke calmly, giving me instructions. 'To you, the magic will give a token. Guard it carefully and keep it by you. And from you, I take a token of my own. It will link us, soldier's boy. What you speak, I will hear. I will taste the food you eat, and in turn I will fill you with my sustenance. All you are, I will share and learn.

'To you I will give a great task; you will stop the spread of the intruders. You will turn back the tide of encroachers and destroyers from our lands. Of you I will make a tool to defeat those who would destroy us.' As my mind reeled with pain and I attempted to understand, she lifted her voice again. 'He serves my magic and me now, Kidona man. And you gave him to me! Go back and tell your leather-skinned folk that! You *gave* your weapon into my hand! And now I take it!'

Her words made no sense to me and I had no time to ponder them. My panic increased as I felt her grip tighten on my hair. She pulled suddenly upward and I felt my hair ripping out of my scalp. The pain shot down my spine. I twitched like a gaffed fish. Deep inside me, something important gave way and was dragged out of me, like a strand of thread drawn out of a piece of weaving.

Suddenly her face was so close to me that I could feel her breath on my lips. The only thing I could see were her grey green eyes as she said, 'I have you now. You can let go.'

I did. I fell into blackness.

FIVE

The Return

Somewhere close by, my parents were arguing. My mother's voice was very tight but she was not crying; that meant she was extremely angry. Her words were clipped, the corners sharp. 'He is my son, too, Keft. It was . . . unkind of you to keep me uninformed.' Obviously, she had rejected a much harsher word than 'unkind'.

'Selethe. Some things are not a woman's concern.' From the timbre of my father's voice, I knew he was leaning forward in his chair. I imagined his hands braced on his thighs, elbows out, his shoulders hunched against her rebuke, his stare intent.

'When it comes to Nevare, I am not merely a woman. I am his mother.' I knew that my mother had crossed her arms across her bosom. I could almost see her, standing arrow straight, every hair in place, spots of colour high on her cheeks. 'Everything that concerns my son is *my* concern.'

'Where he is your son, that is so,' my father agreed blandly. But then he added sternly, 'But this concerned Nevare as a soldier son. And where he is a soldier, the boy is mine alone.'

I felt that I had passed through many dreams to reach this place and time. But this was not a dream. This was my old life. I had found my way home. The moment that realization came to me, the other dreams faded like mist in the sunlight. I forgot everything in my haste to rejoin my life. I tried to open my eyelids but they were stuck fast. The skin of my

119

face felt thick and stiff. When I tried to move the muscles of my face, it hurt. I recognized the feeling, from many years ago. I had been badly sunburned and my mother had coated me entirely with agu jelly. I took a deeper breath and smelled the herb's tang. Yes.

'He's waking up!' My mother's voice was full of hope and relief.

'Selethe. It was just a twitch. Nerves. Reflexes. Stop tormenting yourself and go get some rest. He will either recover or he won't, regardless of whether you wear yourself out by keeping watch at his bedside. Your vigil does neither of you any good, and it may become neglect of our other children. Go and busy yourself about the house. If he awakens, I will call you.'

There was no hope in my father's voice. To the contrary, it was heavy with resignation. I felt he rebuked himself as well as her. I heard him settle back, and recognized the creak of the reading chair in my chamber at home. Was that where I was? At home? I tried to remember where I had thought I was, but could not summon a memory of it. Like a dream examined by daylight, it had faded away to nothing.

I heard the rustle of my mother's skirts and her light footfalls as she walked quietly to the door. She opened it, and then paused there. In a lowered, husky voice, she asked, 'Will not you at least tell me why? Why did you entrust our son to a savage, to a man who had reason to hate you personally as well as with the tenacity of his vicious race? Why put our Nevare in harm's way deliberately?'

I heard my father breathe out threateningly through his nose. I waited, as he did, for her to leave. I knew he would not reply to her accusation. Strangely, I recall that I wondered more about why she did not leave than I did about how he might answer her questions. I suppose that I believed so firmly that he would not reply that I did not think any reply was possible.

120

Then he spoke. Quietly. I had heard the words before, but somehow there, in my mother's house, they were more freighted with meaning. 'There are some things that Nevare can't learn from a friend. Some lessons a soldier can learn only from an enemy.'

'What lesson? What thing of value could he have learned from that heathen, other than how to die pointlessly?' My mother was perilously close to tears. I knew as well as she did that if she broke, if she sobbed, my father would banish her to her rooms until she had regained control of herself. He could never abide a woman's tears. Her voice was tight as she said, 'He is a good son to you, willing, obedient and honest. What could he learn from a savage like that Kidona?'

'To *dis*trust.' My father spoke so softly that I could barely hear him. I could scarcely believe that he spoke at all. He cleared his voice and went on more strongly. 'I do not know if you can understand this, Selethe. This once, I will try to explain it to you. Have you ever heard of Dernel's Folly?'

'No.' She spoke softly. I was not surprised that she had never heard of Captain Dernel. He was not renowned but notorious among the military. He was widely blamed for our having lost the Battle of Tobale to the Landsingers. A messenger had brought him orders from his general, telling Dernel to lead a charge into what was clearly a suicidal situation. Dernel had the advantage of the high ground. He could see for himself that the situation had changed since the order had been issued from the rear. He even said so to the orderly he left behind in his tent. Yet he had chosen to be an obedient soldier. He had obeyed a stale order, and led 684 mounted men to their deaths. He had obeyed, even though he had recognized the folly of the order. Every cavalryman knew about Captain Dernel. His name had become a synonym for an officer who did not lead but merely obeyed orders from above.

'Well. Never mind that tale. I will say only that I do not

wish my son to follow in Dernel's footsteps. Nevare is, just as you have said, a good son. An obedient son. He obeys me without question. He obeys Sergeant Duril. He obeys you. He obeys. It is an admirable trait in a son and a necessary one in a soldier. These last few years, I have waited and watched him as he grew, waiting for him to *dis*obey, to question, to challenge me. I waited for a time when he would be tempted to follow his own will. More, I hoped for a time when he would put his own judgment ahead of mine or ahead of Sergeant Duril's.'

'You wanted him to defy you? But why?' My mother was incredulous.

My father gave a short sigh. 'I did not think you would understand it. Selethe, I want our son to be more than an obedient soldier. I want him to rise through the ranks as much by his own aptitude as by our ability to buy a commission for him. To be a good officer, he must be more than obedient. He must develop leadership. That means making his own decisions, finding his own way out of bad situations. He has to be able to evaluate conditions in the field, and know when to follow his own instincts.

'So, I deliberately put him into a difficult situation. I knew that Dewara would teach him many skills. But I also knew that Dewara would eventually put Nevare in a situation in which Nevare would have to make his own decisions. He'd have to question authority, not just Dewara's, but mine in putting him there. It was a desperate tactic, I know. But he had shown no propensity of his own to grow in that direction. I knew I would have to push him across that boundary between boyhood and manhood. I hoped he would learn when to ignore orders given from the safety of the rear by men who do not know the conditions at the front. To trust his own judgment. To know that every soldier is ultimately in command of himself. To lead. To lead first himself, so that eventually he might learn to lead others.' I heard my father shift in my chair. He cleared his throat again. 'To know that not even his own father always knows what is best for him.'

There was a very long silence. Then she spoke in a voice cold with outrage. 'I see. You gave our son's welfare into the keeping of a vicious savage, so that Nevare would learn that his father did not always know what was best for him. Well. I have learned that lesson tonight. It is a pity that Nevare did not learn that lesson much earlier.'

It was the cruellest thing I'd ever heard my mother say to my father. I had never even imagined they had such conversations as this.

'Perhaps you are right. In which case, he would not have survived long as a soldier anyway.' Never had I heard my father's voice so cold. Yet there was sorrow in his words. Did I hear guilt there as well? I could not abide that my father perhaps felt guilt over what had befallen me. I tried to speak, failed, and then tried to shift my hands. I could not, but I could move them back and forth on my bedding. I felt my fingers scratch shallowly against the linens of my bed. That wasn't enough. I drew a deeper breath, braced myself for a great effort, and lifted my right hand. I trembled with the effort, but I held it up.

I heard my mother gasp my name, but it was my father's rough hand that gripped my bandaged fingers. I had not understood that even my hands were wrapped in lint bandages until I felt his fingers close around mine. 'Nevare. Listen to me.' He spoke very loudly and clearly, as if I stood at a far distance from him. 'You're home now. You're safe. You're going to be all right. Don't try to do anything just now. Do you want water? Squeeze my hand if you want water.'

I managed a feeble compression and a short time later a cool glass was held to my mouth. My lips were swollen and stiff; I drank with difficulty, soaking the bandages on my chin and then was returned to my pillows, where I sank into a deep sleep once more.

Later I would learn that I had been returned to my

mother's house, with a fresh notch cut deeply into my ear beside the first one for my disobedience, just as Dewara had promised. But that was not all he had done to me as I lay helpless. The barking of the dogs alerted my father that someone approached his manor house in the slight coolness of the early dawn. The taldi mare had hauled me up to my father's doorstep on a crude travois made of brushwood. My clothes were in tatters, and some parts of me scraped to meat, for the rough conveyance had not completely protected me from being dragged against the ground. The exposed parts of my body were burned past blistering by exposure to the sun. At first glance, my father thought I was dead.

Dewara sat his mount at a distance from the house. When my father and his men came out into the yard to see what the disturbance was, he lifted a long gun and shot Keeksha through the chest. As she screamed, sank to her knees and rolled to her side, he turned his taldi's head and galloped away. No one followed him, for their first concern was to get my unresponsive body clear of her dying kicks. Other than my doubly-notched ear and the slaughtered taldi, Dewara left no message for my father. I was later to learn that he either never returned to the Kidona or that his people concealed him and refused to surrender him to Gernian justice. His possession of a firearm was, by itself, a hanging offence for one of his folk. That he showed it so blatantly still makes me wonder if it were an act of defiance or one that invited his own death at my father's hands.

My injuries were numerous, though only one appeared life threatening. I was dehydrated and burnt from exposure to the summer sun, and rubbed raw from being dragged home. My freshly notched ear was oozing thick blood when my father received me. A patch of scalp the size of a coin was missing from the crown of my head. The doctor summoned by my father shook his head after examining me. 'Whatever is wrong with him, other than the burns and gouges, is beyond my skill.

Perhaps he took a sharp blow to the skull. That may be the reason for his coma. I cannot tell. We will have to wait. In the meantime, we will do what we can for his other injuries.' And so he picked gravel and dirt from my wounds, suturing and binding as he went, until I looked like a mended rag doll.

I come from a thick-skinned and hardy folk, my father said. Healing was painful and slow, but once I awakened from my long unconsciousness, heal I did. My mother insisted that my body be kept well greased to keep air away from my burns. It did serve to keep my fingers from sticking together as the old skin sloughed off to reveal raw pink newness beneath, but lying on greased linen when every inch of my body's surface stung was a sensation I have never forgotten. The pungent agu kept most infection at bay, but left a reek that lingered in my bedchamber for weeks afterward. The wound on my scalp healed over, but no hair grew there.

Talking was painful, and for two days my father spared me any questions. My family had feared for my life, and I was uncomfortably aware, despite my usually bandaged eyes, that for every hour of the day either my mother or one of my sisters sat vigil by my bedside. That this duty was not entrusted to a servant was a sign of the depth of my mother's concern.

Elisi was keeping the watch one afternoon when my father arrived. He shooed her from the room and then sat down heavily in my reading chair. 'Son?' he asked me, and when I turned my head slightly toward the sound of his voice, 'Would you like some water?'

'Please,' I whispered hoarsely.

I heard him pour water into the glass by my bedside. I lifted my hand and nudged aside the greasy poultice across my eyes. My entire face had been blistered from the sun and the healing skin itched. My father watched as I very carefully levered myself into a more upright position. It was awkward to take the glass from him with both my hands in their mittenish bandages, but I saw that he was pleased to see me doing things for myself. That made it worth it. I drank and he took the glass from me quickly as I tried to fumble it back onto the bedside table. Beside it was my only souvenir of the experience. Sergeant Duril had insisted on helping put me to bed. He'd saved one of the rocks they'd dug out of my flesh and set it aside for me. It wasn't much of a rock; some sort of quartz, I suspected, flecked and streaked with other minerals, but his reminder that I had once more cheated death was oddly cheering to me. Duril, at least, expected that someday I would look back on this painful time and find some amusement in this trophy.

My father cleared his throat to draw my attention back to him. 'So. Feeling a bit more yourself now?'

I nodded. 'Yes, sir.'

'Think you can talk?'

My lips felt like burnt sausages. 'A little, sir.'

'Very good.' He leaned back in his chair and thought for a bit, and then leaned toward me again. 'I don't even know what to ask you, son. I think I'll leave it to you to tell me. What happened out there?'

I tried licking my lips. It was a mistake. Ragged bits of skin rasped against my tongue. 'Dewara taught me Kidona ways. Hunting. Riding. How they make fires, what they eat. Bleeding a horse for food. Using a sling to hunt birds.'

'Why did he notch your ear?'

I tried to remember. Parts of my time with him had gone muzzy and vague. 'He had food and water, and would not share. So . . . I left him, to go find water and food of my own. He told me I couldn't leave and I went anyway. Because I thought he'd let me die of thirst if I didn't.'

He nodded to himself, his eyes alight with interest. He didn't rebuke me for disobeying Dewara. Did that mean he thought that I had learned the lesson he'd sought to teach me? Was what had befallen me worth that lesson? I felt a sudden spark of hatred toward him. Resolutely I quenched

126

it and forced myself to hear his question. 'And that was all? For that, he did this to you?'

'No. No, that was just for the first time.'

'So . . . you left him. But then you went back to him for food and water?' Disappointment tinged his question as well as confusion.

'No,' I denied it quickly. 'He came after me, sir. I didn't crawl back to him and beg him to save me. When I rode away from him that first time, he followed me. He chased me on horseback and notched my ear with his swanneck as I fled. I didn't go back to him and stand still for him to mark me like that. I'd have died first.'

I think the vehemence in my voice shocked him.

'Well, no, of course you didn't, Nevare. I know you wouldn't do such a thing. But when he came after you . . . ?'

'I rode a day and a half, and then found water for myself. I knew then that I'd survive. I thought I'd just come home from there. But he came after me, and that night I fought him, and then we talked, and after that, he taught me things, about how the Kidona survive and how they do things.' I took a deeper breath and suddenly felt very, very tired, as if I'd fenced for hours instead of just conversing for a few minutes. I told him that.

'I know, Nevare, and soon I'll let you rest. Just tell me why Dewara did this to you. Until I know, from you, I don't know how to respond to what he has done.' A frown furrowed his brow. 'You do understand that what he has done to you is a great insult to me? I can't ignore it. I've sent men to find him; he will answer to me. But before I pass judgment on him, I must know the full tale of what drove him to this affront. I'm a just man, Nevare. If something passed between you that drove him to this fury . . . if, even unintentionally, you offered him great insult, then you should tell me that, to be an honourable man.' He shifted in his chair and then scraped it across the carpet to come a bit closer to my bedside. He

127

lowered his voice, as if speaking a great confidence to me. 'I fear I learned a greater lesson than you did from Dewara, and one that is just as hard. I trusted him, son. I knew he would be harsh with you; I knew he would not compromise the Kidona ways for you. He was my enemy, never my friend, and yet he was a trusted enemy to me, if those words can ever be spoken together in such a way. I trusted his honour as a warrior. He gave me his word that he would teach you just as he would teach a young Kidona warrior. Then . . . to do this to you . . . I erred in my judgment, Nevare. And you paid the price.'

I considered my words carefully. I'd already thought through my experience. If I ever told my father how close I'd come to 'going native', he'd never respect me again. I found as much of the truth as I thought he could accept. 'Dewara kept his word, Father.'

'He went past his word. To notch your ear . . . I had the doctor put a stitch in each, son. There will be scars, but less than Dewara intended. That I could have accepted, since you admitted you disobeyed him. In truth, I expected you to come home with a scar of some kind. A scar is no shame to a soldier. But to expose you deliberately to the sun when you were helpless, to leave you parched and burning . . . he said nothing of that, nor have I ever heard of it as a punishment applied to Kidona warriors in training. I think he struck you in the head. Do you have any recollection of that?'

When I shook my head, mutely, he nodded to himself. 'Perhaps you would not recall it. Head injuries can erase part of a man's memory. I judge that you must have been unconscious for some time, to burn as you did.'

My thoughts swirled around his earlier admission. I said it aloud, to make him hear it from me. 'You knew I'd disobey him. You knew I'd come home at least with a notched ear if he caught me.'

He paused for some time. I don't think he'd expected to have to admit that to me. 'I knew that might be a conse-

128

quence of your training.' He drew back a bit and looked at me, his head tilted. 'Do you think what you learned from him was a fair exchange for that?'

I thought for a bit. What had I learned from him? I still wasn't sure. Some physical skills in riding and survival. But what had he done to my mind? Had he taught me something, shown me anything? Or only drugged and deluded and abused me? I didn't know but I was certain that my father would be of no help to me in answering those questions. Best not to even raise them. Best to make it possible for him to let it all go. 'Probably what I learned is worth a few scars. And as you've told me before, a soldier must expect scars from his career.' I hoped he would ask no questions when I added, 'Father. Please. Just let him go. I wish this to be the end of it. I disobeyed him. He notched my ear as he said he would. Let it end there.'

He stared at me, torn between bewilderment and relief. 'You know I should not do that, son. This leaving you next to dead on our doorstep . . . If we allow a Kidona to do this to the soldier son of a noble family and take no action . . . well, then we invite other plainspeople to do the same, to other families. Dewara won't understand tolerance or forgiveness. He will respect me only if I command that respect.' He rubbed the bridge of his nose as he added wearily, 'I should have considered that more deeply before I put you in his power. I fear I see what I've done too late. I may have created unrest amongst the Kidona. Having done that, I cannot deny it or step away from it and leave it to others to handle. No, son. I must know the whole tale, and then I must take action on it.'

During his speech, I had begun to scratch gently at the sodden blisters, long burst, on my left forearm. The grease and butter treatment had left me sloughing soggy bits of skin like a river fish at the end of his migration. The temptation to peel it free was as great as it was juvenile. I was nudging gently at an itchy patch, not quite scratching it, and thus avoiding meeting his eyes.

'Nevare?' he prompted me after I had let a moment pass.

I made the decision. I lied to my father. I was surprised at how easily the words fell from my lips.

'He took me up to the plateaus. He was attempting to teach me a manoeuvre for crossing a chasm. It seemed unwise to me, unnecessarily dangerous and I refused to perform it. I was, perhaps, too outspoken. I told him it was stupid, and only a fool would do it. He tried to force me; I struck back at him. I think I hit him in the face.' My father would know that was mortal insult to a Kidona. Dewara's reaction would now seem plausible. I paused, and then decided that was story enough. 'That's the last thing I remember until I woke up here.'

My father sat very still. His silence radiated disappointment in me. I did not wish I had told him the truth, but I did wish I had found a better lie. I waited for him to think it through. The blame for what had happened to me had to fall on either Dewara or myself. I took it upon my shoulders, not because I felt I deserved it, but because even at that young age, I could see far-reaching repercussions if I did not. If Dewara had injured me without serious provocation, my father must be relentless in his pursuit and punishment of the warrior. If I had brought it on myself, then it would be possible for my father to be less vengeful in his hunt. I knew, too, the far-reaching implications of taking the blame on myself; that others must then wonder why my father did not pursue Dewara implacably. There would be a taint of doubt about me; what had I done to the Kidona to deserve such an insult and injury? If my father could tell his associates that I had brought it on myself by striking the Kidona in the face, then it became understandable. My father would be a bit ashamed of me that I had not ultimately triumphed in a physical battle with the warrior. But he could take a bit of fatherly pride in that I'd struck Dewara. Belatedly, I wished

I could revise my lie for I had said I'd refused to cross a chasm, and that did make me sound a bit of a coward. But it couldn't be changed now, so I pushed those thoughts aside. I was in pain and weary and often, during my convalescence, felt that my thoughts were not quite my own.

I did not, for even an instant, consider trying to explain my truth to my father. That was how I had come to think of it in the days of fitful wakefulness since it had occurred. My truth was that, in a dream, I had failed to follow Dewara's command to kill the tree woman. I had disobeyed him, thinking I knew better. I hadn't. He had warned me that she was a formidable enemy. I'd not struck when I had the opportunity to kill her. I would never know what would have happened if I had rushed forward the moment I first saw her and slain her. Now I would live with the consequences. I'd died in that dream place, and as a result, I'd nearly died in this world, too. I wondered if there were any way I could even discuss that 'dream' with my father. I doubted it. Ever since I had learned my father's secret opinion of me, ever since I'd heard him express to my mother his reservations about my fitness to command, I'd felt an odd distance from him. He'd sent me out to be tested by a hostile stranger, with never a word of warning. Had he ever even considered that I might not come back from such a test? Or had that been an acceptable risk? Had he coldly judged that it would be better to lose me now as a son rather than risk disgrace from me when I was a soldier? I looked at him, and felt sick with anger and despair.

I quietly spoke the first words that came to me. 'I don't think I have anything else to tell you right now.'

He nodded sympathetically, deaf to the emotion of my words. 'I'm sure you're still very weary, son. Perhaps we'll talk about this again another time.'

The tone of his words sounded as if he cared. Doubt swirled through me once again. Had I met at least part of his challenge? Did he think I had it in me to command men? Worse, I suddenly doubted my own future. Perhaps my father saw me more clearly than I could see myself. Perhaps I did lack the spark to be a good officer. I heard the door of my room close softly as if I were being shut off from the future I'd always assumed I would have.

I leaned back on my pillows. I took a deep breath and tried to calm myself. But even though I could force my body to relax, the thoughts in my mind only chased one another more swiftly. I felt they had worn a rut in my brain with their endless circling. During the days I lay in bed, strangely weak beyond my injuries, I had handled the memories over and over, trying to make sense of them.

But I couldn't. Logic failed. If it had all been a dream, then I could blame none of it on the Kidona. Obviously, Dewara had drugged me, first with the smoke from the campfire, and then, if truly he had, when he put the dried frog in my mouth. But everything after that had been illusion, of course. It had all been my imagining; none of it had really happened. But why, then, had Dewara been so angry with me? For I was certain of that. He had been so angry that he would have killed me, if he had dared. Only his fear of my father had made him spare my life. But why would he have meted out punishment for an imaginary transgression that he couldn't have known about? Unless it was possible that he truly had followed me into my dream; unless, in some peculiar way, we had entered some plainsfolk world and sojourned there.

That circle of illogic gave way to another conclusion. The dream I'd dreamed hadn't been mine. I was convinced of that in a way I could not dispute with myself. It had been fantastic in a way that was foreign to my thinking. I would not have dreamed of such a peculiar bridge, or such a chasm. I would certainly not have dreamed of a fat old woman as the nemesis I must fight! A two-headed giant or an armoured knight of olden times should have guarded a river ford or bridge, if it

132

had been *my* dream. Those were the challengers of my legends. And my own reaction had been wrong. I felt puzzled, as if I'd read a tale from a distant land and not understood the hero or the ending. I could not even decide why the dream seemed so important to me. I wanted it to fade as my other dreams did when I woke, but this one lingered with me for days.

As the dreary days of my convalescence passed, the dream merged with recollections of my days with Dewara until all of it seemed unreal. It was hard for me to put the events of those days in consecutive order. I could show Sergeant Duril the skills the Kidona had taught me, but I could not recall the precise sequence of learning them. They had become a part of me, something written into my nerves and bones along with breathing or coughing . . . I did not want to carry the Kidona into my life with me, yet I did. Something of him had seeped into my very blood, the way he accused my father's iron shot of staying in his soul. Sometimes I would stand before my rock collection, staring at the coarse stone the doctor had dug out of my flesh, and try to decide how much of the experience had been real. The rock and my scars were the only physical evidence that I had that any of it had been real. Occasionally, I would touch the round bald spot on the crown of my head. I decided that I had been unconscious when Dewara struck me there, and my brain had incorporated the pain into my dream.

Only once did I try to speak of my dream journey to anyone. It was about six weeks after I had been returned to my father's house. I was up and about again and well on my way to full recovery. A few places, such as my forearms and the tops of my cheeks were dappled pink for many months after the rest of my body had healed, but I had progressed to once more rising and breakfasting daily with my family. Yaril, my younger sister, seemed to have a very vivid dream life, and often bored or annoyed the rest of the family by insisting on giving long accounts of her illogical imaginings at the breakfast table. That morning, midway through one such rambling tale of being rescued from the jaws of ravenous sheep by a horde of birds, my father banished her, breakfastless, to the drawing room. 'A woman who has nothing sensible to say should not bother speaking at all!' he told her sternly as he sent her from the room.

After the rest of us were excused from the table, I sought her in the parlour, knowing that she was far more sensitive than her siblings, and wept over rebukes that Elisi or I would simply have shrugged off. My estimate of her temperament was correct. She was sitting on a settee, ostensibly working on some embroidery. Her head was bent and her eyes were red. She would not look up at me as I came in. I sat down next to her, held out the muffin I had filched from the table and said quietly, 'Actually, I was quite looking forward to hearing what came next in your dream. Won't you tell me?'

She took the muffin from me, thanking me with a look. She broke off a piece and ate it, and then said huskily. 'No. It's foolish, as father says. A waste of time for me to prattle about my dreams or for you to listen to them.'

I could not disagree with my father, not to my little sister. 'Foolish, yes, but so are many things that amuse us. I think he feels the breakfast table is not the best place for stories of that sort. But I'd be happy to listen to them, when we have time together, like this.'

My younger sister had enormous grey eyes. They always reminded me of a soot-cat's eyes. Her gaze was very solemn. 'You are so kind to me, Nevare. I can tell when you are just being kind, however. I do not think you have the slightest interest in what I dream at night, or in what I do or think by day. You are only trying to be sure my feelings were not hurt when father dismissed me.'

She was absolutely correct about her dreams, but I tried to soften my practicality. 'Actually, dreams do interest me, mostly because I have so few myself. You, on the other hand, seem to dream nearly every night.'

'I've heard that we all dream, every night, but only some people can remember their dreams.'

I smiled at that. 'And if everyone forgot all their dreams, how could anyone prove such a thing? No. When my head touches my pillow and I close my eyes, all is quiet in my mind until morning. Unlike you. You seem to fill your sleeping hours with all sorts of adventures and fancies.'

She glanced away from me. 'Perhaps I adventure in my dreams because there is so little else in my life to distract me.'

'Oh, I don't think you've got such a hard life, little girl.'

'No. I've hardly any sort of a life at all,' she returned, almost bitterly. When I just looked at her, puzzled, she shook her head at me. A moment later she asked me, 'Then you've never had a peculiar dream, Nevare? One that made you wake, heart racing, wondering which was more real, the dream world or this one?'

'No,' I said, and then added, 'well, perhaps once.'

She focused those kitten eyes on me. 'Really? What did you dream, Nevare?' She leaned toward me, as if such things were truly important.

'Well.' As I pondered where to begin the telling of the dream, I felt a strange sensation. The scar on the top of my head burned, and from there, the hot pain shot down through me, once more running along my spine. I shut my eyes and I turned hastily away from Yaril. I felt faint. The reality of the pain brought my dream back in shattering detail. The smell of the tree woman was in my nostrils and my hands clutched the slicing blade again. I took a shuddering breath and tried to speak. At first, no sounds came out until I said, 'It was a disturbing dream, Yaril. I do not think I will speak of it.' The pain ceased as suddenly as it had begun. It still took me a moment to catch my breath and force my hands to open. I turned back toward Yaril; she was regarding me with alarm.

'Whatever could you have dreamed, that would frighten a man so?' she asked me.

Her childish naïveté that saw me, only a few years her senior, as a grown man, silenced me more effectively than the burst of pain had. For I deemed my sudden pain to be a sort of hallucination, a terrible re-experiencing of the dream that had been my downfall. Despite how badly that brief experience had rattled me, my sister had referred to me as a man, and I would not do or say anything to lessen her opinion of me at that moment. So I merely shook my head and added, 'It would not be a fit topic to discuss in front of a lady anyway.'

Her eyes widened in surprise that her brother Nevare might have dreams not fit to discuss with a lady, but I also saw her pleasure that I had referred to her as a 'lady' rather than as a 'child'. She sat back in her seat and said, 'Well, if it is so, Nevare, then I will not ask you any more about it.'

Such innocents we both were then.

Days piled on days to become months, like dead leaves heaping atop one another to become loam. I set my dream experience aside and forgot it as much as I could. My burns healed, the stitched ear healed more slowly, and the notches became scars I lived with. I kept a small bald spot on the crown of my head, scar tissue where once healthy scalp had been. I moved on with my life and my lessons and training. I carried inside me, small and sharp, the knowledge that my father, despite his encouraging words to me, doubted me. His doubt became my own, a competitor that I could never quite conquer.

I made only one other concession to that experience. Late in the autumn, I told my father that I wished to go hunting alone, to test my prowess. He told me it was foolish, but I persevered in my stubborn request, and eventually he granted me six days to myself. I told him I would be hunting along the high banks of the river, and I did begin my journey in that direction. I first visited the spot where Dewara and his women had been camped when I first met him. The ashes and stones of a cookfire and the disturbances where he had pegged his tent were almost the only marks of his passage. The sheath of my old cavalry sword lay on the ground, the leather slowly rotting in the weather. Of the sword itself, there was no sign. Perhaps a passing traveller had discovered it. But it seemed unlikely that someone would come across a sword and its sheath, and carry off only the bare blade. I didn't think so. I tossed the sheath back onto the ground and walked away from it. A man could not summon a weapon to come to him. Not in my world. I felt a touch of pain in the scar on my head. I rubbed at it, and then turned away from the campsite. I didn't want to think about it just now.

I turned Sirlofty's head inland. The prairie had changed with the season, but I allowed for that, and roughly calculated how long it would take Sirlofty's gentle, long-legged lope to travel the distance the taldi mare had covered in that mad gallop. For the first two days, I rode steadily, pushing Sirlofty in the morning and taking it more gently in the afternoon. The autumn rains had made watering spots more plentiful than they had been when last I crossed this terrain. Tiny rivulets had resumed their task of shaping the plateaus and the gorges. I had expected this lonely journey to bring my memories back and let me put them to rest, but it only made the events of the spring stranger and more incomprehensible.

I found, eventually, the same spot where Dewara had built the final fire we had shared. I was certain of it. I came to it in early afternoon. I stood on the edge of the cliffs and looked out over the vista. The scorched rocks from that last fire were still there, tufts of grass sprouting up around them. I found the burned ends of the Kidona fire-bow I had made under Dewara's tutelage and the leather cup of the sling he had given me to use. It looked to me as if everything he had given to me or had me make had been deliberately consigned to the flames. I thought about that for a time, and also about how he had shot the mare that I had ridden. Did it mean that I had somehow tainted Keeksha, made her unfit for use by a Kidona warrior? Dewara had left me no answers, and I knew that the ones I made up for myself would always remain theories.

Then, risking life and limb, I climbed down and along the face of the cliffs, looking for the entrance to the cave. I had thought it through and decided that there must be a cave down there, and a ledge, a place we had jumped down to and entered, and that there the frog had made me hallucinate. I was certain of that explanation.

I found nothing. I did not find a ledge that I could comfortably stand on, let alone the place I had jumped down to and the cave I had entered. They didn't exist. I climbed back up and sat on the edge of the bluff, looking off to the distant river. All of it had been a dream, then, or a hallucination brought on by the fumes of whatever Dewara had burned on the fire. All of it, every bit of it. I made a fire on the site of our old one, with good flint and steel, and spent the night at the site, but did not sleep. Rolled in my blanket, I stared up at the night sky and wondered about the things that savages believed and if the good god had somehow given them a different truth than he had given us. Or did the good god reign over them at all? Did their old fading gods linger, and had I visited one of the worlds of those pagan deities? That thought sent a shiver up my spine in the dark. Were those dark and cruel worlds true places that existed, but a dream step away?

The good god can do all and anything, the Writ says. He can make a square circle and create justice from men's tyranny and grow hope from withered seed in the desert. If he could do all those things for his people, did the old gods possess a similar power for theirs? Had I glimpsed a reality that was not meant for my kind?

A boy on the edge of manhood ponders such questions and so I did that night. My meditations were not conducive to sleep. The next morning, sleepless but unwearied, I rose with

138

the sun. As the first light touched my campsite, the good god seemed to answer a prayer, for the light played briefly on a rough outcropping of stone. For a moment, the dawn sparkled on trapped flecks of mica, and then the angle changed, and it became only a dusty outcropping. I walked to it, crouched by it, and touched it, feeling its hard reality. This, I was sure, was the mother of the small stone I'd carried in my flesh. That cruel souvenir, at least, had definitely come from this world. I mounted Sirlofty and rode toward home.

The very next night, as if to reward me for my deception of my father, a rustling in the brush at the wet end of a gully where I had decided to camp proved to be a small plainsbuck. I brought him down with a single shot. I cut his throat to bleed him out, slit his hind legs between the tendon and the bone, and hoisted him up into a stunted tree. I gutted him as he hung there and propped the chest cavity open with a stick to let the meat cool. He wasn't large and his rack was no more than a set of spikes, but he was sufficient excuse for my expedition.

I don't think I was exceptionally surprised when Sergeant Duril rode into camp while I was cooking the liver. 'Nothing better than fresh liver,' he observed as he dismounted. I didn't ask if he had been following me for long, or why he was there. Our hobbled horses grazed together and we shared the meat as the stars came out. Autumn was advanced enough that we welcomed the fire's warmth.

We had been in our blankets for some time, silent and pretending to sleep when he asked me, 'Do you want to talk about it?'

I nearly said, 'I can't.' That would have been the honest answer. And it would have led to all sorts of other questions and probing and worries. I would have had to lie to him. Duril wasn't a man to lie to. So I simply said, 'No, Sergeant. I don't think I do.'

And that was what I learned from Dewara.

SIX

Sword and Pen

I have spoken to men who have suffered sudden severe injuries, or endured torture or extreme loss. They speak of those events distantly, as if they have set them out of their lives. So I attempted to do with my experience with Dewara. Having proved to myself that none of my encounter with the tree woman had even the most tenuous tie to reality, I moved on with my life. I resolutely left that nightmare vision behind, along with childish fears of hobgoblins under my bed or making wishes on falling stars.

It was more than the tree woman I attempted to vanquish from my thoughts. I also banished my father's secret doubt of me from my ruminations. Dewara had been a test, to see if I could, when circumstance demanded it, question my father's wisdom and resist the old plains warrior and become my own leader. I had only briefly defied Dewara before becoming submissive again to his guidance. I had never defied my father. But I had lied to him. I had lied to try to make him think I'd found the backbone to stand up to the Kidona. If I had thought that lie would buy me new respect from my father, it hadn't. His attitude toward me had not changed at all that I could detect.

For a short time, I strove desperately to win his regard. I re-doubled my effort, not just at the fencing and cavalla techniques that I loved, but also on the academic studies that were my demons. My scores soared, and when he discussed the monthly reports of my progress, he praised me for my efforts. But the words were the same ones I had always heard from him. Having never suspected he doubted me, when obviously he had, I now found I could no longer believe in his praise. And when he rebuked me, I felt it doubly-hard, and in private my own disgust with myself magnified his disappointment in me.

Some part of me realized that I could never do anything that would guarantee my father's approval. So I made a conscious decision to set those experiences aside. Spirit journeys to tree women and lying to my father did not fit with the day-to-day understanding of my existence, and so I discarded them. I think it is how most men get from one day to the next; they set aside all experiences that do not mesh with their perception of themselves.

How different would our perception of reality be if, instead, we discarded the mundane events that cannot co-exist with our dreams?

Yet that was a thought that only came to me many years later. What remained of my sixteenth year demanded the full focus of my mind. My recovery from my injuries was followed by a growth spurt that astonished even my father. I ate like a starved beast at every meal. It all went to height and muscle. In my seventeenth year, I went through three pairs of boots and four jackets in eight months. My mother declared proudly to her friends that if I did not soon reach my man's height and stop growing, she would have to hire a seamstress just to keep me decently clad.

Like almost all youths at that age, I and my own concerns seemed of the utmost importance to me. I scarcely noticed my younger brother being packed off for his first indoctrination into the priesthood, or my sister Yaril graduating to long skirts and pinned-up hair. I was too intent on whether or not I could ever make first touch on my fencing master, or improve my target scores with a long gun. I consider those years to be the most selfish of my life, and yet I think such selfishness and self-focus is necessary for a young man as deluged with lessons and information as I was.

Even the events of the greater world seldom touched me, so involved was I in my own learning and growing. The news that reached my ears was filtered through my vision of my future. I was aware that the King and the so-called Old Nobles wrestled for power and tax money. My father sometimes discussed politics with my elder brother Rosse after dinner, and even though I knew that politics were not the proper concern of a soldier, I listened. My father had a right to be heard in the Council of Lords, and he regularly dispatched messages that contained his views. He always sided with King Troven. The Old Nobles needed to lift their heads and see the King's new vision of a realm that extended east across the plains rather than west to the sea. The Old Nobles would have cheerfully renewed our ancient strife with Landsing, all in the name of trying to win back the coastal provinces that we had lost to them. My father's attitude was that the King's way was wiser; all his New Nobles backed him in his eastward expansion. I gave little attention to the details of the strife. It might have to do with us, but all the debating and posturing occurred in the capital, Old Thares to the west. It was easy and fitting that, as a solider son, I nod my head and adopt my father's opinion as my own.

I was more enthusiastic about news from the eastern borders. Tales of the Speck plague dominated. The awareness of plague had slowly permeated all our lives during the years I grew toward manhood. Yet, dreadful as the tales of decimation were, they remained stories of a distant disaster. Sometimes it reached in amongst us, as when old Percy came to my father, to ask for time to travel east to visit his sons' graves. A soldier himself, both his boys had gone for troopers, and died of plague before they could sire sons to carry on Percy's line and his calling. His daughter's sons would be shoemakers like their father. He confided this to my father as if it grieved him. His personal loss made the ravages of the plague a bit more real to me. I had known Kifer and Rawly. They had been but four and five years older than I, and now they rested in distant graves near the border. But for the most part, the plague stayed where it belonged, confined to the military outposts and settlements in the foothills of the Barrier Mountains. It was but one of the many dangers of the border: snakes and poisonous insects, the erratic and irrational attacks by the Specks, the great cats and savagely aggressive humpdeer. Wariness of the disease surged in the hot summers when it flared up, consuming men like kindling. It ebbed only when the gentler days of winter arrived.

My eighteenth summer was filled with marching troops. Weekly we saw them moving past our holdings along the river road. These were solid ranks of replacements for men fallen to disease during the summer rather than the steady trickle of new soldiers off to their first assignments on the border. Westward bound funeral processions, black-draped wagons full of coffins drawn by sweating black horses, clopped and creaked past our homes on their mournful journey back to the civilized west, bearing the bodies of men from families sufficiently wealthy or noble to require that they be returned home for burial. Those we watched from a distance. My father made little noise about them, but my mother feared contagion and strictly forbade any of us to loiter along the river road when such sad processions were moving along it.

Each summer when the plague returned, wave after wave of it consumed our soldiers. My father estimated the mortality rate at between twenty-three and forty-six percent amongst able-bodied soldiers, given the information he had access to. Among the elderly, the women and the very young, the scythe of death swung even more efficiently, leaving few standing in its wake. It wasted a healthy man to skin and bone in a matter of days. Of those who survived, some recovered to lead nearly normal lives, though most were unfit for the heavy duty of a horse soldier. Some suffered an impaired sense of balance, a terrible loss for a cavalry man. The survivors that I met were unnaturally thin. The soldier sons of my father's friends, they stopped in to visit and dine with us on their long journeys back to Old Thares. They ate and drank as any men did, and some even pushed themselves to consume more than a normal amount of victuals. Yet they could not seem to regain the strength and vitality they had once possessed. Broken bones and torn muscles seemed to befall them easily. It was a terrible thing to see young officers, once hale and hearty, now thin and listless and retiring from the military just when they should have been rising to command. They seemed weary beyond the stress of a long day in the saddle. They spoke of frontier towns full of widows and children, their common-soldier husbands fallen not to war but to plague.

Autumn came, and the wet winds of winter quenched the plague fires. The end of the year brought both my eighteenth birthday and the Dark Evening holiday. The latter was not much observed in our household. My father regarded Dark Evening as a pagan holiday, a superstitious holdover from the days of the old gods. Some still called it Dark Woman's Night. The ways of the old gods said that a married woman could be unfaithful to her husband on that one night of the year and not be held accountable for it, for on the night of the Dark Woman, a woman must obey no will save her own. My mother and sisters did not hold with any such nonsense, of course, but I knew that they envied some of the other households in our area who still celebrated Dark Evening with masked balls and opulent feasts and gifts of pearl or opal jewellery wrapped in starry paper. In our home, the longest, darkest night of winter passed with little fanfare.

My mother and sisters would set tiny boats afloat on our pond with candles on them, and my father always gave each of his women a small envelope containing a gift of money, but that was the extent of it.

I had always suspected that my birthday was so well celebrated simply because my father had forbidden a lavish Dark Evening in our household, and so my birthday became the mid-winter celebration by default. Often my mother gave a special dinner in my honour, and invited guests from neighbouring holdings. But that year, my eighteenth year, my birthday marked my entrance into manhood, and so the party was more solemn and restricted to our immediate family.

It made the occasion more formal and portentous. My father had brought Vanze home from his studies in the western monastery to preside. His voice had not even changed yet, but still he was so proud to hold the family book and wear his priest's vest while he read aloud my verses from the Writ:

'The second born son of every noble man shall be his father's soldier son, born to serve. Into his hand he will take the sword, and with it he shall defend the people of his father. He shall be held accountable for his actions, for it is by his sword and his pen that his family may have glory or dwell in shame. In his youth let him serve the rightful king, and in his old age, let him return home, to defend the home of his father.'

As my brother spoke those words, I held up my father's gifts to me for my family to see. In one hand I gripped my new cavalla sword, sheathed in gleaming black leather. In the other, I held aloft a leather-bound journal, with our family crest stamped on the front. One was my weapon, the other my accounting for my deeds. This second gift marked a significant moment for my entire family. It was not just that I had reached an age when I was expected to behave as a man; it also marked the passing of a family torch to me.

My father was a New Noble, and the first to bear the title of Lord Burvelle of the East. That made me the first soldier son of this new line of nobility. For the first time in my life, the place of honour at the head of the table was mine. The book I held had come all the way from Old Thares, and my father's crest had been imprinted on the cover by the King's official press.

In that moment of silence, I looked down the long table at my family and considered my place in it. To my right was my father, and sitting just beyond him, my mother. To my left was my elder brother, Rosse, the heir who would inherit my father's house and lands. Just beyond him stood my younger brother, Vanze, home to read the Holy Writ in my honour. Next to Vanze on one side of the table and next to my mother on the other side were my two sisters, elegant Elisi and kittenish Yaril. They would marry well, carrying off family wealth in the form of dowries but enriching the family with the social alliances they would bring. My father had done well for himself in the begetting of his children. He had fathered all the family that any man might hope for, and an extra daughter besides.

And I, Nevare, was the second son, the soldier son of the family. Today it became real to me. Always it had been so down the years of my bloodlines: the eldest son to inherit, the third son a gift to the good god, and the second son a soldier, to bring honour and fame to our family name. And to every nobly born soldier son on his eighteenth birthday was given such a journal as I now held in my hands, bound in good calfskin, the pages stitched firmly in place, the creamy sheets heavy and durable. My own words would hold me 'accountable' as the Writ said. This book and the serviceable pen kit that buckled inside it would travel everywhere I did, as surely as my sword did. The journal was made to open and lie flat, so that I could write easily in it whether at a desk or camped by a fireside. The pen kit held not only two sturdy pens and an ink supply and tips but also pencils with various weights and colours of leads for sketching terrain and flora and fauna. When this volume was filled, it would return to Widevale, to be placed on a shelf in the library as part of my family's permanent record, alongside the journals that told of our crops and cattle and recorded births, marriages and deaths. The journal I held in my hands now would become the first volume in the first record of first soldier son to wear my father's crest. When this book was filled and sent home, I would immediately begin my new entries in the next volume. I would be expected to record every significant event in my duty to king, country, and family.

In my Uncle Sefert's mansion in Old Thares, an entire wall of his grand library was given over to tall shelves that held rank upon rank of such journals. Sefert Burvelle was my father's elder brother, the eldest son who inherited the family home, title, and lands. To him came the duty of preserving the family history. My own father, Keft Burvelle, had been the second son, the soldier son of his generation. Forty-two years before my eighteenth birthday, my father had mounted his cavalla horse and set out with his regiment for the frontier. He had never returned to live at Stonecreek Mansion, his ancestral home, but all of his military journals had. His writing occupied a substantial two shelves of his brother's library, and was rife with the telling of our military's final battles with the plainspeople as King Troven had expanded his holdings into the Wilds.

In time, when my father had gained rank and been offered private quarters at the fort, he had sent word home that he was ready for his bride to join him. Selethe Rode, then twenty but promised to him since she was only sixteen, had travelled to him by coach, wagon and horseback, to be wed to him in the regiment chapel at Fort Renalx. She had been a good cavalry wife, bearing child after child to the lieutenant who became a captain and eventually retired as a colonel. In their youth, they had believed that all their sons would go for soldiers, for such was the destiny of the sons of a soldier son.

The battle of Bitter Creek changed all that. My father so distinguished himself in the final two charges that when King Troven heard tell of it, he granted him a holding of four hundred acres of the land so painstakingly and bloodily won from the plainspeople. With the land grant went a title and a crest of his own, making him one of the first elevated into the new nobility. The King's new lords would settle in the east and bring civilization and tradition with them.

It was my father's crest, not his older brother's, sharply stamped into the fragrant leather of my new book, which I held up for my brothers and sisters to see. Our crest was a spond tree resplendent with fruit beside a creek. This journal would return here, to Widevale Mansion rather than being posted to our ancestral home at Stonecreek in Old Thares. This book would be the first volume on the first shelf set aside for the soldier sons of my father's line. We were founding a dynasty here on the former edge of the Wilds, and we knew it.

The silence had grown long as I held the journal aloft and savoured my new position. My father finally broke it.

'So. There it is. Your future, Nevare. It awaits only you, to live it and to write it.' My father spoke so solemnly that I could not find words to reply.

I set my gifts down carefully on the red cushion on which they had been presented to me. As a servant bore them away from the table, I took my seat. My father lifted his wine glass. At a sign from him, one of the serving men replenished all our glasses. 'Let us toast our son and brother, wishing Nevare many brave exploits and opportunity for glory!' he suggested to his family. They lifted their glasses to me, and I raised mine in turn, and then we all drank.

'Thank you, sir,' I said, but my father was not finished.

Again, he lifted his glass. 'And.' He spoke, and then waited until my eyes met his. I had no idea what might come next but I desperately hoped it would be a cavalla horse of my own choosing. Sirlofty was a wonderful mount, but I dreamed of a more fiery horse. I held my breath. My father smiled, not at me, but the satisfied smile of a man who had done well for himself and his family as his gaze travelled the full table. '*And* let us toast to a future that bodes well for all of us. The negotiations have been long and very delicate, my boy, but it is done at last. Show Lord Grenalter three years of honourable service on the frontier, earning a captain's stars on your collar, and he will bestow on you the hand of his younger daughter, Carsina.'

Before I could say a word, Yaril clasped her hands together in delight and cried out, 'Oh, Nevare, you will make Carsina and me sisters! How wonderful! And in years to come, our children will be both playmates and cousins!'

'Yaril. Please contain yourself. This is your brother's moment.' My mother's rebuke to my lively younger sister was soft-spoken, but I heard it. Despite her words, my mother's eyes shone with pleasure. I knew that she was as fond of young Carsina as my sister was. Carsina was a lively, pleasant girl, flaxen-haired and round-faced. She and Yaril were the best of friends. Carsina and her elder sister and mother often came of a Sixday, to join the women of our house in meditation, needlework, and gossip. Lord Grenalter had served alongside my father, and indeed won his lands and family crest in the same engagements that had led to my father's elevation. Lady Grenalter and my mother had attended the same finishing school and had been cavalla wives together. As the daughter of a New Noble, Carsina would be well schooled in all that was expected of a soldier's wife, unlike the tales I had heard of old nobility wives, near suicidal with despair when they discovered they were expected to cope with a home on the border and plainspeople on

149

their doorstep. Carsina Grenalter was a good match for me. I did not resent that whatever dower of land she might bring would enrich my brother's estate rather than come to Carsina and me. That was how it had always been done, and I rejoiced for how it would expand my family's holding. In the dim future, when I retired from the cavalla, I knew we would be welcomed home to Widevale, to finish raising our children here. My sons would be soldiers after me, and my brother Rosse would see that my daughters married well.

'Nevare?' my father prompted me sternly, and I suddenly realized that my musing had kept me from replying to his news.

'I am speechless with joy at what you have won for me, Father. I will try to be worthy of the lady, and show Lord Grenalter the full nobility of my bloodlines.'

'Very good. I am glad you are conscious of the honour he does us in trusting one of his daughters to our household. To your future bride, then!'

And again we all lifted our glasses and drank.

That was my last night as a boy in my father's house. With my eighteenth birthday, I left behind all childish pursuits. The next morning, I began a man's schedule, rising with the dawn, to join my father and brother at their austere breakfast and then ride out with them. Each day we rode to a different part of my father's holdings, to take reports from the supervisors. Most of them were men my father had known in his cavalry days, glad to find useful work now that they were too old to soldier. He housed them well, and allotted each a garden patch, pasturage for a cow or two milk goats and half-a-dozen chickens. He had aided many of them in acquiring wives from the western cities, for well my father knew that although the sons of such men must go for soldiers, their daughters might very well attract cobblers or merchants or farmers as husbands. Our little river-town needed such an influx of tradesmen if it was to grow.

I had known my father's men all my life, but in the days that followed, I grew to know them even better. Although they held no rank now, having given up their titles with their uniforms, my father still referred to them as 'corporal' or 'sergeant', and I think they enjoyed that acknowledgment of their past deeds.

Sergeant Jeffrey oversaw the care of our sheep in their rolling, riverside pasture. That spring we had had a bumper crop of lambs, with many ewes dropping twins. Not all of the ewes had the milk or patience to care for two lambs, and so Jeffrey had had his hands full, recruiting plainspeople nippers from the tamed Ternu villagers to help with the bottle feedings. The youngsters came to their tasks with enthusiasm, happy to work for a penny a day and a stick of sugar candy. My father took pride in how he had tamed the Ternu, and was now training their offspring in useful endeavours. It was, he maintained, the duty of the Gernian New Nobles to bring such benefits to the formerly uncivilized folk of the plains and plateaus. When he and my mother hosted dinner parties and gatherings, he often deliberately steered the talk to the necessity of such charity work, and encouraged other New Noble families to follow his example.

Corporal Curf lacked part of his right foot, but it did not slow him much. He oversaw our hay and grain fields, from ploughing to planting to harvest. He had much enthusiasm for irrigation, and often he and my father discussed the feasibility of such an engineering project. He had seen plainspeople employ such tactics to bring water to their seasonal fields in the east, and was eager to attempt an experiment to duplicate their success. My father's stance was to grow what the land would naturally support, in accordance with the good god's will, but Curf burned to bring water to the upper fields. I doubted the question would be resolved in my lifetime. Curf worked tirelessly for my father, trying all sorts of tactics to try to restore the fertility of the land after its third year of use.

151

Sergeant Refdom was our orchard man. This was a new area of endeavour for us. My father saw no reason why fruit trees should not flourish on the hillsides above the grain fields. Neither did I, but flourish they did not. Leaf curl blight had all but killed every one of the plum trees. Some sort of burrowing worm attacked the tiny apples as soon as they formed. But Sergeant Refdom was determined, and this year he had brought in a new variety of cherry that seemed to be establishing well.

Each day we returned to the house by mid-morning. We shared tea and meat rolls and then my father dismissed me to my classes and exercises. He deemed it wise that I learn the basics of husbanding our holdings, for when my soldiering days were over, I would be expected to come home and serve my brother as his overseer in his declining years. Should any untimely illness or mishap befall Rosse before then, he could by law ask the King that his soldier brother be returned to him for the 'defence of his father's lands'. It was a fate that I nightly prayed to be spared, and not just out of fondness for my solid older brother. I knew that I had been born for the cavalla. The good god himself had made me a second son, and I do believe that he grants to all such the fibre of character and adventurous spirit that a soldier must possess. I knew that eventually, when my days of riding to battle were over, I must return to our holdings, and probably take up the duties of Corporal Curf or Sergeant Refdom. All my sons would be soldiers and to me would fall the training of my elder brother's soldier son, but all my daughters would take whatever dower they carried from our family holdings. It behooved me to know the operation of them, so that when my time came to contribute directly to their upkeep, I'd be a useful man.

But my heart was full of dreams of battle and patrol and exploration as our forces pushed ever deeper into the wild lands, winning territory, riches and resources for good King

Troven. In the border lands to the east, our troops still skir-mished with the former inhabitants of the lands there, trying to make them settle and see that the greater good of all demanded that they accept our civilization. My greatest fear was that we would be able to subdue them before I reached my soldiering age, and that instead of battle, I would spend my years of duty in administrational tasks. I dreamed that I would be there on the day when his King's Road finally pushed through the Barrier Mountains to the shores of the Far Sea. I wanted to be one of the first to ride triumphantly the length of that long road, and gallop my horse through the surf of an alien ocean on a foreign beach.

The rest of the mornings of my last year at home were spent at book lessons. The afternoons were completely weapons practice now. The two hours that once had been mine for leisure reading or boyish amusements vanished. My childhood fascination with naming and classifying the stones that had 'killed' me now had to be set aside for a man's pursuits. Spending an hour listening to Elisi practise her music, or helping Yaril gather the flowers for the vases in the parlour and dining room were no longer worthy of my time. I missed my sisters, but knew it was time I focused my attention on the world of men.

Some of the lessons were tedious, but I kept a good disci-pline, aware that both my father and my tutors judged me not only on how well I could repeat my lessons but also on the attitude I displayed. A man who wishes to rise to com-mand must first learn to accept commands. And no matter how high I rose in the ranks, there would always be someone above me to whom I must bow my head and whose author-ity I must accept. It behooved me to display that I could accept the harness of discipline and wear it willingly. In those days, the sole ambition I possessed was the one that had been with me since birth: I would make my family proud of me. I would force my father to hold me in high esteem.

153

In the evenings, after dinner, I now joined my father and Rosse in the study for adult conversation about our holdings and politics and the current news of the realm. As I would not be allowed to either smoke or drink during my Academy years, my father advised me not to cultivate an indulgence for tobacco and to limit my liquor to the wine always served with our meals and a single brandy after dinner. I accepted that as a sensible restriction.

The third weeks of every month of my nineteenth year were to my liking. Those days were given over entirely to Sergeant Duril's 'finishing school' as he laughingly called it. Sirlofty had become my daily mount and I strove to make my horsemanship worthy of that excellent steed. Sergeant Duril now made it his business to toughen me as befitted a cavalryman, as well as to perfect my execution of the more demanding drill movements.

Duril had been a drill sergeant for new recruits at his last outpost, and knew his business well. He worked with me on precision drill until I swore I could feel every set of muscles in Sirlofty's body and knew exactly how to match my body to my horse's as he moved. We did battle leaps, kicks and spins, high-stepping parade prance and the demanding cadence gaits.

We rode out often over the wide prairie wastelands. Now that I had a man's years, Duril spoke to me more as an equal. He taught me the plants and creatures of that region as he and my father's troops had utilized them, for survival sustenance, and gradually reduced my packed supply of water and food until I had learned to go for several days with only what we could scavenge from the land itself. He was a demanding taskmaster, harsher in some ways than Dewara had been, but Duril set the example himself and never let his strictness pass the line into abuse. I knew he carried emergency supplies in his saddlebags, yet he limited himself just as he did me, and proved by example how little

a man could survive on if he employed his own resourceful-
ness. If he required me to learn how to find cactus-borers,
he demonstrated looking for their holes in the spiny palms
of the flathand cacti, and showed me, also, how to cut my
way to the heart of the colony where the fat yellow grubs
could provide a nourishing, if squirmy, meal for a desperate
soldier. He was a natural storyteller and the veteran of many
campaigns. He illustrated his lessons with stories from his
own experience. I often wished that my history books were
more like his anecdotes, for he made the plains Campaigns
the history of his life. He never expected me to do anything
he had not proven that he could do also, and for that my
respect of my gruff teacher was boundless.

Toward the end of my training with Duril, in the beating
hot days of summer, he took me out to prove myself on a
five-day jaunt over the waterless and scrubby terrain of the
rough country to the east of Widevale. On the third day, he
took my hat from me and made me ride bareheaded under
the sun, saying not a word until I finally halted and fashioned myself some head protection by weaving a crude hat
from sagebrush twigs. Only then did a smile break his craggy
face. I feared he would mock me, but instead he said, 'Good.
You figured out that protecting yourself from sunstroke is
more important than saving your dignity. Many a failed
officer put his dignity before the need to maintain a clear
mind for himself so that he can make good decisions for his
troops. It's even worse when those in command won't let
their troops do what they must to survive. Captain Herken
comes to mind. Out on patrol, and a watering spot he'd
been relying upon reaching turned out to be a dry hole. His
men wanted to use their urine. You can drink it if you
have to, or use it to damp your clothes and be cooler. He
wouldn't let them. Said no command of his was going to be
piss-breathed. He chose death for a third of them over a little bit of stink. Far better a sage-hat and a sensible leader

than a bare-head and ridiculous orders from some fool suffering from heatstroke.'

It wasn't the first time he'd told me such rough tales of survival. I never asked my father about them, and of course I'd never repeat such stories about the house. I think I understood that by putting me with this man, my father signalled his approval of whatever harshly won knowledge the sergeant chose to pass on to me. Duril might lack a lofty pedigree, but he was a soldier's soldier, and as such my father respected him.

That night, when we camped around a smoky little fire of resinous branches near a thornbush-ringed water hole, he led the conversation to the history of the cavalla. For him, it was not dates and distant places and the strategy of campaigns. It was the story of his life. He'd joined when he was barely a lad, back in the days when the mounted forces did little more than patrol the existing borders of Gernia and hold the lines against the plainspeople. It had not seemed a promising career choice when he'd joined. I think I alone knew Duril's deepest secret. He was no true soldier son, only the fourth son born to a shoemaker in Old Thares. His family had given him over to the King's Cavalla in a sort of fatalistic despair. A city needs only so many cobblers. If he'd remained in the Old Thares, he'd either have starved at home or become a thief on the streets. He'd told me a few tales of Gernia in those days. The Long War with Landsing had ended in our defeat in the days of King Darwell, father of our present king. Generations of fighting had earned us only the loss of our coastal lands and our best coal-mining region. Landsing had taken our ports, leaving us with no access to the Locked Sea. Bereft of our ports and the rich veins of coal that had been our main export, Gernia was weakening like a fasting man. Our defeated navy was shamed, both ships and seaports gone. Our army and cavalla were little better, shunned and mocked when they abandoned their uniforms to become beggars, despised as cowards and incompetents if they chose to remain in the service of the King. Such was Sergeant Duril's introduction to life as a military man. He began by blacking and polishing boots for cavalla officers who seldom wore them any more, for our former foes were the victors and there were no more battles in which honour might be reclaimed.

Duril had served three years when King Darwell died and King Troven inherited the crown. To hear Duril tell it, the young king had single-handedly stopped Gernia's slide into despair. He mourned his father for three days, and then, instead of convening his Council of Lords, he summoned his military commanders to him. Even as he gathered that group and offered them what remained of the funds in his depleted treasury to rebuild Gernia's might, his nobles muttered that they would not again follow a king into battle against Landsing, that four generations of near-constant war had left them beggared as well as defeated.

But it was not west to Landsing and the lost province that young King Troven turned his eyes. No. King Troven was weary of the plainspeople's incursions against his remote settlements. He had decided that if they would not respect the boundary stones that had been mutually set four score of years ago, then he would not, either. The King sent his cavalla forth with the commands not only to push the plainspeople back, but also to set the boundaries anew and take new territory to replace that lost to the Landsingers.

Some of the King's lords did not support him in that ambition. The plains were despised as wastelands, not fit for agriculture or grazing, too hot in the summer and too cold in the winter. We traded with the peoples of the region, but only for raw goods, such as furs from the northern reaches. They were not farmers and had no industry of their own. Some were nomads, following their herds. Even those who cultivated small fields were migratory, wintering one place and summering another. They themselves admitted that no one owned the land. Why should they or our own nobles dispute our right to settle it and make it productive?

Duril remembered the brief and bloody Nobles' Revolt. Lord Egery had risen before the Council of Lords, asking them why more sons should shed their blood for sand and stone and sagebrush. The traitor had advocated overthrowing young Troven, and allying themselves with our old enemies for the sake of port concessions. King Troven had put the revolt down decisively and then, instead of punishing the rebels, rewarded those families that had given him their soldier sons to send into that battle against their fellow lords. King Troven altered the emphasis of his military, pouring men and money into the cavalla, the mounted troops descended from old knighthood, for he judged that force could best deal with the ever-mounted plainspeople. He dissolved his navy, for he no longer had a port or ships for them. Some folk mocked the idea of putting sailors on horseback and commodores in command of ground troops, but King Troven simply asserted that he believed his soldier sons and their commanders could fight anywhere that their patriotism demanded. His men responded to his confidence.

In that fashion had the Kingdom of Gernia increased by a third of its size since Sergeant Duril had been a boy.

The Plains War had not been a war at first. It had been a series of skirmishes between the nomads and our folk. The plainspeople had raided us, attacking our military outposts and the new settlements that sprang up around them; we had retaliated against their roving bands. The plainspeople had initially assumed that King Troven was merely reasserting his right to his own territory. It was only when we not only moved our boundary stones but started planning and erecting citadels and then settlements that the plainspeople realized that the King was in earnest. Twenty years of war had followed.

The plainspeople counted themselves as seven different peoples, but our records showed there were clearly more than thirty different clans or tribes. They often travelled in smaller bands. They roved and in their own way, ruled the plains, plateaus and rolling hills to the north. Some herded sheep or goats, others their long-necked dun-coloured cattle that seemed immune to every sort of weather. Three of the lesser tribes were simple hunters and gatherers, regarded by the other nomads as primitives. They tattooed their faces with swirling red patterns and believed that they were kin with the barking rats, the rodents of the prairie that sometimes riddled acres of ground with their burrows and tunnels. The Ratmen likewise dug tunnels into the earth and stored seeds and grains in them. They had made little resistance to our eastward expansion, and had actually enjoyed their new fame as an oddity. A number of artists and writers from Old Thares had visited them to document their strange lives, enriching the rat people with fabric, scissors and other trade items.

The Kidona had been the predators, the raiders who lived by attacking the others. The nomadic tribes had moved in a seasonal migration pattern, following grazing for their animals, and the Kidona had followed them, just as predators followed the migratory antelope of the plains. For generations, Gernian traders ventured out to barter with the plateau and hill folk for furs when the tribes came together for their traditional autumn trade gathering, but for the most part, our peoples had ignored one another.

'For generations, they had nothing we wanted, and we knew they would fight like devils to keep it. They had their magic, and the few times we'd crossed swords with them, we'd come out the poorer for it. How can you fight a man who can send your horse to his knees by flapping a hand at him, or wave a bullet aside? So we left them alone. We were a seafaring folk. We had our territory, and they had theirs.

If the Landsingers hadn't bottled us up like they did, maybe we would have ignored the plainspeople forever. It was only when we were pressed for territory that we pressed them as well. We'd always known that iron could stop plains magic; the problem was getting close enough to use iron against them. In olden times, one of the Gernian kings had sent knights out to avenge a murdered nobleman's son. Their magic couldn't knock down an iron-armoured knight or his shielded horse, but we couldn't catch up to them to do them any harm! They just fled. We tried archers, but a shaman could warp their bows with one flick of his finger. Lead ball? They'd slow it, catch it, and keep it for a trinket. But once we learned to use iron pellet in our muskets, well, the tide turned then. They couldn't turn iron shot, and a scatter gun full of round iron pellet shot from ambush could take out one of their raiding parties with one blast. Suddenly we could pick one of their war-shamans out of his saddle at two to three times the distance they expected. You didn't even have to kill him; just put enough iron shot in him that his magic left him. They couldn't even get close to us.

'Yet even then, if ever the tribes had thought to unite and fight us, well, chances were, they could have driven us back. They were nomads, their boys born to the saddle, and horsemen such as we'll never see again. But that was their weakness, too. When drought or plague or territorial disputes struck, why, if they couldn't win, they just up and moved into new territory. And that's what they kept doing, moving away as we advanced, losing cattle and sheep and possessions as they gave ground to us. Some of the smaller bands settled, of course, made peace with us and realized they'd have to live like regular folks now, keeping house in one place. But some just kept on fighting us, until they found the Barrier Mountains at their backs. Forest and mountains are no place for horse troops. That was when the fighting really got ugly. We had crowded the different tribes up against

160

one another. Some of them turned against their own kind. They knew they'd lost almost all their old grazing lands. The best parts of their herds and flocks were forfeit to us or dead behind them. They could look out over the plains from the high plateaus and see our citadels and our towns rising where once their beasts had grazed. The battle at Widevale was one of the worst. They say that every man of fighting age of the Ternu tribe died there. We took in their women and children, of course. It was only the right thing to do. Settled them down and taught them how to live right, how to farm and how to read. That battle was harsh and vicious, but in the end, it worked a kindness for those folks. Your da has done right by them, giving them sheep and seed and teaching them how to make a life in one spot.

'Not like the Portrens tribe. They chose to die to the last soul, men, women, and children. Not a thing we could do to stop them. When it was plain that the battle tide had turned against them, and they'd either have to bow their heads and become good subjects to King Troven or be driven up into the mountains, why, they just turned tail and rode their horses into the Redfish River. I saw it myself. We were trailing the Portrens with our forces, still skirmishing with them. Most of their powerful magic users had fallen to us days before; they couldn't do much more than hold their protective charms around them. We thought we could make them stop and surrender. We knew they'd come up against the river soon, and it was in spring flood from the snowmelt in the mountains. Must have been two hundred men mounted, their striped robes and kaffiyeh floating in the wind of their passage, riding guard around their women and children in their pony chariots. We thought they'd stop and surrender, I swear we did. But they just rode and drove straight into the river, and the river swept them away and that was the end of them. It wasn't our doing. We would have given them quarter if they asked for it. But, no, they chose death and we

161

couldn't stop them. The men stood guard on the bank until every one of the women and children were swept away. Then they rode in after them. Wasn't our fault. But many's the trooper who hung up his spurs after that battle and lost all heart, not just for fighting but for the cavalla life. War was s'posed to be about glory and honour, not drowning babies.'

'It must have been a hard thing to see,' I ventured.

'They chose it,' Sergeant Duril replied. He leaned back on his bedroll and knocked the ash out of his pipe. 'Some as rode alongside me saw it as watching death. A few of the lads near went mad. Not at the moment; at the time we just sat on our horses and watched them do it, not fully understanding that they were choosing death, that they knew they couldn't make it to the other side. We kept thinking there was some trick to what they did, a hidden ford they knew of or some magic of their own that would save them. But there wasn't. It was afterwards that it bothered some of my mates. They felt like we drove them to it. But I swear, it wasn't so. I decided I was watching a free people make a choice, probably one that they'd talked about before they came to it. Would we have been more right to try and stop them, and insist they give up their roving ways? I'm not sure. I'm not sure at all about that.'

'Only a plainsman can understand how a plainsman thinks,' I said. I was quoting from my father.

Sergeant Duril was packing more tobacco into his pipe and at first he didn't answer me. Then he said quietly, 'Sometimes I think being a cavalryman turns you into a plainsman, somewhat. That maybe we were almost coming to understand them too well before the end. There's a beauty and a freedom to riding over the flatlands, knowing that, in a pinch, you and your horse can find everything you need to get by on. Some folk say that they can't understand why the plainspeople never settled down and used the land, never made their own towns and farms and tame places. But if you ask a plainsman, and I've asked more than a few, they all ask the same question in return. "Why? Why live out your life in one place, looking at the same horizon every morning, sleeping in the same spot every night? Why work to make the land give you food when it's already out there, growing, and all you have to do is find it?" They think we're crazy, with our gardens and orchards, our flocks and herds. They don't understand us any more than we understand them.' He belched loudly and said, 'Excuse. Course, now there aren't many plainspeople left to understand. They've settled in their own places, under the surrender terms. They got schools and little stores now, and rows of little houses. They'll be just like us, in another generation or two.'

'I'm sorry to have missed them,' I said sincerely. 'Once or twice, I've heard my father talk about what it was like to visit one of their camps, back in the days when he rode patrol and sometimes they came in close to the boundaries to trade. He said they were beautiful, lean and swift, horses and people alike. He spoke of how the plainspeople tribes would gather, sometimes, to compete in contests of horsemanship, with the daughters of the ruling lords as the prizes. He said it was how they formed their alliances . . . Do you really think those days are gone?'

He nodded slowly, smoke drifting from his parted lips. For a time, human silence held, but the prairie spoke between us, a whispering wild voice, full of soft wind and rustling brush and little creatures that moved only by night. I relaxed into the familiar sounds and felt them carrying me closer to sleep.

'They're gone,' he confirmed sadly. 'Gone not just for them, but gone for us old soldiers, too. Gone, never to come again. We began the change; we swept away what had been here for hundreds of years. And now . . . well, now I fear that we were just the ones at the front of the charge, so to speak. That we may go down with those we defeated, and

163

be trampled under by those who come after us. Once the plainspeople are tamed, what use is an old soldier like me? Change, and more change . . .' He fell silent and I cared not to add any words to his. His thoughts had put a chill in my night that had not been there before.

When the sergeant spoke again, he had moved the topic a little aside, as if he shifted to avoid old pain. 'Sirlofty, he's plains stock. We soon discovered that to fight mounted plainspeople we had to have horses the equal of theirs. Keslans are fine for fancy carriage teams, and no one can beat Shirs for pulling a plough. But the saddlehorses that you'll find out west in the cities are creatures bred to carry a merchant about on his errands, creatures you could trust your dainty daughter to when she rides out with her fancy friends. That wasn't what we needed for the conquest of the prairies. We needed tall and lean, with legs like steel, a horse that could handle uneven ground, a horse with the sense to look after itself. That's what you've got in Sirlofty.' He nodded at my tall mount drowsing in the shadows at the edge of the campfire's circle. Almost reluctantly he added, 'I don't know how he'll do as a mountain horse. I don't know how well our cavalla will do fighting in the forest terrain, if it comes to that. Which I 'spect it shall.'

'Do you think we'll have war with the Specks, then?'

If it had been daylight and if we had been mounted and trotting as we spoke, I think he would have turned my question aside. I think he spoke as much to the night and the stars as he did to the wellborn son of his old commander. 'I think we're already at war there, from the little I've heard of it. We may not know it as war, but I think that's what the Specks would call it.

'And I wish I could prepare you for it better, but I can't. You won't be riding patrol across rolling prairie like your father and I did. You'll be serving at the edge of the wild lands, at the foothills of the Barrier Mountains. It's different there. Cliffs and ravines. Forest so thick that a cat couldn't walk through it, yet the Specks melt in and out of it, like shadows. All I can teach you is the attitude you'll need; I don't know what sort of plants or animals you'll encounter there, no, nor what type of warfare the Specks wage. But if you can bring yourself to dine on lizard legs and cactus flats here, then I think you'll have the sand to make it there. I think you'll make us proud. If circumstances demand that you make a meal of monkey stew, I expect you'll tuck right into it and ride on as strong as before.'

Such praise from the shaggy old sergeant made me blush even in the darkness. I knew that if he said as much to me, he doubtless said more to my father. They had ridden and fought side by side, and I knew my father cherished the old soldier's opinions, for he would not have lightly entrusted me to his care.

'I thank you, Sergeant Duril, for what you've taught me. I promise, I'll never shame you.'

'I don't need your promise, lad. I've your intention, which is good enough for me. I've taught you what I could. Just see you don't forget it when your papa sends you off to that fancy cavalla school back west. You'll be schooled alongside those lords' sons who think that leading a charge is something you do after you've waxed your moustache and had your trousies pressed. Don't let them pull you aside into their Fancy Dan ways. You grow up to be a real officer, like your papa. Remember. You can delegate authority—'

'But not responsibility.' I finished my father's old saw for him, and then added, 'I'll try, Sergeant,' I said humbly.

'I know you will, sir. Look up there. Shooting star. God's your witness.'

SEVEN

Journey

My father never had the good fortune to attend the King's Cavalla Academy in Old Thares. In his youth, it did not exist. He had received a more generalized military education in the old Arms Institute and had expected to command artillery, defending our fortified seacoast towns from foreign ships. That was before Carson Helsey designed the Helsied Cannon for the Landsing Navy. In one shocking summer, this single change to the cannons on their ships reduced our fortifications to rubble while their ships remained safely out of range of our weapons. What exactly Helsey had done to the Landsing cannons to extend their range and accuracy was a military secret the Landsingers jealously guarded to this day. Their sudden and shocking advantage had ended our decades of war with the Landsingers. We had been soundly and humiliatingly defeated.

With the ceding of the coastal territories to Landsing, my father's brief assignment as a cliff-top artilleryman ended, and he had been reassigned to the cavalla. Flung into the foreign environment, he had proved himself a true soldier son, for he learned what he must know by doing it, and ignored the disdain of some of his fellows that he had come to the cavalla but was not descended from the old knighthood. His first few years had been spent in the discouraging task of escorting refugee trains from our captured seaports into the resettlement areas along our borders with the plainsmen. The plainspeople had not welcomed the shantytowns that sprang up along their borders, but our people had to go somewhere. Skirmishes fought with mounted plains warriors formed my father's first experience of fighting from a horse's back. Despite the 'hard-knocks' nature of his cavalla education, he was a staunch supporter of the Academy. He always told me that he had no desire to see any young man learn by trial and error as he had done. He favoured a systematic approach to military education. Some said he was instrumental in the creation of the Academy. I know that on five separate occasions he was invited to travel there to speak to graduating young officers. Such an honour was a sign of the King's and the Academy's respect for my father.

Before the Academy was founded, our cavalla consisted of the remnants of Gernia's old knighthood. During our long sea-war with Landsing, the cavalla had been seen as a decorative branch of our military, displaying the buffed and polished family armour and riding their plumed horses for ceremonial occasions, but doing little more. Footsoldiers manned the Long Wall that marked our land boundary with Landsing, and held it well. On the few occasions when we had attempted to invade Landsing by land, our heavy horses and armoured fighters were less than useless against the Landsing cavaliers with their fleet steeds and muskets. Even so, we had skirmished with the plainsmen for more than two years before the King's advisors recognized that specialized training was required to create a cavalla that could deal with the plainspeople's unconventional fighting style. Our heavily armoured horse could do little against warriors that flung magic at them, and then fled out of range of lance and sword. Our cavalla had to be forced to embrace the musketry and marksmanship that flouted the traditions of old knighthood. Only then did we begin to prevail against a foe that saw no shame in fleeing whenever the battle went against them.

I would be the first member of my family to be educated at the King's Academy. I would be the first student to show our spond tree crest at the school. I knew there would be other first generation new nobility sons, but I was also aware there would also be cadets descended from the old knighthood. I must show well and never disgrace my father or the Burvelles of the West, my Uncle Sefert's family. I was heart-thuddingly aware of this, for my entire family took care that I should not forget it. Uncle Sefert, my father's heir brother, sent me a magnificent gift prior to my departure. It was a saddle, made especially to fit Sirlofty, with the new family crest embellished on the flaps. There were travelling panniers to go with it, such as any good cavalla horse might bear, likewise decorated. I had to copy over my note of thanks four times before my father was satisfied with both my courtesy and my penmanship. It was more than that the note would go to my father's elder brother; it was that my father was now his peer, and I the equal of any noble's soldier son, and so I must conduct myself and be seen by all, but most especially by the members of my own family.

In early summer, the fabric for my uniforms was ordered from Old Thares. The fat fold of cloth in the rich green of a cavalla cadet came wrapped in thick brown paper. In a separate packet were brass buttons in two sizes, embossed with the crossed sabres of a cavalla man. My mother and her women had always sewed all my clothing before then, as they did for the entire household. But for the task of creating my academy uniform, my father sent for a wizened little tailor. He came all the way from Old Thares, riding a sturdy dun horse and leading a mule laden with two great wooden chests. Inside them were the tools of his trade, shears and measuring tapes, pattern books and needles, and threads of every weight and colour imaginable. He stayed the summer with us, creating for me four sets of clothing, two uniforms of winter weight and two of summer, and of course my cavalla man's cloak. He inspected the work of the local cobbler who made my boots and said they were passable but that I should have a 'good' pair made as soon as I could upon my arrival in Old Thares. My sword belt had been my father's. New bridles were ordered for Sirlofty to match the new saddle. Even my small clothes and stockings were all new, and every bit of it was packed away in a heavy trunk that smelled of cedar.

If that were not enough newness, two evenings before my departure I was seated on a tall stool and my father himself sheared off every bit of my hair that could be removed with scissors, until only a fine bristly cap remained on my scalp. My entire head was now almost as bald as my scar. I looked into the mirror when he was finished and was shocked at the contrast between my sun-browned skin and the paleness that his scissors had exposed. The stubble of blond hair was almost invisible against my naked pink scalp, and my blue eyes suddenly looked as large as a fish's to me. But my father seemed pleased. 'You'll do,' he said gruffly. 'No one will be able to say that we've sent a shaggy little prairie boy to learn a man's trade.'

The next evening I donned my green cadet's uniform for the first time since my fittings. I wore it to the farewell dinner gathering that my parents held for me.

I had not seen my mother turn out the house so thoroughly since the formal announcement of Rosse's engagement to Cecile Poronte. When the manor house was built, shortly after my father's elevation to lordship, my mother had argued passionately for a dining room and adjacent ballroom. We had all been small children, but she had spoken then of the necessity of her daughters being shown to advantage when they entertained other nobles in our home, and had fretted much that the dance floor must be of polished wood rather than the gleaming marble she had known in her girlhood home in Old Thares. The cost of bringing such stone up river from the distant quarries to our home was prohibitive. She had been flattered when she discovered that western visitors often exclaimed in amazement at the soft glow of the waxed wood, and proclaimed it a wonderful surface for slippered feet to tread. She was fond of recounting that when Lady Currens, her childhood friend, had returned to her grand home in Old Thares, she had insisted that her husband order the creation of just such a dance floor for her own home.

The guest list for my farewell gathering included the country gentry for miles around. The wealthy ranchers and herdsmen and their stout wives might have been disdained in Old Thares society, but my father said that here in the Wildlands it behooved a man to know who his allies and friends were, regardless of their social rank. Perhaps this sometimes distressed my mother; I know she wished her daughters to marry sons of nobility, new nobility if she could not find matches for them amongst the older families. And so she extended invitations to those of our own rank, despite the distance they must cross. Lord and Lady Remwar and their two sons travelled for a day and a half to accept my mother's invitation, as did widowed Lord Keesing and his son. Privately, I thought my mother was taking this opportunity to see how these noble sons were turning out and to display them to my father as possible matches for Elisi and Yaril. I did not begrudge it to her, for the guest list also included Lord and Lady Grenalter and Carsina. As I thought of Carsina and looked into the mirror, I decided that my shorn head looked oddly small above my dashing cavalla cadet's uniform. But there was nothing I could do to change it, and I could only hope that Carsina would remember me as she had last seen me and not find the change ridiculous or embarrassing

I had seen Carsina perhaps a dozen times since my father had told me that Lord Grenalter had agreed to our match. Theoretically, all of our meetings were carefully chaperoned. Carsina was my sister's friend. It was natural that she would come to visit my sister, natural that sometimes the visit might last a week. Although our engagement had not been formally announced and would not be until I graduated from the Academy, she and I were both aware that we were now destined for each other. There were moments when our eyes met at the dinner table, and my heart would take a leap into my throat. During her visits, she and Yaril and Elisi would play their harps together in the music room, singing the romantic old ballads that the girls seemed to love the best. I knew they did it for their own pleasure, but as I passed the room and saw Carsina the warm wood frame of her harp leaning against the softness of her breast while her plump little hands floated gracefully from the strings at the end of each chord, her words seemed pitched to me as she sang of 'my brave horseman, in his coat of green, who rides to serve his king and queen.' Nor could I help but know, when I saw her walking in the garden or sewing in the women's room with my sisters, that there was the girl who would some day be my wife. I tried not to let it show in my glance when our eyes met across the room. I tried not to hope that she had the same half-formed dreams of a home and children together.

That farewell evening, for the first time, I was allowed to escort Carsina into the dining room. Carsina and my sisters had been sequestered upstairs for the better part of the day, as servants hurried up and down the steps with seemingly endless armloads of freshly pressed linens and lace. When they descended the stairs just before dinner, the transformation was stunning. I scarcely recognized my sisters, let alone Carsina. Often I had heard my mother counsel my sisters that bright colours would suit their pale complexions and fair hair best, and so it was that Yaril wore a blue gown, with a neck ribbon of a darker blue, and Elisi chose a rich dark gold for her attire. But Carsina was dressed in a gown of some material that seemed to float about her, in a pale pink that reminded me of the interior of the conch shells in my father's study.

171

It was barely a shade darker than her skin. The rounding of her breasts was just visible through the frothy lace that edged the neckline of her dress, and made me catch my breath at my first sight of her. The girl promised to me was displayed as a woman before the eyes of every man in the room. It made me feel more protective of her than ever. Whenever I lifted my eyes during dinner, I saw her looking directly at me, and feeling rude to stare at her beauty, I looked aside. As we left the table, I heard her say something softly to Yaril, and their soft laughter made my cheeks burn. I turned aside from both of them, and was unusually grateful when the wife of retired Colonel Haddon greeted me and asked me a dozen questions about my anticipation of the Academy.

Later that evening, when we both moved through the interchange dances thought suitable for young unmarried folk, I tried to hold Carsina's hand or touch her waist as courteously as I did that of any of the other girls in the dance. Yet I could not help thinking, as she came so briefly into my arms, that here was the girl who would share my life. I dared not look down at her, for she kept smiling up at me. The smell of the gardenias in her hair filled my lungs and her eyes sparkled more than the tiny diamond pins that ornamented her hair. Such a tightness came to my chest and a flush to my cheeks that I feared I might unman myself by fainting. I suspect that all who saw us together must have guessed that already the feelings I held for her were ones of pride and tenderness and protectiveness. When, our brief turn completed, I had to pass her on to another fellow, the girl I trod the next measure with undoubtedly found me a clumsy partner.

The gathering was in my honour, and I did my best to fulfil my every duty as a son of the household. I danced with the matrons who had known me since my baby days. I made conversation, and thanked them for their congratulations and good wishes. I had just fetched wine punch for Mrs Grazel, the wife of the stockman who owned a large acreage to the south of Widevale, when I observed both Yaril and Carsina slip out through the fluttering curtains and into the lantern-lit garden beyond them. The evening was warm and we were all flushed with dancing. Suddenly it seemed to me as if a brief stroll through the garden away from the music and chatter of guests might be a welcome rest from the party. As soon as I graciously could, I excused myself from Mrs Grazel's conversation about the blood-purifying bene-fits of adding parsley to her young sons' meals and made my way out onto the terrace that overlooked the gardens.

Lanterns with tinted glass had been spaced along the walks. The last flowers of summer were still in bloom and the evening milder than this time of year usually offered. I saw my brother Rosse seated with his fiancée on a bench in the living arbour of a weeping willow. He was within his rights to steal this time alone with her for their engagement had been announced months ago. I expected to come home from the Academy in the spring to witness their marriage. Roger Holdthrow was strolling the paths by himself. I sus-pected he was looking for Sara Mallor. The announcement of their engagement had not been made, but as their families possessed neighbouring estates, it had been expected since their childhood that they would be paired.

I saw Yaril and Carsina seated on a bench near the pond. They were fanning themselves and talking softly. I longed to approach them, but could not summon the courage until I saw Kase Remwar emerge from the shadows. He bowed gracefully to both of them, and I heard him bid them good evening. My sister sat up very straight and returned him some pleasantry that made him laugh out loud. Carsina joined in their laughter. It was not completely correct for Remwar to be alone with the two young women, and taking a rightful interest in my sister's welfare, I ventured down the steps to join them.

Remwar greeted me jovially and offered me good wishes

for my journey on the morrow and for my studies at the Academy. He was a first son of his family and the heir to his father's title, so I thought it a bit condescending when he said that he wished he were free to go off, as I was, and have great adventures in the wide world rather than have to stay at home and assume the burdens of his rank.

'The good god places us as he wishes us to be,' I told him. 'I would not wish my brother's inheritance, or my younger brother's priesthood. I believe I will be what was destined for me.'

'Oh, the birth order destiny is fixed, of course. But why cannot a man be more than one thing? Think on it. Your own father has been soldier, and now he is lord. Why cannot an heir be also a poet, or a musician? Soldier-sons of nobles keep journals and sketchbooks, do they not? So, are you not also a writer and a naturalist as well as a soldier?'

His words opened a window in my future, one that I had never even considered. I had always wanted to know more about rocks and minerals, yet I had always regarded that as an unworthy thought sent by the great distracter. Could a man be both, without offence to the good god? I pushed the thought away, already knowing the true answer in my heart. 'I am a soldier,' I said aloud. 'I only observe and write what is needed to aid the soldiers who may come after me. I do not hunger for the destinies the good god has granted to my brothers.'

I think Remwar heard my disapproval of his attitude, for he started to frown and began to say, 'I only meant—' when Yaril suddenly interrupted him.

'Angel's breath!' she exclaimed. 'I've lost an earring! One of the new lapis ones that Papa gave me especially for this evening. Oh, what will he think of me, to be so careless with his gift. I must go look for it!'

'I'll help you,' Remwar immediately offered. 'Where might it have fallen?'

'Probably along the walk to the greenhouse,' Carsina

174

offered. 'Remember, you stepped from the path and your hair tangled for a moment against the climbing rose on the trellis there. I suspect that is when you lost it.'

Yaril smiled at her gratefully. 'I'm sure you are right. We'll look for it there.'

'I'll come with you.' I volunteered, giving Remwar a measuring glance.

'Don't be silly,' Yaril rebuked me. 'Carsina came out here to rest a moment from the dancing. She doesn't want to go down to the hot houses again, and we certainly can't leave her sitting here alone. Besides, with your great feet, you'd probably tread my earring into the sod before you saw it. Two of us are plenty to go looking for one little earring. Wait here. We won't be long.'

She had risen as she spoke. I knew I should not let her go off down the shadowy path with Remwar unchaperoned, but Carsina gently patted the bench beside her, suggesting I sit there, and I could scarcely leave her sitting in the garden alone. 'Don't be long,' I cautioned Yaril.

'I shan't be. The earring will either be there or it won't,' she replied. Remwar dared to offer her his arm, but she shook her head in a pretty rebuke, and led him off into the dimness. I looked after them. After a moment, Carsina asked quietly, 'Don't you wish to sit down? I would think your feet would be tired after all that dancing. I know mine are.' She pushed her dainty little foot out from the hem of her dress, as if to show me how weary it was, and then exclaimed, 'Oh, my slipper's come unfastened. I shall have to go inside and fix it, for if I stoop here, I'll surely muddy the hem of my gown.'

'Allow me,' I asked her breathlessly. I went down on one knee fearlessly, for the weather had been dry and the paving stones of the garden path were always kept well swept.

'Oh, but you should not,' she exclaimed as I took up the silk laces of her slipper. 'You'll soil the knee of your fine new uniform. And you look so brave in it.'

'A little dust on my knee will not mar it,' I said. She had said I looked brave. 'I've been tying my sister's slippers since she was a tiny thing. Her knots always come undone. There. How is that? Too tight? Too loose?'

She leaned down to inspect my work. Her neck was graceful and pale as a swan's and a waft of her gardenias enveloped me again. She turned her gaze to mine and our faces were inches apart. 'It's perfect,' she said softly.

I could not move or speak. 'Thank you,' she said. She leaned forward and her lips barely brushed my cheek, a kiss as chaste as a sister's that still caused my heart to hammer in my ears. Then she leaned back suddenly, lifting her fingertips to her lips in surprise. 'Oh! Whiskers!'

I lifted a hand to my cheek in horror. 'I did shave!' I exclaimed, and she laughed, a sound that reminded me of skylarks soaring into a morning sky.

'Of course! I did not mean your face was rough. Only that there is a trace of them, still. You are so fair, that I did not think you would be shaving yet.'

'I've been shaving for almost a year now,' I said, and suddenly it was easy to talk to her. I rose, brushing at my knee and sat down on the bench beside her.

She smiled at me and asked, 'Will you grow a moustache at the Academy? I've heard that many cadets do.'

I ran my hand ruefully over my nearly bald head. 'Not in my first year. It isn't allowed. Perhaps when I'm in my third year.'

'I think you should,' she said quietly, and I suddenly resolved that I would.

A little silence fell as she looked out over the night garden. 'I dread your leaving tomorrow. I suppose I won't see you for a long time,' she said sadly.

'I'll be home for Rosse's wedding in late spring. Surely you and your family will be there.'

'Of course. But that is months and months away.'

176

'It won't be so long,' I assured her, but suddenly it seemed like a very long time to me, also.

She looked aside from me. 'I've heard that the girls of Old Thares are very beautiful, and dress in all the latest fashions from the coast. My mother says that they wear musk and paint their eyelids and that their riding skirts are almost trousers, for they don't care at all that men may see their legs.' Worriedly she added, 'I've heard they are very forward, too.'

I shrugged. 'I don't know. Such things may be true. But I'll be at the Academy. I doubt I'll catch so much as a glimpse of a woman there.'

'Oh, I'm glad!' she exclaimed, and then looked aside from me. I had to smile as her tiny flame of jealousy warmed me.

I glanced at the dim path that led toward the greenhouses. I could not see my sister. I did not want to leave, but I knew my responsibility. 'I'd best go look for Yaril. Finding an earring should not take her this long.'

'I'll come with you,' Carsina offered. As she stood, she took my arm, her hand light as a little bird perched there.

'You should go back inside while I find Yaril,' I said dutifully.

'Should I?' she asked me, looking up at me with wide blue eyes.

I could not bring myself to answer that, and so we ventured down the path together. It was narrow and so she had to walk close to me. I went slowly, for fear she would stumble in the dark. Then we came to the turn in the path, and as I feared, I saw Yaril standing very close to Remwar and looking up at him. As I watched, he stooped and kissed her.

I froze in horror. 'He has no right!' I gasped in disbelief.

Carsina's grip on my arm had tightened. 'No right at all!' she whispered in shocked agreement. 'Unlike us, there is no understanding between the families. They have not been promised to one another, as we have.'

I looked down at her. Her eyes were very big, her breathing rapid through her slightly parted lips.

And then, without quite knowing how, I had taken her in my arms. The top of her brow came just to my nose, so that I had to stoop and turn my head to kiss her mouth. Her little hands gripped the front of my new uniform coat, and when she broke the kiss, she hid her face against my shirt-front as if overcome by what we had done. 'It's all right,' I whispered into the curls and pins of her soft hair. 'We are promised to one another. We've done nothing shameful, save steal a taste of what our lives will bring.'

She lifted her face from my shirt and leaned back from me. Her eyes were shining and I could not resist her. I kissed her again.

'Carsina!' A voice hissed in rebuke. We sprang apart guiltily. Yaril seized her friend by the elbow and looked at me in sisterly rebuke. 'Oh, Nevare, I never would have thought it of you! Carsina, come with me!' Then, like petals blown on a sudden wind, the two girls swept away from us. At the turn in the path, one of them laughed suddenly, the other joined in and then they were lost to my sight. I stared after them for a moment, and then turned to confront Remwar. My eyes narrowed and I took breath to speak, but he laughed lightly and punched me in the shoulder.

'Relax, old man. My father is speaking to yours tonight.' Then he met my gaze as an honest fellow should and said, 'I've loved her for two years. I think our mothers both know. I promise you, Nevare, I'll never let harm come to her.'

I could think of no reply to that, and he suddenly said, 'I hear the music starting again. To the chase, lads!' And he set off down the path in a long-legged stride in pursuit of the girls. I was left shaking my head, dizzied by the kiss and the perfume that Carsina had left clinging to me. I tugged my coat straight and brushed a bit of her powder from the front of it. Only then did I discover that she had tucked her tiny handkerchief into the front of my coat. It was all lace, delicate as a snowflake and scented with gardenia. I folded it carefully into my pocket and hastened back toward the lights and music. Suddenly, the thought of departing on the morrow was nearly unbearable. I would not waste a single moment of the time left to me.

Yet the instant I returned to the dance floor, my mother found me, and suggested that courtesy demanded I partner several of her older friends in dances. I saw my father invite Carsina to the floor, while my sister Yaril looked almost desperate to escape Major Tanrine's plodding performance. The night stretched before me, both endless and desperately short. The musicians had announced the final dance when my mother suddenly appeared at my elbow with Carsina at her side. I blushed as she set my betrothed's hand in mine, for I was suddenly certain she knew of our loitering in the garden and even of the kiss.

I was tongue-tied by Carsina's glowing beauty and the way she gazed up into my eyes. It seemed the dance turned around us rather than that we whirled around the floor. At last I managed to say, 'I found your kerchief.'

She smiled and said softly, 'Keep it safe for me, until we meet again.'

And then the music was ending, and I had to bow to her and then release her hand and let her go. Ahead of me stretched the three years of academy and three more of service before I could claim her. I suddenly felt every day, every hour of that distance. I vowed I would be worthy of her.

I did not sleep that night, and arose very early the next morning. Today I would leave my family home behind me. I was suddenly aware, as I looked around my bare room, that 'home' would be a place I would visit now, during my breaks from the Academy, and that I would not know a true home again until Carsina and I made one for ourselves. My narrow bed and emptied wardrobe seemed but shells of my old life. A single wooden box remained on one shelf. My rocks were in it. I had started to throw them out, but found I could not. Yaril had promised to take custody of them. I opened the box to take a final look at all of my avoided deaths. The rock I thought of as Dewara's stone, the one from my boot, glinted as I opened the box. I stared at them all for a moment, and then selected that one to take with me. I slipped it into my jacket pocket, a reminder that I was always but one caught breath this side of death. It was a thought to make a young man seize his life in both hands and live it to the full. Yet when I closed the door of my room behind me, the snick of the door catch seemed to echo in my heart.

Father and Sergeant Duril were to accompany me on the first stage of my journey. My chest of fine new uniforms was loaded on a cart pulled by a sturdy mule, along with a smaller chest that held my father's wardrobe for the trip. I wore a white shirt and blue trousers, a blue jacket to match, and thought I looked rather fine. My father and I wore our tall hats. I recall that I had only worn mine twice before that, once to Colonel Kempson's anniversary ball at his home, and once to a funeral of one of my mother's friends. Sergeant Duril was attired as humbly as ever, for he was to accompany us only as far as the flatboat to see us loaded.

I had made my farewells to my mother and sisters the night before. I had tried to have a private word with Yaril, but I suspected that she avoided giving me the opportunity. If Remwar's father had spoken to mine, I'd heard nothing of it, and dared not ask my father about it for fear of plunging Yaril into disgrace with him. I had not expected the rest of my family to rise with the dawn to bid me farewell. Even so, my mother, already in her morning gown, descended to kiss me goodbye and offer me her blessing before I departed from her doorstep. I almost wished she had not, for it brought a lump to my throat. I did not want to leave my home with boyish tears on my cheeks, but I narrowly escaped doing so.

The rains of winter had not yet swollen the river. I was just as glad that we would not be travelling when the current was full swift and strong amongst the heavy cargo barges. Instead, it was a time when flatboats plied their trade, carrying families back west to visit relatives and buy the latest fashionable attire for the winter season to come. I confess that I rather hoped our flatboat would hold some of the young ladies from up the river, for I thought it would be pleasant to let them see me in my fine new attire. But the flatboat that Sergeant Duril loaded our trunks on was a simple ship with only four cabins for passengers and most of the deck left open for cargo. The captain and his two crewmen quickly erected the temporary stall walls that almost all the flatboats carried, and Sirlofty and my father's grey gelding Steelshanks were put up side by side in roomy boxes on the deck. The crews of the flatboats were very familiar with cavalla men and their needs when they travelled. Some had become almost too familiar, but I was pleased to see that even though my father was retired, they treated him with the respect due his former rank, as well as the courtesies owed a 'battle lord', as the newer ranks of the King's nobility were sometimes affectionately known. Two of the deckhands were plainsmen. I had never seen such a thing before, and I think Captain Rhosher knew my father disapproved, for he took the time to point out that both of them wore thin necklaces of fine iron chain, a sign that they had voluntarily given up all association with magic. My father pointed out to the captain that there were many Gernian men who would have welcomed the work, and that he could have allowed the plainsmen to remain with their own kind. It was their last exchange on the matter, but in our cabin, my father later commented to me that if he'd known of the plainsmen working the deck, he'd have booked passage on a different flatboat.

Despite this, our journey soon settled into a pleasant routine. The river was low, the current calm but steady, and the steersman knew his business. He kept us well in the channel, and the deckhands had little to do other than keep a watch for snags. The captain was brave enough to keep us travelling at night when the moon was full, and so we made excellent time. The other passengers were two young gentleman-hunters from Old Thares and their guide. The young nobles were returning home with several crates of antlers, horns, and pelts as souvenirs of their Wildlands adventure. I envied them their fine muskets, and elegantly tailored hunting jackets and gleaming boots. They were both first sons and heirs to old names and fortunes. I was a bit shocked to see them out and about in the world, enjoying life and having it all their own way, but they both gave me to understand that in their circles, young heirs were expected to go out and do a bit of adventuring and sowing of wild oats before settling down in their thirties to the serious business of inheriting the family name. When I compared them to my elder brother Rosse, I found them very lacking.

Their guide was a well-seasoned hunter who made our shared meals interesting with his tales. My father enjoyed the man's tall tales as much as any of us did, but privately he warned me that there was little truth to them, and that he had small use for such idle dandies as his clients were. They were only a few years my senior, and although they several times invited me to their cabin for brandy and cigars after dinner, my father had instructed me to find excuses to refuse their invitations. I regretted it, for I would have liked to make friends with them, but my father's word on this was final. 'They are dissolute and undisciplined, Nevare. Young men of their years have no business drinking themselves senseless at night and bragging of their conquests. Avoid them. You will lose nothing by doing so.'

I had made two previous trips to Old Thares. One was

when I was three years old, and I remembered little of it, other than the sight of the river slipping placidly by us and the crowded cobbled streets of the capital city. I had made another journey with my father and brothers when I was ten. We had taken my younger brother Vanze to the Ecclesiastical School of Saint Orton to register him with the priesthood. It was a prestigious school and my father wished to enter his name in the enrolment lists well ahead of time, to be sure he would be admitted when the time came for him to attend.

During that visit, we stayed with Uncle Sefert Burvelle in his elegant townhouse with his gracious family. His wife was a very fine lady, and he had a son and two daughters. My uncle welcomed us warmly, and spent several hours with me, showing me the extensive journals that had been contributed to his library by the soldier sons of the Burvelle line, as well as the numerous trophies won by them. There were not just the jewelled swords of noble adversaries defeated in battle, but the grislier trophies of earlier disputes with the savage Cuerts to the southeast. Necklaces of human neck vertebrae and beads of lacquered hair were among the prizes claimed from them. There were hunting trophies as well, bison pelts and elephant feet and even a wide rack of barbed antlers from a humpdeer that my father had sent back to his ancestral home. My uncle took care to let me know what a valorous family history we shared and that he fully expected me to contribute to it. I think I sensed then his disappointment that he had produced no soldier son of his own. Until his son and heir sired a soldier son, there would be no new journals. For the first time in more than one hundred years, there would be a gap in the Burvelle's military his-tory. No son of his would send back the written record of his exploits, and clearly that saddened him a bit.

Even then, I sensed that my father's sudden change in sta-tus had caused a ripple of discord in the extended family. It had been decades since any Gernian king had established

183

new titles and granted land. King Troven had established a double dozen of new lords at one bestowal. The sudden influx of aristocrats diluted the power of the older houses. His battle lords felt a higher degree of loyalty, perhaps, to the King who had so elevated them. Prior to creating his battle lords, the Old Nobles on the Council of Lords had been muttering that perhaps they deserved more than an advisory status with the monarchy; that perhaps the time had come for them to wield some true authority. The King's newly created nobles diluted and muted that rebellion. I am sure that King Troven was aware he was creating that solid block of support for himself. If there is one thing that military men know how to do, it is to follow their rightful leader. Yet I still believe that King Troven was not merely playing political chess, but was sincerely rewarding those who had served him well in difficult times. Perhaps he recognized, too, that the former borderlands would need nobles who understood the rigours of survival. Nonetheless, I am sure that it had crossed my uncle's mind, and certainly Lady Burvelle's mind, that the King could just as easily have granted those lands to the Burvelle family of the west, that they might fall under his control. It must have been odd for him to look at his soldier brother, the second son born to serve, and see him now as a peer. Certainly it seemed to fluster his lady-wife to greet my father as an equal at her table and introduce him as Lord Burvelle of Widevale in the east to her guests.

My mother had included a packet of gifts for my female relatives. She had chosen plainsworked copper bracelets for my two girl cousins, thinking that they would be unique and interesting to them, but there was no such homely gift for my Aunt Daraleen. For her, my mother had chosen a string of freshwater pearls of the highest quality. I knew the pearls had been costly, and wondered if they were intended to buy me a welcome in my aunt's home.

These were thoughts I mulled as our barge made its

placid way down the river toward Old Thares. I knew I would be expected to call upon my uncle and his wife on a regular basis while I was a student at the Academy. Selfishly, I wished it were not so, that I could have all my time to devote to my studies and to socializing with my fellow students. Many a young officer who had paused on his journey east to share our table had spoken glowingly of his days at the Academy, not just of the lifelong friendships he had discovered there and the demands of the studies, but also of the high-spirited pranks and general good fellowship of the mess and barracks life. Our isolated lifestyle at Widevale rather than any inclination of my own had forced me into a solitary boyhood. I'd always enjoyed my brief opportunities for socializing with lads my own age. I felt some trepidation about being plunged into the communal life of the Academy, but mostly I felt anticipation and excitement. I was ready for a change from my quiet rural ways.

And I knew that the days of my boyish freedom had dwindled to a close. There would be no more long rides with Sergeant Duril; no idle evenings spent listening to my sisters practise their music or my mother read aloud from the Holy Writ. I was no longer a lad to sprawl on the hearthrug and play with lead soldiers. I was a man now, and days of study and work awaited me. Yet even as that thought weighted me, my fingers found the tiny snowflake of lace in my pocket. Carsina, too, awaited me, once I had proven myself worthy of her. I sighed as I thought of her, and the long months that must pass before I even saw her again, let alone the years of duty I must serve until I could claim her. I had not realized that my father had also approached the rail of our vessel until he asked, 'And why do you sigh, son? Do you not anticipate your days at the Academy with eagerness?'

I straightened to stand tall before I spoke to my father. 'With great eagerness, Father,' I assured him. And then, because I feared he might not approve of my soft sentiments

185

toward Carsina before I had rightly earned her, I said, 'But I shall miss my home while I am gone.'

He gave me a look that might have meant he divined the true centre of my thoughts, for he added wryly, 'I am sure you will. But in the months to come you must take care to concentrate your mind on your lessons and duties. If you are homesick and pining, you will not focus, and your instructors might believe that you do not have the devotion to be a good officer. It takes independence and self-reliance to be an officer in the forefront of battle or stationed at our farthest outposts. I do not think you would be content to earn a less demanding post, attending more to bookkeeping and supplies than to actual confrontations with the foe. Let them see your true mettle, my son, and earn the post that will bring you the most glory. Promotions come more swiftly at the border citadels. Earn your assignment there, and you may find that your ambitions are more swiftly satisfied.'

'I will heed your advice, Father, and try to be worthy of all you have invested in me,' I replied, and he nodded to himself, pleased with my answer.

Our river journey was the least eventful part of our travels. It might have even become boring, for that part of Gernia is much the same. The Tefa flows steadily along through the wide plains, and the little towns and villages that cluster at likely landing spots resemble one another so much that most of them have large signs posted along the riverfront to announce the name of the town in no uncertain terms. The weather continued fair, and though the foliage along the more deserted stretches of riverbank grew denser than it did on the prairie, it varied little.

My father saw to it that I did not waste my travelling days in idleness. He had brought with him his copies of the texts he had helped approve for the Cavalla Academy, and insisted that I attempt the first several chapters in each book. 'For,' he warned me, 'the first few weeks of living in a barracks and

186

rising before dawn to rush to breakfast and then classes will be a foreign experience. You may find yourself wearier than usual, and distracted in the evening by the company of other young men at the study tables in your barracks hall. I am told that promising young cadets often fall behind in their first weeks, and never catch up, and hence earn lower marks than might otherwise be expected of them. So, if you are already versed in what you will study in those first weeks, you may find yourself on a more solid footing with your instructors.'

And so we went over texts on horsemanship, and military strategy and the history of Gernia and its military forces. We worked with map and compass, and several times he awoke me late at night to come onto the deck with him and demonstrate that I could identify the key stars and constellations that might guide a horse soldier alone on the plains. On the occasions when our boat docked for a day in small towns to take on or unload cargo, we took the horses out to stretch their legs. My father, despite his years, remained an excellent horseman and he lost no opportunity to share the secrets of his expertise with me.

Early in our journey, there was an incident that disrupted our crew and justified my father's reservations about Captain Rhosher employing plainsmen as deckhands. It happened as evening was creeping over the land. The sunset was magnificent, banks of colour flooding the horizon and echoing in the placid waters before us. I was on the bow of the ship, enjoying it, when I saw a lone figure in a small vessel on the river coming toward us, cutting a path against the current. The little boat had a small square sail, not even as tall as the man himself was, but bellied out with wind. The man in the boat was tall and lanky, and he stood upright, my view of him partially obscured by the sail. I stared at him in fascination, for despite the current being against him, his boat cut the water briskly as he steered up the main channel of the river.

When he saw us, I saw him perform some task that made

his little boat veer to the left, so that he would pass us with a generous space of water between us. As I stared at him and his unusual vessel, I heard heavy footsteps on the deck behind me. I turned to see my father and the captain tamping tobacco into their pipes as they strolled toward the bow for their evening smoke together. Captain Rhosher gestured with his unlit pipe and observed genially, 'Now there's a sight you hardly see any more on this river. Wind-wizard. When I was a youngster, we often encountered such as him, in his calabash boat. They grow those boats, you know. The gourds from such a vine are immense, and they fertilize them with rabbit dung and shape the fruits as they grow. When the gourds are large enough, they cut them from the vine, let them dry and harden and then shape each one into a boat.'

'Now that's a tale,' my father challenged him with a smile.

'No, sir, as I'm a riverman, I'll tell you it's true. I've seen them growing, and once even watched them cutting the gourd to shape. But that was years ago. And I think it's been over a year since I've seen a wind-wizard on this river,' the captain countered.

The little boat had drawn abreast of us as he spoke, and a strange chill ran up my back, making the hair stand up on my neck and arms. The captain spoke true. The man in the boat stood tall and still, but he held his spread hands out toward his little sail as if guiding something toward it. As there was every night on the river, a gentle breeze was blowing. But the wind that the plains mage focused toward his sail was stronger than the mild breeze that barely stirred my hair. His wind puffed his sail full, pushing the boat steadily upstream. I had never seen anything like it, and I knew a moment of purest envy. The solitary man, silhouetted against the sinking sun, was at once so peaceful and so powerful a sight that I felt it sink into my soul. With no apparent effort, one with his magic, the wind and the river, his shell-boat moved gracefully past us in the twilight. I knew I would remember that sight to the end of my days. As he passed us, one of our polemen lifted his hand in greeting, and the wind-wizard acknowledged him with a nod.

Suddenly there was a gun blast from the upper deck behind me. Iron pellets struck the wind-wizard's sail and shredded it. As my ears rang with the shock, I saw the craft tip and the man spilled into the river. A moment later, a cloud of sulphurous smoke drifted past me, choking me and making my eyes water. The angry shouting of the captain and raucous laughter from the upper deck barely reached me through the ringing of my ears. The two young nobles stood on the upper deck, arms about each other's shoulders, roaring with drunken laughter over their prank. I looked back toward the wind-wizard's boat, but saw nothing there but blackness and water.

I turned to my father in horror. 'They murdered him!'

Captain Rhosher had already left us and was running toward the ladder that led to the upper deck. One of our plainsmen polemen was faster. He did not use the ladder, but scrambled up the side of the cabins to the upper deck, where he seized their gun. The poleman threw it wildly away from him, and it sailed over the side of the boat, splashed and sank. A moment later the guide, probably alerted by the gunshot, was on the scene. He seized the plainsman and spoke to him in his own language, forcibly holding him off the two young nobles as the captain hurried up the ladder. Down on the deck, the other poleman was running frantically up and down the length of the flatboat, scanning the river for any sign of the wind-wizard. I ran to the railing and leaned out as far as I could. In the darkness, I could barely make out our wake. 'I can't see him!' I called out.

A moment later my father joined me at the railing. He took my arm. 'We are going to our cabin, Nevare. This is none of our doing, and none of our business. We shall stay clear of it.'

'They shot the wind-wizard!' My heart was hammering with the shock of what had happened. 'They killed him.'

'They shot his sail. The iron pellet destroyed the magic he was doing. That was all,' my father insisted.

'But I can't see him!'

My father glanced at the water, and then pulled firmly at my arm. 'He's probably swum to shore. He'd be far astern of us by now; that's why you can't see him. Come on.'

I went with him, but not eagerly. On the upper deck, Captain Rhosher was shouting at the guide about keeping 'those drunken youngsters under control' while one of the young men in question was complaining loudly about the cost of the gun that had been thrown overboard and demanding that the captain compensate him. The poleman on the upper deck was shouting something in his own language and angrily shaking a fist. The captain still stood between him and the others.

I followed my father numbly to our cabin. Once inside, he lit the lamp and then shut the door firmly as if he could shut out what had happened. I spoke determinedly. 'Father, they killed that man.' My voice shook.

My father's voice was thick but calm. 'Nevare, you don't know that. I saw the pellet shred his canvas. But even if some struck him, at that range it would probably barely penetrate his skin.'

I was suddenly impatient with his rationality. 'Father, even if they didn't shoot him, they caused him to drown. What's the difference?'

'Sit down.' He spoke the command flatly. I sat, more because my knees were shaking than because I wished to obey him. 'Nevare, listen to me. We don't know that any pellet hit him. We do not know that he drowned. Unfortunately, the current is in command of us at the moment. We cannot go back to be certain of his death or his survival. Even if we could go back, I doubt that we could be

190

certain. If he drowned, the river has taken him. If he lived, he has reached the bank and is probably gone by now.' He sat down heavily on his bunk, facing me.

I was suddenly at a loss for words. The amazement I'd felt at the sight of the wind-wizard and the callous way in which the two hunters had ended his remarkable feat warred in me. I desperately wanted to believe my father was right, and that the wizard had escaped lasting harm. But I also felt a strange hurt deep inside me, that they had so thoughtlessly snuffed out a wondrous thing. I had glimpsed him so briefly but in that moment I had felt I would have given anything, anything at all, to know the power that he channelled so effortlessly into his craft. I clasped my hands in my lap. 'I'll probably never see anything like that again.'

'It's possible. Wind-wizards were never common.'

'Father, they deserve punishment. Even if they didn't kill him, they could have. At the very least, they sank his boat and caused him needless injury with their recklessness. For what? What had he done to them?'

My father did not answer my last question. He said only, 'Nevare, on a ship the captain is the law. We must let the captain handle this. Our interference could only make matters worse.'

'I do not see how they could be worse.'

My father's voice was mild as he observed, 'It could be worse if the plainsmen were stirred to outrage over this incident. If our captain is wise, he will swiftly shed those two and their guide, but before he does, he will see that they pay an ample amount of coin to the two plainsmen who witnessed it. Unlike Gernians, plainsmen see nothing dishonourable about being bought off. They feel that as no death can be righted and no insult completely revoked, there is nothing wrong with taking coin as an indication that the culprit wishes he could undo his mistake. Let Captain

191

Rhosher handle it, Nevare. This is his command. We shall not say or do any more about this incident.'

I did not completely agree with his argument, but I could think of no better alternative. At the next town, the hunters, their guide and their trophies were unceremoniously off loaded. I did not see the plainsmen polemen after that, but I never found out if they quit or were discharged or simply took their bribe and left. We picked up two more deckhands and departed within an hour. The captain was obviously disgruntled about the whole incident. None of us spoke about it again, but that is not to say it did not trouble me.

We were the sole passengers for the rest of the journey. The weather turned rainy and cooler. As we slowly approached the juncture where the Tefa River meets the surging flood of the Ister River, the land changed. Prairie gave way to grasslands and then forest. We began to see foothills and beyond them distant mountains to the south. Here the two great rivers converged around a rich isthmus of land to form the Soudana River that flows in a torrent to the sea. Our plan was to disembark at the city of Canby and there change to a passenger jankship for the remainder of our journey. My father was very enthused about this next leg of our trip.

It had become quite fashionable for touring parties to come upriver by carriage and wagon, seeing all the country and staying at inns along the way. Canby was gaining the reputation of being both summer resort and trade centre, for it was said that the best prices in the west for plainsworked goods and furs were there. The jankships that moved slowly upriver by the ponderous processes of poling, sailing, and cordelling went downriver a great deal faster. Once they had been almost entirely sheep and cargo vessels. Now the eighty foot vessels were grandly appointed with elegant little cabins, dining and gambling salons, and deck-top classes in watercolours, poetry and music for the ladies. We would make the final leg of our journey to Old Thares on such a vessel, and my father had emphasized that he wished me to show well in this, my first introduction to society.

We were a few days away from making port at Canby when I awoke one morning to a smell at once strange and familiar in my nostrils. It was scarcely dawn. I heard the lapping of the river against the drifting flatboat, and the calls of early morning birds. It had rained steadily through the night, but the light in the window promised at least a brief respite from the downpour. My father was still sleeping soundly in his bunk in the flatboat cabin we shared. I dressed quickly and quietly, and padded out onto the deck barefoot. A deckhand nodded wearily at me as I passed him. A strange excitement that I had no name for was thrilling in my breast. I went directly to the rail.

We had left the open grasslands behind in the night. On both sides of the river, dark forest now stretched as far as the eye could see. The trees were immense, taller than any trees I had ever imagined, and the fragrance from their needles steeped the air. The recent rains had swollen the streams. Silvery water cascaded down a rocky bed to join its flood with the river. The sound of the merging water was like music. The damp earth steamed gently and fragrantly in the rising sun. 'It's so beautiful and restful,' I said softly, for I had felt my father come out to stand on the deck behind me. 'And yet it is full of majesty, also.' When he did not reply, I turned, and was startled to find that I was still quite alone. I had been so certain of a presence nearby that it was as if I had glimpsed a ghost. 'Or not glimpsed one!' I said aloud, as if to waken my courage and forced a laugh from my throat. Despite the empty deck, I felt as if someone watched me.

But as I turned back to the railing, the living presence of so many trees overwhelmed me again. Their silent, ancient majesty surrounded me, and made the boat that sped along on the river's current a silly plaything. What could man make that was greater than these ranked green denizens? I heard

193

first an isolated bird's call, and then another answered it. I had one of those revelations that come as sudden as a breath. I was aware of the forest as one thing, a network of life, both plant and animal, that together made a whole that stirred and breathed and lived. It was like seeing the face of god, yet not the good god. No, this was one of the old gods, this was Forest himself, and I almost went to my knees before his glory.

I sensed a world beneath the sheltering branches that crossed and wound overhead, and when a deer emerged to water at the river's edge, it seemed to me that my sudden perception of the forest was what had called her forth. A log, half-afloat, was jammed on the riverbank. A mottled snake nearly as long as the log sunned on it, lethargic in the cool of morning. Then our flatboat rounded a slight bend in the river, and startled a family of wild boar that was enjoying the sweet water and cool mud at the river's edge. They defied our presence with snorts and threatening tusks. The water dripped silver from their bristly hides. The sun was almost fully up now, and the songs and challenges of the birds overlapped one another. I felt I had never before comprehended the richness of life that a forest might hold, nor a man's place in it as a natural creature of the world.

The trees were so tall that even from the boat's deck, I craned my neck to see their topmost branches against the blue sky of early autumn. As we drifted with the river, the nature of the forest changed, from dark and brooding evergreen to an area of both evergreen and deciduous trees gone red or gold with the frosts. It filled me with wonder to stare at those leafy giants and recognize the still life that seeped through their branches. It was strange for a prairie-bred youth to feel such an attraction to the forest. Suddenly the wide sweeping country that had bred me seemed arid and lifeless and far too bright. I longed with all my heart to be walking on the soft carpet of gently rotting leaves beneath the wise old trees.

When a voice spoke behind me, I startled.

'What fascinates you, son? Are you looking for deer?'

I spun about, but it was only my father. I was as startled to see him now as I had been surprised not to see him earlier. My conflicting thoughts must have given me a comical expression, for he grinned at me. 'Were you day-dreaming, then? Homesick again?'

I shook my head slowly. 'No, not homesick, unless it is for a home I've never seen until now. I don't quite know what draws me. I've seen deer, and a snake as long as a log, and wild boar coming down to water. But it isn't the animals, Father, and it's not even the trees, though they make up the greater part of it. It's the whole of it. The forest. Don't you feel a sense of homecoming here? As if this is the sort of place where men were always meant to dwell?'

He was tamping tobacco into his pipe for his morning smoke. As he did so, he surveyed my forest in bewilderment, and then looked back at me and shook his head. 'No, I can't say that I do. Live in that? Can you imagine how long it would take to clear a spot for a house, let alone some pasture? You'd always be in the gloom and the shade, with a pasture full of roots to battle. No, son. I've always preferred open country, where a man can see all around himself and a horse goes easily, and nothing stands between a man and the sky. I suppose that's my years as a soldier speaking. I'd not want to scout a place like that, nor fight an engagement there. Would you? The thought of defending a stronghold built in such a thicket as that place daunts me.'

I shook my head. 'I had not even imagined battle there, sir,' I said, and then tried to recall what I had been imagining. Battle and soldiering and cavalla had no place in that living god. Had I truly been longing to live there, amongst the trees, in shade and damp and muffled quiet? It was so at odds with all that I had planned for my life that I almost laughed out loud. It was as if I had suddenly been jarred out of someone else's dream.

195

My father finished lighting his pipe and took a deep draw from it. He let the smoke drift from his mouth as he spoke. 'We are at the edge of old Gernia, son. These forests used to mark the edge of the kingdom. Once, folk thought of them as the wild lands, and we cared little for what was beyond them. Some of the noble families had hunting lodges within them, and of course we harvested lumber from them. But they were not a tempting place for farmer or shepherd. It was only when we expanded beyond them, into the grasslands and then the plains that anyone thought to settle here. Two more bends of the river, and we'll be into Gernia proper.' He rolled his shoulders, stretching in a gentlemanly way, and then glanced down at my feet and frowned. 'You do intend to put on some boots before you come to breakfast, don't you?'

'Yes, sir. Of course.'

'Well, then. I will see you at table, shortly. Beautiful morning, isn't it?'

'Yes, sir.'

He strolled away from me. I knew his routine. He would next check on the horses in their deck stalls, he'd have a sociable word or two with the steersman and then return to our stateroom briefly and thence to the captain's table for breakfast, where I would join them.

But I still had a few more moments to enjoy the forest. I reached for that first consciousness that I'd had of it, but could not reattain that state of heightened awareness. The old god that was Forest had turned his face away from me. I could only see it as I had seen it all my life, as trees and animals and plants on a hillside.

The sun was rising higher; the man on the bow was calling his soundings and the world glided past us. As my father had predicted, we were nearing a slow bend in the river. I went back to our stateroom to put on my boots, and to shave. My hair was already growing out to annoying stubble that could not be combed. I hastily made the bed I had

196

so quickly abandoned at dawn and then headed to the captain's small salon for breakfast.

The captain's salon and table were unpretentious on such a small vessel. I think my father enjoyed the informality. As they did every morning, he and Captain Rhosher exchanged pleasantries about the weather and discussed what the day's travel might bring. For the most part, I ate and listened to the conversation. The meal was not elaborate but the portions were generous and the food was honest. Porridge, bacon, bread, fresh apples, and a strong morning tea made up most of it. I was happy to fill my plate. My father praised the ship's rapid progress through the night.

'It was a good run, with a strong moon to light our way. But we can't expect the same tonight, or even for the rest of the day. Once we go past Loggers, the river will be thick with log rafts. Those are bad enough to get around, but worse are the strays. The river has gone silty, with shallows growing where they never were before. Wedge a stray log in a sandbar, let us run upon it blind, and we'll hole our hull. The lookout and the sounder will work for their wages today, as will our polemen. Still, I foresee that we'll make Canby as scheduled.'

They went on to discuss our disembarkment there and which jankship my father should book our passage on. Our captain made gentle mock of the big vessels, saying that my father was not interested in their speed but only desired the novelty of the experience and the company of the lovely ladies and elegant gentlemen who preferred such distinctive travel to his own simple ship.

As my father was laughingly denying this, I became aware of a very unpleasant smell. Manners required that I ignore it, but it quickly quenched my appetite and soon began to make my eyes tear. With every passing moment, the smoky odour grew stronger. I glanced toward the small galley, wondering at first if something had been neglected on the ship's little oil stove. But no visible smoke was emanating from there. The stench grew stronger. It had the most peculiar effect on me. It was not just that it greatly displeased my nose and irritated my throat. It woke in me a sense of terror, a panic that I could scarcely smother. It was all I could do to stay in my chair. I tried to dab at my streaming eyes discreetly with my napkin. Captain Rhosher grinned at me sympathetically. 'Ah, that'll be the sweet aroma of Loggers getting to you, lad. We'll have thick breathing for the next day or so, until we're past their operations. They're burning the trash wood, the green branches and viney stuff, to get it out of the way so the teams can get up and down the hills easier. Makes for a lot of smoke. Still, it's not as bad as that operation they had going on further down the river two years ago. That company would just set fire to the hillside, and burn off the underbrush. Anything big enough to be left standing, they harvested right away, to beat the worms to it. Fast money, but a terrible lot of waste, that was how I saw it.'

I nodded at his words, scarcely comprehending them. The end of breakfast could not come too soon for me, and as soon as I politely could, I left the table, foolishly thinking to find fresher air outside.

As I stepped out onto the deck, an inconceivable sight met my eyes. The day was dimmed by wood smoke hanging low in the air. The lower half of the hillside on the port side of the boat was stripped of life. Every tree of decent size had been cut. The raw stumps were jagged and pale against the scored earth. The remaining saplings and undergrowth were crushed and matted into the earth where the giants had fallen and been dragged over them to the river. Smoke was rising from heaped and smouldering branches; the hearts of the fires burned a dull red. The hillside scene reminded me of a large dead animal overcome by maggots. Men swarmed everywhere on the hillside. Some cut the limbs from the fallen giants. Teamsters guided the harnessed draught horses that dragged the stripped logs down to the river's edge. The track of their repeated passage had cut a deep muddy furrow in the hill's flank, and the rainfall of the last few days had made it a stream, dumping into the river that here ran thick with muck. The brown curl of it wavered out into the river's current like a rivulet of clotting blood. Stripped logs like gnawed bones rested in piles at the river's edge, or bobbed in the shallows. Men scuttled about on the floating logs with peevees and lengths of chain and rope, corralling the logs into crude rafts. It was carnage, the desecration of a god's body.

On the upper half of the hill logging teams ate into the remaining forest like mange spreading on a dog's back. As I watched, men in the distance shouted triumphantly as an immense tree fell. As it went down, other, smaller trees gave way to its fall, their roots tearing free of the mountain's flesh as they collapsed under its mammoth weight. Moments after the swaying of branches ceased, men crawled over the fallen tree, bright axes rising and falling as they chopped away the branches.

I turned aside from the sight, sickened and cold. A terrible premonition washed over me. This was how the whole world would end. No matter how much of the forest's skin they flayed, it would never be enough for these men. They would continue over the face of the earth, leaving desecration and devastation behind them. They would devour the forest and excrete piles of buildings made of stone wrenched from the earth or from dead trees. They would hammer paths of bare stone between their dwellings, and dirty the rivers and subdue the land until it could recall only the will of man. They could not stop themselves from what they did. They did not see what they did, and even if they saw, they did not know how to stop. They no longer knew what was enough. Men could no longer stop man; it would take the force of a god himself to halt them. But they were mindlessly butchering the only god who might have had the strength to stop them.

In the distance I heard the shouts of warning and triumph as another forest giant fell. As it went down, a huge flock of birds flew up, cawing in distress and circling the carnage as crows circle a battlefield. My knees buckled and I fell to the deck, clutching at the railing. I coughed in the thick air, gagged on it, and coughed some more. I could not catch my breath, but I do not think it was the smoke alone that choked me. It was grief that tightened my throat.

One of the deckhands saw me go down. A moment later, there was a rough hand on my shoulder, shaking me and asking me what ailed me. I shook my head, unable to find words to express my distress. A short time later, my father was at my side, and the captain, his napkin still clenched in his hands.

'Nevare? Are you ill?' my father asked solemnly.

'They're destroying the world,' I said vaguely. I closed my eyes at the terrible sight, and forced myself to my feet. 'I . . . I don't feel well,' I said. Some part of me didn't wish to shame myself before my father and the captain and crew. Some other part of me didn't care; the enormity of what I had glimpsed was too monstrous, and suddenly too certain. 'I think I'll go back to bed for a while.'

'Prob'ly the stink from all those fires,' Captain Rhosher said sagely. 'That smoke's enough to make anyone sick. You'll get used to it, lad, in a few hours. Stinks a lot less than Old Thares on an early morning, believe me. We'll be past it in a day or so, if all those damn log-rafts don't block our way. A menace to navigation, they are. Time was, good stone was the only thing a rich man would build with. Now they want wood, wood, and more wood. 'Spect they'll go back to honest stone when this last strip is gone. Then we'll see the quarries bustle again. Men will do whatever brings in the coin. I'll be glad when they've cut the last timber on that hill and the river can run clear again.'

EIGHT

Old Thares

I lied to my father again that day. I told him that something I had eaten had disagreed with me. That excuse let
me keep to my bed for three days. I could not bear to
look out the window. The stink of burning branches, the
particle-laden air and the cursing of the deckhands as they
yelled warnings to the sweepsman and fended us away
from the floating log rafts with long poles told me all that
I did not wish to know. I felt as aggrieved as I had when
the hunters had shot the wind wizard. I had glimpsed
something immense and wonderful, and in the next
instance had seen its destruction. I felt like a child, shown
a most desirable plaything that is then whisked away. I
could not discard the feeling that I had been cheated. The
world I had expected to live in was vanishing before I
could explore it.

At Canby, we disembarked and bid Captain Rhosher
farewell. Trade goods and waters converged here where the
rushing Ister River met the languid Tefa. The joined rivers
flowed west as the mighty Soudana River. Wide and deep
and swift, the Soudana was a major trade artery, as well as
our boundary with Landsing. The Soudana would make its
swift way past Old Thares, our destination, and continue
without us to Mouth City and the sea. Mouth City had once
been a Gernian town and our best seaport; it had been ceded

201

to the Landsingers at the end of the war and was still a bitter loss for any loyal Gernian to contemplate.

I felt overwhelmed by the masses of people in the street, and walked at my father's heels as if I were a cowed puppy. People thronged the walkways, hurrying to and fro and dressed in stylish city clothes. Vehicles of every imaginable sort fought for space in the crowded streets. I was impressed with how my father threaded confidently through the crowds to the booking office, and made arrangements for our tickets on the jankship, the conveyance of our luggage and our evening stay at a hotel. It felt strange to be jostled by strangers, and to take a meal in a large room full of people talking and laughing as they dined. Music played and the black-aproned waiters hurried from table to table, behaving in such a grand and proud manner that I felt shabby and rustic and out of place, as if some mistake had been made and *I* should have been serving *them*. I was glad to retire to our room for the evening, and gladder still to take ship on the morrow.

Once our horses and luggage were aboard the immense jankship, I reassured my father that I had recovered from my illness. The jankship's passage down the swift currented river felt much different from our flatboat's placid journeying, for the wind in our square sails encouraged the ship to outstrip the current's pace. The horses did not like the creak and rock of the hastening vessel and neither did I, when it was time to sleep. But during my waking hours, I scarcely noticed it, for there was so much else to claim my attention.

Our accommodations were much grander than those we'd had on the humble flatboat. We each had a private cabin, with an iron bedstead that was bolted to the deck and ample room for our trunks. There was a dining salon with white-clothed tables and gleaming silver, and a gaming room for cards and dice, and the company of other travellers to cheer us. My father had chosen a vessel whose captain had a reputation for daring and speed. It had become a point of pride among the captains on the Soudana to compete with one another for the swiftest trip down the river. During the day, I enjoyed the thrilling view of the landscape that seemed to race past us. The meals were meticulously prepared and every evening there was some sort of entertainment, be it music or singing or a play. My father made himself affable and sociable and quickly made the acquaintance of most of the other twenty passengers. I did my best to follow his example. He advised me to listen more than I spoke, and that did seem to be the charm that made my company attractive to the ladies aboard. There was only one awkward moment. A young woman had just introduced me to her friend. At the name Burvelle, her friend had started, and then asked me with great interest, 'But surely you are not related to Epiny Burvelle, are you?' I replied that I had a younger girl cousin of that name, but I did not know her well. The woman had burst into laughter and remarked to her companion, 'Fancy having to own up to Epiny being your cousin!'

'Sadia!' exclaimed my acquaintance in obvious embarrassment. 'Have some courtesy! Surely no one can help who they are related to, or I would not have to introduce *you* as *my* cousin!'

At that, the second woman's smile faded and she even became a bit cold despite my assurances that her remarks had not offended me in the least. But for the most part, my interchanges with the other passengers were courteous and interesting, and improved my sophistication, as I am sure my father had intended.

As we travelled west on the river, the land became more settled. Soon the dawns were showing us prosperous farms along the riverbanks, and the towns we passed were populous and large. Fishermen plied the river in their small rowing boats, setting nets or fishing with poles. Our captain, determined that our ship would slow down for nothing, often bore down on them, forcing them to scuttle like water bugs to stay out of our path. The young ladies watching from the upper deck would gasp with trepidation and then laugh with delight as the little boats reached safety.

For the final two days of our journey, there was never a time when I could look out at the riverside and not see signs of human habitation and industry. By night, the yellow lights of homes lit the shores, and by day the rising smoke from chimneys feathered up into the sky. I felt a sort of wonder as I thought of all those people living so close together, and on its heels followed a tinge of fear; soon I must live amongst all those people, day in and day out, with never a respite from human company. I found the prospect daunting. My once-glad anticipation dimmed to a grim foreboding.

I recalled the flatboat captain's warning that Old Thares would smell far worse than the timber fires had. When I asked my father about it, he shrugged his shoulders.

'Much coal is burned in Old Thares, and it has been a city for hundreds of generations. It is bound to smell like a city. Old Captain Rhosher probably hasn't left the river in twenty years. He can't smell the smells of his own boat and crew, but he's happy to tell you that the city stinks. It's all in what one is accustomed to, Nevare, and a man can become accustomed to almost anything.'

I found myself doubting that. My father read my misgivings. He stood beside me as I leaned on the railing, staring glumly across the river toward the rows of smoke-blackened stone buildings that crowded the river's edge. Scarcely any natural land remained. Stonework lined the banks of the river and the rise and fall of the water was marked plainly by the slime. At intervals, foul coils of thick water oozed into the river from open trenches or gaping pipes, discharging their stench into the air and their filth into the river. Despite this, ragged hooligan youths fished and fought and wandered dazedly along the reinforced banks of the river. Stunted bushes and thick water plants blanketed the muck at the river's edge. Above and beyond the hunched ware-houses and factories was an undulating roof of housetops and smoking chimneys. It was as dreary and forbidding a sight as any I had ever seen, and more ominous to my eyes than any arid stretch of desert or harsh prairie land.

The aromatic smoke from my father's short pipe was a welcome mask for the lingering odours in the air. After a time, he knocked the husk of burnt ashes from the bowl. 'I never went to the Academy. You know that.'

'I know that it didn't exist when you were my age, sir. And that you had a great deal to do with its creation.'

'That's true, I suppose,' he replied modestly as he tamped more tobacco from his pouch into his pipe. 'I was educated at the Arms Institute. I attended at a time when those of us who expressed a desire to join the cavalla were regarded as somewhat . . . above ourselves. Cavalla assignments were the rightful domain of the families who had served the old kings as knights. Even though those families had dwindled, leaving our mounted forces undermanned, some felt it was almost against the will of the good god for a young man to want to be what his father had not been before him. Yet, a soldier is a soldier and I had persuaded my father that I could serve my king as well on horseback as I could on foot. I will admit that I was sorely disappointed when I was marked to be an artilleryman. It seemed the touch of the good god himself when that changed and I was sent off to the cavalla. Well.' He put the stem of the loaded pipe to his lips, gave flame to it from a sulphur match, and took several encouraging puffs to get it going well before he continued. 'Here in this city, I fear you will live, as I did during my years at the Arms Institute. No open air, not enough space to run, mediocre food, and living cheek by jowl with your fellow cadets. Some of them will be all a good officer should be, already. Others will be brutish louts and you will wonder why the good god made them soldier sons, let alone destined them to be officers. But when your days here are done, I promise you that you will return to living like a free man again, to roam and hunt and breathe the fresh air of the wild spaces. Think of that, when the city smoke and endless grey nights become oppressive. It may give you heart.'

'Yes, sir,' I replied, and tried to find relief in the thought, but it was elusive.

We docked in Old Thares late that evening. My uncle had sent a man with a wagon. He hoisted our baggage into the bed of the wagon and tethered Sirlofty and Steelshanks to its tail. I rode alongside my father on the spring seat of the rather humble wagon and tried not to wonder if this was an affront to my father's status. The night was chill with a warning of damp in the air that promised that winter would soon arrive. We left the docks and rumbled through the poorer sections of Old Thares, then through a commercial district, quiet in the darkness save for occasional watchmen.

Finally we emerged from the town's clutter and climbed into the gentle hills to an enclave of manors and estates. When we arrived at my uncle's home, the great house was dark save for one yellow lantern at the main entry and a single set of windows alight above us. Servants swiftly appeared, including a groom who took our horses. My uncle's man greeted my father, and told him that his mistress and my cousins were long abed, but that my uncle had had word of our imminent arrival and awaited us in his study. We followed my uncle's man into his house and up a richly carpeted staircase while behind us servants struggled with our heavy trunks.

At the double doors of my uncle's study, his man rapped lightly, then opened the door for us and stood to one side as we entered the warmly lit room. There any doubts I'd had about my uncle's welcome of us were dispersed. Not only were wine, cold meats, cheese and bread set out on a table to welcome us, but also tobacco for my father. My uncle, clad in an elaborate smoking jacket and silk lansin trousers,

206

rose and came to greet my father with an embrace. Then he stood back from me, pipe in hand, and feigned amazement at how I had grown. He insisted that we sit down immediately to the late night repast he had had prepared for us, and I was glad to do so.

Their conversation flowed over my head as I ate. I was glad to be seen and not heard, for it afforded me the uninterrupted opportunity to enjoy the best food I'd faced in some days, and also to see my father and my uncle as I'd never witnessed them before. In the next hour I realized what had always escaped me, that my father and my uncle were close and that my Uncle Sefert not only rejoiced in my father's elevation but had genuine affection for his younger sibling. I had been a child the few previous times I had seen them together, and on those occasions they spoke and behaved with the reserve appropriate to their stations. Perhaps it was the lateness of the hour or the casual setting, but tonight they spoke quickly, laughed heartily, and generally behaved more like two boys than two peers of the realm.

As if to make up for lost time, they discussed a dozen topics, from the health of my father's crops and the product of my uncle's vineyards to my uncle's marriage plans for his daughter and my father's selection of prospects for Yaril's hand. My father spoke of my mother's gardens, and that he wished to visit the flower market and take new dahlia tubers home with him, to replace the ones devoured by rodents earlier that summer. He talked about my mother's pleasure in her garden and home, and how his daughters grew all too swiftly and would soon leave his protection. In contrast, my uncle spoke of his wife's discontent and ambition with painful honesty, acknowledging that she was ill-pleased with my father's elevation in status, as if somehow his rise had compromised my uncle's position. 'Daraleen has always been jealous of her position. She was a younger daughter in her family, and never thought to be wed to a first son. It is almost

207

as if she fears that some of her honour will be taken from her if others rise to share the same footing. I have tried to reassure her, but alas, her mother seems to share her daughter's apprehension. Her family behaves as if the new nobles sprang from common stock, but every one of the soldier sons King Troven elevated had a noble father. Nonetheless, my wife's family shuns contact with the new nobles as upstarts and frauds. It is without foundation, but, there it is.'

My father commiserated with him on this, taking none of it personally, as if they spoke of a house with a cracking foundation or a field suddenly prone to root-rot. He did not condemn the woman, nor was there any discomfort in how frankly they discussed her jealousy. It was a flaw they both acknowledged, but did not allow to affect their relationship. Daraleen went to great pains to cultivate her friendship with the Queen. She put their daughters before her majesty at every opportunity, and hoped to see them invited to court for an extended stay. To that end my younger cousin, Epiny, had begun to study the occult, for spiritualists and séances and other such nonsense fascinated the Queen. My uncle was plainly displeased by this. 'I have told her she is to regard it as studying pagan beliefs or plainsmen legends. At first, she seemed to share my opinions of it, but the longer she studies that claptrap, the more she babbles of it at table and the more validity she seems to give it. It troubles me, Keft. She is young, and unfortunately behaves even younger than her years but I think the sooner she is settled with a solid man, the better it will be for her. I know that Daraleen has high ambitions for her, and hopes to marry her above our station. Nightly she reminds me that if Epiny finds favour with the Queen and is invited to court, she will be seen by the finest young nobles of the realm. But I fear for my daughter, Keft. I think she would be better off studying the scriptures of the good god than researching crystal chimes and telling fortunes with silver pins.'

'She does not sound so different from my own Yaril. It seems to me that Elisi, too, went through a flighty period at about that age. All she wanted to babble about was what she had dreamed the night before, and although she knows I don't approve of the old holy days, she sulked for a week when I would not allow her to go to a friend's Dark Evening ball. Give Epiny a year or so, brother, and I expect her father's common sense will come back to her. Girls need those flights of fancy and time to indulge them, just as boys pass through a reckless time of measuring their courage by challenging themselves.'

I was a bit surprised to think that fathers took so much thought over their daughters. Then, as I pondered it, it seemed that of course it must be so, and I wondered if some day Carsina and I would have daughters that we must safely shepherd into marriages. I wondered if I would ever sit with Rosse and discuss my children's prospects. I was jolted from my thoughts when Uncle Sefert suddenly addressed me. 'Nevare, you have a pensive look. What are you thinking?'

I spoke honestly, without giving thought to my words, saying, 'I was hoping that some day Rosse and I will sit at table together and discuss our plans for our children with as much fondness and pleasure as you share with my father now.'

I had not intended to flatter either of them, and yet my father gave me the warmest smile I had ever seen on his face. 'Such is my wish for you also, my son,' he assured me. 'When all is said and done, family is what counts for most in this world. I hope to see you have a distinguished career in the cavalla, just as I hope to see Rosse manage my lands well and to see your sisters well wed, and young Vanze honoured as a pious and learned man. Yet above all, I hope that in the years to come, you will remember one another fondly, and always do whatever you can for the honour and well being of your family.'

209

'As surely my younger brother has done for our family over the years,' my Uncle Sefert added, and was rewarded by the slight blush that suffused my father's face at his elder brother's praise.

I perceived my uncle then as a very different man from what I had previously supposed him. I decided that their free discussion in front of me marked, perhaps, their recognition that I was now a man and more worthy of confidences than I had been as a child. As if to confirm this, my uncle then asked me a number of polite questions about our journey and my preparation for the Academy and its rigours. At the news that I had brought Sirlofty, he smiled and nodded his approval, but cautioned, 'Perhaps you should stable him with me until you reach the state in your training where they will allow you a personal mount. I have heard that the officer in charge of the young cadets has instituted a new practice of putting all of them on uniform horses to begin with, so that pace and stride and appearance are matched for each regiment.'

'I had not heard of that,' my father frowned.

'It is quite recent,' my Uncle Sefert assured him. 'The news of it likely has not reached the eastern frontiers yet. Colonel Rebin has recently chosen to retire; some say his wife importuned him, others that the gout in his knees and feet has become so painful that he can scarce bestride a chair, let alone a horse. There are also less kind whispers that he somehow offended the King and found it wiser to leave the post before he was relieved of it. Whatever the cause, he has left the Academy and Colonel Stiet has taken it over.'

'Colonel Stiet? I don't believe I know him,' my father observed stiffly. I was alarmed at how unsettled he seemed to be at this sudden news.

'You would not. He isn't a frontierman, or even cavalla, but I've heard he is a good military officer for all that. He had risen through the ranks here at home, by diligence and long years rather than field promotions. Yet the gossip is that he is more given to show than Colonel Rebin was, and his insistence on well matched horses, all of a colour, for each regiment is but the tip of it. My wife's family knows the Stiets well. We have often dined together. He may not be a soldier's soldier, but he will have the Academy's best interests at heart.'

'Well, I'm not opposed to a bit of spit and polish, I suppose. Attention to detail can save a man's life in a ticklish situation.' I could hear that my father was speaking for my benefit, and suspected he was trying to make the best of a bad situation.

'He's more than polishing uniform buttons and shining boots.' My uncle paused. He stood up, paced a turn about the room, and then continued. 'This is gossip, pure and simple, and yet I think I'll pass it on. I have heard he favours the soldier sons of the established nobles over King Troven's battle lords, as some call you.'

'Is he unfair?' My father asked the question bluntly, his voice going low with concern.

'Strict. Strict, but not unfair, is more what I've heard. My wife is a close friend of his lady, and knows them well. There is talk that . . . well. How to put this? The cavalla is ultimately commanded by the King, of course, as is all our military. But some fear that too many battle lords' sons rising to officer status will shift the military to, to a, well, to a loyalty to the King that might be unhealthy for the rest of the kingdom. The Council of Lords already saw its power diluted when the New Nobles were granted equal seats with them. It is much easier for the King to have his way there. And some say that if ever it came to, well, to an outright rebellion by one lord or another, the King might use the power of his army against the rebel lord. And that an army led by the sons of battle lords might be less dismayed by that than an army commanded by Old Nobles' sons would be.'

An awkward silence fell as my uncle seemed to run out of words rather than stopped speaking. My father asked him, somewhat stiffly, 'Is there, in fact, any danger of such a rebellion? Do you think any of the old lords might rise against our king?'

My uncle had been standing near the fire. He crossed to a chair and sat down in it heavily. 'There is talk, but I think it will never go beyond talk. Some say he favours his new nobles too much. His push to the east benefits them, and fills the King's coffers, but does nothing for noble families who lost their most profitable holdings when the coastal stretch was ceded to Landsing. Some say that we have recovered from our long war with Landsing, and that now, with a determined military, we could defeat them, and take back what is rightfully ours.'

My father was silent for a long time. Then he said quietly, 'I do not think such decisions are for the lords, but for the King, whom the good god put over us. I mourn as much as any Gernian, soldier or lord, for the lost coastal provinces. King Troven did not relish doing what he must to gain an end to that long war. Have they forgotten all we endured, that long last decade of war? Do they forget that once we feared to lose not just the coastal provinces, but all the lands along the Soudana as well? King Troven did not do so badly for his old nobles. He did better than his father had done, beggaring us with a war we long knew we could not win. But, come. Enough of chewing on old bones. Tell me more about Colonel Stiet?'

My uncle considered before he spoke. 'He is the soldier son of an old nobility family. Politically, his heart lies with the Old Nobles in this divide. Some of them say that we have far too many New Nobles' sons attending the Academy now. In the last two crops of first-year cadets, the New Noble sons have outnumbered the old. This year, the ratio is even more skewed. You battle lords seem a vigorous lot

212

when it comes to fathering sons.' He smiled at my father as he said it. I held very still. I wondered if it pained my uncle that his younger brother had fathered three sons to his one.

My father put my uncle's unspoken warning into words. 'You think that Stiet's family and friends may urge him to balance that ratio.'

'I do not know. I think pressure will be applied. I do not know Stiet well enough to say if he will give way to it. He is new to his post. He has promised to hold *all* the cadets to a high standard. He may hold that standard more tautly with the soldier sons of battle lords than he does with those of the old guard.'

My father gave me a sideways glance, and then nodded to himself. 'Nevare can bear that sort of scrutiny, never fear.'

I felt pride that my father had such confidence in me, and tried not to let anxiety find any lodging within me. They moved from the table to their comfortable chairs by the hearth. It was early in the season for a fire, and yet after our long journey and damp wagon ride, the warmth felt good to me. I was honoured to sit with them while they smoked and talked, and tried to pay attention to the conversation even if I knew it was not my place to join in. Several times my uncle addressed me directly to include me in their conversation. From family matters they passed to general discussion of the political climate. Landsing had been quiescent of late, even negotiating favourable trade exchanges and allowing our king generous passage to Defford, one of their best seaports. Uncle Sefert felt that Landsing encouraged our eastward expansion, for it kept our military busy and our king's acquisitive eyes away from them. My father did not think King Troven was overly greedy, only that he saw the benefits of having a generous border of territory that he controlled around our populated areas. Besides, all knew he had brought civilization, trade and other benefits to the plainsfolk. Like as not, even the Specks would eventually be

213

better off thanks to our assimilation of the Wilds. They made no use of the forests, farmed no lands, and harvested no timber. Let them learn from Gernian example how to use those resources wisely and surely all would benefit.

My uncle countered with one of the 'noble savage' sentiments that had been so popular of late, more, I slowly realized, to nettle my father than because he believed such nonsense. I think he was surprised when my father expressed an affection for natural people, such as the plainsmen and even the Specks, but pointed out that unless civilization reached out to embrace and uplift them, they would likely be trampled beneath its ongoing eastward march. My father's view was that it was better we reach and change them sooner rather than later, so that they might have a chance to emulate us rather than fall victim, in ignorance, to the civilized vices that natural people were so vulnerable to.

It was late and despite my interest in the conversation, I was battling my heavy eyelids before my father and uncle had finished catching up with one another. My uncle did not summon his man, but carried a branch of candles himself and showed us up to our adjoining bedchambers, where he bid us goodnight. Our trunks were already there, and in my chamber, my nightshirt was already set out across the opened bed. I was glad to disrobe and hang my garments on a chair, pull on my nightshirt and then burrow into the soft bed. The linens smelled of sweet washing herbs, and I settled into them, certain of a deep and restful sleep.

I was leaning over to blow out my candle when there was a soft tap-tap, simultaneous with my bedchamber door opening. I expected perhaps a servant, but certainly not a maid in her night robe and mobcap peeking in at me. 'Are you awake?' she asked me eagerly.

'So it would appear!' I replied uncomfortably.

A smile spread over her face. 'Oh, good! They kept you so long, I thought you would never get to your bed.' With that she bounced into my bedchamber, shut the door behind her and sat down on the foot of my bed. She curled her legs up under her and then demanded, 'Did you bring me anything?'

'Should I have?' I was completely taken aback by her peculiar behaviour and had no idea what to expect next from her. I had heard tales of how forward maid servants were in a big city, but I had never expected to encounter such brazen behaviour in my uncle's house. She looked young to be a maidservant, but in her night robe and with her hair bundled up in a cap, it was difficult to guess her age. I wasn't accustomed to seeing women in such garb.

She gave a small sigh of disappointment and shook her head at me. 'Probably not. Aunt Selethe sends us little presents from time to time, so I hoped perhaps you had brought one with you. But if you haven't, I shan't be offended.'

'Oh. Are you Epiny Burvelle, my cousin?' Suddenly this midnight encounter had become even stranger.

She looked at me for a moment in shock. 'Well, who else did you think I might be?'

'I'm sure I had no idea!'

She stared at me a moment longer, perplexed, and then her mouth formed a scandalized 'O'. She leaned closer to me and spoke in a whisper, as if she feared to be overheard. 'You thought I was a wanton maid, come to warm your bed, and demanding your largesse in advance. Oh, Nevare, how depraved young men from the east must be, to expect such things.'

'I did not!' I denied hotly.

She sat back. 'Oh, don't lie. You did so. But forget that. Now that you know that I'm your cousin Epiny, answer my first question. Did you bring me a present?' She was eager and tactless as a child.

'No. Well, not exactly. My mother sent presents for you and your mother and sister. But I don't have them. My father does.'

'Oh.' She sighed. 'Then I suppose I shall have to wait until morning before I get it. So, tell me. Did you have a good journey coming here?'

'It was good, but wearying.' I tried not to say the words too pointedly. I was very tired and this bizarre re-introduction to my cousin was straining my courtesy. She didn't notice.

'Did you get to ride on a jankship?'

'Yes. Yes, we did.'

'Oh!' She all but collapsed with jealousy. 'I never have. My father says they are frivolous and dangerous and a hazard to sane navigation on the river. Last week, one collided with a coal barge. Six people were lost and all the coal was spilled in the river. He says they should be outlawed, and their reckless captains clapped in irons.'

'Really.' I made my voice flat with disinterest. I felt that her comment criticized my father and me for arriving by jankship. 'I am really very tired, cousin Epiny.'

'Are you? Then I suppose I should let you go to sleep. You're a bit disappointing, cousin Nevare. I thought a boy-cousin would have far more endurance than you seem to. And I thought someone from the east would have interesting things to tell.' She clambered off my bed.

'Perhaps I do, when I'm not so tired,' I said sharply.

'I doubt it,' she said sincerely. 'You look very ordinary. And you sound as dull as my brother Hotorn. He is very concerned with his dignity, and I think that prevents him from having an interesting life. If I were a boy, and permitted to have an interesting life, I would have no dignity at all.'

'You don't seem to be overly burdened with it as a girl,' I pointed out to her.

'Well, yes, I've discarded it as being useless to me as a girl, also. But that doesn't mean I can have an interesting life. Although, I do aspire to one. I do. Good night, Nevare.' She leaned closer as if she would kiss me on the cheek, but stopped short, staring at the side of my head. 'Whatever did you do to your ear?'

'A plains warrior cut it with his swanneck. A swanneck is a long, curving blade.' I was glad to say it. Her remark that I was ordinary had stung me sharply.

'I know what a swanneck is, cousin.' She sounded very patronizing as she paused with her hand on the doorknob. 'And you are my dear cousin, and I will love you no matter how boring you are. So you needn't make up wild tales about savage plainsmen. You probably think you can easily deceive a city girl like me, but I know such stories are rubbish. I have read a great deal about the plainsmen, and I know they are a natural and gentle folk who lived in complete harmony with nature. Unlike us.' She gave yet another sigh. 'Don't tell lies to make yourself seem important, Nevare. That is such a wearying trait in a man. I'll see you in the morning.'

'He cut my ear twice. I had to have it stitched!' I tried to tell her, but she shushed me furiously as the door closed behind her. Before her visit, I had been wearily relaxed and ready for sleep. Now, despite my fatigue, I could not drift off, even after I blew out my candle. I lay in the big soft bed and listened to the rain hitting the window glass and wondered if I were ordinary and boring. Eventually I decided that Epiny was too eccentric to know what ordinary was, and thus I was able to fall asleep.

Only my youth, I am sure, made me jolt awake at the chambermaid's timid tap at my door early the next morning. Unthinking, I bade her come in, and then stayed where I was, blushing beneath my covers, as she fetched warm wash water and then bundled away my travelling clothes for freshening and brushing. I was greatly unaccustomed to being cared for in such a way, and even after she had left, it took me some little time before I dared venture from my bed, lest she return unannounced. When I did, I washed and

217

dressed hastily. Habit made me tidy my room, and then I wondered if the maid would think me odd and rustic that I had spread up my bedding myself. Then I became irritated with myself that I would worry so much about what a maid might think of me. Having pushed that concern from my mind, I began to consider nervously all that my uncle had said of the Academy the night before. Had I had any more time by myself, it is likely I would have worked myself into a fine lather, but luckily for me, another knock at my door summoned me to an early breakfast with my uncle and father.

Both were up, shaved, and neatly attired for the day despite our late night. I had expected to see my aunt and cousins at table, but there were no extra settings and my uncle made no mention of them. We were served a hearty breakfast of kippers and a mixed grill, with tea and toast. Sleep had revived my appetite, until my uncle observed, 'Eat well, Nevare, for I've heard that a young man's first meal at the Academy is a hurried one. I doubt that your noon meal will please you as well as this breakfast does.'

At his words, my appetite fled, and I asked my father, 'Am I to go directly to the Academy today, then, Father?'

'We think it best that you do. Your uncle has agreed to keep Sirlofty here until such time as you are allowed to have your own mount. We'll make one stop for a boot fitting with a cobbler Sefert recommends, and then I'll escort you to the Academy. You'll be a day ahead of most of the others. Perhaps it will give you a chance to settle in before your classmates arrive.'

And so it was done. Breakfast was scarcely finished before a footman came to announce that my trunks had been loaded onto my uncle's carriage. My uncle bid me farewell at the door and advised my father that there was to be an excellent venison roast with wild plum sauce for dinner.

We were walking to the carriage when Epiny suddenly hastened down the steps after us. She was still in a nightgown with a robe flung over it, but now her curling brown hair was loose about her shoulders. By daylight, I estimated her to be only a few years younger than me. Yet she seemed childish when she cried out, 'Nevare, Nevare, you cannot leave when you have not even said farewell!'

'Epiny! You are much too old to be running about in your nightclothes!' my uncle rebuked her, but there was suppressed mirth in his voice, and from it I suspected that she was her father's favourite.

'But I must bid my cousin good luck, Father! Oh, I told you I should have stayed up last night. I knew it! Now we've had no time at all to talk, and I had so looked forward to doing a reading for him, to foretell his success or failure at the Academy.' She stepped back from me, lifting her hands to frame my face as if she were planning to paint my portrait. She narrowed her eyes to slits and said in a hushed voice, 'Perhaps I misjudged you? How could I have thought you ordinary? Such an aura. Such a magnificent aura, twice what I've seen on any other man. It burns red with a man's vigour close to your skin, but a second corona of green says you are nature's child, and a loving son to her—'

'And that sort of nonsense is exactly why you were not allowed to stay up to greet him! Bid him the good god's blessing, Epiny, and then he must be on his way. Nevare cannot let a silly little girl and her play-pretend nattering delay him on an important day like this.' True impatience and perhaps a bit of embarrassment had crept into her father's voice. I stood still as she pattered up to me, her little slippers peeping from beneath her robe. She stood on tiptoes to kiss me on the cheek and bid me god speed. 'Come to dinner soon! I regularly die of boredom here!' she whispered hastily, and then she let me go.

'Blessings of the good god be on you, cousin,' I managed

to say, and bowed again to my uncle before climbing into the carriage. Epiny stood on the steps, holding her father's hand and waving to us as the footman held the carriage door open for us. I scarcely knew what to think of her, but decided my uncle was correct to be concerned. No wonder the young woman on the jankboat had seemed so amused to find Epiny was my cousin. I felt a belated blush over that.

My uncle's carriage was a much grander transport than the wagon that had carried us the night before. His crest, the 'old crest' of my family, gleamed on the polished wood door. There was a driver, attired in my uncle's colours of maroon and grey, and a fine team of grey geldings with maroon touches on their harness and headstalls. My father and I climbed into the carriage while a footman held the door for us. We climbed in and took our seats on the plush grey upholstery. There were little burgundy cushions with soft charcoal tassels in each corner of the seat and window curtains to match. I had never been inside a conveyance so fine, and despite the fact that only my father accompanied me, I sat up very straight.

The driver cracked his whip to start the team, which made me leap in my seat. My father allowed himself a small smile and I found myself grinning back. 'Don't be so tense, son,' he counselled me gently as we set off. 'Show the alertness of a fine spirit, but do not make Colonel Stiet think the Burvelle family has sent him a Nervous Nellie.'

'Yes, sir,' I replied, and forced myself to sit back on the seat. The carriage rolled thunderously over the cobbled streets of Old Thares. At any other time, I would have been fascinated at the sights outside the window, but today they could scarcely hold my attention. We first passed other fine houses with manicured grounds, not very different from my uncle's domain. Beyond the well-kept walls and gates, I had glimpses of tall oaks and fine lawns, pathways and statuary. Then we wound down into the merchants' districts, and trees and open space were left behind. Commercial establishments stood wall to wall, with residential quarters above them. We stopped at the cobbler whom my uncle had recommended. He made swift work of measuring my feet and promised my new boots would be delivered to my rooms at the Academy within a fortnight.

Then we were on our way again. It was now full morning and more people were astir. Wagons of merchandise and hurrying apprentices crowded the streets, slowing the passage of our carriage. In one busy street, a clanging bell warned us of a streetcar drawn by a stout team of horses. Women in hats with extravagant feathers and men in their morning coats gazed from its open windows as they enjoyed the leisurely ride to their day's errands. Prosperity ruled in this part of town, and I suspected that many of the folk I saw strolling the street did so only to show they had fine clothes and the leisure to display them.

Gradually we left the heart of the town behind. The streets grew narrower and the shops smaller. Slowly the houses changed, becoming first unkempt and then decrepit. The coachman shook the reins and we went more swiftly through noisome streets past cheap taverns and houses where painted sluts lounged in the open windows. I saw a blind boy singing loudly on a corner, his begging pan at his feet. On another corner, an itinerant priest preached loudly, exhorting the straying souls of these slums to turn their minds and heart to the next world. The coach passed them and his voice faded behind us. Somewhere, a bell tolled, and then another took up the solemn telling of the morning-prayer hour. My father and I bowed our heads silently.

Finally we turned onto the river road. It was wider and better kept, and yet there again we were forced to go more slowly, for traffic of every kind flowed into it. I saw wagons full of logs freshly unloaded from the waterfront, and loads of newly cut timber. A traveller's wagon and a string of nags for sale fell in behind our carriage. In our turn, we followed a coal-man's cart.

'Have we far to go, Father?' I asked when it seemed that several days had passed in the space of one morning.

'It's a good drive. When they decided to build a separate school for the Academy of Cavalla, they looked for a location that offered space for horsemanship drills, as well as ready access to pasturage and water. That placed the Academy somewhat outside of Old Thares. But that, too, we considered an advantage. You young men will focus more on your studies if you are well away from the distractions and vices of the city.'

It seemed a rebuke that he felt I must be kept away from such temptations in order to stand strong against them, and I said as much.

My father smiled gently and shook his head. 'I fear more for your companions than I do for you, Nevare. For I do not know what strength of character they bring with them, nor how they have been taught at home. But this I do know of men, both young and old. When they are in groups, they are likelier to sink to the lowest acceptable behaviour rather than rise to the highest possible standards. And this is especially true if there is no strong leader holding his men firmly accountable for their behaviour. You will be living among your peers, and it will become easy for you to believe that your ethics are, perhaps, provincial or outdated if the young men around you are dissolute or self-indulgent. So, I caution you, beware of those who mock goodness and self-discipline. Be wise in choosing your friends. Above all, be true to what you have been taught and to the honour of your family.'

And those were the words on his lips as our carriage left the main road and turned up the long tree-lined drive that led to the arched entry of the King's Cavalla Academy.

NINE

The Academy

My father left me too soon in that place.

The memories of that first day whirl and mingle in my mind now, for so many things happened so quickly. At the end of the long gravelled drive, we passed under a stone arch that bore the inscription *King's Cavalla Academy*. Marble sculptures of mounted knights flanked the entrance. A tall wall of worked stone surrounded the property, and within it, groundskeepers were at work everywhere with rakes and barrows and pruning hooks to prepare for the new term. Lush green lawns were studded with old oaks and bounded by tall laurel hedges. We stopped before the Administration Building, which was made of red brick and was several storeys high with a white portico. Well-tended footpaths led away from it across grassy swards to classroom buildings and dormitories. To the east of the residence halls, I saw a stable and several paddocks, and beyond that, an exercise arena.

I had only a moment to look about and get my bearings, for our driver had climbed down and opened the door for us. I followed my father out of the carriage and he instructed the driver to wait, then led me up the steps of the imposing central building. Before we had reached the top of the stairs, the door swung open and a lad emerged smiling and greeted us. He could not have been more than ten years old, yet his head was cropped in a military style and he was

223

attired in clothing that mimicked a cavalla uniform. He bowed to my father and asked in a clear voice if he could be of service.

'Perhaps you can, young man. I have brought my son, Nevare Burvelle, to enter him into the Academy.'

The lad bowed again. 'Thank you, sir, I shall be glad to assist you. Allow me to escort you to Colonel Stiet's office. May I arrange for your son's possessions to be taken to his dormitory for him?'

'You may.' My father was clearly impressed with the boy's manners and self-possession, as was I. He held the door for us to pass before him, and then quickly came to show us the way to the colonel's office. The vestibule of the building was panelled in dark wood, its floor covered with thick grey Antoleran tiles. Our boots rang on their gleaming surface. The boy led us through an arch to an adjutant at a desk in the colonel's anteroom. He nodded us through at the sight of the boy. The lad paused at his desk and asked, 'Please look up "Burvelle, Nevare" and arrange to have his trunk taken to his dormitory. His carriage is outside.' Then the lad advanced to the next door, knocked firmly on the mahogany panel, waited for a response, and then entered to announce us. When the colonel replied that he would see us immediately, the boy came back to usher us into the room, bowed again, and told my father that with his leave he would now go to ascertain that the young man's trunk was correctly delivered.

'You may, and my thanks to you,' my father told him gravely. As he hurried out of the door, Colonel Stiet rose to come around his desk and greet us. His family resemblance to the lad was unmistakable, and my father marked it as well. 'There goes a youngster that any father could be proud of,' my father observed.

Stiet replied coolly, 'He does well enough. Time will be the proof. Good blood and early training; those are my criteria for choosing young men of potential. I'm very pleased to meet you, Lord Keft Burvelle.'

'And I to meet you, Colonel Stiet. May I introduce my son, Nevare Burvelle?'

I stepped forward and gravely shook hands with the colonel, meeting his gaze as I had been taught. His grasp was warm and dry, but somehow unwelcoming. 'How do you do, sir?' I said. He made no reply. I released his hand, bowed slightly and stepped back, feeling uncertain. He spoke to my father.

'When young Caulder returns, I'll have him show your son to his dormitory. Sometimes I offer a brief tour of our Academy to the parents of new students, but surely with your history of association with our institution, that would be redundant.'

Something in his tone made me wary. I could not be sure if he was rendering my father an insult or a compliment. I was sure my father was aware of it as well, but he smiled affably and said firmly, 'Redundant or not, Colonel Stiet, I am sure I would enjoy a tour, if only to see how our Academy prospers under your hand. Lord Sefert Burvelle, my brother, has spoken to me of some of the changes you've wrought. I'm sure I'd enjoy seeing them for myself.'

'Has he?' Colonel Stiet cocked his head. 'How strange that he would take an interest in my institution, when he has no soldier son of his own. Still. If you are sure you have the time . . .?'

'I will always have the time when our cavalla is concerned.'

'And where your son is concerned, I suppose.' Colonel Stiet smiled narrowly.

My father's expression was calmly affable. 'As from today my son is a member of the King's Cavalla, I trust that if I concern myself with the best interest of the cavalla, the cavalla will, as it always has, look after its own.'

There was a moment of silence. 'Indeed,' said Colonel Stiet, and that was not the affirmation of fellowship that I had hoped for, nor did I think his lukewarm response pleased my father.

Caulder Stiet re-entered the room quietly, to stand at parade rest behind his father's shoulder. He had not made a sound, and yet Colonel Stiet seemed immediately aware of him. He spoke to his son without looking toward him. 'Show Cadet Burvelle to his quarters. Let my secretary know that I will be occupied for a short time, showing Lord Burvelle about the Academy grounds.'

'Sir,' the boy agreed, and then turned to me and with a gesture invited me to precede him from the room. Outside Colonel Stiet's office, we paused while Caulder passed on the colonel's message to the young lieutenant there. The young man acknowledged it with a brusque nod and continued opening and sorting a large stack of envelopes on his desk. I wondered briefly if it bothered him that his commands were passed on to him by a mere boy.

I followed young Caulder as he led me out of the Administration Building and across the grounds of the Academy. We kept meticulously to the well-groomed footpaths. The boy was silent and walked swiftly, but my longer legs easily kept up with his. He glanced back at me once, but the sunny friendliness had left his face. He was all business now.

He marched us swiftly to cadet housing. There were several dormitory houses, all fronting on a central parade ground. Two were of new red brick with many windows. The other three were older buildings of grey stone, and had obviously been adapted to function as dormitories. Caulder led me to one of the older structures. Noting the davits and freight hooks still attached to the upper storey, I guessed that they had begun their existence as warehouses. I followed him up the worn steps.

A wide door admitted us into the foyer. Battle trophies

and war flags decorated the panelled walls. In the centre of the room, a grey-haired sergeant in cavalla uniform sat behind a polished desk. Before him was a spotless blotter, inkpot and pen stand, and a sheaf of paper. Behind him, a wide staircase led to the upper reaches of the building. The sergeant regarded us steadily as Caulder approached him. There was no warmth in his grey eyes; rather he reminded me of a weary shepherd dog given yet another task.

'Cadet Nevare Burvelle for you, Sergeant Rufet. He's a New Noble's soldier son. He is to be billeted on the fourth floor.'

Sergeant Rufet's gaze slid past the boy to meet my eyes. 'Are you a mute, Cadet?' he asked me in a falsely kind voice.

I stood straighter. 'No, Sergeant, I am not.'

'Then I suggest that you report in for yourself, Cadet. Unless you plan to keep your little friend at your side for your entire Academy career.'

A flush heated my cheeks. 'Cadet Nevare Burvelle reporting, Sergeant Rufet.'

'Very good. Now, let me see where I've got you bedding down.' His blunt fingers travelled down the list before him. I noticed then that his right hand had only half a thumb. 'Ah. Yes. I believe your trunk was already delivered.' He lifted his eyes from his sheaf of paper. 'And it's taking up more than your share of space in the quarters you'll be sharing. Fourth floor. First door to the left. Your trunk is at the foot of the bed assigned to you. See that you move your necessary possessions to your allocated space, and then place the trunk and all unnecessary items in the lowerground storage area. Pick up your bedding from the quartermaster after that, and make your space tidy. Meals commence five minutes after the bell sounds and are served in the mess. You will march there with your patrol. Be on time, attired properly and in your place, or go without a meal. Any questions?'

'Where do I find the quartermaster, Sergeant Rufet?'

'Down that hall, second door on the right.'

At my side, young Caulder fidgeted restlessly, impatient at being ignored. I wondered if the sergeant disliked the boy or if his rudeness was simply part of his nature. 'Any other questions?' the sergeant barked at me, and I realized I had not responded to him.

'No, Sergeant. Thank you.'

'You're dismissed then.' He lowered his eyes back to his papers.

'Am I dismissed, also?' Caulder asked. His tone was snide, as if he wished to provoke a response from the sergeant.

'As you're not a cadet here, I can neither dismiss you nor detain you.' The sergeant didn't even look up from his work. He reached for a pen and made a notation. I realized I was still standing there, watching them, and turned smartly on my heel and left.

I went lightly up the flights of gleaming wood steps, past the open parlours on the second and third landings to the fourth and highest floor and emerged into an austere room, well lit by tall windows, furnished with a fireplace and several long tables lined with straight-backed chairs. The study area, I decided. I crossed to the windows and looked out at the view, charmed to be at such a height. Paths radiated from the central dormitories through the landscaped grounds to the various classroom buildings, the stables, paddocks and the drill ground. Beyond the drill grounds I glimpsed the targets of a musket range, and beyond them, the brushy banks of the river. From the opposite window, I could see the Academy chapel with its tall belltower, the whitewashed infirmary building a bit further on, and finally the wall of the Academy grounds and the outskirts of Old Thares beyond it. A haze hung over the city. It seemed a magnificent view to me. Later I would discover that these rooms were deemed the least desirable in Carneston House.

228

They were stifling in summer and chill in the winter, not to mention the endless tedium of running up and down the steps several times every day. Upper floor residents were invariably at the end of the dinner line. But for now, my provincial soul was delighted with my lofty new quarters.

After I had gazed my fill and oriented myself, I went to the first door to the left of the staircase. It was ajar, but nonetheless I tapped before entering. No one replied, but when I opened the door I saw a tall, slender boy with very black hair reclining on his bed and regarding me with some amusement. Another youth, his blond hair cropped as short as my own, gazed at me over the top of a book.

'Nice manners!' the latter observed, in a way that might have been a jibe. But in the next instant, he had bounded to his feet and advanced, holding out a large hand to me. The book he had been reading dangled in his free hand, his finger holding his place. 'I'm Natred Verlaney. Glad to see the rest of our roommates are finally arriving. I've been here three days already. Father said it's always better to arrive early for a formation than to be last to fall in.'

'Nevare Burvelle,' I greeted him, shaking his hand. His fingers engulfed my own and he stood half a head taller than I. His companion also stood, waiting his turn to offer his hand. His eyes were as black as his hair, his skin coarse and swarthy. 'I'm glad to be here. And my father, too, thought it better we arrive a day or two early than late.'

'Well, of course. Kort's father told him the same. What do you expect? The soldier sons of soldier sons are soldiers before they are sons.'

It was an old saying, but it still made me grin. Alone, in a strange place, it was good to hear someone utter an adage I'd grown up with. I felt a little less out of place. 'Well, I suppose I'd best do as Sergeant Rufet suggested and unpack my trunk.'

Kort gave a friendly snort of laughter. 'That won't take

you long. Most of what's in there will have to stay in there. Here's your closet.' He stepped to the wall and opened a narrow cupboard. There was space at the bottom for a pair of boots, and room to hang two sets of extra clothing. Above that space was a small shelf. When Kort opened his own closet, I saw that he had stowed his shaving mug and toilet articles there.

I copied his arrangement, and then was shown my hook on the coat-rack, and the shelf in the room allotted for my books. That was all. I looked into the trunk at all the small comforts my mother and sisters had so lovingly packed for me; the various home remedies, the carefully crocheted sweater, the bright scarf, the small trove of sweets and all the other touches that might have made the room a homelier place. I set most of them aside, except for the sweets that I put out to share. I added my prayer book, Dewara's stone and my new journal to my shelf of books. Then I reluctantly shut the lid of my trunk, latched and strapped it, and hoisted it to my shoulder to take down to the storage area.

Kort accompanied me, for friendship as much as to show me the way. He seemed a good fellow, quick to smile, but not talkative. From the quartermaster I received a set of linens, a very flat pillow, and two green wool blankets. When we returned to our room, we discovered that our fourth roommate had arrived. Spink Kester was small and wiry as a weasel, with bright blue eyes that were surprising in his darkly tanned face. He shook hands hard and too fast; I surmised that he was a bit nervous at being the last one of us to arrive, but we soon had him ensconced and his battered trunk hauled down to storage. He was the most poorly turned out of the four of us. Only when I realized that did I also recognize that I was the best. My uniforms and books were new and of the best quality. Kort's clothing was new but his books looked secondhand. Natred had the opposite situation. His books were pristine, but I could see that his uniform had been altered to fit him. Spink's uniform had obviously been cut down to fit him, and his books were scarred and scruffy. Yet, in his personal grooming and the precise way that he stored his meagre possessions and made up his bed, I saw both good breeding and training. If anything, his obvious dearth of wealth made me wish even more to be his friend.

All four of us perched on our beds, getting to know one another. I learned that Kort and Natred had known each other since they were children and had often visited one another's homes. Their fathers, like mine, were new nobility, hammering estates from the raw land of the plains. They had travelled together to Academy, and in all likelihood would wed one another's sisters, a prospect that did not seem to dismay either of them.

In contrast, Spink, whose real name was Spinrek, had grown up closer to the frontier than any of us. His family estate was far to the south and east, and he had travelled the first leg of his journey here by mule, skirting the Red Desert. He and his escort had faced down one party of bandits, killing one man and wounding, he thought, two others before they fled what they had doubtless thought easy prey. Spink had a good way of telling a story; he was not boastful, for he gave full credit to his accompanying mentor, Lieutenant Geeverman, for driving off the robbers.

He had just finished his tale when my father entered the room. Reflexively, we all leapt to our feet. He gazed searchingly around the room, and then gave us a measuring stare. For some reason, I could not bring myself to speak. Then he smiled and nodded his head approvingly. 'I am pleased to see you in such company, Nevare, and to see that your quarters are as tidy as any trooper's should be. Will you introduce me to your companions?'

This I did, stumbling a bit when I realized I didn't know Kort's surname. It was Braxan, and he supplied it quickly

231

when I hesitated. My father shook hands with each of them in turn. I introduced Spink last, giving his proper name of Spinrek. At this, my father cocked his head, and then asked carefully, 'You would be Kellon Spinrek Kester's son, then?'

'That I would, sir,' and a faint blush of pride crept into Spink's cheeks that my father would know his father's name.

'He was a fine soldier. I served alongside him in the Hare Ridge campaign. I was not with him at Bitter Springs, but I heard how he died. He was a hero, and you should be proud of his name. Your mother, Lady Kester, does she fare well?'

I think Spink nearly gave a polite and untruthful reply. He took a breath and then said, 'Things have been difficult for her the last few years, sir. Her health has not been good, and a dishonest overseer brought us to the edge of ruin. But he has met his justice, and my older brother Roark is learning the full running of our holdings now. I am sure that things will improve.'

My father nodded gravely. 'And your father's regiment? They do well by her and your family?'

'Very well, sir. Lieutenant Geeverman escorted me here, to be sure I would arrive safely. My mother's pride forbids that we rely on them too much. She always thanks them for their many offers, but tells them that her husband would, she is sure, wish to see his sons learn to stand well on their own in paucity rather than rely on the charity of others to live in comfort.'

'I am sure he would, Cadet Kester. Just as I am sure you will bring honour to the name you bear. Hold to your father's values and you will be a fine officer.'

I perceived then that my father had already known these things, but that by asking about them in front of us, he had given Spink the opportunity to share his family's straitened circumstances without making it seem that he sought our pity. Only later did I learn the tale of his father's death. Going to the aid of a wounded comrade, Captain Kellon Kester had

232

been captured by the plainsmen. The tribe that took him was the Ebonis, well known for their utter ruthlessness toward any enemy. When Kester saw that he'd been drawn into a trap baited with his wounded comrade, he shouted to his fellows not to come after him, no matter what.

Even the Ebonis honoured him for what came after that. Their warriors did every vile thing they could devise to Kester, hoping to wring from him the screams that might torment his comrades into attempting a rescue. He bore it silently. They tortured him to death that night, making a long, slow business of it. Yet as dawn arrived, they discovered their mistake, for while they were thus occupied, the cavalla scouts had marked well their location, and the trap that the Ebonis had set turned into an encirclement that resulted in the slaughter of nearly every warrior there. Kester's second-in-command decreed that five of them be allowed to live, but with their bowstring fingers severed. He sent the mutilated and defeated warriors back to the Ebonis, so that the tale of Captain Kester's courage might be told around their campfires. Less than a year later, what remained of the Ebonis came in under a treaty flag and agreed to resettlement in the north. Kester's silence under torture, and the discipline of his lieutenants who heeded his order not to risk his men by charging in after him, no matter what, is often cited as an example of the chain of command working exactly as it should and the solid requirement of coolness in desperate circumstances that a good officer must always possess. The telling of that campaign takes up a major portion of chapter four of the text *Fit for Command* by General Tersy Harwood.

But at the time, I knew nothing of that, only that my father had judged all three of my roommates to be worthy companions. He bade me walk him down to the carriage to say good-bye. We stood beside it for a time, talking. I was torn, not wishing for him to go and yet anxious to begin my new life and return to my new friends. My father cautioned me, as any father must on bidding farewell to a son, to remember all I had been taught and to cling to the rules of my childhood. Then he added a further warning.

'Be above reproach, son, especially for the first few months of your education. There is a good reason I did not recognize Colonel Stiet's name. He's not from a cavalla family, although his wife is. Our good king, for reasons I shall not question, has seen fit to put a regular army officer in charge of the Cavalla Academy. Moreover, even as an army officer, he has not served in warfare, but here at home, keeping track of numbers and enforcing petty regulations about uniforms and weapons ordnance. Most recently, he was in charge of organizing parades for state occasions. And he trumpets this as an accomplishment! I will not speculate that his wife's connections had more to do with him receiving this appointment than his own record.' My father shook his head. In a lower voice he added, 'I fear he will be more concerned that his troops look good on a drill field than that they be able to shoot from a moving horse or keep their heads cool in a tight situation.

'Now you look shocked, and well you should to hear me speak so of a fellow officer. But there it is; it is how I have judged him, and though I pray to the good god that I may be proved wrong, I fear I shall not. I have seen the horses he bought for his cadets. Pretty little things, all of a size and colour, that will doubtless look well in a parade but would jolt a man to death on a long day's ride and die after two days with no water.' My father paused abruptly and took a deep breath. I do not know what else he had thought to say, but whatever it was, he seemed to change his mind.

'I think that your uncle was correct when he said that Colonel Stiet has little love for the sons of the new nobility. I wonder if he has any love for the cavalla at all. We are expensive, if all a man looks at is the flow of coins it takes to keep us horsed and equipped and does not reckon up the lives that would be lost if we did not. He does not understand our place in the military; I think he believes we are but a showpiece, an entertainment and a spectacle, and thus he will build his career on fostering that image of us.' He drew breath again, and then he said what I think he had hesitated to say before. 'Remember that he is your commander. Respect and obey his orders. Do things as he wishes them done, even if you think you know a better way to do them. Perhaps *especially* if you think you know a better way to do them.

'Stay true to your upbringing. Avoid bad companions and remember that you were born to be a soldier. The good god has granted you that. Let no one steal it from you.'

And with those words he embraced me tightly. I knelt for his father's blessing. I know I must have watched him get into the carriage and drive away, and certainly we must have waved farewell to one another. But all I recall is standing on the edge of the drive, looking after the departing carriage and feeling more alone than I had ever felt in my life. I felt suddenly cold and hollow, and nearly queasy as I turned and hurried back to my new quarters.

My fellows awaited me, and let me know that my father had left a fine impression. 'There's no mistaking a cavalry man; it's in his walk. Your father is the genuine item. I'd wager he's spent as many hours in the saddle as he has on foot in his life.'

'More, I think,' I replied to Kort's compliment.

We spent the rest of the early afternoon settling ourselves into our room. Three fellows from across the hall came and introduced themselves. Trist, Gord, and Rory were all the sons of new nobility. Gord was a slab of a boy, pale and fat, his neck bulging over the collar of his uniform and his brass buttons tight on his belly. He stood, smiling awkwardly and saying little, at the edge of our group. Trist was tall and golden, with the bearing and charm of a young prince. Even so, it was squat affable Rory who claimed all our attention. 'I heard that they put us all together a'purpose,' Rory told us solemnly.

235

'Because we're not good enough to associate with the soldier sons of the old nobility?' Kort was both astounded and offended.

'Nar. So's we won't make their lads feel bad.' Rory grinned as if it were a fine jest. 'They may be soldier sons, but they h'ain't been raised by soldiers like we were. Half of them never had a leg over a horse, save for riding a pony in the park. You'll see when we get to drill. My uncle's soldier son was fostered with us, 'cos that's how we do it in our family. First sons always give their soldier sons to their soldier brothers to raise, so the boy gets a good start on his training when he's still a little feller. My cousin Jordie was through the Academy four years ago and wrote me letters every month about it. So I've got a pretty good idea what to expect here.'

That brought us clustering around him. For the next hour or so, we sat at the study tables in our common room, and Rory held the floor with tales of strict instructors, cadets working off demerits by mucking out the stables, hazing from older cadets, and every other Academy tale that he could dredge up for us. He was a born storyteller, swaggering as he spoke of young officers and cowering as he mimed us junior cadets. He held us spellbound when he theatrically warned us of 'cullings'. 'Commander declares one, anertime he feels like it. Could be a drill exercise, could be a jography test. Every cadet who falls lower'n a certain score, Whist! He's gone. Culled like a spindly lamb. They send you home, with just a note that says "failed to meet Academy standards, thanky all the same for sending 'im." And you know what comes after that for a soldier son. It's goodbye officers' mess, hello chow-tent and life as a foot soldier. Only thing a soldier son can do if he fails here is go for the common enlistment. Those cullings are murder, and they give no warning a'tall. It's one way t'keep us on our toes with our noses in our books.'

He spoke with a Kenty twang that I secretly found amusing. At the time, I did not know that several of the others

236

thought my 'plains drawl' just as humorous. More cadets drifted in from the other rooms on our floor to join us as we listened to Rory's tales, until there were eleven of us there, almost our full patrol. We were a mixed lot, but all sons of new nobility, as Rory had predicted. In a short time it seemed as if we had all known one another for years instead of hours. Oron had red hair, large teeth and a pleasant, contagious laugh. Caleb joined our group with four *Penny Adventure* folios under his arm, which he immediately offered to share with us. I had never seen one before, and the lurid covers on the cheap booklets were a bit shocking. Caleb assured me they were mild compared to others that he owned. Jared had only one older brother and six younger sisters, and claimed he wasn't accustomed to talking much as he got so little opportunity at home. He said it would be a huge relief to have only male companionship for a while. Trent was a slight youth with an anxious air. He had arrived with three trunks full of clothing and household goods and seemed very particular about his wardrobe and bedding. He bemoaned the limited living and closet space allotted to him. In the midst of our yammering, a twelfth cadet arrived to round out our dozen. His name was Lofert. He was a tall, gangly fellow who seemed a bit dim. He didn't have much to say beyond his name. Gord helped him find the last empty bunk in their room and they soon rejoined us. Every one of them seemed like a good fellow to me and I felt a sudden elation that my first year of Academy was off to such a good start. But I am sure I was not the only one listening anxiously for the dinner bell. Somehow I had missed the noon meal and by the time the longed-for bell finally clanged I felt cramped with hunger.

Hungry as hounds, we rushed down the stairs together, only to be thwarted in our headlong race by a flood of other boys pouring out from the lower floors onto the same staircase. Obviously, more students had been arriving hourly while we conversed upstairs and we were forced to descend sedately, a single riser at a time.

'I hear the food's bad here. Same stuff every day,' Gord observed brightly. He was breathing loudly through his nose, as if even going down the stairs was an exertion.

I could think of no reply, but Rory said, 'If it sits still on the plate, likely I'll eat it. Bet you will, too. You don't look like you've been too picky in the past!'

Several of the others laughed aloud and I grinned. Even Gord smiled sheepishly. I took another step down and resisted the urge to push past the cadets in front of me. Even when we finally reached the ground floor, we could not race off to the mess hall. On the walkway in front of our dormitory, we found older cadets – red sashes and striped sleeves proclaiming their authority – who sternly reminded us to keep to the paths and not jostle one another, and move in unison to our goal as befitted military troops. These supervisors who bunched us into groups were Academy students one year ahead of us, Rory informed us before he was ordered to stop talking in the ranks. They formed us up by floors, which suited us well, and our shepherd, Corporal Dent, marched us off in our new patrol. Dent put Gord next to me. The portly cadet puffed as we marched, lurching along as he strove to stretch his stride to match our pace.

We were not at the very end of the line as we filed into the mess hall, but close enough to it that it taunted my hunger. We could smell the food, and I heard Gord's stomach rumble loudly. Within the hall, Dent herded us to our laden table and directed us to stand behind our chairs until each table was granted leave to sit down and begin eating. There were covered tureens of soup, platters of sliced meat, thick slices of dark bread, and heaped bowls of boiled beans on each table. Even when all the occupants of our table had arrived Dent kept us standing a time longer as he lectured us perfunctorily that every officer sees to the well-being of his men

238

before he takes care of himself. This waiting until our fellows were ready to dine alongside us was our first reminder that the cavalla flourished only when the needs of every rider were given equal consideration. Dent's eyes seemed to linger on Gord as he spoke.

It seemed a completely unnecessary lecture to me, for I had always been taught that basic dining manners demanded that one wait until the entire party had arrived and been seated but I held my tongue and stood in place behind my chair until we were given permission to sit. And again, I found myself surprised that our shepherd seemed to think we needed instruction in basic manners. Speaking simply, as if we might not understand, he informed us gravely that each dish of food would be passed around the table, allowing each man an opportunity to serve himself, but that we were to refrain from eating until every man had his rations. He cautioned us also that there was enough food for each of us to have generous servings, but that we should serve ourselves in moderation until we had seen that each man had a fair portion of every dish. I exchanged a glance with Kort and Natred. Kort rolled his eyes toward Gord, as if to indicate he was the intended recipient of Corporal Dent's words. Gord's eyes were downcast, but I could not tell if he stared at the food or avoided Dent's gaze.

Later, as we sat around the study tables in the relative peace of our dormitory, Natred grinned and said, 'I half-expected him to be shocked that we used cutlery instead of eating with our hands!'

Spink shrugged. 'He probably thinks that those of us from the frontier were raised rough and crude. I suppose I have been, in many ways. Many's the night when I've shared a common pot of food with our hired men when we're camping with the flocks to keep the wild dogs off the new lambs. It doesn't mean that I don't know how to behave when there's a cloth on the table, but perhaps he thought it better to tell us ahead of time, and keep some poor sap from embarrassing himself by having to be corrected.'

Our conversation was interrupted when Caleb and Rory commandeered our table for an arm-wrestling match. Very soon we were all involved in trying our strength against our fellows. The contest between Rory and Natred quickly escalated into a wrestling match on the floor. We had not realized how rowdy we had become until the study table overturned with a crash. That sobered us, and we had righted it and resumed our seats when we heard hurried footsteps on the stairs. Seconds later our red-sashed shepherd thrust himself into our room. 'What's going on up here?' Corporal Dent demanded as we came to our feet. His freckles had nearly vanished in the angry flush on his face.

'Just some horseplay, sir,' Natred replied after a few moments of silence. 'Good-natured. Not a fight.'

Corporal Dent scowled. 'I might have known,' he muttered, as if he had been foolish to expect civilized behaviour from us. 'Well, settle down and stop romping like boys. The men on the floors below you are trying to enjoy some peace. The lot of you had best get yourselves ready for lights-out. When the horns blow at sunrise, you'll be expected to assemble – washed, shaved and in uniform – on the central parade ground. Don't make me come and roust you out. You won't be pleased by how I'll do it.'

With that, he turned himself about smartly and marched out of our common room. As he went down the steps, over the angry clacking of his boots, we heard him fume, 'Just my luck. Saddled with a bunch of New Noble oafs!'

We exchanged glances, some of us shocked, others puzzled as we slowly resumed our seats. Natred seemed amused, Kort offended.

'It's how they'll do us,' Rory informed us lazily. He stood, scratched his chest, and then stretched. 'My cousin's an Old Noble's son. Made no difference. He said the corporals will find a reason to pick on us all, as a group. He says it's supposed to teach us group loyalty and make us hang together, to improve as a patrol. Next couple of weeks, no matter how hard we try, they'll ride us hard, find little things to fault us on, and hand out extra duties or make us march demerits or roust us out of our bunks in the middle of the night for nothin'. And Dent won't be the only one. Expect some harassment from every cadet with a second-year stripe on his sleeve. In fact, tonight will probably be the last good night's sleep we'll get for a time. So I'm going to take advantage of it.' He yawned hugely and then grinned at us sheepishly. 'Country boy, me. I go to bed when the birds stop singin'.'

His yawn had set me to yawning, also. I nodded at him. 'Me, too. It's been a long day.'

'No one wants to stay up for a game of dice with me?' Trist asked invitingly. He alone seemed undaunted at Corporal Dent's rebuke. He leaned his chair back on two legs, his arms crossed on his chest as he grinned his broad, white grin. Trist was the handsomest of us, with his hazel eyes and short thatch of curly, sandy hair. He exuded charm like a flower gives off scent. I surmised that he'd quickly become our leader, and eventually a charismatic officer. His invitation was tempting.

'I'm in,' Gord announced eagerly. His fat cheeks wobbled with enthusiasm.

I steeled my will and spoke into the quiet room. 'Not me. I don't play dice.'

I turned to go to my bed as Spink reminded Trist seriously, 'Dice are against the rules. No cards, no dice, no games of chance allowed in the dormitories, on pain of expulsion. Didn't you read the rule book?'

Trist nodded lazily. 'I did. But who's going to tell?'

I turned back slowly to the group, knowing that my honour would require me to report any breaking of the rules. I suddenly liked Trist a lot less than I had a few moments ago.

241

I tried to find the courage to say that I would report it, that I'd have to. My mouth was dry.

Spink shook his head. He crossed his arms on his chest but it didn't help much. He still looked small, almost childish compared to the lanky, lounging Trist. 'You shouldn't be putting us on the spot like this, Trist. You know we'll be held accountable for your behaviour, even if we're not part of it. You know that the honour code would require us to report it.'

Trist brought his chair back flat on the floor with a thump, and then stood slowly. The blond cadet towered over small, dark Spink. 'I was just joking with you, Spink. Are you always this serious? God's breath, what a stiff neck you are!'

Spink stood his ground, his feet slightly apart as if setting his weight for a fight. 'And that's blasphemy, to speak the good god's name other than in prayer. And also against Academy rules.'

'Your pardon, O saintly one. I'll go to my room and make reparations now.' Trist rolled his eyes and sauntered from the room. Spink refused to notice it or to look after him. After a moment, Oron and Gord followed him, closing the door behind them.

I felt sad at that first little crack in our unity, even though a part of me recognized it as inevitable. Sergeant Duril had spoken to me of such things, though he had been speaking from his experience in the field rather than at an Academy. Despite the differences, I recognized that his words would hold true here as well. 'Whenever a new group forms, or an old group takes in new members . . . don't matter if it's a regiment or a patrol, nor even if it's troopies or officers . . . there'll be some shoving to see who's first to the trough. They'll try each other's strength, and it's rare that there's not a fistfight or three before the dust finally settles. Just keep your cool and remember it's got to be, and do your best to stay clear of it. Don't back down, lad, that's not what I'm saying. But hang back, calm like, and make them shove the challenge at you before you take it up. So no one ever doubts that it wasn't you that started it. You just be the one that finishes it.'

'Nevare?' Kort nudged me, and I jumped. I realized I'd been staring at the closed door. 'Forget about it,' he advised me quietly.

I nodded. 'I think I'm ready for bed, too,' I excused myself. But that was sooner said than done. There was only one washstand in our room, and I had to wait my turn for it. Rory wandered into our room in a homespun nightshirt. He perched on the foot of my bed beside me and spoke quietly. 'Think there'll be trouble 'tween Trist and Spink?'

'Spink won't start it,' I said after a moment of pondering.

'I guess that's right. But I'm thinking that if there's a fight, we'll all have to pay for it. That's how they do things here. One screws up, we all pay the toll.'

It was my turn for the washstand, and as I stood, Rory said quietly, 'Maybe you could talk to Spink. Tell him to take it easy until we all settle in. It's goin' to be bad enough with Corporal Dent chewing on us without us bitin' each other.'

'Maybe Trist is the one we should talk to,' I offered.

Rory's dark eyes met mine and he gave his bullet head a shake. 'Na. Trist isn't one to listen. Well. I'd best get back to my room.'

I wanted to ask him if Trist had sent him to talk to me, and wondered, too, if they were playing dice in there. Then I decided I didn't want to know.

Shortly after that, Kort blew out the lamp and we all knelt by our beds to say our prayers. I prayed longer and more earnestly than I usually did, asking the good god to show me the middle path through strife. Then I got into my narrow bed in the darkness and tried to fall asleep listening to the breathing of the others in the room.

TEN

Classmates

In the dead of night, someone was drumming. I rolled over and fell out of my bed. It was much narrower than my one at home, and this was the third time I'd fallen out of it. I groaned as I sprawled on the cold floor. I heard a door open and close and someone came into the room carrying a candle. In that instant, I was awake. I sat up wearily. 'That can't be the drums for dawn. It's black as pitch out there.'

'Not if you open the curtains,' Kort observed dryly, as he walked to the window and pulled back the drapes. There was a faint pearliness to the night sky. 'That's the drum for rising. We have to be up, dressed, and on the parade ground by the dawn horn. Remember?'

'Vaguely.' I yawned.

Spink was sitting up on his bed, blinking owlishly. Natred had his pillow over his head, and was holding it down with both hands. I saw an opportunity to be first at the washstand and seized it. Kort unceremoniously jostled me aside to share it as we shaved. As he passed Natred's bed on the way to his closet, he kicked the end of it. 'Get up, Nate! Let's not be the ones to give Dent an excuse to harangue us today.'

I was struggling into my boots before Natred rolled out of his bunk. Nonetheless, he was ready to go when we were. Nate patted his downy cheek happily as he left the washstand. 'I love being fair. My father told me I'll be in my twenties before I have to start shaving!'

Spink had made up his bunk for him, even as he promised ominously that it was the first and last time he'd ever do it and that Natred now owed him a favour. We were immensely proud of how tidy we left our room and how well turned out we all were. We left our floor, calling to the laggards who remained to hurry up, lest we all get in trouble. As we clattered down the stairs, uniform hats clutched under our arms, cadets from the other floors joined us until we spilled out of our dormitory to join a green-clad flood of students cascading onto the parade ground in the dimness of pre-dawn.

The dawn horn had not yet sounded, but Corporal Dent was there before us. He demanded to know where the rest of his patrol was, but gave us no time to answer before informing us that he expected us to arrive as a group, for we'd soon learn that the men in a cavalla patrol look out for one another. He used the minutes before the others arrived to disparage our appearances. He asked Spink if he'd slept in his uniform and then demanded that Kort describe a boot brush to him and tell him what it was used for. He told me to put my hat on straight and warned me that if I continued to show the wrong attitude, he'd find a cure for it that I wouldn't like. He walked all round Natred several times, regarding him as if he were an exotic animal before asking him how long he'd been walking on two legs and when he thought he might learn to stand up straight. As a scarlet-faced Natred groped for a reply, Gord arrived. He came trotting in alone, cheeks red and one of his buttons already giving way to his girth. Dent appeared to forget all about Nate as he turned to a new target. 'Look at yourself, Gorge!' he commanded, and Natred gave a snort of laughter that Dent ignored. 'Stand up straight and suck that gut in! What? That's the best you can do? Who's in there with you? Or have you a baby on the way?'

Dent went on for some time in that vein as Gord squirmed

in humiliation and Natred nearly suffocated trying to keep from laughing. I was torn between sympathy for my fellow cadet and my own suppressed amusement. The more Gord tried to hold in his gut, the redder his cheeks grew. I think he might have burst if he had not been rescued by the arrival of the rest of our patrol. They dashed up, out of breath, and Rory's shirttail was only half-tucked in. Corporal Dent sprang on them like a big tomcat on a nest of new mice.

He didn't have a single kind word or encouraging comment for any cadet. Not one of us met his standards and he doubted that any of us would survive our first term as cavalla cadets. If he couldn't think of some fresh insult for a man, he simply roared, 'And you're no better!' before proceeding to his next victim. He pushed, prodded, and bullied us into ranks until he was either satisfied or too frustrated to try any more. He took his position in front of us when the dawn horn finally sounded.

Then we stood there. I knew we were supposed to keep our eyes straight ahead, but I risked a glance at the others. In the dawn light, we all looked alike: forest green uniforms, tall hats, black boots, and wide eyes. Only the lack of stripes on our sleeves distinguished the first-years from the upper classmen. Each dormitory had formed up separately. We were Carneston Riders, named for our dormitory Carneston House, and our colours were a brown horse on a green field. Each dormitory housed cadets from all three years. I noticed that two of the first-year patrols were substantially larger than the other two. I wondered if this were a breakdown of New Nobles' versus Old Nobles' sons. The cadet officers had formed up their own separate ranks off to the right. I envied them the dress swords that hung at their sides.

I don't know how long we waited. Eventually, four junior officers came to inspect us. Each one took two of the patrols, moving down our lines and criticizing us as the corporals hovered, wincing at each derogatory comment as if it applied to him personally. It dawned on me that it probably did, that we were most likely Corporal Dent's first command, and his ability to whip us into shape would be considered the measure of his leadership capability. I felt a pang of sympathy for him, and stood a bit straighter and focused my eyes straight ahead.

After the rough inspection was finished, the junior officers moved to the front of our ranks, quietly and mercilessly told our corporals all that they had done wrong, and then formed a line of their own. Again we waited. Eventually, we were rewarded with the sight of Colonel Stiet making his way toward us. He walked briskly. The cadet commander of the Academy walked on his left side, while young Caulder struggled to match their strides on the right.

They halted crisply in front of our troop. Colonel Stiet ran his eyes over his ranked charges and gave a small sigh that seemed to say we were no better than he had expected. We stood at attention while a small cadet band of brass instruments played 'Into the Fray' as the Gernian colours were hoisted, with the Academy banner displayed below them.

Then Colonel Stiet made a speech welcoming us to the King's Cavalla Academy. He reminded us that the cavalla was not one man on one horse, but a hierarchy of patrols, troops, regiments, brigades, and divisions. Every patrol was only as good as the weakest man in it, and every troop only as effective as the most ineffective patrol. He expounded on this for some time, and I grew weary, for it seemed to me he was stating the obvious. He urged each of us to help our fellows to be the best cadets they could be, in studies, in honour, in manners, and in skills. Our military careers, and indeed our lives might eventually depend on other cadets that we had helped to shape in these Academy years. In closing, he took great pains to tell us that he regarded us all as equals, with equal potential to rise in the ranks and graduate well. It did not matter if we had come to the Academy from the city, the country or the frontier. It did not matter if our fathers were the true cavalla sons descended from the old knighthood or soldier sons of the old nobility or the soldier sons of battle lords. All would be treated the same here and offered the same opportunities. His words were welcoming and assuring, and yet somehow they increased my awareness that some here might see the New Nobles' sons as uncouth upstarts and pretenders.

After Stiet had spoken to all the assembled first-years, the senior cadet commander addressed us. He had plainly memorized his speech of welcome and his list of cautions and warnings. The grumbling of my belly distracted me from his words. By the time the commander of the Carneston Riders spoke to us, it was difficult to stay focused. His name was Cadet Captain Jeffers. He and his staff of third-year cadets lived on the lower floor of Carneston House and were ever ready to attend to both our needs and our discipline. He discoursed far too long on the rules of Carneston House and its proud history. I tried not to roll my eyes at that. I had more 'history' than the Academy did; it had been founded less than ten years ago! But each cadet captain appeared to be delivering the same sort of lecture to his standing troops. Even Colonel Stiet looked bored and impatient to be gone. When they finally finished, we continued to stand until Stiet and the senior officers had departed. By the time our captain commanded that we should march off to our breakfasts, I was famished and aching from standing still for so long.

They fed us well; I'll give them that. The dining hall was more crowded this first official day of term. The routine of our meal was the same as yesterday's, with Dent reminding us yet again of our basic manners before allowing us to fall on to the porridge, bacon, boiled beans, fried bread and coffee. After we had finished eating and given thanks for our food, he briefed us on the rest of our day. All first-year patrols followed the same schedule. He cautioned us that there would be no easing of standards for those of us who were the soldier sons of New Nobles. We would be expected to live up to the gentlemanly example of those who were the offspring of old nobility, and he advised us that we could learn much simply by emulating their behaviour.

I think we might have muttered amongst ourselves at this if muttering had been permitted at the table. Instead, he quick-marched us back to Carneston House to get our texts and other supplies and then herded us to our first class before hastening off to his own. Military History shared a long, low brick building with Languages and Communication. We filed into the classroom and took our seats, straight-backed chairs arranged along long tables. Rory was to one side of me and Spink was on the other. Gord walked slowly past us, looking as if he wished to sit by us, but the row was full and he went to the next row along with Natred and Trist. Spink spoke quietly. 'It can't be easy for Dent to have to herd us around and then rush off to his own classes.'

'Don't expect me to feel sorry for that little popinjay,' Rory growled and then we all jumped in our seats as our instructor shouted, 'Stand up! Don't you know you're to stand when your instructor or any superior officer enters the room? On your feet, this instant!'

Captain Infal was our Military History teacher. He kept us standing while he quickly listed the daily work for the class. He spoke in a clear, precise voice that carried, as if he were accustomed to addressing people in the open air rather than within a classroom. We were to keep silent and sit straight, take notes as he lectured, and read twenty-five pages of the text every night. There would be daily quizzes and weekly tests. Three consecutive scores of less than seventy-five percent on the tests would result in mandatory study halls. Five consecutive scores of less than seventy-five percent on the quizzes would be grounds for Academy probation. The patrol of a man on probation was expected to assist him in raising his scores by diligent studying. Absence from class would be excused only with a note from the Academy Infirmary. A trooper was useless if he did not have robust health. Here he glared at Gord and then shifted his disapproval to a young man who was coughing in the second row. Three medical absences were grounds for Academy probation. There would be no talking amongst students. Cadets were not allowed to either borrow or lend supplies during the class hour. 'Be seated now, silently, no scraping of chairs, and pay attention.'

And with that, he launched into his first lecture. I barely had time to take out pencil and paper. He gave us no opportunity to ask questions, but lectured continuously for the next hour and a half. From time to time, he noted dates or the correct spellings of names and places in a large, flowing hand on the chalkboard behind him. I took notes frantically, trying not to be distracted by my sympathy for Rory, who did not have a pencil but sat with blank paper before him. Beside me, Spink scratched along steadily. At the end of class, the captain again ordered us peremptorily to our feet and then departed without a backward glance.

'Can I . . .?' Rory began desperately, and before he could finish, Spink replied, 'You can copy mine tonight. Do you need a pencil for your next class?'

It impressed me that he among us who seemed to have the least material goods shared what he had so readily.

We had no time for further talk. A red-sash I didn't know was standing in the door of the classroom, bellowing at us to fall in outside immediately and stop wasting his precious time. We obeyed with alacrity, and he marched us off with no more ado. Halfway to the maths building, he dropped back, to march beside Gord and harangue him to keep in step, stretch his legs and try, for the good god's sake, *try* to look like a cadet and not a sack of potatoes bumping in a market bag. He told Gord to count the cadence for us, and then shouted at him to raise his voice and be heard like a man when the plump cadet could scarcely get his words out for shortness of breath. I am ashamed to say that I felt a sneaking relief that Gord was there to hold the corporal's attention so that his sniping was not aimed at me.

Maths and science classes were held in an old building that resembled Carneston House in that it seemed to have once been a warehouse, too. Built of irregular stones, it crouched along a riverbank. Several docks with small boats moored to them ventured into the river's sluggish flow. We were marched to the shore side of the building, and directed to a classroom on the second floor. A mouldy smell greeted us as we entered the dank building. We clattered up the steps, only to discover that we were already late.

'Come in, sit down, and shut up!' ordered Captain Rusk, a round bald man scarcely as tall as my shoulder. Before we latecomers were even seated, he had turned his back on us and was once more scratching numbers onto the board. 'Work it through, raise your hand when you think you have an answer. The first five with an answer will be invited to come to the board to show their work.'

Our patrol hastily found some seats, and I quickly copied down the equations he had written on the board. It seemed a fairly straightforward problem, though Spink was scowling over it. I had the answer quickly enough, but continued to scratch with my pencil on my paper, unwilling to be called to the board. Gord was the third cadet to raise his hand. Captain Rusk called him down along with four others. As they worked their proofs on the board and presented their answers, the captain wrote a page number on the board and announced, 'All those who did not raise their hands with an answer are responsible for completing the following remedial exercises by tomorrow. The practice should sharpen your calculation skills. Very well, now, let us see how your fellows did at the board.'

I sat in my seat, a cold rock of disappointment in my belly, reflecting on how my simple act of cowardice had already repaid me as I deserved. Four of the five cadets at the board got the correct answer. Kort was one of them. I didn't know the fellow who made a simple addition error in the final step. Gord's proof was the best, simple and elegant, written in a firm, clear hand, and taking an alternate route to the answer that eliminated two steps of calculation. Captain Rusk worked his way across, using his pointer to demonstrate the progression to a correct answer, pointing out the one fellow's error and chastising another for his sloppy handwriting and uneven columns. When he got to Gord's work, he paused. Then, he tapped the pointer once on the board and said, 'Excellent.' That was all. He moved immediately to the next cadet, and Gord, dismissed, went back to his seat beaming.

I noticed that Spink's hands had balled into fists on the edge of the desk. I glanced over at his face. He was pale. I looked down at the page before him, where he had attempted to solve the first problem. His small neat figures filled half of it, but had carried him no closer to a solution. His hands suddenly spread flat over his paper, and when I glanced up at him, his face had turned red. I didn't meet his eyes; it only would have embarrassed him more. It would be better if I pretended not to know that he had no grasp at all of any maths beyond arithmetic.

Captain Rusk erased the board, and then immediately wrote another problem on it. He paused, tapped his chalk on the board and said, 'Of course, for most of you, this is a review of ground you know well. But I know a tower cannot be built upon a shaky foundation, and so I choose to test your foundations before we begin to add to your knowledge.' Beside me, Spink made a very small sound of dismay in the back of his throat. By an effort of will, I didn't glance at him. Captain Rusk solved the problem on the board, step by step, for us. He wrote up three more, each of increasing complexity, and moved precisely through their resolutions, step by step. He was a good teacher, making his reasoning clear. Beside me, Spink's pencil scratched frantically as he struggled to write an explanation of each step beside the problems he had copied. He was in over his head, drowning in concepts he'd never glimpsed before now.

I felt almost ashamed, as if I flaunted my knowledge cruelly before him, as I was the first to raise my hand for the next problem, and the one after that. Each time, Gord had a place at the board beside me. Each time, his proof was leaner and more elegant than mine, though we had both arrived at the correct answer. And each time, as we returned to our seats, Captain Rusk assigned another set of problems to those who had not been among the first five to complete the problem. By the time he dismissed us, most of the class was groaning under an onerous burden of work that would be due by this hour tomorrow. We stood as our instructor left. Then, in the shuffle of students gathering their papers and books, I made my offer to Spink. 'Let's work through these problems together tonight.'

He did not protest that I obviously did not need the practice. Instead, he said quietly, his eyes downcast, 'I would appreciate that. If you have the time.'

The other patrols left quickly. We waited impatiently for Dent, but another corporal arrived to take command of us and quick-marched us to our next class. I suddenly felt overwhelmed. It frustrated me that our destination was the same building we'd left only an hour and a half ago. Why couldn't they have scheduled our Varnian class to follow our Military History class, instead of making us rush back and forth across the campus? Only the thought that this was our last class before our noon meal sustained me.

We joined another patrol of first-years waiting in the classroom. It was our first unsupervised encounter with first-years outside of our own patrol, and after a few moments, we began chatting and discovered that they, too, were New Nobles' sons. Their patrol was fifteen strong. We felt lucky to be in Carneston House when we heard that they were barracked in the top floor of Skeltzin Hall, where they shared one large open room with a single window at each end and gaps in the eaves large enough to admit pigeons and bats. They had been promised repairs before winter, but for now the evening winds off the river blew very chill.

We sat and talked, teacherless, for a quarter of an hour, before Corporal Dent, very red-faced, came charging into the room, demanding to know what we were doing there and why we hadn't waited for him. As we followed him into the hall and up a flight of stairs to the correct classroom, the other patrol's corporal found his charges as well. They lectured us angrily about stupidly following a cadet we didn't even recognize, and I came to realize that this had been a prank played upon Dent and his fellow, with us as ancillary victims.

We were late for the class and we received the blame for it. Mr Arnis spoke to us in Varnian, saying that it was the only language we could use during the class, to force us to become fluent more quickly. He added that if we thought we could disrespect him because he was not a military man, he would soon teach us our error. I understood the gist of what he said to us as he ordered us to take the last available seats in the back of the room. Only Trist seemed completely comfortable. He sat two chairs down from me, his pen moving effortlessly over his paper as he took notes. Before the instructor dismissed us, he had assigned us to translate the introductory passage of Gilshaw's *Journal of a Varnian Commander* into Gernian, and to compose a letter in Varnian to send to our parents, telling them how much we had enjoyed our first day of Academy life. Because we had been late, he gave us the additional assignment of writing a formal apology for disrupting the class schedule. Someone

254

in the back of the classroom groaned and our instructor permitted himself a small smile, the first sign of humour that any of our teachers had displayed.

As we had arrived late, so he kept us late, and thus any thoughts of a walk back to Carneston House or a leisurely meal were dashed. Corporal Dent was waiting for us, very annoyed that he, too, would be late for his meal. He would not let us run but formed us up and marched us back to our quarters. Before he dismissed us to take our books upstairs, he informed us, with sadistic glee, that we had all failed our first inspection of quarters. A list had been left for us and we should correct our deficiencies before going to the dining hall. After this, our inspection of quarters would take place every morning before we left for breakfast.

I was shocked at the length of the list. Our floor had not been swept and mopped, our window was dirty and the windowsill dusty. Our clothing was to be hung in our closets with all buttons fastened, facing to the left. This, I supposed, explained why each of our closets was now empty, our clothing heaped on the floor outside it. Natred's bedding was dumped on the floor beside his bunk; evidently, it had not been spread up as tidily as required. Our lamp should have been refilled with oil, its chimney wiped and the wick trimmed. The list even specified the order in which our books were to be placed on our shelves.

We hurried through our tasks. Some we shared. I swept, Nate mopped, Kort cleaned the window and windowsill while Spink took care of the oil lamp. When our books had been neatly arranged on our shelves, we departed as a group, merging with the others as they came, complaining, out of their rooms. Trist's room had drawn care of the common room, so they had had the task of replenishing the firewood and kindling as well as sweeping, dusting, and setting the chairs at precise intervals around the study tables. Trent had to make two trips down to his trunks in storage, carrying the extra clothing that he had tried to store under his bunk. We clattered down the stairs in a herd, but before we had even emerged from the doors, Corporal Dent was shouting at us to hurry up, he didn't relish having to wait for fools.

We were not quite the last patrol to enter the mess hall. The patrol of New Nobles' sons from Skeltzin Hall looked as harassed as we felt as they followed us in. As we gathered around our table, Corporal Dent cautioned us yet again about our manners. I do not think any of us really heard him. Our attention was fixed on the thick slices of roast pork, the large bowl of mashed turnips, and the curling strips of bacon in the molasses baked beans. Sliced bread, a large pot of butter, and several carafes of coffee also awaited us. I do not recall if there was any conversation at that meal other than the polite necessities of asking that more food or coffee be passed. We all ate, as my father would have phrased it, 'like troopers', and left not a crumb or a scrap on any platter. By the end of our meal, the welcome food weighted my belly and I thought longingly of a nap. It was not to be. Instead, there was a brisk march back to our house, where we were dismissed to gather our books and supplies for Engineering and Drawing.

These two subjects were taught as one by the same instructor. I immediately liked him the best of any of our teachers. He was certainly the eldest of our instructors, a tall man whom age had whittled down to bones and tendons. He still had the proud posture of an excellent horseman. Captain Maw warned us that he did not think we could learn these topics best from a book, but must apply the concepts immediately if they were to be fixed in our mind. His classroom was filled with a beckoning assortment of models of bridges and embankments, topography of famous battle sites, ancient ballista, pontoons, carts, and earthworks of all sorts. He did not force us to sit still through a long lecture, but invited us to leave our seats and explore his collection,

256

assigning us to sketch three items amongst them before the class was over. I was pleased and glad on Spink's behalf that Captain Maw had a large collection of miscellaneous drawing supplies and encouraged us to make use of them, for Spink had nothing, no compass, rule, nor even any variety of leads. These Maw furnished to him, matter-of-factly, saying that careless former students who had left them behind had scarcely appreciated them nor would notice their absence.

I budgeted my time carefully and created three drawings of various catapults and ballista. I was well satisfied with my attempts, for I had always excelled at drafting and had designed a bridge for a steep-banked stream near our home when I was only twelve. Spink, as engrossed with the drawing tools as if he were a boy with new toys, spent the entire period attempting an ambitious rendering of one of the topographical battle scenes. Yet I noticed that, at the end of class, when we each submitted our final works, Captain Maw made no mention that Spink turned in just one sketch, saying only, 'I can see you are inexperienced, yet enthusiasm and dedication can make up for much, young man. If you need additional assistance, come and see me in my office after hours.' After his humiliation in maths, I think this encouragement meant much to Spink and certainly warmed my heart toward Captain Maw.

I left the building relieved to be finished with academics for the day. Even Corporal Dent seemed in a better mood as he formed us up in our ranks and marched us back to Carneston House. He still fell back beside Gord and criticized him, referring to him again as Gorge and promising him that he'd shave him thin as a rail before his first year was through. Gord strove to keep pace with us, but in truth, his legs were short, so that he lurched and jounced along rather than marched. Dent harangued him all the way back to our dormitory, winning not a few smiles and sniggers from some of the other cadets. Dent did have a clever wit and the sharp observations he made about Gord, how his cheeks kept cadence with the jiggling of his belly and, how he breathed through his nose like a blown horse were piercingly accurate and delivered in such a wondering yet sarcastic tone that even I could not keep my lips from crooking.

Yet when I stole a glance in Gord's direction to see how he was taking it, I felt a creeping shame about my secret smile. Gord soldiered on manfully, sweat already streaming down the side of his fat face. The folds of his neck bulged red above his tight collar. His eyes stared straight ahead and his face showed no expression, as if he had long been schooled to mockery. I think if he had looked flustered or embarrassed, I might have been able to smile without shame. But that he took it in stride, with dignity, even as he manfully attempted to force his body into compliance, somehow made Dent's taunts childishly cruel. Gord was doing the best he could; there was nothing he could have done to please Dent. All amusement went out of me, and for the second time on that first day of Cavalla Academy, I discovered a worm's trail of cowardice within my soul.

Dent dismissed us outside Carneston House, allowing us to racket into the building and up the stairs. Or so we thought. A roar of outrage from Sergeant Rufet brought us all to a sharp halt. The war veteran actually rose from his desk to confront us, and the way he reduced us to cringing puppies with two dozen words showed that Dent had a long way to go to develop the lashing tongue and acid vocabulary of the true sergeant. When he released us, we went upstairs quietly, exhibiting the self-control that we'd some day be expected to display as cavalla officers.

Our respite was brief. We were allowed just enough time to put our books and supplies away and straighten our uniforms. Then it was time to once again fall in on the parade grounds, this time for drill.

I had expected that we would go straight to the stables and the horses, and in truth I had looked forward to being in a saddle again and seeing what sort of mounts our new Academy commander had procured for us. Instead, in our small patrols, we spent the better part of the afternoon with Dent, practising the basic drill. His inexperience at teaching was as great a handicap to us as our inexperience at marching. I knew the fundamentals of drill, for Sergeant Duril had taught them to me, just as he had schooled my normal stride to twenty inches, the standard for marching troops. But I had never drilled with a group of men, where one must watch one's fellows from the corner of one's eye and match both pace and stride to the patrol.

Some of the others did not know even how to do an 'about face'. We repeated these over and over, with those of us who knew them standing like oxen in harness while Dent harangued those who did not and made them endlessly shift from 'attention' to 'parade rest' and back again. It was almost a relief when he decided to get us into motion. He marched us back and forth, back and forth, seeming to become more discontented and more distraught with our ragged lines and uneven response to his bellowed commands. Those of us who quickly caught on to drill could do nothing for those who did not, nor could we make our entire patrol look better than the worst soldier in it. Gord took a heavy share of Dent's abuse, as did Rory, for he walked with a rolling gait and bent elbows. Kort had a longer stride than the rest of us, and when he attempted to shorten it, he appeared always on the verge of stumbling, while gangly Lofert could not seem to master the difference between right and left on any of the commands. He was always a second behind the rest of us as he strove to go in the correct direction by spying on the cadet beside him.

Dent cursed us all roundly but without Sergeant Rufet's skill. I could not understand why he could not teach us calmly, until I spied Cadet Captain Jeffers and Colonel Stiet standing to one side of the parade ground. Jeffers had a notebook in his hands and seemed to be critiquing each patrol under Stiet's watchful eyes. Caulder Stiet stood just behind his father and to his left, scrutinizing us as well. I wondered if he contributed comments to our critique. I was beginning to understand Sergeant Rufet's apparent intolerance for the boy. It was annoying that this pup seemed to have his father's ear on all facets of the Academy, and yet, were I his father and in a similar position, would not I try to teach my boy by my example? Even as I tried to justify his presence that way, I knew that my own father would have expected me to exhibit far more humility and would not have suffered me to wear a cadet's uniform until I had truly earned it.

Such thoughts occupied my mind and made me perform a 'column left' turn when the command had been 'left flank'. I threw our entire patrol out of stride, and was given a demerit to march off before I could go to my study hours.

I was not alone in my punishment. When Dent finally dismissed us after a final dressing down, almost every cadet on the ground had a demerit or six to march off. These consisted of marching the perimeter of the parade ground, pausing to salute every direction of the compass at each corner. I had never before experienced such a useless discipline, and resented this waste of time that would have been better spent with my books. Rory, Kort, and Gord were still marching when I finished my single demerit and left them to go back to Carneston House.

I had hoped for a time of quiet alone with my books. My upbringing had been in many ways solitary and the constant companionship and noise were beginning to grate on me. But there was no peace when I returned to my quarters. The long tables in our central room were already crowded with cadets, books, papers, and inkwells. A corporal I did not recognize presided over us as a study mentor. He circled the table like a dog at dinner, making comments and answering questions and providing help to those who needed it. I quickly fetched my books and found a place at the corner of the table next to Spink.

I was grateful for my father's foresight in preparing me for my lessons. I knew the material and had only to endure the drudgery of writing out information I was already familiar with. Many of the others were not so fortunate. Writing arm cramped tightly to my side, I finished my language and history assignments and then took out my maths. The set of exercises Captain Rusk had given were basic calculations, not difficult at all, which made doing them even more tedious. At least I'd only earned the first set of problems in addition to the regular review assignment. A few of the other fellows had four sets to complete tonight. Trist was finished before any of us, and bid us a cheerful farewell as he headed off to the quiet and relative comfort of his room. Beside me, Spink laboured with many blotches through his Varnian translation exercise and then composed the letter to his mother.

I had nearly finished my maths when he took out his book and opened it reluctantly to the very first page. I watched him as he studied the given examples and then headed his paper for the first set of problems. He took a deep breath, as if he were about to dive off a bridge, and began. Our proctor came and stood behind him. Midway through Spink's second problem, he leaned over him. 'Six times eight is forty-eight. That's your error, on this and on the first problem. You need to drill yourself on your basic arithmetic facts or you'll not get far at the Academy. I'm shocked that you don't know them already.'

Spink became even quieter, if that were possible, keeping his eyes fixed on his paper, as if he feared to face mockery if he looked up from it.

'Did you hear me?' the corporal prodded him. 'Go back and fix the first one before you continue.'

'Yes, sir,' Spink replied softly and began carefully rubbing out the error on his paper as the corporal continued his circuit of the table. The arrival of Rory and Kort took up his attention for some time. He had just given them places at the table when a very red-faced Gord came puffing up the stairs. Perspiration had left wet tracks down the side of his face into the rolls of his neck. He smelled of sweat from marching off his demerits, not clean man's sweat, but a sour spoiled-bacon stink. 'Whew!' someone exclaimed in soft disdain after he had passed through the room on his way to hang up his coat and get his books.

'I think I've finished,' Natred announced in a way that left no doubt he was actually fleeing Gord's arrival. He gathered up his books and papers, leaving an empty chair on the other side of Spink. As Natred left the room, Gord entered, his books under his arm. He sank down gratefully in the vacated chair and put his books on the table. He grinned at me past Spink, obviously relieved to be off his feet. 'What a day!' he exclaimed to no one in particular, and the proctor rebuked him with, 'We are here to study, Fats, not socialize. Get to work.'

I saw it again, as if Gord had donned a cold mask. His face stilled, his eyes went distant, and without a word, he opened his books and bent to his task. I do not know what made me keep my place at the table. I longed to be alone, and yet there I sat. I saw Spink begin his third problem. He wrote it out carefully and then began to set it up. I touched his hand lightly. 'There's an easier way to set that up. May I show you?'

Spink reddened slightly. He glanced toward the proctor, expecting a rebuke. Then, deciding to forestall it, he raised his hand and said, 'May I request that Cadet Burvelle be allowed to assist me with my assignment?'

I mentally cringed, expecting a scathing onslaught from the corporal. Instead, he nodded gravely. 'Assist, not do it for you, Cadet. Assisting a fellow cavallaman is well within our traditions. Go to it.'

So we did, whispering quietly together. I showed him how to set up the problem, and he worked it gravely, arriving at the correct answer with only one prod from me, again on his calculation. But when he said, 'It's much easier. But I don't understand why I can set it up this way. It seems to me we're skipping a step.'

'Well, it's because we can,' I said, and then paused, perplexed. I knew what I had done, and I'd done similar problems a hundred times. But I had never thought to ask my maths tutor why it could be done that way.

Gord's hand softly came down on Spink's paper, covering the problem. We both looked at him hostilely, believing he was going to complain about our whispering. Instead, he looked at Spink and said quietly, 'I don't think you understand exactly what exponents are. They're supposed to be a short cut and once you understand them, they're easy to use. Shall I show you?'

Spink glanced at me as if he expected me to be irritated. I turned a palm up to Gord, inviting him to go ahead. He did, speaking softly, his own books ignored on the table before him. He was a natural teacher. I saw that. It made him want to help Spink before he began his own work, despite his late start at it. He didn't do Spink's work for him, or even work the problem himself to demonstrate it. Instead, he explained exponents in a way that enlightened me. I was good at maths, but I was good at it in a rote way, just as a small child recites 'nine plus twelve is twenty-one' long before he knows what numbers are or that they signify quantities. I could manipulate numbers and symbols accurately, because I knew the rules. Gord, however, understood the *principles*. He explained exponents in a way that made me understand that I had been looking at a map of mathematics and Gord knew the countryside of it. That is an inadequate explanation for such a subtle awakening, but it is the best I can do.

Gord's mathematical expertise woke a grudging admiration for him in me; grudging because I still could not condone how he maintained his body. My father had always taught me that my body was the animal the good god had settled around my soul. Just as I should be shamed if my horse were dirty or sickly, so should I be shamed if my body were unkempt or poorly conditioned. All it required was common sense, he had taught me. I could not understand how Gord could tolerate life in such an ungainly body.

Curiosity kept me at the table as Gord walked Spink through each set of exercises and explained why and how the numbers could be manipulated. Then he turned to his own books and lessons. We were nearly alone at the table by then. Even the proctor had pulled a chair over by the fire and was dozing, a military history book open before him on his lap.

Spink was a quick study. He worked rapidly through the exercises, only occasionally asking for help when a problem presented a variation, and even then, it was most often to confirm that he had correctly solved it. Spink did suffer from weakness in his command of his basic maths facts. Several times I quietly pointed out small errors to him. I had my grammar book open before me with the letter I'd composed, as if I were checking it a final time, out of loyalty to Spink, I suppose. He and Gord had just finished their work when the proctor suddenly snapped his bobbing head upright and then glared at us as if it were our fault he'd dozed off. 'You should be finished by now,' he informed us curtly. 'I'll give you another ten minutes. You have to learn to use your time wisely.'

In less time than that, we had packed up our books and

papers and shelved them. The three of us had only a few moments to ourselves before it was time to go down the stairs and form up for our march to the mess hall. This evening meal differed substantially from the welcoming dinner of the previous night. Tonight we were given a simple repast of soup and bread and cheese, for our noon meal was expected to be our major nourishment for the day. We all ate heartily. I would have enjoyed a more substantial dinner and I do not think I was the only man at the table who felt that way. 'Is this all there is?' Gord asked pathetically, both alarmed and disappointed at the modest meal, and there was some jesting and laughter at his expense over it.

After dinner, we returned to the parade ground. After a brief flag-lowering ceremony by an honour guard of older cadets, Dent dismissed us, cautioning us that we had best tend to our uniforms and boots and extra studying that we needed for the morrow rather than wasting our time in frivolous socializing.

We did both, of course. Our floor was a jostle of cadets cleaning their boots, comparing impressions of the day with each other, waiting in line for the washbasins, and speculating on what tomorrow would bring. Dent was correct, however. When he came up to give us our ten minutes to lights-out warning, half of us hadn't finished those basic tasks. We all used up what time we had left as best we could, and then Dent ordered lights-out immediately, regardless of how any of the cadets were engaged. There was much stumbling and muttering in the dark as we made our blind ways to our rooms and beds. In the darkness, I knelt by my bedside to say my prayers. My roommates did likewise, each confiding his own thoughts to the good god and then climbing wearily into bed. I remember thinking that I would have a hard time falling asleep, and then nothing more until the drum awoke me to the dim dawn of another day at the Academy.

ELEVEN

Initiation

That first day at Academy set the indelible pattern for the days that followed. Five days a week we had classes and drill. On Sixday, we had chapel and religious study, followed by mandatory recreation in the forms of music, sport, art, or poetry. On the Sevday of each week, we ostensibly had the day to spend as we wished. In reality, it was a day for study, laundry, and haircuts and any other personal chores that had been crowded out of the frantic schedule of academics and drill. On that day, too, we received mail and occasional visits from family or friends. First-year cadets were only allowed to go into town on holidays, unless it was a necessary errand for laundry or a seamstress or the like. But as the year progressed, we came to know some of the second-years, and they would, for a small fee, bring back tobacco, sweets, spicy sausages, newspapers, and other luxuries for us.

It sounds a rigid and bound existence, and yet, as my father had foretold, I formed friendships and found life both exciting and pleasurable. Natred, Kort, Spink, and I got along famously, and our comfort with one another made our dormitory room a pleasant place. We shared the chores without shirking. It did not mean that we passed inspection effortlessly, for those who inspected us delighted in finding forgotten tasks: we had not dusted the top of our door, or perhaps there were a few drops of water on the sides of our washbasin. It was virtually impossible to pass an inspection unscathed, but we did our best. Marching off demerits became part of our routine. There was no shame associated with earning the demerits, only annoyance. Strange to say, the hardships we endured did unite us, as I am sure they were intended to. We shared the same complaints about the food, the early hours, the unreasonable inspections, and the stupidity of marching off demerits. Just as an old leather shoe can distract high-spirited puppies from chewing on one another, so I think the unnecessary hardships the Academy meted out to us kept quarrels from fomenting amongst ourselves. We became a patrol.

Even so, within our group, we had our special friendships and our rivalries. I was probably closest to Spink, and through him, to Gord. Life at the Academy did not become easier for our portly friend, for despite drilling and the marching of his numerous demerits he grew no leaner, though he did seem to become both stronger and gain more endurance, both for physical exercise and the routine harassment that came with his girth. Gord was something of an outcast even from his bunkroom. Sometimes he sought sanctuary in our room for evening conversation, but just as often he would sit by himself in a corner of our common study room, reading letters from home and replying to them. Trist disdained him, and Caleb followed Trist's example when the golden boy was present. Rory was affable to everyone, and he often joined us at studies or conversation in our room, and sometimes Caleb came with him. Both Rory and Caleb were weathervanes, courteous enough to Gord on their own, but apt to laugh riotously at Trist's mockery of him, and to needle Gord with apparent disregard for his feelings.

Trist remained somewhat aloof from my roommates and me. He seemed to think us beneath him. Oron trotted at Trist's heels like a pet dog, and when he was not present, Rory snidely referred to him as Trist's red-headed orderly. Trist continued to bend rules, as much to defy Spink's iron code of conduct as to enjoy his misdeeds, I think. He was more worldly and sophisticated than the rest of us, and sometimes used that to his advantage. Early in the year, he proposed that we hire a laundress to do our shirts for us. We all contributed money, and Trist volunteered to be the one to take our shirts in and to pick them up as well. To volunteer to do such a menial task was unlike him. The first week, the neatly folded shirt I received back from him looked no cleaner than when I had turned it in. The second week, a smudge on the cuff made me wonder if it had been washed at all. But it was Trent, the clothes dandy, who finally spoke out his criticism of Trist's laundress. Trist laughed out loud at us, and then asked if we had seriously thought that he cared enough about laundry to make a weekly trip into town with it. It turned out we had been paying for his whore. The reactions within the patrol ranged from Spink's outrage to fervent curiosity from Caleb, who rattled off questions that Trist answered so wittily that he soon had all of us roaring with laughter. We forgave him his ruse, and it was Spink who sought a reliable laundress' name from Sergeant Rufet and took over seeing to our clean shirts. Only later did I discover that Rory, Trist, Trent and Caleb continued to 'take their laundry' by turns to Trist's laundress.

Despite Trist's deception, he had such a high-spirited and pleasing personality, I knew that in other circumstances, I would have quite enjoyed his company and temperament, and probably followed him willingly. But I had met and been friends with Spink first, if only by a few hours, and I did not feel I could be Trist's friend without offending Spink, and so I did not attempt it.

It was strange to watch our alliances and rivalries build, and I was grateful for the insights that both Father and Sergeant Duril had given me, for I was able to see the interactions almost impartially. I knew it was Trist's natural leadership clashing with Spink's that made them antagonistic toward one another, rather than any real flaw in either fellow. I could even see that, as a future commander, Spink might have to learn to bend his will to accommodate the real conditions of life while Trist might have to curb his own satisfaction with himself lest it lead him into prideful risks for the men under his command. I wondered, too, if I lacked leadership because I did not feel obliged to challenge either of them. More than one night I lay awake and pondered this. My father had often said that an officer's ability to lead was based not only on his drive for it, but also on his ability to make others wish to follow him. I ached for an opportunity to arise that would let me show I could lead, yet knew, in my heart of hearts, that fellows like Trist did not await a chance to lead. They simply led.

As if the pressures of a new life away from home, stiff classes, and long study hours were not enough, we had six weeks of initiation to endure as well. During that time, we had to bow our head to whatever tasks or humiliations the older cadets chose to heap on us. Some of it took the form of pranks. At other times, it was simple harassment, unreasonable orders and silly demands that we were forced to obey. That kind of teasing came most often from older cadets of other houses, but the second- and third-years of Carneston House did nothing to shield us from it. Some of the ridicule was harmless and even humorous, especially if it was happening to another fellow, but at other times, the pranks were almost vicious. The bar of soap that found its way into our pot of coffee one morning only sickened two of our cadets; the rest of us tasted it and set our mugs aside as soon as we realized something was wrong with it. I do not know who was more annoyed, the cadets who spent the days out of class, or those of us forced to forgo our morning coffee. The doors of our study room were booby-trapped one afternoon with buckets of filthy water that drenched Nate and Rory as they charged through them. Sticks of stinkwood mixed in with our regular firewood drove us out of the room another evening. A trip-wire stretched across our stairs combined with the landing lamps blown out bruised Rory, Lofert and Caleb badly. For three days running, we were sabotaged immediately before inspection, with our closets emptied onto the floor and our bunks over-turned. Another night, we all found our bedding liberally doused with very cheap and very strong perfume. 'Whorehouse in June', Rory dubbed it, and the pervasive fragrance was something we had to live with for the week.

The second- and third-year cadets who lived on the lower floors of Carneston House seemed to consider us their 'personal property' during our initiation period, and enjoyed relegating us to the status of servants. Our patrol blacked boots, carried firewood and endlessly polished anything wood or brass an older cadet pointed to. They found ways to steal any free time any of us might have. Third-year cadet officers had the power to issue demerits, and did so liberally.

The endless demerits we had to march off cut deeply into our study and sleep time. I felt I could never completely relax, and often arose in the morning feeling as weary as when I had gone to bed. When I found dirty leaves and a stone in my bedding one morning, I thought at first it was another prank, and wondered not only how it had been done without waking me, but why I had been singled out. Several nights later, I had my answer. I jolted out of a dream I could not recall to find Sergeant Rufet's hand on my arm. He was speaking in an uncharacteristically calming voice as he said, 'Easy now. Easy. No harm done. You're sleepwalking, Cadet, and we can't have that.'

I took a shuddering deep breath and a startled look around. I was in my nightshirt, in the little edge of woods at the far side of the parade ground. I looked at the sergeant and he grinned at me in the faint lamplight from the empty parade ground. 'Awake, are you? Good. Then I'll tell you this is the third time I've seen you wandering out and about

270

at night. The first time, I thought it was some damn-fool command you'd been given and let it go. The second time, I was determined to put a stop to it, but you turned about and went back up to your bed, and never awakened at all that I could tell. I would have let you go this time, too, but you were headed for the river's edge. It's not too far beyond that belt of trees. Can't have no drowned cadets, you know.'

'Thank you, Sergeant.' I spoke in a subdued voice. I felt disoriented, as much by his gruff kindness as the strangeness of awakening outside and so far from my bed.

'Don't mention it, lad. I see it more often than you might think, especially in the early months of school. Were you a sleepwalker at home?'

I shook my head dumbly, and then remembered my manners. 'No, sir. Not that I recall.'

The sergeant scratched his head. 'Well, like as not you'll get over it and stop doing it. If it gets too bad, just tether your wrist to your bedpost at night. I've only had one cadet who had to do that, but it worked just fine. Woke him up when he started dragging his bed behind him.'

'Yes, sir. Thank you, sir.' The dream that had captured me and taken me outside seemed to linger at the edges of my consciousness, like a fog that would recapture me if it could. I felt drawn to it, but I also felt embarrassed to be out wandering about in my nightshirt, and even more so that the sergeant had had to rescue me.

'Now don't be troubled, Cadet,' he said as if he could read my thoughts. 'This isn't a disciplinary matter. It remains between you and me. And I doubt you'll keep it up. It's the pressure of the first few months that brings it out in some cadets. Likely when initiation is over, you'll go back to sleeping all night in your own bed, and no harm done.'

By then, we were walking back up the steps of Carneston House. My feet were bruised from the gravel and I was wet to the knees from the tall grass I'd waded through. I climbed the

271

stairs and got back into my bed, grateful for its warmth, but also with a strange sense of regret for the dream that had been interrupted. I could not recall a moment of it, but a sense of wonder and pleasure from it still echoed in my sleepy mind.

We all knew that initiation 'officially' ended after the first six weeks of classes, when the 'survivors' were judged to have been introduced properly into Academy life. I looked forward fervently to our lives becoming simpler. Some of us hated the bullying to the point of depression and even weeping, such as Oron. Rory, Nate, and Kort seemed to take the clashes as a personal challenge, and they endeavoured to gallop through it as if it bothered them not at all. Told he must eat six hard-boiled eggs, Rory swallowed down a dozen. I resented how the inane tasks given me devoured my time for study and sleep. Nonetheless, I tried to keep a game attitude about it, for I did not wish to be seen as a bad sport.

Then a single incident changed my view of the initiation. I was walking alone back to Carneston House after marching off my demerits. The light was fading rapidly from the sky and the fall day was getting chilly. I was looking forward to getting in out of the cold and settling down to my studies for the night. When I saw two third-years coming toward me, I groaned inwardly. As protocol demanded of me, I stepped off the path, came to attention and, as they passed, snapped them a salute. I prayed they would just keep walking, but they halted and looked me up and down, smiling. I kept my eyes straight ahead and my face expressionless.

'Nice uniform,' said one. 'Was it tailored especially for you, Cadet?'

'Yes, sir, it was,' I replied promptly.

'Good boots, too,' the other observed. 'About face, Cadet. Yes, all seems in order from the back, too. All in all, a well-turned-out cadet. My compliments, Cadet.'

'Thank you, sir.'

The first spoke again, and I suddenly perceived that this

was a well-rehearsed routine for them. 'But we cannot be sure that he is truly well-turned-out. A book may have a fine cover, but soiled pages within. Cadet, are you wearing regulation undergarments?'

'Sir, I do not understand.' But I did, and my heart was sinking.

'Off with your coat and trousers and boots, Cadet. We cannot have you out of uniform even when you are out of uniform.'

I had no choice but to obey. There, on the path, I took off my jacket, untied my boots and set them aside, and then stepped out of my trousers as well. I folded them neatly and set them to one side and came back to attention.

'Oh, and your shirt, too, Cadet. Didn't I mention his shirt, too, Miles?'

'I thought certainly you had. An extra demerit for you, Cadet, for not obeying promptly. Shirt off, sir.'

I hoped an instructor might venture by and put an end to their pleasure in tormenting me, but I had no luck there. By a series of commands, they reduced me to my underwear. I stood barefoot on the cold gravel, trying to maintain a pose of attention without shivering, and blessed my good fortune that my smallclothes were new and free from holes. Rory would not have been so fortunate. They had added three more demerits to my original one, and now charitably suggested that I could immediately work them off by marching round them in a circle, singing my House song at the top of my lungs. Again, there was no help for it. Within, I seethed, but outwardly I kept a good-natured air of tolerance for this silliness as I began my circuit. The cold gravel bit into my bare feet, every inch of my skin was up in gooseflesh and I had two tests that I desperately needed to study for. Instead, I marched around them, singing the Carneston House loyalty song at the top of my lungs as they exhorted me to 'Get your knees up,' 'March faster,' and 'Sing louder, Cadet.

Are you ashamed of your good house?'

They were standing in the centre of my orbit, enjoying my discomfort and embarrassment when another cadet came hurrying along the pathway. The stripes on his sleeve proclaimed he was a fourth-year, and I braced myself for him to heap some new ignominy upon me. Instead, as he approached, I saw the faces of the two cadets who had been afflicting me darken into antipathy. He came abreast of us, and I was forced to halt my silly circuit, come to attention and salute the newcomer. But his attention was not fixed on me but on my tormentors.

'I'll trouble you for a salute, gentlemen,' he said coldly to them, and I heard the frontier in the way he stretched his words and softened the ends.

They came grudgingly to attention and saluted him. He left them standing that way and turned to me. There were not many fourth-year cadets at the Academy. Those who stayed on for that extra year did so by invitation only, due to academic excellence and potential that could not be fully developed in a field situation. Technically, he had already graduated from the Academy and achieved a lieutenant's rank, though he would wear the uniform of a cadet until the end of his schooling. I noticed the gear emblem on his collar, the sign of the Engineers Regiment. That was where he would be bound upon his completion of this extra year, and he'd probably wear a captain's insignia soon after he got there. He looked me up and down and demanded my name.

'Cadet Nevare Burvelle, sir.'

He nodded to himself. 'Of course. I've heard of your da. Put on your uniform, Cadet, and be about your business.'

Honesty demanded that I tell him, 'I've three more demerits to march off yet, sir.'

'No, you don't, Cadet. I've cancelled them, and any other silly waste of time these two were imposing on you. Stupidity.'

'It was just a bit of fun, sir.' The words were marginally

respectful. The tone was not. The engineer glared at the third-year who had spoken.

'And you only wring your "bit of fun" out of New Nobles' sons, I've noticed. Why don't you go pick on your own, Cadet Ordo?'

'We're third-years, sir. We have authority over all first-year cadets.'

'No one spoke to you, Cadet Jaris. Keep silent.' He turned away from them and looked at me. I was tying my bootlaces as fast as I could. The tormentors were eyeing me with cold hatred that I had witnessed their humiliation. I wanted to be away from them as swiftly as I could. 'Cadet Burvelle, are you dressed yet?'

'Yes, sir.'

'Then I order you to go directly to your dormitory and commence your studies.' He glanced at the two still standing at attention. 'If you are stopped again by either of these two cadets, you are to respectfully inform them that you are already on an errand for Cadet Lieutenant Tiber. That's me. Then you are to continue about your business. Is that clear, Cadet? Your command from me is that you are not to waste your time by participating in this foolish "initiation".'

'Yes, sir.'

He turned back to his captives. 'And you two, are you clear that you are not to haze Cadet Burvelle?'

'We are permitted, until the sixth week, to initiate the first-years.' A moment passed, then, 'Sir.'

'Are you? Well, I am permitted, for this entire year, to issue commands as I see fit to third-years. And my command is that you are no longer to participate in the "initiation" of any New Nobles' sons. Are you clear on that, Cadets?'

'Yes, sir,' was the sulky response.

'Cadet Burvelle, you are released to follow my orders. Dismissed.'

As I walked away and left them there, Lieutenant Tiber

kept the other two cadets at attention. I was grateful that my torment was over, but feared also that his actions would make me a target of the third-year cadets.

His intervention and subsequent comments had given me much to think over, but it was late that night before I found a chance to talk to Rory. It was after lights-out, and technically against the rules, but our patrol was already making its own adaptations of the rules for our floor. Our proctor, as was his custom, had extinguished the light precisely on time, ignoring those of us who were still at minor tasks. He left us to bumble our way to bed in the dark. Instead, we congregated on the floor of the study room by the dying embers on our hearth. Speaking in a hushed voice, I recounted my mishap and also my rescue by Lieutenant Tiber. After they'd finished snickering at my embarrassment, I asked Rory, 'Did your cousin ever tell you anything about hostility between the New Nobles' and Old Nobles' sons?'

In the shadows, he lifted one shoulder carelessly. 'He din't need to tell me much, Nevare. Course it would be toughest between Old Nobles and first-years that are New Nobles' sons. They're at the top of the top here, and we're at the bottom of the bottom. Not only first-years, but New Nobles' sons, too.'

'But why does that put us at the bottom of the bottom?' Spink asked earnestly.

Rory lifted his open hands, lost for words, 'Just because we are, I guess. 'Cause it's always been that way. Old Nobles' sons know the ropes and they're going to know each other from balls and dinners and all that social stuff. So they'll look out for the Old Noble first-years, and not ride 'em so hard. But us, well, they just have at us. You don't hear much about any Old Nobles' sons in the infirmary from initiation.'

'That's so,' Gord agreed.

'Someone ended up in the infirmary?' I hadn't heard of this.

Natred nodded soberly. 'A first-year from Skeltzin Hall. Their third-years marched them out into the river fully dressed, up to their chests, and made them stand there for an hour. When they finally gave them the command to come in, one of the cadets slipped and went under and didn't come up. He was cold, the river rocks were slippery and his uniform was heavy with water. I guess he couldn't get back on his feet. I heard some of the older cadets laughing about it, that he'd nearly drowned in four feet of water.'

'And he went to the infirmary for it?'

'Not him. One of his friends lost his temper, and shouted that they were trying to kill him and charged at the third-year who had started it. The third-year and the other second-years jumped him and beat him up pretty badly. Now he may be discharged from the school. For insubordination.'

'That's one New Noble's son gone,' Kort said quietly. 'They don't bully their own first-years like that. Oh, they have to scrub the steps or sing a song for an hour. But they don't feed them soap or trip them on the stairs. Or half-drown them.'

'But it's not fair,' Spink said. He sounded both hurt and bewildered. 'Our older brothers are heirs and will be lords, just like theirs. By the King's own word, we have as much right to be here. If it hadn't been for our fathers and their deeds, this Academy wouldn't even exist! Why should we be treated so badly?' I could hear the anger building in his voice.

I heard Rory's puzzlement, too, when he objected, 'Aw, Spink, it's only six weeks. Another two weeks to go and we'll be past it. Besides, I think they've slacked off after the river incident. They didn't hurt Nevare. Just chilled him down a bit and made him sing. I don't even know why that Lieutenant Tiber stepped in. It was just fun for them, and test a first-year's mettle. That's all. You aren't hurt, are you, Nevare?'

'No. It wasn't that drastic. But it seemed important to Tiber that he stop it.'

'Well, he's touchy about such things,' Trist said softly as he joined our group. He had glided up behind us in the darkness, already dressed for bed. He sank down on the hearthstones

277

beside me, putting his back to the warmth of the fire. He spoke so knowingly that he immediately gained all our attention.

'Why?' I asked him when he'd let the silence stretch.

'Well, he's like that. I don't know him that well, but I've heard my brother's friends talk about him. He's a New Noble son, like us, but he's dead brilliant at engineering, and that's what he gets by on. Even before Stiet came, when it was Colonel Rebin in charge, he came close to being kicked out. And Rebin really liked him and knew his family well. But Tiber just likes to stir things up. He's always saying that the New Nobles' sons aren't treated fair, here or when we go out into the cavalla. He says we draw the bad postings and move up slower than Old Nobles' sons. And because it's how he is, he made up this big chart on paper to prove it, and presented it to Rebin last year as part of his project in military law.'

'Is it true?' I asked.

'I wouldn't lie about it!' Trist declared angrily.

'No, I don't mean *that*. Is it true that we get the bad posts and don't move up as fast?' Suddenly, the disparity was personal to me. Carsina awaited me only if I showed her father I could win rank quickly.

'Well, of course it is, for most of us. I even heard that when Roddy Newel's family tried to buy him a captain's commission, the regiment declined to have him. There's a lot of political stuff like that, Nevare. I guess you don't hear about it much, out on the frontier. But those of us who grew up in Old Thares know.' He leaned closer to me. 'Haven't you noticed? Our corporal is old nobility. So are all the cadet officers. They never put us with our own kind, or let us have officers from amongst the second- and third-year New Nobles. All the second-years and third-years in Carneston House are old nobility. Next year, when we're second-years, do you think we'll be here again, or in one of the nice, new houses? No. They'll put us across the grounds in Sharpton Hall. It used to be a tannery, and still stinks of it. It's where all the

278

second- and third-year New Nobles' sons are housed.'

'How do they fit them all?' Gord asked wonderingly.

'All?' Trist said snidely. 'Listen up, Gord. Rory told us about culling at the beginning of the year. What do you think it's about? It's about having more Old Nobles' sons go on as officers than New Nobles' sons. Come the end of the year, a lot of us won't be here any more. It was bad enough when Colonel Rebin was in charge. I've heard that Colonel Stiet would be just as happy to find ways to clear all of us out.'

'But that's not fair! He can't exclude us or kick us out of the Academy just because we aren't from Old Noble stock.' Spink was shocked and angry.

Trist stood up, tall and lean, and stretched casually. 'You keep saying that, Spink, lad. But the fact is, fair or not, he *can* do it. So you'd best find ways to make it less likely it will happen to you. That's what my father advised me before I left. Make the right friends. Show the right attitude. And don't make trouble. Or be seen with trouble-makers. A little free advice: Going about whining "that's not fair" isn't going to endear you to Colonel Stiet.' He rolled his shoulders and I heard his spine crack.

'I'm off to bed, children,' he informed us archly. I liked Trist, but his superior manner at that moment grated on me. 'I have to be up early, you know.'

'So do we all,' Rory observed cheerlessly.

We dispersed from our hearth into the chill of the bunkrooms. I said my prayers and got into my bed but could not fall asleep. Spink seemed to share my insomnia for he whispered into the quiet, 'What happens to us if we get sent home from Academy?'

I was surprised he didn't know. 'You're a soldier son. You enlist as a common soldier and do the best you can from there.'

'Or, if you're lucky, some rich relative buys you a commission and you go off as an officer anyway,' Nate added into Spink's despairing silence.

279

'I don't have any rich relatives. At least, I don't have any who like me.'

'Me, neither,' Kort observed. 'So perhaps we'd better sleep tonight and study hard tomorrow. I don't like the idea of marching for the rest of my life.'

We all fell asleep to that thought, but I think I lay awake longer than the rest of them. Spink's family had no money to buy him a commission if he were culled from the Academy. My father did, perhaps. But would he? He had never intended that I should overhear his doubts of my ability to be a leader and hence an officer. But once I knew that he had them, it had made my golden future shine a little less brilliantly. In the back of my mind, I had been consoling myself that graduating from the Academy virtually guaranteed I would be at least a lieutenant, and both my father and Sergeant Duril had said that even the most idiotic lieutenant could usually make captain, by attrition if by no other means. But what if I were culled? Would my father judge me, after that failure, worth the cost of a good commission? The positions in the best regiments were very dear, and even in the less desirable ones, they were not cheap. Would he think I was worthy of that expense or would he consider it good money thrown after bad, and leave me to enlist as a common soldier? Ever since I had been old enough to realize I was a second son and meant by the good god to be a soldier, I had thought my future assured. On my eighteenth birthday, I had thought I grasped it in my hands. Now, I perceived that golden future could be lost, and not even through my fault, but purely by the politics of the day. Prior to the Academy, I had given little thought to the prejudice I might encounter as the second son of a New Noble. During my training with Sergeant Duril it had seemed a thing I could easily overcome by dint of solid effort and good intentions.

I hovered at the edge of sleep. I think I dozed. Then I felt a sudden sting of outrage. I sat up in the dark. As if from a distance, I heard myself speak. 'A true warrior would not

280

put up with continued humiliations. A true warrior would find a way to strike back.'

Spink shifted in his bed. 'Nevare's talking in his sleep again,' he complained to the quiet room.

'Shut up, Nevare,' Kort and Natred said in weary chorus. I lay back in my bunk and let sleep take me.

The few weeks of initiation that remained seemed an eternity to me. The pranks grew rougher. One night, we were all roused out of bed in our nightshirts and forced outside in a cold, driving rain and told to stand at attention. Sergeant Rufet had been lured from his desk for that one; he found us when he was doing one of his regular rounds of the building, and angrily ordered us back to bed. I could no longer, as Rory did, shake such humiliations off as a challenge to toughen me. I now saw them as a small place where the Old Nobles' sons could unveil how they truly felt about us. When they taunted me or forced me to behave foolishly or wasted my time with unnecessary tasks, it now burned in my soul. It created a little well of anger in me, one that they fed, drop by drop. I had always been a good-natured fellow, able to take a joke, able to forgive even the roughest of practical jokes. Those six weeks taught me why some men carry grudges.

I began, foolishly perhaps, to take small vengeances. When I blacked the second-years' boots, I took care to get blacking on the laces so they'd dirty their hands. They caught me at that, of course, and angrily warned me to be more careful the next time. I blacked the boots meticulously, but pushed a thumbful of pine-tar up into the treads of several random boots. They tracked the sticky mess all over their floors the next morning as they left their dormitory, and reaped the punishment for a sticky floor at the noon inspection. That, they blamed on each other, and had demerits of their own to march off. That pleased me. Far better to make their misfortunes seem accidental.

A few nights later, I rose from my bed after I judged the

281

others were asleep. I walked silently through the study room, but just as I reached the door, Rory spoke.

'Where you going, Nevare?'

He and Nate had been sitting in the dark, talking quietly. I hadn't noticed them.

'Out. Just for a minute.'

'What you got there? More tree gum?'

When I made no reply, Rory gave a snort of laughter. 'I saw you gatherin' it the other day. Pretty smooth, Nevare. Actually, pretty sticky. And I wouldn't a thought it of you. What are ya doing now?'

I was torn between reluctance and a certain amount of pride in my cleverness. I came back to the hearth, blew briefly on the coals to wake a feeble flame, and then showed them what I held in my hand.

'Wood chips? What are you going to do with wood chips?'

'Wedge them into a door frame.'

Nate was shocked. 'Nevare! That's not like you. Or is it?'

I shook my head, a bit surprised at his question, and taken aback for a moment. It wasn't like me to play such tricks. More like Dewara, I thought to myself. It was a plainsman tactic, this subtle revenge, and probably unworthy of a gentleman. I tried to care about that, and could not. It was almost as if I had discovered a second me inside myself, capable of such things.

Rory leaned closer to my hand to peer at the chips, and then shook his head. 'They're too little to make any difference. They won't hold.'

'Want to bet?' I asked him.

'I'm coming with you. I got to see this.'

Rory and Nate followed me as I crept down the stairwell to the next floor. The second-years had a door that opened out from their study room onto the stairwell. They closed it at night to hold the heat in their rooms. I crouched down. The dim lantern in the stairwell barely illuminated my work

282

as I carefully stacked the wood chips into a series of wedges under their door. 'Do some in the sides, too,' Rory suggested in a whisper.

I nodded, grinning, and worked them in just above the hinges, pressing them firmly into the crack and pushing them flush to the frame.

The next morning we hastened our fellows out of the room and down to the parade ground, ignoring the pounding and shouting from the second-years' door as we passed it. There, we assembled without Corporal Dent, and were innocently awaiting our corporal when the third-years and the cadet officers arrived. All the second-years were late to the parade ground and awarded demerits as a result. It was easy for most of us to look innocent, for Nate, Rory and I had kept our secret to ourselves. I don't know if Nate or Rory whispered, but by noon, all my fellows had, in one way or another, conveyed subtle congratulations to me. Our corporal suspected us and did his best to make us miserable that day. Yet his best efforts did little to dampen our spirits, and that, I think, infuriated him all the more.

I should not have been the instigator of such a trick, for I should have known that Rory would only escalate the war of mischief. I think it was he who pissed in their water ewer and left it by their washbasin, but I have no way to be certain. Day after day, the second-years bullied us, and every day, we found some small way to strike back. We were far more adept than they were at subterfuge, and more creative. Flour and sugar rubbed into their bed sheets meant they awoke as sticky as dumplings. A hollowed stick of firewood, packed with horsehair from the stables, drove them out of their study room one night. They cursed at us and accused us, but could prove nothing. We marched off the demerits, kept our eyes down and seemed to submit to them, but at night, after lights-out, we often gathered to whisper and rejoice in our defiance. All good-natured tolerance for our

283

'initiation' was gone. We waged a war of endurance, now, to prove we would not be run off.

The six-week initiation culminated in a grand mêlée on the parade ground. Traditionally, it was some sort of mock battle, a wrestling competition or a tug-of-war or footraces or other sport challenge between the houses that theoretically dispersed any ill-feeling that had built up during the initiation. All were to emerge from it peers and equals, Academy cadets one and all. But in my first-year, it all went wrong, and to this day, I do not think what happened was entirely an accident. How naive we all were! We had been brought to the edge of a boil and held there by bullying and pressure. We should have known better to put any trust in anything a second-year from our house told us. Yet when Corporal Dent came pounding up the stairs, shouting at us to rally, for Bringham House had stolen the flag of Carneston House and was defying us to take it back, we all slammed our books shut and left our Sevday afternoon study to pelt down the staircase out onto the parade ground.

Across the parade ground, to our fury, we beheld our cherished brown horse flying upside-down from Bringham House's flagpole, below their own flag by a substantial margin. The base of their flagpole was guarded by their first-years. On seeing us emerge like bees from a kicked hive, they roared at us their challenge to come and prove who was the better house. The Bringham House second-years stood on the steps, cheering them on.

I think the upper classmen had misjudged the temperament of the Carneston House first-years. Or perhaps they had not. We charged into the fray, Rory in the forefront, bellowing like a bull. I heard someone shout from behind me, 'Champions. You are supposed to choose champions to fight for each house!' But if that had been the plan, no one had told us about it beforehand, and now it was too late. The first-year cadets of Carneston House hurtled, barehanded, into the ranks of Bringham House first-years. We thought that we battled for the honour of our houses. In reality, the second-years of both houses had manoeuvred us into providing them some free entertainment. They roared and cheered and cursed us from the sidelines. We were scarcely aware of them. At first it was only pushing, shouting and standing wrestling as we tried to win through to the base of the flagpole to reclaim our colours. Then fists started to fly. I do not know who struck the first hard blow. Bringham House accused our cadets, and we accused theirs. I think that all the frustration of all the first-years at the bullying we had endured as well as the pressures of the Academy suddenly burst like a swollen boil.

There were a dozen of us from Carneston House. There were only eight first-years in Bringham House, but when their second-years saw that we were getting the better of them, enough of them waded in to more than even the odds. Even so, the triumph came to us. Most of us were frontier-lean and leathery while the Bringham House first-years were town boys. Gord, for all his tubbiness, was in the thick of it, red-faced and shouting and flailing away. I saw three Bringham House cadets try to bring him down, but he just hunched his head into his shoulders and ploughed on toward the flagpole. Trist was ever the best of us, for he fought as if he were in a ring, throwing punches and ducking and gracefully sidestepping his opponent's wild swings. There were perhaps twenty-five of us battling at the base of the flagpole, but at the time, it seemed like hundreds. I fought with none of Trist's refinement or economy of motion. I brawled, shoving men aside, kicking the feet out from under one who came at me, rolling another off my shoulders as he jumped on me. He landed badly and I didn't care. I stepped over him, shoving my way closer to their flag.

I don't even know who finally reached the lines and pulled our flag down within our reach. Theirs came down as well, and we seized it gleefully. We were falling back across the parade ground, in possession of both flags and heading toward our own house when third-years on horseback led by the house sergeants from all four houses on foot clattered onto the parade ground. The sergeants waded into us, tossing cadets aside as if we were children. Once they had roughly separated us, the third-years rode their horses in between us. We were standing apart, breathing hard and caught between shock and triumph at what we had done when Colonel Stiet himself was suddenly there, bellowing at us to form up in ranks.

The elation we had felt at winning Bringham's colours evaporated. We came to order in two ragged lines, facing one another. My nose was bleeding, my knuckles were raw and one sleeve was half-torn from my shirt. Trent was holding his arm across his chest. Jared's features were hidden by a mask of blood flowing down his face from a scalp wound. My only satisfaction was that the Bringham House cadets facing us were in far worse condition. One of them was being held up by two of his comrades. His eyes were dazed, his jaw hanging slack. One had lost his entire shirt in the battle, and the red blossoms of what would be bruises were all over his chest and upper arms. In the middle of the parade ground, the Bringham House flag stirred in the dust as a slight wind picked up one of its corners.

I had no time to see more than that. A corps of third-years was coming down the rank on foot, roughly hustling us into a straighter line. Sergeant Rufet came behind them, quickly checking to see which of his charges were severely injured. Trent and Jared were hustled off to the infirmary, each escorted by two third-years, as if they were criminals under arrest. Despite the anger and buried fear we saw in the eyes of those evaluating us, Rory was unabashed. His battle lust was clearly unabated, regardless of a bloody abrasion high on his cheek. He elbowed me joyously in my sore ribs and pointed to five cadets from Bringham House being escorted to the infirmary, one of whom was being carried. The rest of us were judged fit to stand and take our punishment.

Stiet spared none of us. He held us all responsible, not just the brawling cadets, but also the second-years who had incited us, the third-years who had not stopped the second-years, and the house sergeants who had ignored the brewing mischief. He promised us severe repercussions before dismissing us to our houses, with the stern order that we were all confined to barracks until further notice.

We did not break our ranks to return to our rooms, but were marched all the way up to our quarters, where a furious Corporal Dent ordered us into our respective rooms. As soon as his footfalls were no longer audible, we all crowded to the doors of our bunkrooms, to talk quietly across the short hallway that separated us.

'We done 'em good!' Rory exclaimed in a hoarse whisper.

'Think we'll get kicked out?' Oron asked in a far more subdued tone.

'Nar!' Rory was certain of it. 'It's like a tradition. Every year, the new cadets mix it up a bit down there on the parade ground. I'm just surprised it was only two of the houses instead of all four. We'll march a lot of demerits, and have a lot of extra duties. Prepare to man those manure forks, men! But then it will all settle down and we'll be in our regular harness the rest of the year.' He patted his cheek cautiously, winced, and looked philosophically at the blood on his fingertips. 'You'll see.'

'I'm not sure about that,' Trist said quietly. 'One of theirs looked badly hurt. If he is, then someone is going to have to pay. No Old Noble family is going to send their boy off to Academy, and then be bland about it when he's sent home an invalid. We may be in for some hard times.'

'Count on it,' Gord said quietly. 'Count on it. What got into us? I've never even been in a real fight before in my life. I should have known better, I should have known we were being set up.'

287

'So should we all,' Spink said solemnly. I hadn't seen him in the battle, but one of his eyes was starting to blacken and blood crusted his nostrils.

Trist rolled his eyes at them. 'Yes, little saints all, that is what the cavalla wants us to be. Come on. It happens every year. Don't you think it was a test of our mettle? If we'd all said, "oh, sorry, fighting won't solve anything, let them keep our flag, it's only a rag" do you think we'd have had any respect from anyone the rest of the year?'

'What happened to our flag, anyway?' Natred asked with a smile. There was a sheen of blood on his teeth.

We looked at one another for an answer. But it was Nate himself who pulled our brown horse out from under his shirt. He grinned as he showed it to us. 'You don't think I'd leave our colours in the dirt, do you?' he asked.

Rory crossed the hall to pound him on the back, and then lift our flag and proudly wave it for all of us. Despite my desperate fear of what punishment might befall us, I could not help but grin. In our first engagement, our patrol had won, we had saved our colours, and seen only two of our men wounded. It seemed to me that it boded well for the future. And yet, in the next instant, I wondered how harshly we would be judged for the five fellow cadets we had injured. We talked for a time longer in our hallway, and then retreated to our rooms again.

There, we sat on our bunks or did small chores. I rinsed some blood from my shirt with cold water, and then sat down to mend the sleeve. Natred dozed. I stared at the ceiling. Spink and Kort talked quietly about their families, and how they would react if bad reports on them were sent home. I didn't want even to speculate on what my father would say about such a thing.

The dinner hour came and went, and the light faded outside our window. Trent and Jared were returned to us. Both were so dosed with laudanum that they could not complete

288

a sentence. The neat row of black stitches on Jared's brow and the splint on Trent's arm spoke for them. They went to their cots and closed their eyes. The long evening dragged on. I made a brief foray to the study table and brought back my books. We sat on the floor and dispiritedly completed the lessons we had abandoned when we went to battle. A gloom settled over us. We had been told nothing, and I think that brooding silence was more threatening than any pronouncement could have been. When Sergeant Rufet bellowed 'Lights out!' up the stairwell, we obeyed promptly, and then sought our beds without a word to one another.

I didn't sleep well. I doubt that any of us did. I bounced from one vivid, incomprehensible dream to the next. All were disturbing. In one, I was a woman, wandering the Academy grounds by night and crying out, 'But where are the trees? What has become of the ancient forest of the West? Is all wisdom lost to these people and that is why they have gone mad? What can be done for such a folk? What can stand against their madness, if they have done this to their own forest?'

I woke myself tossing restlessly in my bed, and then lay there with that question wedged in my mind. It made no sense to me but some part of me urgently desired an answer. Why was the city better than the forest that had once stood there? That was what I wanted to know, and yet the question itself seemed to make no sense.

I sank back into sleep as if I were sinking into a tar hole. I dreamed I walked on the logged off hill above the river, and that a presence walked at my side. Every time I tried to turn and look at him, he was always just a few steps behind me, always at the corner of my vision. I glimpsed his shadow on the ground. His shoulders were wide and above his head, I saw the shadows of antlers. We walked up the burned and scarred hillside. Everywhere, men in rough work clothes plied their axes and saws, oblivious of our passing. They shouted genially to one another, and sweated as they hacked and chopped all through the chill day. When a horn sounded, they all hiked down the hill to a noon meal of soup and bread. Finally, I turned to my companion and answered his unspoken question.

'You will find no answer here. They don't know why they do it. They are told to do this by others who give them money for their work. They have never lived here or hunted here. They only came here to do this task. And when it is done, they will leave and not look back. It never belonged to them, and so what they destroy is no loss to them.'

I saw the shadow of the antlered head nod slowly. He did not speak, but I heard a woman's voice say heavily, 'As they do here, so will they do in every place that they go. It is worse than I feared. You see that I am right. We must turn them back.'

And again I woke, sweating as if I had just broken a fever. Bleakness settled over me as I recalled the pale stumps like broken teeth, and the old scar on the top of my head pounded. I felt sick with someone else's sorrow. It was a moment before I could find my own foreboding over the mêlée on the parade ground. My own concerns seemed foreign and petty. When I tried to refocus my mind on them, I drifted into a restless sleep.

I stood before a tribunal, at attention, in my uniform. I was not allowed to speak. Light from a high window fell on me, right into my eyes, dazzling me. The rest of the room was in shadow. I felt cold stone under my feet. I could do nothing save stand in cold dread while voices from above discussed my fate. The voices echoed so much that I could not distinguish the words, but I knew they judged me. A cold fear filled me.

Suddenly a voice came clear. 'Soldier's boy.'

The voice had sounded feminine. I was confused. 'Yes, ma'am.'

The voice was gravid with solemnity. 'Soldier's boy. It was given to you to turn them back. Did you?'

I lifted my eyes to my judges and tried to pierce the dimness. I could see nothing of them. 'I got caught up in the moment, sir. When they called us, I ran out with the others and joined in the fight. I am sorry, sir. I failed to think for myself. I showed no leadership.' A deep shame flooded me.

As I stood there, desperately trying to defend my actions, I heard a drum beating in the distance. I turned my head to see where it was coming from and fell, to awaken on the cold floorboards of my room. The morning assembly drum was sounding. I got up off the floor, feeling as if I hadn't slept at all. Every bruise on my body ached, a grim reminder of my foolishness the day before.

My head was still filled with foreboding from my dream. The others were rising from their beds as slowly as I was. Uncertainty filled me. Were we still confined to barracks? My stomach betrayed me with a loud rumble. Disgraced or not, my body wanted food. I dressed and shaved despite the swollen places on my face. Spink finally voiced our question aloud. 'Do you think we just go down to breakfast like nothing happened, or wait up here until we're called?'

We had not long to wait for an answer. A rumpled-looking Corporal Dent came pounding up the stairs to demand that we immediately assemble in the square. It was earlier than usual, but we managed to be fairly presentable, even Jared and Trent. Trent had to button his coat around his splint, and Jared still seemed half-dazed, but we worked together to get our entire patrol out onto parade ground.

It was a chill, dark morning. We stood in the pre-dawn blackness and waited. We heard the horn sound and still we stood in our ranks. I was cold, hungry and above all else, frightened. When Colonel Stiet finally appeared, I did not know whether to be relieved or even more frightened. For an hour or more, he lashed us with a lecture on the traditions of the cavalla, the honour of the Academy, and the responsibility of each soldier to uphold the honour of his regiment and how badly all of us had failed. He promised again that there would be serious repercussions of our riot yesterday, and that the ringleaders responsible for it would be leaving the Academy forever in shame. When he finally dismissed us, all hope and appetite were dead in me.

We marched soddenly to our breakfast, and filed into an uncharacteristically quiet mess. We served ourselves a breakfast that was typical of every breakfast we had eaten there. It seemed more tasteless than usual, and despite my night's fast, I had quickly had enough. We spoke little at the table, but exchanged many sidelong glances. Which ones of us would be judged ringleaders and dismissed?

When we returned to our dormitory to gather our morning texts, we had the answer. Three trunks, already packed, waited in our study room. Mine was not among them, and the relief I felt shamed me. Jared stared at his dully; I think they had overdosed him with the sedative, and he could not quite comprehend the full depth of his misfortune. Trent went over and sat down on his and buried his face silently in his good hand. Lofert, a gangly, dim lad who seldom spoke did now. 'It's not fair,' he said hopelessly. He looked round at all of us for confirmation. 'It's not fair!' he said more loudly. 'What did I do that was any more than any of you did? Why me?'

We had no answer. Rory looked stricken, and I think we all secretly wondered why he had not been sent packing. Corporal Dent came up the stairs angrily to roust us out. He callously told Jared, Trent and Lofert that they'd be moved to a rooming house in the city. Messages had already been sent to their fathers detailing their disgrace. It felt horrible for the nine of us to form up where there had previously been twelve. He marched us double-time to our first class and left us at the door. Trist spoke quietly as we entered the classroom. 'Well. That was our first culling, I suppose.'

'Yah,' Rory agreed stoically. 'And all I can say is, damn glad it wasn't me.'

I felt the same, and it shamed me.

TWELVE

Letters from Home

Life at the Academy went on. Our routine closed up around us like a healing wound and after a time, the empty bunks in our quarters and our smaller formation when we marched did not seem so foreign. Outwardly, little changed, but inwardly, all my feelings about the Academy and even the cavalla had subtly altered. Nothing seemed certain; no future could be taken for granted, no honour or fellowship assumed. In the space of a day, I had seen three boys have all their dreams dashed. I now had to believe that it could just as easily befall me.

If that culling had been intended to build a fire in my belly, it succeeded. With single-minded concentration, I poured myself into my academics. I pushed homesickness aside. I even buried my outrage at how the Old Nobles' sons were treated in comparison to us. We soon learned that none of the latter had been sent home in disgrace. On even flimsier excuses, four of the first-years from Skeltzin Hall had been culled. The first-years from Bringham House received demerits to march off, as did a number of the second-years. Our own Corporal Dent had dark circles under his eyes for a month, for he had to rise an hour early each day to discharge his punishment. But that was the worst that befell any of them. In time I came to believe, as Rory heavily observed one evening, 'We were set up for that culling. We were chumps, friends. Chumps.'

The strange part was that once the culling faded in our minds, I truly began to enjoy my days at the Academy. Life was both busy and demanding, and yet uncomplicated. All elements of my day were predetermined; I rose when told to do so, marched to my classes, did my work, ate what was put before me, and slept when the lights were extinguished. As my father had foretold, my friendships deepened. I still felt a divide between Spink and Trist. I liked them both, Spink for his ethics and earnestness and Trist for his elegance and sophistication. If I could have, I would be friends with both of them, yet neither seemed inclined to allow that to happen.

I think the differences between the two showed most in how they treated Caulder, for the commander's son became very much a part of our lives. I recall the first time that he showed up in our common room, uninvited and unannounced. It was at the end of our second month in the Academy, and on that Sevday evening, the proctor had left our study room early to take himself off to an evening in town. It was the first time we had been left unsupervised for a full evening, and a welcome respite from the grindstone. Ostensibly, we were applying ourselves to our lessons to be ready when classes resumed on the morrow. Certainly Spink was, with faithful Gord at his elbow as he laboured through page upon page of maths drills, for that remained his most challenging class. I had finished my written work, but had my Varnian grammar book open before me, going over some irregular verb forms. As my father had intended, I was ahead of the column in most of my classes and fully intended to retain that lead.

The other residents of our floor sat at the tables or sprawled before the empty hearth, books and papers scattered on the study tables or on the rug. The quiet buzz of desultory conversation filled the room. All our previous inclination to horseplay had been worn away by the long day of classes and drill that we had endured.

Rory, who seemed to have an endless supply of bawdy tales and ribald jokes, was lounging at the table and in the midst of recounting a long tale about a whore with a glass eye. Caleb was in his corner with his latest penny dreadful, reading aloud to Nate and Oron about an axe murderer who preyed on loose women, when a young and disapproving voice loudly exclaimed, 'I thought you were all supposed to be studying here tonight. Where is your proctor?'

Rory stopped in the midst of his tale, his mouth agape, and we all turned our attention to the lad who stood in the doorway looking in at us. If it had not been for the tenor of his voice, I might have mistaken his utterance for the disapproval of a senior officer, so confident did he sound of his right to rebuke us. There was a moment of silence in which all of us exchanged glances. If anyone else had been there to witness, they might have thought it comical to see a room full of physically prime young men fall to a hush at a rebuke from a mere boy. But I am sure the thought flashed through everyone's mind: 'Is he here on his own, or at his father's behest?'

Nate found his tongue first. 'Our proctor isn't here at the moment. Have you a message for him?'

It was a guarded response, and I knew immediately that Nate was putting himself on the line for our study proctor. Was it possible that he was not supposed to have left us that evening? I admired his courage and loyalty even as I doubted his wisdom.

Caulder advanced into the room like a rat that has discovered the cat is away. 'Oh, aye, I've a message for him. Someone should tell him that he'll get the dick-scald if he doesn't stay away from Garter Anne's girls.'

Rory gave a great 'hah!' of laughter at this unexpected pronouncement and the rest of us joined in. Garter Anne's was a cheap brothel at the edge of town closest to the Academy. We had all been sternly warned away from it and like establishments in the first Sixday service we had attended, and heard tales of Anne's wild girls from every upper classman on every day since then. Caulder stood grinning, a bit pink on the cheeks, well pleased with the effect he had wrought. Later I would come to know that this was a pattern with the lad. He would first fling about his father's authority, to see who was impressed, and, if that did not bring him welcome, he'd next sink down to some crude jest to see whose interest that would win. Had I been older, I would have recognized it as a boy's floundering attempt to win approval and acceptance with any coin he could muster. At the time, caught off-guard, I laughed along with the rest of them, even as I was appalled at Caulder's words. In my home, at his age, they would have earned me a severe whipping from my father or tutor. Here, having earned his entry into our company, Caulder advanced into the room.

'Well, I can see you're all hard at work here!' he said, his tone conveying exactly the opposite. Eyes bright, he wandered through the room as if he had a right to be there. Most of the cadets watched him curiously. Kort put a blank sheet of paper over the letter he had been composing. Caleb opened a book to conceal his pamphlet. Across from me, Spink's pencil continued to scratch its way through another set of exercises. As if drawn to him by this very lack of attention, Caulder stopped at Spink's elbow and rudely peered over his shoulder at his work.

'Eight times six is forty-eight, not forty-six! Even I know that!' He stabbed at Spink's error. Spink's lifted arm casually blocked him. Without even looking up from his work, Spink asked, 'And do you know that this is the study room for Carneston House first-years, not a playroom for little boys?'

The mocking smile melted from Caulder's face. 'I'm not a little boy!' he declared angrily. 'I'm eleven years old and the first son of the commander of this institution. You don't seem to realize that my father is Colonel Stiet!'

Spink lifted his gaze from the page before him and looked at the boy flatly. 'My father was Lord Kellon Spinrek Kester. Before that, however, he was Captain Kellon Spinrek Kester. I am his soldier son. As your father was a soldier son, and not a lord, all his sons are soldier sons. That would make us peers and equals, *if* you were old enough to be a cadet here. And if, as the son of a soldier and not the son of a noble, you were guaranteed entry to the Academy.'

'I . . . I am a first son, even if I will be a soldier. And I will go to the Academy: when my father took over this post, he asked that of the Council of Lords and they granted it. My father has promised to buy me a good commission! And you, you are just, just a second son of a second son, an upstart battle lord's son, jumped up to the status of a noble's son! That's all you are!' Caulder had lost not only all his charm, but also his veneer of maturity. His name-calling unmasked him for the child he was, even as his rash reply revealed what he truly thought of all of us. The words were scarcely out of his mouth before he realized what he had done. He looked around at all of us, and seemed torn between attempting to mend fences and defiantly putting us all in our places. He drew breath to speak.

Trist saved him. He had been reading a book, his chair tipped back to lean against the wall by the hearth when the boy came in. Now he tipped it forward so that the front legs landed with a thud on the floor. 'I'm going out for a chew,' he announced to no one in particular. Caulder looked at him in puzzlement. At first I thought Trist was announcing it aloud just to irritate Spink further. Trist had recently discovered that although the smoking of tobacco in 'paper, pipes, water tubes, or containers of any sort' was expressly forbidden by Academy rules, the chewing of it was ignored. Some said it had been forgotten when the rules were drawn up; others said it was well known that the chewing of tobacco could stave off certain diseases that bred in close quarters, and thus it was tolerated, although spittoons were forbidden in our rooms. For whatever reason, Trist interpreted that whatever was not specifically forbidden was allowed, and openly indulged in the habit. It annoyed Spink, who regarded it as a churlish sidestep of gentlemanly behaviour. He had grown up in an area where tobacco was not commonly used, and seemed to find any use of it disgusting. As predictably as the sun rising, Spink observed, 'A filthy habit.'

'Undeniably,' Trist agreed affably. 'Most manly pleasures are.' He won a general laugh for that, and then I perceived his true target as he turned his inclusive grin on Caulder. 'As befits an indulgence of "battle lord upstarts". Don't you think, Caulder Stiet? Or have you never been exposed to tobacco chewing?' Before the boy could reply, Trist answered himself, 'No, doubtless you are too well-born to have ever even heard of the simple pleasures a cavallaman may carry in his own pocket. A bit too rough for a gently-reared lad like yourself.' Casually, Trist took a plug of tobacco from his pocket. He peeled back the bright wrapper and then the waxed paper to reveal the dark brown brick of dried leaf. Even from where I sat, I could smell the harsh tobacco. It was cheap, rough snoose, something a sheep farmer might chew.

Caulder looked from the plug to Trist's smiling face and back again. I could almost feel the charismatic pull myself. He didn't want to be seen as ignorant, nor as 'too genteel' to enjoy the manly pleasures of a cavallaman. Too genteel was only one step away from being a sissy. I didn't envy him his dilemma. If I had been a boy burning to distinguish myself in front of a room full of manly young cadets, I'd probably have taken the bait also.

'Seen it before,' he said disdainfully.

'Have you?' Trist's reply was lazy, and he let it hang a moment before he asked, 'Ever tasted it?'

The boy said nothing, but only stared at him.

'A demonstration,' Trist offered affably. 'Like so, lad.' He

298

made a show of breaking a corner off the plug. 'Now, it doesn't go into your mouth on your tongue. Rather, it tucks into the lower lip. Like this.' Snugged into place, the plug barely showed as a lump in Trist's lip. He nodded his head sagely. 'A man's pleasure. Rory?'

'Don't mind if I do,' Rory replied enthusiastically. I had known that he chewed, also that he had been too short of coin to bribe a second-year to buy him snoose in town. He stepped forward to receive the offered plug, broke off a share, and tucked it into his lip. 'Aw, that's the stuff!' he exclaimed when he had it in place.

'Caulder?' Trist asked, extending the bar of pressed tobacco.

All eyes were on him. Except for Spink's, of course. His pencil had not paused in its scratching. His diligence was a rebuke to the rest of us, but even Gord seemed transfixed by Trist's seduction of the boy. Trist was so golden, so relaxed as he leaned an elbow on the mantel of the fireplace. He was one of those rare men on whom a uniform looks unique. Every one of us in the room was dressed in the same green jacket and trousers and white shirt, but Trist looked as if he had chosen the garb rather than donned it by default. His shoulders were wide, his waist trim, and his gleaming black boots hugged the calves of his long legs. Our severe haircuts made most of us look like shorn sheep, or, as Rory had aptly put it, 'bald as scalded pigs'. But Trist's dense blond curls hugged his skull in a golden cap rather than, as my own hair did, standing up in a forest of coarse bristle. If ever a young man exemplified a cavalla cadet, it was Trist. How could any lad who longed to distinguish himself turn away from such an offer of camaraderie?

Caulder couldn't. A hushed silence held as the boy advanced, saying with bravado, 'I don't mind saying that I'll try it.'

'There's a lad!' Trist exclaimed with approval. He broke

off an overly generous chunk of the harsh stuff and handed it to the boy. Caulder tucked the whole wad into his lower lip, and then tried to smile bravely around the bullfrog bulge of it.

'Well, let's outside for a stroll about before curfew shuts us in, shall we?' Trist invited him and Rory. Caulder was already turning pinkish about his eyes as they walked out of the room. Rory and Trist, well experienced in the way of chew, were chatting about the day as their boots clattered down the stairs. For a time, the silence held in the room. Then suddenly Oron, and a couple of other cadets were suddenly inspired to rise and tiptoe down the stairs after the trio, barely managing to contain their mirth as they went.

'Bet he don't even make it to the second landing,' Nate said quietly. Kort lifted one dark eyebrow sceptically, then drifted across the room and moved silently to where he could watch the descent.

Someone chuckled, and then silence filled the room again. We listened to the regular cadence of boots descending the stairs. Then suddenly we heard a desperate rush of footsteps down the stairs. A truly impressive bellow of retching reached our ears, echoed almost instantly by Sergeant Rufet's roar of outrage, and drowned in the hoots of laughter and cruel applause of Caulder's audience. Kort reappeared and announced solemnly. 'Vomited down two flights of stairs. I've never seen one plug of tobacco go quite so far.' We all burst out laughing. Spink lifted his eyes from his books and slowly shook his head at us. 'Picking on a lad,' he shamed us solemnly.

'Oh, and you were so kind to him earlier,' Gord rebuked him good-naturedly.

A smile crimped one corner of Spink's mouth. 'I wasn't so harsh. I spoke to him just as I would my own little brother. No, actually, a bit gentler. If Devlin had come in here as Caulder did, mincing about and showing off to try to win

300

our attention, I'd have loosened his head a notch on his shoulders. It's a brother's duty to teach his younger brother humility.' He allowed himself a grin. 'And I learned lots of humility from my eldest brother, so I have a great deal of it to pass along.'

'Well, from the sounds of it, he's had more than an ample lesson from Trist. Imagine a lad of his age not knowing better than to swallow snoose.'

Rory re-entered the room. 'Sergeant Rufet told him to clean up after himself. Caulder refused and ran out of the hall crying. Rufet's not so hard a stone. He sent Trist after him to see to him. He gave mops and buckets to the others. I was behind, and played innocent.' He was smirking, well pleased with the prank and his evasion of punishment.

'It should have fallen on Trist,' Spink said quietly, and I found myself agreeing with him silently. I thought Trist had taken things a shade too far, and despite feeling that Caulder was insufferable, I felt a twinge of sympathy for him as well. I'd had my own harsh experience with chewing tobacco when I was only seven. The memory had never dimmed. Caulder might have fled Carneston House, but I doubted he'd gone home. Probably he'd found a quiet place to be horribly sick.

Several hours passed before Trist returned. Most of the other cadets had cleared out of the common room, but Spink and Gord were just finishing up his maths, while Rory and I lounged back in our chairs, talking of our homes and the girls who waited for us there. Trist came in whistling just before lights-out, and looked so pleased with himself that I could not help but ask him what he'd been up to.

'I've been invited to dinner at the commander's house,' he said cheerily.

'What?' Rory demanded, outraged and grinning. 'How'd you pull that off, after poisoning his son with plug tobacco?'

'Me? Poison Caulder?' Trist struck an aggrieved pose, his

301

hand to his breast. Then he flung himself in a chair and thrusting his long legs out before him, stacked his boots one on top of the other. He grinned. 'Who went after the poor lad and wiped his mouth and cleaned him up? Who was astonished at his reaction to the tobacco, and said it must be an allergy he had, for I'd never seen anyone else puking after chewing tobacco? Who sympathized with him for all those rotters who laughed and mocked him when he retched? And who gave him peppermints to settle his stomach and take the nasty taste away, and then walked him safe to his daddy's door? Trist Wissom, that's who. And that is who young Master Caulder has invited to his father's table, next Sevday.' He stood and stretched gracefully, well pleased with himself.

'And you don't think the boy will ever discover that almost everyone vomits the first time they chew tobacco? Don't you think he'll eventually realize that you set him up for that humiliation and hate you for it?' Spink's voice was cold.

'Who would he ask? And who would tell him?' Trist asked calmly. 'Good night, fellows. Pleasant dreams!' He sauntered from the room.

'Some day, that will come back to haunt him. See if it doesn't,' Spink said angrily.

But, as with all risks that Trist took, it never seemed to take a toll on him. Trist remained a favourite with the lad in the early months of our schooling, often inviting him to our rooms and making time for him, for all that the boy irritated the rest of us. I soon came to share Sergeant Rufet's attitude toward him; I found Caulder annoying and presumptuous. He seemed to think himself a small extension of his father, for whenever he encountered a first-year he was very outspoken in giving his opinion of him. Even when Corporal Dent was marching us in formation to one of our classes, if we encountered Caulder on the way, the lad felt free to tell Rory that his uniform shirt needed tucking in, or criticize the shine on Caleb's shoes. Spink, with his ill-fitting garb, was

302

often a target of the boy's snide criticism. Spink did not take kindly to it, and often righteously seethed that Dent never told the lad to be off about his own business and leave us alone. Caulder always had a cheery and comradely greeting for Trist, almost as if he wished to be sure that we knew he favoured the fair cadet.

Worst was when the boy chose to invade our living space, often under the guise of delivering a message or issuing some unnecessary reminder to us. I soon learned that we were not the only house troubled by his visits. He patronized all of us, new nobles and old alike. Some cadets muttered that he spied for his father, looking for hints of drinking, gambling, or women in our barracks. Others, more accurately I felt, pitied the boy, saying he sought from us the companionship that his father did not offer him, for never had we seen him treat the lad as anything other than a small soldier. It was said he had two younger sisters and a mother, but as yet, none of us had ever seen any sign of them. He had no friends of his own age that we ever saw. He lived in the commander's quarters on the campus, and was tutored in the morning hours. In the afternoons, he seemed to run free, and often into the early evening he could be seen wandering about the campus alone.

He did seem to be in search of something. He began to seek Trist's company, often invading the sanctuary of our upstairs common room. Trist would share contraband sweets with the lad if he had them, and unlikely tales of encounters with plainsmen and their beautiful women when his pockets were empty. It was a tactic that seemed to pay off, for as Trist had bragged, he was one of the first cadets invited to share the commander's table in his own quarters, a rare honour that Colonel Stiet extended only to those he considered of glowing potential. It did not escape my notice that Trist was the only New Noble son to be thus distinguished, even though the dinner invitations were handed out on a regular basis. It singed my competitive soul that I was not so honoured, and

303

yet I stoutly refused to compromise my pride or my friendship with Spink by courting the little boy's regard.

Due mostly to my father's foresight in preparing me, I achieved solid marks in my academics as the year advanced toward winter. Not all my fellows fared as well. Spink continued to struggle with his mathematics. His faulty arithmetic foundation was an added hindrance to him, for even when he mastered algebraic concepts, his answers still depended on his ability to calculate accurately. Rory struggled with his drafting, Caleb with language. We all helped one another from our strengths and learned there was no shame in baring a weakness to our friends. Despite the chafing between Spink and Trist, we became, all told, a tightly knit group, just as our officers had intended we be.

For myself, I most enjoyed our afternoon class in Engineering and Drawing. Captain Maw seemed to me to be an even-handed instructor who paid no attention to Old Noble or New Noble differences. He seemed genuinely fond of Spink who made great efforts in our class, but I quickly became something of a favourite with him as well. My tasks on my father's holding had given me a generous dose of practical engineering. I glowed with pride on the day that Captain Maw referred to me as 'a muddy-boots engineer like myself' meaning that my skills had come to me with practice rather than from books. He often enjoyed setting us tasks that demanded non-standard solutions, and he often threatened us that 'there may come a time when you must throw up earthworks without shovels or create a bridge without lumber or worked stone.'

I distinguished myself one afternoon by constructing a model of a raft built from 'logs' and string alone. Captain Maw created a set of rapids on a water table from a bucket of water poured down a ramp. Mine was the only raft to successfully negotiate the rapids and bear its cargo of lead soldiers to a safe landing at the bottom. I earned high marks for the class that day and was still flushed with success when he asked me to stay behind.

After the others had departed, and we were left alone to tidy away the rafts, soldiers and buckets, he shocked me by asking me solemnly, 'Nevare, have you ever considered becoming a cavalla scout?'

'No, sir!' I replied in quick and honest horror.

He smiled at my disdain for the position. 'And why is that, Cadet Burvelle?'

'Because I, well, I want to be an officer and distinguish myself in service to my king and make my family proud of me and . . .'

My words dribbled away as he cut in quietly with, 'And you could do all that as easily as a scout as you could as a lieutenant in uniform.' He cleared his throat and spoke quietly, as if sharing a secret with me. 'I know a number of good men stationed in the border forts. A recommendation from me would take you far with them. You wouldn't have to remain here at the Academy with your nose shut in a book for most of the day. Six weeks from now, you could be free and on the open land, serving your king.'

'But, sir!' I halted, realizing that I should not argue with an officer, nor even offer an opinion until he sought it.

'Speak freely,' he encouraged me. He went back to his desk and sat down. As I spoke, he toyed with a small model of a catapult.

'Captain Maw, a scout does not have the status of a regular officer. He commands no men save himself. He operates alone. Often he is a ranker or a man disowned by his family. They are expected to know the conquered folk intimately, their language, their habits . . . Sometimes scouts even take plains wives and have children with them, and only come into the forts sporadically to report for duty. They are not . . . they are not gentlemen, sir. I am sure that being a scout is not what my father intends for me.'

305

'Perhaps not,' he conceded after a few moments. 'But I will tell you this plainly, young man. You have a talent for innovation and independent thinking. Those abilities are not prized in a lieutenant. On the contrary, your commander will do his best to quash those gifts, for a freethinking lieutenant is not an asset to a smooth chain of command. Cadet Burvelle, you are not meant to be a cog in a gear drive, nor a link in a chain. You will be unhappy there, and will make those above and below you unhappy in consequence. I think the good god made you to act on your own. Soldier son you may be and, by the King's word, your father may be a noble. But take it as no shame that I say this to you: I do not see an officer when I look at you. That is not an insult. It is my honest appraisal. I think you are brilliant, capable of landing on your feet no matter what tricks life plays you. But I do not see you as a line officer.' He smiled at me kindly and looked more like an uncle than an Academy instructor as he asked me, 'Do you, honestly, see yourself as an officer five years from now?'

I squared my shoulders and forced my words past a lump of disappointment in my throat. 'Yes, sir. I do. With all that is within me, it is what I aspire to be.'

He left off playing with the catapult and leaned back in his chair. He raised his bushy grey eyebrows and sighed with resignation. 'Well, then. I suppose that is what you will do your best to be. I hope you find it to your liking, Cadet. I hope the cavalla does not lose you when you discover that the limits of such a role are greater than you thought them to be.'

'I am cavalla, sir. Born and bred.'

He nodded gravely. 'I suppose that you are. Remember something for me. Remember that your raft passed through the rapids with its cargo because you were wise enough to engineer some flexibility into your structure. Do the same with yourself and your ambitions, Cadet. Leave room for them to bend without breaking you. Dismissed.'

306

And with that he sent me out into the fading afternoon to ponder his offer. I could not decide if his words had been complimentary or a warning to curb my ambitions. I didn't discuss it with any of my fellows.

After the first two months of classes, those of us who had performed well were allowed a day of liberty every second Sevday to visit relatives. It was a welcome change from the previous 'holidays' we'd been offered in our schedule. All the first-years had been given a Sevday of leave once before, but it was a sham. We'd been ordered to spend our 'free day' in attending a musical performance given by Lady Midowne's Historical Society. A score of noble ladies and their daughters sang original compositions that told of significant events in Gernian history. It was interminable, with extravagant costumes and sets and mediocre singing that scarcely reached our ears. At the end, we dutifully applauded, and only then learned that first-years were not even allowed to attend the tea that followed it to mingle with the young ladies. Instead, we were sent back to our dormitory to 'enjoy the rest of our day of freedom'.

I was fortunate among the New Nobles' sons in that I had nearby relatives willing to welcome me to their home for my free afternoons. Trist, Gord, and myself were the only ones who could count on a dinner invitation. The others most often stayed in the dormitory. My uncle always sent a carriage to pick me up, and provided me with a hearty meal at his home. I came to know my aunt and my cousins Hotorn and Purissa a bit better. Aunt Daraleen did not lose her stiffness toward me, but I perceived, as my father had observed, that there was nothing personal in it. As long as I did not presume on our relationship, she felt unthreatened by me. I did enjoy the long talks with my uncle in his study, in which he often asked how my lessons progressed and discussed language and military history with me. Sometimes Hotorn, his heir son, joined us there. He was older than me by four years, and enrolled in a university. Sometimes he spoke of his studies there, and I confess I somewhat envied that literature and music and art were amongst his subjects. My younger girl cousin, Purissa, took enough of a fancy to me that with her governess' help, she would bake little cakes and sweets, and pack up a basket of such treats for me to take back to my friends at the Academy. But Epiny, my older girl cousin, was always absent whenever I visited. In some ways, this was a relief for me, for my first impression of her had been a rather strange one.

Thinking to make polite conversation at the table one afternoon, I once observed to my aunt, 'It is unfortunate that Epiny is always occupied elsewhere when I visit.'

My aunt gave me a look even cooler than her usual formal regard and said, 'Unfortunate? I do not follow your thought. Why would you think it unfortunate?'

I instantly felt unsure of myself, as if I were riding a horse over unsound ground. 'Why, I meant only that it was unfortunate for me, of course. I am certain that I would enjoy her company and the opportunity to get to know her.' I thought those words would smooth whatever had ruffled my aunt's feathers, but I was wrong.

She stirred her cup of tea for a moment and then smiled at me without warmth. 'Oh, I am certain that you are wrong about that, Nevare. You and my daughter would have absolutely nothing in common, and could scarcely be expected to enjoy one another's company. Epiny is quite a sensitive young woman, and very refined. I cannot imagine what you might find to talk about. I am sure it would be very awkward for both of you.'

I lowered my eyes to my plate and murmured, 'Of course, I am sure you are correct.' I would have done anything in the world to cool the blood that flushed my face at her smoothly worded rebuke. Obviously, she thought I had been forward to hint that I might speak to her daughter. Just as obviously, it was no accident of scheduling that Epiny was never present in her father's home when I was. My aunt deliberately kept her daughter apart from my company. I belatedly realized that when I was their guest, I was always the sole guest. The next thought that rushed into my mind was that perhaps my uncle, too, considered me too socially inept to associate with family friends. I was sharply reminded of how my own father had kept my mother and daughter away from Captain Vaxton when the rough old scout had come to call. Did my aunt see me in a similar way? Did my uncle?

As if he could hear my thoughts, my uncle sought to disarm the hurt that hovered. 'In some ways I agree with your aunt, Nevare, but not for the reasons you might think. Although by her years Epiny is almost grown, she behaves so childishly that I have not thought to expect the social duties of a young woman from her yet.' He drew breath to say something more, but my aunt cut in, outraged.

'Childishly! Childishly? She is a sensitive, Sefert! Guide Porilet, the queen's own medium, has seen great potential in her. But she must be allowed to unfold slowly, as a blossom opens to the sun or a butterfly opens her new wings, damp with the waters of her birth. Force her too soon into the worldly duties a woman must bear and that is what she will become: a worldly woman, shallow and cow-like, bearing the yoke of insensitive men! Her gifts will be lost, not just to her, but also to all of us. Childish! You do not see the difference between innocence and spiritual awakening and babyish behaviour.' Her voice seemed to get shriller with every word.

My uncle abruptly pushed his chair back from the table. 'I am sure I do not see the difference between this "sensitivity" and childish behaviour. And thus I am sure that Nevare cannot, either. So, I think I shall spare him exposure to it. Nevare, will you join me in my study?'

I was mortified. I had precipitated this barely-concealed

quarrel between them. I stood as gracefully as I could and bowed to Lady Burvelle as I left her table. She turned her gaze away from me, and gave a disdainful sniff as I left. It was the most awkward moment I'd ever endured in my young life.

Once we reached the study, I stammered out an uncomfortable apology to my uncle, but he shrugged his shoulders as he took out a cigar. 'If something you did hadn't offended her, she would have found something in my behaviour to offend. Epiny has begged, several times, to be allowed to see you. I still think it may be arranged, despite the busy schedule her mother contrives for her. But I warn you, she is exactly as I said: a girl with a child's ways. Sometimes I think Purissa is more mature than her older sister.'

I could not very well tell him that my expressed desire for my cousin's company had been a polite bit of conversation rather than a sincere desire to see her. In truth, Epiny had impressed me as flighty and foolish. I felt no need to spend time with her. But all I could do was smile and assure my uncle that I would look forward to it, while ardently hoping that it would not come to be and that I could thus avoid any conflict with my aunt.

After that Sevday interlude, it was almost a relief to return to the Academy and the company of my fellows. That week, to my delight, mounted drills replaced marching in our schedules. The beasts they gave us to ride were sedate, brown, and so uniform in both temperament and appearance that there was scarcely anything noteworthy between one and another of them. They were numbered, not named. My mount was Seventeen C, for Carneston Riders. The care of the beasts also fell to us, crowding yet another task into our busy days. Warhorses they were not, nor cavalla chargers, but I suspect we looked very pretty as we performed our choreographed manoeuvres on them. They were undemanding creatures, unquestioningly obedient, and completely unsuited to any challenge of endurance or speed. We sat on their backs and they went through their paces with precision but no spark. When there were errors, it was usually the fault of the cadet rather than the horse. Gord proved himself an apt horseman, to my surprise, but Oron slouched in his saddle and Rory was over-enthusiastic in 'controlling' his horse, reining him sharply and kicking him harder than was needed, prompting the animal to fidget and baulk.

Even so, our small troop looked better on horseback than the other first-year patrols. The Carneston House first-years were not only the soldier sons of soldiers, we were one and all the sons of cavalry officers, and none of us lacked saddle experience. That was obviously not true of the old nobility-bred soldier sons. On our breaks, we would watch them drill. Rory put it into words for us. 'Them're why we're all mounted on these mealy-spirited hobby horses. Put a real horse between their legs, and half those lads would wet themselves.'

A few rode like true horsemen, but for the most part their inexperience was apparent. Their ignorant fellows botched the efforts of those with skill. The horses knew the commands but their riders did not. I saw one fellow sawing on his reins with his elbows held wide of his body, causing his mount to veer from one side to the other and occasionally shoulder into the horse beside him. Another rode with one hand gripping the horn of his saddle. At the trot, he looked as if he might be unseated at any moment. It gave us some amusement, but it was short-lived. Our drill instructor, Lieutenant Wurtam, was old nobility and would not suffer us to mock them as we desired. Instead, we were given demerits to work off with stable mucking. Wurtam lectured us that when we mocked the men of other troops, we were mocking the cavalla itself and defiling the age-old custom that the cavalla took care of its own. The diatribe did not sit well with any of us. We already well knew the difference between good-natured teasing and ignoring a fellow in need. The punishment was yet another blow to the wedge that the cadet cavalla officers seemed intent on driving between old and new nobility cadets.

I often thought of Sirlofty and missed him, though I knew he would be well cared for in my uncle's stable. A boyishness in me looked forward to my third year. Then the emphasis of our education would leave the classroom and be founded on fieldwork. Then I could have my own mount in the Academy stables and show off the quality of both horse and horsemanship that I was accustomed to displaying.

Two months into my first year, those hopes were dashed when Colonel Stiet proclaimed that all privately-owned horses in the stables would be returned to their owners' homes, and replaced with Academy-owned mounts. The long announcement about it cited cost advantages due to the uniformity of tack, veterinary care, and the use of a horse through several classes, and made much of the concept that all cadets would be equally mounted. To me, it well and truly proved that Colonel Stiet had no concept of what it meant to be a cavalla trooper. It undermined morale in a way that perhaps only a horse soldier could understand. A cavalla trooper is half-horse; unmounted, he becomes an inexperienced foot soldier. Mounting us on uniform but mediocre horses was tantamount to giving us medium-grade weapons or tatty uniforms.

This was the subject of one of the letters that I sent to Carsina. I judged it neutral enough that her parents would not disapprove, and that her father might find it of interest also, as Carsina's younger brother would one day attend the Academy. Twice a month, I sent correct missives to her, in care of her father. I wrote them with the knowledge that they would be paternally perused before she received them. It was frustrating not to be able to share all that overflowed my heart, but I knew that her father must consider me a purposeful cadet and a man of focus if I wished to win her. Flowery phrases and reminders of how I cherished that tiny lace handkerchief would not win me his respect. The brief missives I received from her in response were very unsatisfactory. She always inquired after my health and told me that she hoped I was doing well in my studies. Sometimes she mentioned some useful pursuit of her own, such as learning a new embroidery stitch or supervising the kitchen girls as they put up berry preserves for the winter. I cared very little for embroidery or preserves, but those stiff little notes were all I had to sustain me.

I carried her token with me always, folded carefully and wrapped in a sheet of thin paper to preserve its scent. At first, I spoke little of my love to my fellow cadets, for fear of teasing. Then one evening, I walked in on a conversation between Kort and Natred. They were speaking of home and loneliness, and one another's sisters. Kort was holding a tiny square of linen with a forget-me-not embroidered on it. Natred's token from Kort's sister was a cross-stitched bookmark in the Academy colours. I'd never seen him use it and suspected that he probably regarded it as too precious for such a mundane task.

There was a strange relief and pride in presenting my own lady's token and speaking of how it had been given to me. I confided to them that I, too, missed my sweetheart more than was seemly in one who was promised but not formally engaged yet. In the course of discussing how carefully I must tread in that situation, each of them sheepishly produced a small packet of letters. Kort's was bound with a lavender ribbon and Natred's was scented with violets. They were in league with their sisters, who received letters from their brothers and then exchanged them. Thus Kort and Natred could not only write of how they truly felt but were privileged to hear from their darlings without any parental censorship.

The obvious solution to my dilemma immediately presented itself, but for several weeks I procrastinated. Would Yaril go to my mother with my request? Would Carsina think less of me for trying to evade Lord Grenalter's monitoring of my correspondence? Most difficult of all was the ethical question of whither I was leading my sister in my attempt to enlist her in my plot. I was still agonizing over it when I received a peculiar letter from Yaril. My family took turns writing to me, so that I had a good chance of receiving at least one letter a week. Yaril's notes had been dutiful and rather perfunctory up to that time. The missive that came that week was fatter than usual. I weighed the envelope in my hand, and when I opened it, I caught a waft of scent that was at once unusual and yet delightfully familiar. It was gardenia, and I was instantly transported back to my last night at home and my stroll through the garden with Carsina.

Inside was my usual dutiful missive from my sister. But folded within that letter was a second letter. The borders of the notepaper had been painstakingly decorated with butterflies and flowers. Carsina had used violet ink, and her penmanship was almost childishly large and very ornate. Her spelling errors would have been laughable in almost any other setting, but somehow they only added to the charm of her message as she told me that 'every momint seems an age until I shall puruse your face agen'. The intricacy of her illustrations spoke to me of hours spent on the two pages she sent me, and I studied every tiny picture. She had a wonderful eye for detail, and I could name the various flowers she had so carefully reproduced.

Yaril had committed no guilty word of her own to paper, and so when I replied to her, as I did immediately, I made no direct mention of the enclosure. I did mention that I had heard that first-years were sometimes given a day's liberty in town at the turn of the semester, and that I would be happy to buy her some lace or other trinkets if she told me what might please her, for it always delighted me to be kind to a sister who had in turn done so many kindnesses for me. Mindful that, even though Carsina's father might not see it, it was very possible that my sister might be tempted to read my letter before passing it on to Carsina, I spent an agonizing two days composing my first missive to my love.

I tried to balance manliness with tenderness, respect with ardour, and passion with practicality. I spoke of our future together, the children we'd have, the home we'd establish together. I stopped when I realized I had run to five pages of finely written script. I folded it inside my letter to my sister, and sealed it separately from my letter to her, hoping that my parents would notice neither the uncharacteristic length nor promptness of my response. Feeling extremely guilty, I then composed an equally long and detailed missive about classes and the Academy's decision regarding our mounts and sent it off to my father, hoping that it might prove a distraction from the letter I sent Yaril.

I had never thought that receiving and then replying to a letter from Carsina would prove such a distraction to me. After it was posted, I could not stop thinking about it, and wondering how many days it would take to travel to her on the mail boat, and if it must dawdle long with my sister before a visit brought them together and Yaril could pass it on. At night, I lay awake, imagining her receiving it, wondering if she would open it while Yaril was there or wait for a quiet time alone. I longed for both, for if she wrote a response while they were visiting, Yaril could immediately send it along to me, yet I also hoped she read it privately and kept its contents to herself. It was a delicious agony and a serious distraction from my studies. It became my nightly ritual; evening ablutions, night prayers, and then staring into the darkness, listening to the deep breathing of my slumbering roommates and thinking of Carsina. I often dreamed of her. One night, as I hastened myself toward sleep with thoughts of Carsina, I dreamed, vividly, that a letter had arrived from her. The detail of that dream was extraordinary.

Sergeant Rufet distributed our mail to us. Often we returned from our morning classes to find whatever we had received set precisely in the centre of each bed. In my dream, there was a letter addressed to me in my sister Yaril's hand, but I immediately knew that it held tidings from Carsina. I slipped it inside my uniform jacket, resolving to open it alone and unobserved so that I could privately savour whatever she had written to me. In the golden last light of the afternoon, I slipped away from the dormitory to a peaceful copse of oak trees that graced an expanse of lawn to the east of Carneston House. There, I leaned against the trunk of a tree and opened my long-awaited letter. Light filtered down through the canopy of autumn leaves. A light layer of fallen leaves on the ground shifted softly in the evening breeze from the river.

I drew the longed-for pages from the envelope. My sister's letter was a large, golden leaf. As I looked at it, it turned brown, the inked lines fading with the colour change. The edges of the leaf curled in, until it resembled the dry husk of a butterfly's cocoon. When I tried to unfurl it, it crumbled into tiny brown bits and blew away on the wind.

Carsina's letter was written on paper. I tried to read it, but her handwriting, once so large and looping, crawled into tiny spidery letters, the characters becoming so ornate they defied my eyes. But within the page was a pressed trio of violets. They were carefully enfolded in a sheet of fine paper. When I opened them and put them on my palm, I could suddenly smell their fragrance as strongly as if they were freshly bloomed. I put my nose close to them, breathing in their perfume and knowing, somehow, that Carsina had worn this tiny bouquet pinned to her dress for a day before she had pressed them and sent them to me. I smiled, for the scent of the flowers was the air of her love for me. I was so blessed, that the woman destined to be mine regarded me with affection and anticipation. Not all arranged partners were so fortunate. My future was gold before me and assured. I would be an officer and I would lead men and acquit myself well in feats of war. My lady would come to me, to be my wife and to fill my home with children. When my days as a cavalla officer were done, we would retire to live out our years in Widevale in a gracious home on my brother's holding.

As I thought these thoughts, the violets in my hand began to grow. They budded and more blossoms joined the three, and the three eldest blossoms formed tiny seeds, which dropped on the palm of my hand. There they germinated, sinking tiny roots into the lines of my palm and opening small green leaves to the sunlight. Flowers with the faces of children began to open. I watched over them, cherishing them, as I leaned on the trunk of a great oak.

I do not know what made me look up from them. She made no sound. She stood, unmoving as a tree, looking at me with great determination. Tiny flowers bloomed in her hair. The robe that draped her was the gold of birch leaves in autumn. The majestic tree woman shook her head in slow denial. 'No,' she said. Her voice was quiet and not unkind, but her words reached my ears with absolute clarity. 'That is not for you. That may do for others, but a different fate awaits you. There is a task to be done and you were chosen for it. Nothing and no one shall lead you away from it. You will go to it, even if you must go as a dog that flees from flung stones. It is given to you to turn them back. Only you can do it, soldier's boy. All else must be put aside until your task is done.'

Her words horrified me. It could not be so. I looked back at the future I held so securely. Cupped in my hand, the foliage of the tiny offspring of our love thrived briefly then, horrifyingly, yellowed and shrivelled. The little faces closed their eyes and grew pale and wan. The blossoms bent, withering, and then suddenly subsided into rotting foliage in the palm.

'No!' I cried, and only then felt how the oak had taken me in. Its bark had grown over my shoulders and engulfed my torso. Years before, my brother and I had left a rope swing tied to the branch of a gully willow. As time had passed, the tree's limb had swelled up around the rope until the constricting line was invisible. So was this tree engulfing me, growing around me and taking me inside it. It was too late to struggle. Bemused by the flowers in my hand, I had been unwary.

I lifted my head and opened my mouth to scream. Instead, soundlessly, I vomited forth a cascade of green tendrils. They dived into the earth at my feet, and then rose again as saplings. On the lawn before me, a forest sprouted, and I felt them drawing sustenance from my body. As Nevare, I dwindled to nothing, and became instead a green awareness. My tree-selves grew and first encroached on the campus buildings and then enfolded them. My roots buckled the walkways and cracked foundations. My branches thrust into glassless windows. I sent wandering yellow tendrils across the dusty floors of empty classrooms. The Academy fell before me, and became a forest, a forest that slowly began to climb over the walls of the grounds and spread out into the streets and byways of Old Thares.

I felt nothing about all this. I was green, alive and growing, and that meant all was well. Everything was safe. I had protected them all. Then I felt footsteps pacing slowly through me; someone moved through the forest I had become. Slowly I became aware of her. With great fondness, I turned my attention to her.

The immense tree woman of my spirit dream turned her

318

face up to the lances of sunlight that shafted down onto her through my many leafy branches. Her grey-green hair cascaded down her back. She smiled up at me and the flesh that wreathed her face echoed her smile. 'You did it. You stopped them. This is your success.' I felt a surge of pride in myself. I understood. The healing of the earth that I worked in my world would be a healing of this other world as well.

A moment later, a wave of horror replaced it. My enemy had corrupted me. I did not love her and her forest. My love was for my homeland, my loyalty to my king. I saw her as she really was. She was fat and disgusting, her many chins wobbling like a frog about to croak. I could not give my life to *that*.

I woke to Spink gripping me by the shoulders and shaking me roughly. 'Wake up, Nevare. You're having a bad dream!' he was shouting at me as I became aware of the darkness of the dormitory. I fell back into my crumpled blankets gratefully.

'A dream. Oh, thank the good god, just a dream. A dream.'

'Go back to sleep!' Natred pleaded in an agonized groan of weariness. 'It's still a couple of hours before reveille. I need all the sleep I can get.'

In a few moments, the room was quiet around me again, save for the heavy breathing of my roommates. Sleep was a very precious commodity to cadets; we never seemed to get enough of it. Yet the rest of that night, it eluded me. I stared into the dark corner of my dormitory room and told myself over and over that it had only been a dream. I wrung my hands together, trying to eliminate the itching feeling that the roots had left on my palms. But worse was the burning in my heart. I had fretted before that I did not possess the natural leadership that Spink and Trist manifested so plainly, but I had never doubted my courage. Yet in my dream, I had clearly chosen to ally myself with the tree woman. Was my dream a truth from my soul? Did cowardice lurk in me? Could I be a traitor? I could conceive of no other reason that I would turn away from patriotism for king and family.

The next day was torture for me. I could scarcely keep my eyes open, and earned demerits for myself in Varnian and maths classes. I was both exhausted and ravenous when we returned to the dormitory at noon. I could not decide which I wanted more, my lunch or a brief nap, until I spied the envelope awaiting me on my bunk. Spink and Natred had also received mail, and tore into it joyously. I realized I was standing and staring at mine when Kort nudged me. 'Isn't that something you've been hoping for?' The smile he gave me was both warm and yet teasing.

'Perhaps,' I said guardedly. He was looking at me expectantly, so I picked it up. It was addressed to me in my sister's familiar hand, but it weighed more than one of her perfunctory messages would have. Kort was watching me avidly. I couldn't send him away, for I realized belatedly that I had watched him with the same envy when he had received mail. At any other time, I would have resented his vicarious sharing of this moment, but it was suddenly comforting to have him there. Last night had been a dream, and Kort standing next to me anchored me in reality. This envelope might well hold a message from Carsina. A message from my future bride and the woman who would be mother to my children. I tore open the envelope and coaxed out the contents.

A dutiful letter from my sister, several pages longer than usual, enclosed another written on fine onionskin paper. I forced myself to read my sister's missive first. She did, indeed, know of several things I could send her from Old Thares, should I have the opportunity to get into town. Her list was quite specific and occupied two pages of her letter. Beads, in certain colours, sizes and quantities. Lace, no more than one inch wide, in white, ecru and the palest blue I could find, in quantities of at least three yards each. Buttons shaped like berries, cherries, apples, acorns or birds, but not like dogs or cats, please. At least twelve of each, and if they came in two sizes, an additional four in the smaller size. After the sewing notions, there followed a list of drawing pencils and then several nibs she would like to have. I had to smile at her cheerful avarice. I suspected she well knew that I would do my best to get her some, if not all, of her heart's desires.

Shaking my head, I refolded her letter and turned my attention to the packet of fine paper within it. A drop of crimson wax sealed that missive, and lacking a ring to seal it, the delicate imprint of a small finger. I tried to leave it intact as I opened it and failed utterly. It cracked into red crumbles. As I unfolded the pages, a fine dust of brown flakes cascaded from them onto my bunk.

'Look at that! His girl has sent him snuff!' Kort exclaimed in amazement. Several heads turned to see what he was talking about. I was already making my way through the maze of Carsina's looping handwriting. The fallen fragments did, indeed, resemble snuff, but I could not imagine that she had sent me such a gift.

I read through two flowery pages of endearments and loneliness and anticipation before I solved the mystery. 'And herein I enclos several pansies from my garden. These are the largest and brightest blooms I have ever rased, and I have presed them carefully for you so that they held their colours. Some people fancy that pansies have little faces. If these ones do, then each one holds a kiss for you, for I have plased them there myself!'

I smiled. 'She has sent me pressed flowers,' I said to Kort.

'Oh, posies for her sweetheart!' he mocked me, but even in that mocking, there was an acknowledgment that we shared something, and I felt manlier for him knowing that there was a girl who waited for me. I slit the other side of the envelope and spread it open carefully, looking for my keepsake. But all I found was brown dust that dribbled out to float on the air before settling on to the floor. I looked at it in dismay.

'The flowers must have dried away to nothing.'

Kort raised one eyebrow. 'How long ago did she send them to you? Has the letter been delayed?'

I checked the date. 'Actually, it's travelled quite rapidly. It has taken only ten days to reach me.'

He shook his head at me, a smile on his face. 'Then I think your lady is having a bit of a joke with you, Nevare. Nothing decays that fast. Now your dilemma: do you thank her for her pretty posies, or ask her why she sent you a thimble-full of compost?'

Others of my schoolmates had overheard now. Rory had come into the room and brayed out his laugh with, 'I'm thinkin' that she's testing you to see how honest you are, brother!'

I brushed the fine debris from my bed. It clung to my palm. My hand tingled strangely. I resisted the urge to stare at it and managed a weak smile. 'We're going to miss our meal if we don't leave now.'

'And we're going to fail our inspection if you don't sweep up your "flowers"!' Spink added heartlessly.

I did as Spink advised, and then hastily washed my hands as they all waited on me. By late evening, I had convinced myself that it was silly to think my dream had foreshadowed this or that there was any significance to it at all. It was awkward to write to Carsina and tell her that her gift had arrived in the form of dust, but I was determined to be ever honest with her. I read her letter over several times before I slept that night, fixing each phrase in my mind and surreptitiously kissing her looping signature before I slipped it under my pillow for the night. I fell asleep determined to dream of my future bride, but if I dreamed at all, I did not recall it.

THIRTEEN

Bessom Gord

I entered my third month at the Academy with the expectations that my life would now settle into a predictable pattern. Initiation was behind us, and I had survived the first culling. The shock of that experience was followed by a period of gloom that engulfed us all. But it eventually dissipated, for no group of young men can remain down-hearted for long, and all of us seemed determined to set it behind us and get on with our schooling. My marks in all my classes were better than average, and I excelled in my engineering course. Whenever Carsina visited my sister, she managed to send me a warm note. I enjoyed my friends, and my problems seemed limited to occasional recurrences of sleepwalking and the fact that I was growing again and my new boots now seemed a bit tight. Winter was on our doorstep. There were bright blue days of snapping cold interspersed with grey skies and icy rain. Our fireside studies seemed almost cozy when we gathered near the hearth every evening. For a brief time, all was peaceful in my life.

The convening of the Council of Lords, scheduled for that month, was a double disappointment to me. All the patrols, new and old alike, competed in horse drill to see who would be in the honour parade to welcome the nobles to Old Thares. The Carneston House Riders were not chosen. As first-years, our chances had been slim, but we had hoped for that distinction. A second disappointment was the news that my father would not make the journey to the Council of Lords this year, for he had pressing problems at home. It seemed our tame Bejawi had been poaching cattle from a neighbour's herd, and could not grasp why that was unacceptable to my father. My father had to stay and sort it out, both with our plainsmen and the irate cattleman.

I envied the other cadets who would enjoy visits from fathers and elder brothers or other extended family come to Old Thares for the gathering. We were to be given several days off to leave the Academy and visit with relatives. But not all of us had invitations to go anywhere. Gord would be so favoured, as would Rory. Nate's and Kort's fathers were journeying together, and bringing their families for a brief stay in the city. The friends were light-headed at the thought of seeing their sweethearts, no matter how brief and well chaperoned the visit might be. Trist's uncle lived in Old Thares, and he saw him often, but he was excited at the thought of his father and elder brother sitting at table with them. Trist's family had invited Nate's and Kort's fathers to accept their hospitality for a dinner, and the three cadets were looking forward to a convivial Sevday dinner. Oron's and Caleb's fathers did not expect to come to the Council meeting, but Oron's aunt lived in Old Thares, and she had invited him and Caleb to come and spend their extra days off with her. Nobly born, she still led what we regarded as an eccentric lifestyle. She had been married to a noble's youngest son, a musician, and the couple was renowned throughout Old Thares for the musical gatherings they hosted. Oron and Caleb both looked forward to a lively break from their school routine. Spink had not a prayer of seeing anyone from his family; the journey was too arduous and expensive. So he and I commiserated on being abandoned and anticipated a couple of days on our own in the dormitory. We fantasized about sleeping in and hoped we could get leave to visit some of the small shops in town. I still had to make good on my promise of buttons and lace for my sister.

As the Council's opening day drew closer and nobles both new and old flocked to Old Thares, their political differences came to the fore in the press and on our campus. The friction between Old and New Nobles' sons that had died down stirred again in small, unpleasant ways. There were several thistly decisions facing the Council of Lords at this gathering. I refused to bother my head with them, and only by a forced osmosis of overheard discussions did I know that one had to do with how the King would raise funds for his road building and his forts in the far east. I was also vaguely aware that there was a large disagreement about some sort of tax revenue which the Old Nobles said traditionally belonged to them, a percentage of which was now being claimed by the King. Although politics were not discussed in most of our classes, there were plenty of hallway debates and some of them became heated. The sons of the Old Nobles seemed to consider such issues as personal affronts, and said such things as, 'The king will beggar our families building his road to nowhere!' or 'He will use his pet battle lords to vote in a law allowing him to siphon our income away.' None of us liked to hear our fathers referred to as 'pets' and so the discord was awakened between us again. It grew as the end of the week approached, for many of the cadets eagerly anticipated their first night away from the dormitory since we had arrived. The fortunate ones would be allowed to leave the campus on Fiveday afternoon and could be away with their families until Sevday evening.

The coming break was on everyone's mind as we queued up for mid-day meal that Threeday. The mess had always been 'first come, first serve' in the sense that as each patrol arrived, it was allowed to join the line for entry. As we had to enter in an orderly and quiet manner, it could sometimes entail what seemed a substantial wait to hungry young men.

325

Worst were the days when chill rain fell on us as we waited. A cadet could not even hunch his shoulders, but must stand with correct posture. That day, a chill wind was blowing and the sleet that pelted us was trying to turn into wet snow. Thus we were not pleased when Corporal Dent abruptly ordered us to move aside of the main line to allow another patrol to precede us. Disgruntled as we were, we still had the sense to keep quiet, except for Gord. 'Sir, why do they have priority over us?' he asked almost plaintively from the ranks.

Corporal Dent rounded on him. 'I'm a corporal. By now, you should have learned that you do not call me "sir". You do not, in fact, call me anything when you are in ranks. Speak when spoken to, Cadet.'

For a moment, we were properly cowed. My ears were starting to burn with the cold, but I told myself I could endure it. But when another patrol likewise passed us to join the queue, Rory muttered, 'So, we're supposed to starve in silence? And not even ask why?'

Dent rounded on him. 'I don't believe this! Two demerits for each of you for talking in ranks. And if I must explain it, I will. Those men are second-years from Chesterton House.'

'So? That makes them hungrier than us?' Rory demanded. Rory was always antagonized by punishment rather than cowed. He'd keep it up now until he had an answer that satisfied him, even if it meant a dozen demerits for him to march off. I shook my head to myself, hoping I would not have to share the punishment he earned. A mistake.

'Two more demerits for you, and one for Burvelle for supporting your insubordination! Did any of you read your booklets "An Introduction to the Houses of King's Cavalla Academy"?'

No one answered. He hadn't expected an answer. 'Of course you didn't! I shouldn't even have bothered to ask if you had. I'm quickly learning that you've done the least you could to prepare yourselves for the year. Well, let me enlighten you. Chesterton House is reserved for the sons of the oldest and most revered of cavalla nobility. They are descended from the circle of knights who were the first lords under King Corag. The nobles were the original founders of the Council of Lords. Learn this now and it will save you a lot of social disasters later. The cadets of that house expect and deserve your special respect. You can either give it to them, or they will demand it of you.'

I could feel both confusion and simmering anger from the cadets to either side of me. Not for the first time, I wondered why there was not a house solely devoted to our kind. New Nobles first-years were housed on the upper floor of Carneston House or in the frigid attic floor of Skeltzin Hall. Second- and third-year New Nobles' sons were housed well away from us in Sharpton Hall, a converted tannery that was a joke among the cadets. I had heard it was run down past the point of discomfort and verging on dangerous, but had accepted that without pausing to think much about it. Chesterton House, by contrast, was a fine new building, plumbed for water closets and heated with coal stoves. Surely the third-years of the new nobility deserved such lodgings as much as any other. Lowly first-years that we were, we were always being either taunted or tempted by the freedom and better lodgings that awaited us in our gradua- tion year. Slowly it was dawning on me that such comforts were never meant for the sons of new nobility. What I had been accepting as the lowly status endured by any first-year cadets went deeper. I could expect it to last through all my time at the Academy. I suddenly felt queasy as I saw all the lines that had been invisibly drawn to divide us into differ- ent levels of privilege. Why had not the Academy given us officers from our own stratum if there was such a difference amongst the level of nobility? And if this was how they seg- regated us in the Academy, what did it foretell for when we were issued our graduation assignments?

As I pondered all this, Dent held us there, letting yet another patrol go ahead of us, mostly to engrave on us his authority over us. We held our tongues and he finally allowed us to join the queue.

After we were seated and served we were allowed conversation at our table. Casual conversation, beyond polite requests to pass food, was a new privilege for us. Corporal Dent, who was still required to share our table and supervise us, obviously did not enjoy it, and was inclined to stifle our talk at every opportunity. Of late, we had been united in refusing to be daunted by him. I was too hungry and cold that day to think about further defying Dent. I was grateful to wrap both my hands around a mug of hot coffee and hold them there to thaw.

Gord was the one who foolishly brought up the sore topic as he passed the bread to Spink. 'I thought all cadets entered the Academy on an equal footing, with equal opportunity to advance.'

He did not address his words to any individual, but Dent seized the comment like a bulldog latching onto a shaken rag. He gave a martyred sigh. 'I was warned that I'd find you an ignorant lot, but I thought surely a simple process of logic would have shown you that, just as your fathers are lesser nobles, their gentility only conferred on them by a writ, so are you at the bottom rung of the aristocracy of command and least likely to rise to power. True, if you manage to complete your three years here, you will begin your military careers as lieutenants, but there is no guarantee you will ever rise beyond that rank, nor even that you will retain it. I don't have to mince words with the likes of you. Many here at the Academy feel that your presence among us is awkward. But for your fathers' battlefield elevations, you'd be enlisting as common foot soldiers. Don't tell me that you are not aware of that! We will tolerate you at our king's whim, but do not expect us to lower our standards of academics or manners to accommodate you.'

Corporal Dent was quite out of breath by the time he finished this diatribe. I think only then did he realize that, ravenous as we were, we were all sitting still and silent. Gord's face was scarlet. Rory's hands were clenched into fists at the edge of the table. Spink's shoulders were tight as steel. Trist managed to speak first, all his elegance and usual laconic style erased from his voice. He looked around our table, meeting the eyes of as many of his fellows as he could and thus making it clear he spoke to us rather than replying to Dent. At first, he seemed to be genteelly changing the topic of conversation. 'The son of a soldier son is a soldier before he is a son.' He took a sip of coffee and then added, 'The second son of a noble is also a soldier son. But perhaps, such soldier sons are nobles before they are soldiers. So I have heard it said. Perhaps that is the good god's way of balancing the advantages a man is born with. To some are given the ability to remember always that their fathers are nobles, while others are soldiers to the marrow. For myself, I'd rather be the son of a soldier first, and the son of a noble second. As for those who are nobles first? Well, I've also heard it said that many of them die in battle before they learn to fight first as a soldier and primp like an aristocrat afterwards.'

There was nothing humorous about his words; I had heard them before, from my own father, and judged them wisdom, not wit. Yet every one of us laughed and Rory was so carried away as to bang his spoon on the table edge in rough applause. All laughed, that is, save Dent. The corporal's face first went white then scarlet. 'Soldiers!' he hissed at us. 'That was all you were ever born to be, every one of you. Soldiers.'

'And what's wrong with being a soldier?' Rory demanded bellicosely.

Before Dent could reply, Gord softened the discussion. 'The scriptures teach us that the same is true of you, Corporal Dent,' Gord observed mildly. 'Are not you a second son, and destined to serve as a soldier? The Writ says to us also, "Let every man take satisfaction in the place the good god has given him, doing that duty well and with contentment".' Either the man had excellent control of his features or Gord sincerely meant his words.

The colour rushed up to Corporal Dent's face again. 'You, a soldier!' Scorn filled his voice. 'I know the truth about you, Gord, at least. You were born a third son, and meant to be a priest. Look at you! Who could imagine you were ever born to soldier? Fat as a pig, and more fit to be preaching than brandishing a sabre in battle! No wonder you argue by quoting holy Writ at me! It was what you were meant to know, not fighting!'

Gord gaped at him, his wide cheeks hanging flaccid for an instant, his round eyes opened wide. Dent's words were deep insult, not just to Gord but also to his family. If the allegation were true, it would be shocking.

Gord knew it. He knew his status amongst us hung by a thread. He looked, not at Dent, but around the table at the rest of us. 'It isn't true!' he said hotly. 'It's a cruel thing even to speak of it to me. I was born a twin, and due to my mother's size, both priest and doctor attended our birth. The doctor cut my mother's belly to lift us from the womb. He took out my brother first, but he was blue and lifeless and small. I was hearty and strong, and the priest pronounced that by my size and heartiness, I was clearly the elder of the babes my mother bore that day. I am a second son, a soldier son. My poor little brother who died before he drew breath should have been the priest for our family. Both my father and my mother wonder daily why the good god did not bless them with a priest son, but they accepted his will. As do I. I bowed my head to the good god's yoke and came here to serve him as I am fated to do. And I shall!'

He spoke with vehemence, and for the first time, I wondered if, free to choose his own road, Gord would have chosen differently. Certainly his ungainly body did not look as

330

if the good god had meant him to be a soldier. Could the priest who had attended him after his birth have been mistaken about the relative ages of the twins? I had seen enough of stock to know that when sheep dropped twins it was not always the largest that came first. I do not think I was the only one who suddenly harboured a tiny doubt of Gord's fitness to be my fellow.

Gord knew it. He offered what further proof he had. 'My family does not circumvent the laws of the good god. I have a younger brother. My father has not named him as priest son to replace my twin who died. No, Garin will be our family artist. Much as my father would love to have a priest son, the good god did not bless our family with one, and my father has never ignored the will of the good god.'

The silence that followed his words betrayed that some of us still wondered, and Corporal Dent grinned, rejoicing evilly in the suspicions he had sown. If he had stopped there, I think he would have retained a great deal of power over us, but he pushed it one step further. 'Five demerits more for every man at this table for your earlier mockery of me. Subordinates should never laugh at the man who commands them.'

Some of us would now be marching off demerits until sundown, and we knew it. Inwardly, I snarled at the little popinjay, but I kept my eyes down and my tongue still. Across from me, Kort picked up his fork and began eating. A wise move. If we had not finished by the time the order came to clear off all tables, we would simply go hungry. Gradually, the rest of us took up our utensils and began to eat. My hunger, so pressing just a few minutes ago, seemed to have fled. I ate because I knew logically that it was a good idea, not from any eagerness. Dent looked around at all of us and probably decided that we were well cowed. He had just taken up a spoon full of soup when Spink shocked me by speaking.

'Corporal Dent, I do not recall that any of us here mocked you. We enjoyed a remark that Cadet Trist made, but surely

you do not think you were the butt of any joke amongst us?'
Spink's face was solemn and without guile as he asked his
question. His earnestness caught Corporal Dent off-guard.
He stared at Spink, and I could almost see him searching his
memory to find the insult that he had claimed to himself.

'You laughed,' he said at last. 'And that offended me.
That is sufficient.'

A strange thing happened then. Spink and Trist exchanged
a look. I almost pitied Corporal Dent at that moment, for I
suddenly knew that, all unknowing, he had forged a brief
alliance between the two rivals. Trist spoke, his sincerity
almost as convincing as Spink's had been. 'Your pardon,
Corporal Dent. From now on, I am sure we will all endeavour
to save our laughter for when you are not present.' He looked
round at all of us as he spoke, and we all managed to nod
gravely and with great apparent sincerity. It was as if a chain
of resolve suddenly linked us. No matter how we might clash
elsewhere, from now on we would be united against Dent. He
rewarded our deception of him by nodding solemnly and saying, 'Even as it should be, Cadets,' completely unaware that we
had now secured his permission to mock him behind his back.

That thought gave me comfort that evening as our entire
patrol marched off our demerits together. It even somewhat
sustained me during the next day of classes. All of us had been
too weary to do more than a cursory job on our assignments,
and we were soundly berated by our instructors and given an
extra heavy load of study work as punishment. The egalitarian
injustice that we laboured under seemed to unite us as we stood
straight despite Corporal Dent's efforts to grind us down.

Yet it did not extend as widely as I'd hoped. United
against Dent we might be, but Spink and Trist still chafed
one another. They seldom challenged each other directly for
our loyalty; the division was now most plain in how they
treated Gord.

Gord continued to tutor Spink in his maths, and gained

for his efforts a solid friend. Spink's scores were not astounding, but his marks were solid and passing. We all knew that without Gord's help, Spink would have been on probation if not expelled from the Academy. Gord was generous with the time he gave Spink, and most of us admired him for it. But after Dent's accusation about Gord's birth, Trist began to needle Gord in sly ways. He began to refer to Gord's drilling of Spink on his basic maths facts as his 'catechism lesson'. Occasionally, he would refer to Gord as 'our good bessom', a term usually reserved for a priest who instructs acolytes. The nickname spread throughout our patrol. I think that Spink and I were the only ones who never jestingly called him 'Bessom Gord'. On the surface, it was just a play on Gord's role in drilling Spink on repetitive facts, but the undercurrent was that perhaps, just perhaps, Gord had been intended for the priesthood rather than the military. Every time someone called him Bessom Gord, I felt a small prick of doubt about him. I am sure Gord felt the jab of the possible insult more keenly.

Gord was stoic about it, as he was about almost all the teasing he endured. Stoic as a priest, I one day found myself thinking, and then tried to stifle the thought. He had an almost inhuman capacity to tolerate mockery. I think that even Trist regretted his cruelty the next day when he unthinkingly asked 'Bessom Gord' to pass the bread at table, for Corporal Dent immediately seized on the name, and used it at every opportunity. It spread like wildfire from the corporal throughout the second-year cadets who would call mockingly for Bessom Gord to come and bless them as we were marching past them on our way to classes. When that happened, it felt as if the mockery fell on all of us, and I could almost feel the ill will building toward Gord. It was hard not to resent him for the mockery that included us.

However stoically Gord might endure his torment, Spink betrayed his anger at every taunt. Usually it was subtle, a

333

scowl or a tightening of his shoulders or fists. When it happened within our own chambers, he would sometimes speak out angrily, bidding the teaser to shut his mouth. A number of times, he and Trist almost came to blows. Slowly it became obvious to me that when Trist needled Gord, Spink was the actual target. When I spoke to Spink about it, he admitted he was aware of that, but could not control his reaction. If Trist had attacked him directly, I think Spink might have been a better master of himself. Somehow, he had become Gord's protector, and every time he failed in that role, it ate at him. I feared that if it ever led to blows, one of us would be expelled from the Academy.

Each day seemed longer than the last in that final week before our holiday. The cold and the wet and the early dark of afternoon seemed to stretch our class hours and even our drill times to infinity. The weather always seemed to flux between drizzle and snow when we were drilling. Our wool uniforms grew heavy with damp and our ears and noses burned with cold. When we returned to our dormitories after our evening soup, our uniforms would steam and stink until the air of our rooms seemed thick with memories of sheep. We would take our places around the study table and try to keep our eyes open as our bodies slowly warmed in the ever-chilly room. Our study mentors regularly prodded us to stay awake and do our lessons, but more than one pencil went rolling out of a lax hand, and more than one head would nod and then abruptly jerk upright. It was a slow and headachy torture to sit there, burdened with the knowledge that the work must be done but unable to rouse any interest or energy to do it. It left tempers frayed and sharp words flew more than once because of spilled ink or someone wobbling the table when someone else was writing.

It began that night with just such an incident. In moving his book, Spink had nudged Trist's inkwell. 'Careful!' Trist sharply rebuked him.

'I did you no harm!' Spink retorted.

A simple thing but it set all our nerves on edge. We tried to settle back into our studies, but there was the feel of a storm in the air, a hanging tension between Spink and Trist. Trist had spoken glowingly several times that day of the carriage that would come for him early tomorrow morning, and of the days off that he expected to enjoy with his father and elder brother. He had mentioned dinner parties they would attend, a play they were going to and the well-born girls he would escort on his various outings. All of us had envied him, but Spink had seemed the most downhearted at Trist's crowing.

Then Spink, vigorously rubbing out some errors in his calculations, vibrated our table. Several heads lifted to glare at him, but he was furiously intent on his work and unaware of them. He sighed as he began his calculations again, and when Gord leaned over to point out a mistake, Trist growled, 'Bessom, can't you teach catechism elsewhere? Your acolyte is quite noisy.'

It was no worse than any of his usual remarks, save that he had included Spink in his name-calling. It won him a general laugh from those of us around the table, and for a moment it seemed as if he had defused the tension that had gathered. Even Gord only shrugged and said quietly, 'Sorry about the noise.'

Spink spoke in a flatly furious voice. 'I am not an acolyte. Gord is not a bessom. This is not a catechism. And we have as much right to study at this table as you do, Cadet Trist. If you don't like it, leave.'

It was the last phrase that did it. I happened to know that Trist himself was struggling with his maths proof and I am certain that he was every bit as weary as the rest of us. Perhaps he secretly wished he could ask Gord's advice, for Gord had swiftly and tidily completed his maths assignment an hour ago. Trist rose from his bench and leaned his palms on the study table to thrust his face toward Spink. 'Would you care to make me leave, Cadet Acolyte?'

At that point, our study mentor should have interfered. Perhaps both Spink and Trist were relying on him to do so. Certainly they both knew that the penalty for fighting in quarters ranged from suspension to expulsion. Our mentor that night was a tall, freckly second-year with large ears and knobby wrists that protruded from his jacket cuffs. I do not know if he swallowed a great deal or if his long neck only made it seem so. He stood quickly and both combatants froze, expecting to be ordered back to their studies. Instead, he announced, 'I've left my book!' and abruptly departed from the room. To this day I do not know if he feared to be caught in the middle of a physical encounter or if he hoped that his leaving would encourage Trist and Spink to come to blows.

Bereft of a governor, they glowered at one another across the table, each waiting for the other to make the first move. Spink had come to his feet to face Trist across the table and the differences between the two could not be more apparent. Trist was tall and golden, his face as classic as a sculpted idol.

Spink, in contrast was short and wiry and had not shed his boyish proportions. His nose was snub, his teeth a bit too large for his mouth and his hands too large for his wrists. His uniform had been home-tailored from a hand-me-down and it showed. His hair had begun to outgrow its most recent cropping and stood up in defiant tufts on his head. He looked like a mongrel growling up at a greyhound. The rest of us were wide-eyed in silent apprehension.

Gord's intervention surprised all of us. 'Let it go, Spink,' he counselled him. 'It's not worth getting disciplined over a fight in quarters.'

Spink didn't look away from Trist as he spoke. 'You can take the insults lying down if you want to, Gord, though I'll own I don't understand why you eat the dirt they throw. But I'm not about to smile and nod when he insults me.' The suppressed anger in his voice when he spoke to Gord shocked me. It made me realize that Spink was just as angry at Gord as he was at Trist. Trist's acid mockery of the fat boy and Gord's fail-ure to react were eating away at Spink's friendship with Gord.

Gord kept his voice level as he answered Spink. 'Most of them don't mean anything by it, no more than we mean harm when we call Rory "Cadet Hick" or when we mock Nevare's accent. And those who intend it should sting are not going to be changed by anything I might say or do to them. I follow my father's rule for command in this. He told me, "Mark out which non-commissioned officers lead, and which ones drive from behind. Reward the leaders and ignore the herders. They'll do themselves in with no help from you." Sit down and finish your assignment. The sooner you sit, the sooner we'll all get to bed, and the clearer our heads will be in the morning.' He swung his gaze to Trist. 'Both of you.'

Trist didn't sit down. Instead, he flipped his book shut on his papers with one disdainful finger. 'I have work to do. And it's obvious that I won't be allowed to do it here at the study table in any sort of peace. You're being a horse's arse, Spink, making a great deal out of nothing. You might recall that you were the one shoving inkwells about and shaking the table and talking. All I was trying to do was get my lessons done.'

Spink's body went rigid with fury. Then I witnessed a remarkable show of self-control. He closed his eyes for an instant, took a deep slow breath and lowered his shoulders. 'Nudging your inkwell, shaking the table and speaking to Gord were not intended to annoy you. They were accidents. Nonetheless, I see they could have been irritations to you. I apologize.' By the time he had finished speaking, he was standing more at ease.

I think all of us were breathing small sighs of relief as we waited for Trist to respond with his own apology. Emotions I could not name flickered across the handsome cadet's face, and I think he struggled, but in the end, what won out was not pretty. His lip curled with disdain. 'That's what I would expect from you, Spink. A whiny excuse that solves nothing.' He

337

finished picking up his books from the study table. I thought he would walk away and he did turn, but at the last moment, he turned back. 'Once pays for all,' he said sweetly, and with a graceful flick of his manicured fingers, he overturned the inkwell onto not only Spink's paper but also his book.

Gord righted the inkwell in an instant, snatching it away from the table. It was good that he did so, for in the next moment, books, papers, pens and study tools went flying as Spink took two giant steps over the table to fling himself on Trist. Momentum more than the small cadet's weight drove them both to the floor in front of the hearth. In half a breath, they were rolling and grappling. We ringed them, but there was none of the shouting that would ordinarily mark two men fighting in a circle of their fellows. I think every one of us who watched knew that we suddenly had been catapulted into a place of decision. Spink and Trist were breaking Academy rules by fighting in quarters. And those rules dictated that at least one of the combatants must be expelled and the other suspended, if not both expelled. The rules stated that anyone witnessing such a fight must immediately report it to Sergeant Rufet. By not immediately going to report it, we were participating in the fight. Every one of us standing there suddenly risked his entire military career by doing so.

I expected Trist to end the conflict quickly. He was taller and heavier than Spink, with a longer reach. I braced to see Spink go flying and hoped there would be no blood. I think if Trist had ever managed to get to his feet, he would have made short work of my friend. But to my astonishment, once Spink had Trist down, he quickly restrained him. Trist, shocked to be borne down and then held face down on the floor, first thrashed and then flailed like a landed fish. 'Let me up!' he bellowed. 'Stand up and fight me like a man!'

To this, Spink made no reply, but only spread his legs wide and tightened his grip about Trist's neck and one of his shoulders. The smaller cadet clamped on like a pit dog and gripped

338

his own wrists to lock them around Trist's neck and shoulder while Trist heaved and bucked beneath him, trying to throw him off. Trist's boots crashed against the floor and he kicked over two chairs as he struggled. Every time Trist tried to pull a knee under himself to come back to his feet, Spink kicked it out from under him. Both their faces were red.

No blows were struck, save for a few flailing and forceless ones by Trist. Watching Spink get a hold on him and then immobilize him reminded me of a battle I had once witnessed between a weasel and a cat. Despite the difference in size, the weasel had quickly dispatched the cat before I could intervene. Now Spink, despite his smaller size, mastered Trist, half-choking him. The tall cadet was running out of wind; we heard him wheeze. Spink spoke for the first time. 'Apologize,' he panted, and then, when Trist only cursed at him, he said more loudly, 'Apologize. Not just for the ink but for the name-calling. Apologize, or I can hold you here all night.'

'Let him up!' Oron cried in a voice shrill as a woman's. He sounded outraged and distressed. He sprang forward as if to attempt to drag Spink off. I stepped between them and him.

'Leave them alone, Oron,' I advised him. 'Let them settle it now or it will plague us all year.' Then I stood where I was to be sure he did so. For an instant, I half-feared that he'd lift a hand to me; I was fairly sure that if he did, the struggle on the floor of our study room would turn into a full-fledged brawl involving all nine of us, for Caleb had stepped forward to back Oron while Nate and Kort were rallying behind me. Rory looked completely distressed and ready to fight anyone. Fortunately, Oron stepped back, glowering at me.

'Don't fret about it, Oron,' Caleb sneered at me. 'Trist will finish him in a minute. See if he don't.'

Trist thrashed about more wildly at that, but Spink only spread his weight, set his jaw and held on as grimly as a terrier on a bull. I saw him tighten the arm around Trist's throat. Trist's face went redder, his eyes bulged and he gasped out a foul name. Spink's face showed no change in emotion but his grip tightened relentlessly and then, 'I give. I give,' Trist wheezed.

Spink relaxed his grip, but not completely. He let Trist draw in a gasping breath before he spoke. 'Apologize,' he commanded him.

Trist was very still for a moment. His chest heaved as he sucked in a larger breath. I thought it was a trick and that he would resume the struggle. Instead, 'Very well,' he said in a tight, grudging voice.

'Then apologize,' Spink suggested calmly.

'I just did!' Trist spoke into the floor, clearly furious that Spink continued to pin him. I think the loss of his dignity pained him more than the chokehold.

'Say the words.' Spink replied doggedly.

Trist's chest heaved, and he clenched his fists. When he spoke, it was only words with no sincerity behind them. 'I apologize for insulting you. Let me up.'

'Apologize to Gord, too,' Spink persisted.

'Where is Gord?' Rory suddenly asked. I had been so caught up in the drama before me that I'd almost forgotten the other men ringing the combatants.

'He's gone!' Oron exclaimed. And then, without even a breath between, 'He's gone to report us, I'm sure of it. That treacherous bastard!'

In the stunned silence that followed his accusation, we heard boot steps coming hastily up the staircase. It sounded like more than one man. Without uttering another word, Spink freed Trist and they both leapt back to their places at the study table. The rest of us followed their example. In less than two seconds, we were all apparently busy at our studies. Scattered pages and dropped books had been restored. Save for Trist's reddened face and rumpled appearance, and a slight puffiness on the left side of Spink's jaw, we looked much as we usually did. Spink was blotting haplessly at the spilled ink and ruined book when Corporal Dent and our freckled monitor entered the room.

'What's going on here?' Dent demanded angrily before he'd even got all the way into the chamber. We made a fair show of innocence as we lifted our heads and stared at him in perplexity.

'Corporal?' Trist asked him in apparent confusion.

Dent gave a furious look to our erstwhile monitor, then glared around at us. 'There was an altercation here!' he asserted.

'That was my fault, Corporal,' Spink said earnestly. He looked as if butter would not melt in his mouth. 'I've made a bit of a mess. Knocked over my ink; fortunately, it's only my own book and work that I've ruined.'

I could almost feel how keen Dent's disappointment was. He salved himself with 'Five demerits for disrupting study time, to be marched off during your Sevday, Cadet. Now back to your books, all of you. I've better things to do than come rushing up here to settle you.'

He left the room, and after a disconsolate stare at all of us so meekly occupied, our monitor followed him. We heard him say, 'But, Corporal, they were—'

'Shut up!' Dent rebuked him crisply, and then, several stairs down, we heard a flood of angry whispering, interspersed with our monitor's whiny protests. When he returned to us a few moments later, his freckles were lost in his angry flush. He stared around at us and then said, 'Wait a moment! Where did the fat one go?'

We exchanged baffled looks. Rory attempted to rescue us. 'The fat one, Corporal? You mean the dictionary? I have it here.' Rory helpfully lifted the hefty volume for him to see.

'No, you idiot! That fat cadet, that Gord. Where is he?'

No one volunteered an answer. No one had an answer. He glared round at us. 'He's going to be in big trouble. Big, big trouble.' The proctor stood, working his mouth, perhaps trying to come up with a more specific threat or a reason why Gord would be in trouble simply for not being there. When he could not come up with anything and we continued to stare at him like worried sheep, he slapped the table. Then, without another word, he packed up the rest of his books and papers and stamped out of the room. Silence held amongst us. I don't know about the others, but that was the moment when I realized what we had done. By collusion, we had deceived those in command of us. We'd witnessed fellow cadets breaking an Academy rule and had not reported it. I think our collective guilt was seeping into the awareness of my fellows, for without speaking, the others were closing their books and carefully putting their work away for the evening. Trist was humming to himself, a small smile on his face, as if he were enjoying Spink's attempt to salvage his book. Spink looked grave.

'You fought like a plainsman, grabbing and strangling and rolling around on the floor. You're no gentleman!' This belated accusation came, unsurprisingly, from Oron. He looked both disgusted and triumphant, as if he had finally discovered a legitimate reason for disliking Spink. I glanced at the small cadet. He didn't look up from blotting ink from his book. It was ruined, I thought to myself, the print obliterated by the soaking ink and well I knew he had no money for a new one. What was a minor mishap to Trist, little more than an impulsive prank, was a financial tragedy for Spink. Yet he didn't speak of it. He only said, 'Yes. My family had no money to bring in Varnian tutors and weapons instructors. So I learned what I could from whom I could. I learned wrestling and fighting alongside the plainsboys of the Herdo tribe. They lived at the edge of our holding, and Lieutenant Geeverman arranged for me to be taught.'

Caleb made a sound of disgust. 'Learning to fight from savages! Why didn't the lieutenant teach you to fight like a man? Didn't *he* know how?'

Spink folded his lips and his face got that mottled look it

342

did when he was angry. But he spoke calmly when he replied. 'Lieutenant Geeverman was a noble's son. He knew how to box and yes, he taught me. But he also said I would be wise to learn the wrestling of the Herdo. He had seen it useful in many circumstances, and as I did not look to grow to be a large man, he judged it would work especially well for me. He also counselled me that it was a good form to know, for when I only wanted to immobilize someone and not to injure them.'

And that was a sting to Trist's pride and he was happy to seize on it as an insult. He slapped his last book shut. 'If you'd fought me as a gentleman instead of as a savage, the outcome would have been different.'

Spink stared incredulously at him for a moment. Then a stiff smile spread over his face. 'Doubtless. Which was why, free to choose my tactics, I chose one which allowed me to win.' He tapped a textbook that had escaped the spill of ink. 'Chapter twenty-two. Selecting Strategy in Uneven Terrain. It pays to read ahead.'

'You've no concept of fair play!' Trist insulted him ineffectually.

'No. But I've a good one of what it takes to win,' Spink shot back unrepentantly.

'Let's go. You'd be better off talking to the wall. He can't even grasp what you're trying to tell him,' Oron huffed. He took Trist's arm and tugged at it. Trist shrugged him off and walked away from the table, his neck flushed. I think Oron's words had only embarrassed him more.

When Trist slammed the door of his room behind him, the flush of victory left Spink's face. He looked down at the table and his ruined book in dismay. He put his intact books away and then came back to the table with a cleaning rag to scrub at the ink stain on it. I realized that I was the only one still sitting there. I shut my books and gathered my papers to be out of his way. I closed Gord's books and set them

343

aside. I couldn't think of anything to say to him. Then he spoke, a very soft question.

'Do you think Gord went to report us?'

His voice was full of dread and pain. I had been so busy with my own thoughts, I hadn't even worried about where Gord had gone. I considered what must have been going through Spink's mind: that alone of all his fellows, Gord had betrayed him, by upholding the honour code that we were all sworn to. And if Gord had done so, Spink might very well be sent home from the Academy, for he had, indisputably, struck first. And then the cowardly thought followed: if we all stuck up for Spink and Trist and said there had been no fight, Gord would appear to be the liar. Only he would have to leave.

And there we all were, stretched tight between loyalty to our patrol and the honour of the Academy. Which side would I stay with? Spink? Gord? I suddenly saw that all of us could be expelled over this. I felt weak and sick. There was no possible way to be completely honourable, to keep my oath to the Academy and to keep faith with my friends. I dropped back into my seat at the table. 'I don't know,' I said. And added, 'But if he had, surely they would have come up here by now. So perhaps not.'

'Then where did he go? And why?'

'I don't know. I don't even have any ideas.' Worry crept through me. Where could he have gone? The rule for first-years was clear: evenings should be spent in study and house-keeping tasks followed by an early bed. Outside, the barracks the weather was intemperate and walking about the grounds that we traversed several times each day on our way to classes offered little attraction. The physical rigours of the day sapped our interest in visiting the gymnasium in the evenings. Occasionally we had guest lecturers or poets or musicians who performed for us in the evening, but attendance at those events was mandatory and not regarded by any of us as recreational. Nothing like that was scheduled tonight. Surely Gord

344

would not have attempted to venture past the guards at the gates of the Academy? I could only picture him walking by himself about the grounds in the evening drizzle. It was a sad image, and yet I felt little sympathy for him. More than half the evening's disaster was his fault. If, from the beginning, he had stood up to Trist's taunting, it would never have come to blows between Trist and Spink. For that matter, I seethed to myself, if he could simply control his appetite at table, he would lose the girth that made him such a target for mockery.

Such were my thoughts as I prepared for my evening's rest. My bookwork was not complete, and I felt out of sorts about that. I'd probably be punished with extra assignments tomorrow, to be completed over the days off. The others were expecting a fine holiday away from the Academy. I'd looked forward to at least having plenty of idleness. Now even that was taken from me. I sighed as I entered our bunkroom. Natred and Kort were already in their bunks, asleep or pretending to be so. Spink was at the washstand, holding a cold cloth against his bruised face. The night quiet was uncharacteristic of our room, the uneasy silence that followed a fight. It set me on edge.

As I shelved my books, I nudged my Dewara rock off the shelf. I caught it one-handed before it hit the floor and stood there, hefting its roughness and thinking. Some part of me was aware that I was being unfair to Gord as I fumed at him. It was still easier than being angry with Spink or even Trist. Gord, I thought to myself, was a much easier target for blame. I looked down at the rock in my hand, and for some reason I found myself thinking of all the stones I had left at home in my collection. How many times had I been a potential target for Sergeant Duril? What had he really been trying to teach me with all those stones? Or was I investing meaning into something that the sergeant had intended only as a simple exercise in wariness?

I was still holding the stone in my hand when the door to

345

our room was flung unceremoniously open. We all jumped at the intrusion. Nate opened his eyes and Kort leaned up on one elbow. Spink was caught half-bent, his fingers dripping a double handful of water halfway to his face. I turned, expecting Gord. It took a moment for me to realize that it was not a cadet officer, but only Caulder standing in our doorway. Rain had beaded on his hat and dripped onto our clean floor from his cloak. His nose was red with cold. He had a grinning sneer on his face as he said pompously, 'I'm to bring Cadets Kester and Burvelle to the Infirmary. Right away.'

'What for?' Spink demanded.

'We aren't sick,' I added rather stupidly.

'I know that!' Caulder was properly disdainful of our ignorance. 'You're to come and fetch that fat cadet back to Carneston House. The doctor has certified that he's fit to return for duty.'

'What? What happened to him?'

'What I said!' Caulder said disgustedly. 'Come on. I'll take you to him.' Then, as I obediently placed my rock on my bookshelf and prepared to follow him, he demanded suddenly, 'What's that?'

'What?'

'That rock. What's it for? What is it?'

I was sick of this youngster, for his lack of manners and the way he flung about his father's authority without any regard for his elders. 'The only thing you need to know about it is that it isn't yours,' I responded tartly. 'Let's go.'

If I'd had younger brothers rather than younger sisters, perhaps I would not have been so shocked by what happened next. Caulder shot out his hand and snatched the rock off the shelf.

'Give me that!' I exclaimed, outraged that he had taken what was mine.

'I want to look at it,' he replied, turning away from me with the rock in his hands. He reminded me of a little animal trying to hide a piece of food while he devoured it. He seemed to have completely forgotten his mission.

'What happened to Gord?' Spink demanded again.

'Someone beat him.' A note of satisfaction was in this announcement. I could not see Caulder's face but I was certain he was smiling. A flash of anger went through me. I reached over his shoulder, seized his wrist and squeezed it. He released the rock and I caught it and restored it to my shelf in one motion.

'Let's go,' I told him as he looked up at me, caught between incredulity and anger. He cradled his arm to his chest, rubbing his wrist and glaring. His voice was venomous as he said, 'Don't ever put your filthy hands on me again, you peasant bastard. This adds another strike to my tally against you. Don't think others don't know about how you poisoned me with that "tobacco" and then laughed at me. Don't think I don't have friends who can help me take revenge on you.'

I was shocked. 'I had nothing to do with that!' I blurted out angrily before I could realize that keeping silent would have been better. I'd all but admitted that his tobacco experience had been a cruel prank, not an accident.

'It happened here,' he said coldly, turning away. 'It was your patrol. All of you were in on it. Don't think I don't know that. Don't think my father doesn't know how you misused me. It's as the Writ says, Cadet: "Evil befalls the evildoer in its time, for the good god is just." Now why don't you follow me and get a good look at justice?'

Still cradling his bruised wrist, he stalked away. I paused only to put on my winter cloak. Spink had dressed hastily for the weather and was waiting for us. He glanced back at me as we went down the stairs and his face was pale. 'Were you told to fetch us specifically?' he asked Caulder in a neutral voice.

Caulder spoke disdainfully. 'Fat Gord seemed to think you were the only ones who'd turn out to help him back to the dormitories. Not a surprise, really.'

We did not speak after that. Sergeant Rufet lifted his eyes to watch us leave but said nothing. I wondered if he already knew our mission or was giving us enough rope to hang ourselves.

We stepped out into a cold, persistent rain. My cloak had not dried completely from its earlier use. The wool kept the warmth in but grew heavier with every step I took in the downpour. Caulder turned up his collar and hastened ahead of us.

I had not been to the infirmary before, having had no occasion to go there. It was a wood-framed building, set well away from the classroom structures and busy pathways of the Academy campus, tall and narrow and tainted a garish yellow by the oil lamps that burned in front of it. We followed Caulder up onto a porch that creaked beneath our steps. He opened the door without knocking and without pausing to put off his hat or cloak, took us through an antechamber where a bored old man dozed at his desk. 'We're here for the fat one,' he said. He did not wait for a response from the orderly but crossed the room briskly to open a second door. It led to a corridor, unevenly lit by badly spaced lamps. He marched down it, entered the second doorway and even before we reached the threshold, we heard him say, 'I've brought his friends to take him back to Carneston House.'

Spink and I crowded through the door and into the small room. Gord sat on the edge of a narrow bed. He was dressed, but his buttons were not fastened, and he sat with his upper body tilted forward and his head drooping. The knees of his uniform trousers were wet and muddy. He did not look up at us as we came in but the man attending him did. 'Thank you, Caulder. You should probably go home now. Doubtless your mother will be wondering where you are, out so late.' The man's words fell somewhere between a polite suggestion and a steel command. I judged that he was not fond of Caulder and anticipated an argument from him.

348

He got it. 'My mother has not ruled my hours since I was ten, Dr Amicas. And my father—'

'Will, I am sure, be very glad to see you and to hear how helpful you were in letting us know that you had found an injured cadet. Thank you, Caulder. Please give your father my regards.'

Caulder stood stubbornly a moment longer, but as we all kept silent and avoided looking at him, he soon realized that he would witness nothing interesting by staying. 'Good evening, Doctor. I shall convey your regards to Colonel Stiet.' He added his last words pointedly, as if we could somehow have forgotten that his father was the commander of the Academy. Then he about-faced smartly and left the small room. We listened to the clacking of his boots as the sound receded, and then heard the door shut behind him. Only then did the doctor look at us.

He was a spare old man with a fringe of trimmed grey hair around a bald pate. He wore rimless spectacles and a white smock over his uniform shirt. A spattering of faded brown on the smock showed that it was well used. The hand he held out to each of us in turn was veiny but strong. 'Dr Amicas,' he introduced himself gravely. He smelled strongly of pipe tobacco. He nodded his head almost continuously. He looked at us more over than through his spectacles when he spoke. 'Young Caulder came racing in here close to an hour ago, abrim with the news that he'd found a New Noble cadet trying to crawl back to Carneston House.' The doctor worked his mouth for an instant as if wishing for a pipe that wasn't there. He seemed to choose his words carefully. 'He seemed to know a mite too much about this cadet for someone who'd just chanced upon him. Of course your friend there hasn't said anything different from Caulder's tale, so I'll have to take it at face value.' He gestured at Gord as he spoke, but Gord still didn't look up at us. He hadn't made a sound since we entered the room.

349

'What happened to him, sir?' Spink asked the doctor, almost as if Gord weren't sitting there.

'He says he slipped on the steps of the library and fell all the way to the bottom, and then tried to crawl back to his dormitory.' The doctor gave in to himself. He took a pipe from one trouser pocket and a pouch of tobacco from the other. He loaded his pipe carefully and lit it before he spoke again, and his tone was clinical. 'However, it looks to me as if he was attacked by several men and restrained while someone hit him. Repeatedly, but not in the face.' The doctor took off his glasses and rubbed the bridge of his nose wearily. 'I'm afraid that in my years here, I've become an expert in the bruises that a bushwhacking leaves. I'm so tired of this sort of thing,' he added.

'Caulder told us that Gord was beaten,' I said. At my words, Gord lifted his head and gave me a look that I could not interpret.

'I suspect he witnessed it,' the doctor said. 'Caulder is often the first one to run and tell me of injuries to first-year cadets. Lately he has reported several "accidents" befalling new nobility cadets, accidents he claims to have witnessed. The first-years from Skeltzin Hall seem to be remarkably unlucky about falling down stairs and walking into doors. I'm distressed to see that clumsiness spreading to Carneston House.' The doctor set his glasses firmly back on his nose and clasped his hands in front of himself. 'But no one ever contradicts what that little gossip-monger lad says. Thus I have no basis on which to attempt to put a stop to it.' He looked pointedly at Gord, but the fat cadet was working at his buttons and didn't meet the doctor's gaze. Gord's knuckles were scuffed and grazed. I folded my lips, guessing that he'd got in a few licks of his own before he went down.

'New Noble first-years are being beaten?' Spink sounded far more shocked than I was.

Dr Amicas gave a brief snort of bitter laughter. 'Well, that

350

is what I would say, based solely on my examinations. But it's not just first-years experiencing this plague of "accidents". My written reports speak of everything from falling tree branches to tumbling down a rain-soaked riverbank.' He looked at us severely. 'That second-year cadet nearly drowned. I don't know what makes all of you keep silent as you do; will you wait until one of you is killed before you make complaint? Because until you speak up on your own behalf, there is nothing I can do for any of you. Nothing.'

'Sir, respectfully, this is the first we have heard of this. I hadn't heard of any cadets having such accidents.' Spink was appalled. I held my silence. I had the most peculiar feeling of hearing something that I'd already known. Had I truly suspected such things were going on at the Academy?

'No? Well, I've had to send two lads home this year already. One for a badly shattered leg and the fellow who ended up in the river with a punctured lung came down with pneumonia. And now this young man, with fist-sized bruises all over his chest and belly from "falling down the steps".' He snatched his glasses off again, and this time polished them furiously with the edge of his smock. 'What do you think? That the bullies who do this will respect you for not reporting them? That there is some sort of honour or courage to enduring this sort of abuse?'

'I hadn't heard anything about it, sir,' Spink repeated doggedly. An edge of anger tinged his voice now.

'Well. You do now. So think about it. All three of you.' He had been leaning against the bunk that Gord sat on. He straightened suddenly. 'I was born to be a healer, not a soldier. Circumstance puts this uniform on my back, but I cover it with the smock of my vocation. Yet sometimes I feel that I'm more of a fighter than you lads born to soldier. Why do you take this? Why?'

None of us attempted to answer. He shook his old head at us, and I suspect he felt disgust for our lack of spark. 'Well, take your friend back to your dormitory. There's nothing broken and nothing bleeding, and he should be able to get through the day tomorrow. In two or three days, he'll feel like himself again.' He swung his attention more directly to Gord. 'You drink one of those powders I gave you tonight, and another in the morning. They'll make you a bit woozy, but you'll probably manage to get through your classes. And eat less, Cadet! If you weren't fat as a hog, you'd have been able to put up a better fight, or at least run away. You're supposed to look like a soldier, not a tavern keeper!'

Gord made no reply, but only lowered his head more. I winced at the harshness of the doctor's last words, even as I had to agree with them. Gord moved slowly to get off the bed; I could almost feel his pain as he stood. He grunted softly with pain as he shouldered into his jacket. It was caked with mud and pine needles. He hadn't picked up that dirt from the library steps. He fumbled at his jacket buttons as if to do them up and then let his hands drop to his sides.

'You didn't have to send for them. I could have got back by myself. Sir.' Those were the only words that Gord spoke. When Spink and I tried to help him stand, he waved us away. He came to his feet, lurched slightly, and then walked toward the door. Spink and I followed him. The doctor watched us leave.

Outside the infirmary, the rain had stopped but the leafless trees were still swaying to the storm's wind.

'What happened to you? Where did you go, why did you leave?'

When Gord didn't answer, Spink added, 'I beat Trist. He apologized to me. He would have apologized to you, too, if you had been there.'

Gord had never been a fast walker. He lagged between us, as ever, and when he spoke in a low voice, I had to turn my head and look back at him to hear his answer in the night wind. 'Oh. And that solves everything, doesn't it? I'm sure

352

that has put an end to his mockery and resentment of me forever. Thank you, Spink.'

It was the first time I'd ever heard Gord speak sarcastically or bitterly. I stopped and so did Spink. Gord walked on, both arms crossed protectively over his unbuttoned jacket and gut, and passed between us without pausing.

Spink and I exchanged glances and then hurried after Gord. He caught at Gord's elbow. 'I still want to know what really happened,' Spink demanded. 'I want to know why you just left the room like that.'

It suddenly occurred to me that perhaps I wouldn't like the answers to those questions.

Gord shrugged off Spink's hand. He kept walking as he spoke, but he sounded short of breath. 'I left because I didn't want to witness anyone breaking an Academy rule. Because, by the honour code, I would have had to report it.' His voice was tight, from anger or from speaking past pain. I could not tell which. 'And what happened to me was that I went to the library. I found it closed. Then, I "fell down the steps". And afterwards, Caulder ran and reported it, and some orderlies were sent to pick me up and take me to the infirmary. When the doctor asked me for the names of two cadets who might be willing to walk me back to my dormitory, I gave him yours. But only because if I had not, he would not have released me tonight. And I'm very much looking forward to my family carriage coming for me tomorrow evening.' He did not look at either of us. We matched our pace to his.

'Why are you angry at me?' Spink demanded in a low, tight voice. The question I wanted to ask was what had really happened to him, but I bit it back, knowing that until those two sorted things out between them, I was not going to get any response.

'You don't know?' It wasn't really a question. Gord just wanted to make Spink admit it.

'No, I don't! I'd think you'd be grateful to me, for

353

standing up for you when you hadn't the spine to do it for yourself!' Spink's anger flashed from him.

For ten steps, Gord kept silent. When he did speak, I judged he had spent that time mastering his temper and ordering his words. 'I'm a man grown, Spink. I'm fat, and perhaps that is a fault or perhaps it is just the way the good god made me. But it does not make me a child nor does it make me any less in command of my own life. You think that I should fight those who are cruel. The doctor back there thinks I should change myself so they would have less excuse to be cruel to me. But what I think is that I should not have to do either.'

Gord halted. Then he abruptly left the gravelled pathway and walked across the frozen lawn to an oak tree. He leaned on its wet black trunk, catching his breath. We were silent, and the heavy drops from the branches above us dripped down on us. Looking at him, some memory of a memory teased at the corner of my awareness. He reminded me of something, or someone. Then Gord spoke again, and the half-recalled image fled my mind.

'I think that the ones who taunt are the ones who should be pressured to change. I have no delusions about myself. In a physical fight, Trist would best me easily. And, having won it, he would then use that superiority to justify however he treated me afterwards. He is saying that my physical condition should determine how he treats me. And you think that because you have bested him in a physical struggle, you have proved something to him. But you haven't. All you have done is shown that you agree with him, that the man who can physically defeat another is the man who should make the rules. I don't agree with that. If I attempt to live by those rules, I will be beaten, and I do not intend to be beaten. So I will not be goaded into a physical confrontation with Trist or anyone else. I will win another way.'

A silence fell among us. There was such a sharp contrast between the bravery of Gord's words, and the fat boy leaning on a tree and puffing. I think Spink saw the same contradiction because he grudgingly pointed out, 'We are military, Gord. What is a soldier about if not besting another man physically? It's how we support our king and defend our country.'

Gord pushed away from the tree. We followed him back to the path and resumed his slow pace. The wind was building and the first wild drops warned that another squall was on the way. I wanted to hurry but did not think that Gord could keep up with us. In the dormitory buildings nearby, lights were starting to go out. If we came in after lights-out, Sergeant Rufet would have a few choice questions for us. I didn't want any more demerits to march off. I gritted my teeth and put it down to the cost of my friendship with Spink.

'On the lowest, simplest level, the military and the cavalla are about physical might. I'll concede that. But the King made my father a noble, and when my father made me, he made me a soldier son with the opportunity to serve as an officer. And that isn't about physical strength, Spink. No officer could prevail if his troops turned on him. An officer leads by example and intelligence. I have the intelligence. I won't set the example that I can be beaten physically and cowed that way. And I won't let you set it on my behalf. If you fight Trist again, know that you are not fighting for me, but for yourself. You seek to salve your own bruised pride, that you have to accept help from someone who is fat. Somehow, you think that reflects badly on you, and that is why Trist can goad you to fight. But my battles belong to me, and I'll fight them my own way. And I shall win.'

A terrible silence fell then, and it seemed to bring on the rain that suddenly drenched us. I longed to sprint for shelter. Gord seemed to share my impulse for he clasped his belly more firmly, lowered his head to the storm and walked faster. I finally felt I could speak. 'What did happen to you, Gord? Caulder said you were beaten.'

Gord was puffing more heavily now, but he managed an answer. 'Caulder can say whatever he likes to whoever he likes. I fell down the library steps. That is the truth.'

Spink figured it out before I did. 'Part of the truth, you mean, and that's why you can hold to it. You hold the honour code above all else. When did you fall down the steps, Gord? When you ran from them, or after they had beaten you?'

Gord stumped stolidly on. I looked over at Spink, blinking raindrops from my lashes. 'He's not going to answer you.' I felt stupid for only now realizing what should have been obvious to me. By sticking to his story, Gord kept the battle on his territory. Those who had beaten him could not openly boast of it. Doubtless, their friends would know of it. But if Gord refused to admit that he had been beaten, if he refused to acknowledge a defeat from them, he took some of their triumph away.

I walked more slowly, falling somewhat behind them as I pondered. In bemoaning the fact that both Spink and Trist seemed to have a natural leadership that I lacked, I had over-looked something. Trist based his ability to attract followers on his golden charisma. I had already seen its effect on young Caulder, with disastrous results. Spink was tough and stubborn and the son of a war hero. He gave and demanded great loyalty. Those of us who followed him were swayed by those things, but the more I thought about it, the more it seemed to me that he did not always look far enough ahead and reason out where his actions might lead. Tonight, I had admired that he had stood up to Trist, despite the differences in their sizes, and I had been impressed that he used unconventional tactics to bend the larger man to his will. But now I had to consider the far-reaching consequences of those actions. He and Trist, by taking their rivalry to blows, had put all the lads in our patrol into a compromising position. We had all witnessed an Academy rule being broken, and none of us had kept our honour vow to report it. It bothered me, even though I knew that I would have felt more truly disgraced if I had raced off to report the infraction.

Only Gord had had the foresight to save himself from that. Even now, battered and facing a hellish day tomorrow, he forced his body to be subject to his intellect. I had considered him weak because of his girth. But in truth, now that I pondered it, he did not seem to indulge his appetite any more than the rest of us did. Perhaps he was simply born to be a portly man and always would be.

And perhaps he was demonstrating a quiet leadership that I had not witnessed before. Even if his only follower was himself, I admired his foresight. Then, my mind suddenly transposed an idea that I'd assumed. I had thought that Gord had attached himself to Spink because of the small cadet's leadership. But perhaps, in offering his help to Spink, Gord had been, not following him, but offering his leadership. So, then, if Spink followed Gord, and I followed Spink, was it not Gord whom I was actually accepting as my commander?

We had almost reached the walkway to Carneston House when Caulder ran past us, headed back toward the infirmary. He paused, and spun, skipping backwards as he shouted at us, 'Seems to be an unlucky night for New Nobles' sons! I'm off to fetch the doctor again.' Then he turned and ran off into the darkness.

'I don't like the sound of that,' I said to Spink.

'He came from the direction of the carriageway,' Gord gasped. 'We should go see who is hurt.'

I shook my head. 'You're done in, Gord. Go up to bed. Spink, make sure he gets there while I go find out what Caulder was talking about.'

I had expected Spink to argue with me, or for Gord to say he could get back to the dormitory alone. Instead, Gord nodded miserably, and Spink said, 'If you don't come back soon, I'll come looking for you. Be careful.'

That was a strange admonition to receive on the campus

of the King's Cavalla Academy. I wished I hadn't said I'd go, but I couldn't turn back now. I nodded to Spink and Gord and ran off toward the carriageway. The wind gusted and the rain slapped my face as I ran. I saw no one, and I was beginning to hope that Caulder had lied. I had actually turned back and was hurrying home to Carneston House when I heard someone groan. I stopped and looked back. In the shadows of the trees by the carriageway, something moved. I ran back to find a man lying prone on the wet earth. He was wearing a dark cloak, and the deep shadows of the trees had hidden him from me. I was surprised Caulder had found him.

'Are you hurt?' I asked him stupidly as I knelt down by his side. Then the reek of raw spirits hit me. 'Or just drunk?' I amended my question. My disapproval must have been in my voice. Cadets were forbidden to drink on campus, and surely no instructor would be falling down drunk on the grounds.

'Not drunk,' he said in a faint hoarse whisper. The voice was familiar. I leaned closer, trying to make out his features. Mud and blood caked them, but I recognized Cadet Lieutenant Tiber, who had rescued me from humiliation during initiation. I decided not to argue with him about being drunk.

'But you're hurt. Lie still. Caulder's gone to fetch the doctor.' It was too dark for me to know what sort of injuries he had, but I knew better than to try to move him. The best I could do for him was to keep vigil by him until Caulder sent help.

Despite my words, he scrabbled faintly at the ground, as if he would get up. 'Bushwhacked me. Four of them. My papers?'

I looked around. A few feet away, I saw a dark shape on the ground. It proved to be a satchel. Near it I found a muddied book and a handful of trampled papers. I gathered them up by touch and brought them back to him. 'I have your papers,' I told him.

He made no response.

'Lieutenant Tiber?'

'He's passed out,' a voice said. I nearly jumped out of my skin. Sergeant Duril would have done more than hit me with a rock if he'd been there. I'd been completely oblivious to the three figures who had walked up on me in the pouring rain.

'Drunk as a beggar,' said the man behind me and to my left. I turned my head to see him but he took a couple of steps back. I couldn't make out his face, but his voice was almost familiar. I'd caught a glimpse of his jacket under his coat. He was a cadet. 'We saw him arrive here. Carriage brought him from town. He staggered this far and passed out.'

If I hadn't been kneeling by Tiber, I don't think I would have made the connection. I was coldly certain of it now. The cadet talking to me was a second-year, Jaris, the one who had ordered me to strip during initiation.

I said a foolhardy thing. I only realized it when the words were out of my mouth. 'He said he was ambushed by four men.'

'He talked to you?' Dismay was clear in the voice of the third man. I didn't recognize his voice at all. It was shrill with alarm.

'What did he say?' demanded Cadet Ordo. The pieces of the puzzle were fitting in all around me, and I didn't like the picture they made. 'What did he tell you?' Ordo demanded, coming closer. I don't think he cared if I recognized him or not.

'Just that. That four men had jumped him.' My voice shook. I was shivering with cold, but icy fear was also creeping up my spine.

'Well, but he's drunk! Who could believe a thing he said? Why don't you run along, Cadet? We'll get help for him.'

'Caulder's already gone for help,' I pointed out. I was almost certain they knew that. 'He's the one who sent me here,' I added more boldly, and then could not decide if that was a wise thing to say or not. I doubted Caulder would give witness against them if they dragged me off, killed me and threw me in the river. In the pouring rain and cold wind, with Tiber dead or unconscious before me, it did not seem such an impossible thing that they might kill me. I wanted so badly to stand up, brush the mud from my knees, and tell them I was going back to my dormitory. Yet if I was not coward enough to leave Tiber there, I was also not brave enough to voice what I suspected. They'd seen him get out of the carriage, noticed he was drunk, and known that in that condition, he was no match for them.

'Go home, Cadet Burvelle,' Ordo quietly commanded me. 'We have things under control here.'

Coincidence saved me from having to decide if I were a man or a coward that night. I heard the rasp of hurrying feet on the walkway. Through the rain and dark I made out the figure of Dr Amicas. He was carrying a lantern and it made a small circle of light around him as he came. Two brawnier men followed him, carrying a stretcher between them. The relief that surged through me weakened my knees, and I felt lucky I wasn't standing. I waved my arm over my head and called out loudly, 'Over here! Cadet Lieutenant Tiber is hurt.'

'We think he got beat up in town and then came home here in a carriage and passed out. He's drunk.' All of this was volunteered by Cadet Ordo. I expected to hear the others confirm it, but when I looked around, they were gone.

'Out of the way, boy!' Dr Amicas commanded me. I moved to one side, and he set his lantern on the ground beside Tiber. 'This is bad,' he said at first sight of Tiber's face. The doctor was still puffing from his trot here. I turned aside, thinking I might be sick. A blow from something had split his scalp and it was sagging open over his ear. 'Did he speak to you?'

'He was unconscious when we found him,' Ordo volunteered quickly.

360

The doctor was not a dull-witted man. 'I thought you said he came here in a carriage. Surely the driver didn't carry an unconscious cadet over here and dump him before they left?' Hard cold scepticism was in his voice. It made me brave enough to speak.

'He talked to me a little bit, when I first got here. When we were taking Gord back to Carneston House, Caulder ran past us. He said someone was hurt. So I came here, thinking I might be able to help. Tiber was conscious when I got here. He said he wasn't drunk. And that four men had attacked him. And he asked me to be sure his papers were safe.'

The doctor lowered his face, sniffed at Tiber suspiciously, and then drew back. 'Well, he certainly doesn't smell sober. But drinking doesn't lay a man's scalp open either. And he didn't get this sort of mud on himself in town. He's damn lucky not to be dead after a blow to the head like that. Load him up on the stretcher and let's get him back to the infirmary.'

The doctor stood and held the lantern for the two orderlies who carefully edged Tiber onto the stretcher. In the lantern's feeble light, the doctor looked older than he had in the infirmary. The lines in his face seemed deeper and his eyes were flat.

'He might have got muddy here after he fell trying to walk back to his dormitory,' Ordo suddenly volunteered. We all turned to look at him. The reasoning sounded laborious to me, and the doctor must have agreed, for he suddenly snapped at him, 'You'll come with us. I want you to write down everything you saw and sign it. Burvelle, you go back to your dormitory. And Caulder! Get yourself home this instant. I don't want to see you again tonight.'

Caulder had been holding back at the edge of the circle of light, staring at Tiber with an expression of both fascination and horror. At the doctor's words, he startled, and then scampered off into the night. I stooped and picked up Tiber's satchel and papers.

'Give those to me,' the doctor commanded me brusquely, and I passed them over to him.

Dr Amicas's path led in the same direction as mine, so I walked on the other side of the stretcher from him. The swaying light of the lantern made the shadows travel over Tiber's face, distorting his features. He was very pale.

I left the miserable cavalcade at the walkway to Carneston House. The windows in the upper floors were all dark, but a lantern still burned by the door. When I went inside, I took the last of my courage and reported to Sergeant Rufet. He stared at me as I stammered out my excuse for coming in after lights-out. I thought he would take me to task over it, but he only nodded and said, 'Your friend said you'd run off to see about someone who was hurt. Next time, come here first and report it to me. I could have sent some of the older cadets with you.'

'Yes, sir,' I said wearily. I turned to go.

'It was Cadet Lieutenant Tiber, you said.'

I turned back. 'Yes, sir. He'd been beaten up pretty badly. He was drunk. So I don't think he put up much of a fight.'

Sergeant Rufet knit his brows at me. 'Drunk? Not Tiber. That boy doesn't drink. Somebody's lying.' And then, as if he suddenly realized what he had said, the sergeant snapped his jaws shut. 'Go to bed, Cadet. Quietly,' he told me an instant later. I went.

I found Spink waiting for me by the hearth in his night-shirt. He followed me into our room, and as I undressed in the dark, I quietly told him everything. He was silent. I shook out my damp uniform but knew that it would still be wet when I donned it again tomorrow. It was not a pleasant thought to take to bed with me. I tried, instead, to focus my mind on Carsina, but she suddenly seemed far away in both time and distance; girls, perhaps, did not matter as much as deciding how I would make it through the rest of my first year. I was in my bed before Spink asked his question.

'Was the liquor on his breath?'

'He reeked of it.' We both knew what that meant. As soon as he recovered, Tiber would be suspended and face discipline. If he recovered.

'No. I mean, was he breathing the smell at you? Or was it just on his clothes?'

I thought about it for a minute. 'I don't know. I didn't think to check anything like that. I just smelled spirits, very strong, when I got close to him.'

Another silence followed my words. Then, 'Dr Amicas seems very sharp. He'll know if Tiber was really drunk or not.'

'Probably,' I agreed, but I wasn't sure I believed it. There wasn't much I had faith in any more.

I fell asleep, and dreamed deep. The old fat tree woman sat with her back against her tree and I stood before her. Rain was falling on both of us. Although it drenched me, it did not wet her. As soon as it touched her, it was absorbed as if her flesh were thirsty earth. I didn't mind the rain. It was gentle and soft, and its chill touch was almost pleasant. The forest glen felt very familiar, as if I had been there often. I was not dressed against the weather, but sat bare-limbed in the rain, enjoying it. 'Come,' she said. 'Walk and talk with me. I need to be sure I understand what I have seen through your eyes.'

We left her tree, and I led the way, walking on a winding path through a forest of giants. In some places, the overhead canopy of leaves sheltered us completely from the falling rain. In others, the water plashed down, from leaf to twig to branch to leaf and then down, to soak into the forest floor. It did not bother either of us. I noticed in passing that although she seemed to walk freely with me whenever I glanced at her she appeared to be in some way part of the trees. Her hand would touch the bark of one, her hair would tangle against another. Always, always, she was in contact with them. Despite the swaying bulk of her body, her heavy walk had an odd grace. She was strength and opulence in my dream. The pillows of flesh that softened her silhouette to curves were no more repulsive to me than the immense girth of a great tree or the vast umbrella of its branches and foliage. Her largeness was wealth, a mark of skill and success for a people who lived by hunting and gathering. And this, too, seemed familiar.

The deeper I went into her forest, the more I recalled of this world. I knew the path I followed, knew that it would lead to the rocky place where a stream ran down from a stony cleft to suddenly launch itself in a glittering silver arc into the forest below. It was a dangerous place. The rocks close to the edge were always green and slick, but nowhere else was the water so cool and so fresh, even when the rain was falling. It was a place I cherished. She knew that. Letting me go there in the dream was one of my rewards.

Rewards for what?

'What would happen, then,' she asked me. 'If many of the soldier sons who are to be the leaders were slain, and never ventured east to bring their people against the forest? Would this stop the road? Would it turn these people back?'

I had been thinking of something else. I came back to her question from my distraction. 'It might slow them for a time. But it would not stop them. In truth, nothing will stop the road. You can only delay it. My people believe that the road will bring riches to them. Lumber from the forest, meat and furs. And eventually, a way to the sea beyond the mountains, and trade with the people there.' I shook my head in resignation. 'As long as wealth beckons, my people will find a way to it.'

She scowled at me. 'You say "my people" when you speak of them. But I have told you. You are no longer of those ones. We have taken you and you belong to The People, now.' She cocked her head and stared deep into my eyes. I felt she looked inside me and out the other side, as it were, to some other eyes I did not know I had. 'What is it, son of a soldier? Do you begin to wake to both worlds? That is not good. Not yet should you do that.' She set her hand fondly on the top of my head.

It was a comforting touch that dispelled all anxiety. Some worry I had felt had slipped away from me. All would be well.

She lifted both her hands to her face and hair. She smoothed them over her head as if to ease the anxiety I knew she felt. Then she looked at me through her plump fingers. 'You still have not spoken of your magic, soldier's son. At the moment it was given to you, it began to work through you. What have you done for us? The magic chose you. I felt it take you. All know that once the magic of the god touches a man, he does his task. You were to turn the intruders back and make those who are here leave. What did you do?'

'I do not understand what you are asking me.'

Both her question and my response were as familiar to me as my evening prayers, learned at my mother's knee. She tried again to explain. 'You would have done something. Some action of yours is supposed to begin the magic that you will finish when you are a great man. Telling me will not stop the magic. It will only ease my fears. Please. Just tell me. Put my mind at ease, so I may tell the forest that the beginning of the end of waiting has begun. The guardians cannot dance much longer. They weary. They die. And when they all die, there will no longer be a wall. It will fall, and nothing will remain to hold the intruders at bay. They will walk freely under the trees, cutting and burning. You know what they will do. We have seen it.'

We were nearly to the waterfall. I longed to see it. I tried to see it through the forest, but the trees leaned together, blocking my view. 'I do not understand your words.'

She sighed, like wind in the trees. 'If such a thing could be, I would say the magic chose poorly. I would say that one of The People would have known better how to use the given gift.' She shrugged, lifting the soft roundness of her shoulders and then letting them fall. 'I will have to do what is within my power to do. I do not do it lightly. My time for doing things should be past. This should be only my time for being. But I fear you cannot turn them back by yourself. My strength is needed, still.' She sighed and then she brushed her fat hands together. Dust, fine brown dust, fell from the surfaces of her palms as they passed one another. 'I have thought of a thing, and now I have decided I will do it. I will send one of the old magics to you. With it, we can harvest from the intruders some of what they are. No knife is sharper than a man's own turned against him. Perhaps it will give us more time to discover what it is you have done to help us.' She lifted her hand and waved it oddly at me. I sensed immense power in the simple gesture. 'When the magic finds you, it will signal you. So. Then it will begin. Do not struggle against it.'

I felt a terrible fear. She stared at me, the colour of her eyes going darker in disapproval. 'You should go now. Stop thinking about these things.'

I awoke with a start to deep darkness, and the sounds of rain beating on the roof above me and the stentorian breathing of my fellows around me. The rags of my dreams hung about my mind. I touched them and tried to pull them together, but they went to threads in my fingers. I felt dread unlike the fear I might feel from a nightmare. This was the dread of something real, something I could not recall. The wind gusted, and the rain suddenly pattered harder and swifter against roof and windowpane. It lulled, then gusted again. I listened to that, sleepless, until morning, and then rose wearily to face another day.

FOURTEEN

Cousin Epiny

I don't know how Gord staggered through his classes the next day. As I feared, I earned punishment exercises for my incomplete maths assignment. My spirits were low. When I heard the rumour that Cadet Lieutenant Tiber had been found disgustingly drunk and was not to be suspended but simply expelled from the Academy for conduct unbecoming an officer, my misery was complete. I suspected his punishment was undeserved, but had no real proof to offer on his behalf. I still wondered if I should not take my suspicions to Dr Amicas, and wondered, too, if my reluctance to do so was cowardice or pragmatism.

The news of Tiber's disgrace eclipsed all curiosity about what had befallen Gord. I was a bit disillusioned with my roommates, for most of them accepted unquestioningly the tale that he had taken all those bruises tumbling down the library steps. He had developed a fine black eye from his 'fall' and limped as we marched to and from our classes, yet seemed quietly pleased about something. I decided I didn't understand him at all.

I was feeling bleak and downhearted when I returned to Carneston House at noon, and found an unexpected missive from my uncle. In it, he mentioned the upcoming days of freedom, and assured me that he would come to get me on Fiveday evening so I would not have to spend my time in the dormitory. Spink, to his credit, tried to look happy for me when I shared the news with him, though we both knew it condemned him to remaining behind alone there.

'I need the study time,' he declared. 'And I know you'll enjoy yourself there. Don't worry about me. Bring me back some of those cinnamon cakes your little cousin baked for you last time, and have a good time.'

Nate and Kort had also received letters. To their dismay, they found that the plans had been changed. They would spend the night at Nate's great-aunt in Old Thares. Their sisters and sweethearts would be housed in Kort's uncle's home. The evening tryst the four had secretly planned was abruptly doomed, and Nate's younger sister was soundly denounced as a tattletale.

We completed our afternoon classes, and then hurried back to our barracks to pack. As we were climbing the stairs up to our room, Gord actually passed me on the steps. By the time I reached the study room, he was coming out the door with his previously packed bag slung over his shoulder. A broad grin dominated his fat and swollen face.

'What are you so chipper about?' I demanded.

He shrugged. 'I'll see my parents over the break. My father has come to town for the Council meeting. And I always enjoy staying with my uncle. And Cilima will be visiting there as well. She lives only a few miles from my uncle's house.'

'Who is Cilima?' I demanded, and all around me, the other cadets paused to hear the answer.

'My fiancée,' Gord asserted, and suddenly blushed a deep red. There was some scepticism and mockery, but he quietly produced a miniature of a raven-haired girl with large black eyes. Her beauty stunned me, and when Trist archly asked if she knew the fate that awaited her, Gord replied with dignity that her affection and belief in him were the keystone to his persevering through difficult times. Again, I was struck by the realization that there seemed to be more to Gord than any of us had imagined. He was the first of us to leave, and the others followed soon after, for they had all packed the night before.

Spink followed me to our room and watched woefully as I packed, and then bravely accompanied me down to the drive to await my uncle's carriage. He stood beside me, talking as we waited. Other carriages and conveyances were coming and going, bearing off cadets. I could tell he was eaten up with envy that I would escape the Academy routine for a full two days, but he was covering it well, saying only that I should enjoy food cooked for the pleasure of eating it rather than the convenience of feeding.

I had expected only that my uncle would send a carriage for me. Thus I was taken aback when the driver pulled in his horses and I saw that not only my uncle but also my Cousin Epiny had come to fetch me. The coachman descended to open the door and my uncle emerged to greet me. I introduced him to Spink, of course, and Uncle Sefert graciously shook hands with him and asked him several questions about how he was enjoying the Academy and how his studies were progressing. Epiny, left unattended in the carriage, immediately climbed out without assistance. I watched her from the corner of my eye as she wandered a short distance down the walk, studying the grounds and the Administrative Building with her direct, inquisitive stare. She looked like a stick in a large lace collar. I was accustomed to seeing women and girls of her age in the voluminous flounces and bustles and hoops or whatever it was under their skirts that made them bell out so. Epiny's dress was a childish style in a stiff, shiny fabric of diagonal navy and white stripes. It was short enough that I could see she wore little black boots instead of slippers. Her hat looked like a cock-eyed tower with lace and three blue flowers sprouting out the top of it as if it were a vase. It was so ugly that I was certain it was extremely fashionable. She had some sort of shiny charm on a string around her neck, which she held between her teeth. When she came closer, I realized it was a whistle shaped like an otter. Her breathing blew it very softly as she carried it. She came to stand at my uncle's elbow. She listened for a short time to Spink detailing his current project for drafting and then sighed out through the whistle, rather loudly.

My uncle gave her a sideways glance. I was embarrassed for her. I expected him to rebuke her, as my father surely would have done if either of my sisters had so put herself forward in the company of men. Instead, he made a slightly sour face at Spink and said, 'My rather spoiled daughter is hinting that I should introduce her to you.'

Spink glanced at me, and then reached his own decision. He made a very polite bow and said, 'I should be delighted to meet her, sir.'

'I'm sure,' my uncle replied dryly. 'Cadet Spinrek Kester, I am pleased to present to you my daughter, Epiny Helicia Burvelle. Epiny, take the whistle out of your mouth. I have never so regretted buying any trinket for you as I have that one.'

Epiny spat out the whistle so it dangled about her neck. She dropped an elegant curtsy to Spink. 'I am so pleased to meet you,' she said, quite correctly, and then spoiled it when she asked with a smile, 'And may I presume that you will be joining my cousin for his visit to our home?'

Spink glanced at my uncle in confusion tinged with alarm. 'Uh, no, Miss Burvelle, I was merely here to see your cousin off.'

Epiny swung her direct blue gaze to me and demanded, 'Why isn't he coming with you, Nevare? How could you be so stupid as not to have invited your friend?' Before I could even frame a reply to her accusation, she turned pleadingly to her father. 'Papa, please invite him now. It would be perfect. Then we'll have enough hands for a good game of

Towsers. Right now, we're short a player, and it is far too easy to deduce the cards if there are only two of us. Please, Papa! If you don't, then you shall have to be the one to round out the game for us.'

'Epiny!' her father rebuked her, but he sounded more abashed than angry.

'Please, Papa! I've been so bored and you told me you no longer approve of Mistress Lallie spending every week's end with us. I shall die of ennui this Sevday if we do not have some company to amuse me. Please, Papa! Mama will not mind! She is gone to wait on the Queen, so she will not complain of too much company and noisy games giving her a headache. Please!'

I had never heard a woman of her years whine and beg like a little child. I think I would have been more humiliated by Epiny's wheedling if a flush of forlorn hope had not passed over Spink's face. It was gone almost before I had seen it, but I knew my uncle had perceived it when he said gently, 'Epiny, my dear, I would be glad to invite Nevare's friend, but I fear we have left it too late for this visit. I would need to request permission of Colonel Stiet, and Cadet Kester would need time to pack a bag. Perhaps when the first-years are next given leave, we can invite him.'

She gave a harrumph and then crossed her arms stubbornly. 'Papa, it is not a problem, really. You can tell the colonel now that we are taking him, and while you are doing so, he could run back and quickly pack a few things. Men need very little in the way of clothing and such; I am sure he could be ready in no time at all. Couldn't you, Spinrek?' She smiled most charmingly as she unabashedly helped herself to his first name.

He was like a bird paralysed by a snake. Epiny and Spink were of a height and she cocked her head and smiled as she awaited his response. He looked into her open gaze and knew he must offer a reply and that the only polite response

371

would be to agree with her. 'I suppose I could,' he said, and then, as if suddenly aware that he had put my uncle in a difficult position, hastily added, 'But I doubt that Colonel Stiet would give me permission on such short notice.'

'Oh, Colonel Stiet? Don't fret about him. My mother knows his wife, and the colonel's lady would just die to do anything that might please her. I'll go with Papa and say that my mother would take it as such a personal favour if you were allowed to visit. Run and get your things so you don't keep us waiting when we come out. Come, Papa, let us go and see the colonel.'

'Epiny, you are impossible!' To my shock, my uncle was laughing at her deplorable behaviour.

'No, Father, I am certainly not! What is impossible is trying to remain amused when the house is as still as a tomb. Just look at how Nevare is already frowning at me! I do not think he will be very amusing at all. Purissa is too little to be any use at all in serious games . . . unless *you* will take time to play with us? Oh, would you, Papa? I can never guess your finish card when I play Towsers with you. Will you play?'

My uncle just looked weary at the question, and I found myself wondering how many hands of Towsers he'd had to play recently. I well recalled when my sisters had become infatuated with table marbles and made the game the focus of their lives for an entire summer. My father had tolerated it for a month, then exiled it to the schoolroom and finally banned it outright when my mother complained that chores and lessons were being shirked. Uncle Sefert seemed willing to try a different tactic. In a moment of decision, I saw both Spink and myself offered as sacrifice to Epiny's caprice. 'I'm sure I won't have to mention your mother to get Colonel Stiet to release Cadet Kester to me for the free days.' He paused to look at both of us severely and add, 'I trust you young men will bring your study materials so as to be well

372

prepared for Firstday. I do not want the colonel to think that my home is an undisciplined place of folly and leisure.'

'No, sir. I shall not neglect my books.' Spink's pleasure at the thought of two days away from the routine of the Academy shone in his face. He beamed as I had never seen him smile before.

I think that such an honest display of warm anticipation pleased my uncle, for he gruffly ordered us to 'put my nephew's bag in the boot, and then hurry off to fetch Kester's pack. Epiny, wait in the carriage. I will not be long.'

'But I want to go with them, to see Nevare's dormitory, Papa!'

For one horrifying moment, I thought my uncle would accede to this also. Instead, he held out his arm to her and patted it firmly with the fingers of his other hand. After a moment, she sighed in resignation, and obediently set her hand atop his arm. He escorted her back to the carriage, and then he himself went up the steps of the Administration Building. As the door closed behind him, she scowled at us from the window of the carriage and gestured imperiously that we should be on our way.

I loaded my bag into the boot and then Spink and I risked a demerit by running full tilt back to Carneston House. As Epiny had predicted, it took very little time for him to stuff his necessities into a small bag, and then we were off, again at a run. Although we had hurried, my uncle and Epiny were both waiting beside the carriage when we returned. Caulder was there too and despite my uncle's disapproving grimace, he seemed to be trying to strike up a conversation with Epiny. At that moment, it dawned on me that it was very likely that my cousin knew Caulder, if her mother and his mother were actually friends.

We caught the end of some admonition that Epiny was delivering to him as we hurried up, out of breath. '. . . just tell him you won't wear it, Caulder. Has your father no idea of how silly you look, all dressed up as a cadet when it will be years and years until you are really old enough to be one? It's as if you are playing dress-up in your nursery! Look at me, now. I'm *years* older than you are, and yet you don't see me all dressed up as if I were already a lady of the court or a married woman!'

Caulder's cheeks were very pink. He sucked in his lower lip, almost as if he feared it would tremble, and glared at Spink and me as if it were our fault we had overheard his friend's remonstrance. He brought his heels together and bowed to Epiny, saying only, 'I shall look forward to seeing you at Lake Foror for the spring holiday.'

'Perhaps,' she said vaguely, and then turning aside from him, she lifted her whistle to her lips and tweeted it at us inquiringly.

'We're ready,' I told her, almost defensively. The way Caulder was staring at us promised trouble for Spink and me later. I felt it unwise to ignore the boy completely, so I bid him a stiff farewell, as did Spink. I suddenly wanted, more than ever, to be away from the Academy.

On the long ride to my uncle's home, he and I dominated the conversation. I do not think Spink had ever been in so fine a carriage. He touched the leather of the seat, fingered the tassel on the cushion and then abruptly folded his hands on his lap. He looked out the window for most of the journey and I did not blame him, for Epiny stared at him frankly, breathing lightly and speculatively through her whistle. I thought her behaviour quite childish for her years and wondered that her father tolerated it, but he seemed caught up in quizzing me about my studies, routine, classmates, and teachers, and ignored his wayward daughter.

At one point, in the midst of my uncle telling me a story about his days at boarding school, she took the whistle out of her mouth, pointed it at Spink and said accusingly, 'Kellon Spinrek Kester. Am I right?'

Spink, startled, only replied with a sharp nod. When my uncle looked at me quizzically, I said, 'Spink's father was a war hero. He was tortured to death by plainsmen.'

'He lasted over six hours,' Epiny enlightened us, and then added for our benefit, 'I adore history. I much prefer our family's soldier son journals to the watered-down places-and-dates history in the schoolbooks. Your father's journal mentions Spink's father, Nevare. Did you know that?'

'Not until now, *Epiny*,' I said, deliberately using her first name, as she had made so free with Spink's nickname. Then I inwardly winced, wondering if my uncle would think me ill-mannered, but in truth, I do not think he even noticed. I was shocked when Spink said, very quietly, 'I should like to read those entries if I might, Lord Burvelle.'

'Of course you may, Cadet Kester,' my uncle replied warmly. 'But I fear that we shall have to rely on Epiny to find them for us. My brother, Nevare's father, sent us more than twenty-five volumes during the course of his service for the King. He was a very prolific writer in his soldier son days.'

'I can find it easily enough,' Epiny promised. 'And if you wish, I can copy out those passages for you. They might make a lovely introduction to your own soldier son journals.' She smiled at him warmly as she said this and Spink returned her a tentative smile of his own.

When we arrived, Epiny scrambled out of the carriage ahead of even my uncle, saying over her shoulder, 'I'll see that they set an extra place for Spink at the table. I am famished, for all I ate this morning was an apple and a rasher of bacon, I was so excited to be going to pick you up.'

My uncle descended more sedately and we followed him in. A servant came to take my bag and took Spink's worn leather case as well. My uncle directed that we should be put in adjoining rooms. He added to us, 'You'll be in the room that I had as a boy, Nevare. And your friend will be in your father's old room. The rooms share a sitting room that used to be our schoolroom. I think a lot of our old things are still in there; you may find them amusing. I think I'll leave you both in Epiny's capable hands and see you at dinner. Is that agreeable?'

Of course it was, and I thanked him sincerely before we followed the servant up the stairs. I settled my things quickly and then walked through the connecting room to Spink's chamber. I found him standing, his valise at his feet, staring around himself as if he had never seen a bedchamber before. His mouth was slightly ajar as he looked at the carved bedstead and matching wardrobe, the embroidered hangings, the heavy curtains and the ornate and well-stocked desk. He turned to me and said, 'I had no idea your family was so grand!'

I grinned. 'We aren't. My bedroom at home is far humbler than this, and a third the size, my friend. This is a lord's house, built over generations.' I ran the toe of my boot lightly over the thick rug on the floor. 'The value of this rug alone would more than equal all the furniture in my bedroom at home. But surely you have old nobility relatives of your own. Have you never visited the house your father grew up in?'

He shook his head. 'They have very little to do with us. My father was given his title posthumously, you know. My uncle looked at my mother, a widow with young children, and perhaps thought that she would make too many demands of them if they offered her any help at all. So they did not. When our first overseer absconded with so much of the money, we heard that my father's family said, "Well, that is what happens when a soldier's widow tries to live like a great lady." Which was not the case at all, but my mother was not about to spend time and money travelling to Old Thares to prove them wrong. They live here, you know, somewhere in this city. Your uncle probably knows them. But I don't, and I don't think I ever will.'

I was trying to think of something to say when there was a tap on the door. Epiny walked in almost simultaneously, saying, 'Well, here you both are! What is the delay?'

'Delay in what?' I asked her.

She looked at me as if I were slow and shook her head a bit. 'Coming downstairs, Nevare. Dinner isn't for hours yet, but I've managed something to sustain us until then. Come on.'

Her tone was imperative and she didn't wait to see if we would obey, but simply walked out of the room. Spink looked at me, and then followed her meekly. I trailed them with less grace. My cousin was embarrassing me. She was certainly old enough to behave as a lady. I wanted Spink to feel welcomed into my gracious and dignified ancestral home rather than assaulted by a spoiled little girl.

She somewhat atoned by leading us to a small room off the pantry where she had fashioned an indoor picnic for us. Dishes of cold food and napkins were set out on a bare kitchen worktable. She helped herself to a cold chicken wing with her fingers and then stood eating it, and we were only too happy to follow her example. There were also a pot of black tea, a loaf of bread, butter, jam, and little vanilla cakes. We ate without ceremony, catching the crumbs in napkins. After our months of Academy fare, the simple food was ambrosia. I had never seen a girl eat like a boy before, biting meat off bones and then wiping the grease from her lips. I had not realized how hungry I was until I started eating. Then I concentrated on it, and let Spink and Epiny do all the talking. She swiftly had the names and ages of all his siblings and a brief history of his life out of him; in short, she learned more about him in that hour than I had in all our months of Academy.

We helped her clear away the evidence of our furtive feast and then she took us out walking in the gardens. The stables were a short stroll from there and I was very pleased to have the chance to show Spink my horse. 'That is the finest animal I've ever seen,' he told me, his envy plain in his voice as he looked up at Sirlofty's proud head.

'And he has the temperament of a kitten,' Epiny responded, as if my horse were hers. 'Father told me that he would never go in a side-saddle, but I tried it, and he does. He was a bit surprised at first, but willing and now I'm sure I could ride him anywhere, but Father will not let me. He says I would first have to ask Nevare, and I told him, "How silly! Do you think Nevare will trust him to some stable boy to exercise, someone he has never even met, and then say 'no' to his cousin whom he knows, his own flesh and blood?" But Father insisted that I cannot take him out of the ring without your permission, and so I am asking. Nevare, may I ride your horse on the promenades in the park?'

All the while Epiny spoke, Sirlofty was whuffling her shoulder and nudging her to be stroked. She petted him with familiarity and that firm competence that marks a good horseman. Or horsewoman, I thought sourly. She could not have manoeuvred me better and I was certain she had engineered it so. I wanted to forbid her to ride him, but could not say so in front of Spink without appearing selfish and unreasonable. The best I could hedge my permission was by saying, 'I think we shall leave it up to your father. Sirlofty is a lot of horse for someone your size.'

'My Celeste actually tops him by a hand, but he is smoother-gaited than my mare. Would you like to see her?' And with that she left Sirlofty's stall and took us two doors down to a grey mare with a silky black mane. As Epiny had said, she was taller than Sirlofty, but far more docile. I knew instantly that Sirlofty's fire was what attracted her, not his smooth gait, but held my tongue as she and Spink were chatting away. Spink had never owned a horse all to himself and had been relieved to know that he would not need to furnish his own mount until the third year. But he did find our little cavalla mounts insipid and his descriptions of the spiritless beast that was his daily mount soon had Epiny choking with laughter.

We left the stables and followed an ornamental walk through a landscaped orchard of miniature trees. It was late in the year and the trees were long bare of fruit or leaves, but Epiny insisted that we see it all. The wind was rising and I could not understand Spink's enthusiasm for the stroll. Even the statuary looked cold to me, and the ornamental pond was mossy and depressing; the fish hid under a layer of floating weeds and fallen leaves. As we tried in vain to see the ornamental fish in its murky depths, a light rain began to fall. Just as we were abandoning the pond, and I hoped, bound for the house, we were accosted by a small girl in a pinafore and black pigtails. She marched up to Epiny, pointed a skinny finger at her, and admonished her, 'You are not supposed to be walking around alone with young gentlemen. Mother said so.'

Epiny pointed a finger right back at her and bending slightly at the waist informed her, 'These are not young gentlemen, Purissa. This one, as you know, is your cousin. You didn't even say "how do you do" to our cousin Nevare! And this one is a cadet from the Academy. Curtsey to Cadet Kester.'

The little girl obeyed each of Epiny's commands in turn, quite charmingly and with more maturity than Epiny had shown. 'It's a pleasure to see you again, Purissa,' I told her, and her smile crinkled her nose when I bowed to her.

Epiny was not charmed. 'Now run along, Purissa. I'm showing them around until dinnertime.'

'I want to go with you.'

'No. Run along.'

'Then I shall tell Mother when she gets back.'

'And I shall have to tell her that you were trotting about in the gardens alone during the hour when you are supposed to be studying Holy Writ with Bessom Jamis.'

The child did not look the least bit daunted. 'He fell asleep. He's snoring and his breath smells like garlic. I *had* to run away.'

'And now you have to run right back. If you are wise, you will be there, head bent over your books when he awakes.'

'His breath makes the whole school room stink!'

I was horrified at both my cousins' blunt discussion of their tutor. I had never imagined that girls had such discussions among themselves. But despite myself, I was grinning. I tried to smother my smile. Spink had laughed openly and even Epiny looked moved by the child's plight. She pulled a tiny handkerchief out of her pocket and gave it to her, instructing her, 'Go to the lavender beds and fill this with leaves. Then sit at your school table and hold it before your nose while you read. It will fend off the garlic.'

'The lesson today is boring. It is the second chapter of the Dutiful Wife.'

Epiny looked dismayed. 'That *is* boring. It is beyond boring. Put your finger in at that spot, but read the Book of Punishment instead. It is all about what happens to people for various sins in the afterlife. It's very gory and quite amusing, in a horrid sort of way. When Bessom awakes, just flip the book open to where you should be.' She leaned closer and added in a whisper, 'You should see what it says will befall wayward and harlotrous daughters.'

Purissa's face lit up as if she had been promised candy. I felt slightly scandalized, but when I looked at Spink to see how he had reacted to my unruly cousin, he was grinning. He winked at Purissa, adding, 'I remember that book. The retribution for sons who did not respect their elder brothers as they ought gave me several sleepless nights.'

'You can watch us play Towsers after dinner if you run off and behave yourself now,' Epiny offered.

'No. I want to play, too. Or I won't leave now.'

Epiny sighed. 'Perhaps. But only a few games!'

That bribe was enough to tip the balance. Purissa snatched the handkerchief and trotted off toward the lavender beds. As soon as she was out of sight, Epiny turned back to Spink. 'Shall we continue our tour, Cadet Kester?' she asked him, sweetly formal.

'If the lady pleases, then we shall!' he replied with mock gravity, and bowed. As he straightened, he offered his arm, and she took it, laughing. They walked off down the path together. As I followed, I was beginning to feel a bit annoyed with both of them. Evening was rapidly darkening the sky and the rain was growing stronger. I suddenly recognized what was annoying me. Epiny dressed like a little girl and behaved like one in her lack of restraint and deportment. But there she was, her hand on Spink's arm as if she were a young woman, taking advantage of Spink's manners. Perhaps it was harsh of me, but I decided to force her to declare herself one way or the other. I caught up to them and said coolly, 'Epiny, a young girl like you should really not be accepting escort from a man you've only met today. Give me your hand.'

I reached to move her hand from Spink's arm to mine. I saw her bridle and thought she would resist. Then everything went strange. The moment I touched her arm, skin to skin, my vision doubled. In the most peculiar moment I'd ever experienced in my life, I saw everything around me as foreign. Epiny was not my cousin, but a young woman, unknown to me in every way. Her clothing, her stance, the way she wore her hair, the scent she wore, even her silly hat seemed outlandish and vaguely threatening. I smelled the familiar scents of the rainy garden as exotic perfumes, and Spink looked menacing to me, as if I faced a warrior of unknown skills and customs, who might attack me with no provocation at all. Nothing had changed, and yet everything that was around me had lost every trace of familiarity. I was abruptly a stranger, standing in cold rain, gripping hard the forearm of an unknown and dangerous rival.

And Epiny? Epiny looked at me with eyes that went wide and then wider still. She leaned closer to me, a pin drawn by a magnet, her eyes locked to mine. 'Who are you?' she panted as if the words took great effort. I felt something flow between us, as if she tried to force a response from me. I gasped.

'Nevare. Nevare! Let her go, her hand is turning red! What ails you?' My friend had raised his voice and was shouting at me, I recognized dimly. Then Spink parted us, not roughly, but not gently either. He knocked my hand from Epiny's arm, and both of us sprang back from one another, as if we had been straining to break free but only his touch had parted the cord. I let out a shuddering breath and looked aside from them, embarrassed by whatever had just happened.

'What was that?' I exclaimed, and did not know whom I asked.

But Epiny answered. 'That was strange. And more than strange.' She leaned closer to me, turning her head to gaze up into my averted face. 'Who are you?' she repeated her earlier question earnestly and with great passion, as if she did not recognize me at all.

At that moment, a freak bolt of lightning cut across the stormy sky overhead. The brightness flashed the world to white and black, and when it was gone, my eyes held the after-image of Epiny's stark face staring at me. The thunder that boomed came almost immediately and rattled my bones to the marrow. For an instant, I could neither hear nor see. Then the heavens opened, letting loose a drenching cold downpour and all three of us ran for the shelter of the house.

FIFTEEN

Séance

As soon as we reached the house, Epiny excused herself to go change for dinner. Spink and I retired to our rooms. I hung up my damp jacket, cleaned my shoes of garden mud, and used a brush to freshen the cuffs of my trousers. Then, lacking anything else to do until dinner, I decided to explore the schoolroom. I wandered about the space where my father and uncle had taken their lessons, and wondered what it must have been like to grow up in so grand a house. I discovered my father's initials carved into the edge of one table. Well-worn books shared shelf space with several models of siege engines and a stuffed owl. A rack held fencing foils and sabres. I was sitting at the table, examining one of the siege engines when Spink entered. He looked around the room and crossing to the window, stared out over the grounds of my uncle's estates. He quietly asked me, 'Did you think I was being too forward with your cousin, Nevare? If so, I wish to apologize, to you and to her. I did not mean to take advantage of her.'

'Advantage of her?' I laughed aloud. 'Spink, man, if I were trying to protect anyone, it was you! My cousin is taking advantage of *your* good nature with her outrageous manners. One minute she is tooting a whistle at us like a street performer, and the next she's claiming your arm to escort her as if she were the Queen herself. No. You've given no offence. She is just so odd. Truth to say, she embarrasses me.'

'Embarrasses you! Nevare, there's no need for that. I find her oddness, well, charming. I've never before met a girl who is so direct, so honest. She puts me at my ease. And so, I thought, perhaps I had become too relaxed with her, to offer to escort her down the path without first asking your permission. I do beg pardon if I presumed too much familiarity.'

'There is no need, Spink. If anything, she is the one who presumes too much familiarity. She started calling you by your first name almost the moment she met you. I just thought to put Epiny in her place, and show her that if she behaves like a spoiled child, I intend to treat her as one. And now I will offer to beg your pardon, if I offended you with what I said to her.'

'Me, offended? No, not at all. It was just, well, you acted so strangely for a time. You gripped her arm as if you intended to hurt her, and the way she looked at you, as if she'd never seen you before – I was quite frightened, to tell you the truth. I feared you'd do an injury to one another.'

I was aghast. 'Spink! You know me well enough, I think, to know that I'd never harm a girl, let alone my own cousin!'

'I do! Yes, I do, Nevare. It was just that, for a time there, you did not seem like the Nevare I know.'

'Well . . . It was odd. For an instant, I didn't feel like myself at all, either, in all honesty.'

And my admission of that stunned us both into an awkward silence. Spink moved away, looking everywhere except at me. He touched the books on the shelves, the much used school table, and then wandered to the windows. He rested his hands on the sill and looking out into the night asked me, 'Do you ever wish that you could own a home such as this? With rooms like this for your sons to learn in?'

I was a bit shocked at his words. 'I never thought of it. I'm a soldier, Spink. All my sons will be soldiers. I'll teach them what I know, as they grow, and I hope they'll be bright enough to rise quickly through the ranks. Maybe, if one of them excels, I'll ask my brother to speak for him and try to have him admitted to the Academy or purchase a commission for him. But, no, I don't ever expect to own a home like this. When I'm old and can no longer serve my king, I know my brother will make me welcome on his holdings, and he'll help arrange solid marriages for my daughters. What more could a soldier son ask?'

He turned from his contemplation of the darkening grounds and gave me a rueful smile. 'You have deeper roots than I, I think. This beautiful home is your ancestral estate and you are still welcomed here. And the way you speak of Widevale makes me think that in a generation or two the house and grounds there will rival this place. But for me, the only home I recall is Bitter Springs.' He smiled wryly. 'I love the land there. It's home. But when your father was given his lordship, he chose lands that bordered the river, arable land and pasture land. Land that could generate the monies to enable him to live like a noble. My mother chose with a different purpose. She chose the land that surrounded the area where my father was killed. His burial site was lost; his troops covered him hastily, for they still feared they might be over-run by the plainsmen and did not want them to have his bones as trophies. So they buried him and hid the grave and we have never been able to discover it. But she knows it is somewhere on the land that she claimed, and says that all we build or do there is memorial to him. But the problem is, the land is not good for much else. You can't shove a spade into it without hitting a stone, and when you remove that, you find two more stacked under it. You can hunt and you can forage there, but you can't till a field or even graze sheep. My brother is trying hogs and goats, but they swiftly strip the land and leave only stirred rocks behind them. I do not think they are a good idea; but he is the heir, not I.'

He said this so wistfully that I had to ask, 'And if the land were yours, to develop as you chose?' I felt I was tempting him to the sin of ingratitude for order, and yet I could not forbear to pose the question.

He gave a brief, bitter laugh. 'Stone, Nevare. Stone is what we have. The idea first came to me when one of my father's soldiers came to retire with us. He looked over our land and asked another fellow if we were growing rocks as a crop or for pleasure. And it came to me then, if stone is what we have, then stone is what we should prosper on. Our house, small and humble as it is, is built all of stone, and the walls between our so-called fields are of stone. I've heard that the King's Road building goes slowly for lack of proper stone. Well, we've stone in plenty.'

'Exporting stone sounds difficult. Are there roads in your region?'

He shrugged. 'There could be. You asked me for my pipe dream, Nevare, not for the reality. It would take years to bring it to fruition. But my family will be there for generations so why not begin the task now?'

I had made myself uncomfortable with the discussion. All knew that a man's career was determined by his birth order. To question it was to question the will of the good god himself. All knew the tales of what came of trying to quarrel with your fate. A son must be what he was born to be. My family was strict in the matter. It was true that some of the other noble families were less observant of the law. In one notorious case, when the House Offeri heir son died, Lord Offeri had moved each of his sons up a notch, so that the soldier became the heir, the priest the soldier, and so on. All were failures in their careers. The new 'heir' was too militant with the estate serfs, and many of them fled the land, leaving crops to rot in the fields. The priest son did not have the constitution to endure the arduous life of a soldier, and died before he had even faced a battle. The artist forced to become a priest was too creative in his copying of scripture and nearly faced charges of heresy from the archor of his order. And so it went. The story was often told as a warning to any families considering such an extreme measure. I should not be tempting Spink or myself to pretend we would ever be anything but soldiers. I changed the subject.

'Why is your home called Bitter Springs? As testament to your father's death there?'

'Well, that is a bitter memory for my mother, but no. There are several large springs not far from our home. The water that comes to the surface there tastes terrible, but several plainsmen tribes revere the spot and hold that people can be cured of disease or granted marvellous visions or increase their intelligence by bathing or drinking the waters. They offer my family trade goods in exchange for being granted passage to the springs. I think it is my mother's sole act of revenge that she will not allow any member of the folk that killed my father to visit the springs. It angers them greatly, for they say the springs are sacred and were always a truce place and open to all. To which my mother replies, "You changed all that when you killed my husband." Over the years, there have been a few clashes over that, with warriors attempting to make sorties to the springs to steal water. My father's old soldiers always repel them. They take pride in that.'

I barely heard the last few sentences. I had become aware of an odd sound. At first, I had thought it a distant birdcall from the garden, but now I realized that the soft trilling matched the cadence of breath. The door of the old schoolroom was ajar. I thought I had latched it. I crossed the room silently and pulled the door suddenly open. Epiny stood outside it, her otter-whistle between her lips despite the fact that she was dressed for dinner. She grinned at me, clenching the silver toy between her teeth and letting it wheeze as she did so. 'It's time to come down to dinner,' she said around the whistle.

'Were you eavesdropping?' I asked her severely.

She spat her toy into her hand. 'Not really. I was just

standing outside the door listening, so that I could wait for a break in the conversation to announce dinner rather than interrupting you.'

She said it so blithely that I almost believed her. Then I decided that I would follow through on my earlier resolution about my cousin. If she were going to act as if she were an errant ten year old, I would speak to her as such. 'Epiny, listening outside of rooms for any reason is impolite. At your age, you should know better.'

She cocked her head at me. 'I do know when it is rude to listen at doors, dearest cousin. And now it is time for us all to go down to dinner. Father enjoys his food and hates to have it served at less than the correct temperature. You do know, don't you, that it is rude to keep your host waiting for his dinner?'

I could control my temper no longer. 'Epiny, you are close to my age, and I know my aunt and uncle have taught you manners. Why are you acting like an ill-mannered child? Why can't you behave as if you were a young lady?'

She smiled at me as if she had finally forced me to recognize her. 'Actually, I am one year and four months younger than you are. And the moment I begin to behave as if I were some suffocatingly correct young lady, that is how my father will start to treat me. Not to mention my mother. And that will be the beginning of the end of my life. Not that I expect you to understand what I am talking about. Spink. Would you care to escort me to dinner? Or do you find me too childish and spoiled?'

'I should be glad to,' Spink declared. To my astonishment, he crossed the room with alacrity and offered Epiny his arm. He blushed as he did so and she seemed likewise ruffled. Nonetheless, she accepted his offer and they preceded me out of the room. Epiny's long, pale blue skirts rustled against the marble steps as they descended the staircase. Her hair had been brushed and simply confined to a gold lace net at the base of her neck. Spink's back was straight as a ram-rod; he was not much taller than she was. As I followed them, it struck me that they looked like a couple.

Then, abruptly, Epiny ended that illusion. She snatched her hand back from his arm, gathered up her skirts and bustled down the stairs ahead of him, leaving Spink looking confused. I caught up with him as Epiny was disappearing into the dining room.

'Don't mind her,' I told him. 'It's as I told you. She's a very silly little girl at this point. My sisters went through a similar time.'

I did not add that my father's reaction to my sisters' flightiness had been far more severe than my uncle's tolerance of Epiny's eccentricity. I recalled his stern admonition to my mother: 'If we do not settle them soon into a becoming and womanly calm, they will never find appropriate husbands. I am a New Noble, madam, as you are aware. Some of their opportunities to rise in society they must create for themselves, and they will best do so by being sedate, tractable, and demure young women.'

'As I was,' my mother had filled in, and there was an edge to her voice, bitterness or regret, that I could not understand.

I do not think my father even heard it. 'As you were, my lady, and continue to be. A fine example of all a noble-woman and wife should be.'

When we entered the dining room, Epiny was standing behind her chair. My uncle was at the head of the table. Purissa waited at his left elbow. The child looked far more groomed than she had earlier. Someone had tidied her hair and put a clean pinafore on her. Spink and I rapidly took our places and I murmured an apology that we had kept my uncle waiting.

'We are short on formality at family meals, Nevare, and that is what we will enjoy this evening, for you are definitely

389

family, and you appear to regard your friend as if he were almost a brother. I regret that your Aunt Daraleen and cousin Hotorn cannot be here as well. He is away at his schooling, and she has been summoned to serve our queen at court for the days of the Council of Lords. They will not convene it until Firstday, but the women of the court must have at least a dozen days to be dressed for it. And so she has departed, leaving us here to get by on our own. But we shall make do here as well we can in their absence.'

With that, we took our seats and a servant entered almost immediately with the soup. The meal was the most excellent one I had had since arriving in Old Thares. The food had been cooked to be consumed by individuals rather than stirred up in vats for hundreds. The difference in taste and texture seemed marvellous after so many meals produced for the masses. I felt almost honoured to be presented with a single chop cooked to my liking rather than a ladled serving of meat chunks in watery gravy. I ate well, trying to control my greed, and finished the meal with a large serving of apple pan dowdy.

Spink kept pace with me, but also managed to hold up his end of the conversation with Uncle Sefert. He expressed great admiration for my uncle's home, and asked a number of questions about the house and the estate in general. The gist of his questions seemed to be that he wondered how long it took a noble family to establish such a grand ancestral seat. The answer seemed to be 'generations'. My uncle spoke proudly of the innovations that he had introduced in his lifetime, from gas piping and lights to his remodelling of the wine cellar to allow for better temperature control. Spink followed his answers with enthusiasm, and I saw my uncle warm toward him.

When dinner was over, my uncle suggested that we might retire to his den for tobacco and brandy. My brief hope of a peacefully masculine retreat was shattered when Epiny protested with, 'But Papa! You said I might have them to play Towsers! You know how much I've been looking forward to it!'

Uncle Sefert heaved a tolerant sigh. 'Oh, very well. Gentlemen, instead of my study, we shall retire to the sitting room, for sweet biscuits, soft wine, and several hundred rousing games of Towsers.' He looked ruefully amused as he announced this, and what could we do save smile good-naturedly and agree? Purissa seemed to share her sister's delight, for she jumped from her chair and ran to catch hands with her. They led us away from the table and into a pleasant room where a little iron stove enamelled with flower-patterned tiles was keeping a teakettle puffing out steam. The floor was layered with bright woven rugs from Sebany. Upholstered cushions in the vibrant colours of that exotic land littered the room. Pot-bellied oil lamps with painted shades flickered in their alcoves despite literally legions of fat yellow candles of all shapes and sizes on holders of all heights throughout the chamber. There were several low tables, little higher than my knee, and on one of these were several platters of biscuits and a carafe of watered wine. A large wicker cage held half-a-dozen tiny pink birds that hopped from perch to perch, twittering as we entered. White curtains had been drawn for the evening across the tall windows.

'Oh, I should have showed you our sitting room earlier, while there was still daylight!' Epiny exclaimed in sudden disappointment. 'You can't see our new glass curtains at all properly at night!' Despite this announcement, she went to a corner and drew the white curtains back with a pulley arrangement. Between the night and us a threaded fabric of tiny glass beads hung on thin filaments of wire. 'When the sun shines, you can see that there is an entire landscape there worked in beads. Tomorrow, perhaps you can see it better,' she announced, and swept the white curtains across once more.

Spink and I were still standing, for the room lacked chairs of any kind. My uncle folded his long legs to sink down on one of the immense cushions that littered the carpeted floor. Purissa was already sprawled on one, and Epiny returned to likewise ensconce herself on one. 'Do sit down,' she directed us as she produced a brown wooden game box from a drawer in a low table. 'My mother has followed the Queen's example in furnishing our sitting room. Our queen has been quite taken with Sebanese décor of late. After a court dinner, she retires with all her favourites to her own lounging room. Just sit down anywhere around the table and be comfortable.'

Both Spink and I settled uneasily. Our trousers had not been tailored for this sort of sitting, nor did our boots allow much bend to the ankles, but we managed. Epiny was setting out a game with brightly coloured cards and ceramic chips and an enamelled board. She seemed to delight in the musical clacking of the pieces as she arranged it all.

'I'm afraid I don't know this game,' Spink said sociably as she assigned a colour to each of us.

'Oh, never fear on that account. All too soon, you will know it too well,' my uncle predicted with a wry grin.

'It is such fun, and terribly easy to learn,' Epiny assured him earnestly.

Such proved to be the case. For all its shiny and elegant pieces, the game was idiotically simple. It involved matching colours and symbols, and calling out different words if one had a red match or a blue match and so on. Both girls were constantly leaping to their feet and doing little dances of triumph when they secured winning pairs of cards. I rapidly tired of leaping to my feet to declare that I'd scored a point. Epiny insisted it was a rule and that I must comply. For the first time, my uncle interfered with her wilfulness, and announced that neither Spink nor I nor he would leap up, but would merely raise a hand. Epiny pouted about this for a time, but the dreary little game proceeded anyway. Is there anything more tedious than a pointless pastime?

Uncle Sefert managed to escape with the excuse that little

Purissa was not allowed to stay up late. Her nanny had come to the door to find her, and surely he could have sent the child off with her. I think he insisted on accompanying them simply to escape the dreadful game.

With two players gone, the game proceeded even more rapidly, for the element of uncertainty as to who held what markers was greatly reduced. We played two more rounds of it, with Spink courteously pretending to enjoy himself before I could stand it no longer. 'Enough!' I said, throwing my hands up in mock surrender. I tried to smile as I added, 'Your game has exhausted me, Epiny. Shall we take a brief recess?'

'You tire too easily. What sort of a cavalla officer will you be when you cannot stand up to the demands of a simple game?' she asked me tartly. Smiling, she turned to Spink. 'You are not weary yet, are you?' she asked him.

He smiled back. 'I could play another hand or two.'

'Excellent. Then we shall!'

I had expected Spink to side with me. Deprived of my ally, I conceded and we played another three hands. Midway through our second hand, my uncle looked in on us. Epiny immediately and enthusiastically welcomed him back to the game, but he firmly declined, saying he had some reading to do. Before he retired to that, he reminded us that the next day was the Sixday, and that we should all get to bed early enough that we could easily rise for the daylight services he always attended.

'We're just going to do a few more hands,' Epiny assured him to my dismay, for I was very willing to retire from her and her game and seek a good night's rest. My uncle left and we finished yet another round of the tedious game. Then, as Epiny gathered the markers to set them up afresh she asked us, 'Has either of you ever been part of a séance?'

'A science?' Spink was puzzled, then helpfully offered, 'Nevare appears to enjoy geology as a hobby.'

'No. Not a science.' Epiny continued to set up the playing

393

pieces for the game. She was sending us only furtive glances, gauging our reactions from under her eyelashes. 'A *séance*. A summoning of spirits, often through a medium. Like me.'

'A medium what?' I asked her. She laughed aloud.

'I am a medium. Or so I believe, for so the Queen's medium said to me the last time I attended a séance at my mother's side. I've only begun to explore my talent in the last four months. A medium is someone with the power to invite spirits to speak through her body. Sometimes the spirits are the ghosts of those who have died, but who earnestly wish to convey some final bit of information to the living. Sometimes the spirits appear to be elder beings, perhaps even the remnants of the old gods who were worshipped before the good god came to free us from that darkness. And sometimes . . .'

'Oh. Those. I've heard some talk about them. People sitting in a circle in the dark, holding hands and playing at bogey-frights on one another. It sounds unholy, and completely unfit for a girl to be interested in,' I told her sternly. In my heart, I was full of curiosity and longing to hear more, but I did not wish to tempt my own cousin to corruption.

'Indeed?' She gave me a disdainful look. 'Perhaps you ought to tell that to my mother, for tonight she assists the Queen at her weekly séance session. Or perhaps the Queen herself would like to hear your notions of what is "unholy and unfit for girls".' She turned to Spink. 'The Queen says that much of what is judged "unfit for women to pursue" are the very sciences and disciplines that lead to power. What do you think of that?'

Spink glanced at me but I had no help for him. It struck me as an entirely peculiar conversation, not unlike Epiny herself. He took a breath, and the expression on his face was the same one he wore when an instructor called on him in class. 'I have not had much time to reflect on that, but on the surface, it would certainly seem true. Women are not encouraged to study the exact sciences or engineering. The complete texts of the Holy Writ are forbidden to them; they only study the writings given specifically for women. The arts and sciences of war are judged unfit . . . if those be the paths to power, then, yes, perhaps women are denied those paths when they are denied those disciplines.'

'Why should it matter?' I spread my hands. 'If there are disciplines that are unfit for girls, then it is only natural that those disciplines would lead to inappropriate ends. Why would any father put his daughter on a path that can only lead her to unhappiness and frustration?'

Epiny swivelled her gaze to me. 'Why would a powerful woman be unhappy and frustrated?'

'Because she wouldn't, well, a powerful woman, would not, have, well, a home and family and children. She wouldn't have time for all the things that fulfil a woman.'

'Powerful men have those things.'

'Because they have wives,' I pointed out to her.

'Exactly,' she said, as if she had just proven something.

I shook my head at her. 'I'm going to bed.'

'You're leaving me alone here with Spink?' she asked. She feigned being scandalized, but the look she shot Spink was almost hopeful. He shook his head at her regretfully.

'No, I'm not. Spink is going to bed, too. You heard your father. We have to waken early for Sixday services at dawn.'

'If the good god is always with us, why must we worship him at such an awful hour?' Epiny demanded.

'Because it is our duty. It's a small sacrifice he asks of us, to demonstrate our respect for him.'

'That,' she told me archly, 'was a rhetorical question. I already know its conventional answer. I just think it's a good idea for all of us to think about it now and then. For just as the good god makes rather strange requests of how men must show their respect, so do men make peculiar demands of women. And children. Are you truly going up to bed already?'

'I am.'

'You won't stay and hold a séance with me?'

'I . . . of course not! It's unholy. It's improper!' I throttled a terrible curiosity to know how a séance worked and if anything real ever happened in one.

'Unholy? Why?'

'Well, it is all trickery and lies.'

'Hmm. Well, if it *is* all trickery, then it can scarcely be sinful. Unless, of course . . . ' she paused and looked at me quite seriously, almost as if alarmed. 'Do you think those mimes that pester people in the Old Square are sinful? They are always pretending to climb ladders or lean on walls that aren't there. Are they unholy, too?'

Spink choked back a laugh. I ignored him. 'Séances are unholy because of what you are trying to do, or pretending to do, not just because they are all fakery. And they are a most improper activity for young ladies.'

'Why is it improper? Because we hold hands in the dark? The Queen does it.'

'Nevare, surely if the Queen does it, it cannot be improper.' This, from Spink of all people.

I took a breath, resolved to be calm and logical. I felt a bit affronted that they were united against me. I spoke coolly. 'Séances are unholy because you are trying to take a god's power to yourself. Or at least, pretend to have such. I've heard something of séances: foolish people sitting in the dark, holding hands, listening for thumps and knocks and whispers. Why do you think they hold them in the dark, Epiny? Why do you think nothing about them is ever clear or straightforward? All is mumble and mystery. We are of the good god, Epiny, and we should set the superstition and trickery and magic of the old gods behind us. Soon, if we ignore them all, they will fade to nothing, and their magic will be no more. The world will be a better, safer place when the old gods have passed away completely.'

'I see. And is that why you and Spink both do that little finger-wavy, charm thing over your cinches each time you go to mount your horses?'

I stared at her, astonished. The keep-fast charm was something I had learned from Sergeant Duril when I first learned to saddle my own horse. Before then, he or my father had made the charm. It was a cavalla tradition, a tiny bit of the old magic that we had kept for ourselves. I had once asked the sergeant where it had come from, and he had said, in an off-hand way, that most likely we had learned it from the conquered plainsmen. Then he had mentioned that there had used to be other little charms, a string charm to find water, and another to give strength to a flagging horse, but that they did not seem to work as well as they once had. He suspected that all our iron and steel was the cause of the magic fading. And then he added that it was probably not wise for a cavallaman to be using too much of the magic that we had learned from our enemies. A man who did that might end up 'going native'. At the time, I had been too young to fully understand what was meant by the phrase, other than that it was very bad. So Epiny talking about that magic to me suddenly made me feel both exposed and ashamed. 'That's private!' I exclaimed indignantly, and glanced at Spink, expecting him to mirror my outrage.

Instead he said thoughtfully, 'Perhaps she has a point.'

'She does not!' I retorted. 'Answer honestly, Epiny. Don't you think séances are an affront to the good god?'

'Why? Why should he care?'

I had no ready reply to Epiny's question. 'It just seems wrong to me. That's all.'

Spink turned to me, his hands palm up. 'Go back, Nevare. Let's talk about the keep-fast charm. You know it's a small magic we use. And everyone says it works, when they say anything about it at all. So either we are as ungodly as Epiny is for tampering with such things, or there is no sin in investigating it.'

Spink was taking her side again. 'Spink, you should know séances are a lot of nonsense. Otherwise, why would there be all those rules about holding them in the dark, and keeping silent, and not being able to ask questions during them, and all that silliness? It's to cover up the trickery, that's all!'

'You seem to know a great deal about them, for one who has never taken part in one,' Epiny observed sweetly.

'My sisters went away for a spring week at a friend's house. When they returned, they spoke of holding a séance there, because a visiting cousin from Old Thares had told them about one. They'd heard a wild tale of floating plates and unseen bells and knocking on tabletops, so they all joined hands and sat in a circle in the dark and waited. Nothing happened, though they scared themselves silly waiting. Nothing happened because there was no charlatan there to make things happen and pretend the spirits were doing it!'

I think my irritation had daunted even Epiny, for she sounded subdued when she said, 'There is a lot more to it than floating plates and mysterious knocks, Nevare. I don't doubt that there could be fakes and charlatans, but the séance I attended was real. Very real and a bit frightening. Things happened to me there . . . I felt things that no one could explain. And Guide Porilet said that I had the same skill that she did, but was untrained. Why do you think I was left here with Father this time? It was because I interfered with the trained medium and she could not summon the spirits to herself while I was there. They all wanted to come to me. I suppose I cannot blame you for doubting me. I could scarcely believe it myself at first. I found all sorts of ways to deny it and explain it away. But it wouldn't stay gone.'

This last she said in a very soft, uncertain voice. I capitulated to her feelings. 'I'm sorry, Epiny. I'd believe you if I could. But all my logic and reason tell me that these "summonings" are simply not real. I'm sorry.'

'Are you, Nevare? Truly?' She straightened slightly, a flower refreshed by a gentle rain.

I smiled at her. 'Truly, Epiny. I'd believe you if I could.'

She grinned in response and jumped to her feet. 'Then I'll make an offer to you. Let's just turn down the lampwicks, extinguish all but two candles, and sit around it, holding hands, in a circle. Perhaps you are right and nothing at all will happen. But, if things do start to happen, you can tell me stop and I'll stop it. Now what could be the harm in that?'

She had acted as she spoke. By the time she finished, she had darkened the room except for two fat yellow candles burning on what had been our game table. Their wicks were short and the flame guttered shallowly in the fragrant wax. Epiny sat down in the dimness, folding her legs under her skirt. She extended one hand to Spink. For the first time, I noticed how slender and graceful her fingers were. He took her hand without hesitation. With her free hand, she patted a cushion next to her and extended her hand in invitation to me. I sighed, recognizing both that it was inevitable, and that, deep down, my own curiosity was urging me on.

I settled on the cushion beside her. There was a mildly uncomfortable moment as Spink took my hand. Epiny's waiting hand hovered in the air between us. I reached for it.

Suddenly, I again felt that distortion of my senses. The room was closed and suffocating, the scent from the yellow candles so foreign that I could scarcely breathe. And the girl reaching for my hand had eyes deeper than any forest pond and fingers that could sink roots into me before I could draw a breath. Something deep inside me forbade this contact; it was dangerous to touch hands with a spirit-seeker, and unclean besides.

'Take my hand, Nevare!' Epiny spoke impatiently, as if from a great distance. In my dream, I reached for her fingers, but it was like pushing my hand through congealed jelly. The very air resisted the motion, and when Epiny reached her eager hand toward mine, I saw her encounter the same barrier.

'It's like ectoplasm, but invisible!' she exclaimed. Her voice was triumphant with curiosity, not fear. She continued to push her pale white fingers toward me like seeking roots that could burrow into my heart.

'I . . . I feel something,' Spink said. I heard his embarrassment at admitting it. I knew, as clearly as if he had spoken it aloud, that he had thought this 'séance' all a sham, but an excellent excuse to hold Epiny's hand in his. He had not bargained on whatever it was that was happening. It frightened him but a part of me noticed that he had not released Epiny's hand.

'Stop!' I suddenly commanded them. My voice came out cracked like an old woman's. 'Stop, you little witch thing! By root, I bind you!'

My hand tried to do something it did not know how to do. I was shocked, shocked at my words, shocked at how my fingers danced frantically in the air between Epiny and me. I watched my hand, powerless to stop it. Epiny stared at me and Spink's eyes were big as saucers. Then Epiny suddenly leaned forward and blew out both candles.

We were plunged into darkness. At least, my mortal eyes were. My 'other' eyes, the ones that saw Epiny as foreign and strange, suddenly looked out at the dense forest in front of me. For an instant, I smelled rich humus, even felt the tendrils that bound me to the tree at my back. Then someone yelped, a cry blended from surprise, fury, and yes, a touch of fear.

The 'other' left me. Suddenly I was sitting on a cushion in the dark. A tiny spark still gripped the end of one candle's wick. It illuminated nothing, but gave me a place to fix my eyes. I heard the scratch of a sulphur match and smelled its familiar stink. I saw Epiny's hand in the small circle of light the match made. She re-lit the two candles and looked from me to Spink and back again. She looked shaken, but her words were arch. 'Well. As you see. It's all people sitting in a circle in the dark, holding hands and playing at bogey-

400

frights on one another. Still, it can be amusing, all the same.'
A small smile came to her pale face. 'I think you can stop
holding Spink's hand now. If you wish.'

I became aware of the bruising grips we had on each
other. We dropped hands. I sheepishly massaged my crushed
fingers.

'Are you all right?' Spink asked Epiny gently.

She was pale. By the candlelight, her eyes looked hollow.
'I'm tired,' she said. 'Tired as I've never been before. Guide
Porilet, the Queen's medium, is often exhausted after a session. I thought it was just because she was old. Now I understand better what she feels.' Dismissing herself, she turned to
me. 'Do you recall what I said to you that morning, when
you were departing for the Academy? I told you that you
seemed to have two auras. You do. But only one belongs to
you. There is something in you, Nevare. Something strong.
Something very old.'

'And evil,' I added, feeling sure it was true. I ran my hand
over the top of my head. My bald spot stung like a fresh
injury. I pulled my hand away from it.

Epiny pursed her lips for a moment. I watched her, thinking how silly and impossible this conversation would have
seemed only a short time before. 'No. I would not call it evil.
It is something that wants to live, desperately, and will stop
at nothing to keep on living. It feared me. It fears even you,
but continues to inhabit you. Even now, when it has retreated,
I know you are still bound to it. I feel it.'

'Don't say that!' Spink begged this, but I would have said
the words if I had thought of them first.

'We will not talk of it right now. But before you leave, we
must try this again, I think. I must learn what it is that has
touched you and taken you. I've never heard of anything like
this before,' Epiny said earnestly, gripping my hand once more.

'I think we shall leave it alone,' I said firmly. I did not
sound convincing, even to myself.

'Do you? Well, we shall see. For now, goodnight, sweet cousin Nevare. Good night, Spink.'

With that, she dropped my hand, rose from her cushion and swept out of the room, her exit surprisingly womanly after her behaviour had been so irritatingly childish all day.

I think my mouth was agape as I stared after her. I shifted my stare to Spink. He looked like a pup bird-dog the first time he sees a pheasant lift from the tall grass before him. Entranced.

'Let's go,' I told him, a bit irritably, and after a moment he swung his gaze to me. We rose, and he followed me dumbly from the room. I tried to walk steadily. I was sorting what had happened through my mind. I needed to find an explanation that fit with my life. I was inclined to blame Epiny for the whole bizarre experience. As we went up the stairs, Spink said quietly, 'I've never met a girl like your cousin before.'

'Well, at least there's that to be grateful for,' I muttered, mortified.

'No. I mean, well . . .' He sighed suddenly. 'I suppose I haven't known many girls, though. And I've never before spent an evening almost alone with one. The things she thinks about! I never thought that a girl, well—' He halted, floundering for words.

'Don't worry about saying it aloud.' I excused him from his awkwardness. 'I've never before met anyone like Epiny, either.'

We parted to go to our separate rooms. It had been a taxing day for me in many ways, and despite my weariness, I worried that I would not fall asleep. I dreaded dark dreams of trees and roots, or staring endlessly into the black corners of the room. But I was more drained than I thought. The soft bed and feather pillow welcomed me and I sank into sleep almost as soon as I settled into them.

SIXTEEN

A Ride in the Park

A servant tapped at my door before dawn. Both Spink and I attended the daybreak service with my uncle in the chapel on his estate. Epiny and Purissa were also there, in the women's alcove. I glanced over at them once, only to surprise Epiny in the midst of an immense yawn that she had not bothered to cover. My uncle chose the readings for the men; they focused on duty, valour, and being steadfast. I suspected he chose them with Spink and me in mind. I prayed with an earnestness that I had not had since I was a boy, asking the good god to be with me at all times.

As my aunt had still not returned, Epiny did the women's readings. They seemed very short and I could not detect any common thread in what she chose. One had to do with not wasting her husband's resources frivolously. The next was something about refraining from gossip about her betters. And the last was the horrendous section from Punishments on the afterlife fate of wayward and harlotrous daughters. This moved Spink to a choking fit that left him gasping for air.

After the common services, Spink and I retired with my uncle and the serving men of the household for meditation. The chamber for this was adjacent to one of his hot houses and very pleasant. It was more comfortable than the austere room we used at home on Sixday, and despite my good night's sleep, several times I nearly drowsed off.

At home and at the Academy, the Necessary Tasks that the Writ permitted always followed services and meditation on the Sabbath. To my delight, and Spink's, the Sixday at my uncle's house proved to be a day of relaxation. At my uncle's house, even the servants had an easy time of it. We had a simple cold luncheon, during which my uncle attempted to keep the conversation quiet and pious. Only Purissa repeatedly asking him if the mimes that performed in the city were evil and offensive to the good god marred it. I saw Spink and Epiny exchange a smile and knew that she had primed the child for that question.

After our meal my uncle advised Spink and me to enjoy the library and do our studying, if we were so inclined. I was, and I brought out my books. Spink seized the opportunity to have Epiny guide him through my father's journals to the sections that mentioned his father. She seemed to have an excellent memory and found the entries quickly. Out of curiosity, I joined them for a time, but soon wearied of reading over Spink's shoulder as Epiny pointed out passages. I went back to my schoolwork and rapidly completed two of my assignments.

Dinner that evening was again simple, 'for the sake of our serving folk' my uncle said, but once more, far better than anything we had eaten at the Academy. Only the meat was served hot, but the cold fruit pies and whipped cream that finished the meal almost tempted me to over-indulge. 'Think what Gord would make of this!' I commented to Spink as I took a second slice.

'Gord?' Epiny instantly asked.

'A friend of ours at Academy. One who is inclined to over-indulge in food whenever he gets the opportunity.' Spink sighed. 'I hope he is feeling better when we return. The last few days have been difficult for him.'

'How is that?' Uncle Sefert wanted to know.

We did the stupidest thing possible. Spink and I exchanged glances, and then neither of us spoke. I tried to find a truthful lie, but when one came to me (He has not been feeling well!) it was somehow too late to utter it. Epiny's eyes shone with sudden interest when her father said mildly, 'Perhaps we shall discuss your friend's difficult days in my study after dinner.'

I think Epiny was as surprised as I when her father shut the door before she could follow us into the study. She had traipsed along behind us, apparently confident that she was to be included. Instead, just as she tried to enter, her father stepped to the door and said, 'Good night and sleep well, Epiny. I will see you at breakfast tomorrow.' Then he simply closed the door. Spink looked shocked, but covered it well. My uncle went to his sideboard and poured a brandy for himself. After a pause in which he seemed to be considering it, he poured two very short shots for Spink and me also. He gestured us toward two chairs and took the couch for himself. Once we were settled, he looked directly at us and said, 'Nevare, Spinrek, I think it's time you told me whatever it is that you think you should not tell me.'

'I haven't done anything wrong, sir,' I said, trying to reassure him, but even as I said the words, guilt jabbed me. I had watched Spink and Trist fight and not reported them. Worse, I suspected that Lieutenant Tiber was being treated unfairly, and yet I had not spoken out. My uncle seemed to sense that things were amiss, for he kept his silence and waited. It startled me when Spink spoke.

'It's hard to tell where to start, sir. But I think I would value your advice.' Spink spoke hesitantly, and glanced at me as if for permission.

My uncle read his look. 'Speak freely, Spink. Honesty should never seek permission of anyone.'

I cast my eyes down before my uncle's rebuke. I was reluctant for Spink to talk to my uncle, but there was nothing I could do about it now. With no embroidery or excuses, he told of his fight with Trist, and then went on to tell how we had gone to the infirmary to bring Gord back, and that we were sure that Old Noble cadets had been responsible for Gord's beating. Somehow Gord's tale meandered to include the bullying and humiliation at the beginning of the year, and the flag-brawl and the culling that had followed it. When I did not bring up Tiber right away, Spink prompted me, saying, 'And Nevare fears a worse injustice against a New Noble cadet.'

I had to speak then. I began by saying that I had only suspicions and no real evidence. I saw my uncle scowl at that, and forced myself to recognize my words as a weakling's excuse for keeping silent. Instead, he commented, 'I know Lord Tiber of Old Thares, not well, but I do know he does not drink, nor did his father before him. I doubt that his soldier brother drinks, and hence I doubt that his son would. I may be wrong in this. But either Lieutenant Tiber has broken not only an Academy rule but also his family's tradition, or he has been entrapped by falsehoods. It demands investigation. I am disappointed that you were not called on to tell what you knew before they took such an extreme disciplinary action against him. It must be rectified, Nevare. You know that.'

I bowed my head to that. I did know it, and there was a strange relief in hearing him say it. I expected him to rebuke both of us for breaking the honour code and advise us to turn in our resignations to the Academy. I knew I would have to obey him. Not only was he my uncle, he would only be saying aloud what I already knew was the most honourable course to pursue.

Instead, brows knit, he began to question us about the distinctions made between old and new nobility soldier sons, and how Colonel Stiet ran the Academy and even about his son Caulder. The more we told him, the graver he looked. I had not realized what a relief it would be to unburden myself about the inequities at the school. I had believed the Academy would be a place of high honour and lofty values. Not only had I discovered that was not so, I had

406

besmirched my own honour in my very first year there. I had not realized how troubled I was nor how disappointed until we were given the opportunity to talk freely.

Small things bothered me almost as much as the larger injustices. When I told him that in all likelihood, we had brought Sirlofty all the way to Old Thares for nothing, for I would be forced to use an Academy mount, he did not smile, but nodded solemnly and commented, 'Giving you that horse was a very significant act for your father. He believes that a worthy mount is a cavallaman's first line of defence. He will not approve of this new regulation.' I felt a great relief to know that he, a first son and never a soldier, could grasp the depth of my disappointment.

When both Spink and I had talked our way to silence, he leaned back and sighed heavily. For a brief time, he stared into the shadowy corners of the room as if seeing something there that was invisible to us. Then he looked back at us and smiled sadly.

'Doings at the Academy only reflect what goes on in the wider world of the court,' he told us. 'When King Troven created a second rank of nobility, and gave it equal status to the first, he well knew what he was doing. When he elevated those soldier sons to lords, he won their hearts and their loyalty. The old nobility families could find no grounds to refuse them admittance to the Council of Lords. In ancient days, we of the old families had won our nobility on the battlefields, just as the new lords had. And Troven did not elevate anyone who was not the second son of an old lord. No one could say that the men he raised were of inferior blood without levelling the same accusation against their brother nobles. It divided many a family, as Spink here knows too well. In other families,' he shifted uncomfortably in his seat, 'well, it is not coincidence that I have chosen to invite you to my home when my lady-wife is away. She is one of those who feels that her own status was diminished when others were elevated to share it.'

He sighed again and looked down at his hands folded between his knees. Spink and I exchanged glances. He looked more bewildered than I felt. From my father's conversation with my uncle when we first arrived in Old Thares, I'd had an inkling that the schoolboy politics at the Academy were connected to the larger unrest among the nobles. I still had not expected my uncle to take our account so seriously. And I was surprised that my uncle reacted as if our breaking of the honour code were of little importance. I wondered if he really understood the honour code, if a man not born a soldier son could grasp how important it was. I was tempted to let sleeping dogs lie, but my father's instruction had ground honour into me. I suddenly knew that I could not carry that guilt for the next two years. I lifted my head and met his eyes squarely. 'What about the fight in our dormitory?' I asked. 'Neither Spink nor I reported it.'

He almost smiled. He shook his head fondly at me and shocked me by saying, 'Let it go, Nevare. Among any group of men, there will always be those tussles, the shouldering and jockeying for power. Spink here had the common sense to keep it within bounds. It might surprise you to know that I've seen a few fistfights in my time, and most of them were a lot bloodier and dirtier than what you described to me. I don't think anyone's honour is broken or even tarnished by it. No. What the honour code tries to prevent is the sort of thing that happened to your friend Gord or the young lieutenant. From what you say, they took serious beatings, and not from some individual with whom they clashed, but from a group of cadets who singled them out. What happened to your friend Gord might have been the impulse of the moment, but it sounds as if Tiber encountered a plot against him. That should have been reported; I am still shocked that the doctor didn't take it upon himself to question you more thoroughly. I fear that the second-years that you spoke of may have been more forthcoming as witnesses. That you did not speak differently from what they might have said . . . well. I think I will have a word with him, when I return you two to the Academy.'

I was struck dumb for an instant and looked at the floor. I desperately did not want him to do any such thing, but could not think of any reason I could give to dissuade him from it. An instant later, to my shame, I realized I was afraid that if he confronted the doctor and forced him to investigate it, the second-years would know I was the source of the conflict, and that retaliation might befall me.

I glanced back at my uncle to find him nodding at me. 'You are too honest, Nevare. Your thoughts parade openly across your face. But this is not something that should be up to you and Spink and Gord to solve for yourselves, though I do fear that you may have to face, alone, the repercussions of my attempting to solve it. Yet attempt it I must, and do what I can afterward to protect you. You are students at the King's Academy. If true justice does not prevail there, then what can we hope for when you enter the greater world as soldiers of the King?'

He sounded so solemn and so sad that it sent a chill of premonition up my spine.

'What do you fear?' I asked him, and found I was speaking in a hoarse whisper.

'I fear on a large scale what you are experiencing on a small scale. I fear old nobility facing off against the King's battle lords, in a power struggle that will eventually come to violence, and perhaps even civil war.'

'But why would that happen? Why would it ever come to that?' I asked, startled.

'Even if they dislike sharing nobility with us, why should it come to bloodshed?' Spink asked also. 'It seems to me that there is land in plenty for the King to grant to his New Nobles; and of honour, there is no limited supply that men must fear to receive a lesser share.'

'Not for land, for most of the Old Nobles perceive the lands granted to your fathers as wasteland and desert. Not for honour, for though all nobles should possess that, few think it a goal to be struggled for. No, young sirs, I fear that we speak only of money, of common coin. The King lacks it; old nobility has it, though not in the quantity that we did at one time. If he tries to squeeze it from us, as our families were squeezed through so many years of war and bloodshed, I fear we—that is, some of us, will turn on him. But his battle lords, they would stand with him, perhaps. And in so doing, stand against us, their brothers.'

Spink knit his brow. 'The King lacks for money? How can that be? He is the King!'

My uncle smiled weakly. 'Spoken like a true New Noble, I fear. The final twenty years of war with Landsing beggared the monarchy, and everyone else. King Troven's father did not hesitate to borrow from his nobles. He threw all he had into his war with Landsing, hoping to leave his son a triumph and a treaty. He did neither, but he spent a great deal of money attempting it. The debts the monarchy owes to the old nobility are many and heavy. And, some on the Council of Lords say, long past due for repayment. Troven's father was willing to grant his nobles much greater autonomy in exchange for their "generosity". But the more free rein he gave to his lords, the less inclined we were to tax our vassals for his benefit. When his father died and Troven came to power, one of the first things he did was to end the war that had drained our coffers for so long. We were glad to have the war over, yet those of us with holdings in the coastal regions were dismayed to find ourselves stripped of our estates there. Our ports, our warehouse, our fishery and our trade were all surrendered to the Landsingers. Many Old Nobles still say that in his haste to end the war swiftly, Troven gave away too much, and that much of what he gave was not his to cede.

'Then, when he turned his eyes to the east and began a

determined expansion, we had to ask ourselves, who would pay for this new war? Will the King bully us to lend money again, just as our own fortunes are starting to recover? The Council of Lords were determined it would not be so. We had grown stronger and more resolute in limiting what percentage of our taxes we would turn over to the monarchy. Even when the wars in the east went well, and we began to see the profits of victory, some nobles asked one another, "Why do we need a king at all? Why cannot we govern ourselves?"'

Spink and I had remained as still and silent as children listening to a bogey tale. This was certainly not the history I had been taught. I suddenly wondered if this was yet another of the differences between first sons and soldier sons. The treason of that thought shocked me at first, but I faced it in my heart. Then I wondered at how naïve I had been, that one talk with my uncle could re-order my whole view of the world. I asked my question carefully, fearing he would think me a traitor. 'Does the King deliberately cultivate fractiousness between his Old Nobles and his battle lords?'

'It would be in his best interest to keep them at odds,' my uncle replied carefully. 'If ever all his nobles united . . . well. Some would say, not I, of course, but some would again say "what use do we have for a king?"'

'When King Troven first turned his excursions into the east, they brought fresh wealth to nobles stripped of resources by years of war. Game meat, salted in barrels, came to our tables, and it was a new thing for many of us to have as much meat as we wanted, for our own flocks and herds had dwindled in the war years. The land that was opened up for farming yielded rich harvests, at first. We feared the competition from our battle lord brothers. But now they are finding that even letting those prairie fields lie fallow does not restore their productivity. Our crops are still in demand. In the east, there are new orchards and vineyards and fish from the streams, and more demands for the goods we manufacture as our excess population moves eastward. The only difficulty is moving the goods, and the difficulty of that adds delay, cost and inconvenience. The King anticipates rich revenues if he can finish his King's Road. I am one of the nobles who sees a great promise. The lumber and forest goods that travel intermittently to us now on barges and occasional wagons would become a steady flow, and there is a market for that lumber in Landsing as well as here at home. I can see that all would benefit if the King's Road were finished. But some think it is folly to imagine that might be done in our lifetimes. To finish his road, he must have labourers and coins to pay them. And that is where he runs into conflict with his Old Nobles. For the Old Nobles would like to keep their labourers and their coins to work on our own needs here in the west.'

'I thought the convicts were building the road,' I interrupted.

'Convicts labour much as mules do. A good driver can get solid work out of them, but if the driver is lazy or absent, the mules are useless. In the case of the convicts, they can be worse than useless; they can be trouble of a destructive nature in our new towns and on the frontier. When they have served out their time, few of them wish to settle to peaceful lives of hard work and modest returns. Some become robbers on the highway trade, preying on the very King's Road that they helped to build. Others return to being the drunks, thieves, and whoremasters they were here in the west. When you are stationed to your first posts, you will discover that our cavalla and foot soldiers are used as much to keep order in our border towns, as they are to calm the savages and advance the King's claims. You and Spink are soldiers in a troubled time, Nevare. I understand why my brother has kept you innocent of these intrigues, but soon, as an officer, you will have to navigate those uneasy waters. I think it is best that you know what you will face.'

412

'I thank you, sir, for sharing these things with me, also.' Spink spoke grimly. 'My family's holdings are closer to the borders, and I know that often we have had to defend our people, not from savages but from roving bands of outlaws. To hear the other cadets speak of their homes and peaceful upbringings made me wonder if perhaps we are the only folk so troubled. Now I see that we are not. But I still do not understand why brother should stand against brother in this. Surely the nobles, closely related as they are, could band together to act for the greater good of their king and themselves.'

'Some of us believe that to be true. Obviously, my brother and I have kept our close bonds, and feel it is in our best interests to continue them. But other families felt betrayed when the King stole their soldier sons. Many nobles felt that the lands granted to the soldier sons as their noble portions should have instead been given to the first sons of the families, to hold in trust for their soldier brothers. Why, they wonder, did the King not enrich them instead of their soldier brothers?'

'But the soldiers had earned both honour and estates! They were the ones who shed their blood and risked their lives to gain those lands for the King.'

'So the soldier son sees it, of course. But tradition was that honours and rewards that the soldier son earned were for his family, not himself. There are now noble families who have sons who have openly expressed the ambition that if they do great deeds in battle, they too may rise to the status of lords. And, I fear that not all soldier sons who have risen to noble titles have conducted themselves nobly. Many were ill prepared to deal with wealth and power. They have squandered what was granted to them, and are now in debt or disgrace. Yet even so, they are lords with the option of voting in the Council of Lords. They are vulnerable to those who would buy influence. Thus it is that many old families feel vulnerable to the new nobility in many ways.'

413

'But . . . but how do we threaten them? Or our fathers, I mean.' Spink was genuinely puzzled.

'The new nobility threatens our power and in some cases, our dignity. But most of all, they cripple our ability to advance our own goals, which may be different to the King's. For the King, the benefits of division among his nobles are undeniable. The Council of Lords is seldom able to achieve a majority vote with a quorum on any question, let alone the questions that relate directly to taxation or the king's authority. But even on matters such as boundaries and regulating the trade guilds and constructing works for the good of all, such as building bridges, we now have difficulty in reaching a consensus. Often New Nobles in the outlying areas have no care to attend the sessions or vote on things that seem not to have any impact on them. Why should they be taxed to lay rail lines in Old Thares? Then, to accomplish these things, we are forced to send an advisory to the King, who then commands that things should be so.'

'If the nobles get what they want, why do they care?' I asked. I knew the answer but I was suddenly feeling stubborn. Were these the reasons that soldier sons of new nobility were treated poorly at Academy? Things that we had no control over?

My uncle gave me a long look. Then he answered and did not answer me at once. 'All men long to be in control of their own lives. Even a loyal servant, given authority over his master's business, will soon wish for more authority, and the right to profit when he runs it well. It is human nature, Nevare. Once a man has had authority over his own affairs, he does not surrender it easily.'

Saying that seemed to rouse some strong emotion in him. He stood, rolled his shoulders, and then strode across the room. He refilled his glass of brandy. When he turned back to us, he said more calmly, 'But I remain one of the Old Nobles who is convinced of the wisdom of the King's current

414

ambitions. I think there is wealth to be found in expanding our borders. I think that if we can gain a seaport on the Rustian Sea, on the far side of the Barrier Mountains, we could gain trade contacts and alliances with the people of the far eastern lands. I know his dream seems far-fetched to many, but we live in a time of great change. Perhaps one must have big dreams and take large risks to increase our stature in the world.' He lowered his voice suddenly. 'And here at home, I think we would be wiser to unite and support him in it than oppose him. And I am troubled that this jockeying of first sons has led to a division in the Academy, and trouble amongst our soldier sons. That should not be. It starts with hazing at the Academy, but where does it stop? That I do not even wish to consider.'

I think I learned that evening the difference between how first sons and second sons were educated. My uncle had taken something I had perceived as a problem that existed in the Academy among the students there and extrapolated the consequences of it into the greater world of our military. I am not sure at all that my father would have done so. I think he would have seen it as a lapse of discipline in the school and a flaw in the administrator. My uncle saw it as a grave symptom of something already affecting the larger community, and I could feel the depth of his concern.

I could think of nothing to reply to his remarks and afterward we subsided into more general talk. When he bid us goodnight Spink and I were subdued, and parted to our separate rooms without any further discussion.

Habit awoke me early the next morning, the one day of the week when I could have slept late. I tried to huddle back into my pillows, but my perverse conscience reminded me that today I must return to the Academy grounds and that I had not yet completed my schoolwork. With a groan, I stretched and rose. I was splashing my face at the washbasin when the door opened and Epiny sailed into the room. She was still in her nightgown and wrapper, her hair in long braids past her shoulder. She greeted me with, 'What shall we do today? A séance, perhaps?' Her question was teasing. My reply was not.

'Absolutely not! Epiny, this is completely inappropriate! At your age, you should never enter a man's bedchamber unannounced and still in your nightclothes!'

She stared at me for a moment and then said, 'You're my cousin. You don't count as a man. Very well. If you are afraid to hold a séance, shall we go riding?'

'I have a lot of schoolwork to do. Please leave.'

'Very well. I told Spink that you'd probably prefer to stay behind. That leaves Sirlofty free for me, then.' She turned and started to leave.

'You and Spink are going riding? When was this decided?'

'We had early breakfast together.'

'In your nightclothes?'

'Well, he was dressed, but I scarcely see the sense of getting dressed before we've decided what to do with the day. Now I shall go and put on my riding skirts.'

'That is scandalous!'

'It's eminently sensible. If you knew how long it takes for a woman to dress, you would see that I've saved nearly an hour of my day. And there is no more precious commodity than time.' Her hand was on the doorknob. She opened the door.

I spoke hastily. 'I'm going riding with you. On Sirlofty.'

She smiled at me over her shoulder. 'You'd best hurry then if you expect to eat anything before we leave.'

Despite her claim of how long it took for a woman to dress, she was ready and waiting by the door before I had finished a very hurried breakfast. Spink was likewise eager to depart. He and Epiny stood in the foyer, talking and laughing, she with her annoying whistle clamped between her teeth all the while. Her father bade us a good-natured farewell, for he would not budge from his leisurely breakfast

and morning newspaper. I envied him, but could not tolerate the thought of Epiny showing off my horse to Spink.

Nevertheless, I was a bit disappointed. I had expected a
groom to accompany us, so that Spink and I could safely
gallop off without worrying about Epiny. Instead, we were
her guardians. Spink was mounted on a borrowed white
gelding, a well-trained saddle horse but one completely
unfamiliar with any sort of military manoeuvres. And Epiny
chose that we would ride on the bridle paths parallel to the
Grand Promenade in Cuthhew's Park. I suspected that she
enjoyed displaying herself to the proper young women riding in pony carts with their mothers or strolling the paths in
groups of three or four with an earnest chaperone. And
there was my cousin, her riding skirts barely coming to her
shins, as if she were a girl of ten instead of a young woman,
alone with two young men in cadet dress. I had not considered how we might appear to others when I had agreed to
ride with her, and feared I would bring embarrassment to
my uncle's household. Surely rumours of this outing would
fly back to my uncle's wife. How could any of Epiny's
acquaintances know that I was her cousin and responsible
for her that day? They would simply see her as out riding
with two soldier sons. Epiny's mother already disdained me.
How could Epiny put me in a position where I would appear
to deserve that scorn? I did what I could to present a
respectable appearance. I kept our pace sedate. Several times
she sighed loudly and looked exasperatedly at me. I ignored
her, determined to behave properly in such a public place.

She was the one who suddenly put her grey mare into a gallop, forcing Spink and me to give chase and exciting all sorts
of cries of alarm and consternation as we raced after her.
Epiny clung like a burr to her mount, shrilling wildly through
the otter-whistle that she still gripped in her teeth. I wondered
if she were too stupid to realize that the sound of the whistle
was probably frightening her horse and exciting Celeste to

even greater speed. I kicked Sirlofty to overtake her, but the path had narrowed and Spink and his gelding were in the way. I cried out to him to leave the path and give me clearance, but I do not think he heard me. A cyclist coming toward us wailed in alarm and crashed his machine into a laurel hedge to avoid us as we thundered past him. He shouted angrily after us.

Epiny guided her horse away from the commonly used paths and onto a lesser trail. We left the groomed environs of the park behind and soon raced, single file, down a bramble-choked winding path. Spink had his horse between my cousin and me, or Sirlofty could have easily outrun Epiny's mare and let me catch her. Twice, fallen trees blocked the way, and each time her horse cleared the obstacle in a jump, I feared that I would be bringing her lifeless body home to my uncle. We came to an open area alongside the river, and there it was that she finally pulled in her mount.

Spink reached her first, crying out, 'Epiny, are you hurt?' as he flung himself off his horse. She had already dismounted and was breathing hard. Her cheeks were very pink in the cool air and her hair had come undone from her netted hat and tangled about on her shoulders. As I rode up and dismounted, she reached back to carelessly knot it up again and restore it to the snood it had escaped.

'Of course I'm all right!' She smiled. 'Oh, what a lovely gallop that was. It did both of us much good. Celeste so seldom gets a chance to really stretch her legs.'

'I thought your horse had run away with you!' Spink exclaimed.

'Well, yes, she did, but only because I urged her to it. Come. Let us walk the horses on the path by the river to cool them. It's lovely there, even at this time of year.'

I had had enough. 'Epiny, I cannot believe your behaviour! What is the matter with you, to give us such a scare? Spink and I were terrified for you, to say nothing of the other people in the park. What ails you, that a young woman of your family and years acts like an irresponsible hoyden?'

She had begun to walk away, leading her mare. Now she turned back to me. Her face changed as completely as if she had removed a mask, and I think that in some ways, she had. She leaned toward me as she spoke, and had she been a horse, her ears would have been back and her teeth bared. 'The day I begin acting like a woman instead of a girl, the day I succumb to the manacles and shackles prepared for me is the day on which my parents will auction me off to the highest bidder. I had heard that on the border, women were allowed to have lives of their own. I had expected a more modern sensibility from you, cousin dear. Instead, over and over, you reveal my worst fears for you rather than my fondest hopes.'

'I don't know what you're talking about!' I felt angry, indignant, and strangely hurt at her disparaging words.

'I do,' Spink said quietly. 'My mother speaks of it.'

'Of what?' I demanded. Was he siding with Epiny again? I felt as I did when I first tried to learn Varnian; that people were talking but that their words conveyed no meaning.

'Of women learning to run their own affairs,' Spink said. 'I've told you how our first overseer cheated us, when my brothers and I were little more than children. My mother blames that on her education and upbringing. She says that if she had been able to understand the accounts and how the holdings should have been operated, she would have never lost for us what should have been my brother's fortune. So when she sent for a tutor for my brother, she insisted that she be allowed to sit in on all his lessons. And she has taught my two sisters all that they might need to know, should they ever become untimely widows with small children to defend.'

I stared at him, unable to think of anything to say.

'Exactly,' Epiny said, as if it justified all her strange behaviour.

I found my tongue. 'I would blame more your mother's family, that your uncle did not come to your aid.'

419

'Blaming them will not undo what is done. And even though I doubt that my elder brother would ever abandon my wife and children to such a fate, no one can predict that he would be alive and in a position to help them in such straits. My mother has said that no daughter of hers will suffer as she did, from ignorance.'

I could think of any number of replies to that, ranging from tactless to cutting. Instead, I turned to my cousin and said, 'I cannot imagine what "shackles and manacles" you are so dreading, Epiny. If you behave like a lady, you will marry well and go to a lovely home of your own, with servants to care for your needs. It seems to me that all noble ladies in Old Thares have to do is fix their hair and order new clothing to be made for them. Are those your "shackles" you speak of? It shames you to speak of your parents as "auctioning you off" as if you were a prize cow! How can you say such a cruel thing when your father so obviously loves you?'

'Shackles of velvet, and manacles of lace, dear cousin, can bind a woman as effectively as those of cold iron. Oh, my father loves me and so does my mother, and they will find some noble son of a good family who will be delighted with my dowry and will probably treat me well, especially if I produce children for him in a timely and uncomplicated way. The man they choose for me will become an important political ally, which is where I see all the difficulties arise, for my father and my mother have very different political ambitions, as you undoubtedly know.'

I understood what she spoke of, but I pointed out, 'So it has always been. My parents have chosen my wife for me, and my elder brother's wife as well.'

'Poor things!' she said with heartfelt sympathy. 'Assigned to boys before they are even men, with no more choice in their fates than an orphaned kitten has. When it is my time to wed, I intend to choose my husband for myself. And I will get me

420

a man who respects my mind.' And here she looked directly and very boldly at Spink. Spink glanced away, flushing.

I suppressed my anger and merely shook my head to indicate my disapproval, but Epiny and Spink seemed to think I was commiserating with her.

'Let's walk the horses,' Spink suggested, and they set off side by side. I went to get Sirlofty. When I caught up to them, Epiny was saying, 'Well, I admit that women don't seem to have minds adept at the maths and sciences, but I think we have other talents that men lack. Of late, I've been exploring them.'

'My sisters are at least as good at maths as I am,' Spink told her. I commented to myself that that was scarcely an endorsement, but kept my thoughts to myself.

'Well, perhaps it is because they were set to such studies earlier in life than I was. I had but the rudiments when I was small, and my governess made it seem that learning to calculate was far less important than the ten basic stitches of Varnian embroidery. So I learned them for the week and promptly forgot them. Only later did I discover that even in needlework one needs to understand proportions in order to change a pattern, and ratios to adapt a recipe . . . but that is not what I am speaking about when I mention women's talents.'

The trail had led us down a gently sloping bank to a wide grassy space. Old foundation stones jutted up from the tall grasses and butterfly bushes that grew there. A corner of a demolished building still stood, and last night's rainfall had pooled on the unevenly sunken floor. We let the horses drink there; I judged it better than risking the steep bank and stinking river water. I suspected the structure had been an old brewery. Soil had washed over the old stone floor in a shallow layer and grass had sprouted and died there. Without asking us, Epiny slipped Celeste's bit and let her loose on the brownish tufts.

'We cannot stay long,' I protested, but she ignored me. Epiny

421

seated herself on a wall of exposed foundation stones and stared out over the river. Plainly this was not the first time she and Celeste had come here. I sat down beside her and Spink sat down next to me. She seemed suddenly melancholy and against my better judgment, I felt sorry for her. She was very forlorn and alone. I spoke gently to her. 'Epiny. I don't understand why your future makes you unhappy, but I see it does. And I'm sorry for that. It can be hard sometimes but we must all endeavour to accept the roles the good god has set for us.'

I don't think she even heard me. She gave a sniff and sat up straighter. 'Well. We all know what we must do now, and that is to find out exactly what was going on last night. We should hold another séance.'

'We have no time,' I said quickly. 'Spink and I both have to return to the Academy this afternoon. In fact, we should return to your home very soon. Spink and I have to pack and then return to the Academy before nightfall. There won't be time for a séance this afternoon.'

'Well, of course not. I meant right now, and here. That's why I brought you here, you know. It's very private.'

I was startled and unprepared. 'But . . . it's broad daylight. And I thought . . .'

'You thought I'd have to set up some sort of trick. I don't, Nevare. That is what is so upsetting to me about this talent. Ever since my first séance with Guide Porilet, it has been only too easy. I feel like she opened a window in my mind, and I don't know how to shut it. I feel I must always stand watch between my thoughts and that other world. Those others stand there, right at my shoulder, just at the corner of my vision, waiting for a chance to speak through me. Pressing always against my boundaries.'

'It sounds very uncomfortable,' Spink said. He leaned out around me to speak to Epiny.

She looked a little startled. 'I am surprised you would understand that!' she exclaimed, and then shocked me by saying, 'Oh. I did not mean to be rude when I said that. It is just that I've become so accustomed to people saying, "I have no idea what you are talking about." Even my mother, who first took me to a séance, says that. You know, I am not sure that she believes in what Guide Porilet does. I fear she thinks it is just a game she plays, a pretence she makes to win favour with the Queen.' She, too, was leaning past me to speak to him. I stood up and stepped away, uncomfortable to be in the middle of their exchange. She immediately slid closer to him on the wall and held out a hand to him, adding, 'I know that what we do is real. I think you know it, too. Shall we attempt it here and now?'

'Attempt what?' he asked her. A very foolish smile spread across his face like some sort of creeping rash.

'A séance, of course. Nevare, come here and take hands. No, wait, this won't do. Last night, something very dark and powerful was going on. If I am overtaken by spirits, I don't want to go tumbling off the wall. Let's find a more comfortable place on the grass and make a tiny circle.'

'I'm afraid that we'll be late getting back,' I protested, backing further away from them. I didn't even want to talk about last night or admit that anything had happened, let alone attempt a re-enactment. 'Spink and I do have to return to the Academy this afternoon, you know.'

'And you're afraid. That's natural, Nevare. But you don't need to worry about being late. My father will scarcely leave without you. And you know that we must do this, for our own peace of mind. Here's a good place. Come sit with us.'

She had been moving as she spoke, drawing Spink along after her. She indicated a flat place amongst the ruins that did not look too damp, and then, folding her legs, sat down cross-legged, her riding skirt conforming to her body in a way that was entirely too revealing. She still had not released Spink's hand, and with a tug, she pulled him down to sit beside her. 'Hurry up, Nevare,' she chided me.

'But—'

'If you are so worried about the time, do sit down and let us get this over with.'

I eased myself down across from them. She immediately held out her free hand to me. I looked at it without enthusiasm. Honesty took me. 'I'm not that worried about the time. I didn't like what happened last night, whatever it was. Quite frankly, whatever it was, I'd prefer to ignore it and go on with my regular life. I've no desire to repeat that experience with another séance.'

'Ignore it? You could just ignore it?' she demanded of me.

'Exactly what did happen last night?' Spink asked almost at the same moment.

'I don't know, and I don't want to know,' I told them both. To Epiny I said firmly, 'Whatever you did to me, I didn't enjoy it. No more séances.'

Epiny stared at me for a moment. 'You thought that was a séance? You thought that – whatever it was – was something I did? I beg your pardon, cousin dear. Whatever happened last night was all *you*. All that strangeness came from you. I'm only asking you to let me find out what it was by asking the spirits. Because whatever it was, I think you need to know. I don't think ignoring it will make it go away. That's like saying of an ambush, "Oh, just keep riding and ignore those enemies. Hope for the best, that they'll let us pass". You need to stand your ground and face it, Nevare. Better to do it now while you have friends with you than to face it alone later.'

'I'm not sure I agree with you,' I grumbled. Her advice applied too well to what I was facing when I returned to the Academy. I wondered unhappily how much Spink had told her. Both she and Spink held out their hands to me, and I surrendered. I settled myself and unwillingly held out my hands. Epiny seized mine immediately. I was relieved that the unearthly resistance we had encountered last night was gone. Perhaps that meant nothing peculiar would happen

424

this time. I clasped hands with Spink as well. We sat in a circle like children beginning some nursery game. I was almost immediately uncomfortable. The ground was uneven and stony. 'Now what do we do?' I asked, somewhat irritably. 'Do we shut our eyes and hum? Or bow our heads and—'

'Hush!' Spink replied, his voice commandingly intense.

I glared at him but he was staring, mouth ajar, at Epiny. I followed his gaze and felt repelled. She had allowed her mouth to fall half-open and her face to slacken. Her eyeballs were visible beneath her half-open lids and they were jittering back and forth like marbles rattled in a can. She drew in a long, raspy breath through her nose and let it out through her mouth. A tiny bubble of spittle rode it.

'Disgusting!' I said in quiet dismay, appalled at my cousin's shameless theatrics. This was far worse than whatever she had subjected me to the night before.

'Be quiet!' Spink hissed. 'Can't you feel the change in her hand? This is real!'

Her small hand in mine was very warm to the touch compared to Spink's cold and callused one. I had not noticed before how warm it was. Then, as Epiny's head first lolled back and then rolled laxly forward on her neck, her hand in mine grew cooler. In two heartbeats, it was as if I held hands with a corpse. I exchanged worried glances with Spink. Epiny spoke. 'Don't let go,' she begged us. 'Don't let me get lost here in the wind.'

I had been at the point of dropping her hand. Now I held it firmly. Her small fingers clutched at mine as if her very life depended on it.

'Let's stop this,' Spink said quietly. 'Epiny, I thought you were playing a game with us. This is . . . Let's stop this. I don't like it at all.'

She made a sound, an ugly noise somewhere between a retch and a sigh. She seemed to struggle to control her own voice. Then, 'Can't,' she muttered. 'I can't shut the window. They're here all the time.'

'Enough!' I said. I tried to let go of Epiny's hand, but she held on to my fingers with unnatural strength.

'Someone's coming,' she whispered. Her head dropped, sagging to her breast. Then I felt something change in her. I still cannot explain what happened. Perhaps it was something like looking through rain on a dusty windowpane, and seeing a shape and then suddenly recognizing the person outside. Up to then, I had thought her sounds and grimaces a selfish and ugly little game she was playing to mock us. At that moment, it became something much more dangerous. She lifted her head, but it wobbled on her neck. She looked at me but someone else was looking out of her eyes. The gaze she turned on me was tired and worn and old.

'We weren't dead,' she said quietly. The voice wasn't Epiny's. She spoke with the accent of a frontier woman. She closed her eyes tightly for a moment, and then tears ran from their corners. 'I wasn't dead. My little boy wasn't dead. We'd just been sick so long. I could hear them talking but I couldn't rouse myself. They said that we were dead. They sewed us up together in a burial bag. They'd run out of coffins. We woke up under the ground. We couldn't get out. I tried. I tried to free us. I tore my nails against the canvas. I bit it until my teeth bled in my gums. We died there, in that sack, under the ground. And all around us, in that burying ground that night, we heard others dying the same way. We died. But I didn't cross their bridge.'

Her voice didn't sound angry, just flat with sorrow. She looked at me earnestly. 'Will you remember that, please? Remember it. 'Cause there'll be others.'

'I will,' I said. I think I would have said anything to give that poor soul comfort. Epiny's eyes went dull and the woman's expression faded from her face, leaving her features soft and unformed.

I breathed a huge sigh of relief it was over. 'Epiny?' I said. I gave her hand a little shake. 'Epiny?'

Something or someone else took her. It didn't slide into

426

her as the woman had. It seized her so that her body jerked sharply in its grip. Her hold on my hand tightened painfully and I heard Spink gasp at her grip. When she lifted her face and looked me in the eyes, I recoiled as if her gaze burned me. Tree woman looked at me from my cousin's face. A pain tingled, then burned through me, from the top of my head down to the base of my spine. I felt immobilized by it.

'I did not summon you!' she said disdainfully. 'You are not welcome here until I call you. Why do you try to come to me? Do you seek to give my magic to her? Do you think you can touch our magic and not be touched by it? Magic touches back, soldier's boy. Magic may give, but it always takes. You send this little one into my world, with no thought for her. What if I decide to keep her, soldier's boy? Would that teach you not to play with my magic? Hold fast, do you say, and make our sign to invoke it? Hold fast indeed.'

Epiny abruptly let go of my hand. I felt dizzy when she did so, as if I dangled over a chasm with only Spink's hand to grip. To my shock, her freed hand made the little charm sign over her own hand where she clasped Spink's, the sign every good cavalla-man makes over his cinch to make it hold. Tree woman looked back at me through Epiny's eyes and smiled her knowing smile. 'When the time comes, I will show you what "hold fast" means, soldier's boy.'

Then Epiny suddenly wilted, her softened hand pulling loose from Spink's as she collapsed. He released my hand and caught her by the shoulders before her face struck the ground. He pulled her back to lean against him and looked at me with anguish.

'Is she dead?' I asked dully. I was surprised the words emerged from my mouth. Control of my body came back to me slowly, like a numbed hand buzzing back to usefulness.

'No, no, she's breathing. What happened, Nevare? What was that? What did she mean?'

'I don't know,' I said, and I was not lying, for I did not

know any way I could explain it to him. A creature I had dreamed seemed to have reached out and threatened me through my cousin. I felt dizzy. I put both hands to the sides of my head as if that would still the whirling of the world. One of my fingertips brushed the old scar on my scalp. It was hot and pulsed with pain. My recollection of the injury flared fresh in my mind. I closed my eyes and shook my head. I tried to push the knowledge away from me, but it would not leave. It threatened to put a crack in my ordinary and logical life. Only a crazy man could have made any sense from the events. I did not want to be crazy, and so I could not think seriously about these things or permit them to have meaning in my life. I lumbered to my feet and panting, staggered away from them both. I was suddenly angry, with Epiny and myself, for allowing any of my strange dreams and experiences to take that one step closer to my reality. I was angry that Spink had witnessed it. 'I wish I had never let her talk me into this séance nonsense!' I snarled.

'I don't think that was fakery, Nevare,' Spink said firmly, as if I had asserted it was. He still held my cousin in his arms. His face was pale, his freckles standing out sharply on his face. 'Whatever happened here was, well, not real but . . . not pretend, either.' He finished his sentence lamely. 'She's not waking up, Nevare! What did we allow her to do? I should have listened to you. I know that now, I should have listened to you. Epiny? Nevare, I'm so sorry. Epiny! Please, wake up!'

I looked away from the misery on his face. Spink, like me, was an eminently sensible man. If we started believing that my cousin could summon spirits that talked through her, well, where would that belief carry us? Yet if we did not believe it, we must decide that either she was insane, or an unrepentant liar making fools of us. I stubbornly rejected every theory, and turned my back on Spink's dilemma in order to ignore my own. 'This should never have happened!' I said savagely. I think Spink took it as a rebuke to him. He had begun to timidly pat at Epiny's cheek in an effort to bring her around. He looked frightened, almost as if he wanted to cry.

I went and wet my handkerchief in the river and came back to dab at her wrists and temples. Epiny roused quite slowly. Even when she could sit up by herself, she still seemed dazed. Finally, she looked at me and said, 'I want to go home now. Please.'

I caught our horses and helped my cousin to mount. Our ride back was far more sedate than our journey there. I did not speak at all. Spink essayed several bland pleasantries, and after his third effort, Epiny said she would like to listen to the birds' song for the rest of the ride. There were no birds that I saw or heard. I think she knew Spink was unnerved by our experience and was trying to make her feel better, but could not summon the energy to reward him. I wanted to dismiss the whole incident as her dramatic ploy to get Spink's attention. I could not. If it had all been a pretence, why didn't she take advantage of his concern now? Instead she looked straight ahead, unspeaking, and I wondered how much of the séance, if any, she remembered. She dismounted at the door, and I allowed Spink to escort her inside while I took the horses around to the stable.

When I came in, Spink told me that Epiny had a severe headache and would not be joining us for luncheon. When we saw my uncle at the table and I passed on this message, he nodded calmly and said that she was often plagued with headaches. He seemed to find nothing odd about it, and turned the talk to plans for when we might next come to visit. Spink could not seem to find a response or an appetite. He pushed his food about on his plate and when I said that we had been warned that our studies would soon become more difficult and that we should save our free time for our books, Spink nodded unhappily.

SEVENTEEN

Tiber

The carriage ride back to the Academy was a quiet one. It seemed to pass very quickly, as time does when one is dreading something. Both Spink and I were subdued, and my uncle very thoughtful. The bizarre séance and Epiny's abrupt withdrawal after it filled my thoughts. I struggled with whether or not it was my duty to tell my uncle of all that had transpired. The worst was that I could not in good conscience talk about it without revealing to him my subjective experience of it. I dissected the 'séance', trying to recall every word that Epiny had said to me. Slowly, I began to see that it was my interpretation of her words that was so otherworldly and strange. She had never said, 'I am Tree Woman, reaching for you from your past!' I had supplied all those connections myself. All she had done was look at me with a strange expression on her face and mutter some vague references to magic and 'hold fast' charms.

I felt swept by a tide of revelation. I had created it all in my mind. That was all. Nothing had really happened. Charitably, I decided that Epiny did believe that spirits were invading her mind and making her say and do strange things. She was not a conscious fraud. I had been drawn in by her play-acting or delusion, and I had provided the unspoken details that had made the séance so alarming. If, as a rational and modern man, I looked at what she had said and done, there was really very little to it. I drew in a deep breath, and with great relief, rejected my fears. All my anxiety was of my own making, the penalty I must pay for having indulged in her ungodly game of séance. The next time, I would know better. I was older and a man. I had set her a bad example by participating. I would not make that error again.

Spink, too, was silent and withdrawn, staring out the window wordlessly at the passing scenery. I think my uncle mistook the cause of our gloom. As we drew closer to the Academy gates, he took a deep breath and then warned us that he had sent a messenger ahead that morning, to request 'an hour of the commander's time'. Then he added, 'I know you two are dreading what your honesty may have brought down upon you and your fellows. If Colonel Stiet is any kind of true officer, then he will appreciate knowing that there are abuses going on within his command. Lieutenant Tiber deserves to be treated fairly, as do all first-years of any parentage. Stiet should take steps to assure equity, and I intend to ask him to keep me informed of his progress in dealing with the offenders. If what I hear does not satisfy me, then I will write to your father, or go directly to the board that oversees the Academy. If it comes to that, you both may be called on to testify. I don't think it will go that far, but I want to be honest with you. Through no fault of your own, you have entered difficult waters. Nevare, I want you to write to me daily and with honesty. If letters do not arrive from you as expected, I will be visiting here again, so see that you do not neglect this task.'

My heart sank at his words, but I dutifully replied, 'Yes, Uncle.' To have him remind me that there were other, weightier matters hanging over my head dampened my spirits even more thoroughly.

We bade him farewell at the entrance to the Administration Building. Spink and I watched him as he strode up the steps and entered. I thought I caught a brief glimpse of Caulder when the door was opened. I hoped not. I'd seen as much of that youngster as I wanted, and desired still less to have anything to do with him after I had seen how Epiny disdained him. I wished I had not witnessed the scene between them; Caulder would not forget that I had seen his humiliation. Spink and I shouldered our bags and headed back toward Carneston House. Halfway there, Spink spoke up suddenly but quietly.

'Epiny stays in my mind. She . . . defies comparison.'

I felt myself flush slightly. 'That's a kind way to put it,' I replied gruffly. I felt it a bit unfair of Spink to point out just how oddly she had behaved. Surely he could see that it was not my fault, and that I had suffered just as acutely as he had.

Then he said shyly, 'She's so sensitive, and so lovely. Like a butterfly, wafting on the wind. I think she feels things much more keenly than the rest of us.'

For a time, I was quiet. I was shocked. Sensitive and lovely? Epiny? I had felt mostly irritated and embarrassed by her. But Spink had *enjoyed* her company? Strange thoughts were suddenly unfolding in my mind. To be certain, I asked him, 'You liked her, then?'

A wide and foolish grin spread across his face. 'Oh, more than liked! Nevare, I am smitten with her. Smitten. I always thought that was a silly word. But now I understand completely what it means.' He took a deep breath and gave me a sorrowful look. 'And now you will say that you are sorry, but that she is promised already and has been since she was a child.'

'If you asked me, I would say she is still a child. If she is promised, I do not know of it, and I doubt it would be so.' There was a much larger obstacle, one that I was loath to point out to him, but I was equally reluctant to leave him ignorant. I gathered my courage. 'The problem would not be that she was spoken for, Spink. It might be that my aunt would be unwilling to consider an offer from a new nobility family. My uncle did not speak of it directly, but it is an

432

open secret within our family that she resents my father's elevation and allies herself only with old nobility.'

He shrugged, almost dismissing my concern. 'But her father seemed to like me, and Epiny herself . . . well . . .' He stopped short before he said anything indelicate.

'Epiny obviously likes you,' I admitted. 'I thought her rather too forward about indicating that to you.'

His face and tone lightened, as if I had just given a brother's consent to his courtship. 'Then if I could win your uncle's regard and good will, I might have a chance with her.'

I doubted it. I suspected that my aunt had a will of steel. Seeing how Epiny had ridden roughshod over my uncle, I doubted that he would stand up to my aunt well. And even if my uncle were well disposed toward Spink himself, all he had told me of his family made me sure that he was a poor prospect as a match for my cousin. No money, no influence, new nobility . . . 'You might have a chance,' I heard myself concede, simply because I lacked the courage to point out to him that his odds of success were less than a whisper's chance against storm winds.

He looked at me oddly, as if he had somehow managed to hear my mental reservation. 'Speak to me plainly here, my friend. Do you feel I set my sights too high? Would you oppose my courting your cousin?'

I laughed out loud. 'Spink, no, of course not! I can think of nothing I would like better than to call you cousin as well as friend. But what I might oppose is my cousin courting you! My friend, in temperament and manners, I think you could do far better than Epiny. Even if you were thinking of taking a plains wife.'

He looked shocked and then gave an odd laugh. 'A plains wife? My mother would kill me. No, she wouldn't have a chance. My brother would do it first.'

Our steps had carried us to the door of our dormitory. We checked in with the sergeant and then went up the steps to our room. Spink asked me not to speak too much of Epiny before the other fellows, and I was only too happy to comply. We greeted Oron and Caleb. They were both finishing their assignments at the study table. They kept us listening for some time as they recounted their stay with Oron's aunt. She had hosted a musical gathering at her home, and they were full of stories of ribald songs, risqué dancing, and a young woman who had bedded both of them on the same night with neither the wiser to it at the time. Even now, they were astonished, scandalized and delighted to have such a wild adventure to tell. It made the tales from Caleb's penny adventure books pale by comparison.

I was almost relieved that they gave us no room to talk of our own time away from the dormitory. Spink and I were talking of settling down and getting our assignments finished before the evening meal when we opened the door to our room. There we halted, filled with dismay that rapidly turned to anger.

My bunk had been overturned and all my books strewn about the floor. My carefully pressed and brushed uniform parts were scattered around the room. It looked as if someone had thrown them down and then trampled and kicked them about. There was a dusty footprint clearly outlined on the back of my jacket. Spink's things had suffered similar vandalism. The bedding from the other bunks in the room had been flung about, but Natred and Kort's belongings still rested on their shelves. Whoever had done this had targeted Spink and me for most of the mayhem. Spink recovered first, beginning to curse savagely in a low voice very unlike his normal tone. I stepped back into the common room and called Oron and Caleb. They came quickly, wondering what could be wrong, and then stood in shock when they saw the mess in our room.

'Any ideas on who might have done this?' I asked them.

Oron spoke first. 'We only returned to Carneston House about an hour ago. And I had no reason to come in here.' He looked at Caleb.

Caleb was as mystified. 'Our room was fine when we unpacked. Nothing was touched in there.'

'Check the other room,' Spink suggested brusquely.

In the room that Gord shared with Rory and Trist, Gord's bedding and possessions were the only ones that had been disturbed. The mess in there was even worse than in our room; Gord's books and personal items had been heaped on top of his bedding on the floor, and someone had urinated on them. In the closed room, the smell was overpowering. We quickly backed out.

'I'm reporting this to Sergeant Rufet,' I announced.

'Do you think that's a good idea?' Caleb asked me. The gangly cadet looked even more anxious than usual.

'It's going to be seen as tattling,' Oron added, scowling. 'And no one likes a snitch, Nevare.'

In one sense, I knew he was right. A deep dread surged in me. This was how they reacted simply because we knew what they had done. This was how they sought to cow and silence us. When they discovered that we had talked to my uncle and that he had taken the matter to the commander, what would they do then? Abruptly, I knew that keeping silent about this and accepting their abuse would not stop it. My uncle's complaint to Colonel Stiet might stir them to worse things, but keeping silent hadn't made them leave us alone. Reporting this was the only way I could stand up to them. Difficult as it was, even though my fellow cadets might see me as weak, I held myself to what my uncle had said I must do. 'It's not "snitching".' I told Caleb and Oron. 'It's a cadet reporting vandalism to the dormitories while we were gone.' They just stared at me, unconvinced. Why was this so difficult? My uncle had said it was the right thing to do. 'I'm going downstairs now. Leave this mess alone until Rufet has seen it.'

'Should I go with you?' Spink offered quietly.

'I think one of us is enough,' I told him, but he knew I was grateful for his offer.

With every step I took down the stairs, doubts assailed me. Reporting it seemed a whining and babyish thing to do, running to the sergeant to tattle. I knew the others might speak with disdain. Were we too soft to take a bit of pranking in stride? Yet the early months of school were past, and what had been done to our rooms went beyond ordinary hazing.

I stood before the sergeant's desk until he looked up at me. Then, in as calm a voice as I could muster, I reported the damage to our rooms and possessions. He heard me out, his face darkening with anger. Then he led the way back up the stairs to survey the mess for himself. He questioned Oron and Caleb, but they had nothing to tell. The mess could have been made at any time. When he realized there would be no easy discovery of the culprits, his orders were terse. 'Clean it up. Have Cadet Lading report to me. I'll see that you get fresh bedding. There isn't much more I can do.'

Spink and I set to work on our area immediately. As our other roommates trickled in, they expressed various levels of outrage or amusement at our predicament.

'It isn't just the time lost when we should be doing assignments,' Spink complained as he pulled the bedding tight on his bunk. 'It's the feeling of invasion, and of being the butt of a joke with no chance to hit back.'

Rory had come into the room. Without anyone asking him to do it, he began to put Natred's and Kort's bedding back on their bunks as he spoke to us. 'At least your stuff is just tossed about. Our room reeks like a sty and it's freezing in there. Oron says he just about passed out from the smell when he first walked in, so he opened our window. That didn't help much. Trist is furious with Gord; he says if he don't come back soon and clean up the mess, he's just going to toss all his stuff. And I'll be there lending a hand!'

'It's not Gord's fault!' I said. 'No more than this is our fault. Trist should be mad at whoever did it.'

'Well, I sort of see it both ways,' Rory replied obstinately.

436

'Obviously, you and Spink and Gord made someone really mad at you that night. Gord's never said what happened, but I don't believe he fell down the steps. Now they're getting their own back at you all, but Trist and I are the ones who are paying for it.'

'You're paying for it? How?' Spink was incensed.

'Our whole room reeks, that's how! And Gord isn't even here to clean it up, so we have to put up with it until he gets back. I don't even want to go in there.'

'You could clean it up for him.'

'It's his stuff. It's his mess.'

'You just made Natred's and Kort's bed up. Why is that different?'

Rory grinned good-naturedly, but still could not completely admit his hypocrisy. 'Well, their stuff isn't covered in piss, for one thing. And for another, I like them.'

'And you don't like Gord?' I was surprised.

He looked at me in disbelief that I could be so stupid. 'Not much.' He sighed. 'Look, Spink, I know he helps you a lot, and I guess you and Nevare both like him well enough. But you two don't have to live with him. He smells awful when he comes in from marching, like bacon gone bad. And he's always sweaty. And he's noisy; his bed creaks under him at night, and he lies on his back and snores like a pig. He's so damn big that every time he walks in the door, the room feels crowded. I've seen you two stand side by side and shave at the same basin when you have to hurry. Can't do that with Gord. There's no room. And he's just, well, annoying. He's always trying to be too friendly. He invites the things that happen to him with the way he calls attention to himself. Why does he have to be so huge? The first time I saw him nekkid, I just about got sick. He's all pale and wobbly and . . . Well, it was Trist first said it, but I'll admit I laughed. With the gut he has, we wonder if he even knows he has a cock. He prob'ly hasn't seen it in a couple of years at least.'

Rory laughed at his own joke. Spink and I didn't. A week ago, I would have, I realized. But now it seemed a personal affront, as if a rough joke about Gord were mockery of us as well. Why? Not because we were his friends; I still did not feel that great a personal attachment to him. It was because whoever had targeted him had attacked us as well, and somehow made the three of us into a single entity now. Like it or not, when they mocked Gord, it was mockery of us as well. I didn't like it at all.

Rory threw up his hands at our silent stares and shrugged defensively. 'Well, take it that way if you want to. It's not personal, not with me. I like you fellers.' He took a shallow breath as if daring himself to speak. He lowered his voice. 'When I was leaving for the Academy, my father said, "Son, choose your friends well. Don't let them choose you; you be the one who decides who your pals are. The needy and weak ones will always be the first to try to become close friends with those they perceive as strong. In the cavalla, a man needs strong allies who will stand back to back with him, not weaklings who shelter in his shadow." When I first met you fellers, I knew you were strong, and that I could count on you at my back. And when I first met Gord, I knew that he didn't have the stamina or strength to be a real officer. He's a liability to those who befriend him. That's why he's always trying to be everyone's buddy, and doing everyone favours; he knows he'll need pals to protect him if he ever gets into a tough situation. You know that's true.'

I put the last book back on my shelf and then stood silent, thinking over what Rory had said. By having Spink as a friend, I'd also chosen to be associated with Gord. And, by default, that cut me off from being friends with Trist. If I had not befriended both Spink and Gord, I could have been one of Trist's companions. I liked Spink and instinctively knew that in many ways our values were more compatible than if I had followed Trist. Yet I also knew that Trist was more charismatic, more social, and more . . . I searched for a word, and nearly laughed aloud when I found it. Fashionable. Trist was making connections and winning friends among the older cadets, even those of old nobility blood. He'd eaten at the commander's table, and even now, when Caulder scorned most of the new nobility, he still greeted Trist warmly. If I had been Trist's friend, those connections and associations would have been open to me as well. But I had met Spink first, and at my father's recommendation, had chosen him as a friend. Had my father been wrong?

Even as doubt and guilt for feeling that doubt assailed me, I realized that something was missing. 'My rock's gone!'

Rory and Spink looked at me as if I were slightly mad.

'The rock I brought from home with me. I always kept it on that shelf. It was a, well, an important keepsake.'

'Your girl gave it to you?' Rory asked, even as Spink suggested pragmatically, 'Did you look under your bunk?'

I was on my knees, looking under every bed and in the corners of the room when I heard Gord return. He was greeted with an uproar of voices, some telling him what had befallen him even as others demanded that he immediately clean it up. I reached the door just in time to see peace and relaxation fade from his face to be replaced by his usual expression of resigned caution. It struck me for the first time how much he had changed since the first day of Academy. We all followed him to the door of his room, to gawk at his shock and dismay.

I think the others were disappointed at his reaction. He walked into the room, looked down at the ruined books, soiled clothing, and sodden bedding and made not a sound. He did not curse or stamp or whine. He only drew in a deep breath that swelled his back against the tightness of his coat. It reminded me of a beetle's carapace as he lowered his head into his shoulders. 'What a mess,' he said finally. Then he hung up his greatcoat in his cupboard and set his weekend satchel on the floor beside it. There was a posy pinned to the lapel of his greatcoat, and I wondered if the girl he was promised had put it there. Could she love him, fat and unlovely as he was? Was that where he got the strength to go to the urine-soaked blankets and tug them off his books and notes? As he picked it up, the sodden blanket sprayed yellow drops on the floor. There was a collective chorus of groans of disgust and one or two chuckles of that horrified laughter that comes over men in bad situations.

I stepped forward. 'Sergeant Rufet said to tell you that he would issue you clean bedding.'

Gord glanced up at me and for a moment the opacity in his eyes melted. I saw the pain this insult had dealt him. But his voice was flat when he spoke. 'Thanks, Nevare. I guess that is where I'd better start then.'

'I've got to get to my assignments. Spink and I didn't get our work finished during our time away.' I was making an excuse not to help him and I knew it. I left him and got my books and went to the study table. Spink came and joined me a while later. When I glanced up at him, he said, 'There's not much I can do in there. He's made up his bed and dried off his books as best as he can.' He opened his books. Without looking at me, he added, 'All his drafting notes are ruined. He asked if I thought you'd let him copy yours onto clean paper, and I said you probably would.'

I nodded and bent my head back to my studies. A time later, I heard the swishing of a scrub brush at work.

That incident was a turning point in my first year at the Academy. After that, the division was so plain within our rooms that we might have been wearing different uniforms. Spink, Gord and I were seen as a unit, with Kort and Natred in a separate orbit around us. They spoke to us in our room in the evening, and never shunned us, but neither did they go with us to the library or spend free time with us. Kort and Natred seemed a self-sufficient duo, not needing any other alliance. Trist ruled the roost for the rest of them. Oron was probably closest to him, or gave every sign of wishing to be. He always sat beside Trist, nodding to his every word and laughing the loudest at his jests. Caleb and Rory followed the golden cadet without question. Sometimes, Rory came to our room to visit and talk, but not as often as he had. And when we sat at the study table or at the mess table, we sat divided by our loyalties.

We did not find out who had invaded our rooms, nor did I find my precious rock. It was strange for it to vanish, for there had been a small amount of money in a coat pocket, and that had not been taken. It became common knowledge that I had reported the incident to Sergeant Rufet. The day after we returned, I was called out of Drafting class. A third-year marched me silently to the Administration Building. I was immediately guided to an upstairs chamber. My escort tapped on the door, and then waved me in. Heart hammering, I entered the room. I saluted, and then stood silently. The room was panelled in dark wood, and the winter daylight from the tall, narrow windows did not seem to reach me. There was a long table, and six men seated around it. Cadet Lieutenant Tiber, bandaged and pale, was seated to one side in a straight-backed chair. His posture was very stiff, either from nervousness or the pain of his injuries. Beside him, standing at parade rest was Cadet Ordo. I recognized Colonel Stiet and Dr Amicas among the men seated at the long table. A figure moved near the windows, and I realized Caulder Stiet was there as well, observing. I directed my salute to the colonel. 'Reporting as ordered, sir,' I said, trying to keep my voice steady.

Colonel Stiet did not mince words. 'And if you had not waited to be ordered to report, things might have been made clear much sooner, Cadet. It will not look well on your records that you had to be summoned to speak here, rather than volunteering your information immediately after the incident.'

He had not asked me a question, so I could not venture a

reply. My mouth was suddenly dry, and my heart hammered so loud I could hear it in my ears. Cowardly. Here I was, facing no more than a room full of men, and I feared I might faint from terror. I took a deep breath and steadied myself.

'Well?' the colonel demanded of me, so suddenly that I jumped.

'Sir?'

Stiet took in a deep breath through his nose. 'Your uncle, Lord Burvelle of the West, had to come to me personally to divulge to me that you had not reported all you saw on the night Cadet Lieutenant Tiber was injured. You are now here to tell us, completely and in your own words, exactly what you witnessed. Proceed.'

I took a deep breath and wished desperately for water. 'I was returning to my dormitory, Carneston House, from the infirmary, when I saw Caulder Stiet running toward us—'

'Stop there, Cadet! I think we all need to know why you were out of your dormitory at such an hour and wandering around the campus.' Stiet's voice was severe, as if I had tried to conceal some wrongdoing.

'Yes, sir,' I replied mildly. I began again. 'Caulder Stiet came to Carneston House to summon Cadet Kester and myself to the infirmary, to help Cadet Lading home.'

I paused, to see if this was a good starting place. The colonel nodded at me irritably, and I spoke on. I tried to tell my story simply, but without subtracting anything. I spoke of the doctor's words to me, hoping I did not betray him. From the corner of my eye, I saw him nodding, his lips pinched flat. When I spoke of him sending Caulder home, and the boy's response, Colonel Stiet scowled, and his scowl became deeper when I spoke of my second encounter with the boy that night. I was careful as I recounted all that I had seen and heard when I found Tiber. I dared one glance at him. He stared straight ahead, his face expressionless. When I mentioned Cadet Ordo, a man at the table nodded slightly, but when I added Cadet Jaris, I saw Stiet start, as if surprised. So his name had not been included in this, I decided. I wished I could have seen Tiber's face, but didn't dare to look. I wondered if he had known his attackers, and if he did, if he had volunteered or kept to himself their names. I even included, as I finished my report, that Sergeant Rufet had said that Cadet Tiber was not a drinker. I hoped I was not bringing any trouble down on the sergeant by doing so, but felt it was the only way I could cast doubt on Tiber's drunkenness. I had been meticulously careful to say only what I had observed and to make no mention of the conclusions I had known.

When I was finished, Colonel Stiet let me stand some time in silence. Then he shuffled some papers before him and said sternly, 'I will be sending your father a letter, Cadet Burvelle, about this incident. I will let him know that I think he should encourage you to be more forthcoming in the future if you witness something untoward on the Academy grounds. You may go.'

There was only one possible response. 'Yes, sir.' But as I began my salute, a man at the table said, 'A moment. Surely I can ask the boy a few questions if I wish?'

'I am not sure that would be appropriate, Lord Tiber.'

'Damn what is appropriate, sir. I'm after the truth here.' The man stood suddenly and pointed a finger at me. 'Cadet. Do you think my son was drunk? Did you see him arrive back at the campus in a carriage? Do you know of any reason why he'd be carrying his schoolbooks with him if he'd gone into Old Thares to get drunk? Did the manner of the other cadets make you think they wished you would leave, so they could finish what they had started?' His voice rose on every question. I had heard of people 'shaking in their boots'. I was doing it now. I think if the table had not been in the way, he would have advanced on me. I stood my ground but it was difficult.

'Lord Tiber! I must ask you to sit down. Cadet Burvelle, you are dismissed. Return to your classes.'

'Damn it, Stiet, my son's career is on the line here! The rest of his life. I want the truth. All of it.'

'Your son's career is in no danger, Lord Tiber. If Burvelle had come forward immediately, I would never have considered dismissing him from the Academy. He is restored to the Academy and to his rank, and the incident will be expunged from his record. Does that satisfy you?'

'No!' the man roared. 'Justice would satisfy me. Punishment for those who ambushed my boy and stole the journal of the abuses to New Noble cadets that he had been keeping. Cleaning out the corruption that you are allowing to spread through this institution would satisfy me.'

'Cadet Burvelle, you are dismissed! You should not need to hear a command twice.' The anger Colonel Stiet could not direct at Lord Tiber had found a target in me.

'Yes, sir. Sorry, sir.' I finally found my legs and walked from the room. As I went out the door, I heard the shouting continue. Even after I shut it, the sounds of the altercation followed me. I walked down the hall, around the corner and then stopped to lean briefly on the wall. Of course I should have gone immediately to the doctor with what I had seen. It seemed obvious to me now, but at the time, it had seemed all guesses and suspicions, with no real facts to base them on. Now I had earned myself a letter of complaint to my father, a note in my record, the reputation of a snitch among the Old Noble cadets and the reputation of a coward among the New Noble cadets. I was sure that was how Tiber and his father must see me; I had held back when I could have cleared his name, because I was afraid to oppose those who had beaten him. That was how it must look to them. That was how it looked to me, now. And Caulder would be sure to let all his New Noble friends know that I had named names when Tiber evidently had not. I trudged back to my classes and went through the rest of my day in a daze.

In the days that followed, Spink, Gord, and I all seemed to

share the shame of being a snitch, for often there were low catcalls when we walked somewhere, or spit-wads that seemed to come out of nowhere when we studied in the library. Once, studying alone, I left my book and paper on the library table while I sought a reference book. I came back to find my assignment torn to pieces, and filthy names scrawled across the pages of my text. It dragged my spirits down and I began to feel that I had made a sorry mess of my Academy years, one that would follow me for the rest of my career. While others were forming lifelong friendships, I had committed myself to having, it seemed, only two close friends. And one was someone that I didn't even like all that much.

I wrote nightly to my uncle, as he had requested, and received frequent missives in return. I was honest, as he had bade me be, and yet it made me feel that I whimpered. He constantly told me to stand firm with my comrades and know that we acted in the best interest of the Academy and the cavalla by reporting such misdeeds, but it was hard to believe his encouraging words. I felt that at any time, I might be the victim of a sneaking attack: a flung snowball, more ice than snow, and the destruction of my model in the drafting room, and once, a crude name scrawled across the back of one of my letters. Nothing further happened to our rooms, for Sergeant Rufet had tightened his watch upon his domain, but that was a small comfort. Still, I looked forward to my uncle's daily note as if it were a lifeline to keep me connected to a world outside the Academy. I had written my father my own letter of explanation, and my uncle assured me that, he, too, had told my father what he knew of the incident. Nevertheless, I soon received a very cold letter from my father, reminding me of my duties to be honest and above reproach in all I did, lest I shame the family name. He said that we would discuss the matter in detail in the spring when I came home to witness my brother's wedding. He also wrote that I should have consulted him rather than my uncle on these matters. My uncle was not, after all, a soldier and did not know how matters such as these were handled within the military. Yet, even so, he did not write exactly what I should have done, and I did not have the spirit to keep the discussion alive in a second letter to him. I let the matter drop.

Spink, too, began to receive mail much more often than he had. I thought at first that the letters were from my uncle as well, but then I noticed that he never opened them in the bunkroom as the rest of us did our letters. Yet I only learned the truth the first time I encountered him in the library, reading a letter. As I sat down beside him at the study table, he hastily turned aside from me, sheltering the pages with his body.

Some part of me must have suspected the truth before that, because I instantly found myself asking him, 'And how is my cousin this week?'

He laughed embarrassedly as he hastily folded the pages and slipped them inside his jacket. He was blushing as he admitted. 'Lovely. Amazing. Intelligent. Enchanting.'

'Strange!' I interjected, and then lowered my voice. I glanced about the library. There was another cadet two tables away, intent on his own studies, but other than him, we were alone.

I envied Spink for a moment; I had not heard from Carsina in two weeks. I knew she could only send me a letter when she visited my sister, but still I wondered if her interest in me was waning. In a shocking moment, my envy turned greener. Spink had met a girl, and on his own decided that he liked her. And she liked him in return. I thought of Carsina, and she suddenly seemed a sort of hand-me-down, a connection passed on to me born of my father's alliance and my sister's friendship. Did she like *me*? If we had met one another casually, would we have felt any attraction? How much, really, did I know of her? I suddenly recognized Epiny's insidious influence on my thinking. Her ideas about choosing your own mate, modern as they might

446

be, had nothing to do with my needs. I was sure my father had selected a good cavalla wife for me, one who would understand her duty to her mate amidst the hardships that we might have to face together. What would Epiny know about the characteristics of a stable husband? Would Spink find that strength in Epiny, if he did manage to win her? How would her séances and glass curtains and foolish ideas sustain her in a border home with her husband often away on patrol? With that thought, I pushed my envy aside and said to Spink, 'I've been wanting to talk to you about Epiny. I think I should speak to my uncle about her interest in séances and spirits and her experiments. For Epiny's own sake, he should know what his daughter is meddling in, before she harms her reputation. What do you think?'

Spink shook his head at me. 'It would only incite a battle between them, to no good end, I think. Your cousin is a strong-willed woman, Nevare. I don't think she is "meddling" in anything. She has touched something that frightens her, and yet she does not retreat from it. She has written to me of how terrifying both experiences were. But instead of fleeing, she girds herself against it and plunges into battle again, to find out what it is. And do you know why she is now so intent on it?'

I shrugged. 'Is it one of the "paths to power" she spoke about? A way to gain unnatural influence over others?'

Spink looked as insulted as if she were his own cousin. Little sparks of anger danced in his eyes, as he said, 'No, you moron! She says it is because she fears for *you*. She. . . She says—' He unfolded the letter and began to quote from it. '"I do not know with whom he battles for control of his soul, but I will not leave him to face her alone." Those are her very words. And she sends me a long list of books she is trying to find, ones that she does not have easy access to. She asks that I look within the Academy library for them. Most have to do with anthropological studies of the plainspeople and discourses on their religions and beliefs. She is

447

convinced that a plainswoman has cast some sort of spell over you or cursed you and seeks to bend you to her will with her magic.' He stopped and swallowed, then looked at me from the corner of his eyes, as if reluctant to admit he'd been playing a silly game. 'She says . . . she writes that a part of your aura has been captured, and walks in another world. That possibly you do not even realize that you no longer belong completely to yourself, but are partially controlled by this, this "other spiritual entity". That's what she calls it.'

'That's rubbish!' I said hotly, in both embarrassment and sudden fear. Then I realized that the other cadet was staring at us in annoyance, his work neglected before him. I lowered my voice to a whisper. 'Epiny is just playing a game, Spink, to make herself fascinating to you. It's all pretend, every bit of it. And I would be remiss in my duty as a cousin if I did not speak to my uncle about it. She is still just a child, and my aunt should not be exposing her to such things. The awkward part, for me, is that it's really my aunt's fault that she has been allowed to pursue such nonsense.'

'I cannot stop you from writing to your uncle about it,' Spink said quietly. 'Just as I can only ask you that you do not tell him that Epiny is sending me letters. If it makes you feel any better, I will admit that as of yet, we have not found any way for me to send responses to her. I've never written back to her. You know that my intentions toward her are entirely honourable. I've already written to both my mother and my brother to ask them to approach your uncle on my behalf.'

I was speechless for a moment. I could only imagine the courage it must have taken for him to approach his older brother with his desire to choose his own wife. Then all I could say, quite heartily, was, 'You know I am on your side in this, Spink. I will speak well of you at every opportunity. Though I still think you could do better for yourself!'

He grinned even as he narrowed his eyes and warned me,

'Now, speak no ill of my future lady, cousin, or we shall have to take it to the duelling grounds!'

I laughed aloud at that, and then stifled my laugh as I saw Caulder emerge from between two rows of shelved books. He did not glance at us and walked quickly out of the library. Only my abrupt silence and stare alerted Spink to his presence. 'Do you think he overheard us?' he asked me worriedly.

'I doubt it,' I replied. 'If he had, it would be very unlike Caulder simply to walk away. He'd have to say something.'

'I've heard his father has told him he isn't to have anything to do with the Carneston House first-years.'

'Really. Now that would be the greatest kindness Stiet has done us this year.'

We both laughed at that, and earned ourselves a glare and a 'sshhh' from the cadet at the next table.

Our studies only became more demanding as the year progressed. The grind of drill, classes, dull meals, and long assignments completed by lantern light carried us into the dim corridor of winter. Winter seemed harsher here in the city than it ever had out on the good, clean plains. The smoke of thousands of stoves filled the winter air. When snow did fall, it was soon speckled with soot. The melting water could not find the drains fast enough; the lawns of the Academy were sodden and the pathways became shallow canals that we splashed through as we marched. Winter seemed to wage a battle against the city, blanketing us with fresh snow and cold freezes, and then the next day giving way to wet fogs and slush underfoot. The snow that fell on the paths and streets of the Academy were soon trampled to a dirty sorbet of ice and mud. The trees stood stark on the lawns, their wet black branches imploring the skies to lighten. We rose before it was light, slopped through the slush to assembly, and then slogged through our classes. Grease our boots as we might, our feet were always wet, and in between inspections, damp socks festooned our rooms like holiday swags. Coughing and sneezing became commonplace, so that on the mornings when I woke with a clear head, I felt blessed. It seemed that our troop no sooner recovered from one sniffling onslaught than the next came along to lay us low. Sickness had to be extreme before we were either excused from classes or permitted into the infirmary, so most of us dragged through the days of illness as best we could.

Even so, all those miseries would have been bearable, for they fell on all of us alike, first-years, upper classmen, officers, and even our instructors. But shortly after Spink and I returned from our days away from the Academy, our fellow New Noble first-years and we became the targets of a different sort of misery.

There had always been differences in how the 'New Noble' first-years were treated compared to the sons of the older families. We had joked about being given the poorest housing choices, endured Corporal Dent making us eat later than our fellows, and hunched our shoulders to the fact that we received a rougher initiation than that inflicted on first-years of old nobility. Our instructors had seemed aloof from it, for the most part. Occasionally they remonstrated with us to uphold the dignity of the Academy despite being new to its traditions. It made us bitterly amused, for no son of any Old Noble could say that his father had ever attended any sort of military academy, yet many of our fathers had graduated from the old War College. The traditions of a military upbringing were in our bones, while our Old Noble fellows learned them only now.

Our classes had been scrupulously segregated for the first third of the year. We always sat in our patrols. New Nobles' sons did not fraternize with the sons of Old Nobles, despite sometimes sharing the same classrooms. Now our instructors began, not to mingle us, but to make us compete against one another. With increasing frequency, our test scores were listed by patrol and were posted side by side outside the classroom doors, where all could see that the New Noble

450

patrols consistently lagged behind the old nobility first-years in academics. The exceptions were Drafting and Engineering, in which we often excelled them, and in drill and on horseback in which they could not best us.

As our instructors began to encourage the rivalry between the two groups, I saw healthy competition take on a darker character. One afternoon we raced into the stables, sure that we would triumph over our rivals in an equestrian drill exercise, only to discover that someone had crept in and smeared dung stripes down the sides and flanks of our mounts and filled their tails with burrs. The hasty grooming we had time for was inadequate, and left our horses looking ill-kempt. We were marked down for that, and though we won for precision, we lost for overall appearance, and thus the cup and the half-day of liberty went to the old nobility troop.

We muttered at the unfairness of it. Then several of the scale models that belonged to Bringham House old nobility first-years were ruined immediately before a judging, leaving Carneston House the winners. Foul play was suspected, and I found it hard to take joy in the victory. My construction of a suspension bridge had been, I felt, so superior that we would have been assured the win without the sabotage. It was very difficult to write my letter to my uncle that night, for I felt that I had to be honest in stating my suspicions of my own fellows.

At about that time, I had a final encounter with Cadet Lieutenant Tiber. Rumours about him had died down at the Academy. I had heard little about him and seen even less. Thus I was a bit surprised to encounter him one evening as I returned from the library to Carneston House. We were both bundled in our greatcoats as we approached one another in the semi-darkness. He walked with a marked lurch to his gait now, probably as the result of his still healing injuries. His head was down, his eyes on the snowy path before him. I was tempted to pretend I didn't recognize him and simply hurry past. Instead, as was right, I stepped to the side of the path and snapped a salute to him. He returned my salute in passing, and kept going. An instant later, he rounded on his heel and came back to me. 'Cadet Nevare Burvelle. Is that correct?'

'Yes, sir. That's my name.'

Then he let a silence fall. I listened to the wind and felt dread build within me. Then he said, 'Thank you for coming forward with those names. I didn't know who jumped me. When Ordo claimed to have seen me drunk and staggering, I suspected, of course. But your saying Jaris' name aloud was what made it certain for me.'

'I should have come forward sooner, sir.'

He cocked his head at me. 'And why didn't you, Nevare Burvelle? That is something I've been wanting to ask you.'

'I wasn't sure . . . if it was honourable. To speak suspicions without having any facts. And . . .' I quickly forced the truth past my lips. 'I was afraid they'd take revenge on me.'

He nodded, unsurprised. Nothing in his face condemned me. 'And did they?'

'In small ways. Nothing I can't endure.'

He nodded again, and gave me a small, cold smile. 'Thank you for facing up to your fear and coming forward. Don't think yourself a coward. You could have never mentioned it to your uncle, or when the time came, lied and said you'd seen nothing. I wish I could tell you that you'd be rewarded for it. You won't. Remember, you were right to be cautious of them. Don't underestimate them. I did. And now I limp. Don't forget what we've learned.'

He spoke to me as if I were his friend. His words made me brave. 'I trust you are recovering well and that your studies go well?'

His smile grew stiffer. 'I've recovered as much as I'm likely to. And my studies have come to an end, Cadet Burvelle. I've received my first posting. I'm off to Gettys. As a scout.'

It was a bad post and a worse assignment. We stood facing one another in the cold. There was no polite congratulation

I could offer. 'It's a punishment, isn't it?' I finally asked hopelessly.

'It is and it isn't. They need me there. The building of the King's Road has come to a virtual halt there and I'm to move among the Specks in their forest and find out why. Ostensibly, I'm well suited for the task. Good at languages, good at engineering. I should be able to scout out the best route for the road and make friends with the wild people. Maybe I'll find why we can't seem to make any forward progress. Everyone gets something they want out of it. I get work I like and I'm good at. The administration gets me out of the way and in a position where I can never hope to rise to any appreciable rank.'

I found I was nodding to his words. They made sense. Reluctantly, I told him, 'Earlier this year, Captain Maw said I'd make a good scout.'

'Did he? Then I expect you will. He said the same thing to me when I was a first-year.'

'But I don't want to be a scout!' The words burst from me. I was horrified at his prophecy.

'I doubt that anyone does, Nevare. When the time comes, try to recognize that Maw means well by intervening in that way. He'd rather see promising cadets serve in some capacity of worth, rather than being culled or sent to useless posts to count blankets or buy mutton for the troops. It's his way of saying you're worth something, even if you are a battle lord's son.'

The silence that followed his words hung between us. Finally, he broke it, saying, 'Wish me luck, Burvelle.'

'Good luck, Lieutenant Tiber.'

'Scout Tiber, Burvelle. Scout Tiber. I'd best get used to it.' He saluted me and I returned it. Then he walked away from me into the cold and the dark. I stood still, shivering, and wondered if I was doomed to follow in his footsteps.

EIGHTEEN

Accusations

Winter deepened and we drew ever closer to Dark Evening. At my father's house in Widevale, Dark Evening had been a night for prayers and meditation and floating candles on the pond or the river, followed by the celebration the next morning of the lengthening of the days. My mother had always given each of us a small but useful gift in celebration of the turning of the year, to which my father added a yellow envelope containing spending money. It had been a minor but pleasant holiday each year.

Thus I was astonished to hear my fellows speak of Dark Evening with enthusiasm and anticipation as it drew near. The Academy itself would offer a feast to us on Dark Evening's Eve, followed by two days of liberty for all cadets in good standing. There were also plays in the playhouses, and the King and Queen gave a grand ball in Sondringham Hall in Old Thares, to which the senior cadets were invited. For the younger cadets, there would be carnival and street performers and dancing in the guildhalls. We were sternly admonished that we could attend such events only in uniform, and thus must be on our best behaviour, not just for our own reputations, but also for the honour of the Academy. I looked forward to it as something I'd never experienced before.

Caleb was shocked to hear that I knew so little of Dark Evening. I thought he was teasing me when they told me that on Dark Evening all whores went masked and gave away their favours for free, and that some ladies of good houses sneaked out into the streets on that night, and pretended to be women of pleasure, so that they might sample the favours of strange men without danger to their reputations. When I challenged the truth of this, he showed me several lewdly illustrated stories in some of his cheap folios of Adventure Tales. Despite my better judgment, I read the accounts of women seduced by one wild night in the city and thought them as appalling as they were unlikely. What sane woman would leave her safe and comfortable home simply to indulge in one night of licentiousness?

Privately, I asked Natred and Kort if they had ever heard such a thing. To my surprise, they assured me that they had. Natred said that his older cousins had told him of it. Kort added that his father said it was a vestige of one of the old god's celebrations. 'It's mostly a western custom. The temples of the old gods are still standing in a lot of the older cities, and people remember a lot more about those gods and their customs. Especially the celebrations they had. Dark Evening used to belong to a women's god. That was what I heard. My mother used to tell stories about Dark Evening to my sisters. Not about running around acting like a whore, but old tales, of girls meeting masked gods at Dark Evening celebrations, and being granted gifts by them, like spinning straw into gold or being able to dance two inches above the floor. Just pretty stories.

'Then one year my father caught my three sisters dancing in the dark in the garden, in just their knickers. He was very upset about it, but my mother asked him what harm could it do, so long as there were no young men about. He said it was the idea of it, and forbade them from ever doing such a thing again. But,' and Kort leaned closer to us, as if fearing that someone else might hear, 'I think they still keep the holiday that way.'

'Even my Talerin?' Natred asked intently. I could not tell if he was scandalized or delighted.

'I do not know for sure,' Kort cautioned him. 'But I have heard that many women have rituals and rites of their own for Dark Evening. Sometimes, I think that there is much about our women that we do not know.'

Such talk made me wonder about Carsina. For an instant, I imagined Carsina dancing near naked in a darkened garden. Would she? I suddenly did not know if I hoped she did or didn't. Were there rites and rituals that women observed and we men knew nothing about? Were they all in the service of the good god or did women secretly still worship at some of the old altars? Such questions whetted my curiosity for Dark Evening in Old Thares. To be turned loose in the great old city with my fellows, a man among men on a wild festival night, was something I had never imagined. I counted up my allowance that I had hoarded and felt that the holiday would never come.

In the middle of that week, what began as a good-natured snowball fight with the old nobility first-years from Drakes Hall turned into a nasty pitched battle, with ice and rocks replacing the earlier missiles. I had been at the library, and only learned of it through Rory's retelling when our patrol gathered at the study table that night. Rory had a black eye and Kort a swollen lip to show for it. The skirmish had dissolved when several older cadet officers had come upon the scene. Even so, Rory was rejoicing over making an antagonist 'bleed some of that fine old blood out of his fine old nose.' Trist had also been a participant, as had Caleb. Oron had only witnessed it and yet seemed more upset than Rory. Twice he said aloud, 'I just don't understand it. We are all cadets here. What could have made them hate us so suddenly?'

The second time he said it, Gord shut his book with a sigh. 'Don't any of you read the newspapers?' he asked, and did not wait for the reply before adding, 'The Council of

Lords has just voted on taxation for the King's Road. The Old Nobles opposed it, arguing that they need their monies for roads and improvements in their own territories rather than "the road to nowhere" as Lord Jarfries called it. The old nobility had expected to easily defeat the proposal to channel a portion of their tax income to King Troven's coffers for the road. I even read that some of them laughed aloud when a New Noble named Lord Simem first proposed it. Yet when the ballots were counted, three times and no less, the vote was in favour of taxation for the King's Road.'

He said this as if it were of immense importance. We all stared at him silently.

'Puppies!' he said at last in disgust. 'Think about what it means. It means that enough Old Nobles crossed the line to vote with the New Nobles, secretly, that the King is regaining a stronger hand in the country. The Old Nobles who thought that power was coming slowly but surely into their hands have suffered a major setback. They resent it, and because of that they and their sons resent us all the more. They thought they were on the path to running this country, with the King as little more than a figurehead. But for our fathers, it would have come true. The old nobility would have continued a slow march upon the monarchy, taking more power and control for themselves, retaining more taxes, building more wealth . . . Don't any of you see what I'm talking about?' Sudden frustration broke in his voice.

'The good god put King Troven over all of us, to rule us justly and well. All of holy writ tells us that the lords should serve their king as a good son serves his father; in obedience, respect and gratitude for his guidance.' Oron said this so solemnly that I nearly bowed my head and signed the air with the good god's sign. He sounded more like a bessom at that moment than Gord ever had.

Gord snorted. 'Yes. So we have all been brought up to believe, every soldier son of us, every son of a New Noble father. But what do you think the Old Nobles have told their first sons and their soldier sons? Do you think they have been taught their first duty is to the King, or to their own noble fathers?'

'Treason and heresy!' Caleb said angrily. He pointed a finger at Gord accusingly and said, 'Why do you say such things?'

'*I* don't! I serve the King as willingly as any man here. I only say that perhaps we have been brought up not to question and, as a result, you do not understand those who *do* question. You do not see how our loyalty might offend those who are not so blindly loyal themselves.'

'Blindly loyal!' Rory was incensed. 'What's blind about knowing that we owe the King our loyalty? What is blind about knowing our duty?'

Gord sat back in his chair. Something hardened in his face. He had changed in the last couple of weeks, in a way I could not clearly define. He was still as fat; he still sweated through drill and panted with the effort of heaving his bulk up the stairs, but there seemed to be something of steel in him now. When he had first joined us he had laughed along with his mockers when people made jokes about his weight, and sometimes even made fun of himself. Now he kept silent and merely stared at those who baited him. It seemed to make some of the fellows angry, as if he had no right to stand on his dignity and refuse to accept their mockery as his due. Now he looked round the table at those of us gathered there, and I suddenly perceived that it was not just maths that he was good at. There was more intellect behind those piggy little eyes than I had credited him with. He licked his plump lips, as if deciding whether to speak or not. Then the words seemed to break forth from him, not in a torrent, but in a deliberate cascade of derision.

'I said blindly, not stupidly, Rory. I don't think it's stupid for us and for our fathers to give loyalty to a man who benefited us greatly. But we should not be blind to what he gains by it, nor to what it does to others. Did none of your fathers ever discuss politics with you? When we take our history lessons, do any of you listen? We are to be officers and gentlemen when our schooling is done. Loyalty is fine, but it is even better when it is backed up with intellect. My dog is loyal to me, and if I sicced him on a bear, he would go with no questioning of whether I knew what was best for him. But we are not dogs, and though I believe a soldier must go where he is ordered and do as he is told, I do not think he must march forth in ignorance of what propels his commander's decisions.'

Caleb had never been especially quick-witted, and that day he decided that Gord's words had insulted him. He came to his feet and loomed over the table. His long, skinny frame made it difficult for him to look threatening but he knotted his fist and said, 'Are you saying my father is ignorant just because he didn't talk politics at me? Take it back!'

Gord did not stand up but he didn't back down. He leaned back in his chair as if to disarm Caleb's aggression, but spoke firmly. 'I can't take it back, Caleb, for that isn't what I said! I was speaking in generalities. We all came here, I hope, knowing that our first year is a winnowing process. We expected to be hazed and to have strict teachers and boring food and a burden of assignments and marching and tasks that no sane man would ever make his daily regimen. Yet we undertake it, knowing full well, I trust, that they deliberately make it more difficult and stressful than it needs to be. They are hoping that the weak and even the not-very-determined will be dissuaded by the process and turn away. Better to cull them out now than to have a battle whittle them away, with other men losing their lives in the process! So, we do obey, but we do not obey blindly. That is what I am saying. That we endure what we endure here because we know the reason for it. And when I am a cavalla officer in

459

the field, I expect that I will do the same there. I will obey my commander's orders, but I hope I will remain intelligent enough to discern the reasons behind my orders.'

He looked round at us all. Despite ourselves, we were hanging on his words. He nodded, as if in appreciation of that, and went on, almost as if he were lecturing us, 'And thus we come back to Oron's question: what makes the old nobility first-years dislike us so much if we are all cadets here? And the answer is, they are taught to. Just as we are subtly schooled to resent them. It probably began as a way to wring the best out of us, just as they encourage each house and troop to compete against their fellows. But the politics of our fathers have infected it now, and made it something uglier.'

'But why? Why does someone want us to hate each other?' Oron clasped his cheeks and practically wailed the words.

Gord gritted his teeth for a moment and then sighed. 'I didn't say that anyone had deliberately set us against each other in a serious way. I *am* saying that what the Academy began as healthy competition between us has changed to something more ominous because of the political situation in the streets. That it may even be getting out of control within our walls, becoming something far more vicious than our superiors ever intended. It is in the King's best interest to have his cavalla officers enjoy solid camaraderie. It is certainly in the cavalla's best interest, and hence the Academy's. But there will still be some, Old Nobles and New, who think we should despise each other because our fathers vote against each other in the Council of Lords. And if someone deliberately wanted to damage the power of the New Nobles, if someone wanted to find a way to weaken our fathers' alliance, they'd find a way to turn us against each other. That hasn't happened yet, but it will be very interesting to see what pressures are applied to us. That is all I'm saying.'

460

'Oh, that was so enlightening,' Trist said. He had been silent up until then, though I had twice seen him roll his eyes during Gord's discourse. 'Do you honestly think there's a man in this room who hasn't already seen what is going on and given thought to it?'

Instantly, it seemed that every cadet at the table was nodding, though I seriously doubted that any of us had pondered it through as Gord had.

'Not all of us must take a beating before we understand what the currents are in the Academy,' Trist added, somehow making it seem Gord's own fault that he had been attacked.

I took a deep breath to say my piece on that, but closed my lips as I heard a too-familiar voice say, 'Perhaps you shouldn't blame a beating on politics. Some of your fellow cadets think having a pig in their midst is bad for the Academy.'

I wondered how long Caulder had been standing out of sight beside the door before he chose to enter.

'What do you want here?' Spink asked him waspishly.

Caulder smiled nastily. 'You, actually. Not that I want you; quite the contrary! But for some reason, my father wishes to see you. Immediately. You are to report to him at his office in the Administration Building.' His gaze slid from Spink to Trist. I thought I saw a shadow of pain in his eyes, and he sounded almost like a scorned lover as he said, 'Still laughing over your fine jest on me, Trist? How stupid of me to trust someone like you and think you might want my friendship.'

Trist should have been an actor, not a soldier. He looked puzzled. 'A jest between us, Caulder? I don't recall one.'

'You poisoned me. With chewing tobacco. You knew very well how sick it would make me. Doubtless you all sat up here laughing about it afterwards.'

We had. I tried not to look guilty. Trist made it seem

461

effortless. He opened his hands as if to show he had no weapons. 'How could I, Caulder? You might recall that I was with you. I walked you home afterwards.'

'You made me puke on purpose. In front of everyone. To mock me.' Caulder's voice was very tight, and I felt a small twinge of sympathy. He yearned so badly to be wrong about Trist.

Trist looked mildly wounded. 'Caulder, I've told you this already. I have never seen anyone get as sick as you did from a simple plug of tobacco. Where I come from, mere children are known to nibble a bit, and suffer no bad consequences. Truth to tell, it's supposed to have medicinal values. I once saw my mother give some to my little sister. For colic.'

Did some subtle cue pass between Trist and Oron? The redheaded cadet chimed in with, 'I cannot understand it, either. I've chewed tobacco since I was eight, with no ill effects.'

'Cadet Jaris told me that chewing tobacco makes nearly everyone sick the first time it is tried. He said you deliberately made me sick, and that it served me right for trusting a New Noble's son. He said you did it to mock me. And he, and the others with him, laughed at me.' Caulder fought to keep his voice steady as he spoke. In the silence that followed his words, he stood very still, obviously divided. I could see the boy wanting Trist to be upright and sincere in his offer of friendship. I felt sad for him, so young and so needy, and yet I also felt vindictively satisfied to see him mistreated. I was certain he had been involved in Tiber's and Gord's beatings. He was treacherous, and as the Writ says, the treacherous one earns only treachery from his fellows.

Trist spread his hands helplessly. 'What can I say to you, Caulder? I will not speak ill of a fellow cadet and cavalla man, so I cannot make you see that perhaps others would lie and slander to make you mistrust me. All I can say is, quite sincerely, I am sorry that something I gave you made you so ill. And here is my hand on that.' And the golden cadet stepped forward, hand outstretched to the lad.

Caulder looked as if the sun had suddenly risen just for him. He stepped forward eagerly to clasp Trist's hand, even as Spink muttered disgustedly, 'May the good god witness all you do.' It's a saying that my father once called as much a curse as a blessing, for few of us would willingly call the good god to witness all we do every day. I wasn't sure if Caulder even heard what Spink said, for he turned a quick snarl at him, saying, 'My father does not like to be kept waiting!'

I saw Spink struggle not to respond to that, and win. He stood, closing his books and tidying his space. 'It seems odd for the commander to still be in his office at this hour,' I observed, and Caulder looked nearly triumphant as he said, 'For matters of discipline, where else would he meet with the cadet in question?'

'Discipline?' Spink looked alarmed, as well he might. To be called directly to the commander's office for discipline, after class hours, bespoke an extreme violation of Academy rules, one that might well lead to suspension or dismissal.

Caulder smiled sweetly. 'Of course, I know nothing of what it is all about,' he said, in a sugary voice that implied exactly the opposite. He glanced out the window. 'I do suggest you hurry, however.'

'Do you want me to come with you?' I asked Spink. Curiosity and dread were devouring me.

'He could hold your hand,' Caulder suggested slyly.

'I'll be back soon enough,' Spink said with a venomous glance at the boy. He went for his greatcoat, and moments later disappeared down the stairs.

'Did he finish his maths before he went?' Gord asked me quietly. Spink's understanding of the theory was as good as any cadet's, but his weakness in calculations still undermined his marks.

'I don't know,' I replied.

'We've section tests next Fiveday,' Gord commented, and I groaned, for I had pushed that dread to the back of my mind. Section tests meant that we'd be tested in every one of our subjects, and our marks posted to our records. We'd weathered one section test so far that year. I had not done as well as I had expected, but then, no one had. This time I intended to be better prepared.

'Well, all we can do is the best we can do,' I muttered philosophically. I opened my maths book again.

'And you New Noble sons had best do well at your sections!' Caulder interjected. I hadn't even been aware he was still there.

'We expect to,' Gord returned mildly.

'Why must we do well?' Trist asked suddenly.

The boy smiled at Trist. 'No one is supposed to know,' he said. He glanced around the room, pleased with our suddenly rapt attention. Even Caleb looked up from his latest Dreadful Crimes folio. Caulder licked his narrow lips and added almost in a whisper, 'But you could say a lot of futures may depend on the posting of the final grades for the half-year.'

'Will the commander do a culling?' Rory asked bluntly.

Caulder raised one eyebrow. 'Perhaps. But you didn't hear it from me.' And with that chill remark, he turned to leave the room. Both Oron and Rory shot desperate looks at Trist.

'Hold up, Caulder!' Trist jumped to his feet. 'I was just going out for a bit of air. Perhaps I'll walk a ways with you.'

'If you wish,' the boy acceded smugly, and waited for Trist to join him. After we had heard their boots descend the stair, Rory spoke. 'I don't like the sound of that. I warned you fellers about cullings before, just like my cousin warned me. They had an exceptionally large class the year he came into Academy. The commander that year did three cullings.

464

He'd choose a test or an exercise of some kind, without any advance notice to the cadets, and those who fell below a certain score were simply dismissed.'

'That's brutal,' gasped Oron, and the rest of us nodded grimly.

'It is. But the commander then said that it was as fair as an ambush; that those who were always ready and alert survived, and those who were lax did not.'

I was suddenly reminded of Sergeant Duril's rocks. I didn't like the idea of a sudden culling, but the commander was right. It was fair in the same way that battle odds were fair. I scowled. I still hadn't found the rock that I'd kept on my shelf. It was a minor thing, but it irritated me.

I shook it from my thoughts and opened my maths book again. I had been solid on the lesson; now I resolved to be absolutely in command of it. At the table, other cadets were doing the same. Gord sat silent, staring straight ahead. When he noticed me looking at him, he said quietly, 'I hope Spink gets back soon.'

I nodded. Spink had passed his last section test, but not by much. I breathed a silent prayer to the good god that Spink's efforts at study would be rewarded, and then hastily added myself to that petition as well. I bent my head over my books and tried to concentrate.

I looked up immediately when I heard boot steps on the stairs. Trist came in. His cheeks and forehead were red with cold from the outside, but his mouth was pinched white with fury. He looked round at us and seemed to be strangling on his news.

'So? What did you find out? Did he tell you anything?' Oron demanded of him.

'It's not fair! It's not fair at all, and there's no reason for it!' Trist spoke through gritted teeth. He walked over to our hearth and stood with his back to us, warming his hands.

'What is it?' Rory demanded.

'It's not just an individual culling!' Trist turned back to face us. 'It's going to be based on averaged patrol scores. Lowest patrol is out. One man with a bad test score could lose the Academy for his entire patrol.'

'But why?' The cry burst from several of us.

Trist tore off his gloves and slapped them down on the table. 'Because the Academy overspent on horses and costs must be cut. So the colonel is looking for a way to get rid of some of our class. That's what I think. Caulder gave me some lofty speech about how each patrol should lift individuals to a higher standard, and if we haven't done that by now with our weaker members then we never will as troopers.'

Rory knit his brows. 'That's something like what Colonel Stiet said in that first speech he gave us at the beginning of the year. But I thought it was just inspirational, not that he'd actually hold us to it.'

Oron looked around wildly. 'This means that no matter how well I do, no matter how hard I've studied, any one of you could bring me down tomorrow. I could be dismissed from the King's Academy for something I had absolutely no control over.'

'Spink.' Caleb spoke the name like a curse. 'Spink could do us all in. Where is he, anyway? Why isn't he here and studying, like he should be? Doesn't he care at all?'

'He was summoned to the colonel's office. Don't you remember?' I spoke the words dully. It came to me that alone of us all, Gord had acted on the colonel's words from our welcoming speech. He had tried to lift Spink's mathematical capabilities up to match his own. And then, in a wash of near despair, I thought of what else Gord had just said: that if anyone truly conspired to weaken the New Nobles in the Council of Lords, he would find a way to turn us against each other. If Spink's failure sent all of us home, with the only future option of enlisting as common soldiers,

466

how would our fathers feel about one another? Who would they blame?

'Well, he'd best get back soon! I don't want my career ended because some frontier lad didn't know what eight times six was. You'd best drill him well, Gord, or it's the end for all of us!' This was Rory.

'We're counting on you. Make sure he passes,' Trist added in a tone I didn't like.

Gord lifted his head and looked at him steadily. 'I'll do all I can, in that I'll offer him as much help studying as we both have time for.'

He lowered his eyes to his books again. After a moment, the silence in the room passed back to the normal shuffling of papers and scrubbing out of mistakes. Trist went to his room and came back with his own books. We made room for him at the table. He asked to borrow Oron's grammar book to look up a Varnian verb. He did so, and jotted it down. Trist didn't look up from his own work as he quietly observed to Gord, 'You always sit next to Spink in maths class. And he's left-handed.'

Every head at the table lifted. I looked at Trist in disbelief. 'Are you suggesting they should cheat? That Gord should let Spink copy off his test?'

Trist didn't look up at any of us. 'Gord corrects all his work every night before Spink turns it in the next day. How is that so different?'

Gord strangled for a moment, then said tightly, 'I'm not a cheater and neither is Spink. I tell him when he has the answer wrong, and show him what he did wrong. He still has to rework all the calculations himself.'

Trist's voice was very calm. 'So, if he could see your answers, and if he had time, he might be able to go back to the ones that didn't match his and re-work them for the correct answer. That's not cheating. It's just, well, checking facts. Confirming calculations.'

'I won't. I won't suggest it to Spink and I won't enable him to do it. I won't break the Academy honour vow.' Gord's voice grated low and furious.

'The Academy honour vow also says that every cadet will do all he can to help every other cadet succeed. And your little quibble about letting Spink check his answers off your paper might end the career of everyone in this room. I'd say that's breaking the honour vow in a major way.'

'You're twisting things,' Gord replied, but he did not seem as certain as he had with his earlier responses.

'No. I think this is a test they're giving us. To see how well we hang together and protect our own. I think Caulder knowing about the culling is a fair sign that others will know, too. I think it's a rumour that was meant to get out. To see how resourceful we'll be about protecting our fellows.'

Trist made it seem so plausible. I glanced around at the others, and found in their eyes mostly acceptance of Trist's reasoning. Natred seemed to share my doubt and there were furrows between Rory's eyes, but the rest of them were nodding. I looked at Gord. He was not meeting anyone's eyes. Instead, he began to stack his books. He gathered them in his arms without a word and rose to leave the table.

'We're counting on you, Gord. Everyone's career is at stake here!' Oron called after him. His tone was the friendliest I'd ever heard him use to the fat cadet. Gord made no response.

I stayed at the table long after my studying was done, waiting for Spink to come back. Finally I gave it up. The others had gone to their bunks. I left a single candle burning for him and went to my bed. I tried to sleep, but worry chased my thoughts in circles. Was Spink in trouble? Had he done something I didn't know about? Had the commander called him in to give him bad news from home, such as a death in his family? I thought I would never fall asleep, but

I must have dozed, for I woke when someone opened and shut the door to our dark room. There were soft footfalls and then Spink's bunk creaked as he sat down on it. I heard it creak again as he bent down to pull off his boots.

'What was it?' I whispered into the darkness.

His voice was husky. 'I'm on probation. For immorality.'

'What?' I spoke louder than I meant to.

'Quiet. I don't want the others to know.'

'Tell me!'

Spink came and sat down in the dark on the floor by my bed. He spoke in a hushed voice. 'I was so shocked I thought I would pass out when Colonel Stiet accused me. He was shouting at me and I couldn't understand what he was going on about. He accused me of leading an innocent girl astray, of corrupting a mere child with lecherous advances. I finally understood he was talking about Epiny. I didn't know what to say, so I just kept my mouth shut. The more I just looked at him, the angrier he got. He started shouting at me, Nevare, saying that as long as he was commander, no cadet in his charge would be so corrupt. He asked me how I could be so depraved as to make advances to a mere child, the precious daughter of a respected family. And he told me that when she was of an age for courting, she already had other prospects, much better prospects than a frontier-bred New Noble whelp. He means Caulder. I just know he means that Epiny is for Caulder.'

I gaped at him. I couldn't believe that, at that moment, he was more concerned over who might get Epiny than over the unjust charges against him. He didn't notice my expression.

'He must have roared at me for half an hour before he gave me a chance to speak. When I said I didn't know what he meant, he shook a letter in my face. Then he read it out loud to me.' He took a ragged breath. 'It was from your aunt. She had the housemaids keeping watch over Epiny while she was gone. They've distorted everything about

469

every moment that I spent with her. It's all lies and innuendo, but they're taking it as golden truth.'

I felt a horrible lurch in my stomach. 'No,' I pleaded, knowing it was true.

'Yes.' His voice hitched. I didn't like to think he was weeping, but knew he was. 'Your aunt found a letter Epiny was writing to me. It was . . . affectionate. I am sure it was no more than that. But she wrote that she is certain that I attempted to seduce her, a little girl still new to long skirts. She claims that she questioned the servants, and could prove that I had spent a long morning alone with her daughter. When the colonel asked me if that was so, I could not deny it. We did sit and talk in the morning room. And she wasn't, well, she wasn't yet dressed for the day. But, well, you know Epiny. That didn't feel improper, only, well, unorthodox. I meant no wrong, Nevare. I meant no shame on your family. I am sorry, so sorry. And I'm so afraid I'll be sent home from the Academy. And worst of all, I know that when my family's letters arrive, asking permission for me to court Epiny, it will only be proof to everyone that I've behaved shamefully. Yet it didn't feel that way. I thought I was doing everything correctly. I thought I had been honourable.'

'You were! You did! It's my stupid cousin's fault! Epiny is the one sending letters to you. You haven't written back, have you?'

'I have. I've written reams and reams of letters to her, but I haven't been able to send them. There was no way to do so without, well, without your uncle and aunt knowing. So there you are, Nevare. I did know it was wrong, or I wouldn't have been hiding it from them.'

'Spink, stop being so dramatic! Think this through. It's Caulder behind it. He *did* hear us that day in the library! And this is his perfect revenge, not just on you, but on my uncle for coming to the Academy and complaining about how we were treated. I'm sure Caulder is behind this; he probably wrote to my aunt, or said something to his mother to get the rumour started. Then my aunt would have gone looking for evidence.'

'I never should have let her write to me.'

'Spink, how could you have stopped her? You didn't do anything wrong. It was all Epiny! She was the one traipsing about the house half the day in her nightgown, she was the one making her horse run off and writing you lots of letters. How could you have stopped her? It isn't fair. And—' A slow realization was dawning in my sleepy brain, 'I'll wager my uncle knows nothing of my aunt's letter. He liked you: I know he did. He wouldn't write a letter accusing you of seducing Epiny. If he had any notion that you had behaved improperly toward her, he'd have bluntly told us when we were there. And if he'd heard accusations that you had done something improper, he would have come here and confronted us both. He's direct; that's his way. I'm sure of it. This hasn't got back to him yet.'

Spink sat by my bed on the floor, breathing raggedly. When he spoke, his tone said this was obviously the worst news of all. 'They've sent her away, Nevare. Colonel Stiet told me so. I won't see Epiny again.'

'What? Where did they send her?'

'It's done. They sent her to a finishing school, way out on the edge of the city. Colonel Stiet didn't say which one, only that he wanted me to know that she was forever out of my reach.'

I had only the most vague concept of what a finishing school was. My elder sister had spoken of them with longing, as a place where women could learn music and poetry and dancing and manners, in the jolly company of other well-bred girls. A finishing school taught a girl all that she might need to hold graciously an exalted place in society. To send a girl to a finishing school did not sound like such a dire fate to me. I said as much.

'Epiny will hate it there. And it's all my fault, so she'll hate me, too.'

'Stop wallowing in it, Spink!' I hated to hear him taking all the blame on himself. 'Yes, she'll hate it, but maybe they'll teach her how to conduct herself like a lady. Maybe they'll grind all this séance silliness out of her. Now listen to me. Tomorrow, I'm writing to my uncle about this. I write to him every day anyway, and I'm sure when I tell him what happened he'll straighten it out and let Commander Stiet know that you haven't done anything wrong and shouldn't be punished. Besides, we have much worse things to worry about.'

Hastily I told him about the test, the culling to follow, and Trist's suggestion to Gord. I had expected him to get angry at the suggestion he might cheat. Instead, it just plunged him deeper into despair. 'I'm going to ruin everything for everybody. Oh, Nevare, it's like a curse called down on me.'

'Enough of curses! Don't be silly, Spink. We need to focus on what is real and important. Forget about Epiny until after I've written to my uncle. The most important thing you can do in the next day or so is study your eyes out.'

But he was in no mood to hear or heed me. 'I'll try. But I can't forget about Epiny or forget that I am at fault for her unhappiness. And now I endanger all of you.' His clothing rustled as he stood up. 'The best thing I could do would be to resign from the Academy immediately. Then they couldn't count my low scores against the rest of you.'

'Spink, don't be an idiot!'

'Too late. I've been that, and more. The colonel told me that I've exhibited every fault that he has come to expect in New Nobles' sons. That my behaviour is far more suited to a common foot soldier than a cavalla officer, and shows that in elevating soldier sons to noble status, the King has usurped the good god's will in what I was meant to be.'

472

'He said that to you?' I was outraged. I was not alone. I heard Natred sit up in his blankets. I suspected that Kort was awake and listening in, also.

'He said it. That, and a lot of other, uglier things.'

Nate spoke from the darkness in a furious whisper. 'If you quit, you just prove him right. And if you fail, you prove that they have always been right about New Nobles' sons: that we are fit only to be common soldiers not officers. Spink, you cannot do either. For the dignity of your father's name, you have to prove him wrong. Stay on. Pass the damned test. Do whatever you must to pass it. And let Nevare help you clear your name. Have him go to his uncle on your behalf. I have not heard you speak one degrading word about this Epiny. You have not dishonoured her. Fight to clear your own name, and hers. If you cut and run now, everyone will think you did it because you were ashamed.'

Silently I blessed Natred. He had so quickly and clearly seen how best to sway Spink to courage. What he would not do for himself, he would do for his father's honour and Epiny's good name. I could almost hear him thinking. He walked to his bed and I heard him undress in the dark. Just as I was giving up on him and sliding off into sleep, Spink spoke again. 'I'll try,' he said. 'I'll try.'

NINETEEN

Intervention

There were only three days left until the section test and the culling that would follow. As Gord had predicted, we were not the only first-years to have heard the rumours. Perhaps they had been deliberately sown, perhaps not. All I knew was that the campus was suddenly a far more sombre place. There was no talking or jesting in the meal lines any more, and conversation at table now consisted of discussing our studies and what might or might not be on any of the examinations.

All of us studied harder, but some of us had our own particular demons to wrestle. Rory's was Varnian grammar. Natred and Kort worked endlessly on drafting. Mine was Captain Infal's Military History class. He'd spent the last two weeks on sea battles from King Jurew's War. I failed to see how sea tactics and strategy applied to cavalry officers, and had a hard time keeping the names of the various captains and the military capabilities of their various ships fixed in my head. Now I re-read my notes, desperately trying to memorize every stage of each battle. I was furious with the instructor, certain that I'd never use any of this knowledge that I so painfully pounded into my memory.

And Spink struggled with his maths. It was awful to watch him. There was a safety lamp that was kept burning in the stairwell at all times, even after lights-out. In the ferocity of his drive to find more hours to study, Spink would furtively creep out on the landing with a chair, and stand on top of it to bring his book close enough to the dim lantern to continue studying the equations and how they were manipulated. In the mornings, he rose with bloodshot eyes and a sagging face to begin the day.

Spink's efforts did not escape notice by Trist. He only spoke of it once to him, and he sounded almost kind when he did. 'We all see how hard you're trying, Spink. And we, well, whatever you have to do to get a good score, we'll know that you're doing it as much for us as for yourself.'

Spink lifted his head to stare at Trist and said quietly, 'I don't cheat. Not for anyone.' Then he had turned his gaze back to his books. He had not looked up again after that, not even when Trist shoved his chair back from the table and stamped out of the room.

If the culling had been all that we had to worry about, that would have been enough. But for Spink and me there were other concerns. The day after Spink was put on probation, there was no letter from my uncle. I had written to him of Spink's situation, and posted the letter that same day. The first missed letter worried me, but I persuaded myself that he just needed time to think. The second day with no response conveyed a chill message to me; he blamed me for bringing Spink into his home. What would he write to my father about it? I tried to put a brave face on it for Spink, saying that perhaps his letter to me was delayed, or that he had not yet received mine that explained everything. Spink didn't believe it any more than I did. It was not reassuring when that evening, just when I most wanted to study for the exams I'd face the next day, I was summoned to the commander's office.

I hurried across the winter-dimmed campus, dread a cold weight in my belly. It had snowed the night before, but the day had melted the snow to slush. Now it was hardening into uneven ice on the pathways. I slipped several times, trying to hurry. When I finally reached the stone steps of the Administration Building, I forced myself to ascend them carefully. My uncle's carriage and man awaited outside the building. Anticipation warred with dread as I went up the steps. At least, I would soon know where I stood.

Caulder admitted me and walked me silently to the door of his father's office. He met my gaze with a smirk that I hated. I did not thank him for opening the door for me. I did notice that when it closed it did not latch behind me. I walked forward, saluted and then waited, ever mindful that Caulder's ear was most likely pressed to the door crack.

Colonel Stiet sat behind his desk. Uncle Sefert sat in a comfortable chair to one side of it, looking anything but comfortable. Colonel Stiet spoke to me. 'Your uncle is concerned that you have not written to him lately. Have you anything to say for yourself, Cadet Burvelle?' Clearly Colonel Stiet regarded this as a trivial and annoying complaint. I could almost hear him thinking of his home and lady waiting for him. I kept my eyes on him as I replied.

'I have written and posted letters to my uncle daily, sir. I, too, have been concerned that he has not written to me for several days.'

I saw my uncle sit up straighter in his chair, but he did not speak. Colonel Stiet pursed his lips. 'Well. It seems to me that we then have the answer to our little puzzle. Something has interrupted the post. Letters have gone missing. Certainly this should not cause any of us much distress, however. I do not feel it has been worth this "emergency" meeting tonight at the end of a long and arduous day.'

I could not think of a reply but my uncle answered for us.

'Ordinarily, it would not,' my uncle replied. 'Save that I have had some concerns about young Nevare of late. And thus I made him promise to write to me daily. When he appeared to be ignoring that request, I naturally felt concern.'

'Naturally,' Colonel Stiet agreed, but his voice was flat with scepticism. 'And now that you are reassured that all is well with him, I trust we can put this incident behind us.'

'Certainly,' my uncle agreed. 'So long as Nevare continues to write to me daily. I shall have one of my men deliver my messages and pick up his to me, to be sure that the post does not fail us again. I have promised my brother, Nevare's father, that I would watch over him as closely as I would my own soldier son. I intend to keep that promise.'

'As a man of honour, certainly you must.' The words were correct, but there was still that odd flatness to his voice. The colonel looked at me as if he just realized I was there. 'Dismissed, Cadet. Lord Burvelle, would you care to join me at my home for a glass of wine before you depart?'

I had already turned to go when my uncle spoke. 'Actually, Colonel, I fear I should be getting back to the city. Things are a bit unsettled at my home of late. I shall walk Nevare back to his dormitory, I think, before I leave.'

The colonel was silent for a few moments. Then, 'The walks are icy tonight, Lord Burvelle. I strongly recommend against this.'

'Thank you for your concern, Colonel Stiet.'

And my uncle left it there, neither saying he would take the colonel's advice nor that he would ignore it. It left the colonel little more to say except 'good night'. And that he did, and my uncle returned it to him. Then he joined me as I opened the door for him. As I had suspected, Caulder was lingering in the foyer. I walked immediately to the outer door, but my uncle greeted him kindly and asked him how he had been of late. Caulder responded with faultless courtesy, and a smiling familiarity with my uncle that roused an unreasoning fury in me. I suppose I felt as if Caulder were somehow claiming my uncle. I deliberately held the door open for my uncle, admitting the cold wind into Colonel Stiet's foyer while they chatted. When my uncle finally bid

Caulder good night and preceded me out the door, I was glad to let it close on the building and all it contained.

I think my uncle sensed my upset, for he followed me carefully down the icy steps and then paused to wrap his scarf more closely around his neck. 'My wife's family has close ties with Lord Stiet. That is how we know his brother, Colonel Stiet, and Caulder of course. They have been guests in my home.' He paused as if to let me reply, but I could think of nothing to say. 'The wind has a bite in it tonight,' he observed. 'Shall we sit in my carriage and talk for a bit?'

'I should like that, sir,' I said, but then added, 'If you do not think it would be too hard on your coachman.'

He cocked his head at me. 'A good point, young Nevare. You show your father's concern for folk of lesser station. It is what made him such an excellent officer, and so beloved of his troops. Gaser!' He raised his voice to call to the man. 'I'm going to walk Nevare back to his dormitory. If you get too chilled, you may sit inside the carriage.'

'Thanky, sir,' the man replied, gratitude in his voice. As we walked away, I felt warmed, not just by my uncle's praise, but that he had acted on my concern for his coachman. My uncle took my arm as we walked.

'Well, Nevare, if you had to guess, where do you think our letters have gone astray?'

'I'm sure I've no idea, sir.'

'Oh, lad, you don't need to dissemble with me. I suspect that if I went to my wife's little writing desk and broke the silly lock on it, I'd find them all neatly stacked there. I don't think even Daraleen would have the gall to destroy them completely. No doubt she will say it was an oversight of some sort. It would not be the first time she had tampered in my affairs.' He sighed. 'So. Why don't we cut to the heart of it, and you tell me what you think made her do it.'

His easy acceptance of his wife's fault should have made it easier for me to speak. Instead, it only seemed harder. I suddenly wished that I had been forthright with him from the beginning, and told him not only about the séances but also that Epiny was writing to Spink. To tell it now made me feel I had been a party to his daughter's deception, as indeed I had. He listened in silence as I told the tale, passing lightly over Epiny's efforts at being a medium and dwelling charitably on how impressed Spink had been with her. My uncle lifted his brows in surprise when I told him that Spink's mother and elder brother would surely write to him any day now to ask permission for Spink to court Epiny. It was only surprising that he had not already received their letter.

'Perhaps I did,' he said when I paused. 'Perhaps it is in my wife's secretary, with our correspondence. Perhaps it is what triggered this whole incident. Let me be blunt with you, Nevare. Marrying the soldier son of a New Noble and living hundreds of miles away from Old Thares and the court is not what my wife has in mind for her elder daughter. She takes Epiny into situations that I think ill-advised, to try to advance her socially. This séance nonsense, for instance . . . if only the girl were not so childish. Other girls her age are already young women, formally presented to the court and already spoken for. But Epiny . . .' He sighed and shook his head. In the darkness, I caught his rueful smile. 'Well, you have seen how she is still a little girl in all the important ways. I tell myself that, in her own good time, she will grow up. Some flowers bloom later than others and some say their fragrance is sweetest. We shall see. I have forbidden Daraleen from rushing Epiny into womanhood. Childhood is too brief and precious a thing to waste.' He cleared his throat. 'I thought that my lady wife had come round to my way of thinking when she suggested that Epiny be sent off for some time with other girls her age. Epiny objected, with one of her harangues about being trained to be an ornament for a rich man's mansion.' He glanced at me and his smile was small and a bit bitter. 'I suppose I should have guessed that she was already imagining herself dominating a poor officer's quarters instead.'

I walked on with him, arm in arm, and my tongue felt thick with ashes. Epiny deceived her father, and by my silence, I contributed to it. Yet what was I to say? That when she was alone with Spink and me, she behaved not only as a young woman, but also as something of a coquette? I kept my silence and my guilt.

'So, I can see how your friend's infatuation with her and his prompting of his family to seek permission to court would have been upsetting to Lady Burvelle. She has not even had a time to display her precious treasure at court, and some New Noble upstart is trying to claim her and carry her off to a life on the wild frontier!' My uncle almost made a joke of it. He sounded amused, but regretful that it had happened.

I took a breath and plunged in. 'Spink is very taken with my cousin, Uncle. That is true. But he has not written to her. The correspondence has been one-sided. It is true that he asked his mother and brother to speak for him, but surely, that is what any honourable man would do; first, to attempt to secure permission before he began any courtship of the girl.'

I thought I had carefully led him up to seeing the truth of it: that Epiny only pretended to be childish. But he would not drink of that idea. Instead, he said, 'Well, at least my little girl has had her first childish infatuation. Surely I can take that as a sign of her growing up. And she chose a handsome soldier lad in a bright uniform with shiny buttons. I suppose I should have expected it. But I had no sisters, you know. Your father and I and our two younger brothers were like a den of bear cubs growing up. My mother despaired of ever teaching us anything about young women and how they should be treated. Epiny and Purissa are delightful but mysterious to me. They play at dolls and tea parties. . . it is an enchanting thing to watch, but how, I ask you, can that consume hours of their time? But doubtless you think me indulgent. I suspect your own father takes a firmer line with his offspring.'

'He does, sir, in some ways. And in others, he is indulgent. Once, when Elisi asked him to bring her back blue hair ribbons from his trip to the city, he brought her, not two, but twenty, in every shade of blue that the millinery had offered him. I do not think it a fault for fathers to dote on their daughters.'

We had drawn near to my dormitory. We halted on the walk. The tips of my ears and my nose stung with cold, but I sensed my uncle had not said all he wished to say.

'Let me change the subject, Nevare. Your letters were very detailed, and I assure you that your keen observation of how cadets are treated here will benefit those who follow you. But bring me up to date on yourself. How have you fared over the last week?'

'Oh, it has been nothing out of the usual, I suppose. The last few days have been a bit frantic. We've heard there is to be a culling, not by student but by patrol, based on our upcoming exams. It has all of us a bit worried, for there is not a cadet here who does not have a weakness of some kind. A failure by any of us could bring all of us down.'

'A what? A culling? Explain this to me, please.'

And so I did, as best I could, adding several times that it was only a rumour, but one spread by Caulder himself. My uncle's expression only grew darker as I explained it to him. At last he spoke. 'I, myself, think this is a useless and destructive way to "cull" weak cadets from the ranks. That the good and solid should perish with the lazy and the weak simply because of how your rooms were initially assigned seems but random cruelty to me! I know two members of the Academy board. I will use what authority I have to persuade them to look into this. As I have no soldier son in attendance, they may wonder why I take such an interest.

Worse, I fear they may see that I am trying to advance the cause of the battle lords' sons over their own soldier sons. At the best of times, the board does not move swiftly. Any action they take may be too late to save you this time. All you can do is study, pray and, of course, encourage your fellows to do the same. At least you've a holiday to look forward to when exams are done. You'll have a few days of leisure over the Dark Evening observances. Shall I come and fetch you to my house for them?'

I squirmed a bit. I enjoyed visiting my uncle, but I'd been looking forward to an opportunity to see Old Thares in holiday guise with my fellows. After a moment, I admitted that to my uncle, who laughed genially and said, 'Of course! How could I be so forgetful of what it is like to be a young man? Enjoy your time, then, but be cautious as well. Pickpockets and worse will be out and about on Dark Evening.'

I hesitated, dared myself and then blurted out, 'Is it true, what the lads have been telling me about women and Dark Evening?'

That made him burst out with a ringing laugh that turned the head of the night watchman on his early round. A blush warmed my wind-chilled face. I was certain my schoolmates had played a prank on me. When my uncle could speak, he replied heartily, 'It's true and it's untrue, as most holiday traditions are. At one time, generations ago, the Long Night had several pagan rituals attached to it, and women who served the old gods as priestesses were said to seek out the favour of any man they wished. There was some old legend . . . what was it? That on that night of the year, they were the goddesses incarnate and thus not bound by the rules that bind mortals from day to day. We all serve the good god now, and a day does not pass that I do not thank him that we are freed from ritual sacrifice and scar oaths and sacrificial floggings. Those were bad days, and if you go far enough back in our family history and read the soldiers' logs, you will see that even then, the common men regarded those practices as a burden and a scourge. Some, however, will make out those to be "the good old days" and speak of freedom and the power of the old gods. I think they are fools. Licentiousness and drunkenness and whoring and public floggings were the order of the day. But, I'm lecturing you, when all you want is a simple answer.'

I nodded, mute.

He smiled at me. 'It's mostly a joke now, lad. Sometimes a ribald jest between man and wife. She may disappear for that evening, to try to prick her husband with jealousy. Or sometimes a man's wife will come to him, masked and mysterious, on that night, as a way to bring back a bit of the romance to a marriage become commonplace. It is a night for masks and pretence and wild whims. People take to the street costumed as the kings and queens of old, or as heroes from the old myths or as the nightshades who served the old gods. But do respectable women actually wander about and offer themselves like common whores? Of course not! Oh, one or two perhaps might tempt themselves with that fantasy, but I am sure it is a rarity. Any women you encounter on that night will be professional, and I very much doubt they will offer their services for free!' He laughed again, and then, growing suddenly sober, asked me hastily, 'You have been warned, have you not, that whores may carry vermin and disease?'

I quickly assured him that I had, and had received many lurid and stern lectures on that topic. On that note, he bid me good night. He had turned away and started off down the path before I gave in to an impulse and ran after him. I called to him and he halted to wait for me. 'Uncle. About Spink. Will you . . . do you feel he deserves to be on probation for receiving letters from Epiny? After all, there was little he could do to prevent that from happening.'

He grew suddenly more sombre. 'It is unfair in some ways, Nevare. I know that. To be absolutely correct, he should have returned her letters, unopened, to me. To have read them and to have them about the barracks, well, it exposes her reputation to dispute. I'm a bit surprised that he would accept such tokens of affection from a mere child. But it does speak well of his intentions that he asked his brother to approach me.' He paused a moment, considering the matter.

'I will do this for you. I will get our letters, yours and mine, from Daraleen. And I will, if they are there, get the letters from your friend's mother and brother. The very least I owe young Lord Kester is a response to his request that his soldier brother be allowed to court my daughter. But I will also demand to see what sort of missives Epiny has been sending to young Spink, to incite such a battle frenzy in Daraleen. I should have sensed there was something behind her sudden demand that Epiny be sent off to a finishing school. And Mistress Pintor's Finishing Conservatory at that! It is very expensive, despite its remote location. And I shall sit down with Epiny as well, to explain to her the courtesies that are proper between a girl and a young man, for I'm sure she has no concept of what she has done. Doubtless she thought to befriend him and no more than that. If all is as I expect it is, I myself will contact Colonel Stiet, to see that Spink is restored to his good standing at the Academy. Does that put your mind at ease?'

I scarcely could say yes, for I feared what he might find in Epiny's letters to Spink. I had not yet known my cousin to mince words, even when she was trying to persuade her father that she was far too young to be considered a young lady. But I kept that thought to myself and only thanked my uncle and shook his hand. Before he released my hand from his, he added, 'If Epiny were of a suitable age, I might even look favourably upon a suitor of Spink's quality. He seems a level-headed young man, and that is a trait I think Epiny will sorely need in a husband.' But even as my spirits rose with hope, he added, 'But he would not fit at all with my lady's political ambitions, I fear. I doubt she would ever assent to Epiny becoming engaged to any New Noble's son.'

I was incredulous. 'My aunt has political ambitions? I do not understand.' How could a woman hope to compete in the harsh world of nobles and influence? 'I thought she would seek a wealthy suitor for Epiny, or someone of a fine old family—'

I think my uncle sensed the whole of my question for he shook his head at me. 'And you think that is social rather than political? You have much to learn, Nevare. Or would, if you were a first son. Soldier sons are blessedly immune to such machinations. Here in Old Thares and especially at court, the wives of lords have a society of their own, with a hierarchy of power and alliances that seem far more complicated to me than the simple politics of the Council of Lords chamber. Epiny and Purissa are the coin my lady will spend to secure her position, if you wish to put it crassly. With them, she will buy alliances with other noble houses. There have already been enquiries about both my daughters. I have made it plain that I choose to wait until they are women before I decide. I would have them marry well, but also to men who I can trust to protect them, and even to men that they may grow to love. Colonel Stiet has made no secret that he would take either of my girls as a match for Caulder. But Lady Burvelle hopes to find first sons for both of them, and as determined as she is, I suspect she will succeed.'

'But—' I began, but my uncle held up a hand.

'It's too cold out here to discuss anything more tonight, Nevare. I have kept you far longer than I intended, and you've given me much that I need to think over. You should be getting to bed. If I'm not mistaken, it will soon be lights-out in the halls. Clear your mind of your worries for now, or

485

rather, think only on preparing for your exams, for that is the only thing you can really do anything about. Write to me, and rest assured that if I do not hear from you on a daily basis, I'll be back.'

And with that he was gone, stamping his feet to warm them as he took the path back to his carriage. I became aware that my own toes had gone numb. I hurried up the steps of Carneston House and reported to Sergeant Rufet on the desk, for I was returning to the dormitory a bit late. He excused me when he heard I'd had a family visitor, and I hurried up the dimly lit stairs. At the final landing, I found Spink perched on his chair, holding his maths text to the wall sconce. He looked ten years older than he had at the start of the year.

'My uncle summoned me,' I said without preamble. 'He came to the Academy because he hadn't been receiving my letters.'

'Does he despise me?' Spink asked immediately.

I told him all that had transpired. I spared him nothing, thinking it was better to let him know that he had small chance of ever winning my cousin. He nodded at my account, and a ghost of hope came into his face when I told him that my uncle might speak for him to the colonel. But then it slipped away as he confided, 'Her letters to me are very affectionate. I doubt he will read them and think she would write such things if I had never encouraged her. But I swear that is the truth, Nevare.'

'I believe you,' I said. 'But I also fear that he will think that you incited Epiny.'

'Well. There's nothing I can do about that,' he said. His words were philosophical but his voice was despairing.

'You should go to bed, Spink. Get one solid night of sleep this week. This endless studying will make you a wraith by week's end.'

'I need to keep at it. I just have to fix the equations in my mind. Where I cannot master it by understanding, plain rote may suffice.'

I stood a moment longer. 'Well. I'm going to bed.'

'Good night.' He was not to be dissuaded from his vigil.

In the darkened study room, my books were on the table as I'd left them. I gathered them up in the dark and carried them back to my room.

I put them away by touch and undressed by my bed, letting my clothes drop to the floor. I was suddenly too tired to deal with them. I listened to my friends' breathing for a moment, then fell into my bed and let go of consciousness.

The remaining days to the section exams both lagged and sped past me. I thought it cruel that Captain Infal did no review with us, but simply kept on introducing new material right up to the day of the test. I felt my brain was crammed with dates and facts and names but little understanding of how the battles had flowed or what the overall strategy had been.

A long anticipated letter from Carsina arrived enfolded in a bare note from my sister. I tore it open and for the first two pages her flowering phrases and curly handwriting cheered me. But by the third page, the charm of her innocent affection and her girlish fantasies about the wonderful life we would have suddenly wore thin. What, I abruptly wondered, did she actually know of me at all? What would she think of me if I failed my history exam and condemned my entire patrol to Academy expulsion? Would she still find me as attractive if I were facing the prospect of enlisting as a common soldier? Would her father? Or did her parents, like my aunt, have ambitions and plans, and their daughter was merely a valuable item to be bartered for alliance and advantage?

I tried to shake myself free of my dismal thoughts and forced myself to read to the end of her letter. There was, I realized, nothing new in it. She had sewn a sampler and baked two loaves of pumpkin bread from a new recipe. Did I like pumpkin bread? She so looked forward to cooking for our darling children and me as they came along. She had already begun to fill her hope chest. She enclosed a drawing she had done of our initials intertwining. It was what she was embroidering on the corners of the good linen pillowcases that her grandmother had given to her for her future home. She hoped I liked it. She closed with the wish that I would think of her, and that I would send her some blue lace like I'd sent my sister if I had the opportunity to get to town.

It suddenly struck me that what I knew of Carsina was that she was pretty and well mannered, laughed easily, danced well and got along excellently with my sister. In the short time I'd spent with my cousin, I'd come to know Epiny better than I knew Carsina. I suddenly wondered if Carsina might be as eccentric and strong-willed as Epiny, but more adept at covering it up. I wondered if Carsina would ever want to hold a séance or spend half the morning wandering about the house in her nightgown. I felt very unsettled as I folded up her letter. It was all Epiny's fault. Before I had met her, I had assumed that women were rather like dogs or horses. If one came of good bloodlines and had been properly trained, one had only to let her know what was expected of her, and she would cheerfully carry it out. I don't mean that I thought women were dumb animals; quite the contrary, I had believed them wonderfully sensitive and loving creatures. I simply did not understand why any woman would wish to change her station or do otherwise than her husband's or father's wishes. What could she stand to gain by it? If a true woman dreamed of a home and family and a respectable husband, did she not betray that dream and undermine it when she defied the natural authority of her father or husband? So it had always seemed to me. Now Epiny had shown me that women could be sly, self-indulgent, deceptive, and rebellious. She made me doubt the virtue of every woman. Did even my sisters conceal such wiles behind their bland gazes?

The sudden uncertainty I felt about my wife-to-be, coupled with my anxiety about the upcoming exams, put me in a foul temper. I said little at our noon meal and could scarcely bear to watch Natred and Kort exchanging comments about their most recent missives from their sweethearts. It did not help my mood to see how longingly Spink followed their conversation. He looked a wreck. His uniform, never well-fitted to him, hung on his thin frame, unbrushed and rather spotted with mud about the cuffs. His eyes were red, his hair unruly, and his skin gone sallow from too many sleepless nights. The rumour of his probation had spread throughout the Academy, though not the reason for it. It made him an object of curiosity and speculation, and if he had had the spirit to pay attention to the stares that followed him, I'm sure he would have been annoyed.

The night before exams, Spink was ill. I couldn't tell if it was nervousness or if the prolonged lack of sleep had made him genuinely sick. Half way through our final cramming session, he simply gave up. He closed his books and without a word, only a doleful glance around at us, went off to bed. Our mood, not bright to begin with, sank into the depths. Gord was the next to surrender. 'Suppose I'm either ready for them or not. I've done the best I can,' he observed. He heaved himself to his feet and began to stack up his books.

'Done as much as you can for now, and will do as much as you should, tomorrow,' Trist observed. He made it a statement, not a question. His meaning was clear to all of us. Gord didn't rise to it.

'I'll do all I can to pass every one of my exams well and keep our patrol safe from culling. More than that, none of us can do.'

'One of us could do more, if he had the balls to do it. If he really cared about the rest of the patrol.' Trist raised his voice on the last sentence, to be certain that Gord had heard it. The closing of the bedroom door was his only response. Trist uttered an obscenity and sagged back in his chair. 'That fat bastard is going to do us all in with his phoney honour. He's probably hoping we'll all be culled. Then he can go home to his trough, say it wasn't his fault and forget about being a soldier. I'm going to bed.'

Trist slammed his book shut disdainfully, as if there were no use in further studying, as if all hinged on Gord and Spink, and none of us could do anything to change our fates.

Rory closed his books more quietly. 'I'm done in,' he said with resignation. 'My head is as stuffed as it can get. I'm going to bed and dream about Dark Evening. Our scores won't be posted until after the break. So I'm going to go out and enjoy myself in Old Thares. Might be the only opportunity I ever have. Night, fellows.'

'He's got a point,' Caleb declared. 'I, for one, am going to give myself a night such as I'll never forget. I've heard the whores will be free that night, but just in case, I've saved two months' allowance. I'll leave them limping, I will.'

'You'll be the one limping, after you come down with the dick-scald. You hear what happened to Corporal Hawley from Shinter House? Dick-scald so bad he couldn't even piss without screaming. Don't take a chance on the whores, friend.' This from Rory, over his shoulder as he left.

'Ha! Hawley was too cheap to go to a good house. Took alley girls, is what I heard. Not my idea of fun, standing up and thrusting while some poor girl knocks the back of her head against a brick wall.'

'I'm for bed.' Kort's voice betrayed his amused disgust with them both. 'Good luck, everyone.' As he stood, Natred did, too. I began stacking my books, as did every other man at the table.

Tomorrow, I knew, would determine my entire future. It burned in my heart that even if I scored perfectly on every test tomorrow, one of my fellows could bring me low. I looked round at them and for a moment, I knew hatred for Colonel Stiet and the Academy and even my fellow cadets.

Later, as I lay in bed, I closed my eyes and tried to grope my way toward sleep, but could not reach it. Eyes closed, body relaxed, my mind hovered in the place between wakefulness and rest. I felt I dangled, helpless, over an abyss and that I had no power to save myself from falling. The feeling was doubtless responsible for my nightmares about the tree woman.

Yet my dream began not with terror, but comfort. I was in my beloved forest, at peace. Sunlight broke through the canopy overhead and dappled my skin and I smiled as I looked at it on my bared arms and legs. The rich smells of humus rose around me. I picked up a handful and considered it. It was a layer from yesterday's leaf, down to the black loam that had flora five years ago. Busy little insects toiled in it. A tiny worm coiled and uncoiled desperately on my palm. I laughed at his fears and restored all to the forest soil. All was well. I said as much to my mentor. 'The world lives and dies as it should today.'

The tree woman nodded to me, making shadows shift over my flesh. 'I am pleased that you have come to understand that the dying is a part of the living. For too long, you clung to the notion that each life was significant and too important to perish for the whole. But now you see it, don't you?'

'I do. And it comforts me.' And it did. At least it comforted the part of me that sat on the forest floor at the feet of the great tree, his back to its rough bark. That part of me saw no woman, only felt and heard her speaking to me.

Yet the part of me that stood in the shadowy space between dreams and waking was horrified at my behaviour.

I consorted with the enemy. There was no other way to look at it. My worst fears were confirmed when I heard her say, 'It is good that you have come to the understanding. It will make it easier for you.'

'Did you ever have doubts when the magic first claimed you?' I asked her.

I felt her wistful sigh in the gentle rustling of the leaves above me. 'Of course I did. I had plans for my life, and dreams. Then came a time of drought. I thought that we would all die. I made a spirit journey, just as you did. A choice was offered to me just as it was offered to you. I chose the magic and the magic chose me. The magic used me and my people survived.'

Unbreathing in the shadow, I heard my traitor self ask her, 'The magic will use me, also?'

'Yes. It will use you as you use it. It will give to you and, in the process, it will take from you. You may mourn what is taken. But the loss will make you stronger and truer to your task.'

My dream self made a gesture with his hands. I sensed it signified acceptance. I felt impotent fury that this other self would passively accede to such a fate. And in my fury, I was somehow separate from him, and could observe him. He filled me with contempt. He leaned back, naked and smiling in the gentle balm of the sun. His skin was evenly browned, as if he had never known a scrap of clothing. He had dirt under his fingernails, and his bare feet and ankles were permanently grimed. He was a man turned into a beast of the forest. Yet, he was pleased with himself, content in whatever life this was he lived. I hated him, hated myself and my weakness with a terrifying passion. Then, as he shifted, I felt a thrill of fear strengthen me. I had thought that dream self was my twin, but now I saw he was not. What I had taken for a head as shorn of hair as my own was actually a bald pate. At the crown of his skull, sprouting like a rooster's tail, was a sheaf of hair. I knew with sudden certainty that his crop of hair would exactly match the missing piece of scalp on my scarred head. This was the stolen self that Epiny had spoken about with Spink.

The tree had continued to speak to my dream self. 'It is good that you are prepared, for soon I will reach out to you with the magic. I have considered long whether it was wise for me to take action on my own. Usually, when the magic takes a vessel, the magic soon acts through the vessel, and the events that will make all right for The People are set into motion. But you say you have done nothing; that the magic has not acted through you. Of this you are certain?'

I watched my dream self. He sat silent a moment and then shrugged eloquently. He did not know. I sensed that he had reached for me, perhaps trying to know my thoughts and what this self did in the real world, yet he could no more truly comprehend who and what I was than I could understand him. Perhaps Epiny's summoning had broken my dreams and made me aware of him. His topknot of hair, I now saw, was braided at the base and tarred with something that made it stand up from his scalp. A bit of green vine wrapped it like a schoolgirl's ribbon. It looked silly to me, as foolish as one of Epiny's hats.

The tree sighed, a heavy rustling of wind through her branches. 'Then, act I shall, though I am full of misgiving at taking this upon myself. Old as I am, wise as I have become through the many seasons, I still do not see as the magic sees. The magic sees to the end of all permutations. The magic knows which falling grain of sand will escalate into a landslide. I see more clearly than any living member of The People. But even so, I tremble at what I will do.'

Indeed, a curious shiver did run through the tree, a quivering of the leaves that seemed independent of any stir of air. My dream self folded his hands and bowed his head in submission. 'Do as you must, Tree Woman. I will be ready.'

'I will do as I must, never fear! The dance is no longer sufficient. We trusted to it, but it is failing. Our trees fall and with every tree that dies, wisdom is lost. Power is lost. The forest is what binds our worlds together. As the intruders cut the forest, they are like mice nibbling at a rope. The bridge between the worlds grows weaker. The magic feels itself weakening, and knows it must work quickly. I feel it as I feel the sap of spring that rushes through me. I know we must make a bridge of our own. So, there is no time for you to thrash and blunder your way. There is no time to let you make your own mistakes. Tomorrow, you must pass the test.'

Test. Was that the word that woke me once again to my second, observing self. Suddenly, I knew that I existed as my true self in another place, and in that true self, would face a real test tomorrow. In the curious way of dream logic, knowing that the scalp-locked self before me was a stolen part of me suddenly gave me power over him. I spoke with his mouth. 'This is a dream. Just a dream. You are not real, and this self is not real. I am the real Nevare. And tomorrow, I will pass the test that will let me go on to be a soldier for my people.'

The bark of the tree opened. Creepers sprouted from the cracks and wrapped me. She seized me and held me fast. When she spoke, I knew she spoke to my real self. 'You speak more truly than you know. Tomorrow you face a test. You will pass it and make the sign and you will then fight for The People.'

'Let go of me! Leave me alone! I am a horse soldier, as my father was before me. I serve King Troven and the people of Gernia. Not you! You are not even real!'

'Aren't I? Aren't I? Then wake up, soldier's son, and see how real I am!'

And she flung me away from her. Suddenly I was falling, falling into the crevasse I had so perilously crossed on the flimsy bridges. Her creepers bound my arms tightly to my sides. I tried to scream, but I was falling so fast I could not get my breath.

I've heard it said that although dreams of falling are common, the dreamer always wakes before he hits the bottom. I did not. I hit the rocks. I felt my ribcage give on impact, felt my arms and legs rebound from the slam and then slap the earth again. Everything went black and spun around me. I tasted blood. I groaned and forced my eyes open. I dared not move at first, for surely every bone in my body must be shattered. I lay still, trying to make sense of what I saw.

Moonlight came in faintly at the window. I made out the outline of Spink's bed next to mine. I was on the floor of the dormitory, I gradually realized. My tangled bedding was all that bound me. I wallowed out of it and managed to sit up. I'd had a nightmare and fallen out of bed. I had been right. It had all been just a dream. A very strange dream, but only a dream, and probably the result of the nervousness I felt about the test I faced tomorrow and Epiny's strange notions about me. My head hurt. I put my hand up, and for a moment I could have sworn I felt a tarred scalp-lock standing up from the crown of my head. I brushed my fingers against it, and then it was gone and I felt only the scar on my scalp. My fingers came away damp with blood. My fall had broken it open again. Groaning, I crawled up off the hard floor and back onto my bed. Finally, I slept.

TWENTY

Crossing

I must have wakened a dozen times before dawn, in that dreadful cycle of being horribly tired but fearing I would oversleep and thus rousing myself over and over. The room was colder than usual. My blanket was inadequate against the chill and I ached all over from shivering. My fitful dozing had left me wearier than if I had stayed up all night. At last, I admitted to myself that I could not return to sleep. Around me in the darkness, I could tell from the squeaking of springs and the rustling of blankets that my fellows were as restless as I was. I spoke into the darkness. 'So we might as well get up and face the day.'

Kort replied with an obscenity that I'd never heard him use before. Natred chuckled bitterly. Those two had seemed almost immune from the tension; I now realized that they were just as anxious as the rest of us. I heard Spink sit up without a word. He sighed heavily and made his way through the dark to our lamp. He lit it. The yellow light made him look jaundiced. Despite his longer sleep, he still had dark circles under his eyes. He scratched at his cheek, and then went to the washstand to peer blearily at himself. 'It would almost be a relief to fail,' he said quietly. 'To be sent home and to know that it had all fallen to pieces and that no one would have any expectations of me any more.'

'And take us all down with you?' Natred asked, outraged.

'Of course not. That would haunt me to the end of my days. And that is why I've studied so hard, and I won't fail. Not today. I won't fail.'

But even to me, he sounded more determined than convincing.

The room was colder and the lamp seemed dimmer than usual as we dressed. While waiting my turn for the washbasin, I went to the window and looked out. The Academy grounds were cold and still. The sky was still black overhead, with the last stars fading. The day would be clear, then. Clear and cold. A shallow crust of snow, trampled in places, caked the lawns and tree branches. I looked at the reaching black branches of the tree and a vague memory stirred. When I tried to recall it, the bits fled. I shook my head, at myself and at the Academy grounds before me. They looked the most dismal place in the world. It was strange, but the snow appeared abused and out of place in that city world. If I had wakened to a similar morning in the open countryside it would have felt like a crisp, clean winter day. In Old Thares, it felt like a mistake.

No one spoke much. There were mutters and grumbles of complaint, but I think each one of us was too caught up in his own fears to say much of anything to his fellows. We mustered in the usual place where Corporal Dent appeared to curse and blame us for his miserable life. I felt dull and discouraged and wondered briefly why I had ever wanted so desperately to be here. This was not the golden future I had imagined for myself. This was misery, pure and simple. I wondered if Spink had been right. Maybe it would just be a relief to be sent home, with all expectations of me vanished forever. I gave myself a shake, trying to dispel my gloominess. Dent gave me a demerit for moving in ranks. I scarcely noticed.

We waited in the cold and the dark until our cadet officers

came by and reviewed us. Surprisingly, they found little to scorn us for that day. Perhaps they, too, dreaded the day's exams, even though the upper classmen were immune from the culling process. Or perhaps they looked forward to Dark Evening's holiday and felt merciful to us. Maybe it was simply too dark for Jaffers to see that I had not brushed my jacket and that my trousers had spent the night on the floor, not on a hanger. In any case, Cadet Captain Jaffers allowed how we appeared and we were dismissed from our inspection.

We marched off to a breakfast I had no stomach for. I forced myself to eat, reminding myself of Sergeant Duril's saying, 'The soldier who doesn't break his fast when he can is a fool.' At the table, only Gord seemed to eat with a will. Spink pecked at his food. Trist heaped his plate, ate five bites and then pushed at the rest as if he were poking a dead animal with a stick. Ordinarily, Corporal Dent would have demanded that he eat whatever he took, and lectured us all that a man who took supplies greedily and then wasted them was a liability to his whole regiment. Dent, however, had found as many possible excuses as he could of late to leave us alone at table, so there was no one to rebuke us for the half-eaten meals that day.

We fell in and marched off through a cold day that was just now turning grey to our first class. In Military History the entire chalkboard was already covered in questions written out in Captain Infal's sloping hand. He greeted us with, 'Come in, leave your books closed, and start writing. I will collect your papers at the end of class. No talking until then.'

And that was it. I set out my paper and began writing. I tried to pace myself, to be sure that I would write at least some sort of answer to each question and did well enough at that. I left space at the ends of some answers to allow myself to add more detail if I had time. I struggled with dates and with the sequences of the sea battles. I wrote until my pen was slick in my fingers and my hand ached. And suddenly

Captain Infal was announcing, 'That's it, Cadets. Finish the sentence you are writing and put your pens away. Leave your papers on your desk. I will take them up. Dismissed.'

And that was it. The day outside had warmed a bit, but not enough to melt the ice on the walkways. The closer we got to the river, the more bitterly the wind blew. The dilapidated maths and science building creaked in the cold. There were coal stoves in each classroom, but their warmth did not seem to extend more than a few feet beyond their sullen iron bellies. We took our customary places, with Gord sitting on one side of Spink and me on the other. Captain Rusk saw us seated, then went to the board and began writing the first problem. 'Begin as you are ready,' he instructed us. I gave Spink a reassuring smile but I don't think he saw it. His nose was red with cold, and the rest of his face white with weariness and perhaps fear.

I recognized Rusk's first problem as one directly out of the textbook examples. I could have simply written the answer, but he demanded that all work be shown. I worked steadily, taking down each problem as he wrote it, and several times blessed my father for seeing me so well prepared for my first year of Academy.

Midway through the test, it happened. I heard a small crunch, and then Gord's hand shot immediately into the air. Rusk sighed. 'Yes, Cadet?'

'I've broken my pencil, sir. May I ask to borrow one?'

Rusk sighed. 'A prepared soldier would have an extra one with him. You cannot always depend on your comrades, though you should always be in a position to let them depend on you. Has anyone an extra pencil that Cadet Lading may use?'

Spink lifted his hand. 'I do, sir.'

'Then lend it, Cadet. Please continue with your tests.'

Gord leaned over to accept the pencil that Spink offered. As he did so, his desk bumped against his sizeable midsection and then lurched against Spink's. Both their papers cascaded to the floor under Spink's desk. Spink leaned down, gathered the papers and handed Gord's back to him, along with the extra pencil. I watched this from the corner of my eye. And I could not be certain that Spink gave Gord back every sheet that truly belonged to him.

Captain Rusk made no comment on it. He continued his slow pace around the room. I heard my classmates groan when he announced, 'You should have finished with these problems by now,' and erased the first set on the board. He immediately began to write more problems. And I sat there, feeling paralysed and sick, not by the maths, which was well within my abilities, but by my uncertainty. Had they cheated? Had they planned that manoeuvre? Did I have an honour duty to raise my hand and inform Captain Rusk that they possibly had cheated? But what if they hadn't? What if it was coincidence? I would have doomed the nine men of my patrol to expulsion from the Academy. We would all be culled, because I had had a suspicion. I felt a sudden wave of loathing for Trist, so busily scratching away at his own paper. But for his horrid suggestion, I would never have considered Gord or Spink capable of cheating. I could not move until Captain Rusk asked me, 'Cadet Burvelle? Finished already?'

His words jolted me back to my own situation, and I immediately replied, 'No, sir,' and bent my head over my own paper and my mind back to the task before me. Despite my delay, which had seemed an eternity but had likely been only a minute or two, I finished well within the hour and had time to go back and check my work. I found several errors, probably due to my rattled state. Nonetheless, when Captain Rusk announced, 'Time! Pass your papers to the cadet on your right. End cadets, bring the papers forward to me,' I felt as queasy as if I had failed every problem.

I kept my eyes to myself and spoke not a word as we left our classroom and formed up for our march across campus.

A few of the others whispered to one another about two of the knottier problems on the test, but both Spink and Gord were as silent as I was. Despite the cold air, I felt sweat trickle down my back.

My test in Varnian is a hazy memory to me. We were given a technical passage from a cavalla strategy text to translate into Gernian, and then had to compose an essay in Varnian about how to care for a horse. I handed in my papers feeling I had done well enough. The trick of the essay was, of course, to keep to vocabulary and verb forms one was certain of.

Our mid-day meal was next. We went first to Carneston House, to exchange our morning books and notes for our afternoon materials, and then straight to the mess hall. I didn't speak a word to anyone. No one seemed to notice my silence. They were all preoccupied with the tests we had completed and dreading the ones still to come. If anyone else had noticed what had happened between Gord and Spink, they chose to keep as quiet about it as I did. The cooks had prepared a hot and hearty bean soup containing chunks of fat ham and plenty of fresh bread to go with it. It smelled good, much better than their usual concoctions, but I scarcely tasted it. Spink seemed lighter of spirit, as if he had faced his most feared demon and the rest of the day could not daunt him. I avoided meeting his eyes for fear of what I might read there. Would I know if my best friend had forsaken his honour and cheated on a test? And with the next breath, I traitorously wondered if that would be such a bad thing, if he had done it so that his fellows, including me, could continue at the Academy? Did the ends justify the means? Was the culling, as Trist had suggested, a cruel way to test our loyalty to one another as well as our learning? And then my mind came back to Rusk's comment about Gord needing to borrow a pencil – that one cannot always depend on his comrades but should always be in a position

501

to let them depend on oneself – and wondered if there had been some hidden meaning there.

I entered the Engineering and Drawing classroom with trepidation. I feared a lengthy session with callipers and straight edge and ruler, dissecting and analysing some ancient construction. Instead, we found Captain Maw triumphant over four disorderly heaps of miscellaneous building materials. He wore a heavy coat and hat. He grinned at us all, clearly pleased with himself. It filled me with dread.

'Quickly organize yourself into your patrols. I've decided that we will have a practical test of what you have learned. In a few moments, we'll be carrying our materials outside and across the campus to Tiler's Creek for a realistic demonstration of what you have learned so far in my class.

'Often a cavalla patrol will find itself faced with an obstacle that must be crossed: a river, a ravine, a desert or some other rough piece of terrain. Then all the spit and polish and book learning in the world cannot avail you unless you can put both your minds and your bodies to work. My test is a simple one. Your objective is to transport your patrol across Tiler's Creek. I've furnished you with an ample supply of materials and tools, far more than you would have with you on the average horse patrol. The rules are simple. You must cross Tiler's Creek. You may use only the items from your own supply dump, but you may barter with other patrols for what you think you may need. Barter carefully, for once you have given something away, you cannot demand it back. You will pass or fail this test on the basis of your patrol crossing the creek. I will now give each patrol five minutes to select a leader for this exercise. Only the leader can barter and his decision is final. Choose now.'

Instantly I hated it. Not the construction aspect: I appreciated the chance to prove my skills and knowledge in a practical way. No, I dreaded having to choose between Spink and Trist, for I was certain that they would be my only

502

choices. And once we had selected one or the other, I feared the divided loyalties within our patrol would hamper our efforts to get anything done. As I dreaded, Trist immediately smiled round at us and announced, 'How about it, fellows? You know I can get this done.'

Oron and Caleb immediately nodded, but Gord held up a warning hand. 'Wait. I want to propose a different man for the job.'

'Not Spink,' Oron said decisively.

'No, not Spink,' Gord shocked me by saying. 'I propose Nevare. His marks have been excellent and more than once he has shown that his father gave him a practical grounding in this sort of work. Isn't that true, Nevare?'

Only a week ago, I would have flushed with pleasure at Gord's praise, and at the newly appraising stares that my fellows gave me. Today, I only felt intensely uncomfortable. Did I want praise from fellows who would cheat or suggest cheating? So I only said, grudgingly, 'I've built a cattle bridge or two. And helped with the footbridge for my sisters' garden.'

There was a very long moment of silence. Trist looked shocked, not just that Gord had proposed someone other than Spink but also that he had chosen me. But Rory, Nate, and Kort were all nodding vigorously, and after a moment, Spink did also. Trist just shrugged. 'If that's what you fellows want,' he said, as if he didn't care at all. Caleb immediately nodded also. Trist seemed to think it rather generous of himself to concede, and I suppose it was. As it was, we were still standing about uncertainly when Captain Maw announced, 'Time is up. Name your commanders.'

'Cadet Nevare Burvelle,' Trist announced before I could say anything. Then, quietly, to me he added, 'You best do your job, Burvelle. If you fail this, then we all go down.'

His words changed my warmth at my comrades' support to a liquid fear in my belly. Was that why neither Spink nor Trist had given me much challenge for this post? Because a failure now would be such a spectacular defeat? It chilled me, but Rory, grinning like a frog, tilted his head at me and jovially commanded me to, 'Lead on, Commander Burvelle.'

I think that, even said in jest, it does something to a man the first time someone actually calls him 'commander'. I thought about it as Maw ordered all of us to follow him outside into the raw weather. Each of us gathered an armful of supplies from our pile and followed him. In that moment, I decided I would step up to the challenge rather than, as I had first considered, insist that Trist take it on. Maw was whistling as he led us out into the cold and the wind. We tramped through the caked and icy snow on the lawns to the edge of campus. There he motioned us to set down our loads and invited us to survey the creek.

When I stood by the stack of supplies Maw had given our patrol, my heart sank. Tiler's Creek seeped along, a muddy gash at the edge of our landscaped Academy grounds. The trees that grew along its steep, mud-flanked banks were pole-sized saplings, now bare in winter's grip. The gap we had to cross was not especially challenging. Once, perhaps, Tiler's Creek had been a real creek. I suspected that nearby households siphoned off most of its water and dumped waste into the small trickle that remained. At the bottom of its muddy ravine, the 'creek' was little more than a seep of slime under a coating of ice, and only about eleven mucky feet wide. It was immediately obvious that we had only one wooden plank that was long enough to span the creek. We had a quantity of shorter boards, rope, canvas, stakes, a mallet, several knives, a hammer, a saw, and some nails. My heart sank.

'Let's sort out our materials and see what we have,' I suggested.

That was a mistake. Trist immediately added, 'Let's see if that one long piece will reach across the creek.'

Spink then chimed in, 'Looks like we only have one. We may have to trade to get more.' I suddenly saw how it could go. I would ostensibly be in charge, while the two natural leaders actually made the decisions and set the tasks. I felt the familiar lurch of uncertainty that always plagued me when I wondered if I had the ability to be a good officer. I was too solitary, too independent, too accustomed to doing it all myself, my own way. Perhaps my father had been right about me; I did not have what it took to lead.

The rest of the patrol began to move to obey Spink's and Trist's instructions. I realized my error in not being more forceful. I would not err so again. I tried to put my father's steel into my voice. 'No. That's not how you start a bridge. I'm not worried about spanning it now. The span is no good if we don't have anything to support it. Foundation first.'

Everyone turned to look at me. The other patrols were talking and moving pieces of wood and shaking out lengths of rope. In the circle around me, a small silence reigned. I felt the cold of the day and the chill of my small command's doubt. I suddenly knew they wouldn't follow me, and worse, that neither Spink nor Trist had the real knowledge of how to build a bridge. We were all going to fail, because I had failed my one chance to lead. Then, 'Let's get sorting,' Spink said to Kort. As they moved to obey my command, Spink gave me a wink. It both reassured and annoyed me. It seemed to say that he was with me, and that with his backing, I could command. I was grateful for his support, but I wanted to be able to lead regardless of whether I had it or not. I longed to know how he and Trist made others want to follow him. What did I lack?

There was no time to ponder it. Captain Maw had given us a motley pile of resources. As Trist had noted, there was only one piece of lumber long enough to span the creek. One patrol was already taking the easiest and most obvious solution. They set the single board on the ground so it reached from bank to uneven bank. But the board bowed under the weight of the first cadet who tried to cross it and spilled him into the half-frozen muck. The cadet who had fallen into

505

Tiler's Creek clambered back out, coated in filth, wet, even colder now than he had been, and dispirited. His fellows hooted at him as he rejoined them. Maw, who was sitting silently on a nearby bench reading a book, lifted his eyes, pursed his lips, and shook his head at them. I thought he fought back a smile. Without a word, he took a pipe from his coat pocket and began to fill it with tobacco.

I, too, shook my head. Maw, I suspected, had a different solution in mind. What had seemed so easy when we were building models now seemed almost insurmountable. How easy it was to reach down from above a model and carefully fix a tiny plank into place. I suddenly saw the real first step of the problem. 'We need at least two men to cross to the other side,' I announced. 'We can't build a bridge working just from this end.'

No one wanted to go. It was a steep climb down, a mucky slog across, and then a tough scrabble up the other side. Whoever went was going to get his uniform and boots filthy. I glanced up and down the creek. There were no bridges in sight. Through the muck was the only option. 'Two of us, at least, have to wade across.'

'Not me!' Trist announced with a grin. 'Not right before Dark Evening. I have plans for the days off and they don't include fussing about with my laundry. Make Rory go.'

I'd already forgotten the lesson I'd just learned. I should have issued orders to two of the cadets, not opened it up for discussion. I didn't want to set a good example by wading across myself. For one thing, I had the very same reasons for wishing to stay clean that Trist had. But just as important to me was that I wanted to stay where the materials were so that I could come up with a credible building plan. I took a breath and tempered my remark. 'No one has to go just yet, Trist. We have to determine what materials need to cross with that part of the team. Sending two men across empty-handed won't do us much good.'

'The others have already started, and we're just standing here talking,' Oron complained.

He was right. I saw that one patrol was busily nailing crosspieces to their long plank. Did they think that would make it stronger? Another group had succeeded in trading so that they had two long planks. I looked at ours again, stood it up and shook it. It wavered. Even two of them would not have the load-bearing capacity to be the foundation for a successful bridge. 'There's no sense in doing anything until we have a definite plan,' I told the others. 'And somehow, I don't think that this one long plank is at the heart of it. I think it's a distraction. What if we didn't have this piece of wood? What would we be doing?'

We all looked at our pile of supplies with new eyes. 'Rope bridge,' Rory announced.

I nodded. 'We'll anchor it to those saplings. But we still need a team working at the other end.'

Rory knelt down and began to unfasten the rope from its coil. The others made similar 'busy' motions. I took a breath. It was time to command, and I had no faith that anyone would follow my orders. Not unless I physically led the way. 'Spink and Caleb. You're wading across with me. Rory, give me one end of that line.'

'What do you need us for?' Caleb demanded piteously.

I refused to answer. He shouldn't have been questioning orders and I wasn't going to indulge him. Rory shook out the line and gave me an end. 'Let's go,' I told them.

I started down the steep bank, and despite my attempts to pick good footing, I slid most of the way. I had tried to pick a spot on the bank that was well coated with snow. Even so, there was mud up the back of my trousers before I reached the bottom, where my boots sank into the ooze, but only a few inches. 'Spink, Caleb. Come on,' I told them, and then turned my back, refusing to watch them hesitate. I crossed the mucky creek, breaking through the shallow ice

507

at every step. I scrambled up the opposite bank, using exposed roots and tufts of grass as handholds. By the time I stood on the other side, I was filthy. Spink, to my surprise, was right behind me. Caleb watched us for a moment, then, as we ignored him, he crossed. He had to use the rope to pull himself up; he had height but no real muscle on his frame. We reached down, hauled him to his feet, and then stood up, brushing off our hands. I realized that Captain Maw was watching us, a peculiar smile on his face. I wondered if this was his idea of a practical joke on all of us. I grinned back at him and gave a wave to show I could take it. Then I turned back to our task.

I had never built a rope bridge, but I'd seen pictures of them. I called out that we were going to go for the simplest form: a single rope strung across to walk on and another line above it to hang onto as we crossed. I saw the other three patrols immediately halt in their efforts and look at one another as if trying to decide if that was the plan they should have pursued.

Half an hour later, I had proved to myself that we did not have enough rope to make a bridge. The saplings that grew close to the edge would not take our weight; we had torn three of them up by the roots. The ones that were further back were too far away; we didn't have enough rope. I had made at least four trips back and forth across the mucky creek, trying to find a way to anchor the rope to the bank itself. Trist, to my surprise, had turned to with a will. He had not ventured into the muddy creek, but he was almost as dirty as I was from anchoring the rope to various shrubs that we then uprooted. Gord had served mostly as an anchorman, trying to hold the rope bridge by his own weight; it hadn't worked. Oron had fallen in the creek once and Rory twice. Our time was running out. The only consolation we had was that the other patrols were faring just as badly as we were. If I had not spoken my rope bridge plan aloud, I might have been able to trade our long board for another patrol's coil of line, but it was too late to do so now.

I sat down for a moment to catch my breath. Even putting four men on each end of the line to anchor it and using the long board as a balancing pole, we hadn't been able to get Spink across. That was ignoring the problem of Gord's massive weight, and the larger problem that as soon as a man had crossed, he could no longer act as an anchorman on the home bank.

I glanced at Maw. He was bundled on his bench, reading his book and smoking. He had given up even watching us. I was tired, cold, and muddy, but the frustration was the worst. I did not think Maw would give us a task with no solution. I tried to think back over all our constructions in his class, trying to come up with something that would be a clue to the solution.

'We're running out of time!' Trist announced.

'Does anyone have any ideas?' Spink begged. I heard him throwing it open to anyone to take the command from me and save our patrol. That felt like a knife in my back. I lifted my eyes to stare at him. And there, twirling down from the sky above, shed from some unseen bird that had flown overhead, was a perfect black wing plume. It spun as it came down, shaft first, and neatly twisted itself into some soft snow to stand upright. It stirred slightly in the chill wind.

The memory crashed back into me. I stood with Dewara at the edge of the abyss. What had anchored those flimsy magical bridges? Only feathers driven into the sand, and twists of spider web. I had wood for stakes, a mallet for pounding them in, and stout rope. I could anchor my bridge to the earth itself. There might be just enough rope to do that. I slogged across the creek one more time to whisper my plan to my fellows. If it succeeded, I wanted the success to be ours.

We worked feverishly, cutting our stakes and sharpening them, pounding them into the earth and securing our lines.

Our limited supply of tools meant that I had to wade across several more times, ferrying tools back and forth. We ended up with two parallel lines that barely spanned the divide. We had untwisted our short piece of remaining rope into twine and used it to fasten the crosspieces we had cut from our remaining lumber. We kept one fairly long piece as a balancing pole. I stood back and looked at our 'bridge' and wondered if even a rabbit could cross it safely. We had barely finished it when Captain Maw stood, took out his pocket watch, looked at it, and shook his head. ' Five minutes, gentlemen!' he announced to us. There were shouts of dismay and frustration from the other patrols.

'Go for it, Nevare. Take a chance,' Trist urged me in a whisper. 'If no one else crosses and we do, it may be a clear enough victory to save us all from culling.'

I tried to look as if I hadn't heard him. I made my voice as strong as I could and announced, 'Sir, we are ready to cross!'

'Are you?' He looked at me oddly, and again I had that impression that he wanted to laugh out loud. 'Well, I've been waiting for this. Nevare's patrol, cross!' He barked it out as an order.

Spink, Oron, and I waded across the creek one final time. We did not want to stress our creation any more than we must. I suspected we would only be able to use it once before it gave way. I only hoped the good god would favour us enough to make it last that long. To that end, I lined up my men by size. Spink would go first and Gord last. I saw the decision register in Gord's eyes, but as always, he said nothing about it.

Spink went across lightly, almost dancing from board to board. When he reached the opposite side, he sent the balance pole back to us as if it were a javelin. Oron crossed next. He was less graceful and slower. As Caleb crossed, one of our crosspieces came loose and fell to the muck below. We lost two more when Nate went across. Kort crossed without incident. When it came my turn, I waved the others to go ahead. I had decided that I would go last. My father had often told me that an officer can delegate authority but not responsibility. If my bridge gave way, this might be my only experience of being an officer. I'd do it right.

And thus I stood on the home bank, my feet planted on top of the ropes to give them extra anchorage and told Gord, 'Go ahead. It's held so far. We have to trust our work.'

He nodded gravely to me. Beads of sweat already stood out on his brow. He took the balancing pole and stepped out onto the bridge.

I should have sent him across first, I thought to myself, when our construction was strongest and all the steps were in place. The other patrols had given up any effort to finish their constructions and had come to gape at Gord's crossing. There were muffled snickers as he started out, for the ropes creaked and stretched under his feet. The bridge sagged sharply as he ventured further from the bank, and two of the crosspieces snapped off and flew as if flung from a slingshot.

'Nothing improves pork like hanging it for a few days!' someone gibed and I saw Gord's ears go scarlet.

'Keep your mind on your task!' I barked at him. He gave a slight nod. He went three more steps, four, five . . . On the opposite bank, our entire patrol was trying to stand on the end lines to help anchor them. I could feel the lines straining under my feet. Gord stepped wide over one gap in the footboards, made it to the next one, and then suddenly, it turned under his weight. He fell badly, sprawling across the ropes and then tipping off to land face first in the muck. He gave a muffled cry as he hit, and I knew a sudden jolt of fear that he had broken his back. That pang was as sharp as my knowledge that we had failed. Failed. We'd be culled. I suddenly knew it as clearly as I knew my own name. And so I fulfilled my final task in my very brief career as an officer. I scrabbled down the muddy bank again and waded out into the slime to see if my trooper was injured.

When I reached Gord's side, he had already managed to sit up. Mud and frost were sliding down his face. He tried to wipe it off but only smeared it more. He was groaning, but in response to my query, said he didn't think anything was broken. I helped him stand and glanced up at Captain Maw. The man was still standing on the bank, looking down at us. As I watched him, he again glanced at the pocket watch he held flat in his palm. And suddenly I grasped it.

'Get up the bank!' I shouted at him. Gord looked at me as if I were mad. He tried to turn around and go back to our home bank. I grabbed the back of his jacket and pulled at him. 'No. Get up there. We have to cross. We have to get our patrol across the creek. That was the objective. Not to build a bridge. *To cross the creek*!'

I'd spoken my revelation aloud. Suddenly, all the other patrols saw it as clearly as I had. They hesitated, still, for the filthy and cold water was a daunting barrier. As they did, Gord started his heavy scramble up the bank. Clumps of grass came loose in his hands, and he pulled out the roots that he grabbed. He slid back toward me. Then Spink and Rory reached their hands down to clutch at his wrists. I planted my shoulder in his ample backside and shoved as they heaved at him. His feet slid in the mud, but he moved up and then as the other cadets in my patrol seized his arms and pulled, he moved up the bank. I heard one of the shoulder seams of his uniform give and the pop of a button. Then my other troops had him. I stopped my shoving and scrabbled up beside him. We both reached the top of the opposite bank just as Maw held up his watch and called out, 'Time! Stand where you are, Cadets.'

And we did, panting and bedraggled. 'We're the only ones,' Nate whispered. I moved only my eyes to confirm that what he said was so. We were the only patrol to have reached the opposite bank. The remains of our bridge hung in woeful tatters, but I had got my patrol across. I waited to hear what Maw would say to us. I needed to hear that we had done well.

'Cadets. Gather up your gear and tools, and return them to the supply room. Put the lumber near the kindling supply for the Sciences building. After that, you are dismissed for the day. I hope you enjoy your Dark Evening holiday.'

We looked at one another, trying to decide what his words meant. The patrol of Skeltzin Hall first-years looked devastated. The two Old Noble patrols looked apprehensive. Had they failed? As he walked away, Maw called over his shoulder, 'Marks for this exercise will be posted on my door in three days. Cadet Burvelle, see me in my office. After you have cleaned yourself up, of course.'

And so my triumph was very brief. The other patrols had an easier time of gathering up their materials than we did. The bridge that had proven so frail for crossing was quite tenacious when we tried to take it down. I said little as I did most of the work of dismantling it. It was cold and dirty work, and a thankless task. I had to climb down into the ravine to get the stepping boards that had fallen. When I climbed back up, I found that only Gord was waiting for me, a coil of muddy rope slung over his shoulder. The others had already taken their share of the mess and carried it off. I pushed down a rueful smile; my 'command' had not even waited to be dismissed by me.

Gord and I spoke little as we walked back to Carneston House. As we drew closer to the steps, he said, 'I'm going home for the Dark Evening holiday. My uncle's family is going out to our hunting lodge near Lake Foror. It's frozen by now, and there will be skating.'

'I hope you have a good time,' I said without interest. I wondered if I should have accepted my uncle's invitation, then decided that a holiday with Epiny and my wrathful aunt might be more stressful than one spent alone. I now felt little inclination to go into town with the other cadets. I felt I'd failed them.

'I could take your uniform with me. We have servants, you know. They do quite a good job at cleaning things.'

He didn't look at me as he made this offer, and for a moment I didn't know what to reply. He took my silence for surliness, I think, for he then said, 'I want to apologize, Nevare. I broke the bridge with my damnable weight. But for me, we would have crossed in good order.'

My jaw dropped and I stared at him. It had never occurred to me to blame anyone but myself for what had happened. I said so. 'I thought the bridge would work for us. After most of the patrol was across, I realized I should have sent you first, when it was most intact. But at the time, it seemed more important to me to get the most men across first.'

'And in a battle or patrol situation, you would have been right. You've a good instinct for command, Nevare.'

'Thank you,' I said awkwardly. And then, even more awkwardly, I asked him, 'Is that why you suggested me for leader today?'

He met my eyes and his face was full of guilt. He blushed suddenly, his cheeks turning a hot red and then said, 'No. I'd no idea that you could pull it off. I . . . was following an order, Nevare. From Maw. I had no idea what was coming today, but last week, as we were leaving the classroom, he pulled me aside and said, "A time will come when I tell you to divide in groups and choose a leader. When that time comes, you are to suggest Cadet Nevare Burvelle. Do that, and I'll overlook the hash you made of today's assignment. Fail to do that, and take a failing mark for today." I, well, I didn't know what else to say except, "yes, sir". And today, when he told the patrols to select leaders, he looked right at me. So I suggested you.'

'I don't get it,' I said quietly. What Gord had told me was terribly upsetting but I couldn't quite understand why. 'I don't know why he wanted you to do that. Did he think I'd be a failure, as I was, and that he could cull us all? Don't look so horrified, Gord. You had to do it. He gave you an order. But, I wish . . .' I halted my own words, not sure what I wished. I was suddenly certain that neither Trist nor Spink would have seen the answer to Maw's riddle. If, indeed, it had been a riddle. I shook my head. 'I was so certain that I'd deduced what today's test was all about. That the objective was to get the patrol across the ditch, not to build a bridge.'

'I think you were right. As soon as you said it. I was sure you were right. It made so much sense to me; if we had come across an obstacle like that on a real patrol, would we stop and build a bridge or just find a way across it?'

'We'd just cross,' I said absently. I suddenly knew what was upsetting me. I'd wanted at least one of my friends to see me as a true leader. Even Gord. I wondered suddenly if Trist had also received an order from Maw. Was that why he had given way to me so easily? I felt as if my guts had fallen to the bottom of my belly. Heavy-hearted. Was that what those words had always meant? None of my friends had ever looked at me and seen the potential for command. Because they all knew it just wasn't there.

We walked the rest of the way in silence. I changed into my spare uniform, and decided to accept Gord's offer of taking my other one home to have it cleaned. My bleakness was at odds with the rest of my fellows. Despite the culling still hanging over us, they seemed to have set aside their uncertainties. They were dressing for an evening out in Old Thares and excitedly discussing their plans for Dark Evening. There was to be a night market in the Grand Square, with all sorts of things for sale, at the very best prices. On the adjacent green, a circus with a sideshow had set up its tents and booths. There were acrobats and tumblers, jugglers, and wild animal tamers, and all manner of freaks in the sideshow. Everyone was putting on his best clothing and counting up his spending money. I felt like a stranger among them as I left Carneston House and started back toward Maw's office. No one seemed to notice me leaving or wonder why I'd been summoned.

The sun had gone down behind the distant hills, its meagre warmth fleeing with the night's arrival. The campus was a landscape of grey snow and black trees. The irregularly spaced pole lanterns made pools of feeble light; I felt I travelled from island to island, and suddenly it reminded me of my journey from column top to column top in the dream where I had first met the tree woman. Such a thought on Dark Evening was enough to send a chill up anyone's spine, and I shivered.

Maw was in his office adjacent to the classroom, waiting for me. The door stood ajar. I tapped and waited until he told me to come in. I entered, saluted, and remained standing and silent until he waved me into a seat. The office was as chill as the rest of the building, but Maw appeared comfortable. He set aside some papers stacked on his desk and looked up with both a sigh and a smile. 'Well. Cadet Burvelle, you look a bit cleaner than when I last saw you.'

I couldn't find a smile to match his. I felt a sense of foreboding. 'Yes, sir,' was all I said. He glanced at me, and then looked back at the papers on his desk. He tapped them a bit more into alignment and then said, 'Do you remember our little talk earlier this year?'

'Yes, sir.'

'Has the idea gained any appeal for you?'

'I can't say that it has, sir.'

He wet his lips and sighed yet again. Suddenly he leaned back in his chair and met my gaze squarely. I felt as if he had dropped a curtain between us as he said, 'A man faces many difficult tasks in his life, Burvelle. And when he is given charge of promising young men, and he knows the decisions and choices he makes can affect their futures, their entire lives, well, those are the hardest choices of all. I'm sure you know from rumour that a culling is on the horizon. The

516

cadets always know these things. I don't know why we pretend they are secret or a surprise.'

I made no response, and after a moment he went on. 'The military has changed, Burvelle. It had to. Your own father was instrumental in the first part of the change, when he supported the founding of this Academy. An Academy such as this, as a foundation for becoming an officer, says that education may be more important than bloodlines. That was a very unpopular idea, you must know. We were badly beaten in our war with Landsing. Badly. We had clung to our traditions too firmly; we deployed our men, ships, and cavalla as if we were still fighting with swords and spears and catapults. Soldier sons were born soldiers, we said; we thought the idea that they must be *taught* to fight a foolish one. And of course the soldier sons of nobles were born officers, with no need of instruction in that task. In those days, all commissions were bought or inherited. The education we gave our officers was intended more to form an attitude than to instruct in strategy. Six months of polishing and off we sent our young lieutenants. The War College! Was ever an institution so poorly named? It should have been called the Gentleman's Club. Knowing how to critique a wine or play a good hand of cards were considered more important than knowing how to deploy a regiment across different types of terrain. So we educate you now, and we send you forth. And we see the sons of New Nobles promoted over their better-bred cousins. We see common soldiers rising up through the ranks, and assuming command over nobly born soldier sons. General Brodg, named commander in the east, is the son of a common soldier. It goes against the grain, Burvelle. It rasps the sensibilities.'

I was shocked at what he was saying to me. Nevertheless, I nodded once, wondering where this was leading.

'So, we have changed,' he said, and sat back in his chair with a sigh. 'And it has brought us success, at least against the plainsmen. It remains to be seen how well we would do

517

against the Landsingers, if we were ever allowed to try. Some think we should. Some think the King wastes his time in looking east at the barren lands, and building a road that leads only to impassable mountains. Some think we should turn around and bring our forces against the Landsingers, and take back our coastal regions and our seaports.'

I was silent. He prodded me. 'What do you think, Cadet Burvelle?'

'I don't think it is my place to disagree with my king, sir. The road will go to the mountains, and eventually through them to the sea beyond.'

He nodded slowly, his mouth pursed in a sour smile. 'Spoken like a true New Noble's son, Cadet. That road, that possible port, that theoretical trade, all taken together, could well enrich your family beyond your father's wildest dreams. But what of the Old Nobles, who lost important holdings when King Troven's father surrendered and ceded their coastal holdings to the Landsingers? What of the Old Nobles who live in genteel poverty now, deprived of the taxes that used to fund their families? Do you ever think of them?'

I hadn't. I suppose that showed in my face, for Maw nodded to himself. Then he spoke very carefully. 'We here at the Academy see that a balance must be kept. The King is the King, of course. The military answers to him. But it is commanded by the sons of his New and Old Nobles. There are only a certain number of vacancies to be filled every year. Too many Old Nobles' sons, and the army will sway one way. Too many New Nobles' sons, and it may sway another. We here at the Academy do not attempt to influence politics by our actions. Rather, we strive to keep the military in a neutral balance. I promise you this is true.'

I spoke slowly, knowing my words were not respectful, knowing I could be expelled from the Academy for them. I knew, also that it didn't matter. 'And that is why you will cull one patrol of New Nobles' sons. To be sure that this year's class will not outnumber the Old Nobles' sons.'

He nodded slowly. 'You have a mind for putting things together, Nevare. Just as you did today. That was why I made my suggestion to you earlier this year.'

'And you will cull my patrol rather than the New Nobles from Skeltzin Hall.'

He nodded once, slowly.

'Why? Why us and not them?'

He leaned back in his chair, one fist resting on his chin and took a breath through his nose. Finally, he spoke. 'Because that was what we decided at the beginning of the year. When Colonel Stiet took over the Academy, he put the decision in the hands of the advisory board. Quietly, of course. It's always done quietly. Look at your patrol, and you can see the criteria. Some are the sons of New Nobles who have no power at all. Others are the sons of New Nobles who seem to be gaining too much power. You, I'm afraid, were a special request. A favour between old friends.'

'My aunt, Lady Burvelle requested it of Colonel Stiet. Didn't she?'

He raised his eyebrows. 'You *do* put things together, don't you, Burvelle? I saw that in you. That's why I tried to divert you from the Academy, early in the year.'

My ears were buzzing in shock at all of it. 'It isn't fair, sir. Because I *did* put things together. And I *did* get my patrol across the creek. And if an Old Nobles' sons' patrol had crossed as we did, you would have announced that they had deduced the correct answer, that the objective was to cross the creek, not build a bridge.'

'That's true,' he said, and there was no apology in his voice. 'I wish I could have congratulated you in front of your fellows. But I could not. So I called you here, privately, to let you know. You were right. And you did well. The manner in which you achieved it showed that you will never be a typical line officer, however. That is why I still believe that as a

519

scout, you would excel. And that is why, regardless of what marks are posted a few days hence, I will still recommend you for that position.'

'But I won't continue here at the Academy, will I? Nor will Spink or Trist or Gord or Kort or any of the others. Will they? You will recommend me, and I suppose I should thank you for that. My father's shame and disappointment will not be complete. I'll nominally have an officer's rank. But what of those others? What of them?'

He looked past me now when he spoke and his voice was stiff. 'I've done what I can, boy. Some will come up the old way. Their families will simply purchase commissions for them rather than seeing them earn them here. Trist, I am sure, will become an officer. Gord's family certainly has the wealth to place him well.'

'Spink's family doesn't. What becomes of him?'

Captain Maw cleared his throat. 'I suspect he will be a Ranker. He'll enlist as a common soldier, for he will remain a soldier son. And on the basis of his talents, he will rise. Or not. The military has always provided those alternate paths for men of talent and determination. Not all officers are born of nobility. Some come up through the ranks.'

'At the cost of years of their lives. Sir.'

'That's true. That has always been true.'

I sat there, no longer liking a man whom I had admired for most of the term. A private congratulation on working out his puzzle, and a recommendation to a scout's life was all he was offering me. I'd be a leader without troops, an officer who rode alone. I thought of Scout Vaxton and his rough manners and worn uniform. I thought of how my father had invited him to our table, but kept my mother and sisters away from his company. That was my fate. It was already determined that that was the best I could do. I could not force them to keep me at the Academy. I had done my best, and passed every test they had given me. Yet I would still be discarded, because the tight ranks of the old nobility feared that the King was becoming too strong.

I dared a question. 'And if I go out now and tell what I know?'

He looked at me sadly. 'Now you sound like Tiber.' He shook his head. 'You wouldn't be believed, Burvelle. It would sound pitiful, as if you tried to make excuse for your own failure. Go quietly, son. There are worse things than being culled. You're leaving with an honourable discharge. You don't have to go home with your tail between your legs. You could leave here with a posting to one of the citadels in the east.' He suddenly leaned toward me and tried for a smile. 'Think on it for a night. Come back to me tomorrow morning, and tell me that you've decided you *do* want to be a scout. I'll see that your transfer papers are written up that way. There will be no mention of a culling on them.'

He waited for me to reply. I could have thanked him. I could have said I needed time to think. Instead, I said nothing at all.

Captain Maw spoke very softly. 'You are dismissed, Cadet Burvelle.'

I heard it as my sentence. I rose without acknowledging his words and walked out of his office, out of the Engineering Building and into the cold of Dark Evening. Tonight, in Old Thares, people caroused and celebrated the longest night of the year. Tomorrow, they would breakfast together and exchange good wishes for the first lengthening day of the year. Before the week was out, Sirlofty and I would be on our way back to my family home. All the years my father had prepared me had been for nothing. The golden future he had promised me was dross. I thought of Carsina and tears pricked my eyes. She would not be mine. Her father would never give her to a cavalla scout. I suddenly knew I would die childless, that the soldier son journals I sent home to my brother's house would be a story that dribbled away with no ending at all.

TWENTY ONE

Carnival

Carneston House was deserted. An unhappy cadet corporal sat in Sergeant Rufet's chair behind his desk. Surely that was a punishment duty. I surmised he had been given the night shift so that even our dour sergeant could partake of the pleasures of Dark Evening. He gave me a dispirited stare as I trudged past him. I could not find the energy to hurry up the steps. All around me, the dormitory was unnaturally quiet.

Upstairs, my bunkroom showed all the signs of a hasty departure. No one had waited for me. They'd all racketed off together for a wild night of town freedom without even a thought for Nevare Burvelle. I suspected that all the hire carriages would be gone from the cabstand. Even if I'd wanted to go, it was too late now. But I was hungry. I decided I'd leave the Academy grounds and walk to a nearby public house for a beer and sup. Then I'd simply come back to the dormitory and go to sleep. If I could.

I took my greatcoat from its hook, and as I thrust my arms down the sleeves, a folded bit of notepaper fell out. I picked it up from the floor. My name was on the outside of it, in Spink's handwriting, blotted as if he'd done it hurriedly. I unfolded it and stared at the horrible words that sealed my fate. 'I've gone to meet Epiny. It was none of my doing, Nevare. She sent me a note by messenger, saying she would

find me on the green by the Great Square so we could celebrate Dark Evening together. I know I'm a fool to go to her;
it will seal your aunt's opinion of me. But I dare not leave
her alone there amongst the types of men that will be roving
the streets tonight.' The note was signed with a sloping 'S'.

I crumpled up the paper and thrust it into my pocket.
Now I had to go to Dark Evening, even if I had to walk all
the way into the city's centre, for Epiny's reputation would
be completely ruined if she were to spend Dark Evening
alone with Spink. I wasn't sure that my presence could make
it any better, but resolved that I would do what I could.
Spink would be culled in the coming week, just as surely as
I would. For Epiny to be out with him, and for him then to
be dismissed from the Academy would ruin both their
names. I took my hoarded allowance out of its hiding place
behind my books and left. I wrapped my muffler round my
throat as I ran down the steps.

The path from the Academy gates to the cabstand had
never seemed so long. When I reached it, there were no carriages, but an enterprising boy with a pony cart was waiting
there. The pony was spotted and the cart smelled of potatoes. Given a choice, I never would have ridden in it. I handed
over to the boy the ridiculous fare that he demanded and
mounted the splintery seat beside him. We set out through
the chill streets. The cold wind burned past my ears as the
pony trotted along. I pulled my hat down and turned my
collar up.

The closer we got to the centre of the city, the more evident the holiday became. Streets that would ordinarily be
deserted in the cold and dark were thronged with people.
Holiday lanterns with cutouts of capering nightshades, the
lustful and mischievous sprites said to serve the old gods,
hung in the windows or beside the doors of almost every
establishment. The intersections were jammed with pedestrians and the traffic thickened as every conveyance in Thares

seemed bound for the same destination. Long before we reached the Great Square, I could hear the noise of the crowd and see the haze of light that it put into the night sky. I smelled food cooking, and heard the wheezing notes of a calliope competing with a shrill soprano singing about her lost love. When our pony cart wedged for the third time into standing traffic, I shouted over the din to the driver that I was getting out and left them there.

I moved a little faster on foot but not much. The crowd eddied and swirled around me, and I was often carried sideways with the flow of people. Many of the merrymakers were masked and wigged. Gold chains made of paper and glass jewels sparkled on wrists and throats. Others had painted their faces so extravagantly that the lights glistened off the thick layers of greasepaint. I saw all manner of dress, and a great deal of undress, too. Muscular young men, usually masked as nightshades, went bare-chested through the crowds, making suggestive remarks to women and men alike, much to the merriment of all within earshot. There were women, too, bare-armed even in the cold, their breasts bulging out the tops of their gowns like mushrooms erupting from moss. They wore masks with voluptuous red lips and lolling tongues and arched brows over gilded almond-shaped eyeholes. The crowd nudged and shoved me along until I felt like I swam through the morass of merrymakers.

A vendor bumped into me, rather deliberately. When I turned to confront her, she grinned wildly up at me with a garishly painted mouth and urged, 'Sample my fruit, young sir? It's free! Take a taste.' A domino mask of silver paper and her red painted lips were her only disguise. She held her tray with both hands at chest height. Dark grapes, red cherries, and strawberries surrounded two immense peaches. She leaned toward me, thrusting the tray at me, jolting it against my chest.

I stumbled back from her, confused by her wide smile and

aggressiveness and foolishly said, 'No, thank you, madam. The peaches are large but they are surely well past their season.' Everyone around me roared as if I had made a fine jest while she pursed her lips and then stuck out her tongue at me.

A masked man in a gilt crown and a cheap cloak of thin velvet, his nose red with drink, pushed past me to the vendor. 'I'll taste your fruit, my dear!' he bellowed, and to my shock, he lowered his face into the tray and made loud slurping and gobbling noises while the woman squirmed and laughed delightedly. A moment later, my eyes made sense of the gas-lit scene. The bodice and sleeves of her dress were painted onto her skin, with a collar and cuffs of lace to complete the subterfuge. The 'peaches' on her 'tray' were actually her powdered and painted breasts surrounded by wax fruit on a ledge of stiffened fabric. She was as good as naked. I smothered an exclamation of astonishment, yet could not help laughing along with the gawking crowd. The woman wiggled and shrieked, offering him first one breast and then the other. He gently pinched the nipple of one in his teeth and shook it playfully as she squealed delightedly. Never had I seen such a display of wanton licentiousness, nor witnessed folk gleefully encourage it. Suddenly I thought of Epiny in such a place and the smile faded from my face. A moment before, I had nearly forgotten Epiny in the pageantry of the Dark Evening holiday. Now I turned and pushed my way out of the knot of spectators. I knew I must find Epiny, and quickly.

But where?

The streets were thick as porridge with people. I could not lift an elbow without touching someone. The crowd was in motion, and we all edged forward in a mincing lockstep. I was taller than most, but the extravagant hats and tall wigs worn by many of the festival-goers were a bobbing, swaying forest around me. I could see no open space and so I allowed myself to be carried along, flotsam on a tide of debauchery.

The Great Square was at the heart of Old Thares. All around it, the merchant houses and businesses were the tallest and finest in the city. Lights glowed in many a white-framed window, and music and laughter exploded out of the doors each time they were opened. Despite the cold night, people stood on balconies, glasses of wine in their hands as they stared down at the sea of frivolity below them. The entire city was in the mood for a wild celebration to cheer on the passing of the longest night of the year. The wealthy had gathered in their fine houses for balls and masquerades and sumptuous dinners while outside in the streets the rest of the populace celebrated as only the poor and the working-class know how.

The closer we came to the main square, the louder grew the noise. Thousands of voices competed with all sorts of music, noisemakers, and the shouting of hawkers. I smelled food and was suddenly hungry to the point of nausea. When the river of people around me reached the square, the pressure slackened somewhat. I managed to join a crowd clustered around a stall selling skewers of hot meat, roasted chestnuts in newsprint cups, and hot potatoes baked in their jackets. I bought some of each for three times what I should have paid, and ate standing in the midst of the pushing, shouting crowd. Despite all that had befallen me that day, they were delicious, and if I had had the time, I would have wasted more coin on a second helping of each.

There are seven fountains in the Great Square. I made my way toward the closest one and clambered up on the rim. From that vantage, I got my first full view of Dark Evening in Old Thares. It frightened me and filled me with the contagious excitement of the mob at the same time. The throng filled the immense square and pushed out into the surrounding streets that radiated from it. The heat of the massed bodies banished winter's chill while badly spaced street lamps shed yellow circles of light onto the crowd. In one section of the square, music was playing and people were dancing wildly. In another, some sort of gymnastics contest was going on. People were stacking themselves up into pyramids, higher and higher. Surely when those on the bottom gave way, there would be injuries for those at the top. Even as I watched, it happened, to wild cries of dismay and shouts of triumphs from their rivals. A few moments later, another pyramid was rising.

Beyond the square was the green that sloped gently down to the river, dotted with bright tents that billowed in the winter wind. Spink's note had said that Epiny would find him there. I doubted it. I had never seen or even imagined so many people packed so closely and still filling such a large space. Nevertheless, I jumped down from the fountain's edge and began a deliberate trek toward the green. The crowd did not give way to me. I edged between people and sometimes went around tightly packed knots of folk gathered to watch a performer. I did not move quickly; I could not. All the while, I kept my eyes open, hoping to spot either Spink or Epiny. The lighting was erratic, the masked and hooded people always in motion, and the din of voices and instruments pressed on my ears and wearied me.

The green had become the brown, the tended lawns already trampled to thick mud in this one night. The lamplight did not reach this far and the circus folk had lit their own lanterns. The lights gave colour to the parts of the tents that it touched. Torches illuminated garish posters and wildly attired barkers who perched on their stands and shouted their cant to lure the folk into the tents. The roars of caged beasts emanated from one flapping tent door, its sign promising me that within I would find *Every Large Predator That The World Has Ever Seen!* The next tent had a barker who shouted in a hoarse whisper that no man was truly a man until he had seen Syinese dancers perform the

Dance of the Blowing Leaves, and that the next performance would start in five, only five, a mere five minutes from now, and that I should hurry before all the front seats were gone. I walked past, feeling sure that Spink and Epiny would not be in there.

I halted, staring hopelessly around me and praying for a clue. In that instant, I saw a hat go by. I could not see the face of the woman who wore it, for she was masked, but I recognized the foolish hat I had seen Epiny wearing the day she came to the Academy with my uncle. 'Epiny!' I shouted, but if she heard me over the din, she did not pause. I tried to push my way through the crowd, only to have an angry drunk threaten me for jostling him. By the time I got around him, the hat had vanished into the mouth of a dark blue tent decorated with painted snakes, stars, and snail shells. When I got close enough to read the poster beside the entry, it proclaimed that this tent held *Freaks, Grotesques and Wonders of Humanity!* Well, that would certainly attract Epiny, I thought. I joined the line of people waiting to go in. A few moments later, I was surprised when Trist, Rory, Oron, and Trent joined me. They hailed me heartily, slapping my back and asking how I was enjoying Dark Evening so far. I think their loud greetings were to make it clear to the people who were already waiting behind me that they were my fellows and intended to join the line where I was. In truth, I was very glad to see them. I immediately asked if they had seen Spink.

'He came with us!' Rory shouted over the general hubbub around us. 'But he shied off on his own dam' near soon as we got here. H'aint seen him since.' Drink had brought out Rory's accent.

'Caleb went looking for free whores,' Trist enlightened me, as if I'd requested the information. 'Nate and Kort went looking for ones that took money.'

I looked at their faces, flushed with drink and carnival,

and thought of what I could tell them. The words rose like bile in the back of my throat. I swallowed them down. Soon enough they would know we had all been culled. I felt old as I decided that I would let them have this last holiday, merrily ignorant of their fate.

The line shuffled us along as Rory told me that, truly, I did need to see the Syinese Dancers perform. 'I'd no idea a woman could bend like that!' he enthused, to which Oron sourly observed, 'No proper woman can, fool!'

In the midst of the argument that followed, Trist poked Rory in the ribs and said, 'Look at that! I doubt he was given leave to be here. I'll bet Colonel Stiet thinks little Caulder is home and tucked up in his trundle bed right now!'

I had but a glimpse before the crowd closed off the sight. There was Caulder, his hat on crooked and his cheeks very red. There were several Academy cadets with him, Old Nobles' sons, and most of them second-year cadets. Two I recognized immediately. Jaris and Odon had linked arms and were whooping and shouting back at the barker who was trying to persuade them to come inside his tent and see the Juggling Hidaspi Brothers from Far Entia. The other cadets were passing a bottle amongst themselves. I saw it reach Caulder's hands. He took it and at their urging, tipped his head back for a drink. I saw his face as he lowered the bottle. He did not relish it, but he swallowed it anyway. He grinned weakly afterward, and I wondered if he clenched his teeth against his belly's load.

'They're giving that boy strong drink!'

Rory guffawed. 'If he thinks chawin' bacco made him sick, wait till that hits his belly. He'll be shitting through his lips until the morning light!'

Trist and Trent laughed uproariously at the crudeness of Rory's comment. Oron pursed his lips primly and looked disapproving.

'Someone should stop them,' I said, but the line suddenly began to move more quickly and I was carried along with it. The man at the tent door snatched the admission price from my fingers and reached for the next man's coin. I told myself that Caulder would be all right, and that if he got sick as a dog, he well deserved it. A moment later, I entered the world of the circus sideshow.

The circus folk knew their business. The tent floor was coated thick with straw to keep the walkways from turning to mud. Lanterns hung from supports and the walkways circled through the tent's interior, leading from one display to the next. Low canvas walls or cage mesh forced us to keep our distance from the attractions. Ostensibly, we could wander where we willed, but the push of folk behind us propelled us to the left. In a few moments, I am shamed to say I had nearly forgotten that I was trying to find Epiny in the midst of the chaos.

The first sight that met our eyes was a slender girl dressed in a short vest secured only by a chain across her breasts. The pleated skirt she wore came barely to her knees. Even so, her body was well covered, for it was draped in coil after coil of a monstrous snake that was lapped around her and the throne that she sat on. She held the snake's wedge-shaped head between her hands and stroked it as she spoke softly to it. The snake's tongue fluttered forth and the girl extended her own pink tongue to meet it, earning a collective gasp from the audience. Rory especially would have stayed there, entranced, but the push of the crowd moved us on.

We saw the goat-faced man, with his protuberant yellow eyes, long teeth, and goat's beard. He was tethered to an upended crate and he bleated at us as we passed, but I judged him a fraud. Next was the horrific sight of a man sitting bare-chested on a box, with the body of his half-formed twin hanging from his ribs. I stared at that and could not look away until Rory took me by the upper arm and hurried me on.

The poster had promised true. We saw freaks, grotesques and wonders. A strongman bent an iron bar, passed it round the crowd for us to inspect and then straightened it before our very eyes. The skeleton man stood, bent, and turned round that we might see every vertebra in his back push out against his skin. Three midgets dressed in red, yellow and blue scampered around a ring, turning somersaults and cart-wheels. They then advanced to shake hands round the crowd and win their tips of coins. A cone-head sat rocking on a tall stool, his tongue extended as he amused himself by shaking a large rattle at the crowd. A pretty little girl with long golden curls and flippers instead of arms stood on a chair and sang a song about the heartless mother who had abandoned her. 'The poor little thing!' Rory exclaimed with heartfelt pity. Coins rang as we tossed them into the big china bowl at her feet.

We saw the reptile man with his scaled body, and the tat-tooed lady whose skin was covered in images of flowers. A pincushion man drove long needles through his cheeks, and then stuck a nail far up his nose. I had to look away from that. Twin boys ate fire. In a murky tank, a mermaid sur-faced briefly, waved her webbed hands, flipped her tail at us and then vanished again beneath the greenish water. An albino girl blinked red eyes within her hooded cape. A man swallowed a sword and drew it out again.

On and on we trudged, past wonder after wonder. Three tall warriors from distant Marrea danced in a circle as they flung knives at one another, plucking them out of the air before the blades could reach their targets. In the next cage, a bear-boy snuffled and snorted through his feed. Hair was thick on his arms and down his back, and his little black eyes were devoid of human intelligence.

In the next enclosure, three Specks from the distant

mountains huddled together under a blanket inside a large wooden crate turned on its side. At first, I could see only their mottled faces and oddly striped hands as they peered out at us from the crate's shelter. They all had long, unevenly coloured hair that hung untended around their shoulders. They looked cold and uncomfortable, and showed no signs of enjoying displaying themselves as the mermaid and skeleton man had. It was only when Rory took a plug of chewing tobacco from his pocket that they stirred to life. Then they threw aside their blanket and raced to the edge of their cage, thrusting their hands out through the bars beseechingly. There were two men, one of them old, and a woman. The men wore rags about their loins, the woman nothing at all. The old man moaned piteously, but the woman spoke clearly. 'Tobacco, tobacco. Give some to me. Please, please, please. Tobacco, tobacco!'

She smiled sweetly as she spoke, her voice reminding me of a clamouring child. It was an unsettling contrast to the way she shamelessly pressed her body against the bars of the enclosure to enable her to reach toward us. We stared, transfixed. Her breasts were full and round, her haunches sleek. The markings on her skin wrapped her flesh and were echoed in her multicoloured hair. From where I stood, I could see the dark stripe that ran up her spine, and the mottled stripes that radiated from it. She was not piebald like a horse, not spotted like a jungle cat. The stripes varied in colour from pale yellow to almost black, yet were obviously the pigments of her own skin, not an applied cosmetic. Black lined her eyes as if she had applied kohl, but when she licked her lips eagerly, I saw that her tongue was also banded with colour. An extraordinary thrill ran through me; she was woman and wild animal, all in one, and the abrupt desire I felt shamed me. Her childish begging seemed innocent and natural in contrast to her tempting body. Rory held the tobacco out of her reach; with his free hand, he reached through the bars to stroke her haunch. She made no objection, but only giggled and tried to reach the tobacco in his other hand. He laughed drunkenly, as focused on her as if they were alone. I watched fascinated by desire as he slipped his hand over her knee and began to slide it up her inner thigh. She grew very still; her lips parted and she breathed through her mouth.

The keeper, who had been sitting bored on an upended keg beside the cage, stood suddenly. He was a scraggly fellow in a soiled striped shirt and rough canvas trousers. He hurried over to us, pushing his way through the crowd. He elbowed Rory back and jabbed at the Speck woman with a prod, ordering her angrily, 'Back, back!' Then he turned on us and commanded us, 'Step back from the bars. Don't give them baccy, fella! It's how we train them. Don't you reward them for actin' up. Get back, Princess. Gimpy, get back!'

The young female had completely captured my attention. For the first time, I noticed that the younger male had a shattered foot. Gimpy drew back warily from the keeper's prod. He had not spoken a word. But when the keeper jabbed Princess, she turned on him, hissing. Then, in unaccented passion, she unleashed a stream of the foulest invective I'd ever heard. She finished it with, 'A worm crawled up your mother's hole and laid an egg in her womb, and that was you! Your trees have no roots and your dead do not speak to you! You lick yourself and think your vermin a fine meal! You—'

Before she could mouth another insult, the uncrippled male slapped her. 'Quiet, quiet, quiet! Be good. Show the gennlemun your breasts.' Then, as she staggered back from the blow, he turned to the keeper. 'I'm good. I'm good. Baccy, baccy? Some for good Beggar?'

'A bit,' the keeper conceded. From his pocket, he took a black plug of crude leaf. I could smell the molasses mixed with it. He broke off a tiny crumble and put it into Beggar's hand. Before he could carry it to his mouth, Princess attacked him. They tumbled to the straw on the floor of the cage, wrestling over the prize. The crippled Speck looked on, rocking from his good foot to his unsound one, but not intervening. The surrounding crowd gave up a mixture of cries of alarm and applause. The keeper gauged it as general approval and let them fight. The male seemed intent mostly on getting his hand up to his mouth and wriggled away from the female's blows and scratches. The sight of the two, near naked and struggling supine, was both disturbing and arousing.

'Let's leave,' I said to my fellows. They did not even turn to hear me. But in the crate in the back of the cage, something stirred. A moment later, an old man tottered out. I had not noticed him before. He had wrapped the blanket around his shoulders. Beneath it, he wore a robe of rough cotton. He had long greying hair, the stripes fading in it, and his face was lined as deeply as a crumpled leaf. I thought the elder would rebuke the fighting couple. Instead he came to the bars of the cage and looked round at us with rheumy eyes. He coughed, and then spat dark spittle into the straw. He said something in his native tongue. It was a strange language, flowing, with few consonants that I could detect. The crippled Speck came to stand beside him. He replied in the same tongue and pointed in our direction. The old Speck leaned close to the bars, sniffing loudly. His gaze suddenly met mine. He smiled with brown teeth, and nodded as if we were acquaintances meeting on the street. He held his hand toward me, palm up and open, as if inviting or requesting something.

'Whatturu doin?' Rory demanded of me suddenly. ''zat a charm?'

I looked down in horror. Of its own volition, my hand was moving, my fingers weaving the air. Dream words echoed in my mind. 'Tomorrow you face a test. You will

534

pass it and make the sign and you will then fight for The People.' I seized my right hand in my left and massaged the fingers. 'Just a cramp,' I told Rory.

'Oh,' he agreed.

Inside the cage, the aged Speck nodded at me. Then he took a step back. He slapped one hand on his chest, cupping the hand to make a larger sound than I would have expected. At the noise, the struggle on the cage floor instantly ceased. Both combatants came to their feet. The male hastily clapped his hand to his mouth as he did so, and I saw his tongue work, tucking his nubbin of tobacco into his cheek.

The old Speck said something to them. The girl replied negatively, almost angrily. The old man repeated himself. He did not raise his voice or sound more insistent, but suddenly all three of the other Specks cowered from him. The girl stood up straight then and announced loudly, 'I speak, I speak. Quiet. Listen.'

'Hey, then, what are you up to?' the keeper demanded angrily. He shook his prod at them, but all of the Specks had stepped back, out of his reach. The girl, her face reddened and one arm bleeding from a long scratch, still manifested a sudden, savage dignity. It clothed her nakedness better than any garment. She tossed back her streaky mane and spoke clearly.

'Tonight, we dance. Right now. The People dance the Dust Dance. For you all. Come close, come close. See us dance. Only one time! Watch it now.' She beckoned us, waving her arms to urge us closer.

Beside the cage, the keeper's jaw dropped open. 'What's this, what's this?' he demanded angrily, but the Specks were no longer paying him any attention. He seized the chain that secured the door to their enclosure and rattled it threateningly, as if he were coming in. Beggar looked over his shoulder at the keeper, and then ignored him as the three males trooped back toward their shelter. The girl positioned herself in the middle of their cage, well out of reach of the keeper's prod. Now she lifted her voice and her arms. Her clear tones rang out. 'Dust Dance! Dust Dance! Gather all for the Dust Dance! You never to see this before! You never to see this again! Come one. Come all. Dust Dance of the People!'

Her tone was a fair imitation of the barkers' outside. My estimation of her innate intelligence rose. As a man, we all pressed closer to the cage, even as the keeper warned us sternly, 'Keep back! Keep back! Do not touch the bars!' When we all ignored him he raised his own voice and began shouting, 'The Dust Dance of the savage Specks of the far east! Gather one, gather all. Only five tallies more to witness the Dust Dance. A mere five tallies to watch what you'll never see again!'

But his efforts to profit went mostly ignored. A few fools dug into their pockets and counted money out to him, which he promptly stuffed into his own greasy purse. Inside the cage, the woman continued to cry her appeal for spectators while the males huddled inside their shelter. In a remarkably short time, they emerged 'dressed' for the dance. Feathers, dead leaves, bits of fur, tassels of shells and a pouch were suspended from strings tied round their waists. Their matted hair had been hastily plaited into queues down their backs. Long earrings of cheap beads dangled almost to their shoulders. I sensed items hoarded for a long time, perhaps in great hardship.

Their keeper had turned barker. 'Never before seen in a city! Never before performed under a tent! The Dust Dance of the savage Specks. Ladies and lords, come now, come now, to see the—'

His voice was suddenly drowned out by an ululation from the Speck woman. Before her cry died out, the Speck men took it up, modulating it to a deep-voiced chanting. They spaced their voices, like children singing a round, producing a strange, echoing sound. Slowly, feet shuffling, they

536

began to circle the woman. She stood, her arms uplifted like a tree's branches, and swayed in place as she sang in a pure, sweet soprano. It did not matter that we did not speak the language. I could hear the wind blowing and rain dripping from leaves in her song. The men circled her slowly, once, then twice. The crowd drew closer to the cage, transfixed by the strange dance and odd song. Each of the men dipped a hand into his pouch and drew forth a handful of fine, dark dust. They began to shake their hands over their heads as they danced around the woman. The dust leaked from between their fingers to float free in the air around them. The woman's voice suddenly rose in a long note that she held for an impossibly long time. Again the men circled her, dancing in close and then out in a larger circle. Again, they dipped their hands into their pouches and shook the dust free in the air as they danced. The woman swayed like a tree in the wind, and the crowd oohed in awe as a ghostly wind shushed through the tent in seeming harmony with the dance. It carried the floating dust over the crowd and several people sneezed, raising brief flurries of laughter from those around them.

The dance went on and on. Long after I had wearied of it, I was trapped there. The crowd behind us pressed us close to the cage bars. Rory especially seemed enraptured by the woman and her song. He gripped the bars with both hands and hung on, as if he were the one imprisoned by her wildness. I saw the keeper look at him twice, and feared the man would come to bang his knuckles but the press of the mob trapped the man as effectively as it did us.

The woman's song and the men's chanting built to a crescendo. Their shuffling dance became a swift walk, then a jog, and suddenly they were running round the edges of the cage, even the old man, even the limping Speck, and they flung their dust in handfuls that drifted out over the crowd. People suddenly cried out as the dust stung their eyes.

Coughing and sneezing, I turned my head away from the dance and tried to push my way back into the gathered folk, to no avail. The dust I had inhaled burned in the back of my throat and left a fetid taste in my mouth. The keeper was shrieking at the Specks to stop, stop! And suddenly they did.

Without a glance at their keeper, all of them gathered silently in the middle of their enclosure. The men upended their little dust bags and shook them, but nothing fell out. The woman stood in their midst and briefly set a hand on top of each of their heads, almost like a benediction. Then they turned, and with no acknowledgment to the crowd at all, nor to the rain of coins that were showering onto the straw, they retreated to their crude shelter and huddled there, showing us only their striped backs. Their heads bent together as they conferred about something.

Almost immediately the crowd began to break up, but it was some moments before we could move away from our spot. 'I never saw anything like that before,' Trist said. He knuckled at his eyes, reddened where the dust had hit them. I turned a little aside from my fellows and spat several times, trying to clear the foul taste from my mouth. I wiped my mouth with my handkerchief, and almost immediately had a violent sneezing fit. Around me, other people were coughing.

Rory clung to the bars still, 'She is, well, she is somethin',' Rory agreed. His mouth hung slightly ajar as he stared at the woman huddling in the shadows of the crate.

'You want her?'

We all turned, startled by the keeper's lascivious offer. Somehow he had crept close to us. Now he spoke to Rory in an undertone. 'I seen her looking at you, fella. Fancies you, she does. Now, I don't usually do this, but—' And here he looked from side to side as if fearful of being overheard. 'I could 'range for you to see her. Alone. Or maybe with a friend or two, long as there's no rough stuff. She's a beauty, and I got to keep her that way.'

538

'What?' Rory asked blankly.

'You know what you want, fella. Here's how it works. You give me the money now, so we know you're the one. Then you come back, around midnight when the crowds are less. I'll take you to her. All she'll want from you is your baccy. Specks do love baccy, something fierce. She'll probably do anything you want. Anything. And yer friends can watch, you want 'em to.'

'That's disgusting,' Oron said. 'She's a savage.'

The keeper shrugged and brushed at his striped shirt. 'Maybe so, fella. But some men, they like a woman a bit on the wild side. Give you a ride you won't never forget. Not an ounce of shame in that one, there isn't.'

'Don't do it,' I said quietly to Rory. 'She's not what she seems.' I could not have explained my foreboding.

He jumped as if I had poked him, and looked startled to find me there. He had been so completely focused on the keeper's base offer. 'Well, course not, Nevare. What sorta fool do you take me for?'

The keeper laughed, low. 'Listen to him, you'll be the fool that missed the chance of a lifetime, young feller. Do it now, while yer young, and the memory will keep you warm even when yer old.'

'Let's get away from here,' Oron said. He didn't seem to care that he sounded prissy. I was just glad that he had said it, instead of me. We all began to turn away.

'Come back later, without your friends!' the keeper called out after us as we pushed our way through the crowd. 'You can tell 'em later what they missed.'

It was not Rory, but Trist who glanced back as we left. Would they go back? I strongly suspected they would. 'Let's see the rest of the freaks and get out of here,' I suggested.

'I need a beer,' Rory countered. 'I got dust down my throat what needs washing out. I'm leaving now.'

And so he left us, and I feared he had gone back to speak

to the keeper. I told myself there was nothing I could do about it. I abruptly recalled I was supposed to be looking for Epiny. As the current of the crowd washed us along, I watched for her chimney hat in vain. By the time we had seen the firewalker, the tall man, and the bug eater, my fellow cadets had somehow melted away from me in the crowd. Despite myself, my mind pictured Rory tangled with the calico woman, and I knew an odd mixture of both envy and disgust. I made myself walk on.

I moved to a less congested area. I spat again, feeling queasy from the foul taste of the Speck dust in my mouth. I tried to clear my throat of it, and ended up coughing instead.

When I caught my breath and looked around me, I found myself standing in a backwater in the freak tent. I'd seen the main spectacles. Here, at the outer edges of the tent were the secondary attractions, the ones that seemed trivial after the greater shocks of the main stages. A woman wriggled her deformed yellow feet at me while she cackled like a chicken. The insect man sat within a tiny tent of mosquito netting while roaches and beetles and spiders crawled about on him. Laughing, he set a caterpillar across his upper lip as if it were a moustache. It was too tame. The crowd shuffled past him, unamused.

The fat man stood up from his stool and wiggled his shoulders to set his naked gelid belly dancing. I stared at him. His bulk dwarfed Gord's. He had greased his pouched flesh to make it glisten in the lamplight. He had hanging breasts like a woman and his bare belly drooped over the waistband of his striped trousers like a fleshy apron. Even his ankles were fat, I noted, the flesh puddling over the tops of his feet. Beside him, an obese woman dressed in a short pleated skirt and a sleeveless bodice reclined languidly on a divan. She had a box of candies on a low table before her. As I watched, she ate the last one, and sent the box to join its empty fellows on the floor around the table. Her face and eyes were painted, and when she lifted her gaze and saw me staring at her, she pursed her lips at me in a kiss.

'Look, Eron. A soldier boy. Did you come to see sweet Candy?' She beckoned to me. The way her arms wobbled put me instantly in mind of the tree woman of my dream. I took an involuntary step backward, making her laugh. 'Don't be scared. Come a little closer, lovey. I won't bite you. Not unless you're as sweet as sugar.'

The fat man had resumed his seat on his stool. He turned his head to look at me and smiled. His face was wreathed in fat; even his brow seemed heavy. I was, for the moment, the sole gawker. He spoke to me. 'Soldier, eh? You a soldier lad? Oh, yes, I can tell. It's in the bearing. What branch are you? Artillery man?'

He spoke in such a friendly way that I would have been an oaf to ignore him. Yet I was suddenly uneasy to have the spectacle turn into a person. I glanced over my shoulder. Most of the crowd seemed to prefer the more lurid offerings of the tent and shuffled past his little stage with scarcely a glance.

'I'm cavalla. I'm a cadet at the King's Academy,' I said, and then I stopped. Was I? In a few more days, I was certain I'd be culled. The fat man didn't even notice my abrupt silence.

'Cavalla! You don't say! I was cavalla myself once, though you're not like to believe it now. Jensen's Horse. I started out as their bugle boy, I did, no taller than a flea and skinny as a whippet. Bet you don't believe that, do you?' He spoke as casually as if we had met at a cabstand, as if there was nothing strange about him chatting with someone who had come to gawk at him as an oddity.

I felt embarrassed for him, and smiled awkwardly. 'It's a bit hard to believe, sir, yes.'

'Sir,' he said softly. Then he smiled, the expression

541

pressing lines into his doughy face. 'Been a long time since a young soldier has called me that. I was a lieutenant when this happened to me. I was on my way up, too. They told me that in a month, perhaps two, there would be a vacancy and I'd be a captain in my father's old regiment. I was so happy. I thought it had all been worth it.' His face was transfigured by some memory, his eyes staring into the distance. He glanced down at me abruptly. 'But you're an Academy lad. Bet you wouldn't think much of some ranker like me. My father had been a ranker before me, but he'd never risen higher than master sergeant. When I got my lieutenant's bars, he was over the moon about it. He and my old maw sold just about everything they had to buy me a commission. I was shocked to hear they'd done it.'

He suddenly fell silent and all the old glory faded from his face. 'Well,' he said, and laughed harshly. 'My dad was always a good trader. I bet he got top dollar out of that commission when he sold it off.' He saw me staring at this revelation, and laughed again, more harshly. He gestured rudely at his body. 'Well, after this happened to me, what was I to do? My career was over. I come back west, hoping my family would take me in; they wouldn't even speak to me. Wouldn't even admit it *was* me. My old dad tells everybody that his son died in battle with the Specks. Close enough to truth, I guess. It was the damn Speck plague that did this to me.'

He lumbered over to the edge of his stage and sat down heavily. The whole process of lowering himself looked awkward. He dangled his legs over the edge. His low shoes were run over and tired, near bursting at their seams. His feet looked fat and run over, too, wider than they should have been. I wanted to leave, but could not simply turn and walk away from him. I wished other spectators would come to distract him from me. I did not like that he was being so friendly and talkative. I had to force myself to look interested in his words.

542

'So I come to the city. Took up begging on the street corners, but no one believes a fat man who says he's starving. I
would have starved, too, if I hadn't taken on this duty. It's
not that different from the cavalla, some ways. Get up, do
your shift, eat, go to bed. Watch each other's backs. Stick
together. That's what they say about the cavalla, isn't it?
That we always watch out for one another. Right, trooper?'

'Right,' I said uneasily. I felt he was building to something, some declaration of brotherhood that I didn't want to
hear. I needed to leave. 'I have to be on my way now. I'm
supposed to be looking for my cousin.' The words came to
me with a sour taste of guilt. They were merely an excuse,
and a stark reminder to myself that I had completely forgotten about Epiny and Spink and the danger that she might be
in.

'Yeah, right, he has to go.' The fat lady spoke from her
divan. From somewhere, she had drawn out another box of
candies and was untying the blue ribbon that bound the
creamy yellow box. She spoke without looking at either of
us. 'He knows you're gonna touch him for some coppers. "I
was in the cavalla, gimme a coin." Bores me to tears. I heard
it too often.'

'Shut up, you fat old slut!' the man told her angrily. 'It's
true! I was cavalla, and a damn good soldier once. Maybe I
was a ranker, but I'm not ashamed of that. Every promotion
I got, I earned. It was never given to me because I was some
noble's son, nor bought for me. I earned it. Earned these
lieutenant's bars. Looky here, trooper. You recognize the
real thing, don't you? And you wouldn't mind giving an old
comrade-in-arms a few coins so I could buy me something a
bit stronger than a beer? Gets cold working in here in the
wintertime. A man could use a good stiff drink after what I
go through.'

The fat man had managed, by much effort and with several grunts, to haul himself back to his feet. Now he took a

folded cloth from his trouser pocket. He opened it carefully, to show me the lieutenant's bars that shone inside it. I stared at them, knowing they might not be real, knowing that, like the jewellery that many folk wore for Dark Evening, they might be paper or enamel over dross. The fat man unpinned the gleaming bars from the rag that wrapped them and polished them a bit. Then, as he refastened them to the rag, he made the 'keep fast' charm over them. I felt a chill up my back. True, he might have learned it from watching others, as Epiny had, but there was something so habitual about the way he did it that I doubted it.

He glanced over at me and saw the dismay in my face. He smiled, and it was a cruel smile, one that mocked himself. 'I'm just an old ranker, son. Never sent to the King's Academy like you; never had the guarantees that you have. If the plague hadn't done me in, I'd be serving out near the far east still. But it did, and here I am. I get food, and work, if you call this work – parading around half-dressed in a draughty old tent so young blighters can look at me and laugh and stare, so sure they'll never be me. I get a bed and blanket every night. But that's about all I get. No extras in this life. But once I was a cavalla man. Yes, sir, I was.'

I found my hand thrust deep in my pocket. I pulled out my money and pushed it into his hands and then turned and fled. He shouted his thanks after me, and added, 'Don't you let them send you to the forest, boy! You find yourself a nice post in the west, counting sacks of grain or keeping tally of horseshoe nails! Stay away from the Barrier Mountains.'

I could not find the exit from the tent. I pushed through a crowd of people packed around a girl juggling knives, not caring how they stared at me, nor even for the one woman who cursed me roundly for stepping on her foot. My path led me back past the Specks' cage, but there was no crowd round it that I could see. The male Specks were there, wandering listlessly about the enclosure. The woman was gone.

I estimated the time at midnight, and guessed that Rory and Trist had returned for her.

I made my way to the tent door. I didn't want to think of them with the wild Speck girl. The fat man and his tales of being a ranker had soured the circus for me. The weight of my recent misfortunes descended on me once more. I was to be culled, for no more reason than to keep the Academy in political balance. It would be seen as shameful, no matter what they wrote on my papers. I doubted my father would buy me a commission. He'd probably sternly tell me that I'd had my chance, and that now I'd have to enlist as a common soldier, alongside all the other common sons of common soldier sons. There would be no arranged marriage for me, no officer's commission, and no glorious future commanding troops for the King. I wondered if I would run back to Maw tomorrow and beg to be a scout.

I emerged from the trapped smells and still warmth of the tent into the cold night air. As the night deepened, the crowds were thickening, not dispersing, and I suddenly knew that I had no chance at all of finding Epiny or Spink or anyone else in such chaos. Even if I found Epiny, there was no saving her reputation now. Best to go back to the dormitory and pretend that I had never found Spink's note. The whole world was sour and cold and dark, without a single friendly face. I looked up at the night sky to try to get my bearings, but the lamplight and torchlight overpowered the feeble and distant stars. No matter. I'd just go back the way I'd come. Somewhere at the edge of the Great Square, I would find a cabstand and get back to the Academy.

TWENTY TWO

Disgrace

It was late. After the confines of the lighted tent, the cold outdoors and the endless sky overhead made me feel oddly exposed and alone despite the milling people. The Dark Evening festival felt tired and finished to me. I just wanted to go home to a quiet and familiar room. But all around me, the crowd shouted to one another and jostled me from my intended path as they rollicked through their festival. I thrust my hands deep into the pockets of my greatcoat, sunk my head into my collar and shouldered my way through the throng as best I could. I had given up on trying to spot Epiny or Spink. The odds of my seeing anyone I knew in a gathering this large were ridiculously small. Almost as soon as I reached that realization, an opening in the crowd revealed several young men in Academy overcoats, their backs turned to me. I veered toward them, thinking they might be my roommates. If they were, I suddenly decided I'd go whoring with them. The tawdriness of carnival had won me over. I had nothing left to lose to it. One yelled out, 'Come on! Finish! Down it like a man!' Three others took up the chant, 'Down it! Down it!' They didn't sound like my friends.

I waited until a gaggle of merrymakers tooting horns had passed, and then crossed the crowded space toward them. When I got closer, I instantly recognized them as the New Noble second-years I'd glimpsed earlier. Jaris and Ordo were among them. I turned aside hastily. Then, behind me, I heard one woeful voice raised. 'I can't! I'm sick. That's enough for me!'

'No, no, my lad!' Jaris was hearty with good cheer. 'Drink it down. Finish it, and we'll get you a woman. Like we promised.'

'But first, you've got to prove you're a man. Drink it down!'

'There's not much left. You're more than halfway there!' I recognized Ordo's voice.

The chorus of voices encouraged him. I knew he'd do it. Caulder could never withstand the prospect of approval. The boy was going to be horribly sick tomorrow. Served him right.

I wanted to keep walking. But something made me halt and turn a little, to witness this as if I had not seen enough grotesque spectacles for one night. A brief opening in the crowd showed me Caulder standing in their midst, bottle clutched in one hand. He was weaving on his feet. But as I stared, he obediently lifted the bottle to his mouth and upended it. His eyes were clenched as if in pain, but I saw his Adam's apple bob repeatedly. 'Down, down, down, down!' the chant rose around him again. And then more people walked between us, obscuring the scene. I started to walk away again. There was a whoop, and a roar of approval from behind me. 'That's a man, Caulder! You've done it!' They applauded him but it was followed immediately by derisive laughter. Jaris laughed and cried out, 'That's done it, lads! He won't be following us any more tonight! Let's off to Lady Parra's. She'll let us in now that we don't have the puppy trailing after us.'

All five of them hurried away, jostling through the crowd, whooping and laughing as they went. I didn't see Caulder among them. He'd probably passed out. It was none of my doing, and I wanted nothing to do with it. I was sure that blame for this would fall on someone tomorrow, and that it wouldn't be Caulder. The farther away from him I stayed, the better for me. Nonetheless, I found myself pushing back through the clusters of people to the spot where Caulder lay flat on his back on the ground.

His out-flung hand still clutched the bottle's neck. It was cheap, strong drink, not wine or beer, and I flinched from its harsh stink. Caulder was lying still. His face in the uneven light of the square was the same dirty white as the trampled ice underfoot. His mouth was ajar, his face set in a frown. A domino mask dangled from its string around his neck. His belly heaved a little and he twitched, half-choking. The rejected liquor rose in his mouth like a dark foul pool, a bit trickling down his cheek. He coughed weakly and drew in a wet, raspy breath. Then he was still again. He already stank of vomit and his trouser cuffs were spattered from an earlier mishap.

I didn't want to touch him. But I'd heard of men choking to death on their own puke after drinking too much. I didn't dislike him so much that I wanted him to die of his own stupidity. So I crouched down and rolled him onto his side. At my touch, he sucked in a sudden breath. He was scarcely on his side before he vomited violently, the spew flying out of his mouth onto the frozen crust of dirty snow that he sprawled on. He heaved twice, and then rolled onto his back again. His eyes didn't open. I was suddenly struck by how pale he was. Pulling off my glove, I touched his face. His skin was cold and clammy, not flushed with drink. Again, at my touch, he pulled in a slow breath.

'Caulder! Caulder? Wake up. You can't pass out here. You'll be trampled or freeze to death.' People were barely stepping around us, uncaring and unmindful of the boy stretched out on the ground. One woman in a fox mask tittered as she went past. No one stopped or stared or offered help. I shook him. 'Caulder. Get up! I can't stay here with you. Get up and on your feet.'

He dragged in another breath and his eyelids fluttered. I seized him by his collar and dragged him to a sitting position. 'Wake up!' I yelled at him.

548

His eyes opened halfway and then closed again. 'I did it,' he said faintly. 'I did it. I drank it all! I'm a man. Get me a woman.' His words ran together, and his voice was little more than a mutter. The colour had not come back to his face. 'I don't feel good,' he abruptly announced. 'I'm sick.'

'You're drunk. You should go home. Get up and go home, Caulder.'

He put both his hands over his mouth, and then dropped them to cover his belly. 'I'm sick,' he groaned, and his eyes sagged shut again. If I had not been holding him upright, he would have fallen back onto the ground. I shook him. His head wobbled back and forth. For the first time, a man stopped and looked down at us. 'Best take him home, son, and let him sleep it off there. Shouldn't have let the lad drink so much.'

'Yes, sir,' I replied reflexively, with no intention of taking Caulder anywhere. But neither could I just stand up and walk away from him. I'd drag him somewhere out of the way and leave him where he wouldn't get stepped on or freeze to death. For it was getting colder as the night grew deeper.

I seized his wrists and stood up, dragging him with me. He lolled like a rag doll. I put one of my arms round his waist and held his other arm across my shoulder. It was awkward, for I was substantially taller than he was. 'Walk, Caulder!' I yelled in his ear and he muttered some response. I dragged him along with me as I cut across the big square towards the cabstands. Sometimes he muttered, and his legs moved as if he took giant strides, but his words made no sense.

The Great Square proved its size to me that long night. We were jostled forward sometimes and sometimes blocked by standing crowds who could not or would not give way to us. We were forced to go around one roped-off area where couples were dancing. The music of the instruments seemed at odds with the cavorting of the masked people, and some of them looked more tormented than festive as they leapt and spun and flung their arms about.

Caulder threw up once without warning, a gushing spew that very narrowly missed a fine lady's skirts. I held him as he heaved and spouted like a bad pump, grateful only that the lady's escort hurried her away instead of challenging me. When he was finished, I dragged him away from his mess. I sat him down on the edge of one of the frozen fountains; I wished in vain for water. I took my damp handkerchief from my pocket and wiped his chin and running nose as best I could, and then threw it away. 'Caulder! Caulder, open your eyes. You've got to get up and walk. I can't drag you all the way home.'

But in reply he only shook. His face was pale, and his skin remained clammy. I got up and walked away from him, leaving him sprawled in a half-sitting heap like an abandoned pile of laundry. To this day, I do not know what made me turn around and go back for him. His situation was none of my making and I owed him nothing. I felt only animosity toward the tattling, tag-a-long brat, and yet I could not leave him there to face the cold awakening he deserved. I went back.

I gave up trying to walk him. I lifted him across my shoulders as if he were a wounded man and carried him through the crowd. It was a better solution, for more people saw us coming and got out of the way. When I finally reached the cabstand, there was a long queue. The streets were still choked with pedestrians and so the wait was tripled as cabs struggled to reach the kerb to disgorge the passengers they had and to take on new ones.

When finally it reached our turn, the cabbie demanded his money up front before he would even open a door for us. I stood there, turning my pockets out for what little money I had left and cursing myself for my free spending earlier in the evening. I heartily wished I had kept the money I'd given the fat man. 'Caulder! Have you any money?' I asked, shaking him. Another couple thrust in front of us, flashing a gold piece, and our cabbie immediately jumped down and opened the door for them with a bow. Despite my angry protests, he re-mounted the box and began trying to force his team out into the crowded street.

Fate intervened then or I do not know what would have become of us. Another carriage pulled into the spot left open by our departing cab. The driver jumped down and opened the door to let a fine couple out. The man wore a tall silk hat and escorted a woman in an embroidered gown topped by a shimmering fur cape. She murmured something in dismay and he said, 'I am sorry, Cecile, but this is as close as the cab can bring us. We shall have to walk to General Scoren's house from here.' It was only when he spoke that I recognized Dr Amicas from the Academy infirmary. He looked much different than he had the night he had tended Gord. I think my Academy overcoat drew his eye, for as he passed he looked at me and then, as his eyes fell on Caulder, he exclaimed in disgust, 'Oh, for the mercy of the good god. Who let that silly whelp run loose on a night like this?'

He didn't expect an answer and I gave him none. I stood, holding Caulder upright beside me and half-hoped he would not recognize me, for I did not wish to be connected to Caulder's misfortune. His wife's face was full of dismay at the delay. Dr Amicas spoke to me harshly. 'Get him home as soon as you can. And put your own coat round him, you great fool! He's far colder than he should be! How much did he drink? More than a bottle, I'll wager, and I've seen more than one young cadet die of too much to drink in too little time.'

His words shocked and frightened me, and I blurted out, 'I've no money for a carriage, Dr Amicas. Will you help us?'

I thought he would strike me, he looked so angry. Then he reached into his pocket with one hand as he grabbed the sleeve of his departing driver's coat with the other. 'Here, cabman, take these two young idiots back to the King's Cavalla Academy. I want you to take them right to Colonel Stiet's door, do you hear me? Nowhere else, no matter what they say.' He pushed the money into the man's hand and then the doctor turned on me.

'Colonel Stiet won't be home tonight, Cadet, and you can thank your lucky stars for that. But don't you dare leave that boy on the doorstep! You see that one of Stiet's serving men takes him up to his bed, and I want two pints of hot broth down him before they let him sleep. You hear me? Two pints of good beef broth! No doubt I'll have to deal with both of you tomorrow. Now get along!'

The cab driver had opened the door for us, reluctantly, for it was a fine conveyance and Caulder still reeked of liquor and puke. I tried to thank the doctor but he waved me off in disgust and hurried away with his lady. It took both the driver and me to heave Caulder into the carriage. Once inside, he lay on the floor like a drowned rat. I perched on one of the seats; the driver slammed the door, and mounted his box. And there we sat for what seemed like a very long time before he could force his team out into the steady flow of carriages, carts, and foot traffic. We moved at a walk through the city streets near the Great Square, and more than once I heard drivers exchanging curses and threats with one another.

The farther we got from the square, the darker the night became and the more the traffic thinned. Eventually, the driver moved his team up to a fine trot and we rattled along through the streets. Light from the street lamps flitted through the carriage intermittently. Every so often, I would give Caulder a nudge with my foot. The groan that resulted comforted me that he was still alive. We were almost to the Academy drive when I heard him cough and then ask sourly, 'Where are we? Are we there yet?'

'Almost home,' I told him comfortingly.

'Home? I don't want to go home.' He struggled to sit up and finally managed it. He rubbed at his face and then his eyes. 'I thought we were going to a whorehouse. That was the bet, remember? You bet me that I couldn't drink the whole bottle, and if I could, you were taking me to the best whorehouse in town.'

'I didn't bet you anything, Caulder.'

He leaned closer to peer up at me. His breath was deadly. I turned my head away. 'You're not Jaris! Where is he? He promised me a woman! And I . . .who are you?' Suddenly he grasped his head in his hands. 'By the good god, I'm sick. You poisoned me.'

'Don't be sick in the carriage. We're nearly at your father's door.'

'But . . . What happened? Why didn't they . . . I . . . '

'You drank too much and you passed out on the ground. And I'm bringing you home. That's really as much as I know.'

'Wait.' He tried to get up on his knees to peer into my face. I leaned back. He grabbed my coat front. 'You can't hide from me. I know you. You're that stiff-necked Burvelle New Noble bastard. The one with the rock. And you ruined my Dark Evening. They said I could go with them! They said they would make me a man tonight.'

I took his wrists and ripped his grip from my coat. 'That would take a lot more than one night and a bottle of cheap liquor. Keep your hands to yourself, Caulder. Call me a bastard again, and I'll demand satisfaction of you, regardless of how old you are or whose son you are!' I pushed him away with my foot.

'You kicked me! You hurt me!' He bellowed the words, and then, as the carriage finally pulled up, he burst into weeping. I didn't care. I had had enough of him. I stepped on his hand clambering over him to reach the door handle. I couldn't stand to wait for the driver to climb down and open it for us. I dragged Caulder out feet first, letting his butt thud onto the pavement. I pulled him sideways, away from the carriage and slammed the door shut. The driver immediately stirred up his horses and left. He, too, wanted nothing further to do with us, and I'm sure he was anxious to return to Dark Evening and the inflated cab fares he could charge.

'Get up!' I said to Caulder. I was suddenly furious with him. He was the perfect target for all my pent-up frustration and rage. There he was, a soldier son like me, but without honour or ethics. Yet his father would buy his way into the Academy, and doubtless purchase him a fine commission after he'd drunk and whored his way through two years of school. Caulder would be commanding while I was grooming my own horse and eating food cooked in a vat and sweating to make my sergeant's stripes. Caulder would get a wife of good breeding and fine manners. Perhaps my own cousin Epiny would be his. At the moment, it seemed a fit fate for them both. I looked up at Colonel Stiet's gracious home on the Academy grounds, and knew this was the only time I'd ever knock on that tall white door. I half-walked, half-dragged Caulder up the marble steps of his father's fine house, and when I released him, he collapsed beside me like a sack of meal. 'All your fault, Nevare Burvelle,' he was muttering. 'You won't get away with this. I vow it. You will pay.'

'*You'll* pay,' I replied harshly. 'Your head will pound like hammers on anvils tomorrow. And you probably won't remember a minute of Dark Evening.'

I banged the knocker a dozen times on the colonel's door before I heard anyone stir within. The man who answered the door had his collar loosened and smelled plainly of mulling spices. I suspected the servants left in charge of the house tonight were having their own Dark Evening celebration. He did not look inclined to end his festivities, even when I stepped aside and showed him a sodden Caulder on the doorstep.

'Dr Amicas said to tell you to see him into his bed, but don't let him sleep until you've put a couple of pints of warm beef broth down him. He's colder than he should be, and he's drunk far too much. The doctor said he has seen young cadets die of drinking this much all at once.'

Just as I finished, Caulder leaned to one side and vomited down the steps. The smell that wafted up turned my stomach. The serving man blanched. He turned his head and bellowed, 'Cates! Morray!' When two younger men appeared, he ordered them, 'Take the young master up to his bed, strip him, and get him into a warm tub. Tell cook to make beef broth for him. One of you get a stable boy to come wash down the steps before that vile mess freezes on them. And you! What is your name, sirrah?'

I had been turning to leave. I turned back reluctantly. 'My name is Cadet Nevare Burvelle. But I only brought Caulder home. I didn't get him into this state.'

The man didn't appear to care. 'Nevare Burvelle,' he said carefully and disapprovingly, as if my name were part of Caulder's bad smell. The other servants had dragged Caulder in, and he followed them, shutting the door behind him without so much as a thanks or a farewell.

I went down the stairs carefully, avoiding the slimed steps, and crossed the foreboding night campus. The cold and the dark both seemed stronger and bleaker here. The only sound was the crunching of my boots on the half-frozen snow. When I reached Carneston House, a single feeble light greeted me by the door. I entered to find the main floor lit only by the embers in the great fireplace. No one was at Sergeant Rufet's desk. I went up the stairs, blessing the lights that burned on each landing. Our rooms were all in blackness. 'Spink!' I called, but there was no response. He hadn't returned, and so whatever misadventure he and Epiny were involved in was continuing.

I found my bunk in the darkness, let my clothing fall to the floor and climbed in. I was chilled through and the layers of bitter disappointment fell over me like heavy blankets that did not warm me but only pressed me deeper into despair. I slept fitfully, twitching from one nightmare to the next. I was naked at the carnival and everyone knew that I had been culled from the Academy. My father was there. 'Be a man, Nevare!' he charged me sharply, and instead I wept like a little child. I dreamed disturbingly of Rory and the Speck woman. I woke once or twice as other stragglers came in. They were laughing and the smell of wine or beer on them made my stomach turn. After my evening with Caulder, I suspected it would be a long time before I wanted to drink again. I rolled over and finally fell into a deeper sleep, and with it, a vivid and carnal dream.

All young men have such dreams. There is no shame in them. My dream was heavy with sensuality and detail. I tasted, I smelled, I heard, I touched, and I saw. Every sense I possessed was inundated with the woman. I rested between her thighs and lazily traced the mottled patterns on the skin of her breasts. Her nipples were dark and erect. Her tongue was dark, too, and her breath smelled of flowers and earthy forest and tasted like sun-ripened fruit on a warm summer day. Her body engulfed mine in female suppleness. We mated as animals mate, without hesitation or inhibition.

She was my reward for betraying my people. I lay on her mountainous softness, nuzzling my face against her soft drooping breasts. I wallowed in her flesh, fascinated with the yielding folds and mounds of her. Afterwards, she held me still inside her, trapping me in her embrace. She kissed me with a sensuality that surpassed all intimacy I'd ever dreamed. Her hands held and caressed my shaved scalp and then clutched my tarred topknot of hair. 'You have crossed the line and you are mine,' the tree woman murmured.

I woke with a gasp. Despite the holiday, the drums thundered the next morning. Briefly, the eroticism of the voluptuous woman lingered in my mind and flesh. The next moment, I felt as disgusted with myself as if my dream had been real. No man can control what he dreams at night. Despite that, I felt shamed that I could even imagine such a thing, let alone be aroused by it. Around me, the others groaned and cursed and put their pillows over their heads. No one got up. I dropped back into a real sleep, and slept until true light came in at the windows, and then grudgingly rose to a cold morning. I was better off than most of my comrades. I was still tired and dejected, but at least I didn't have a hangover. Just before it was time for the noon meal, I got dressed in my uniform, still damp from the night before. The tables in the mess hall were half-empty. Spink was one of the few who joined me there. I had seen little of him before that meal, for he had arisen early and gone out for a walk in the crisp, cold day. He was smiling to himself and humming as he sat down next to me. I asked him quietly, 'Epiny?'

He turned bloodshot eyes to me. He looked tired but cheerful. After a moment he said, 'I never found her. I searched for a time, and then gave it up. Perhaps she had the good sense to stay at home. I went looking for you, but never found you. Too many people. Will you ask after her when you write to your uncle?'

'I will.' I realized I had neglected to send him a letter yesterday. For that matter, I hadn't received a letter from him. Well, bad news will keep, my father always said, and I could not think of one good thing to tell him. I thought of telling Spink about my private conversation with Captain Maw. I thought of telling him that all our dreams were doomed. I pushed that thought aside. Some part of me was still desperately clinging to hope. To speak of us being culled seemed unlucky, as if it were a curse I might bring down on us by speaking it aloud. My mind jumped to a topic only slightly less miserable. 'At least you had a better night than I did,' I told him, and recounted my pleasant ride home with Caulder. I had thought he would laugh, but he looked grave.

'You probably saved his life, but we all know what a little snake Caulder is. He'll never appreciate what you did for him.'

Our conversation was interrupted when Oron belatedly

joined us at the table. He looked paler than usual, save for the dark circles under his eyes. His hands shook slightly as he heaped food onto his plate. He gave us a sick sort of smile. 'It was worth it,' he said to our unasked question.

'Did Rory go back to the Speck woman?' I asked bluntly.

Oron looked down at his heaped plate. 'He and Trist did,' he admitted. He struggled to keep a strained smile from his face as he added, 'Actually, we all did. It was amazing.'

I don't think Spink picked up on what we were discussing. 'Well, all of Dark Evening was amazing!' Spink agreed, surprising me with his enthusiasm. He was in such a good mood that I could scarcely stand to look at him. It was as if he'd forgotten entirely about the culling that still hung over our heads. He went on, 'Never in my life have I seen anything like it. I didn't think there were that many people in the entire world; well, you know what I mean. I've never seen such a crowd, or tasted such amazing food. I saw this woman, and she was dressed only in paper chains! The man with her was dressed like a wild man; he only wore strings with leaves attached to them. They were dancing so wildly, I was shocked! And, oh, did you go to the circus? Did you see the tiger tamer, with his big cats jumping through hoops of flame? And then, the side show . . . that poor little girl with flippers instead of arms. Oh, and while I was there, the Specks broke their usual custom and did the Dust Dance! It was amazing! The man in charge of them said it had never been seen this far west before! And—'

'They did it when I was there, too.' Light suddenly dawned in my mind. 'It was all a trick, Spink. He probably always says they never do it, and they probably do it at every show. That way he makes it seem more special.'

'Oh.' Spink looked deflated.

Oron, across the table from us, nodded sagely. 'Most of the acts in that tent were a sham, I'd bet.'

'I talked to the fat man, and he claimed he'd once been a

558

cavalla lieutenant. Can you believe that?' I asked them.

Oron gave a huff of amusement. 'Right. He'd break a horse's back.'

Spink looked so crestfallen, I almost wished I'd kept my knowledge to myself. He shamed me further by saying quietly, 'He said the same thing to me and I felt sorry for him. We gave him some money.'

'Gullible country boys!' Oron exclaimed and then groaned and put a hand to his belly. 'Maybe I'm not feeling as chipper as I thought. I'm back to bed, lads.'

He left the table, and Spink and I followed him a short time later. Spink didn't look well, and I suspected I was as pale as he was. I followed him back to Carneston House, where we found most of our fellows still abed or moving sluggishly about. I sat down and wrote a long letter to my uncle. I'd begun a second to my father, confiding my fears of being culled, when Sergeant Rufet himself entered our common room. He seldom ventured upstairs outside of inspection times, so all of us came immediately to our feet. His face was grave as he said, 'Cadet Burvelle, come with me. You are to report to Colonel Stiet immediately.'

I quickly gave my letter to Spink to post and fetched my coat. Rufet was kind enough to give me a moment to smooth my hair and straighten my uniform. I followed him down the stairs, and then was shocked when he accompanied me out the door. 'I know the way there, Sergeant,' I said in some confusion.

'Orders. I'm to escort you there, Cadet.'

He sounded as if his head were just as sore as my fellow cadets', and so I walked beside him in silence and dread. I knew this could not bode well for me. Rufet asked the colonel's adjutant to admit me. For a change, I saw no sign at all of Caulder. When the inner door of Colonel Stiet's office opened, Sergeant Rufet remained outside it. It closed behind me.

The room seemed dim after the brightness of the cold winter day. Despite the holiday, Colonel Stiet was in full uniform and seated at his desk. He stared at me, motionless, as I crossed the room. His eyes looked tired and the lines in his face deeper than I recalled them. I walked in the door, stood at attention before his desk and 'Cadet Burvelle, reporting as ordered, sir,' I said.

He looked up at me, cold anger in his eyes. He had been writing something when I came in. Now, without a word to me, he went back to it. He finished it, signed it with a flourish, and then, as he poured drying sand over the ink, said, 'My son could have died last night, Cadet Burvelle. Did you know that?'

I stood very still for a moment. Then I answered honestly, 'Only when Dr Amicas told me about it, sir. Then I did precisely as he told me.' I wanted to ask if Caulder were all right today, but dared not.

'And prior to that, Cadet? What did you do prior to meeting with the doctor?'

A stillness was growing inside of me; I had a sense that everything depended on this answer. Honesty was all I had. 'I tried to keep him awake, sir. He was very nearly unconscious when I found him, and I feared that if he were left passed out at the Great Square, he might freeze to death or be trodden on. So I carried him from the square to the cabstand and brought him home.'

'So I've heard. From both the doctor and my servants. And before that, Cadet Burvelle? What did you do before that? Did you attempt to keep him from drinking so much? Did you think, perhaps, that it was unwise to urge a boy of Caulder's years to consume an entire bottle of rot-gut liquor?'

'Sir, that was not my doing!'

'That isn't what I asked you!' the colonel shouted at me. 'Answer my question! Would you have done the same thing to another boy of his years? Don't you think that pouring liquor down a lad is a poor revenge for childish thoughtlessness?'

I stared at him, unable to comprehend what I was being accused of. My silence seemed to feed his fury.

'He's a boy, Cadet Burvelle. Still just a boy, prone to a boy's mischief. He is my son, but even I will admit that he does not have the best judgment. But what do you expect of a growing boy? Whatever grudge you imagine you have against him, it isn't worth his life. You're older than he is, and a cavalla cadet. He looked up to you, wanted to be like you, and trusted you blindly! And you betrayed that innocent, boyish trust! For what? Revenge for some minor prank on your fat friend? You went too far! Here!' He suddenly snatched up the paper he had been writing on and thrust it at me. 'Those are your discharge papers. You are to be gone from the Academy before classes resume. Pack yourself up and get out of here. There is no room at the King's Cavalla Academy for men like you.'

'I've been culled,' I said dully. I'd been expecting it. I hadn't expected to be the first officially sent packing.

'No! That would be too good for you. You've been dishonourably discharged from this Academy. I trust you know what that means. I intend that you never hold a position of power over any man. You've shown that you are not worthy of it, nor to be trusted with it. Take your discharge and go!'

My head was reeling. I did know, very well, what a dishonourable discharge from the Academy meant. It would disqualify me from all military service. I would not be allowed to enlist even as a foot soldier. Oh, there were romantic tales of young men changing their names and enlisting to prove they had reformed themselves, and it was rumoured that some of the civilian scouts who served the military in the more dismal regions were actually dishonourably discharged soldiers. But I knew what the discharge would mean for me. It meant no career, ever. I would go back to my brother's holdings, and slink about them to the end of my days, a useless son. My father's line would have to wait an extra generation before my brother's second son, if there was one, could redeem our honour. I felt physically ill. I'd done a good deed and lost my future. Too late now to go to Captain Maw and tell him I'd be a scout. Too late for everything except disgrace.

I had nothing left to lose. I disobeyed my commander. I did not take the papers he was waving at me, but spoke, unbidden.

'Sir, I fear you have been misinformed about what happened last night. I did not take young Caulder to Dark Evening. I did not even know he was there until I saw him in the company of some other cadets. I did not give him drink. All I did was to go to him after he had drunk a full bottle of liquor and passed out, and see that he got safely home. I swear to you, sir, on my honour, that I had nothing to do with your son's downfall.'

I felt as if my body were literally burning with my fervour. I know I swayed on my feet and prayed I would not disgrace myself by falling. Colonel Stiet looked at me in disbelief. 'Must you compound your failures by lying about them? Do you think my son is unconscious still? Do you think I don't know everything? He has confessed all to me, Burvelle. All. You were the one who bought the liquor and put it in his hands. You and your friends urged him to drink, even when he told you he had had enough. The others will be discharged as well; they were to be culled anyway.' He looked down at the paper he still gripped in his hand. 'I only wish there were something more severe than a dishonourable discharge that I could inflict on you. I will be notifying your uncle. By this afternoon's mail, he will know of how you have shamed his name.'

'I didn't do it,' I said, but my words sounded feeble and uncertain. My guts seemed to squirm inside me and I felt a tearing cramp in my side. I could not help myself. I clutched at my belly. 'Sir, I'm feeling ill. Permission to leave, sir.'

'You have it. Take your papers with you. I never want to see you in this office again.'

He thrust the paper into my slackened hands. I held it against my complaining stomach as I staggered from the room. In the outer office, the colonel's secretary stared at me as I passed him by without a word. I hastened out the door and down the steps. Sergeant Rufet was waiting for me, his face impassive. I began a quick march back to the dormitory, but after a few steps I faltered. A wave of vertigo swept over me and I halted, swaying on my feet.

Sergeant Rufet spoke in a low voice. 'That must have been some dressing down. Taking it hard, I see. Buck up, Cadet. Be a man.'

Be a man. Stupid, useless advice. 'Yes, Sergeant.' I kept walking. Blackness kept trying to close in from the edges of my vision. I would not faint. Never before had foul news had such a profound physical effect on me. My belly boiled with acid and my head spun. I focused my eyes on the path and staggered on.

'So. How many demerits will you be marching off?' he asked. His tone was genial, as if to make light of whatever had befallen me, but I thought there was an edge of concern in it, too.

I could scarcely find breath to answer. 'I won't be marching at all,' I managed, ashamed of how my voice hitched on the words. 'I've been dishonourably discharged. They're sending me home in disgrace. I'll never be a soldier, let alone an officer.'

The sergeant halted in surprise. I think he thought I would stop too, but I kept on walking. I feared I would collapse if I did not. One foot in front of the other. He caught up with me and asked me in a toneless voice, 'What did you do, Cadet, to merit that?'

'Nothing. It's what Caulder accused me of doing. He said

I'm the one who got him drunk at Dark Evening. I didn't. I was just the one who dragged him home.' When the sergeant said nothing, I added bitterly, 'His Old Noble friends are the ones who took him to town and got him drunk. They wanted him to pass out, so they could get into a whorehouse without him. I heard them talking about it. Those Old Noble bastards left him to freeze on the ground. I picked him up, I obeyed the doctor's order, I dragged him home, and I'm the one to be kicked out. All because I'm a *New* Noble's son.'

'Caulder.' The sergeant growled the word like it was a curse. Then he added, in a low vicious voice, 'New Noble, Old Noble, that's all I hear and not a damn bit of difference do I see between the lot of you. Any noble's son is the same to me, born to lord it over me. Damn lot of you wet behind the ears still, but in three years you'll be polishing your lieutenant's bars while I'm still riding a damn desk and babysitting youngsters.'

A fresh wave of misery washed over me. In all the times I'd walked past the sergeant's desk, I'd never stopped to wonder what he thought of us. I glanced over at him. There he was, a man grown, years of service behind him, and in two years of Academy, I would have outranked him. That injustice suddenly seemed as great as what had just befallen me. I drew a breath against the misery that had swollen my throat shut and tried to speak.

'Shut up, Cadet,' he said coldly before I could get a word out. 'I'm not any kind of a noble's son, but I know an injustice when I see it. Listen. Listen to me. Don't say a damn word about that discharge. Fold it up and shove it in your pocket. And don't do a damn thing until someone commands you to do it. Shut up and sit tight. Caulder's been a thorn in my flesh since he and his old man got here. Maybe it's time I had a word with that pup, and let him know that I know what's what with his trotting about here and there. I see a damn sight more than I say. Maybe it's time I put a word in his ear about what I know. Maybe he'll say something to his father to make him change his mind. But the less people the colonel has to explain that change to, the easier it will be for him to do it. So you, you just lie low and don't do anything for a while. Do you understand me, boy?'

'Yes, sir,' I said shakily. I should have felt better for his words of support. Instead I only felt fainter. 'Thank you, sir.'

'You don't call a sergeant "sir",' he pointed out sourly.

I don't know how I made the rest of that long march back to Carneston House. He left me at the door and went, with a heavy sigh, to sit behind his desk. I still clutched my discharge paper in my hand. I started up the stairs. They had never seemed so steep or so long. Sternly, I ordered my body to behave itself and tried to get a grip on myself. On the first landing I paused to catch my breath. Sweat was pouring down my back and ribs. I crumpled up the paper I didn't have the energy to fold and thrust it into my pocket.

I have climbed cliffs that were less demanding than those remaining flights of stairs. When I reached our rooms at last, I stumbled past Spink sitting at our study table. 'You look awful!' he greeted me worriedly. 'What happened?'

'I'm sick,' I said and no more than that. I stumbled to our room, let my coat fall to the floor, kicked off my boots and lay on my bunk face down. I'd never felt so wretched in my life. Yesterday, I'd learned that I'd likely be culled, and it had seemed the worst possible fate. Today, I knew how foolish I'd been. Culled, I could have been a ranker or a scout. At least I'd been left a chance to prove myself a proper soldier son. Dishonoured, I was nothing except an embarrassment to my family. My guts squeezed inside me. I only knew that Spink had followed me into the room when he spoke.

'You're not the only one sick. Trist is down bad, with something a lot worse than a hangover. Oron went to fetch the doctor. And Natred left an hour ago to go to the infirmary. What did you eat at Dark Evening? Natred said he thought he got some bad meat.'

'Leave me alone, Spink. I'm just sick.' I wanted desperately to confide in him about what had just happened, but didn't even have the energy to unfold the story. Besides, the sergeant had told me to say nothing. Lacking any better source of advice, I'd take his. I tried to take slow calming breaths and regain some sort of control over myself. Nausea surged in my gut. I swallowed and closed my eyes.

I don't know how much time passed before I admitted to myself that I truly was ill. It seemed fitting that I should be as physically miserable as I was mentally. I could hear Trist retching across the hall. I dozed off, and woke to a hand on my brow. When I turned over, Dr Amicas was looking down at me. 'This one, too,' he said tersely to someone. 'What is his name?'

'Nevare Burvelle,' I heard Spink say dully. A pen scratched on paper.

When he saw my eyes were open, the doctor demanded, 'Tell me everything you ate and drank at Dark Evening. Don't leave anything out.'

'I didn't give the liquor to Caulder,' I said desperately. 'All I did was bring him home. Like you told me to. He was passed out on the ground when I found him.'

Dr Amicas stooped and peered into my face. 'Oh. So that was you last night, was it? You still owe me some cab fare, Cadet, but we'll let it pass for now. I saw Caulder early this morning. Worst case of alcohol poisoning I've ever seen in a boy that young. But he'll live. He just won't enjoy it for a while. Now. What did you eat and drink?'

I tried to remember. 'A potato. Some meat on a stick. Something else. Oh. Chestnuts. I had chestnuts.'

'And to drink?'

'Nothing.'

'You won't be in trouble for it, Cadet. I just need to know. What did you drink?'

I was getting very tired of people thinking I was a liar. But instead of getting angry, I felt weepy. I ached all over.

'Nothing,' I said again, past the lump in my throat. 'I didn't drink anything. And Caulder lied about me.'

'Caulder lies about a great many things,' the doctor observed as if that shouldn't surprise me. 'Can you get yourself undressed and into bed, Cadet? Or do you need help?'

I groped at my chest, surprised to find that I was still dressed. When I began to fumble at my buttons, the doctor nodded as if satisfied. I heard someone gag and then begin to retch again. It sounded close by. The doctor scowled and spoke sternly, and this time I realized he had an assistant standing at his elbow. 'And there's another one. I want this whole floor quarantined. No. I want the entire hall quarantined. Go downstairs immediately and tell Sergeant Rufet to post a yellow flag by the door. No one comes in or out.'

I think the assistant was happy to leave judging by how quickly he fled. I sat up to take off my boots and the room spun around me. Nate and Kort were both lying on their bunks. Nate was hanging, head down, over the edge of his mattress, retching into a basin on the floor. Kort was motionless. A frightened-looking Spink was standing near the window, his arms crossed on his chest. Doggedly, I went to work at getting my shirt off my arms.

'Dr Amicas! What are you doing here? I sent for you an hour ago!'

I flinched at the sound of Colonel Stiet's voice. As he advanced into the room, his boot heels clacking on our floor, I wondered if it were all a dream. The colonel looked both distraught and furious. His face was red with exertion. Plainly he had hurried up the stairs. The doctor spoke flatly. 'Colonel, remove yourself immediately from this building, or risk being quarantined here with me and these cadets. We've a grave situation here, one that I will not approach with half-measures. All of Old Thares is at risk.'

'I've a grave situation of my own, Doctor. Caulder is ill, seriously ill. I sent my first messenger for you more than an hour ago. He came back to say only that you were "busy". When I came to the infirmary to fetch you myself, they told me you were at Carneston House. I find you up here, molly-coddling hung-over cadets while my boy burns with fever. That is not acceptable, sir. Not acceptable at all!'

'Fever! Damnation! I'm too late then. Unless . . .' The doctor paused, and knit his brows. I managed to get my shirt off. I let it fall to the floor beside my boots. I went to work on my belt.

'I want you to come to my son's bedside immediately. That is an order.' Colonel Stiet's voice shook with passion.

'I want the Academy quarantined.' The doctor spoke as if he had pondered all his options and reached a decision. I do not think he had even heard the colonel's words. 'It is essential, sir. Essential. I fear that what we have here is the first outbreak of the Speck plague to reach the west. It matches every symptom I saw in Fort Gettys, two years ago. If we're lucky, we can stop it here before it spreads to the whole city.'

'Speck plague? It can't be. There's never been a case of Speck plague this far west.' The colonel was shocked; the hard tone of command had gone out of his voice.

'And now there is.' The doctor spoke with angry resignation.

I spoke without thinking. My own voice seemed to come from a great distance. 'There were Specks there last night. At Dark Evening. In the freak tent. They did the Dust Dance.'

'Specks?' the colonel exclaimed, appalled. 'Here? In Old Thares?'

The doctor spoke over him, demanding of me, 'Were they ill? Sickly at all?'

I shook my head. The room was swaying slowly around me. 'They danced,' I said. 'They danced. The woman was beautiful.' I tried to lean back slowly into my bed. Instead the room spun suddenly, and I fell. Darkness closed in around me.

TWENTY THREE

Plague

My memories of those days are distorted, like images seen
through a badly ground magnifying lens. Faces came too
close, sound was shocking and light pierced my eyes. I didn't
recognize the room. There was a window opposite my bed
and bright winter light shone directly in my face. There were
other beds in the room and all of them were occupied. I
heard coughing, retching and feverish moaning. My own life
had vanished. I did not know where I was.

'Please. Pay attention.'

There was an orderly by my bed with an open notebook
in his hand. His pencil was poised over it. 'Concentrate,
Cadet. The doctor demands that every patient answer these
questions, no matter what condition he is in. It may be the
last important thing you can do with your life. Did you
touch a Speck?'

I didn't care. I just wanted him to go away. Nevertheless,
I tried. 'They threw dust at us.'

'Did you touch a Speck or did a Speck touch you?'

'Rory stroked her leg.' I thought of that, and my memories spun me back to the sideshow tent. I saw the woman's
mouth soften as he caressed her. I opened my own mouth,
longing to kiss her.

A voice shattered the image. 'So you've told me. Six
times. You, Cadet. You . . .' He flipped over a page and

likely found my name, 'Nevare Burvelle. Did *you* touch a Speck or allow a Speck to touch you?'

'Not . . . really.' Did I? In a dream, I had done far more than touch a Speck. She had been lush and beautiful. No. Fat and disgusting. 'It wasn't real. It didn't count.'

'That won't do. Yes or no, Cadet. Did you have carnal contact with a Speck? Don't be ashamed. It's too late for shame now. We know that several other cadets bought time with the Speck woman. Did you? Answer me, yes or no.'

'Yes or no.' I echoed the words obediently.

An exasperated sigh. 'Yes, then. I'm putting down yes.'

Dr Amicas's guess had been correct. It was Speck plague. It went against all we knew of that disease for it to strike so far west and during winter. Conventional wisdom at the time said that it flared up in the hot dusty days of summer and died down during the cool wet days of fall. But all the other symptoms matched and Dr Amicas, who had seen the disease first-hand, was adamant from the beginning about his diagnosis. It was Speck plague.

Those of us who fell to the first wave of illness were fortunate in a sense, for in the early days of the plague, we got good care. The first circle of cadets to sicken was composed only of those who had visited the freak tent. I have a hazy recollection of a rumpled and unshaven Colonel Stiet striding up and down past our beds, loudly denouncing us as perverts and saying we would all be dishonourably discharged for having unnatural relations. I remember Dr Amicas pointing out that, 'Numerically, it simply isn't feasible that all these lads had relations with the same female on the same night. Even if she'd lined them up like ducks, there simply wasn't enough time. I'm including your Caulder in that line, of course. For him to become infected so swiftly, he, too, would have had to have had congress with her.'

'How dare you think my son could be involved in something like this? How dare you even suggest it? One of the

570

cadets who dirtied himself with that striped whore passed the illness on to my boy. It's the only possible explanation.'

The doctor's voice was tired but insistent. 'Then, unless you are saying that your son had abnormal relations with one of these cadets, we have to admit the plague can be spread by means other than sexual contact. In which case, perhaps only a few of the cadets had intercourse with the whore.'

'They've admitted it! Half a dozen of those New Noble vermin have admitted it!'

'And as many of your fine Old Noble sons have owned up to it, also. Stop haranguing me, Colonel. How the disease got started is no longer a priority. Stopping it is.'

The colonel's voice was low and determined. 'We never had Speck plague in Old Thares before. Is it a coincidence that the first time we have young men patronizing a Speck whore, we get an outbreak? I don't think so. The city officials who banished the freak show don't think so either. Those who patronized the diseased whore are as guilty as the circus that brought her to town. And they should be punished for what they have loosed upon all of us.'

'Very well,' the doctor conceded wearily. 'You occupy yourself with thinking about how to punish them. I'll try to keep them alive so you'll have someone to punish. Would you please remove yourself from my infirmary now?'

'You haven't heard the last of this!' the colonel promised angrily. I heard him storm out, and then drifted off into my fever again.

Dr Amicas's plan to quarantine the Academy and confine the plague there was doomed to defeat. No walls or gates could contain or hold out the enemy that had descended upon us. The reports of sickness in the city were multiplying before the first day of lengthening daylight was over. As it was with the Academy, so it was with the city. Those who had visited the freak show tent were the first to fall ill. But it spread rapidly to their relatives and caretakers, and outward to others. Families such as Gord's who had left the city for the holiday heard the tidings and did not return. Families trapped within the city closed the doors of their houses and waited inside, hoping against hope that the contagion had not already infiltrated their homes. The circus and the freak show were rousted from the city, but the Specks had inexplicably vanished by then. Their keeper was found dead, choked on his prod that had been forced down his throat.

Two days after I fell ill, the second wave of plague swept through the Academy. The infirmary was overwhelmed. There were not enough beds to hold the afflicted, not enough linens and medicines and orderlies. The doctor and his assistants did what they could to take care of the cadets suffering in their various dormitories. There was little outside help to be had, for the Speck plague was raging through the city by then, and all doctors who dared to treat the ill had far more work than they could handle.

At the time, I knew nothing of that, of course. On the second day of my sickness, I was moved to a bed in the infirmary, and remained there. 'Lots of water and sleep,' was Dr Amicas's first advice. I'll give him this; he was an old soldier and knew well how to take action even before the command came down. He recognized the plague and treated it as such from the first outbreak

He'd seen Speck plague before, and had even contracted a mild case of it when he was stationed at Gettys. Knowing what he knew, Dr Amicas did the best he could. His first recommendation, that we drink lots of water, had not been a bad one. No medicine had ever proven efficacious against Speck plague. A man's own constitution was his best resource. The symptoms were simple and exhausting: vomiting, diarrhoea, and a fever that came and went. Day would seem to bring a slight recovery, but with night our fevers rose again. None of us could keep food or water down. I lay on my narrow cot, drifting in and out of awareness of the ward around me.

My cognizance of those days was an intermittent thing. Sometimes when I was awake the room was brightly lit and other times it was dim. I lost all sense of the passage of time. Every muscle in my body ached, and my head pounded with pain. I was hot, then shaking with cold. I was constantly thirsty, no matter how much I drank. If I opened my eyes, I felt as if too much light were in them; if I closed them, I feared to slip off into fever dreams. My lips and nostrils were chapped raw. I could find no comfort anywhere.

When I first arrived at the infirmary, Oron had lain in the bed to my left. The next time I awoke, he was gone and Spink was there. Nate was in the bed to my right. We were too miserable to talk; I could not even tell them of my dishonourable discharge or that they were soon to be culled as well. I drifted between dreams that were too sharply real to give me any rest and a nightmarish reality of foul smells, groaning cadets, and misery. I dreamed that I stood before my father and that he did not believe I was innocent of the false charges against me. I dreamed that my uncle and Epiny came to visit me, but Epiny had the deformed feet of the chicken woman. When she blew her little whistle, it made cackling sounds.

But the most unsettling moments were neither fever dreams nor sickroom glimpses. For me, there was another world, deeper than the fever dreams and far more real. My body lay in the bed and burned with fever, but my spirit walked in Tree Woman's world. I watched my other self there, and recalled clearly the years I had spent with her since first she had seized my hair and pulled me up and into her keeping. My true self was a pale ghost floating in their world, a party to their thoughts but nothing that they feared or considered at all. In that world, my top-knotted self had been her student for many years, and now I was her lover.

Daily, she had taught me the magic of The People, and daily she had strengthened me in that magic and made me more real in her world. We had walked in her forest and I had learned the irreplaceable value of her trees and wilderness. Her world had become mine, and I had come to see that no measure was too extreme in the war to protect it.

And in her world, I loved her with deep and real passion. I loved the voluptuousness of her flesh, and the deep earthiness of her magic. I admired her loyalty and determination to preserve The People and their ways. I shared her dedication to that cause. In those dreams, I walked beside her, and lay beside her, and in the sweet dimness of the forest night, we made the plans that would save our folk. When I was with her, all was clear. I knew that I had pleased her when I had made the sign to the Speck dancers to 'loose' the magic. I knew the performers had not been captives at all, but the most powerful dancers of the magic who could be spared from The People. They had come seeking my soldier's boy self. They had used that 'me' as a compass heading, to find the place where the intruders raised their warriors. And when they had found me, my other self had taken my hand and made the sign, and they had let fly the dust of the disease.

Powdered dung. That was what it was. It was a disgusting magic to my Gernian self, and as natural as breath to Tree Woman's assistant. It was well known to The People that a tiny measure of powdered dung from a sick person ingested by a healthy child would make the child sick, but only in the mildest way, and never again would the child fall prey to the deadly flux. But in quantity, as they had discovered, the dust could sicken an entire outpost of intruders, cutting down their warriors and women alike and exterminating the workers who slashed the road through the forest's flesh.

In her world I accepted, without question, the further

mission I would fulfil. I would enter the flesh of the soldier's son. I would undergo a change and become him. And I would spread the dust of death, not just through the great house where they raised their warriors, but also throughout their stonewalled hives, and even to the crowned ones who ruled them. Thus would I be the magic that turned the intruders back and saved The People.

All this, I knew so clearly when I wandered outside my feverish body. Each time I came back to my tortured flesh as my true self, I was weaker. Each time, vestiges of that other life and the knowledge of that world ghosted through my fevered brain.

On my third day of sickness, I rallied briefly during the day. Dr Amicas seemed pleased to see me awake, but I did not share his optimism. My eyelids were crusted and raw, as were my nostrils. The lingering illness made all my senses preternaturally sharp. The coarse sheets and wool blankets were a torment. I rolled my head toward Spink. I wanted to ask him if Oron had recovered, but Spink's eyes were closed and he was breathing hoarsely. Nate was still in the bed to my right. He looked terrible. In a few short days, the illness had sucked the flesh from his bones and the fever appeared to be devouring him from within. His mouth hung open as he breathed and mucus rattled in his throat. It was a terrible thing to hear, and I could not escape it. The day droned past me. I tried to be manly. I drank the bitter herbal water that they brought me, vomited it up and then drank the next draught they gave me. There was nothing to do except lie in bed and be sick. I hadn't the strength to hold a book, and could not have focused my eyes if I did. No one came to visit me. Neither Spink nor Nate was well enough to talk. I felt that there was something important that I had to tell someone, but I could not remember what it was or whom I was to tell.

I told myself that I was growing stronger, but as the sun

faded into night, my fever returned. I plunged back into a sleep that was neither rest nor true sleep. My dreams swirled like winged demons round my bed, and I could not escape them. I woke from a dream in which I was trapped in the freak tent to find myself in the dimmed ward. I sat up and discovered that Spink had no hands or arms, only flippers. When I tried to get out of my bed, I found that I had no legs. 'I'm dreaming!' I shouted at the orderly who came to hold me down. 'I'm dreaming. My legs are fine. I'm dreaming.'

I woke from that nightmare, shivering with cold, to find that my head was resting on a pillow full of snow. I tried to throw it off my bed, but Dr Amicas came and scolded me, saying, 'It will cool your hot head. It may break the fever. Lie back, Burvelle, lie back.'

'I didn't give liquor to Caulder. I didn't! You have to make the colonel understand. It wasn't me.'

'Of course not, of course not. Lie back. Cool your head. Your fever is burning your brain. Lie still.'

The doctor pushed me back into the cold softness of the fat man's embrace. 'I used to be in the cavalla!' he told me. 'Too bad you can't be a ranker like me. You can't be anything now. Not even a scout. Maybe you can be a fat man in a sideshow. All you have to do is eat. You like to eat, don't you?'

I sat up suddenly. The softness of the cold pillow had wakened a brief connection of memory. It was night in the ward. Dim lanterns burned and in the beds, shadowy figures tossed. I held tight to what I knew, desperate to share it, to avert my future betrayal of my people. 'Doctor!' I shouted. 'Dr Amicas!'

Someone in a doctor's apron hurried to my bedside. It wasn't Amicas. 'What is it? Are you thirsty?'

'Yes. No. It was the dust, Doctor. The dust they used. Dried and powdered shit from a sick man. To make us all sick. To kill us all.'

'Drink some water, Cadet. You're raving.'

'Tell Dr Amicas,' I insisted.

'Of course. Drink this.'

He held a cup to my mouth. It was pure, cool water and I gulped it down. It soothed my mouth and throat. 'Thank you,' I said. 'Thank you.' And I fell back, through fever dreams of an endless carriage ride into that other world.

Tree Woman shook her head at me. We were seated together in a little bower of flowering bushes, not far from the edge of the world. She smiled kindly at me as she warned me, 'You are not strong enough yet. Be patient. You need to consume more of their magic to walk with strength in their world. If you try too soon to cross back with him, you cannot master him. He will betray you.'

We were sitting together in the eaves of a forest. A soft rain was falling. She had brought me a leaf, folded like a cup. In it was a thick, sweet soup, warm and delicious. I drank it and licked the residue from the leaf as she looked on approvingly.

She had a leaf of her own, laden with the same gooey substance. She lapped it slowly from the cup, licking her lips and smiling. Watching her eat made me hungry for her. There was such plenitude to her, such completeness. She was generosity and richness, indulgence and luxury. In her, nothing was denied. I wanted her again. I wanted to be her, full and rich with magic. She saw me watching her and smiled coquettishly.

'Eat more!' she urged me. 'Soon, I will show you how to get it for yourself.' She handed me another leaf of the stuff. 'Let it fill you. It's their magic. Isn't it delicious? Fill yourself with it. Eat and grow full of magic.' She leaned closer to me, offering it, and suddenly it was not sweet. It was foul and thick, congealed like blood, sweet in the rotten way of carrion that draws flies. I jerked back from it.

'I don't want to be full of magic! I want to be an officer

in the King's Cavalla. I want to serve my king, and marry Carsina and send my journals home to my family. Please. Let me just be what I am supposed to be. Let me go.'

'Easy, Burvelle. Easy. Orderly! More water, here, right away. Drink this, Burvelle. Drink it down.'

My teeth chattered against the rim of a glass. Cold water spilled and dripped on my chest. I pried open my gummy eyes. Dr Amicas was easing me back onto my pillows. He had two days' growth of grey and black stubble on his chin and his eyes were bloodshot. I tried to make him understand. 'I didn't give Caulder liquor, Doctor. All I did was bring him home. You have to talk to Colonel Stiet. Or it's all over for me.'

He stared at me distractedly, then said, 'It's the least of your worries, Cadet. But men seldom lie in fevers. I'll put in a word for you with the colonel. If he survives. Rest now. Get some rest.'

'The dust!' I blurted. 'Did he tell you about the dust? The dung. Dung from a sick child.'

The doctor was pushing me back into my bed. I caught at his hands. 'I betrayed us, Doctor. I made the "loose" sign, and by it the Specks knew it was I. They knew they had reached the place where cavalla officers are taught. They loosed the dust and the death upon us. They were waiting for me, waiting for the sign. I'm a traitor, Doctor. Don't let him become me. He means to kill everyone here, every soldier's son. And everyone in Old Thares, even the King and Queen.' I struggled to push his hands away, to escape the bed.

'Easy, Nevare. Rest. You aren't yourself. Orderly! I need some straps here.'

An old man in a spattered smock hurried to my bedside. As the doctor held me, he tied a strip of linen around my wrist. 'Not too tight,' the doctor rebuked him. 'I just want him kept in his bed until the delirium passes.'

'Loose!' I said, and made the sign. The strip fell away from my wrist.

'Not that loose!' the doctor chided him.

'I tied it, sir. Swear I did.' The orderly was indignant.

'Just do it again.'

'Loose,' I said, but I was losing my strength rapidly. I let the doctor push me back into my blankets. I did not try to sit up again.

'That's better,' he said. 'We may not need the restraints after all.'

I tried to hold onto his words, but they were slippery. I slid back into ordinary nightmares. When I awoke, mid-morning, I felt relief at escaping them, and exhausted as if I had battled all night long. An orderly brought me water and I drank, relieved to find it pure water with no medicines fouling its clean taste. Dr Amicas was nowhere to be seen. The bed to my right was empty and an old woman, her face ravaged by drink, was stripping off the linens. I rolled my head the other way. Spink was there, but he slept on, oblivious to the day's light or the muted bustle around us. Several times I asked after Nate and Oron, but the nurses seemed to know no names.

'They come and go too fast,' one man told me. He scratched his whiskery cheek. 'The beds aren't even cold before we're moving someone else into them. Everyone who went to that pagan Dark Evening festival is sick. Whole city has it now, I've heard. 'Cept for me. I've always had a strong constitution, I have. And I'm a good man, blessed by the good god. I stayed at home with my own wife that night, yes I did. Let this be a lesson to you, young fellow. Those that give credence to the dark gods get paid in the dark gods' coin.'

His words rattled me. The feverish mind is susceptible to suggestion. The words danced around in my brain, eventually colliding with something Epiny had said. Or was it something I had dreamed. Something about not being able to use the magic of an older god without making ourselves vulnerable to it. I wondered if I had sinned by going to Dark

Evening, and if this was the good god's punishment of me. Weak as I was, I became maudlin and tried to say my prayers, only to keep losing my place in the verses.

Later I realized that I never saw that man again. My fever-fuddled mind noticed that the people dumping the slop buckets and bringing water to the moaning cadets no longer moved with the precise air of those trained in the military. There were more women working in the infirmary than I would have expected, and some seemed of less than sterling character. At one point, I saw one going through the pockets of a cadet's jacket as he lay unconscious and groaning in his bed. I had not the strength to lift my hand or voice. When next I opened my eyes, the cadet was covered head-to-toe with a soiled sheet. The altercation between the doctor and two old men in earth-stained clothes had awakened me.

'But he's dead!' One of the old men was insisting. 'Ain't right to let him lie there till he stinks, you know. Bad enough stink in here already.'

'Leave him!' Dr Amicas spoke forcefully but without strength. He looked years older and far more frail. 'No bodies are to be removed from this room unless I personally give the order. Cover them, if you feel you must, but let them be. I want at least twelve hours to pass between the time of death and the removal of the body.'

'But it's not right! It's not respectful!'

'I have my reasons. Leave it at that!'

The other man abruptly asked, 'Is it true what I heard? That a woman was put alive in her coffin, and by the time they heard her pounding on the lid, it was too late? She died on the dead cart, there in the cemetery?'

The doctor looked haggard. 'No body is to be removed from this ward without my consent,' he said quietly.

'Doctor,' I said hoarsely. When he did not turn to my voice, I tried to clear my throat. It did little good, but the next time I rasped out, 'Doctor!' he turned toward me.

'What is it, lad?' he asked, almost kindly.

'Did you speak to the colonel for me? Does he know that Caulder lied about me?'

He looked at me in a vague way that told me he had forgotten the matter that still obsessed me. He patted my shoulder absently. 'Caulder is very ill, lad, and the colonel is not well himself. He fears he will lose his only son. This is not a good time to talk to him about anything.'

Then down the ward, a man moaned loudly, and I heard a gush of fluid hit the floor. The doctor hurried away from me, taking all hope with him. Caulder would die. No one would ever be able to prove he had lied about me. Live or die, I was disgraced. If I died, my father could bury his shame. If I died, there could be no further dishonour for my father or me.

This time, as I sank into fever, I sank with a will. I turned my mouth determinedly from the cool cup that someone pressed to my lips. I would not drink.

I died.

I came to a place of blowing darkness and emptiness. I peered about me into a dull and perpetual evening. I wasn't alone. Others milled there, as fortuneless and disinterested as I. It was hard to make out individual features. Faces were blurred and clothing merely shadows, but here and there, a detail stood out. A woman recalled her wedding ring, and it shone golden still on an ethereal hand. A carpenter clutched his hammer. A soldier moved past me, the medals for bravery glinting on his chest. But most possessed no distinguishing features, no treasured memento of a life abandoned. I moved amongst them, with no destination or ambition other than to move. After an indeterminate time, I felt drawn in a certain direction and so I went, giving in to the summoning.

Like water seeking the path of least resistance, I joined the slow river of departing spirits. Eventually, I became aware that we were approaching a precipice. Most of the spirits drifted to the edge, lingered and then simply flowed over, vanishing from sight. I reached the perimeter and looked down. A pool of contained light, glimmering with rainbows, like oil floating on water, waited below. As I watched, a woman drew near. She looked down for a time and then stepped into the emptiness. She drifted slowly away from me, dwindling and losing substance like ink dispersing in water. I could not see if she ever reached the placid pool or not. I contemplated the pool for a time, but was overcome by a strong feeling that it was not for me. No. For me, there was something else.

I drifted along the cliff's edge, vaguely aware that I was leaving the swirling tide of spirits behind me. Eventually, I joined a separate trickle of disembodied folk. We did not speak or look at one another. The bare cliff jutted over another ravine, this one bottomless and empty. A single dead tree loomed over the gathering souls. And a primitive rope bridge, a narrow web of pale twine and twisting green vines spanned the gap. A swanneck driven into the earth secured the end of the fine yellow footrope closest to me. The hand rails were of a twisting vine that culminated in the great tree that overshadowed the cliff. A shiver both of recognition and premonition ran through me.

Soldiers had gathered to cross here. Cavalla soldiers. Cadets from the Academy, limping veterans, retired officers. They patiently waited their turns to cross. Cold wind blew past us, and brought to us the distant cries of the living. 'Papa, papa!' someone called, faint and far away. The aged man next to me bowed his head, ethereal tears streaming down his pallid face. It was his turn. He trudged on to the bridge, head bent as if to a wind I did not feel.

I saw Trist in that gathering, and Natred and Oron. They slowly milled with the others. They did not speak to me or to one another. Silent and grey, they edged forward, interested in nothing except their own slow progress toward death. I calmly realized that was our destination. Like me, they were dying, and here our spirits waited, on the teetering point between death and life. Some lingered here a long time and seemed to resist the draw. Others seemed to decide swiftly, stepping boldly onto the bridge. It was a bridge, I suddenly knew, that did not belong here. Prior to my alliance with the tree woman, it had not existed. She and I had wrought this crossing, twisting its lines from our very beings. I had taken the magic of her people into me and yielded to her the magic of mine. Of these things was this traverse made that lured the spirits of other soldiers like myself to cross. They, too, I suddenly perceived, had touched the magic of her people. 'Keep fast' they had signed over cinches, not knowing that when the time came the magic would hold them fast as well. Yet as the line of people shuffled forward, I flowed with them, unthinking and unresisting. I, too, would cross. When it came my time, I stepped past the Kidona swanneck that secured the footrope of the bridge and out onto it. I shuffled forward with the rest.

I reached the middle of the bridge before I lifted my eyes to see my destination. A dismal hell awaited us. It reminded me of the logged-off hillside I had passed on my river journey toward Old Thares, but it was not the same place. A massacred landscape of rolling hills lay before me. The sheared stumps before me dwarfed me and reordered my concept of the word 'tree'. Giants had flourished here, and were no more. The realm of the forest god had been ransacked and robbed. Cold rain was falling on it, cutting rivulets in its bare flanks. The still-smouldering mounds of slashed underbrush and branches glowed a dark, evil red. Steam and smoke rose from them. The passage of boots and teams of horses had trampled what plant growth and underbrush remained into the muddy earth. The crushed vegetation sprawled like slaughtered children. Only on the tops of the hills did trees still stand, and I knew that their reign was soon to end. A crude roadbed snaked toward them.

'Nevare!' a girl called from somewhere far behind me. 'Come back, Nevare!'

Once, I had known someone named Nevare. I turned my head slowly and looked back the way I had come. Whoever had called me was not there; she had no power to reach me. Other drifting souls were crossing the bridge behind me. Oron was on the bridge, and Natred. Still others milled on the far side. I glanced back the way I had come. I recognized Caulder and then Spink in the waiting crowd. Oh. So they, too, were dying. And they too were called to cross the bridge. I turned forward and walked on.

As the spirits ahead of me reached the stripped and barren hillside, they drifted aimlessly. Their purposelessness seemed a form of torment, as if they had had some important destination they now could not recall. Some went toward the jagged stumps of the dead trees and touched them, pressing against them as if they were doors that would not yield. Slowly those ones sank down beside the stumps, liquefying into a thick white soup of fog at the base of the chopped trees. A wisp of vapour rose from each as they vanished. I saw Sergeant Rufet go that way. He melted at the base of a stump, leaving a larger puddle than most of the others.

I saw Tree Woman then, and my other self. She stood at the crest of the hill where a line of unharvested trees remained, her back close to one of the towering giants, and looked down on us. She judged us from that vantage point, but I also knew, she could not go far from the living forest. My other self did that for her. He hunted deliberately across the bare hillside among the drifting spirits, his concentration making him far more real than the wandering wraiths. He moved purposefully, a predator among prey.

Tree Woman called encouragement down to him. 'Oh, yes, get that one, hurry before he is gone. He had far more power than he knew, far more wisdom. But he had no tree to put it in; the fools never learned to save a place to store their magic. Go, hurry, and consume his magic before it disperses. Your people have little magic to them. You will have to devour many more before you are full. Eat!'

That other self that was somehow still me in spite of the antipathy I felt toward him hurried to obey her. He had grown, and in that place of ghosts, he seemed substantial. He was round of belly, heavy of arm and leg. Leaves were his only garments. His scalp-lock had been smeared with pine pitch and plaited down his back and interwoven with green vines. He rushed to the puddle that had been Sergeant Rufet and dropped to his knees beside it. He scooped up the white liquid before it was sucked into the earth. He used no leaf cup now. Instead, my other self lowered his mouth to his cupped hands, eagerly lapping the thick porridge of what had been Rufet's soul. For a moment, I was he. I felt the stickiness on my hands and chin, and I felt myself grow stronger for having consumed his essence.

Magic. I was filling myself with magic. I would be a great man if I gained enough magic. If I filled myself with the magic, I could turn back the intruders and save The People. For that moment, his ambition was mine, and I understood it in a profound way. I was essential. I was the crossroads. In me, the magic of The People and the magic of the intruders would be combined and joined. From that combination would come the answer. Tree Woman knew that her magic alone could never stop the destroyers. It would have to be mingled with the magic of the intruders, for only a people's own magic understood that people's weaknesses well enough to defeat them. The magic of The People could hold the intruders, but it would take their own magic, the magic that lived in their bones and flesh, but never truly died, to defeat them completely and send them back whence they had come.

That was Tree Woman's ambition.

And it was mine, too, while I shared that other self's

awareness. For he loved The People as I had never loved my own kind.

That thought jolted me, and in my distant body, I felt a twitch and a gasp. I think that tiny vestige of life attracted Tree Woman's attention to me. She had been watching approvingly as my other self devoured Sergeant Rufet. Her eyes scanned the mournful crowd that pushed slowly across the bridge, cattle in a slaughter chute. Then she saw me, still standing upon the bridge. I had nearly reached her side of the crevasse, where, I now saw, that end of the bridge was secured by a cavalla sabre thrust into the stony ground. I knew the weapon. It had been mine. Dewara had shown me how to summon it to his world, and I had. Now it held the bridge fast, anchored my world to hers.

When she saw me, Tree Woman suddenly flung her arms up to the sky. She grew taller until she stood great as any live oak, and then larger still. She soared in size, to fill half the sky over the stripped hill. She pointed toward me, her fingers long as branches. 'Go back!' she commanded me in fury. 'You are not to be in this place. Go back! Inhabit the body until we are ready!'

What gave her such power over me? I felt she seized me by my hair, jerking me from the trudging queue of spirits and hurled me back across the chasm. I landed on my back, and my eyes flew open and I gasped. Wan daylight filled the room around me, pressing painfully into my eyes. Someone seized my wasted hand and gripped it so tightly the bones rubbed together. 'He's not dead! Doctor, come here! Nevare is not dead!'

The doctor's voice was more distant than Epiny's. 'I *told* you he wasn't dead. This plague sometimes mimes death. It's one of the dangers. We give up on people too soon. Get some broth into him. That's about all you can do for him. Then change the sheets on the empty cots. We'll have them filled again before evening, I fear.'

My fever dreams had been so vivid and strange that for a brief time, I simply accepted that Epiny was sitting on a stool between my bed and Spink's. She wore a stained smock over one of her ridiculous dresses. Her cheeks were red and her lips chapped. Her care-worn face and bundled-back hair made her look more womanly than I'd ever seen her. I stared at her and forgot to resist her as she spooned broth into my mouth. When I began to shiver violently, she set the cup and spoon aside and tucked my blankets more securely around me. 'Finishing school?' I said to her. My cracked lips had difficulty shaping the words.

She frowned at me momentarily, and then a sour smile came to her pinched mouth. 'Finished with that!' she said, and managed a small laugh. She leaned closer to me. 'I ran away. And I went to Dark Evening, and had a wonderful time with Spink. And then I went home and told my parents where I'd been. I knew full well my mother would tell me that I was a ruined woman, and "damaged goods", and all those other quaint phrases powerful women apply to women who don't fall under their control. But I also knew, because I'd filched the letter, that Spink's family had already made an offer for me. When she told me no decent man would ever have me now, I set it on the table before both of them, and told them that as it was the only offer they would ever get for me, it was therefore the best and they'd be wise to take it. Oh, what a terrible scene she made.' Her voice went suddenly thick and for an instant she fell silent. I knew her triumph was not free of pain. When she went on, her voice was tighter. 'My parents will have no choice except to take it. No one else will have me now. I made sure of it.'

I was puzzled. 'Spink said . . . he never met with you.'

She looked startled, then smiled. She turned away from me and reached out her hand to touch his face. 'Such a dear little lie. It probably cost him a great deal to lie to you to protect my "honour". He thinks quite highly of you, you know.

He wants our first son to be named for you. We intend to be married as soon as we can, and to start our family immediately.' And with that sentence, she suddenly sounded as girlishly domestic as any of my sisters. 'We will share a wonderful life. I can't wait. I hope we are posted on the frontier.'

'If he lives,' I said huskily. I had seen past her to the lax body in the next bed. The boyish roundness was gone from Spink's face. His mouth hung ajar and his breath came and went unevenly. Yellow crust caked around his nostrils and eyelids. He was as unlovely as anything I had ever seen.

Yet Epiny looked down at him with her heart in her eyes. She took his limp hand in hers. 'He must,' she said decidedly. 'I have gambled everything for him. If he dies and leaves me alone,' she looked at me and tried to hide her fear, 'I will have lost it all.'

I turned my head on my hot pillow. 'Uncle Sefert?'

'He isn't here.'

'But . . . how are you here, then?' The effort of that string of words set me coughing. With a practised touch that told me she had done this before, she braced my shoulders to sit me up while she offered me water from a cup. She did not answer until she let me down again.

'I came here when the reports began to reach my father of how bad things were at the Academy. Your letter came . . . the one about Dark Evening and Caulder, and being culled with only a future as a scout now. Father was furious. He set out immediately to the Academy, but at the gates he saw a yellow banner and guards turned him back. By the time he got back to the house, my mother had had messengers from her friends, warning of sickness in the city that was spreading fast. My mother declared that none of us would budge from the house until the contagion was past. She lived through the black-pox when she was a girl, and still remembers those days.

'I stood it for three days, being shut up in the house with

588

her. When she was not prophesying that we would all die of the plague, she was scolding me for my shameless behaviour, or weeping over how I had ruined my chances and soiled the family name. She vowed she'd never let me marry Spink. She said I'd have to live at home with her the rest of my life, a disgraced old maid. You cannot imagine how awful that future would be, Nevare. I tried to explain to her that she was treating me as her mother had treated her, disposing of her like a commodity, for it has become obvious to me that women are most responsible for the oppression of women in our culture. And when I tried to speak rationally to her, and point out that she was only angry because I had seized control of my own worth and traded my "respectability" for a future I wanted instead of letting her sell me off for a bride-price and a political connection, she slapped me! Oh, she was furious when I said that. Only because she recognized it was true, of course.'

She lifted a hand to her cheek, remembering the blow. 'It's her own fault for educating me,' she added regretfully. 'If she had kept me at home and ignorant as your family keeps your sisters, I'd probably have been quite tractable.'

Epiny's words washed over me like waves against a beach. The sense of them faded in and out of my mind. It took me a time to realize she had stopped talking, without, of course, answering my question. I summoned my strength. 'Why?'

'Why did I come here? I had to! There were dreadful reports that the infirmary here was overcome with so many sick cadets. After the first scare of plague passed, people began to venture out and the newspapers to print again. The Academy is still quarantined. The plague still rages here, as if it has taken root and will not be satisfied until it has consumed all of you. The city leaders decided to send everyone with the plague here, to keep it away from the general populace. The papers spoke of rows of bodies laid out on the lawns, draped only with sheets and a light fall of snow. They are burying the corpses on the grounds, with quicklime to try to control the smell.

'I came when the paper said that the doctors were allowing the bodies to simply pile up in the halls of the infirmary, and hiring beggars off the streets to fill in for the nursing assistants who themselves had fallen to the plague. I could not stand the thought of you and Spink here and sick, with no one to look after you. And I knew you were sick because no more letters came. So I left the house in the middle of the night. It took me most of the night to walk here, and then I had to get past the quarantine guards. Luckily, I found a tree with its branches leaning over the wall. I was up and over in no time. And of course, once I was inside, Dr Amicas had no choice but to let me stay. I'm as quarantined as anyone now. When I pointed out to him that there was no sense in refusing to let me help, he gave me a smock. He told me I could help until I, too, dropped dead of the plague. He's a sensible man but not a very optimistic physician, is he?'

'Go home,' I told her, bluntly. This was no place for her.

'I can't,' she said simply. 'My mother would not let me back in the door, for fear I would bring the plague with me. And under the circumstances, there is nowhere else I could go. I'm not only a disgraced woman, I'm probably a plague-carrier now.' She seemed quite cheery about both fates. Then her voice dropped and she added soberly, 'Besides. You need me here. Both of you, but especially you. Whatever it was that hovered over you the last time I saw you has grown more powerful. When I thought you were dead . . . that was what horrified me. You had no breath I could detect, no pulse at all. You – now do not laugh at me – your aura had faded to where I could not detect it. But the aura of that, that other that is within you, had grown stronger. It raged about you like fire devouring a log. I was so frightened for you. You need me to protect you from it.'

590

No, I didn't. That was the one thing I was sure of. For Epiny to come here, at risk to herself, was the only thing that could have made me feel worse. Bad enough that helping Caulder had condemned me to disgrace. I could die, and my shame would die with me. She would have to live with her dishonour, as would my uncle. A lingering memory of myself as I was in that other world wafted through my mind, like half-recalled perfume. I was suddenly certain that whatever Tree Woman was, I did not want Epiny near her.

She was staring at me, round eyed. I saw then that she was not well. Little crusts were starting at the corners of her eyes. I should have known from her cracked lips and her red cheeks. She already burned with the fever of the plague. Dr Amicas had been right again.

She reached timorously to touch my head, and then jerked back her fingers as if scalded. 'It comes and goes,' she whispered. 'It shimmers around you, weak and then strong. Now it glows above your head. Like flame shows through a sheet of paper before it bursts through and consumes it.'

As she spoke those words, I could feel him. The other self had grown strong. I suddenly saw with his eyes. Epiny was a sorceress, a mistress of the iron magic. He looked at her and gloated, for powerful as she was, she was doomed. As clearly as I could see Epiny herself, I saw the tie of green vine that bound her wrist to Spink's. I recognized Tree Woman's 'keep fast' charm.

As my true self, I mustered my will. I reached for Epiny's free wrist and seized it. I pulled on her as she pulled back from me with a little squeak of alarm. 'I have to free you!' I whispered hoarsely. 'Before it's too late.' With my other hand, I tried to make the 'loose' sign over the twist of vine that bound her. Once the making of that sign had been my betrayal of my people. Now it would free Epiny. But my other self was too strong for me. I could lift my hand, but my fingers would not move as I commanded. He laughed with my mouth, cracking my dry lips.

'Nevare! Let me go! You're hurting me!'

At Epiny's cry, Spink took an uneven gasp of air. Then he sighed it out. Distracted, Epiny turned to him. 'Spink? Spink!'

I waited. The moments ticked past. He made no indrawn breath. Then, as he gave a final sigh, I heard the death rattle in Spink's throat. Epiny sank to her knees on the floor between our beds. I still gripped her wrist. She didn't seem to notice. 'No,' she said quietly. 'Oh, please, Spink, no! Don't leave me. Don't leave me.'

He is on the bridge now. I thought faintly. My mouth was no longer mine to speak with. My other self had that now. I wanted to call to Epiny for help. Now that his taking of my body was real, I would have claimed help from anyone who could offer it.

But Epiny did not even look at me. She had begun to rock back and forth, her free hand cupped over her mouth. Her keening still escaped between her fingers. Tears flowed down her face and over her fingers.

I knew when Spink's spirit left his body. I did not see it go. But I saw Epiny suddenly sit up straight and look at her free hand. I saw the vine tighten on her wrist. Then, as the vine disappeared as if pulled through in invisible wall, Epiny went white. Her mouth gaped and did not close. Linked to Spink by Tree Woman's 'keep fast' charm, her spirit was being pulled into death along with his.

Slowly she collapsed to the floor and became still.

I fought my other self then. Fought him, as I had not before, with fury and hatred and disgust for all he had made me. I tried over and over to make the 'loose' sign over their bodies. He kept me from it. To the nurses running toward us, I must have appeared a mad man, holding tight to Epiny's wrist as if I could hold her back from death, all the while grunting and shaking my free hand in the air as I tried to force my fingers to move as I wished them.

I suddenly recalled the scout's bluff, all those many years ago. I let my control of the hand go lax, as if surrendering. And when my other self lowered his guard against me, I made a sign over my own grip on Epiny's wrist. Not 'loose'.

'Keep fast!' I managed to say through my cracked lips. And then my body, too, crumpled to the floor as Epiny's departing spirit pulled me after her.

Closing my eyes in that world was opening them to the bridge and its moving morass of the dying. Spink was on the bridge and had nearly completed his crossing. Epiny floated above him like a tethered bird. She was terrified, and she fought the bond that joined them. Spink did not even notice her. He moved forward, a step at a time.

The bond that linked me to Epiny was thinner and more tenuous. My charm did not have the strength of Tree Woman's spell. Here, at least, my actions were my own. 'Loose!' I said, and made the sign. I found myself free of Epiny, but dead all the same. I was suddenly on the bridge myself. The gathered crowd hemmed me in and blocked my progress. It edged forward, a slow step at a time. I fought the stolid detachment that wished to take me, fought the magic of the disease that had wasted my body. I had come here to do something. Unlike these others, I had willed myself here. I elbowed and shoved my way through the clustering souls.

It seemed monstrous to me that a plague could be a summoning, that the tree woman had sent this sickness upon us to work magic against us. Bad enough that we should die of it; far worse that our deaths should bring us to a place that our beliefs had not made! This was not the sweet rest the good god promised his followers. It seemed cruel that those who had faithfully believed should be deprived of it.

Determinedly I tried to push my way forward through the

crowding souls. 'Stop!' I called aloud. 'Spink! Come back!'
He did not heed me. Over his head, Epiny floated, moaning
and tugging at the binding on her wrist. Spink left the bridge,
stepped into the tree woman's domain and began his slow
drift up the desecrated hillside. But at my cry, other spectral
faces had turned to me, halting on the bridge to look back at
me. I pleaded with them. 'Come back. That place is not for
you. Return to your bodies. Go back to your loved ones.'

A few wraiths paused, looking puzzled, as if my words
had stirred their already fading memories. But after the brief
consideration of me, they turned back to their sluggish passage. I had no patience with their delaying me. Heedless of
the emptiness below me, I pushed around and past the
trudging souls. On the far side, from her post at the top of
the hill near the line of trees, the tree woman pointed at me.
I feared she would fling me back into my body, and only let
me return to death after Spink and Epiny had perished forever. I seized the guide ropes of the bridge with both my
hands and held on tightly, determined to resist.

A strange thing happened to me then. I could feel the
magic coursing through the bridge, and recalled that it was
made as much from me as it was from Tree Woman. I recognized the yellow strands that were part of its weaving;
they were my own hair. I sensed I could draw strength from
it, if I only knew how. That other self would have known
how. But I did not, and so I could only hold tight to it and
resist her in that way. I did sense that while I held to the
bridge, she could not expel me from her realm. I began to
make my torturous way across the bridge, slowly moving
my grip, hand over hand, to cross it. I barely noticed the
evanescent beings who gave way to my determined crossing.
I passed them, and crept ever closer to my nemesis. 'Spink!'
I shouted again to my friend as I saw him toiling up the hill,
ever closer to Tree Woman. 'Turn back! Bring Epiny back
with you, to life! Don't drag her into death with you.'

Spink halted. He turned. Light flickered a moment in his hollow eyes, and for the first time, I saw something that sparkled silver on his chest. Her silly whistle hung there, the lover's token that he would take even into the after-life with him. He took a step back toward the bridge and my heart soared.

My other self suddenly reappeared on Tree Woman's hilltop. He did not move slowly at all. He strode deliberately down the hill, closing the distance between him and Spink. His jaw was clenched, his eyes furious. Tree Woman shouted at him.

'Go back! I can deal with him! Go back! You must keep the body. You must inhabit it to keep it alive.'

He was as stubborn as I was. I had angered him. I could feel within my own breast the echo of his anger. He ignored Tree Woman as he hurried down the hill to take his personal revenge on me. First, he would devour my friends.

I shouted frantically at Spink as I pushed my way through the slowly moving spirits on the bridge. It was useless. After a moment or two of staring at me, recognition and purpose faded from Spink's expression. He turned as if he had heard someone calling him and began to make his way up the hill toward my traitor self. Spink walked as if captured by deep thought, not even appearing to see where he was going. Epiny was towed along with him. Her face was clenched in irrational terror. 'Epiny!' I finally thought to shout at her. 'Epiny, hold Spink back. Pull him back; go back over the bridge.'

My words seemed to reach her. Her frightened eyes darted to me and then down to Spink. She was as insubstantial as a butterfly here, a spirit caught between two worlds and belonging to neither. Yet she struggled. She called his name and pulled on the vine that bound them together, trying to gain his attention and bring him back.

My other self scowled. He lifted his eyes to me and our

gazes locked. He hated me. He lifted a hand and made a sign, a sign I knew well. 'Keep fast' he signed at the other spectres on the bridge, and they halted where they were, blocking me.

Caught between life and death, on the bridge between the worlds, the phantoms froze still, unyielding to my shoving, and trapping me in their midst. I pushed at them, frantically struggling, yet ever mindful that I must keep one hand touching that hellish bridge. Ironically, it was Caulder who immediately blocked my way. His features were as sullen in death as they had been in life. With my free hand I seized him and shook him. 'Get out of my way! Go back!' I shouted at him.

And to my horror, a glint of awareness came to his eyes. He opened his mouth to speak to me, but no words came. Terror filled his childish face, and insubstantial tears welled in his eyes, to trickle down his translucent face. It horrified me and drove from me all the hatred and dislike I'd harboured for him. I lifted my hand. 'Loose!' I said to him as I made the sign. 'Go back. Go back to your life.'

His gaze met mine, and he blinked as if waking from a dream. Then, with a soundless sob, he turned and tried to push past me, to get back across the bridge. The spirit behind me blocked his way. I turned to him. He was a craggy old man in ragged clothes, probably a cavalla veteran living out his last days on the streets of Old Thares. 'Loose,' I told him gently, and signed the charm. The old man turned back. I lifted my hand higher and waved it, making the charm over all the spirits halted on the bridge. 'Loose!' I shouted at them. 'Go back.' At my word, every spectre stirred, turned, and began that journey back. I fought my way forward past those who now sought to go the other way. Like a fish battling its way upstream, I shoved a passage through them, until I reached the other side.

I came to the end of the bridge, to the sabre that anchored

it to that place. I looked up at the tree woman. She returned my gaze with equanimity. As surely as I knew anything, I knew that she waited for me to step off the bridge. Once my feet touched her world, I would be in her power. She would be rid of me. And that piece of me that she had stolen, my other self, was still intent on devouring my friend.

Spink was walking steadily toward his doom, trudging up the muddy and ravaged slope, unmindful of what he left behind. Epiny had come to her senses. She spoke to him and fought him, but he moved inexorably on. Somehow that made it more terrible, not less. My other self moved forward to meet him. His hands were already cupped, ready to receive Spink's essence.

Epiny stepped between them. She no longer fought her bond. She used it to hold herself in place, between Spink and the being that threatened him.

She looked strange in this place. She was a flickering flame of a girl, less substantial than the ghost she tried to protect. I saw my other self snatch at her, and then turn in surprise to his mentor when his hands passed right through her. I understood. Epiny had known the 'keep fast' charm, but she had not used it daily as Spink and I had. Their magic did not hold her here; only her attachment to Spink. My cousin seemed unaware of me as I hesitated on the bridge. Instead, she shrieked 'Nevare! Please, be yourself! Help us!' at that other creature who wore my features. The look of betrayal on her face as he again snatched at her burned me. She could do nothing here for Spink or me. She would end her existence thinking I had betrayed her.

I reached for the earlier connection I'd felt with my other self. I could feel the magic he'd consumed swelling inside him. He had grown in power and ability and knowledge under Tree Woman's tutelage. I despised what she had made of that part of me. He was her creature, a traitor to me and mine. He loved what she loved, and would do anything within his power to protect it, with no thought of what it would cost me.

But I was not her creature. And in some strange way, the two parts of me were still bound. I dared not leave the bridge to help them. If I did so, Tree Woman could eject me from this world, and then deal with my friends with no interference.

I focused all my being on that other part of myself. Awareness of him slipped and squirmed through my mind. In flashes, I saw through his eyes, tasted the sweetness that still lingered in his mouth, and felt, too, that eagerness that made him grope toward Spink. My tongue licked his lips. My fingers felt the coolness that was evanescent Epiny as his hands passed through her vaporous form. I could share his awareness but I could not control him.

Epiny battered at Spink, trying to push him back from that world, back onto the bridge. They fought like colliding shadows, darkening and merging where they touched. She raged and wept as she struggled to turn him back, the reality of her cries too harsh and loud in the ethereal place. My other self beckoned imperiously to Spink, and he wavered forward another step, moving right through Epiny. She screamed then, a sound of despair such as I'd never heard before.

I do not know if the sound moved me to greater strength, or if it unnerved that other me enough to break his focus. For a moment, my awareness of my other self was complete. I knew him totally, and as he recognized that, he committed a fatal mistake. His hands moved to protect his weakness from me. His hands covered his waxed and braided scalp-lock.

He fought me for control of his hands. I tried to grab the ridiculous tail of hair, but he closed the hands into fists. Frustrated, I pounded at his head with the hands, but could not deal him a blow of any strength, nor force the fingers to open. Spink had drifted past us now, moving toward a tree stump. Epiny floated after him. She fluttered her hands at his face but could not halt him. His eyes seemed sorrowful, as if he sensed her, but the expression on his face didn't change. Sudden inspiration struck me. My other self controlled the hands, but he had done nothing to guard his voice from me. I made him speak.

'Epiny!' I cried. 'Pull out my hair! It will free me. Rip out this topknot!'

She heard what I said. I feared that she would think it odd that I bade her attack me, but without hesitation she obeyed me. Or attempted to obey. She flew at my other self. Her assault on him was as damaging as a flickering light. She seized at his topknot of hair, but it did not even stir as her hands passed through it. In this world, she was the insubstantial spirit, powerless against what was physical here. He laughed then, loud and delighted, and reached through Epiny for Spink.

Futile as it was, I knew I would challenge him. The only weapon to hand was the cavalla sabre thrust into the earth and securing the footrope of the bridge. It was the same weapon Dewara had once bid me use on Tree Woman. How I wished I had heeded him! I set my hand to it and with a tremendous pull, tore it free of the earth and stone that clasped it. I intended to make a futile charge at my other self. I did not doubt that Tree Woman would effortlessly fling me back, but I had to try.

The moment my hand jerked the blade from the ground, a peculiar thing happened. As Tree Woman gave a great shout of dismay, I felt strength shoot through me. Iron magic. The magic of my people was in my hand. Tree Woman had let me bring it here, for her own ends. Now I would use it for mine. As the secured rope sprang free, my other self gave a cry of dismay. He lifted his hands to his scalp-lock, for it had come loose and was unbraiding itself.

In that second, I perceived all. I turned back to the bridge. The golden threads of my hair that had twined around the tree woman's vines were coming free. They looked almost alive as they uncoiled from the greenery and drifted away in the abyss below. The bridge began to fail from this end. Almost all of the spirits that had turned back had now safely reached the other side. I did not know what they would do there; I did not know if they would return to life or seek the peaceful pool that the other spirits had entered. All I knew was that I would destroy the crossing I had inadvertently created. No others of my fellows would be doomed to come to Tree Woman's world. I turned back to the bridge and swung the sabre furiously, hacking through the vines that made up the other supports. Tree Woman screamed, in pain or fury.

As the bridge parted, unravelling, I heard my other self shriek. I turned back to him, my iron magic heavy and cold in my hand. He sagged like an emptying wine-skin, a pale vapour exiting from the spot where his scalp-lock had been. My features faded from his softening face. Tree Woman screamed and strained toward him, but could not reach him. She could not leave the line of living trees. He sagged into a mound of clay and leaves. I felt oddly stronger. Something that had been missing from me for a long time had been restored.

Epiny clung desperately to Spink, her slender, diaphanous arms locked around his neck. 'Nevare!' She looked from me to the heap on the ground and back again. I saw her struggle to understand and then discard that for a more immediate fear. 'The bridge is gone. What will become of us?' she wailed. Spink's face remained impassive.

'Hold tight to him!' I told her. Sword at the ready, I toiled up the hill toward her. As I advanced on Tree Woman, I warned her, 'Send them back!'

She laughed at me. Her laugh was earthy, musical and rich. To my dismay, I loved it. I loved it, and I loved all she represented. The wilds lands and the forests and the great

600

trees were in her eyes. I loved all of her. I suddenly perceived that she was not old, but eternal. She held out her arms to me, and I longed to rush into her embrace. Tears came to my eyes as I spoke. 'Let my friends go. Or I'll kill you.'

She shook her head, and wind rustled through leafy tree-tops. 'Do you think you can kill me here, in my own world? With what, soldier's boy? That little twig of iron? You stand in my world, in the heart of my magic!' She bent down toward me, and suddenly she was tree and woman, all in one. Her leaves rustled as she swayed down at me. Her branches reached to draw me to her.

'You said it yourself!' My voice came shrill. '"Magic touches back." You brought my magic here, through me, and used it. Used it just as I used the magic of your kind. Just as you gained a hold on me when you used my magic, so I think mine has taken power over you!'

On my final word, I sprang to my attack. A sabre is not an axe. It has a cutting edge, but for flesh, not bark and wood. I put all I had into the swing, expecting the shock of hard contact. I thought I had a chance of hurting her. Instead, it was like cutting butter. My sabre slid through her, and then caught and stuck. I let go of it. It had opened a horizontal gash in her soft belly, in her trunk, in all that she was. She screamed, and it cracked the sky. Golden sap, warm as blood, flowed from her wound and onto the earth. She fell backwards from me, just as a tree would have fallen if chopped through the trunk. When she hit the ground, the earth split. Light burst up from it. The goddess of the world had fallen at my feet, my sabre still stuck in the stump of her body. I stood over her, looking down in shock at what I had wrought. I had triumphed. My heart was breaking.

Her eyes, deep as the forest, flickered open. She made a final gesture at me. As her hand fell, I was flung from her world.

TWENTY FOUR

Vindication

I returned to my life slowly, almost reluctantly, over a period not of days, but of weeks. Dr Amicas told me that my case of the plague was unique; that I had passed from the Speck plague into a brain fever that had sent me into a coma. I did not one day 'awake' from it. Rather, I slowly drifted out of it and back into my life. The doctor was surprised to see me live, let alone slowly recover my faculties. By the time I was aware of myself, I found I had been moved to a comfortable room in the guest wing of my uncle's house. Nonetheless, the good doctor came to visit me often during the days of my convalescence. I think he enjoyed seeing me, for I was one of his few successes in a season of terrible failures.

A hired nurse cared for me at first. Either she did not know anything or she had been told to say nothing that I might find distressing. I know that some days of awareness passed before I came to myself enough to know that I should worry about my family and friends. To my halting questions she would only reply that I should not fret, soon I would be better and be able to get about and discover things for myself. If I'd been able to get out of bed, I think I would have throttled her.

But I could not. I suffered a general weakness in my limbs and an aggravating confusion with my speech. When the doctor visited me, I was able to convey both my frustration and my fear to him. He patted my hand condescendingly

602

and told me that I was fortunate, that after a fever such as mine, some men awoke half-wits. He told me to work on my speech, perhaps by reading aloud or reciting familiar poetry. Then he left me and I had to deal with the hired nurse again.

I did not see much of my uncle. Considering the trouble I had brought into his life, I was surprised that he took me into his home at all. My aunt never visited me. Uncle Sefert did not visit me often, and his visits were short. I could not blame him. He was still kind to me, but in the new lines in his face I could see that Epiny's impulsive act had cost him much in sleep and worry, not to mention heartbreak. Under the circumstances, I kept my concerns to myself. He had enough burdens of his own. I would not tell him that I had been culled, and that as soon as I was well enough to travel, I'd be taking Sirlofty and heading home. I tried several times to write to my father, but my wandering handwriting looked like the scrawl of an irresponsible boy or a depraved old man, and my hand always grew too weary to hold a pen long before I found the words to explain to my father how I had fallen. My nurse often exhorted me to take hope for the future in how the good god had preserved me, but most days it seemed to me that continuing my life was the cruellest jest the good god could have played upon me. Whenever I looked at the days of my life that stretched before me, I felt discouraged. What was I to do with them all, now that I'd ruined my prospects?

Epiny herself came at least once a day, to chatter at me until I was exhausted. She herself had been ill for several days with a much milder case of the plague. During recovery, when she had still been too weak to resist him, the doctor had sternly and firmly returned her to her family home. Her mother had reluctantly received her, she claimed.

To me, she seemed completely recovered now. She read the worried letters that my family had sent to me, and took it upon herself to send replies to them, assuring them of my steady

603

recovery and fond thoughts of them. She did not comment that there were no letters from Carsina. That was a small mercy. She told me that during the days of my coma, she had sat by my bedside and read poetry to me for hours on end, hoping that I would take comfort from the sound of a familiar voice and that it would help me to recover. I don't know that it aided my recovery, but it possibly accounted for several rather peculiar dreams from that haunted wandering of my mind.

In her own careless way, she tried to be considerate of me. She made an effort to always be cheery and pleasant in the time she spent with me, but sometimes the rims of her eyes were pink, as if she had been crying, and she now seemed older than her years rather than younger. She wore sedate women's clothing, and kept her hair up and pinned in a style so tidy that it bordered on severe. I think the conflict with her parents over the choice she had made weighed on her more than she wished me to know.

Epiny waited some time before she judged me well enough to have news. She was worse than the hired nurse. She nearly drove me mad by changing the subject whenever I asked for tidings of my friends. One day, when she had provoked me to a coughing fit by refusing to answer my repeated questions, she relented. She shut the door, sat down by my bedside, took my hand in hers and proceeded to sketch in the ten days that had vanished from my life.

She began with what she called 'the mundane'. Spink had survived and was recovering, but the plague had taken its toll on him. He was thin, wasted to bones, and still so weak that he could not stand. He remained in the infirmary. She had not been able to see him, but was able to send and receive letters from him. Her father had forbidden her mother from blocking them. The letters he sent to her were short. His joints were swollen, and even small movements were painful to him. Dr Amicas had told him regretfully that he would probably never have a military career of any kind, for even after full recovery, he doubted that Spink would have much stamina. My friend could look forward to life as an invalid, depending on his brother for sustenance and keep.

Epiny, of course, did not put it that way. She blithely informed me that as soon as Spink felt well enough for the ceremony, they would have a small wedding, and she would then join him for the journey to his home. She had already been in correspondence with his mother and sisters and found them, 'Delightfully modern. They are capable women, Nevare, and I cannot tell you how I will welcome being in their company. It is a great pity that his family cannot afford the journey to witness our wedding. I am sure it would do my mother great good to see that women can do more than gossip, snipe, and plot their daughters' marriages to their best political advantage. And I am sure it would reassure Papa greatly if he could see that I am going to a worthwhile productive life, rather than being sentenced to endless embroidery, small talk, and child-bearing.'

'Epiny,' I ventured to ask her. 'Are you certain you will be happy in such a situation? You will not truly be mistress of your own household. Rather, you and Spink will have to live on his brother's charity. You speak of his mother and sisters doing useful work. I am sure that the harsh demands of frontier life will be taxing to you. And your circumstances will be far reduced from what you are accustomed to. Perhaps you should think carefully before you plunge yourself and Spink into a life of unhappiness.'

I meant my words well, but she wilted before them. She shook her head at me and tears welled in her eyes. 'Must everyone harp on what I already know? I know it will be hard, Nevare, far harder than I first imagined when I cast my lot with Spink's. But I think I can do it. No. I *know* that I *must* do it, and therefore I will find the strength to do it.' She clenched her hands together in her lap. 'I know you think I am impulsive and will live to regret my decision. I know you think I am weak. Perhaps I am, and perhaps I will be miserable. But I know that no matter how hard it is, I will never return here and beg my parents to take me back under their roof.' She lifted her eyes to meet mine and I saw an angry determination burning there.

'The times are changing, Nevare. It is time for men as well as women to assert that they will make the decisions that forever change their lives for themselves. I know that no matter how hard this goes with me, Purissa will see what I have done, and perhaps take strength from it when her time comes to defy tradition and live her own life.'

'Will you tell her if you are unhappy?' I asked cautiously. I was not certain that what she was doing was a good example to set for her young sister.

Epiny straightened her back and squared her shoulders. 'I take responsibility for my own happiness or unhappiness, Nevare. Every morning, when I look at Spink, I will see the man I chose above all others. And he will know the same of me. Will you have that comfort when you look at Carsina after a quarrel or a difficult day? Or will you have to wonder if she would be there if her parents hadn't decided for her?'

She was edging too close to a subject I had lately found painful. I had no future with Carsina. Slowly I was admitting that to myself. When I'd been discharged from the Academy, I'd forfeited her. I shifted the topic abruptly. 'Can you tell me about my friends at the Academy besides Spink? How are they doing?'

'Are you sure you are well enough for such news?' she asked me. I immediately knew it would be far worse than I had thought.

'Perhaps you should let me be responsible for my own happiness or unhappiness and just tell me,' I said, speaking more sharply than I intended.

She looked at the floor and then back at me. 'Spink knew you would want to know. He told me so the last time I visited him. So he told me the names of the boys in your patrol who died and of some others you would want to know about. I wrote them down because I knew I could never remember all those names.' She reached into her dress pocket and took out a much-folded slip of paper. As she opened it, my heart sank. 'Are you ready?' she asked me.

I clenched my teeth to refrain from shouting at her. 'Yes. Please, Epiny, just tell me.'

'Very well.' She cleared her throat, coughed, and then cleared it again. When she read the names, her voice was tight and choked. Tears brimmed and then ran down her cheeks as she recited the names. 'Natred. Oron. Caleb. Sergeant Rufet. Corporal Dent. Cadet Captain Jeffers. Captain Maw. Captain Infal. Lieutenant Wurtam.'

The first three names stunned me. I lay back on my pillows, and as she went on, I felt each name like a fist blow to my heart. So many dead! So many!

'I'll get you some water,' Epiny said abruptly. 'I've been a fool. Father said you were too weak yet for such tidings. I judged that knowing these things would be less trying for you than living in suspense. I was wrong, and now you shall have a relapse and undo all your healing and my father will once more berate me about acting on my own with too little experience of the real world.'

I sipped from the glass she had poured from my bedside ewer. When I could speak, I said, 'No. You were right, Epiny. Like you, I hate it when people try to make decisions for me. Tell me the rest. Now.'

'Are you certain?' She took the glass from my shaking hand and set it on my sick table.

'Very certain. Tell me.'

She again consulted the page she held. 'Of your other fellows, Kort never caught the plague. Rory had only a mild case. Trist took sick and recovered, but like Spink, he will never be as hearty as he was. Spink thinks they will send him home. Gord and his family have still not returned to the city, so they have missed the plague. Colonel Stiet and his son Caulder were both sick for days. Both will recover but the colonel has given up commanding the Academy. Control of it has passed back to Colonel Rebin. Spink has heard rumours that Rebin is glad to have it back and intends to 'put his house in order' as soon as most of his cadets have recovered. There were deaths throughout the city from plague, but it was worst within the Academy walls. My father says that it has depleted the ranks of up-and-coming officers substantially. He thinks that many soldier sons will now forego the Academy and simply purchase commissions as they used to, for the competition for positions will not be as fierce as it was.' She cleared her throat.

'Spink spoke about that, too. He says that the distinctions between Old Nobles' and New Nobles' sons have worn thin, for the sickness made all of them comrades for a time. And he also says that politically, the Academy can no longer afford to be choosy about students. He has already heard rumours that Rebin will recall many of the culled cadets from previous years, to try to rebuild a corps of officers for the future. Spink says there is talk around the Academy that if it does not take action to demonstrate that Academy-trained officers are superior to those who buy their positions, the existence of the Academy itself may be called into question. It is not a cheap institution to run.'

I was silent for a time, absorbing that. It was strange to hear Epiny speak so knowledgably of the Academy and the long-term effects of the plague upon our military structure. I reflected regretfully that she would have made a good cavalla wife. 'Spink must be heartbroken to have his career cut short before it started,' I said to myself.

'It might be easier for all of us if he were,' Epiny said. 'No. He is not heartbroken. He is furious whenever anyone suggests that he will not recover enough to serve. He will go home, as he has small choice in that. But he says that he will recover his health, and when he does, he is determined to return to the Academy. He is a soldier son and will be a soldier, despite what others may do in this difficult time.'

'What others do?' I asked.

'Oh. I forget that you have been isolated. The Academy suffered, but so did Old Thares. A number of noble families lost their heir sons. In some cases, the lord died as well. The hole that creates in the Council of Lords is a gaping one. With the support of the priesthood, many families are naming a younger son as heir rather than bringing in a cousin to inherit. It has caused quite a bit of discord, for many a hopeful cousin is seeing an inheritance snatched right out of their jaws. But in every case that has been challenged, the priests have supported the families in naming a younger son as first son.'

'That's insane!' I could not believe what I was hearing. 'It flies in the face of the good god's will! How can the priests allow it?'

'My father says we must trust that the priests know the will of the good god. But I think—' Epiny halted suddenly, and looked uncomfortable.

'What do you think?' I prodded her.

'I think that, perhaps, large donations were made to various priestly orders. And in a number of cases, priest sons have been elevated to the status of heirs. They will, by a special allowance, serve in both capacities in their lifetimes.' She frowned to herself for a moment. Thoughtfully she took up her whistle and put it in her mouth, much as a cogitating man might light his pipe. She breathed through it, whistling softly, and then spoke around it, 'I think it might be a matter of influence and power and wealth. Even priests are human, Nevare.'

I did not like to think about the implications of that. I gestured at the whistle. 'I thought you had given that annoying thing to Spink.'

She gave another long low whistle through it, and then spat it out. She smiled at me oddly and then leaned closer to my bed. 'And why did you think that?' she whispered to me.

'Because I saw him wearing it,' I replied in annoyance at her sudden air of mystery, and then suddenly recalled where I had seen him wearing it.

'I wondered how much you recalled,' she said softly.

I don't know what you are talking about. That was what I wanted to say, and yet I could not bring my lips to shape the words. That denial, I suddenly knew, was a legacy of the division that Tree Woman had inflicted on me. I *did* know exactly what she was talking about. I was still reconciling the pieces of myself. Sometimes I woke deep in mourning that I had killed my lover and mentor. At other times, I almost wished I could believe it was all fever dream and hallucination.

Epiny smiled sorrowfully at my silence. 'Is it still so hard for you to admit it, Nevare?' she asked me. 'Then I will not force it from you. I will only say that you saved not only yourself, but also Spink and me. It was when you acted that I suddenly perceived that some items were links between this world and that one. For you, it was your hair and your sabre. When you cut the bridge, you cut her off from our world, didn't you? My task was different. Spink and I were already bound. I had to seize and hold fast to the link that bound us to this world. In our case, it was the imaginary whistle he wore in his mind. He held fast to it in that world, and when I came out of my trance, I was gripping the chain around my own neck. But Spink had come with me. I sat up from the floor and discovered, to my great delight, that both of you were breathing, though not well. The nurses were shocked. It was the second time they had declared you dead, you know. I think you had remained longer in the land of the dead than either of you could have survived in ordinary circumstances.' She leaned closer to add, 'I think you did more than you intended. Prior to our return, several cadets

610

in your ward also gasped in breath at almost the same time. I think your severing of the bridge sent the souls on it back to their bodies.'

'That's preposterous!' And I truly did believe it unlikely. But I smiled at her as I said so.

She did not reply for a moment. Then she leaned forward and before I could react, she gave the hair on top of my head a firm tug. 'Not as preposterous as this!' she told me. 'The scar was gone, Nevare, when you awoke. I noticed it immediately. What she took from you, you took back. And now, when I look at you, I see no trace of her aura. Only that your own has grown much stronger. And yes, stranger.' She leaned back and looked at me so consideringly that I almost expected she would tell me how much I'd grown. 'Definitely a strange aura. But then, you are a strange person and you definitely had a strange experience. Or we did.'

I gave in and asked her. 'Does Spink remember any of that?'

She pursed her lips. 'Not that he admits. I wonder about it. I wonder what any of the others on that bridge remember— Oh!' She thrust her hand back into her pocket. 'I nearly forgot this. It is from Caulder. It came for you two days ago. I think perhaps he had a very strange dream that he wishes to discuss with you.' She smiled cattily as she handed it to me.

I took the envelope from her, noting that the seal on it was broken. 'You already read it, didn't you?'

'Of course. As it was from Caulder, I doubted that it could be extremely personal. And I had to read it, to be able to judge whether or not to pass it on to you. But I think you are as ready for it as you will ever be.'

The note inside was on rich and heavy paper, marred only by Caulder's childish handwriting. 'Please come to visit me at your earliest convenience. I have something for you.'

I tossed it down upon my bedding. 'The only thing that I could possibly want from him is an apology, and I very much doubt that I shall get it.'

'I should have thought you would have said you wished him to tell his father the truth. If only Caulder would tell the truth, his father might still rescind your dishonourable discharge.'

I looked at her speechlessly. To hear those two words spoken aloud were akin to having them branded into me. That she knew and had spoken it aloud made the reality freshly horrible to me. When my shocked silence grew long, she confided calmly, 'Well, I found the paper when I hung up your uniform jacket. Someone had to see to your things; some of the nurses they brought in to the infirmary during the worst of the crisis were thieves and worse. They stole anything they could carry off, including the blankets that covered the dead. It was horrible. So I gathered up your things to keep them safe and—'

'And naturally you went through my pockets.' I was offended.

'Yes. Naturally,' she retorted. 'So that if there was anything of value, I could be sure to keep it safe. The only thing I found was that horrid discharge paper. So I burned it, of course.'

'You burned my discharge papers!'

'Of course.' She was so calm.

'Why?'

She shrugged one shoulder and did not meet my gaze. Then she turned back, looked me in the eye and said flatly, 'I'm not a fool. I knew Colonel Stiet was very ill. I saw that those papers were dated the same day that the plague broke out. I judged that in the midst of all that, there was a chance he hadn't recorded his tantrum anywhere else. And if he died, and there was no record of it, then I saw no reason for you to be burdened with it. So I burned it. No one else saw me do it. And as Spink had not mentioned it to me, I judged you had not told anyone else about it, either.'

She sat back in her chair and folded her hands in her lap.

She looked pleased with herself. Then she gave a little sigh. 'Unfortunately, he didn't die. But we can hope that with all else that has happened, he won't have time to trouble you.'

'I don't know what to say,' I said at last.

'Then say nothing!' she advised me insistently. 'Nothing at all. When you are well, go back to the Academy. Resume your life as if it had never happened. I really doubt that Stiet will take time to impart details like that to his successor. Ignore it. And if anyone is stupid and vicious enough to attempt to send you away from the Academy, you should fight it. Tooth and claw.'

I scarcely heard it. I was still mulling over what she had suggested. 'Just ignore it? That seems . . . dishonest.'

'No, you dolt. Dishonest is a spoiled child lying about you and having you dishonourably discharged from the Academy.' She stood suddenly and then shocked me by leaning down to kiss me on the brow. 'That is quite enough for one day. Think about what I've said, and then sleep on it. And for once, do what is sensible.'

She did not give me a chance to agree with her. She walked to the window, drew the curtains to put the room into darkness, and left me there. I didn't sleep. I thought it over. I calculated my odds like a gambler. Sergeant Rufet had known, but he was dead. The doctor knew, but as he had not mentioned it, perhaps he had forgotten my words to him. Colonel Stiet knew, of course, as did Caulder. But would they linger at the Academy or would they swiftly depart and allow Colonel Rebin to move into the living quarters? I tempted myself with the notion that perhaps the colonel had been too distracted to note my discharge down into the daily log of the Academy. Perhaps with all that had happened, he would forget the incident of his son's drunkenness.

Or perhaps not. I decided sternly that it was a foolish thing to hope for. I also decided I would be equally foolish not to attempt to ignore the discharge. What more, after all, could Colonel Stiet do to me than what he had already done? And so as the days passed and I grew stronger, I kept Epiny's counsel and did not speak of the discharge to anyone.

Perhaps the slim hope I felt speeded my recovery. A day came when I could rise from my bed without assistance. The doctor began to allow me regular food instead of the bland soups I'd been subsisting on. My appetite returned with a vengeance, and to my nurse's delight, I ate heartily every meal and put on flesh. I had lost muscle during my wasting illness, and of course that would have to be rebuilt by strenuous exercise. I was not yet up to it, but after another week had passed, I was able not only to stroll through my uncle's gardens with Purissa but also to ride sedately with Epiny in the park. I did not even much mind that she assigned me her docile mare and rode Sirlofty.

My uncle's home was not a happy place in those days. I did not take my meals with the family, but ate alone in my rooms, glad that I had the excuse of my continuing convalescence. My uncle said little of the misery that Epiny had caused her family, but she spoke of it frankly with me, and at greater length than I enjoyed. I was sorry to have been the indirect cause of my uncle's tribulations, and yet in a quiet corner of my soul, I rejoiced that at least Spink would have the joy of a wife who doted on him. I feared his life would offer him little else in the way of consolation.

The wedding was small and so subdued as to feel almost dreary. Spink's older brother had made the journey to witness the ceremony, and also, as Epiny so crudely put it, 'to pay for the bride'. I am sure his family had offered what it could but it was not a substantial amount and of influence they had even less to barter. I went and stood up with Spink's brother and listened to the priest say the words that bound them to one another. Epiny's dress was simple as was the lace veil she wore, and yet it still looked extravagant next to Spink in his even more ill-fitting uniform. Worse, I suspected it would be the last use he would ever have for it. It was the first time I'd seen him since the infirmary. He looked as if a good gust of wind could carry him off. His eyes were still shadowed and his cheeks sunken, yet he spoke clearly when he thanked Epiny's parents for giving her, and still managed to look happier than I'd ever seen him before. So did Epiny, and despite my misgivings, I envied them both.

I had very little time alone with Spink. He wearied easily and Epiny was determined both to baby him and to have him to herself as much as possible. When I found one quiet moment, I gave him my personal good wishes, and then suddenly found myself saying, 'It's strange. Things matter so much, and then suddenly they don't matter at all. On the day of our examinations, I agonized that you and Gord had found a way to cheat. It seemed of such great importance to me then, a life-or-death matter. Well, now I know what a life-or-death matter is. Does everything seem different to you since we came so close to dying?'

He gave me a soul-baring look. 'Since we died and came back, you mean? Yes, my friend. Everything seems different to me. And things that bothered me a great deal then don't matter to me at all anymore.' He gave a small snort of laughter. 'But I will confess the truth to you. Yes. I did cheat. But Gord had nothing to do with it. I wrote "6 x 8 = 46" on the inside of my wrist.'

'But six times eight is forty-eight!' I exclaimed.

For a long instant, Spink just gaped at me. Then he burst into a hearty laugh, and that brought Epiny sweeping up to us to demand how I had managed to win that response from him. Very shortly after that, they left on their wedding trip, which was only to last two days before they journeyed east again with Spink's brother. The little gathering dissolved almost as soon as the bride and groom departed, and I was happy to seek my room under the pretence of being wearied by all the excitement. My uncle excused me easily, and actually looked as if he wished he could go with me. He appeared bedraggled in that harried way of men whose wives are intensely unhappy with them. My aunt was dressed in a severe dress in a grey so dark it was almost black. She had not spoken one word to me and I was able to bow silently over her hand and escape.

In my bedchamber, I sat and stared out of the window until the day faded to night. Then, my decision made, I took paper and pen and wrote a careful but blunt letter to Carsina. I addressed the envelope plainly to her, care of her father. The next day I arose early, dressed meticulously in my uniform and left my uncle's house. The first thing I did was to post my letter. Then, having faced that particular demon, I rode Sirlofty to the Academy where I called at Colonel Stiet's residence, desperately hoping to find that he and his family had already moved out.

But they were still there, and so I forced myself to do what I had promised myself I would do if I ever had the opportunity. I would confront Caulder with his foul lie. I presented the note he had sent me to the servant who answered the door. The man expressed polite surprise and told me that he would first have to seek permission from the boy's mother. She had given orders that he was not to be allowed to do anything that might excite him in any way. His health was still far too delicate.

And so I was kept waiting for some little time in a finely appointed parlour. I looked at the expensive prints on the walls but did not sit in any of the grandly upholstered chairs. I recalled bitterly that in my cadet days under the colonel, I had never been judged worthy to be invited here. I would not sit on his fine cushions now.

I had expected that Caulder's mother might come in to see who was visiting her boy. But it was the servant who came back, with the simple request from his mother that I not weary Caulder nor stay too long. I assured the man that I had no intention of making a lengthy visit, and then followed him upstairs to a sunny sitting room.

Caulder was already there. He was sitting on a lounge with a counterpane over his legs. He looked even worse than Spink. His arms were bony, so that his wrists and elbows looked unnaturally large. A table with a pitcher of water, a glass, and the other accoutrements of a sick room stood handy to him. His knees made mountains beneath the coverlet, and he had perched several lead soldiers on top of them. Yet he was not playing with them, but only staring at them fixedly. The servant knocked gently on the frame of the open door. Caulder started, and two soldiers fell to the floor with a clatter. 'Beg pardon, young sir. You have a guest,' the man told him, crossing the room to gather up the toy soldiers and hand them back to Caulder. The boy took them absently and did not speak a word to me until the man left the room.

Caulder stared at me for a time, and then said hoarsely, 'You don't look like you've been sick at all.' There was wonder in his voice.

'Well, I was.' I stared at the boy who had done me such a monstrous injustice, who had roused such hatred in me, and felt only a great coldness inside me. I had feared I would lose my temper and shout at him. Now, looking at his wasted body and bloodshot eyes, I found that all I wanted was to be away from him. I spoke brusquely. 'You wrote to me. You wanted to see me. You said you had something for me.'

'I did. I do.' The boy had managed to go paler. He turned to his bedside table and rummaged about in the mess there. 'I took your rock. I'm sorry. Here it is. I want to give it back.' And with that, he held it out to me.

I crossed the room in three strides. He almost cowered away from me as I took it out of his hand.

'I know it was wrong to take it. I'd never seen one like it.

I only meant to find out what it was from my uncle. He studies rocks and plants.'

I looked at the rough stone with its coarse veins of crystal and recalled too well how I had come by it. Did I really want anything that reminded me of that? A little shudder ran up my back at the thought of Tree Woman and her world. Well. I was done with that now. Epiny had said so, and although I did not want to believe her about anything else to do with her séances and spirits, I clung to that. Tree Woman's shadow was no longer cast over me. I was free of her. I set the rock back on his table with a loud clack. 'Keep it. I don't want it anymore. Was that the only reason you wanted me to come?' My words came out more coldly than I'd intended. The memory of the tree woman was a chill one. I had loved her. I had hated her. I had killed her.

A tremor shook Caulder's lower lip. For a terrifying moment, I thought he would crumple up and cry. Then he mastered himself, and said in a stiff, almost angry voice, 'I sent you that message because my father said I must. I told him I had lied about who got me drunk. So he said I must write to you personally, and when you came, I must apologize. I do. I apologize, Nevare Burvelle.' He took a deep and ragged breath. As I was still reeling from that revelation, he shook me further when he added in a whisper. 'And I told him the rest about Jaris and Odon. About them beating up that fat cadet, and Lieutenant Tiber. I apologize for that, too. But even though my father made me send you that note, that isn't why *I* wanted you to come. There is something else I must say.'

He stared at me, and the silence grew uncomfortably long. I think he was waiting for me to say something. At last he said in a hoarse whisper, 'Thank you for sending me back across the bridge. If you hadn't, I would have gone on to that place. I would have died.' He suddenly hugged his arms around himself and started to shiver so violently that I could see it. 'I have tried to tell my father about it, but he just gets

618

angry with me. But I know . . . That is—' He halted his words and looked desperately around the room, as if to reassure himself it was there. His shaking became more pronounced. 'What is real? Is this place more real than that one? Can the whole world suddenly give way around you and then we are somewhere else? I think about that all the time now. I cannot sleep well at night. My father and the doctor drug me to make me close my eyes, but that is not the same as sleep, is it?'

'Caulder, calm yourself. You are safe.'

'Am I? Are you? Do you think she couldn't just reach out and snatch either of us back if she wished it?' He began to weep noisily.

I stepped to the door of his room and looked out into the hall for help. No one was in sight. 'Caulder is not feeling well!' I called out loudly. 'Could someone please come and take care of him?' I went back to his bedside and set a hand to his shoulder, feeling nothing of warmth toward him, only alarm. 'She is gone now, Caulder. Forever. Calm down. Someone will be here soon to take care of you.'

'No!' Caulder wailed. 'No. They'll drug me again. Nevare. Please. Don't call them. I'm calm now. I'm calm.' He hugged himself even tighter, and held his breath in an effort to stop his sobs.

I heard a door open and close and then footfalls in the hall. They seemed to be coming very slowly. I scrabbled desperately for a way to distract him from his terror. I did not wish to be blamed for working an invalid into hysteria. Awkwardly I asked, 'Where will you be going now? To a family estate?'

It was the wrong question. 'My father is, and he's taking my mother. But he's sending me away. I'm no good now. He hates me. He says I quiver like a lapdog and see danger in dustballs. A soldier son who will never be a soldier. What use am I in the world?' He picked up the rock and set it down again. 'He was furious that I stole this from you. He thinks he will punish me by sending me to my uncle. Uncle Car has written to say he will be glad to have me and will adopt me so that he has a son to follow him. He says the scholar son has no need of a strong back or great courage, only a good mind. I don't think I even have that any more.'

'What is all this!' Colonel Stiet demanded from the door. But his voice was only an echo of his old bark. When I looked at him, I saw an old man in a dressing gown, leaning on a cane. He had two days' growth of greying stubble on his chin, and his hair was uncombed. When he recognized me, he growled, 'I might have known it would be you. Well. Do you have your satisfaction?'

I held up the letter Caulder had sent me. I did not intend that it slip from my hand, but it did, and it wafted through the air to lie at the colonel's feet. 'Your son asked me to come here. I did. I now understand that you made him extend the invitation.' I was surprised, not at the depth of my anger, but at the cold control I could maintain over my voice. I spoke flatly and met the old man's eyes with a neutral stare.

He looked away from me to his son, and I saw horror and disgust was in his eyes. Then his mouth turned down in anger. 'Well. I see you've had your revenge on him. I hope you enjoyed it, kicking a cringing puppy like Caulder. Are you satisfied, sir?' He repeated the word as if all of this were my fault.

'No, sir, I am not.' I spoke precisely. 'You gave me a dishonourable discharge based on a lie. Am I still under that onus? Will it be a part of the record I must always carry with me? And what will you do about the cadets who were truly guilty of poisoning your son with cheap liquor and beating other cadets?'

He stood silent for a time. The sound of Caulder's ragged breathing as he huddled in his chaise dominated the room. Then I clearly heard Colonel Stiet swallow. In a quieter voice he said, 'No record remains of your dishonourable discharge. You can return to the Academy at any time, although I do not know when classes will resume. That is up to my successor. He is currently searching for instructors to replace the ones who died. Are you satisfied?'

Each time he asked me that, it was like an accusation. Did he think I was greedy, to demand justice and the return of my honour? 'No, sir. I am not "satisfied". What will become of the cadets who were truly guilty of poisoning your son with cheap liquor?' I repeated my question as carefully and coldly as when I had first asked it.

'That is none of your affair, Cadet!' He coughed on his own vehemence. Then he added, 'In my judgment, nothing is to be gained by profaning the honour of the dead. They are both dead of that foul pestilence. The good god will judge them for you, Cadet Burvelle. Will you be satisfied with that?'

I came as close to blasphemy as I ever have in my life when I replied, 'I suppose I will have to be, sir. Good day, Colonel Stiet. Good day, Caulder.'

I walked past Colonel Stiet to reach the door of the room. As I passed out of it, Caulder showed that he did, perhaps, have a glimmer of a soldier's courage in his soul. He lifted his shaking voice to call after me, 'Thank you again, Nevare. May the good god protect you.' Then Colonel Stiet shut the door too firmly behind me. I listened to the sound of my boots as I thudded downstairs and I let myself out of the colonel's fine house.

I rode Sirlofty back to my uncle's home and stabled him myself. I had thought myself well recovered, but the encounter had exhausted me. I went to my room, slept through the afternoon, and then rose wakeful to the evening sky glowing in my window. My trunk had been brought to my uncle's house, probably at the same time they'd delivered me to him. It looked as if everything from my bunkroom had been hastily thrown into it. I repacked it carefully. When I came to Carsina's letters that I had bundled together, I opened them and deliberately read through each of them in order. What did I know of her? Next to nothing. Yet I still felt a sense of loss as I put each missive back in its envelope and once more tied them into a packet. I felt that Epiny and her attitude and her questions had taken something from me and made my life a bit harder. I found I still wished her and Spink the best of luck. I suspected they would need it.

I think that the horseback ride and my confrontation with Caulder and Colonel Stiet taxed me more heavily than my health was ready to bear. The next day, I found myself sweaty and sick again, and I kept to my bed for that day and the two that followed. Epiny and Spink were gone, and though my uncle visited my chamber, it was a brief visit. I believe he thought me moping more than ill.

On the third day, against my inclination, I rose and forced myself to go for a walk in the garden. The following day, I took a longer walk, and by the end of the week, I felt that my recovery was once more on track. My appetite returned with a vengeance that startled me and frankly amazed the kitchen staff. My health came roaring back, and I felt that my body suddenly demanded both exercise and food to restore itself. I was very happy to give it both. When Dr Amicas paid me a surprise visit, he bluntly said, 'You've not only recovered your weight from before your illness, but added a layer of fat to it. Perhaps you should consider controlling your appetite.'

I had to grin to that. 'It's an old pattern in my family, sir. My brothers and I always put on a bit of flesh right before we shoot up in height. I'd thought I was finished growing, but I daresay I'm wrong. Perhaps by the time I return home for my brother's wedding, I'll be the tallest man in the family.'

'Well, perhaps,' he said guardedly. 'But I shall want to see you in my offices every week after classes resume. Your recovery is unique, Cadet Burvelle, and I'd like to document it for a paper I'm writing on the Speck plague. Would you mind?'

'Not at all, sir. Anything I can do to help bring an end to the disease is no more than my duty.'

When, a week later, a servant brought me a letter from the King's Cavalla Academy, I stared at it with misgiving for a long time before I could bring myself to open it. I dreaded that it would contain some final vindictive act from Colonel Stiet, a bad report and a dishonourable dismissal. Instead, when I opened it, it was simply a notice that the new commander had scheduled a re-opening date for the Academy. All cadets were to report to their dormitories and be in residence within five days. He was reinstating military protocol regarding the gates to the Academy, and some cadets would be experiencing a change in quarters. I stared at it for some time, and I think that was when I finally realized that disaster had passed me by. I was alive, my health was returning, and I was still a cadet. The life I had always imagined for myself might still await me.

I went down to my uncle's library and spent the entire night reading through my father's military journals. If he had ever questioned his fate, it was not confided to paper. He wrote as a soldier should, impassively and concisely. He went there, he fought with those people, he won, and the next day he and his troop rode on. There was a lot of war and very little of life in his accounts. I set my father's journals back and randomly pulled down several of the older ones. I found cramped handwriting, fading ink, and more accounts of dealing death. I admired Epiny's ability to read them. Much of it was dull, and it surprised me that the business of killing people could become so commonplace as to be boring.

Toward morning, my uncle came down with a candle and found me there. 'I thought I heard someone moving around down here,' he greeted me.

I finished shelving the journals I had pulled out. 'I'm

sorry, sir. I didn't mean to wake you. I couldn't sleep and so I came here to read.'

He gave a dry laugh. 'Well, if those journals didn't put you to sleep, nothing will.'

'Yes, sir. I tend to agree with you.' Then we stood there, awkwardly.

'I'm glad to see you recovering so well,' my uncle said at last.

'Yes, sir. I plan on returning to the Academy tomorrow. If I may have the use of your carriage?'

'I think you should ride your horse, Nevare. There will be room for Sirlofty in the Academy stables now. Just yesterday, Colonel Rebin held a big auction of the Academy riding horses that Colonel Stiet had acquired.' He actually smiled. 'He advertised them as "suitable mounts for delicate ladies and very young children". I do not think he was impressed with Stiet's choice of horseflesh.'

'Nor I, sir.' I found myself grinning back at him. It was such a small thing, to be able to ride my own horse in our formations, and yet it lifted my spirits tremendously.

My uncle laughed softly and then said, 'Sir this. Sir that. Am I no longer your uncle, Nevare?'

I looked down. 'After the trouble I brought into your house, I was not sure how you felt about me.'

'If you were the one who brought Epiny here, it escaped my notice, Nevare. No. I made my own trouble, and spoiled her as she grew. I was far too indulgent with her and as a result, I have lost her. I wonder if I'll ever see her again. It is a long way to Bitter Springs, and a hard life that awaits her when she arrives.'

'I think she'll be up to it, sir—Uncle Sefert.' I found that I believed my own words.

'I think she will, too. Well. Leaving tomorrow. I know we haven't seen much of each other of late, but I'll still miss you. So I will still expect you to spend your leave days here, visiting.'

'Will your lady wife be comfortable with that, Uncle Sefert?' I asked the question plainly, wishing to put it all out in the open.

'My lady wife is not comfortable with anything these days, Nevare. Let's leave her out of it, shall we? Perhaps the next free day you get, you and Hotorn and I can go out and do some shooting together. I think I would like a bit of a holiday away from this city.'

'I should like that, too, Uncle Sefert.'

He hugged me before we parted for what remained of the night, and saw me off the next morning when I left on Sirlofty. He promised that he would send my trunk by cart within the hour.

I rose early and dressed in my uniform. It seemed snugger than it had when last I wore it again, and I suspected I was due for yet another growth spurt. As I left my uncle's house, a steady winter rain was falling and the gutters of the city ran full, as did some of the streets. I rode slowly, and tried to come to terms with all the changes that I now must face. My emotions teetered between elation and regret. I was going back to the Academy and my career. But of my patrol, only Gord, Kort, Rory, Trist and I remained. I wondered what the Academy would do with us and had to accept that I had no control over it.

When I reached the gates of the Academy, I found that a second-year cadet stood in the sentry box. He shouted a challenge to me when I tried to ride through. I halted, and when I gave my name, he consulted a list and told me the stall number for my horse and gave me a billet slip and had me sign a roster as 'Returning to Duty'. We exchanged salutes and I rode on, feeling as if I had truly entered a military emplacement.

It was the same in the stables. Harried cadets were bustling at work when I arrived. I found Sirlofty's stall and cared for him and my tack before I left him there. He was in good

company. Other horses were arriving – tall, straight-legged cavalla mounts that held their heads high and bared teeth at
strangers and occasionally snapped at each other. Mounted drill,
I suddenly knew, was going to become a different experience.

My billet slip said that I was now in Bringham House. I
wondered if it was an error. I was certain there was an error
when I walked up the steps and found Rory standing just
inside the door. A newly-sewn corporal stripe was on his
·sleeve. He gaped to see me and then grinned. 'Well, here you
are, back again, and healthy as a pig to boot! Look at you,
Nevare – last time I had a glimpse of you, well, I thought it
would be my last! And here you are, back from the dead,
same as me, but fat and sassy to boot!' Then his grin faded
as he asked me, 'You've had the news, haven't you? About
Nate and Oron and everyone?'

'Yes. I have. It's going to be strange. Is this truly where
we've been billeted?'

Rory nodded. 'Yup. Colonel Rebin's a pip for organizing
things. He came through the dormitories like a tornado, day
before yesterday. He says there's not enough of us left to
keep them all open, and that inefficiency kills in the field.
Didn't he swear when he had a good look at Skeltzin Hall
and saw them broken windows and such! He can cuss better than my own da! Said he wouldn't have kept soldiers in
what was obviously meant to be a pigeon house. I guess
when he turned it over to Colonel Stiet, Skeltzin Hall was
scheduled for demolition! Stiet turned it back into housing.
Anyway, here we are, and the colonel mixed us all up good.
Old blood, new blood, he don't care. Says it all runs red
when you get hurt, so we might as well learn to make sure
none of us gets hurt. Hey. A bit of good news. I saw Jared
and Lofert already. They're back and I put your bunk in the
same room as theirs. Gord's back, too. Hey, you'll never
guess. He's a married man now. Him and his girl got harnessed when the plague was at its worst. Their folks said if

they were all going to die, they might as well have a bit of life first. Only no one in their families even got sick out there. You oughtta see him strut now. He looks so happy he almost doesn't look fat any more.'

I shook my head in amazement. Then, 'How'd you get to be a corporal?' I demanded.

He grinned his big froggy grin. 'Field promotion is what Colonel Rebin called it. He says that's what happens when you're one of the few left standing after the battle-smoke clears. He jumped up a bunch of us. Told us that if we proved ourselves worthy, we could keep the stripes. Bet you wish you'd got yerself back here a day or two early.'

'No,' I found myself saying. 'Looks to me like it just means more work for you. You're welcome to your stripe, Corporal Hart. And here's your first salute from me!' The gesture I made was not the military one, but Rory laughed and returned the crude sign in kind.

I had never been in Bringham House before. I still felt like an intruder as I crossed the polished stone floor to the sergeant's desk. An old sergeant I had never seen before had me sign in on a roster, and then handed me a list of my duties to be completed that day. I immediately went to collect the bedding issued to me. It was so clean it still smelled of soap. I hastened up a flight of steps that did not creak or shake under my tread. The smell of lyesoap was everywhere. My billet was on the third floor. Two cadets were on their hands and knees with scrub brushes in the big study room that took up the entire second floor. I grimaced. A glance at my duty slip told me I'd soon be joining them. Other cadets were dusting books and replacing them neatly on bookshelves. I hadn't even known that Bringham House had its own small reference library. No wonder the Old Noble cadets had consistently bested us at academics. The entire third floor was an open barracks, with a row of washstands at one end, flanked by the water closets. It seemed the height of luxury.

I found my bunk easily. A neatly lettered sign on the foot of it gave my name. And on the rolled-up mattress, I found five letters waiting from me. One was from Epiny and Spink. *Mr. And Mrs. Spinrek Kester* she had written on the envelope, in very large letters. I smiled at that. The smile faded when I saw the next envelope was from Carsina's father. And the third was from Carsina herself, carefully addressed to Cadet Nevare Burvelle. A flat fourth envelope would probably hold a letter of rebuke from Yaril. She'd had such high hopes for Carsina and me. The fifth was from my father. I set them all aside for the time and turned to putting my possessions away. I wondered what I hoped the letters would say, and had no idea.

I put my books on my shelf and hung my clothing in my cupboard. My trunk went at the end of my bunk. I worked slowly and meticulously as I put every item in its place. Then I made my bed with the fresh bedding I'd been issued. And all the while, my mind ground through every possible answer I might have to face in those letters.

When my bunk was covered with a tightly-tucked blanket, I perched on its corner and opened Epiny's letter first, as it seemed the least threatening. It had been written on the road and posted from a way station. Everything she saw and did was marvellous and exciting and amazing. They had slept under the wagon during a downpour when bad roads had delayed them from reaching the next town. It had been so cosy, like a wild rabbit's burrow, and they'd heard the howling of wild dogs in the distance. She'd seen a herd of deer watching them from a hillside. She'd cooked porridge over a fire in an open kettle. Spink got stronger every day. Spink had promised to teach her to shoot once he was well enough to hunt again. She had thought she was pregnant, but then her courses came, which was horribly inconvenient when they were travelling, but probably no worse than morning sickness would have been. I blushed at her bluntness and realized that she wrote exactly as she talked. At the end of her long, closely-written letter was a wavering greeting from Spink and an assurance that he was as happy as a man could be. I folded the pages and tucked them back into the envelope. So, they were happy. I let out a breath I hadn't realized I'd been holding. I decided that they would build a fine life together, and that thought eased my heart.

The missive from my father was next. He wrote that my mother had enjoyed Epiny's letters but that he looked forward to hearing from me personally. He was glad to hear I had recovered. He'd had a note from Dr Amicas expressing some reservations about my health and continued attendance at the Academy. The doctor suggested that I take a year's leave from the Academy, return home, and then reconsider my Academy career at that time. That sentence made me frown. The doctor had said nothing of that to me. My father wrote that he had already notified the doctor that he would see me when I returned home for my brother's wedding in late spring, and that my father would decide for himself at that time if my health had been severely compromised. For now, he trusted I would continue to live sensibly, study hard, and trust in the good god. I decided that perhaps he was referring to an earlier missive from the doctor, one that he had sent before my recovery had become so robust. I set my father's letter aside and gave a small sigh of relief. Other than his mention of the doctor, it sounded as if all were well with him.

The letter from Carsina's father was written in a bold black hand. He wished me well for my continued recovery. He said that looking at death, in any form, could make a man question his life's direction, and often that was good. It would also make a man bold. Foolishly bold in some cases. He reminded me that I had yet to earn the right to call Carsina my fiancée, but that he trusted I would, and that he expected all correspondence I sent her to be as honest and honourable as my first letter had been. My parents were well when he had last seen them. His lady wife sent her best wishes as well.

A drop of perspiration trickled down my spine. I wiped my sweaty hands on my shirt and opened Carsina's letter.

Dear Cadet Nevare Burvelle,

I am thrilled to receive your letter and to know that you are recovering from your illness. The news we had from Old Thares was very frightening.

You asked me if, freed of all parental constraints, I would still choose you to be my husband. I must remind you that we are still not formally promised to one another. Yet if the good god blesses us and you strive with dedication and courage, I am sure that soon we will be. Then the answer will be, yes, I would choose you. I trust my parents' judgment to guide me in all things, as I am sure you trust yours.

With great affection and in the good god's light,
Miss Carsina Grenalter

Every word had been spelled correctly. The penmanship looked like something from an exercise book. Without intending to, they had told me exactly what I had bluntly asked. Carsina chose me because she had never had any other choice. Listlessly, I let the letter fall to my bunk. My heart fell with it.

I had all but forgotten my sister's letter. It alone remained. I opened it by rote. She was glad I wasn't sick any more, and could I try to find three more buttons to match the ones shaped like blackberries that I'd sent her. She loved me and wished me well.

And to my shock, there was another page folded within Yaril's missive. Carsina had written to me with pale blue ink on pink paper. I struggled to make out her words.

'My father was so angry, but my mother said it was the most romantec letter she'd ever seen and that he must let me have it to keep. I am so glad. Every girl who has seen it has turned

green with envie. My mother tells me that I did choose well, and that your letter shows it for you wish me to be happy with you. Oh, Nevare, I did choose you. When I was seven, I told both our mothers that I was going to marry you when I grew up, because you picked the ripest plums that I couldn't reach and gave them to me. Don't you remember that? My mother told me when my father wanted to match me with Kase Remwar. Well, that would never do, for I knew that Yaril was sweet on him. I begged my mother to make a plee that I be matched with you, and she did. So you see, my darling and brave cadet, I did choose you!!!! My heart beats so fast when I think of you. I have read your letter a thousand times. Even my father was impressed with how boldly you asked that question. Oh, Nevare, I am so in love with you. When your brother marries in the spring and you come home to be there, you must wear your uniform, for I am having a dress made that is the perfect shade of green to compliment it. And when our fathers give them to one another, you must find a way to stand next to me, for I am sure that we will make a lovely pair.'

I folded the letter, saving the rest of its sweetness for later. I tucked it into my breast pocket, near my heart, and sat for a moment. I had not chosen her. But she had chosen me, freely. Chosen me over handsome Kase Remwar. I smiled at the compliment. I would see her again, in a couple of months, when I went home for my brother's wedding. I suspected that, given all I had learned, I would choose her.

I found myself considering a future that might still be golden. I started when Gord plunked a bucket and scrub brush down on the floor by my feet. He held another bucket in one hand. I had a feeling that I looked as foolishly happy as he did. 'Good to see you back, Nevare. I picked up your supplies for you. It looks as if we have duty together.'

'That it does, Gord. That it does.'

Smiling, I went to my task.

Acknowledgment

The author would like to acknowledge and thank David Killingsworth for providing information and insight on several weighty matters. It was greatly appreciated.